The Story Until Now

Also by Kit Reed

The Story Until Now

A Great Big Book of Stories

KIT REED

WESLEYAN UNIVERSITY PRESS

Middletown, Connecticut

Wesleyan University Press
Middletown CT 06459
www.wesleyan.edu/wespress
© 2013 Kit Reed
All rights reserved
Manufactured in the United States of America
Designed by Katherine B. Kimball
Typeset in Minion by A. W. Bennett, Inc.

Wesleyan University Press is a member of the Green Press Initiative.
The paper used in this book meets their minimum requirement for
recycled paper.

Library of Congress Cataloging-in-Publication Data

Reed, Kit.
    The story until now: a great big book of stories / Kit Reed.
        p. cm.
    ISBN 978-0-8195-7349-0 (cloth: alk. paper)—ISBN 978-0-8195-
7350-6 (ebook)
1. Science fiction, American. I. Title.
    PS3568.E367S76 2013
    813'.54—dc23

                        2012026804

5 4 3 2 1

For Joe,

who's been in this with me from the beginning

with much, much love

Contents

Scoping the Exits

The Short Fiction of Kit Reed

GARY K. WOLFE

There has always been an oddly passive-aggressive relationship between American literature and the fantastic. Almost from the beginning, a familiar myth has been the notion of bringing order to wilderness, of subduing chaos, of constructing a rational society and rational institutions, of building roads and cities and eventually suburbs and high-rises and shopping malls. But the unsubdued aspects of wildness have an unsettling way of reasserting themselves; the cities and suburbs can *become* their own sort of wilderness; the roads can seem to lead nowhere; the rational society can become a dystopia. Fantastic literature, whether it takes the form of the Gothic, of science fiction, or of fantasy, is at its best a literature that explores *implications,* that aggressively excavates the assumptions behind our sunny plans and rational dreams and shows us where they might *really* lead. This is one reason the fantastic has been such a persistent strain in American writing, from Hawthorne and Poe and Melville through Twain and L. Frank Baum up to H. P. Lovecraft and Robert A. Heinlein.

By the time we get to the last two writers on that list, however, an odd thing had begun to happen to American fantastic literature: it had begun to calve off genres, modes of writing that appealed to specific audiences and markets with particular tastes and desires. Usually, when we think of fantastic literature today, we think in terms of those genres, particularly science fiction, fantasy, and horror. But at the same time, there has been a persistent tradition of fantastic writing that doesn't easily fit into convenient categories, but that makes use of their unique resources. This is a broader tradition than we might at first think, and has deeper roots; it's one of the reasons we can find the occasional fantastic tale by Henry James, Edith Wharton, or Willa Cather. Even after the rise of the pulp magazines and paperbacks that helped define the pop genres, this kind of free-range fantastic continued to appear in the literary or general-interest magazines and mainstream publishing lists, and as late as the 1940s we can find examples of it in the work of writers as diverse as John Collier, Truman Capote, John Cheever, Robert Coates, Roald Dahl, and Shirley Jackson.

This, I think, is the sort of literary space that much of the work of Kit Reed occupies. She has not been averse to publishing her stories in genre magazines such as *The Magazine of Fantasy and Science Fiction* or *Asimov's* (along with venues such as *The Yale Review* or *The Village Voice Literary Supplement*—all are represented in this collection), but by the time her career began, toward the end of the 1950s, some of those genre-based magazines had begun to broaden their scope to include the literary fantastic, while many of the mainstream fiction markets either folded entirely (*Collier's* or *The Saturday Evening Post*) or turned to what Michael Chabon has described as "the contemporary, quotidian, plotless, moment-of-truth revelatory story." It may be no coincidence that Shirley Jackson published her last *New Yorker* story in 1953 and her first in *The Magazine of Fantasy and Science Fiction* in 1954—or that it was the latter magazine which published Reed's first story, "The Wait," in 1958. This disturbing tale of a mother and daughter trapped in a strange town with an even stranger ritual might well have appeared in *The New Yorker* nine years earlier, when it published Shirley Jackson's "The Lottery," a tale with which it clearly resonates, but by 1958 *The New Yorker* had largely moved away from any trace of the fantastic.

Reed's near-legendary reputation may have to do in part with the simple fact that her career began with such an accomplished story more than a half century ago, but it has more to do with how she has continued to produce such stories with astonishing regularity ever since, never quite falling into any particular genre but never quite getting trapped by mainstream literary fashions such as the quotidian moment-of-truth tradition that Chabon describes. She has never stopped being a bit of a rebel with a unique and sometimes quirky voice, and this may occasionally have landed her in the interstices between various fictional categories (the term she uses for herself, and possibly invented, is *trans-genred*). It was probably to her advantage that some of the most visionary editors in science fiction in the 1960s and 1970s were actively on the prowl for such distinctive voices—not only Anthony Boucher, Robert Mills, and Avram Davidson at *The Magazine of Fantasy and Science Fiction*, but Michael Moorcock at *New Worlds*, Damon Knight in his series of *Orbit* original anthologies, Harry Harrison in *Nova*, and others.

Reed's mordantly satiric and sharply funny take on beauty pageants "In Behalf of the Product," with its devastating final line, was written for an anthology edited by Thomas M. Disch, a writer whose acerbic sensibility and finely tuned prose sometimes resembled Reed's. He must have found the story absolutely delicious, because up until then no one would have expected a dystopian tale about beauty queens, just as no one expects the Spanish Inquisition. But story after Reed story comes blustering into the room like those Monty Python characters, frequently offering the same sort of ominous-but-absurd comic edge. For a while in the 1960s this sort of thing was called Black Humor, another movement in which Reed both does and doesn't belong. Even some of her more recent stories take such delirious riffs on popular culture and current events that parts of them would hardly be out of place in stand-up comedy. The Sultan of Brunei buys a bankrupt Yankee Stadium in "Grand Opening" (after Americans finally came to realize that baseball is boring) and turns it into a gigantic mall whose grand opening features a ritualized tribute baseball game with an aging Salman Rushdie throwing out the first pitch while being stalked by an equally ancient assassin, apparently the only one who didn't get the memo about the *fatwah* being over. "On the Penal Colony" similarly rams together wildly disparate elements such as ill-conceived correctional systems and tacky historical reenactment tourist traps, with nods to both H. P. Lovecraft and the Kafka story whose title it nearly borrows: here, prisoners are sentenced to serve as historical actors in a Salem-like historical village called Arkham, though some particularly gruesome punishments are part of the system as well. "High Rise High," one of her most famous stories, borrows elements of every school-rebellion move ever made, from *Zero for Conduct* to *Rock 'n' Roll High School,* with elements of *Escape from New York* thrown in: the school of the title is essentially a maximum security prison sealed from the outside world in order to let intransigent students run wild apart from society—until they start in on hostages, kidnappings, and raids into local neighborhoods.

Reed's association with editors and writers such as Moorcock, Knight, and Disch, along with stories that ranged from her similarly dark comic take on weight-loss farms in "The Food Farm" (in Knight's *Orbit*) to an absurdist fable about a poetry-generating pink colt ("Piggy") to a literary jape on Kafka ("Sisohpromatem"). The latter appeared in the British *New Worlds,* and led to her occasional association with science fiction's "New Wave" of the 1960s, a movement spearheaded by Moorcock whose basic purpose, notwithstanding various barricade-storming manifestos and editorials, was simply to expand the scope of what could be done in science fiction. Reed had been doing this quite on her own before the New Wave had taken shape, of course, and would continue to do so long after, but it's not an unreasonable association, and Reed remains one of a handful of still-practicing American writers associated with this influential movement (and one of an even smaller handful of American women; the only others who quickly come to mind are Carol Emshwiller and Pamela Zoline). Both her first collection, *Mr. Da V. and Other Stories* (1967) and her first science fiction novel, *Armed Camps* (1969), with its grim view of a decaying near-future America, appeared when the movement was in full flood, and seemed fully in keeping with its dual interests in literary experimentation and (mostly pessimistic) social consciousness.

As the New Wave either receded or was assimilated—depending on whose view of literary history you accept—the feminist movement in science fiction, at least as an identifiable movement, came close on its heels. But here again Reed both does and doesn't quite fit. Clearly a feminist who often focused on questions of self-image and constructions of gender identity, she wrote about body images not only in that beauty pageant story "In Behalf of the Product," but in "The Food Farm," with its simultaneous satiric takes on fat farms and the cult of celebrity (which she later revisited in stories like "Special" and "Grand Opening"). She could powerfully depict the alienation and sense of entrapment of a suburban housewife in "The Bride of Bigfoot" (which has something in common with James Tiptree, Jr.'s famous story "The Women Men Don't See," with its protagonist making a radical choice in the end). The lonely elderly sisters in "Winter," worried about surviving another harsh winter in their isolated home, may both moon over the promise of lost youth offered by a young deserter who stumbles across their cabin, but in the end a far more practical decision prevails. But Reed's feminism is seldom overtly political and never doctrinaire, and she is as apt to take women to task for their own passivity as men for their insensitive cluelessness. The men are offstage entirely in "Pilots of the Purple Twilight," in which a group of women of different generations endlessly wait in a kind of limbo near the Miramar Naval Air Station for their husbands to return from various wars, until the oldest realizes, "*It was all used up by waiting.*" Probably Reed's most famous treatment of gender alienation is the much-anthologized and controversial "Songs of War," in which the women simply decamp to the hills and set up their own society. While the overreaction of the distraught husbands more than borders on the ridiculous, and the situation escalates into a national crisis, Reed won't entirely let her women characters off the hook, either; internal squabbles break out between different groups (stay-at-home moms at odds with those who put their kids in day care, for example), and eventually most of the women drift away and return to their homes. What emerges from the story is a satirical voice so complexly ambiguous that while many readers view the story as a satire of the extent to which a military-happy male society might go to keep women in their place, at least one feminist critic found herself, because of its ending, unable to view the story as anything other than an *anti*-feminist parable, with the women's revolution simply dissipating at the end.

If Reed can so unsettle proponents of both sides of a debate at once, she might be doing something right.

Perhaps partly because of her own childhood experiences as a self-described "military kid"—her father was a submarine commander who died in World War II—her attitude toward militarism is equally ambivalent, neither uncritical nor unsympathetic. The title character in "The Singing Marine," haunted by an ill-fated military exercise that left most of his platoon drowned or mired in a marsh, finds himself compulsively singing a song from a Grimm's fairy tale, trying to come to terms with his own possible court-martial and his sense of having been "born in blood and reborn in violence." A similar event—or possibly the same one—haunts the memory of an aging veteran trying to come to terms with his wife's mental deterioration in "Voyager," one of Reed's most moving explorations of loss. "In the *Squalus*" describes how that actual submarine disaster in 1939 shaped and shadowed the entire subsequent life of a survivor, while the apparently demented old veteran in a nursing home in "Old Soldiers" is actually coming to grips with a horrific experience that has kept him psychically trapped for decades. And we've already seen her take on the fates of military wives in "Pilots of the Purple Twilight."

The eclecticism of Reed's themes and preoccupations is such that at times they can seem prescient. A trending topic in literary scholarship over the past few years has been animal studies—broadly concerning the role of animals and their relations with humans in literature—but Reed has notably returned to animals and animal imagery in her fiction for many years, from the pink, poetry-producing pony in "Piggy" (whose poems are mashups of everyone from Longfellow to Dickinson) and the robot tiger that gives its owner self-confidence in "Automatic Tiger" to the bug that finds itself made human in "Sisohpromatem" and the pet monkey that writes best sellers in "Monkey Do." Reed revisits the child-raised-by-wolves motif in "What Wolves Know," a story whose title may give us a clue to what Reed finds appealing in animals (the boy's father, determined to make a media sensation out of him, clearly does not know what wolves know, but finds out). A werewolf mother shows up in "The Weremother," Bigfoot shows up in "The Bride of Bigfoot," and in "The Song of the Black Dog" the title animal has the unusual talent of being able to sniff out those about to die, or most in need of attention, during major disasters. All these seem to suggest a world of hermetic knowledge we can access only through our contacts with animals, if we can access it at all. But easily the most bizarre of Reed's animals-as-conduits is the huge alligator that is the title figure in "Perpetua," inside whom the narrator and her family ride out an unspecified disaster in their city with all the comforts of a private yacht, until the narrator makes her own accommodation with Perpetua.

Despite its unusual setting, "Perpetua" also is a kind of family drama, with a father taking drastic steps to protect his family from the outside world, and this brings us to what is perhaps the most consistently recurring theme in Reed's short fiction, which is simply families, and in particular families under stress. This is a concern that Reed has explored through widely different angles, from the essentially realistic fiction of "How It Works" (in which a skeptical daughter must deal with her mother's new fiancé as well as his own mother issues) and "Denny" (in which parents are concerned about their rebellious son turning violent) to the marginally speculative (a son tries to come to terms with his survivalist father in Nebraska in "Journey to the Center of the Earth") to the vaguely macabre ("The Wait," in which a daughter is trapped in a strange town's rituals because of her mother's possible illness) to a kind of horror (as when the exploitative father gets a comeuppance in "What Wolves Know") to science fiction (an overprotective mother during a virulent plague leads her family to tragedy in "Precautions") to pure absurdity ("The Attack of the Giant Baby," in which a baby eats something from its father's lab floor and rapidly grows to the size of architecture).

In a few of these tales Reed employs a favorite technique of using multiple points of view, sometimes to give us contradictory views of a situation, sometimes to avoid privileging a single character, and sometimes (I strongly suspect) because she just likes doing different voices. In "Denny," the effect is particularly chilling, as we shift between the viewpoints of each of the parents and Denny himself, watching an entirely avoidable tragedy of miscommunication unfold toward a bitterly ironic ending. Sometimes the multiple viewpoints may be used for comic effect, as in "Wherein We Enter the Museum," in which we visit the pretentious "Museum of Great American Writers" from the viewpoints of a focus group of ambitious young writing students, a docent who is also an embittered failed novelist, the committee charged with determining the exhibits, and the wealthy philistine donor, who just wants to honor his favorite writers from childhood, like Longfellow, and is outraged when the committee insists that George Eliot was not only not American, but a woman. (Writers and readers come in for Reed's satiric treatment with some regularity, as in "The Outside Event," in which a writers' workshop retreat turns into a kind of reality TV à la *Survivor*). A voice not too far removed from that museum donor, but with a decidedly darker edge, is that of the venal wealthy tourist taking his wife on an ill-fated exclusive tour bus to a remote mountain observatory in "The Legend of Troop 13." Supposedly a Girl Scout troop disappeared into the wilderness near the observatory some years earlier, and the tourist has concocted a fantasy of nailing what he imagines are now nubile young wood nymphs. But as the expedition spirals toward disaster, we also see him from the viewpoints of the resentful bus driver and several of the Girl Scouts themselves, who have formed a kind of self-sustaining society that is at least as functional as that of the rebellious wives in "Songs of War."

It's appropriate that an observatory should be the setting of the penultimate story in this collection, because in a very real sense that's exactly what this book is. Reed may take us into the minds of some decidedly unpleasant or demented characters, she may show us wars, catastrophes, dysfunctional families, werewolves, monsters, feral children, plagues, dystopias, cannibals, zombies, and weird small towns, but always with the cool yet sympathetic intelligence of an observer both outraged and wryly amused by the labyrinths we make for ourselves. Her fiction may, collectively, seem rather dark, but it may also be that by showing us the ways into these labyrinths, she's giving us hints of the ways out as well. Reed has called this attitude "protective pessimism," and it's as good a phrase as any for describing the characteristic tone of her best fiction. "Dealing in worst-case scenarios doesn't depress me," wrote Reed in the introduction to her earlier story collection *Dogs of Truth*. "It makes me hopeful and resilient. Expect the worst and you're always prepared. You scoped the exits when you came in, just in case something comes up. Something comes up and you know the quickest way out. Given a chronic imagination of disaster, I always have a Plan B.

"This is the way lives—and stories—get built."

Author's Note

Combing through more stories than I'd care to admit for this project, I got interested not in chronology, but in the fact that they organized themselves around certain of my—well, preoccupations is a politer word for what drives me than obsessions. Interesting to me to see what shows up in my work, with what kind of frequency. I've arranged the stories accordingly, with notes on where and when they first appeared in print, from back in the day up through this year, including some new and previously uncollected ones.

KR

The Story Until Now

Denny

We are worried about Denny. We have reason to believe he may go all Columbine on us.

Experts warn parents to watch out for signs, and it hurts to say, but we've seen plenty. Day and night our son is like an LCD banner, signaling something we can't read. If he implodes and comes out shooting, the first thing to show up in the crosshairs will be us.

He was cute when he was little but now he's heavily encoded: black everything, hanging off him in tatters—Matrix coat in mid-August, T-shirt, jeans, bits of peeled sunburn and cuticle gnawed to shreds. Black lipstick and blue bruises around the eyes. That glare. Shake him and dirt flies out—grot and nail clippings, crushed rolling papers, inexplicable knots of hair. Stacks of secret writing that Denny covers as you come into the room and no friends except that creepy kid who won't look you in the eye.

Shrinks list things to watch out for, and it isn't just to protect the innocent, sitting in class when the armed fury comes in and lays waste. They're warning us! Some lout killed his parents with a baseball bat not far from here, they were dead before the sleeping neighborhood rolled over and shut off the clock. In addition to knifings and ax murders, I read about deaths by assault weapon or repeating rifle, people executed by their own children on their way out of the house to massacre their peers.

It's awful going around scared, but there you are. Poor Stef and I are forever on the alert.

Our mutant enemy blunders around the house at night making messes and bumping into things, and, worse? We're the ones who apologize for being in the way. Back in our room, my wife throws herself down on the bed and sobs, "I've failed," but, listen! There may be an enemy within but in spite of the cycle of guilt and mutual recriminations, we know it isn't us.

I don't know what's up with Dad. He and Mom are getting all weird and creepy, lurking with their knuckles hooked under their chins like disturbed squirrels, jumping away with uh-oh looks and shifty eyes when I come in. It's not like they're avoiding me. Unless they are.

How did it get so bad? The tiptoeing and the shrinking, the nights when I go to bed in tears? I want to hug my boy and make it better, but it's like making overtures to a porcupine. Every gesture I try goes astray and if I get too close, I get hurt. What's a mother to do? He was a hard person when the doctor dragged him out kicking and screaming, and it's been downhill ever since. Maybe we were too old to be parents, unless we were too young. We had a baby because we were that age and it was expected, but nobody told us what it would be like. The event? The glories of childbirth thing is an atrocious myth. It was painful and scary and astounding. Stan and I spent the first months exhausted and terrified, but that's nothing compared to now. We love our son, but he's not very easy to like.

Denny's always been sweet with me—well, except at certain times, but God it's hard, and I've tried everything. We need to sit down and talk but my son is hooked up to his music like a patient to an IV and I don't even know what's going into his ears. If I ask him to pull out the earbuds so we can have the conversation he gets all weird and hostile and slouches away with a look that frightens me.

Denny, if it's something I did, then I'm sorry. Isn't this punishment enough?

When you're warned about the enemy within, the first thing you do is blame yourself. It must be something you did, like failing to pay attention or hitting, which can make schoolyard assassins of kids. Hit Denny? I just wouldn't, although God knows there were times when I was close. The flip side of guilt is things you failed to do, but on that score Stephanie and I test clean. Believe me, we read all the books and covered all the bases—lessons, therapy, Ritalin or Prozac as indicated, contact lenses and braces, of course. Dermabrasion. Comedy camp. Implants to replace teeth trashed by playground bullies, a trigger parents are urged to report which we dutifully did, which made our son furious, I don't know why.

We brought home video games, tabletop soccer and a Ping-Pong table to help him win friends, but nobody ever comes over. Why, Stef and I spent last summer redoing his room. We've done everything for the kid, and what do we get back? Black polish on the fingernails, a show of teeth so sharp that I could swear he's filing them down to points. We try to give him everything he wants and the hell of it is, he won't even tell us what he wants.

To this day my wife spends hours on the birthday bunny cake with shredded coconut fur and jelly bean eyes and a combed cotton ball for a tail. She does it with tears in her eyes because it pleased him once, and she has hopes. It does no good to remind her that he was two. Nobody's going to tell us that we don't love Denny, especially not him.

Take a letter off Denny and you get: DENY. Stan and Stephanie don't know it but in study hall I am making a tattoo. It hurts but it's easy to do. It isn't a heart, although I drew an arrow through it to represent Diane, from Spanish class. What I put, with a ballpoint and this safety pin? DENY.

Nobody told me what it would be like. One day you're a normal, perfectly healthy woman with a day job, a sense of who you are in life, the next . . .

You wake up the next morning like a slate that God erased. Your baby howls and everything you used to be is wiped away.

For thirty years of my life, Denny wasn't.

Then he was.

I was so scared. He was so small! Breakable! Like a Swiss watch I had been given to maintain with no idea when the maker would come back to check on me, just the knowledge that I was accountable. There was no clear list of instructions, either, just the expectation that I would take care of it. The machinery was complex and mysterious, but I could tell that it wasn't running right. You try, but what do you do when this precious object entrusted to you is congested with rage? Do I pick him up when he screeches or should he learn to put himself to sleep? Should I feed him now or is he not hungry, should I change him even though I just did and, I ask you, who's supposed to be in charge? Which of us is supposed to have the upper hand? What if he gets so mad that he breaks?

Dear God, did I crack something in Denny while I wasn't looking and is that why he grew up withdrawn and angry and sad?

It's like sharing the house with a wild animal. He slinks around like a night-blooming menace, glowering, thinking tainted thoughts. Denny hates me, I'm sure of it, and I don't know why. Still, we are coexisting here until he's old enough to get a life, so I try. I sign his report cards without comment because anything I say will lead to a fight and the last thing we want here is to set him off. Although I don't much feel like it, I make a smile. I go, HELLO, DENNIS. HOW WAS SCHOOL? and he flinches like I slapped him in the face.

I come into a room and they go silent, you can tell they were talking about me. Then Dad gets all stiff and polite and goes: "Well, Dennis, how's school?" and I hackle. *Get out of my face.* How the fuck does he think school is? I'll tell you how school is. It sucks. I have eight guys lying in wait to beat the crap out of me for eight different reasons, Diane Caldwell being only one. Miss Gleeson in English made me come up in the front of the room and read my story that I wrote; I had to read it out loud which is why seven of the guys are out to get me and the eighth, I'm guessing it's about Diane; if I was sitting in the back and forced to listen to me reading this lame story I'd beat the crap out of me too.

But Dad is all up in my face, "How was school?" and he won't lay back and let me walk away quiet until he gets an answer so I go, "OK."

They want you to believe that when they put your new baby in your arms, it's love at first sight, but instant mother love is another myth. I don't know who puts it out there, greedy grandmothers bent on posterity or men who want to see their spit and image popping out of you. You want to love your children but the truth is, you get used to them. You get used to being baffled and helpless and weepy and you accommodate, over time. I went through the first year terrified. Was I giving him everything he needed or warping him for life? Now he's fifteen and the jury's out and it won't come back. You tell me, did I do it right?

God knows I tried. I tried so hard to do it right that I'm afraid I did everything wrong.

She plants fifteen candles on this year's cake. They bristle like armed cannons on a battleship. We knock ourselves out over presents we chose to change him for the better, whatever that means. Nice clothes. A leatherbound book to write his thoughts in, along with a box so he can lock it away from us. Games, maybe we can bond over cribbage, or chess. After he blows out the candles she cuts off the bunny's head and presents it to Dennis with that heartbreaking tremulous smile.

Why, when we tried to give him everything, does he look like he wants to cry?

Over the years we tried everything. Tricycles and Christmas trees. Skateboards, sleds. Rollerblades. I used to throw the ball around with him when he was small! Now my son and I circle like boxers and my wife has to hold it in all night because she's scared to go out in the hall.

In school today I accidentally knocked off Diane's notebook when I accidentally went by her desk which I did so could I pick it up, and when I handed it back, we could talk, at least a little bit. That was an assaholic thing to do but it was cool. She thanked me with this look but when I came out after, eight assholes were lying in wait for me, so does that mean she likes me and they know it or what?

After I finally lost them I stayed back at the foundation to the new gym. Even though I knew the folks would be pissed off at me, I stayed until I was good to go, which took a while. There are times when you just don't want people to see your face, you know? At home I have to hide what I am thinking or they'll ask.

I have to be in the right head so I can walk in strong and tough.

In China a kid killed his folks with a knife because, he said, they neglected him. When he woke them up complaining that he was unwell they exploded and sent him back to bed. What was he thinking, crouching in his room? *Neglect? I'll show you neglect.* Whatever he thought, whatever they did or failed to do to offend him, his father had thirty-seven gashes in his hide. His mother got almost twice that, now what does that tell you?

It tells you that no matter what you think you're doing, they're there to tell you that you did it wrong.

You go along doing what you always did under the illusion that it's OK and nothing changes. Then menace creeps in like a cat when you aren't looking and goes to sleep on the hearth. Every once in a while it wakes up and licks its balls. It settles back down and watches through slits, regarding us with malevolent yellow eyes because unlike you, unlike Stephanie and me, it knows what's coming and it is content to wait.

There is a hidden clock set for an hour not known to us. Something big that we don't know about is counting down to detonation and everything we see and hear tells us that it is Dennis. Our own flesh and blood!

Sometimes mothers have to be Geneva, the neutral party juggling warring factions, trying desperately to make peace. I try, but this is nothing like Switzerland. My house is an armed camp. Stan turns on the boy at the least provocation. Look at him with his jaw set in stone and his shoulders bunched, waiting for the shooting to start.

Why is he all the time going around ahem, Dennis, how are YOU today, like we are friends? Like we were ever friends, when I know the bastard never liked me, hates the sight of me, doesn't want to be caught walking with me anywhere that anybody from the office will see, and when we do go out somewhere big and anonymous, like a basketball game, he's always fake-smiling at me with that tight mouth and a mean little squint. At least thank God he's quit trying to talk baseball or make me play racket ball with him, or fucking tennis, when he knows my hand-eye coordination sucks and if I see a ball coming at me, I flinch. I don't know whether I hate sports more than sports hate me but I'm fucking sick of it and I'm good and sick of being locked in here with the two of them, like we are in jail together, doing life. If I was old enough I'd join the Army and get blown away in some foreign country that parents never go.

Everybody knows the joke about the eight-hundred-pound gorilla, when he talks you listen, or is it, he sits down wherever he wants? We need to be careful with Denny because, until we see the size and shape of the hatred, we can't begin to deal with it. In Canada, I just saw on TV, the cops are hunting for a kid who shot his parents when he asked for money and they didn't cough up. He emptied their wallets and took off.

You bet I am researching these things on the web.

High school junior knifes his dad after a fight over the family car, and this is only last year. Almost makes it to the border before his mother phones 911 and the cops catch up with him, there's a documentary on it scheduled for HBO.

On the web, everybody has a theory. There's the outsider theory, the video-game/TV-violence theory, the suspicion that shooters were abused at home and then there's the chance that it's not something we failed to do, they destruct for no known reason because fate is arbitrary and vicious and it's nothing anybody did.

One psychologist thinks they blow up because the adolescent's brain isn't fully developed until he's twenty-one. So how do we get through the next six years with our big son? I try to get on Denny's good side, but I can make a 360 around the kid and still not know which side that is, unless he's turning as I do, so I'll never see. Sometimes I walk into a room and find him hunched in a corner like a bag of feed that somebody dropped on the floor, and I wonder, *How do I start the conversation.*

Do I say, "Who do you like for the World Series?" Or do I sit down creaking, so he and I are sitting with our backs to the wall, shoulder to shoulder, and go, *ahem?* When I think I have his attention I'll try this. It works on bad TV: "We need to talk."

Like that ever works.

When Stan does try to make nice, being Stanley, he says the wrong thing. Or Denny takes it wrong. One word and my firstborn clenches like a shaken fist. I love him, but, oh. It was OK when his dad outweighed him, but that was a while ago. Denny thinks that as he's bigger than Stan, he's probably smarter too. This is quite possible, but I wouldn't dare suggest it to Stan, who for reasons I can't fathom needs to be the personal best, no contenders, no argument.

They say every son needs to kill his father to become a man, but that's only in books. My men kill each other every single day. I'll admit it, Denny means well but he's a little abrasive. Like a bear cub that hasn't learned to sheathe his claws.

I love them both but my greatest fear is being pushed to the point where I have to pick one over the other. I just know it will happen sooner or later and I will do anything to prevent it. The least little thing sets them off.

What I hate most is the questions. Can't do this without them asking, can't go out wearing that, can't even think about another piercing, she checks my underwear before it goes in the wash and she isn't only looking for blood. Like, do they think I keep snapshots of all the crap things that happen to me? They are always around here, spying, prying, like, what ever happened to personal space? When I do go out they sneak around looking at my private things when all I want from them, all I want in the world is to have friends and be happy and for once, just one time be not bothered, as in, totally left alone.

Just now a boy murdered his parents three counties over, we saw it on the TV nightly news. The cops got out an APB. So, what happens next? Will he throw his girlfriend into the car for a joyride or drive on to wipe out the contents of a college dorm?

We're told to stay on the lookout, but what, specifically, are we looking for? No parent wants to be the sneaky, underhanded snoop who reads diaries and tosses the kid's room as soon as he leaves the house. My wife and I were brought up to respect people's privacy, and besides. We're scared of what we might find. The papers say, if you see a problem, reach out to your child. Easier if you know he won't bite your hand off.

If only he and his father would talk. They have so much in common: quick tempers, those big, fierce heads, the Esterhazy slouch. If they tried I know they could work it out, but they sit at the supper table like rocks and except for would you pass the whatever, they are so stony that it makes me want to weep. Because it is expected Stan will say "How's school" in that routine, doesn't-want-an-answer way. Then Dennis says "OK" just to get Stan to leave him alone. Stan grunts and that's the end of that and on weekends even that goes by. I hate the silence but if they do get talking, they'll fight so frankly, it's a relief.

I look at their hatchet faces and think: I'm so afraid.

They thought I was the one defacing lockers so I got detention, somebody that hates me used my personal hash, I don't care, the way things are right now, detention is the safest place to be. They ran it across a whole bank of lockers outside the girls' bathroom and in a way, it was kind of magnificent, scored into the metal like the one on my arm: DENY, so I don't care what they do to me, and at home if they get all pissed off about me being late, I'm all, so what, and the hell with them.

I'm telling you, the situation is dangerous. Book says sit the kid down for a heart-to-heart and that would solve our problems, but what do you say when you've been warned that the least little thing will set him off? How do you walk free when your wife cries herself to sleep at night and you personally are hanging on like a squirrel in a hurricane, too stressed to know what to watch out for, or which is the least little thing?

Beware root causes, they tell us, *Signs of depression. Talk of death.* So, what if your kid won't talk? Do you count cabalists drawn on his hands and all over his school notebooks? Is the skull gouged in the bathroom windowsill with his fingernails a sign? *Listen to your children.* Well, you don't live here, you psychiatrists and grief counselors. That's easy for you to say.

I try to talk to them, to bring them together, to make it all right but look what happened last night. I reached out to Denny, but he shrugged me off. I called after him, "Are you all right?" He left the kitchen so fast that I don't know what went wrong with his face, only that it was skewed. Stan tried to get through in his own clumsy way but Denny stalked away before he could clear his throat. Maybe if I put flowers and linens on the dining room table I could get him to stay. Instead of eating in the kitchen we'd sit down to candles, lemon slices in the iced water. Would we linger at dinner if I set the table nicely and pulled the dining room chairs close enough to touch?

Push comes to shove and this is intolerable. The waiting. The unfired shot.

Best-case scenario, I go looking for proof. It sounds ugly to say and it's vile to contemplate, but I'd love to shake out his clothes and watch needles or pills come rolling out, roofies or X or heroin, whatever gets authorities on his case because he's just too much for us and I can't do this alone. If I found hard evidence in his diary, detailed lists of future crimes, I could do this. If I saw death threats or a hit list on his hard drive we could move in on him, get it all out and get this over with. Back him up against the wall and have it out with him, and I don't mean intervention, I mean ultimatums that he'll agree to and honor to the death because enough is enough, and I need to lay down the law. Better yet, I find his cache of firearms in the basement or loaded pistols under the bed or blood on the pillowcase, proof that he sleeps with a knife. It would be awful, but at least we'd have a place to start.

Then I could photocopy the evidence or turn the computer over to the authorities or march my son down to the river and stand over him while he deep-sixed every single piece of mail-order artillery he's probably charged on my Discover card and stockpiled over the years. Then I would force Dennis to his knees and not let him up until he apologized.

Then he would know that I am not afraid and we are not to be messed with, not now and not in any other life.

Better yet—sorry, Stef—I could take him and the evidence to the police station and turn the little bastard in.

Meanwhile the papers boil over with news of kids who kill their parents and forget what they did. What did they think they were doing, routing out vermin or swatting flies? Is this all we are to Denny, pests he can exterminate and forget? It isn't safe! Stephanie and I know what to be afraid of, but in the absence of proof, we don't know what to expect.

I hate when people expect you to go around smiling, like it's your fucking job. Yesterday Diane went backstage with Dick Fletcher at play practice and they stayed there the whole time. Mr. Hanraty yelled so they sent a kid back with the message not to bother them, they were busy running lines, yeah, right. It doesn't matter anyway, she can't see me for shit and then I get home and Sunshine Stephanie wants to know did I have fun at play practice yeah well, fuck you too.

I guess I said something that either hurt Denny's feelings or made him mad and I still don't know if it was asking whether he'd eaten or mentioning the ugly scrape on his chin but he snarled and forgive me, I said, "If you're going to be like that, just go away," and he spat some insult I couldn't parse and stomped off to his room in such a rage that it shook the house.

This kid in England murdered his parents, just for the use of the family car, I read about it on the web. Took off on vacation with his girlfriend. Nice people, it's not like they beat him or some damn thing, they just said no. With every kid Denny's age a walking time bomb, what are we supposed to do? Should the wife and I arm ourselves so we'll feel safe coming out of our bedroom? Keep a gun in the bedside table or a shiv in the pocket of our robe? Probably. Every time I come out into the hall at night he's there and every time, it takes me by surprise.

"Agh!"

He sounds outraged. "Dad!"

How did he get so big? I hate surprises. "What are you doing here?"

"Going to pee." *I'm coming to get you.*

"Go to your room!"

I don't have to see his face. I know that look. *And when I get you . . .* but he shouts, "What am I, supposed to piss on the rug?"

If I had the right words I would say them and, zot! He'd disappear. Instead, I threaten. "I don't care what you do. Just go!"

He goes. Which of us wishes the other dead?

To prevent either, we need protection. The only question is whether to use Snuffy's Gun Shop, which means everyone on Broad Street would know, or buy on the Internet. But what if Dennis finds out because he gets off on hacking into my machine? What if he's waiting when the package comes? What if he's standing in the living room, locked and loaded, when Stef and I walk in the door? Or: smashes into our bedroom and blows us away?

Better forewarned, ergo forearmed.

Diane stuck her gum on my desk today, just left it in the corner when she went past, a perfect thumbprint, like a present for me, it's not like proof that she loves me, but my heart went up and stayed there until I saw her and fucking Dick Fletcher humping in the bushes outside the gym.

I love him, and I try so hard. Yesterday I made his favorite, blueberry waffles for dinner, with apple sausages, and he tramped through the kitchen without even looking and went on up to his room. How do you make it up to someone when you don't even know what you did?

You hate me? You hate your mother and you want to sneak in some night and murder us in our bed? Well, not on my watch, buddy. Not on my watch.

At the sight of the neat pistol I bring home from Snuffy's, Stephanie bursts into tears. "You can't," she cries. "This is Denny."

"And this is to keep us safe." Although I stand a little taller, I do not tell her that I really mean: *empowered.*

She whips her head around. Tears fly. "But he's just a baby!"

Now, Dennis hasn't been a baby since that thing when he was three. He claimed the puppy wanted to swim, but I knew. We are cohabiting with danger but to Stephanie, he's still her baby, which may be how things got so bad. When I'm not looking she indulges him, but I don't have proof. I suppose partly it's me, because the kid and I squared off the day she brought him home. Say his name and I bristle. There, it's out.

I'm embarrassed, but I'm not sorry. We know each other for who we are. I know he never liked me but we've survived so far on mutual respect. What does this mean really, when push comes to shove?

When he comes in tonight I will be waiting. One false move out of the little bastard and I tell you, push will come to shove.

When he was small I could take him in my lap and hug him and forgive him, no matter what he did, and I hugged him like that with his head close to me and his legs hanging down until one day he fought me with both fists, shouting, leave me alone, and when I asked him why he started crying and told me: I'm too big. I said, you're never too big, honey, but then I turned my back on the problem and now he is. On good days I can still call him—Denny? And when he comes into the room he stays long enough for me to ask him, Son, is there anything you want to talk about? when what I mean is, Is there anything you're afraid to tell me. I stand there thinking if only I could hug you but he backs away saying, Not really, Mom, and just in case I don't get it, just before he slams the door he says firmly, "No."

The paramedics leave me in the guidance counselor's office after the fight. I'm supposed to lie there until the bleeding stops. Then Miss Feely comes on to me all tremulous and wary, like, are you OK Dennis, you look like you're about to explode and I'm so fucking depressed that it comes out and runs down my face so I'm fucking embarrassed too. Then she starts spitting questions and I can't tell if she's afraid I'm going to walk into school tomorrow and start firing or if she's afraid I'm going to destroy myself but I am grateful for the attention either way, and I dutifully shake my head no when she asks are there problems at home. Then she talks and I sit there waiting for it to end. I'm not convinced but by the time she's done at least I have a thing to do. I won't exactly bring home presents but I'm going to, like, smile and be nice to Mom and Dad when I get there because they are the only people left. Besides, I feel sorry for them. I have a shitty life but at least I'm not old, like them. We could probably be miserable together until I get big enough to go out on my own. Lame, right? But it's a plan.

This is how a mother's heart breaks. As the gun goes off and his arms fly wide, my only son reaches out to me and his voice rips me from top to bottom, so I will be like this, laid open, until I die. My Denny isn't mad, he isn't even reproachful, he is mystified. "Mom!"

—*Postscripts*, 2008

The Attack of the Giant Baby

New York City, 9 a.m., Saturday, Sept. 16, 197-: Dr. Jonas Freibourg is at
a particularly delicate point in his experiment with electrolytes, certain
plant molds and the man within. Freibourg (who, like many scientists,
insists on being called Doctor although he is in fact a Ph.D.) has also
been left in charge of Leonard, the Freibourg baby, while Dilys Freibourg
attends her regular weekly class in Zen cookery. Dr. Freibourg has driven
in from New Jersey with Leonard, and now the baby sits on a pink blanket
in a corner of the laboratory. Leonard, aged fourteen months, has been
supplied with a box of Mallomars and a plastic rattle; he is supposed to
play quietly while Daddy works.

9:20: Leonard, aged fourteen months, has eaten all the Mallomars and
is tired of the rattle; he leaves the blanket, hitching along the laboratory
floor. Instead of crawling on all fours, he likes to pull himself along with
his arms, putting his weight on his hands and hitching in a semisitting
position.

9:30: Dr. Freibourg scrapes an unsatisfying culture out of the petri dish.
He is not aware that part of the mess misses the bin marked for special
disposal problems, and lands on the floor.

9:30½: Leonard finds the mess, and like all good babies investigating
foreign matter, puts it in his mouth.

9:31: On his way back from the autoclave, Dr. Freibourg trips on
Leonard. Leonard cries and the doctor picks him up.

"Whussamadda, Lennie, whussamaddda, there, there, what's that in your
mouth? Something crunches. "Ick ick, spit it out, Lennie. Aaaaa, Aaaaaaa,
AAAAAA."

At last the baby imitates its father. "Aaaaaaaaa."

"That's a good boy, Lenny, spit it into Daddy's hand, that's a *good* boy, yeugh."
Dr. Freibourg scrapes the mess off the baby's tongue. "Oh, yeugh, Mallomar.
It's OK, Lennie, OK?"

"Ggg.nnn. K." The baby ingests the brown mess and then grabs for the doctor's nose and tries to put that in his mouth.

Despairing of his work, Dr. Freibourg throws a cover over his experiment, stashes Leonard in his stroller and heads across the hall to insert his key in the self-service elevator, going down and away from the secret laboratory. Although he is one block from Riverside Park it is a fine day and so Dr. Freibourg walks several blocks east to join the other Saturday parents and their charges on the benches in Central Park.

10:15: The Freibourgs reach the park. Although he has some difficulty extracting Leonard from the stroller, Dr. Freibourg notices nothing untoward. He sets the baby on the grass. The baby picks up a discarded tennis ball and almost fits it in his mouth.

10:31: Leonard is definitely swelling. Everything he has on stretches, up to a point: T-shirt, knitted diaper, rubber pants, so that, seen from a distance, he may still deceive the inattentive eye. His father is deep in conversation with a pretty divorcée with twin poodles, and although he checks on Leonard from time to time, Dr. Freibourg is satisfied that the baby is safe.

10:35: Leonard spots something bright in the bushes on the far side of the clearing. He hitches over to look at it. It is, indeed, the glint of sunlight on the fender of a moving bicycle and as he approaches it recedes, so he has to keep approaching.

10:37: Leonard is gone. It may be just as well because his father would most certainly be alarmed by the growing expanse of pink flesh to be seen between his shrinking T-shirt and the straining waistband of his rubber pants.

10:50: Dr. Freibourg looks up from his conversation to discover that Leonard has disappeared. He calls.

"Leonard, Lennie . . ."

10:51: Leonard does not come.

10:52: Dr. Freibourg excuses himself to hunt for Leonard.

11:52: After an hour of hunting, Dr. Freibourg has to conclude that Leonard hasn't just wandered away, he is either lost or he's been stolen.. He summons park police.

1 p.m.: Leonard is still missing.

In another part of the park, a would-be mugger approaches a favorite glen. He spies something large and pink; it half-fills the tiny clearing. Before he can run, the pink phenomenon pulls itself up, clutching at a pine for support, topples, and accidentally sits on him.

1:45: Two lovers are frightened by unexplained noises in the woods, sounds of crackling brush and heavy thuddings accompanied by a huge, wordless maundering. They flee as the thing approaches, gasping out their stories to an incredulous cop, who detains them until the ambulance arrives to take them to Bellevue.

At the sound of what they take to be a thunder crack, a picnicking family returns to the picnic site to find their food missing, plates and all. They assume this is the work of a bicycle thief but are puzzled by a pink rag left by the marauder; it is a baby's shirt, stretched beyond recognition and ripped as if by a giant, angry hand.

2 p.m.: Extra units join park police to widen the search for missing Leonard Freibourg, aged fourteen months. The baby's mother arrives and after a pause for recriminations leaves her husband's side to augment the official description: that was a sailboat on the pink shirt, and those are puppy-dogs printed on the Carter's dress-up rubber pants. The search is complicated by the fact that police have no way of knowing the baby they are looking for is not the baby they are going to find.

4:45: Leonard is hungry. Fired by adventure, he has been chirping and happy up until now, playing doggie with a stray Newfoundland which is the same relative size as his favorite stuffed Scottie at home. Now the Newfoundland has used its last remaining strength to steal away, and Leonard remembers he is hungry. What's more, he's getting cranky because he has missed his nap. He begins to whimper.

4:45 1/60th: With preternatural acuity, the distraught mother hears. "It's Leonard," she says.

At the sound, park police break out regulation slickers and cap covers, and put them on. One alert patrolman feels the ground for tremors. Another says, "I'd put up my umbrella if I was you, lady, there's going to be a helluva storm."

"Don't be ridiculous," Mrs. Freibourg says. "It's only Leonard, I'd know him anywhere." Calls. "Leonard, it's Mommy."

"I don't know what it is, lady, but it don't sound like no baby."

"Don't you think I know my own child?" She picks up a bullhorn. "Leonard, it's me, Mommy. Leonard, Leonard . . ."

From across the park, Leonard hears.

5 p.m.: The WNEW traffic control helicopter reports a pale, strange shape moving in a remote corner of Central Park. Because of its apparent size, nobody in the helicopter links this with the story of the missing Freibourg baby. As the excited reporter radios the particulars and the men in the control room giggle at what they take to be the first manifestations of an enormous hoax, the mass begins to move.

5:10: In the main playing area, police check their weapons as the air fills with the sound of crackling brush and the earth begins to tremble as something huge approaches. At the station houses nearest Central Park on both East and West sides, switchboards clog as apartment dwellers living above the tree line call in to report the incredible thing they've just seen from their front windows.

5:11: Police crouch and raise riot guns; the Freibourgs embrace in anticipation: there is a hideous stench and a sound as if of rushing wind, and a huge shape enters the clearing, carrying bits of trees and bushes with it and gurgling with joy.

Police prepare to fire.

Mrs. Freibourg rushes back and forth in front of them, protecting the huge creature with her frantic body. "Stop it, you monsters, it's my baby."

Dr. Freibourg says, "My baby. Leonard," and in the same moment his joy gives way to guilt and despair. "The culture. Dear heaven, the beta culture. And I thought he was eating Mallomars."

Although Leonard has felled several small trees and damaged innumerable automobiles in his passage to join his parents, he is strangely gentle with them. "M,m,m,m,m,m," he says, picking up first his mother and then his father. The Freibourg family exchanges hugs as best it can. Leonard fixes his father with an intent, cross-eyed look that his mother recognizes.

"No no," she says sharply. "Put it down."

He puts his father down. Then, musing, he picks up a police sergeant, studies him and puts his head in his mouth. Because Leonard has very few teeth, the sergeant emerges physically unharmed, but flushed and jabbering with fear.

"Put it *down*," says Mrs. Freibourg. Then, to the lieutenant: "You'd better get him something to eat. And you'd better find some way for me to change him," she adds, referring obliquely to the appalling stench. The sergeant looks puzzled until she points out a soiled mass clinging to the big toe of her child's left foot. "His diaper is a mess." She turns to her husband. "You didn't even change him. And what did you do to him while my back was turned?"

"The beta culture," Dr. Freibourg says miserably. He is pale and shaken. "It works."

"Well you'd better find some way to reverse it," Mrs. Freibourg says. "And you'd better do it soon."

"Of course my dear," Dr. Freibourg says, with more confidence than he actually feels. He steps into the police car waiting to rush him to the laboratory. "I'll stay up all night if I have to."

The mother looks at Leonard appraisingly. "You may have to stay up all week."

Meanwhile, the semi filled with unwrapped Wonder Bread and the tank truck have arrived with Leonard's dinner. His diaper has been arranged by one of the Cherokee crews that helped build the Verrazano Narrows bridge, with preliminary cleansing done by hoses trained on him by the Auxiliary Fire Department. Officials at Madison Square Garden have loaned a tarpaulin to cover Leonard in his hastily constructed crib of hoardings, and graffitists are at work on the outsides. "Paint a duck," Mrs. Freibourg says to one of the minority groups with spray cans. "I want him to be happy here." Leonard cuddles the life-sized Steiff rhinoceros loaned by FAO Schwarz, and goes to sleep.

His mother stands vigil until almost midnight, in case Leonard cries in the night, and across town in his secret laboratory, Dr. Freibourg has assembled some of the best brains in contemporary science to help him in his search for the antidote.

Meanwhile, all the major television networks have established prime-time coverage, with camera crews remaining on the site to record late developments.

At the mother's insistence, riot-trained police have been withdrawn to the vicinity of the Plaza. The mood in the park is one of quiet confidence. Despite the lights and the magnified sound of heavy breathing, fatigue seizes Mrs. Freibourg and, some time near dawn, she sleeps.

5 a.m. Sunday, Sept. 17: Unfortunately, like most babies, Leonard is an early riser. Secure in a mother's love, he wakes up early and sneaks out of his crib, heading across 79th Street and out of the park, making for the river. Although the people at the site are roused by the creak as he levels the hoardings and the crash of a trailer accidentally toppled and then carefully righted, it is too late to head him off. He has escaped the park in the nick of time, because he has grown in the night, and there is some question as to whether he would have fit between the buildings in another few hours.

5:10 a.m.: Leonard mashes a portion of the East River Drive on the way into the water. Picking up a taxi, he runs it back and forth on the remaining portion of the road, going, "Rmmmm, Rmmmmm, RMMMMMM."

5:11 a.m.: Leonard's mother arrives. She is unable to attract his attention because he has put down the taxi and is splashing his hands in the water, swamping boats for several miles on either side of him.

Across town, Dr. Freibourg has succeeded in shrinking a cat to half size but he can't find any way to multiply the dosage without emptying laboratories all over the nation to make enough of the salient ingredient. He is frantic because he knows there isn't time.

5:15: In the absence of any other way to manage the problem, fire hoses are squirting milk at Leonard, hit-or-miss. He is enraged by the misses and starts throwing his toys.

The National Guard, summoned when Leonard started down 79th Street to the river, attempts to deter the infant with light artillery.
Naturally the baby starts to cry.

5:30 a.m.: Despite his mother's best efforts to silence him with bullhorn and Steiff rhinoceros proffered at the end of a giant crane, Leonard is still bellowing.

The Joint Chiefs of Staff arrive, and attempt to survey the problem. Leonard has more or less filled the river at the point where he is sitting. His tears have raised the water level, threatening to inundate portions of the FDR Drive. Speaker trucks simultaneously broadcasting recordings of "ChittyChitty Bang Bang" have reduced his bellows to sobs, so the immediate threat of buildings collapsing from the vibrations has been minimized, but there is still the problem of shipping, as he plays boat with tugs and barges but, because of his age, is bored easily, and has thrown several toys into the harbor, causing shipping disasters along the entire Eastern Seaboard. Now he is lifting the top off a building and has begun to examine its contents, picking out the parts that look good to eat and swallowing them whole. After an abbreviated debate, the Joint Chiefs discuss the feasibility of nuclear weaponry of the limited type. They have ruled out tranquilizer cannon because of the size of the problem, and there is some question as to whether massive doses of poison would have any effect.
Overhearing some of the top-level planning, the distraught mother has seized Channel Five's recording equipment to make a nationwide appeal. Now militant mothers from all the boroughs are marching on the site, threatening massive retaliation if the baby is harmed in any way.

Pollution problems are becoming acute.

The UN is meeting around the clock.

The premiers of all the major nations have sent messages of concern with guarded offers of help.

6:30 a.m.: Leonard has picked the last good bits from his building and now he has tired of playing fire truck and he is bored. Just as the tanks rumble down East 79th Street, leveling their cannon, and the SAC bombers take off from their secret base, the baby plops on his hands and starts hitching out to sea.

6:34: The baby has reached deep water now. SAC planes report that Leonard, made buoyant by the enormous quantities of fat he carries, is floating happily; he has made his breakfast on a whale.

Dr. Freibourg arrives. "Substitute ingredients. I've found the antidote."

Dilys Freibourg says, "Too little and too late."

"But our baby."

"He's not our baby any more. He belongs to the ages now."

The Joint Chiefs are discussing alternatives. "I wonder if we should look for him."

Mrs. Freibourg says, "I wouldn't if I were you."

The Supreme Commander looks from mother to Joint Chiefs. "Oh well, he's already in international waters."

The Joint Chiefs exchange looks of relief. "Then it's not our problem."

Suffused by guilt, Dr. Freiburg looks out to sea. "I wonder what will become of him."

His wife says, "Wherever he goes, my heart will go with him, but I wonder if all that salt water will be good for his skin."

COMING SOON: THE ATTACK OF THE GIANT TODDLER

—*The Magazine of Fantasy and Science Fiction,* 1976

What Wolves Know

When you have been raised by wolves people expect better of you, but you have no idea what they mean by *better.*

Happy comes out of the crate panting and terrified.

When you have been raised by wolves, you expect better of people.

Injured in the struggle before the dart bit him and his world went away, Happy blinks into the white glare.

A dark shape moves into the blinding light. Sound explodes, a not-quite bark. "Welcome home!"

This is nothing like home. Then why is the smell of this place so familiar? Troubled, Happy backs away, sucking his torn paw.

He hears a not-quite purr. "Is that him?"

"Back off Susan, you're scaring him. Handsome bastard, under all the filth." The dark shape gets bigger. "Hold still so we can look at you."

Happy scrambles backward.

"Wait, dammit. What's the matter with your hand?"

The not-quite bark-er is not quite a wolf. Pink, he is, and naked, except for fur on top, with all his pink parts wrapped like a package in tan cloth. It's a . . . Hunter is the first thought that comes. Happy has never been this close to one, not that he chooses to remember. He looks down. His body is choking. There is cloth on Happy too! It won't come off no matter how hard he shakes. He tears at it with his teeth.

The not-wolf yaps, "Stop that! We want you looking good for the press conference."

Happy does not know what this means. With his back hairs rising, he gives the wolf's first warning. He *grrrs* at the man. Man. That's one of Happy's words. And the other? Woman. The rest, he will not parse. The man grabs for him even though Happy rolls back his lips to show his fangs. The wolf's second warning. Now, wolves, wolves know when close is too close, and they keep their distance. With wolves, you always know where you are.

Wolves don't stare like that unless they are about to spring and rip your throat out, but unlike the wolf, man has no code. If Happy bolts, will this one bring him down and close those big square teeth in him?

"Hold still! What happened to your hand?"

Happy does as taught; he snarls. The wolf's last warning.

"Now, stop. I didn't bring you all this way to hurt you."

"Brent, he's hurt." The other voice is not at all like barking. "Oh, you poor thing, you're bleeding."

The man growls, "Come here. We can't let the people see blood."

Happy bunches his shoulders and drops to a crouch, but the man keeps on coming. Happy backs and backs. Oh, that thing he does with his face, too many teeth showing. Just stop! The more Happy scrambles away the more the man crowds him. At his back the walls meet like the jaws of a trap. He tips back his head and howls. "*Ah-whooooooo . . .*"

"Quiet! What will people think?"

"*Ah-whoooooo.*" Happy stops breathing. He is listening. Not one wolf responds. There is an unending din in this bright place but there are no wolves anywhere. Even though he was running away when the humans caught him, Happy's heart shudders. He is separated from his pack.

"Shut up. Shut up and I'll get you a present."

There are words Happy knows and words he doesn't know, but he remembers only one of them well enough to speak. "Oh," he barks bravely, even though he is cornered. "Oh, oh!"

"That's better. Now, hold still." When a human shows its teeth at you it means something completely different from what you are taught to watch out for, but you had better watch out for it.

The woman purrs, "Brent, you're scaring him!"

Woman. Another of Happy's words. The sound she makes is nothing like a howl, but he thinks they are kindred.

"Are you going to help me or what?" The man lunges. Should Happy attack? Other words rush in. Clothes. Arms. Clothes cover the man's stiff arms and he is waving them madly. How can Happy tear out the throat with all that in the way? Can he bring the man down before he pulls out his . . .

Another of Happy's words comes back. Gun. It makes him shudder.

"Brent, he's shaking."

"I'm only trying to help him!"

"Oh, you poor thing." Sweet, that voice. She sounds like his . . . Another word he used to know. *Mother.* Parts of Happy change in ways he does not understand. She says, "Look at him Brent, he's shaking!"

"Oh," Happy barks hysterically. "Oh, oh!"

"Come on, now. Calm down or I'll give you another shot."

The man makes a grab for him. In another minute those hands will close in his fur. Grief touches Happy like a feather, for like the man with his grasping fingers and not-quite barking, Happy is more pink than fur. It is confusing.

"Don't be afraid," the woman says. "Come on, sweetie, come to Mother."

Happy will not know exactly who he means when he thinks, *This is nothing like Mother.* It does not explain, but measures the extent of his confusion. In this and every other circumstance, Happy's position is ambiguous.

This is not one of Happy's words: ambiguous. He has been pulled out of a place he can't explain into a world he doesn't understand and it makes him sick with grief.

He doesn't belong anywhere.

"Oh," Happy yelps. Then more words come. "Oh, don't!" Although he has outlived his mother Sonia and half his littermates, in wolf years, Happy is still a puppy.

He does what any puppy does when cornered and outnumbered. He rolls over and shows his throat.

"For God's sake, kid, get up. What will people think? Get him up, Susan, they're staring."

Others come. Men. Women. People with—how does he know this—cameras! People are pointing their cameras. Kept out by the rope that protects the live baggage claim area, strangers jostle, straining to see.

There are words Happy knows and words he does not choose to understand. She growls, "You should have thought about that before you snatched him."

"Not snatched," the man says firmly. He says in a loud voice because they are not alone here, "*Rescued.* This is not what you think," he shouts to the onlookers. "This is my long-lost brother, I went through hell to save him."

"Stuff it, Brent. They don't care who he is or what you did."

"I rescued him from a wolf pack in the wild!"

She says, "They aren't interested, they're embarrassed."

He shouts, "They stole him from our family!" He is trying to get Happy on his feet but Happy flops every whichway, like any puppy. Brent tells the crowd, "When they found him, the police called me."

Happy gnashes at his hand.

"Ow!" Brent shouts over Happy's head, "Olmstead. My name is on the dogtag!"

Dogtag. It is confusing. Is he less wolf than dog?

"Hush, Brent," the woman says. "Let me do this."

Flat on his back with his paws raised, Happy lifts his head.

Unlike the pink man, the woman is gentle and she smells good. Hair. Not fur. Nice hair. Clothes like flowers. "Sweetie, are you all right?

Oh, that soft purr. Happy wriggles, hoping to be stroked, but there will be no stroking. What was that word he used to have?

Ma'am. It doesn't come out of his throat the way it's supposed to. At least this part comes back: if you can't speak when they make a question, you nod. Happy nods. She shows all her teeth ("See, Brent?") and he shows all his teeth right back to her in . . . Oh! This is a smile. You do it because they expect it. You always did. From nowhere Happy can name, there comes a string of words: *Songs my mother taught me.* Now, why does this make his heart break? He doesn't know what it means and he doesn't want to know where it's coming from. *Songs my mother . . .*

She touches his hair. Parts of Happy go soft and—oh! Another gets hard. Smile for her, she is soft in interesting places. At eighteen Happy feels like a puppy, but he isn't, not really.

Then she prods him with her toe. Her voice drops so he will know she is serious. "OK then, get up."

Slowly Happy rolls over and rises on his hind legs, although he is not all that accustomed. Susan shows her teeth at him, but in a nice way, and her voice lightens. "That's better. Let's get him in the car."

With wolves, you are always certain. Your wolf mother loves you. Get out of line and she will swat you. Gray Sonia did it as needed. Get too far out of line and your father will kill you. Happy bears the marks of Timbo's fangs in his tender hide—this torn ear, that spot on his flank where the gash is healing.

If you are male and live long enough, you will have to kill your father. It is the way of the pack.

The wolves aren't Happy's real parents. In a way this is news to him, but from the beginning he had suspicions. Happy's captor—er, rescuer—doesn't know what Happy knows, and what the boy knows is buried so deep in early childhood that it is only now coming to the surface. All his life Happy has run after the hope that the next thing will be better.

He only left the woods after Timbo tried to kill him.

He thought his real family would be kinder, although for reasons he only partially understands, he had forgotten them.

In fact, he was the last child in a big family. Happy made one too many, and the mother put him in clean clothes when they went out but at home he was forgotten, sitting for hours in his own messes. She yelled at him for being in the way. One did things that hurt, but he will not remember which person. When he cried nobody cared. They didn't much notice. He wasn't supposed to hear his mother snap, "And this one's my mistake."

Words are like weapons, no wonder he forgot.

The night the wolves took him, Happy was alone in his little stroller in a mall parking lot, hours after the family car pulled out with everyone else inside. He was so thoroughly combed and scrubbed that it may have been accident, not neglect that found him there in the dark, crying. A central fact about Happy is that he doesn't know.

He cried and cried. Then the wolves swarmed down on Happy in his stroller and the bawling toddler lifted his arms to them. The big males paced, slavering. The child didn't read their watchful eyes but Sonia knew. She turned on them, bunched and snarling. They backed away. Then she nosed Happy. He looked into her yellow eyes and clamped his arms around her magnificent neck. He buried his face deep in her thick white ruff. Timbo picked Happy out of the stroller and dropped him at Sonia's feet. The pack took the message and backed off. He has been running with them ever since.

The first thing Sonia did was rip off his little outfit with her teeth and lick him raw so he would smell of her and not the other pack, the one he quickly forgot. The only thing left of them was the scrap of metal dangling from his neck. Timbo wanted that off too. Even though he was the leader, Sonia rolled back her lips and snarled. It stayed. Happy ran with the wolves but the cold square tap-tapped on naked flesh, a sign that he was different. Sonia fed her new pup off her sagging belly and licked his tears away. Then she dragged him through dirt and rotting dead things until he was fit to run with the other cubs and from that night on she was his mother. The rule of the pack is: never get between a cub and its mother. He knew he was loved.

Timbo did not love Happy, but he protected him.

In time the pack forgot that he was not one of them. Howling to stay in touch, they ran at night, *ah-whooo,* ranging wide, *ah-whoooooo,* and with the knife he found on a dead man, Happy was as good a hunter as any. Even Timbo came to respect him. This, he thought, was all there was to life. The howling and the hunting, Happy and his littermates running free in the night.

When you are raised by wolves but are not one of them, time is never what you think. You do not age at the same rate.

Happy he was, yet living with the wolves, nursing injuries when his littermates grew up and the challenges began, Happy thought: *This can't be my real family. Some day my father the duke and my mother the movie star will come for me.* Where did these words come from? Who were his people, really?

The litters he ran with grew up much, much faster than Happy.

It was a mystery. The other cubs grew tall and rangy while he was still an awkward pup. They flirted and rutted, things Happy thought he understood and longed for vaguely but was not built to do. He was shaped all wrong, too young in ways Sonia would not explain to him; she was, after all, a mother and there are things mothers keep from you until it's time. His littermates frolicked and did things Happy was not yet old enough to do. When he tried to play they snapped: *don't bother me.* In time, he played with their cubs. Their cubs grew up. Sonia got old. Then Sonia died, and with Sonia gone, craggy Timbo began stalking him, licking his chops.

Now Happy was old enough to do all those things he had been too young to do before, and Timbo?

Timbo had to die. Happy had reached the age of kill or be killed. Wolves know that when you are grown, you have to kill your father. Kill him before he kills you.

He thought he could take Timbo in a fight and so he scent-marked a tree, making clear his intentions. The wolf's challenge!

He bunched himself as Timbo circled, snarling. Imagine his surprise. The gouge in his flank goes all the way from *here* down to *here*. Now, a wolf can lick all the hurt places, but Happy wasn't built to reach the places wolves can reach without trying. Pain drove him sobbing out of the woods.

When you have been raised by wolves, you know what to expect.

Foolish to expect better of people.

Nursing the fresh gash in his flank, he watched the building, men walking back in front of lighted windows. He heard a sound like a forgotten lullaby: human voices. He limped out of the woods, whimpering, "Oh, oh, oh." Then, when he least expected it, a word came to him. He pointed his nose at the sky. "Oh, help!"

He expected helping hands, kind words, but big men clattered out shouting, "Stop where you are!" They were nothing like he expected. Happy froze.

Somebody yelled, "What *is* that?"

Somebody else yelled, "Some kind of *animal*."

They were so angry! *This is nothing like I thought.*

Happy did what wolves do when they are in trouble. He howled. *Ah-whoooo.* One by one his brothers responded but the howls were scattered, the howlers far away. Wolves know never to come out of the woods, no matter who is calling. *Ah-whoooooooooo!*

The men pulled shields over their faces and raised their guns. Guns: a word Happy didn't quite know. In the struggle, the chain around his neck parted and the only scrap of his old life fell into their hands. Why did he imagine it made him special?

He limped back into the woods. The other wolves—his brothers!—smelled men on him. He was ruined for life in the woods and there was as well . . . what? The curiosity. When the men fell on Happy, he felt his flesh smacking into human flesh and there was no difference between them. Even clothed, his attackers were more like Happy than Happy was like the wolves. Like the missing limb that hurts at night, he felt the ghost family. Wolves run in packs or they prowl alone; they kill and are killed and that's the end of it. Men have families.

Night after night Happy doubled back on the clearing. He was drawn by half-remembered smells—hot food, the scent of bulky, not-wolf bodies— and sounds: music and forks clattering, the buddabuddabudda of low, not-wolf voices. Circling, Happy yearned for something he missed terribly. As for what . . . He was not certain.

Alone, Happy howled to the heavens. He wanted to bring out Timbo, even though he knew Timbo would kill him. *Ah-whooooo.* If they fought to the death, one way or the other it would end his confusion. Happy's howling filled the woods but not one wolf howled in reply. *Ah-whooooooo!*

The loneliness was intense.

This is why Happy did what wolves never do. For the second time, he left the woods. For a long time, he circled the police station. Then he dropped to his haunches on the front walk and howled to heaven. He howled for all he was worth. Unless he was howling for everything he was losing.

Now look.

The needle Brent used to get him out of the airport left Happy inert, but aware. They are riding along, he and Brent and this Susan, he can smell her. The car is much smaller than the van that took him to the hospital after the fight at the police station. They sewed him up and Brent came. Happy did not know him, but he knew him. He rolled off the bed and fell into a crouch, ready to lunge. Guards came. He struggled but the doctors gave him to Brent anyway. They said he was next of kin. Family.

. . . Brent?

It was on the dogtag. That's Brent's word for it. But why was Brent's name on the dogtag? *Am I his pet?* Happy wonders. *Do I belong to him?* He is no dog. He runs with wolves.

He does not like Brent. Keep your eyes shut, Happy. Keep them closed and he won't know you're in here.

He is riding along between them. The nice soft woman is soft, but not as nice as he thought. She says over Happy's head, "Why in hell didn't you hose him down before we got in the car?"

"It's not my fault he stinks."

"You could have put him in the trunk!"

Smelly breath mists Happy's face as Brent peers at him, but he keeps his eyes clenched. "Lie down with wolves and you smell like one. You hear?"

"Save your breath, he's out cold." The woman riding along next to him, what does this Brent call her? Susan. Susan gives Happy a little shake; his head rolls back and settles on her arm. "If you want him smiling on TV, you'd better revive him."

"Not now, Suze. Live at Five next Thursday."

"Like they aren't already waiting at Chateau Marmont?"

"No way! We can't go public until Dad makes the deal." *Dad.* The word Happy refused to remember. His teeth clash and his hackles rise. It is hard to keep from growling.

"You should have thought of that at the airport. Mr. Show Biz." She goes on in Brent's voice, "'I rescued him.' Like you didn't see the camcorders. Screen shots. Everybody knows!"

"Well, tough. Nobody sees him until the press conference. Dad is talking eight figures."

Happy's insides shift. He is confused. Wolves don't think in figures.

Brent barks, "Driver, get off at National."

"What are you *thinking?*"

"Gonna hide him!"

"Not in this town," Susan says. Distracted, she's let parts of herself flow into Happy. She thinks he is asleep. Parts of him flow back and she lets him.

"Outskirts. Inland empire. The valley."

She says, "Too close." Happy leans a little closer; she shrugs him off, but he slips back and she lets him. It is hard for him to keep from smiling. They ride along like this for a while. At last she says thoughtfully, "Your mom stayed back in Caverness, right?"

"She did," Brent says and then he just stops talking.

The car rounds a corner and Happy leans into the body next to his, but only a little bit. He can feel her voice vibrating in his bones. "Then take him to your mom's."

Warm, she is so warm.

"No way. She hasn't forgiven me for losing him."

Something changes in the car. "You lost him?"

Happy's ears prick.

The woman has asked a question that Brent won't answer. He says instead, "Come on, Susan. What are we going to do?"

"You lost your very own brother?"

"Not really. Well, sort of."

Happy is trying to make his mouth into the right shape to frame the big question. Even if he could, he knows not to bring it out. It is disturbing.

"Brent, what were you *thinking?*"

The fat man whines, "Mom *said* he was a mistake. I thought she would thank me, but she freaked."

Mom. Another word Happy can't parse. Oh. Same as mother. That word. Soft, he remembers. Other things. He will not remember other things.

"She never forgave Dad either."

"So he lives in L.A. Got that." Susan adds drily, "Too bad you can't divorce your kids."

"Could we not talk about this please?"

She stiffens—*is it something I did?* "Back there." Her voice goes up a notch. "Look. Tell me that's not a mobile unit."

"Holy crap, it's TV Eight. Driver, take Laurel Canyon."

The car goes around many curves and up, up, higher than Happy remembers being, and whenever they round a curve too fast he bumps against Susan's soft parts like a sleeper with no control over what he is doing, but in all the uphill and downhill and veering around corners he never, ever bumps Brent, not even accidentally.

He is aware of a hand waving in front of his closed eyes. A pinch. He wants to play dead but he can't stop himself from flinching. The needle bites. The world goes away again. He can't be sure about the days or the nights, which they are or how many.

Happy sleeps and he wakes up, then he sleeps again and in the hours they drive he can never be certain which is which, or whether the woman is touching him by accident or because she intends it.

At last the car crunches uphill and stops for the last time. Happy's head comes up. The smells when Brent hustles him out of the car and hauls him to his feet on the hard, hard street are terrible and familiar. They are climbing steps to a wooden . . . porch. Happy knows almost all the words now. Brent slaps the door and a remote bell rings. Footsteps come.

Terrified, he begins to struggle.

"Brent, he's waking up!"

"Not for long."

Happy yips as the needle goes into his butt. What they do and say when the door opens is forever lost to him.

When he wakes everything is as it was and nothing is the same. Will his life always be like this? Happy is curled up in his room. He knows it is his room because it used to be his room in the old life, and he knows from the sights and smells that nothing has changed here. It feels good and bad, lying in the old place. From here he can see the pretend bearskin rug in the center of the room with its plastic fangs and empty glass eyes, and lodged in the corner, the faded pink volleyball that he remembers from his very first time on the floor in this room and his very last day here.

When wolves quit the lair they stalk away leaving it untouched because they are done with it forever; they do not expect to come this way again. Is this what not-wolf mothers do?

Not-wolf mothers leave the lost son's room exactly as it was in hopes he will come back, but there is no way Happy can know this. He has no idea who he is or why he feels both good and bad about being back here, although he is a little frightened. He doesn't know why all this makes him miss Sonia so terribly or why, on that night so long ago, his hateful big brother slammed the door to the family car and let them drive away without him.

Brother. That's what Brent is.

Oh.

Happy would throw back his head and howl for Sonia but his hideout is constricted, the woods are lost to him and Sonia is dead now. He could howl for this other mother but before, when he was small and crying out lonely, she was a long time coming and when she did . . . There are things you don't remember and things you don't want to know.

Can you want to belong in two places at once and know you don't belong in either?

At least Happy is safe. When he came to, instinct sent him off the bed where they'd dumped him and under here, where they won't see him before he sees them. Holed up, he counts the cobwebs hanging from rusting springs. He wants to weep for the blue dogs and pink teddies cavorting on the plastic mattress cover. He is under his old crib.

When you can't go back to being what you used to be, you go back to what you were in the beginning. You were safe because she loved you, and Happy does not know whether he means the old mother, or Sonia.

The sounds in the house are so different from the crackle and whisper of the woods that it takes time to name them. The hum of the refrigerator, the washing machine grinding because—Happy looks down—they have changed his hospital rags for gray stuff like the clothes—clothes!—he used to wear when he was a . . . The bark of the furnace kicking in. A telephone ringing, ringing, ringing and soft voices: women talking, a strange man's voice downstairs in the hall. Brent is arguing with the other.

The smells in this house at this moment in his life are enough to break Happy's heart. He can smell mold in the foundations, laundry products; dust, in this room in particular; there is the residue of memory and oh, God . . .— *God?*—there is the smell of something cooking. Whatever else is going on in this place he used to know so well and had forgotten completely, *Mom* is baking brownies. Everything waters. Happy's mouth, his nose, his eyes.

It's getting dark, but nobody comes. Cramped as he is, stuck under the crib for too long when he is used to running free in the woods, Happy is restless and twitching. He thought by this time Brent would be in here raging; they could have fought. He could have killed the brother. Unless Brent jabbed another dart into Happy and dragged him out from under here. Instead the shouting stayed downstairs, sliding into the low, grating whine of a long argument. Then doors slammed and the cars roared away. Now there is no more talking. The machines have stopped. There is almost-silence in the house, except for the stir of a body he knows, approaching. What does he remember from the last time he heard her footsteps? Nothing he chooses to remember. Trembling, he pulls himself out from under the crib just long enough to run his hand along the bedroom door. He finds the lock. He loves the click.

There is a long silence in the hall outside his room. Then there is the soft footfall as she goes away.

Alone in the tight space he has created, Happy considers. Wolves are taught to lay back in this situation, and he is more wolf than anything else. He's been out cold for a long time, and there are problems. Wolves wake up ravenous. Happy hasn't fed since he came to in the crate and emptied his dish. Another thing: a wolf never fouls the den where he is sleeping. When the old house has been still for a long time he eases out from under the crib, unlocks the door, and leaves the room.

Where Happy loped along on all fours when he ran with the pack, race memory kicks in, now that he is here. This place he hoped to forget was not built for wolves. He stands and prowls the house on bare feet. She has left food: some kind of meat on the kitchen table, brownies. He empties the plate, pulling strings of plastic wrap out of the half-chewed chocolate squares before he swallows them. Now, the other thing? As Sonia's cub he never fouled the lair. There is a bathroom just off the kitchen. Happy cringes. What was he supposed to do back then, when he was small and trapped in here? Who used to hit him and hit him for forgetting?

He touches the nail where the belt used to hang and the ghost family rises up like the missing limb miraculously restored. Growling, he quits the house.

Can you ever walk out of your old skin and back into the woods where you were so happy, running with the wolves? There are no woods outside this house, just streets and cement sidewalks and metal fences around house after house after identical house; there are few trees and no hillside which means no caves, no undergrowth and no place to dig, where he can pull in brush to cover himself; it is worrisome and sad. The urban sky is like a cup with Happy trapped under it. He relieves himself and goes back inside. The old room is safe, now that he knows he can lock it.

His days don't change.

At night he goes out to eat what she leaves and to relieve himself. One night it was a meat pie, another, a whole ham.

People come. Sometimes they call outside his room, but Happy will not answer. The wolf doesn't howl unless there is another like him out there, howling or yipping the reply. Brent comes, but not Susan. In the long periods he spends curled under the crib, Happy thinks about this. Her body, expanding with every breath as they rode along in the car. The way it felt, and how he misses it.

If he can't do what wolves do, he understands, he wants to do what he *can* do with Brent's woman. How the parts go together remains a mystery; he only knows what he needs. Brent comes with a doctor, a talking-doctor, he says through the locked door. The doctor talks for a long time, but wolves have no need for words. The doctor goes away. Brent comes with a man who promises money. When you have nothing, you need nothing. Brent comes with another man, who makes threats. Wolves will not be threatened. When you are threatened, you go to ground and stay there. They go away. Brent comes back. He shouts through the locked door. "Just tell us what you want and I'll bring it! Anything, I promise, if you'll just come out so we can get started."

There is one thing, but Happy will not say it.

The brother hits a whine that Happy remembers from the time he refuses to remember. Oh. *That* Brent. This one. Same as he ever was, just older.

Brent snarls, "Dammit to hell, are you in there?"

No words needed here, either. None spoken.

Brent comes back with a woman. The scent brings Happy's head up. It is a woman. "He's in there? Why is he in there when he knows I'm out here?" She goes on in a loud, harsh voice. *"Do you know who I am?"*

It's the wrong woman.

"Listen, baby brother. This is your new agent standing out here in the cold. If you know what's good for you, come out and say hello to Marla Parterre. She can make or break you."

Time passes.

"She's from C.A.A.!"

The agent goes away.

The mother comes. *Mhmhmmm.*

Brent shouts. "How can we sell this story if he won't come out? Dammit, Mom . . ."

She says in the old tone that makes Happy tremble, "Don't you dare talk to your mother like that." He knows her voice, but he always did. He just doesn't know what she used to say to him.

"I'm calling Dad," Brent says. "Dad will get him out."

Then his mother says, "Your father is not coming back here, Brent."

"But Mom, he got us front money in six figures, and we have to . . ." Figures. Happy is troubled by the figures. Skaters, he thinks, short skirts, girls gliding in circles, and wonders how he knows. Women, he thinks, trembling. With their pretty figures.

"No." Her voice is huge. "Not after what he did. No!"

Brent brings a locksmith. There is talk of breaking in. She says, No. She says, over her dead body. Will Brent kill her? Happy shivers. They argue. She uses that huge voice on Brent and they go away. She bakes. Sometimes now, she leaves the food outside his door, hoping he'll come out to see. Happy lies low until she sighs and takes the untouched tray back to the kitchen.

At night she lingers in the hallway outside the room. She does not speak. He won't, or can't. Sometimes he hears her crying.

Happy waits. Sooner or later she always goes away. She leaves things on the kitchen table. Meat, which Happy devours. Fruit, which he ignores. Something she baked. She leaves the door to that old, bad bathroom open so he won't have to go outside to relieve himself. What's the matter with her, did she forget? The sight of the toilet, the naked hook where the belt hung, makes Happy tremble.

Outside is worse than inside. Nights like these make Happy want to throw back his head and howl. Alone in these parts, he could howl to the skies and never hear their voices. The other wolves are deep in the old woods, and he is far, far away. He wants to cry out for Sonia, for the past, when everything was simple, but one sound will bring police down on him with their bats and rifles, visors on bug helmets covering their faces.

Happy knows what wolves know. You never, ever break cover.

Wolves know what Happy is only now learning. He can't go back! Happy's feet are soft and his muscles are slack from days under the crib. He'd never make it and if he did, Timbo would outrun him in seconds. Timbo would kill him in one lunge, and even if he could kill Timbo? His parts and the bitch wolves' parts don't match. They have forgotten he was ever one of them.

He sits on his haunches and tries to think. He is distracted by the buzz of blue lights on poles overhead, where he is used to looking up and seeing trees; by a sky so milky with reflected glare that stars don't show; by the play of strident human voices in the houses all around, the mechanical sounds of a hundred household objects and the rush of cars on the great road that brought them here. Looking up at the house, he groans.

He doesn't belong in there.

He doesn't belong out here, either.

He gets up. Sighs. Stands back. Upstairs in the house, there is a single light. She is awake. Now he knows, and knowing hurts somehow. She doesn't go into her lair and sleep after she leaves Happy's door the way he thought she did. She sits up all night waiting. He steals back inside and goes upstairs to his room. Inside, he closes the door. Tonight, he will not turn the lock.

After not very long—did she hear or does she just know?—the bedroom door opens. She says his name.

"Happy?"

He always knew Happy was his name. This is just the first time he's heard it spoken since he joined the wolves and made Sonia his mother. Does Brent not know? The name Brent calls him is different. Is this big, leaden woman who smells like despair the only one who knows who he really is? In the hospital where the police took him, Brent shouted at the doctor like a pet owner claiming a dog that had strayed. "Olmstead. It's right here on his tag! Olmstead. Frederick."

Her voice is soft as the darkness. "Oh, Happy. I'm so glad you came back."

There is another of those terrible long silences in which he hears her shifting from foot to foot in the dark, pretending she's not crying.

She says, "You don't have to come out from under there if you don't want to."

She says, "Are you OK?"

It's been a long time since words came out of Happy; he only had a few when they lost him. He isn't ready. Will he ever be?

She says, "Is it OK if I sit down on the bed? I mean, since you're not using it?"

Words. He is thinking about words. He knows plenty now, all that talk going on outside his locked door. He has heard dozens. He could spit out a word for her if he wanted, but which one? He waits until she gets tired of him waiting.

She says softly, "I'm sorry about everything."

Then she says, all in a rush, "Oh, Happy. Can you ever forgive me?"

This is not a question Happy can answer.

There is a lot of nothing in the silence that follows. She is breathing the way Sonia did before she died. It's a rasp of pain, but the mother smells all right to Happy. Wolves know nothing of the pain of waiting, nor do they know anything about the pain of guilt.

Her voice shakes in a way he is not used to. "Son?"

Son. It does not parse. Happy rummages through all his words, but there is no right one.

The first morning light is showing in the window; Happy sees it touch the fake fur of the ruggy bear; he sees it outlining the hands she keeps folded on her plump knees and he watches as it picks out every vein in her sad, swelling ankles. She says, "It's all my fault, you know."

What should he do now, bare all his teeth the way they do, to show her he's friendly? Beg her to go on? Howl until she stops? He doesn't know.

She says, "I never should have had you." Slumped on the edge of the bed she leans sideways and tilts her head, trying to see under the crib where Happy's green eyes glint. He makes no expression a human could recognize, although Sonia would know it without question. She says, "Poor little thing."

A sound stirs the air, a kind of shudder. He wonders but does not ask, *Mother, did you sob?*

Her head comes up. "Happy?"

Startled, Happy looks inside himself.—*Did I?* There is nothing he has to say to her.

Then she just begins. "You don't know what it's like living with a man who beats you. I was pregnant with Brent and our parents forced the marriage, crazy thing to happen in this day and time, like it ruined his life to marry me, we had too many babies, and who—*who* got me pregnant every time? Do you see what I mean?"

Happy won't speak. The words come so fast that he chooses not to understand them. *Ow, it hurts!*

Never mind, nothing he says or does not say will stop her. "Hal hated his life so he drank, and the more he drank the more he hated it so he drank some more and the more he drank, the madder he got and nothing I could do or say would make him happy. Every little thing I did used to make him mad at me. The madder he got the more he hit me, but he never hit me when I was pregnant. Oh, Happy, do you understand?"

For another long time, they are both silent.

A long sigh comes ripping out of her. "You do what you have to, just to keep it from happening again. When anger takes hold like that, it has to come out somewhere. Look." She holds up a crooked wrist; even from here it looks wrong. She touches a spot on the temple; she doesn't have to tell Happy about the long white scar under the hair.

He tried so hard not to remember, but he remembers. On his belly under the crib, Happy watches her over ridged knuckles.

Again. She says it again. "He never hit me when I was pregnant." Her breath shudders. "So I had you. I'm so sorry!"

Happy strains to make out what she's trying to tell him but there is no way of translating it.

"I tried. I even named you after him!"

Frederick, he supposes. He supposes it was on the dogtag, but Brent says *his* name was on the dogtag, and Happy? Frederick is not his name.

In the still air of the bedroom, her voice is sad and thin. "My four big boys fought back when he hit them, so I had you. Anything to stop him. But this time." That sigh. "He didn't. Forgive me, Happy. I did what you do to make it through. I couldn't take it!"

The story she is telling is sad, but it's only a story. Wolves know that fathers aren't the only ones that hurt you.

"You cried. You cried so much. He got so mad. He came at me. He kept coming at me and oh God, oh, Happy. I put you in front of me."

Happy flinches.

"I couldn't watch. I left him to it." Relieved, she says in a light voice, "And that was it." As if it's all she needs to do.

Fine. If she is done, then, she'll leave. As soon as she leaves he'll get up and lock the door.

Then, just when he thinks it's over and he can forget this, she groans. "I'm so sorry, Son."

There is another of the long, painful pauses that wolves prefer to using words. Silence is clear, where words are ambiguous.

She says, "I never knew what he was doing. I didn't want to know."

She says, "I know, I know, I should have left him, but where can a woman go with four little boys and a baby? I should have kicked him out, but how would I feed my children then?"

The silence.

"So you do forgive me, right?"

Forgive is not a word wolves know.

"Right?"

He won't move or speak. Why should he?"

"These things happen, son. Things happen when people are stretched too far and their love is stretched too thin. Oh, *please* try to understand."

There is a long silence while she thinks and Happy thinks.

Just when he's beginning to hope she's run out of words forever, she says in a voice so light that it floats far over his head, "Then you got lost. And everything changed. He got himself a nice new wife and moved to Hollywood. After everything I did to make him happy. The others grew up and moved away. Until you came, I didn't have anything."

Happy doesn't expect to speak, but he does. The words that have been stacked in his head for years pop out like quarters out of a coin return.

"You didn't look for me, did you." It is not a question.

She sobs. "You don't know what it's like."

He does.

After a while she goes away.

Happy slinks to the door and locks it even before he hears her stumbling downstairs, sobbing.

"Can I come in?" Her voice is sweet. Just the way he remembers her. Even through the door, Susan is soft and he will always remember that body. He almost forgets himself and answers. Happy is stopped by the fact that except for the slip with the mother, he hasn't spoken. There are too many words backed up in him. He can't get them in order, much less let them out. He just doesn't have the equipment.

Instead he hitches across the floor the way he did when he was two and sits with his back against the door, putting his head to the wood. Feeling her. He feels her outline pressed to the other side of the panel, her heart beating. Susan, breathing.

"Don't worry," she says. "I understand. I just want you to come out so we can be together and be happy."

His fingers creep along the door.

"Happy," she says, and he will not know whether she is talking about their future or using his name, which is his secret. "You know, you're really a very lovely man. It's a shame for you to be shut up in there when you could come out and enjoy the world!"

Swaying slightly in time with that musical voice, he toys with the lock. He can't, he could, he wants to open that door and do something about the way he is feeling. With Susan, he won't have to wonder how the parts fit together.

Like a gifted animal trainer she goes on, about his bright hair, about how lucky she felt when she first saw him; she is lilting now. "It's sunny today, perfect weather, and oh, sweetie, there's going to be a party in the garden!"

Then he hears a little stir in the hall. Someone else out there with her, breathing.

"A party in your honor. Cake, sweetie, and champagne, have you ever had champagne? You're going to love it . . ." He does indeed hear music. Someone tapping a microphone. Voices in the garden. Behind Susan, someone is muttering. She breaks off. "Brent, I am *not* going to tell him about the people from Miramax! Not until we get him out of there!"

The brother. Happy shuts down. What else would he do after what Brent did to him? Things in this room, he realizes; Brent was that much older. Brent giving him a mean, sly look on his last night in this world he outgrew, letting their father hit the gas on the minivan and drive away without him.

After a long time, when it becomes clear that there's no change in the situation, Susan gets up off her knees—he can feel every move she makes—and leans the whole of that soft body against the wood. He stands too, so that in a way, they are together. She says in a tone that makes clear that they will indeed lie down together too, "Champagne, and when it's over, you and I . . ."

There is the sound of a little struggle. Brent barks a warning. "Ten minutes, Frederick Olmstead. Ten minutes more and we break down the door and drag you out."

He does not have to go to the window to hear the speech Brent makes to the people assembled. He can hear them muttering. He smells them all. He hears their secret body parts moving. They are drinking champagne in the garden. Then it changes. There is a new voice. Ugly. Different from the buddabuddabudda of ordinary people talking.

"Thank you for coming and thank you for your patience. ok, Brent. Where is he?"

It's him.

Brett whines, "I told you, Dad, I couldn't . . ."

"Then I will."

Another voice. The mother. "No, Fred. Not this time."

There is a smack. A thud. Under the window, the father raises his head and howls, "Two minutes, son. I'm warning you."

Happy's hackles rise. His lips curl back from bared fangs as in the garden under the window the mother cries, "I told you never to come here!"

There is a stir; something happens and the mother is silenced.

Him.

He commands the crowd. "Give me a minute and I'll bring the wolf boy down for his very first interview."

His father comes.

He will find that Happy has unlocked the door for him.

Big man, but not as big as Happy remembers him. Big smile on his face, which has been surgically enhanced, although Happy will not know it. Smooth, beautifully tanned under the expensively cropped hair, it is nothing like the angry face Happy remembers. The big, square teeth are white, whiter than Timbo's fangs. Even the eyes are a fresh, technically augmented color. Blue shirt, open at the collar. Throat exposed, as wolves will do when they want you to know that they do not intend to harm you. Nice suit, although Happy has no way of knowing.

"Son," he says in a smooth, glad tone that has sealed deals and gotten meetings with major players all over Greater Los Angeles. "You know your father loves you."

This is nothing like love.

Caught between then and now, between what he was and what he thinks he is, Happy does what he has to.

He knows what all wolves know. If you are male and live long enough, you will have to kill your father.

It doesn't take long.

Brent finds the door locked when he comes upstairs to find out how it's going. He says through the closed door, "Everything OK in there?"

Although Happy has not spoken in all these days, he has listened carefully. Now he says in the father's voice, "This is going to take longer than I thought. Reschedule for tomorrow. My place."

There is a little silence while Brent considers.

Happy is stronger than Timbo now. Louder. "Now clear out, and take everybody with you."

It is night again. The mother knocks. Happy has mauled the body, as Timbo would, but he will not eat. There is no point to it.

"Can I come in?"

He allows it.

There will be no screaming and no reproaches. She stands quietly, studying the body.

After a long time she says, "OK. Yes. He deserved it."

When you remember old hurts you remember them all, not just the ones people want you to. Therefore Happy says the one thing about this that he will ever say to her:

"He wasn't the only one."

"Oh, Happy," she says. "Oh God." She isn't begging for her life, she is inquiring.

It is a charged moment.

There are memories that you can't prevent and then there are memories you refuse to get back, and over these, you have some power. This is the choice Happy has to make but he is confused now by memories of Sonia. Her tongue was rough. She was firm, but loving. This mother waits. What will he do? She means no harm. She wants to protect him. Poised between this room and freedom in the woods, between the undecided and the obvious, he doesn't know.

What he does know is that no matter what she did to you and no matter how hard to forgive, you will forget what your mother did to you because she is your mother.

—Asimov's SF, 2007

Automatic Tiger

He got the toy for his second cousin Randolph, a knobby-kneed boy so rich he was still in short trousers at thirteen. Born poor, Benedict had no hope of inheriting his Uncle James's money but he spent too much for the toy anyway. He had shriveled under his uncle's watery diamond eyes on two other weekend visits, shrinking in oppressive, dark-paneled rooms, and he wasn't going back to Syosset unarmed. The expensive gift for Randolph, the old man's grandson, should assure him at least some measure of respect. But there was more to it than that. He had felt a strange, almost fated feeling growing in him from the moment he first spotted the box, solitary and proud, in the dim window of a toy store not far from the river.

It came in a medium-sized box with an orange-and-black illustration and the words ROYAL BENGAL TIGER in orange lettering across the top. According to the description on the package, it responded to commands which the child barked into a small microphone. Benedict had seen robots and monsters something like it on television that year. Own It With Pride, the box commanded. Edward Benedict, removed from toys more by income than by proclivity, had no idea that the tiger cost ten times as much as any of its mechanical counterparts. Had he known, he probably wouldn't have cared. It would impress the boy, and something about the baleful eyes on the box attracted him. It cost him a month's salary and seemed cheap at the price. After all, he told himself, it had real fur.

He wanted more than anything to open the box and touch the fur but the clerk was watching him icily so he fell back and let the man attack it with brown paper and twine. The clerk pushed the box into his arms before he could ask to have it delivered and he took it without question, because he hated scenes. He thought about the tiger all the way home on the bus. Like any man with a toy, he knew he wouldn't be able to resist opening it to try it out.

His hands were trembling as he set it in a corner of his living room.

"Just to see if it works," he muttered. "Then I'll wrap it for Randolph." He removed the brown paper and turned the box so the picture of the tiger was on top. Not wanting to rush things, he fixed his dinner and ate it facing the box. After he had cleared the table he sat at a distance, studying the tiger. As shadows gathered in the room something about the drawing seemed to compel him, to draw him to the verge of something important and hold him there, suspended, and he couldn't help feeling that he and this tiger were something more than man and toy, gift and giver, and as the pictured tiger regarded him, its look grew more and more imperative, so that he got up finally and went over to the box and cut the string.

As the sides fell away he dropped his hands, disappointed at first by the empty-looking heap of hair. The fur had a ruggy look and for a minute he wondered if the packers at the factory had made a mistake. Then, as he poked at it with his toe he heard a click and the steel frame inside the fur sprang into place and he fell back, breathless, as the creature took shape.

It was a full-sized tiger, made from a real tiger skin skillfully fitted to a superstructure of tempered metal so carefully made that the beast looked no less real than the steely limbed animals Benedict had seen at the city zoo. Its eyes were of amber, ingeniously lit from behind by small electric bulbs, and Benedict noted hysterically that its whiskers were made of stiff nylon filament. It stood motionless in an aura of jungle bottom and power, waiting for him to find the microphone and issue a command. An independent mechanism inside the thing lashed the long, gold-and-black striped tail. It filled half the room.

Awed, Benedict retreated to his couch and sat watching the tiger. Shadows deepened and soon the only light in the room came from the creature's fierce amber eyes. It stood rooted in the corner of the room, tail lashing, looking at him yellowy. As he watched it his hands worked on the couch, flexing and relaxing, and he thought of himself on the couch, the microphone that would conduct his orders, the tiger in the corner waiting, the leashed potential that charged the room. He moved ever so slightly and his foot collided with something on the floor. He picked it up and inspected it. It was the microphone. Still he sat, watching the gorgeous beast in the light cast by its own golden eyes. At last, in the dead stillness of late night or early morning, strangely happy, he brought the microphone to his lips and tremulously breathed into it.

The tiger stirred.

Slowly, Edward Benedict got to his feet. Then, calling on all his resources, he brought his voice into his throat.

"Heel," he said.

And hugely, magnificently, the tiger moved into place.

"Sit," he said, leaning shakily against the door, not quite ready to believe.

The tiger sat. Even sitting it was as tall as he, and even now, in repose, with glossy fur lying smooth and soft against the body, every line spoke of the coiled steel within.

He breathed into the microphone again, marveling as the tiger lifted one paw. It held the paw to its chest, looking at him, and it was so immense, so strong, so responsive that Benedict, in a burst of confidence, said, "Let's go for a walk," and opened the door. Avoiding the elevator, he opened the fire door at the end of the corridor and started down the stairs, exulting as the tiger followed him silently, flowing like water over the dingy steps.

"Shhhhh." Benedict paused at the door to the street and behind him the tiger stopped. He peered out. The street was so still, so unreal that he knew it must be three or four in the morning. "Follow me," he whispered to the tiger, and stepped out into the darkness. They walked the dark sides of the street, with the tiger ranging behind Benedict, disappearing into the shadows when it looked as if a car might pass too close. Finally they came to the park, and once they had traveled a few yards down one of the asphalt paths the tiger began to stretch its legs like a horse in slow motion, stalking restlessly at Benedict's heels. He looked at it and in a rush of sorrow realized that a part of it still belonged to the jungle, that it had been in its box too long and it wanted to run.

"Go ahead," he said congestedly, half-convinced he would never see it again.

With a bound the cat was off, running so fast that it came upon the park's small artificial lake before it realized it, spanned the water in a tremendous leap and disappeared into the bushes at the far side.

Alone, Benedict slumped on a bench, fingering the flat metal microphone. It was useless now, he was sure. He thought about the coming weekend, when he would have to appear at his uncle's door empty-handed ("I had a present for Randolph, Uncle James, but it got away . . . "), about the money he had wasted (then, reflecting on the tiger, the moments they had spent together in his apartment, the vitality that had surged in the room just once for a change, he knew the money hadn't been wasted). The tiger . . . Already burning to see it again, he picked up the microphone. Why should it come back when it was free again and it had the whole park, the whole world to roam? Even now, despairing, he couldn't keep himself from whispering the command.

"Come back," he said fervently. "Come back." And then, "Please."

For a few seconds, there was nothing. Benedict strained at the darkness, trying to catch some rustle, some faint sound, but there was nothing until the great shadow was almost upon him, clearing the bench across the way in a low, flat leap and stopping, huge and silent, at his feet.

Benedict's voice shook. "You came back," he said.

And the Royal Bengal Tiger, eyes glowing amber, white ruff gleaming in the pale light, put one paw on his knee.

"You came," Benedict said, and after a long pause he put a tentative hand on the tiger's head. "I guess we'd better go home," he muttered, noticing now that it was beginning to get light. "Come on"—he caught his breath at the familiarity—"Ben."

And he started for his rooms, almost running, rejoicing as the tiger sprang behind him in long, silken leaps.

"We must sleep now," he said to the tiger when they reached the apartment. Then, when he had Ben settled properly, curled nose to tail in a corner, he dialed his office and called in sick. Exhilarated, exhausted, he flung himself on the couch, for once not caring that his shoes were on the furniture, and slept.

When he woke it was almost time to leave for Syosset. In the corner, the tiger lay as he had left him, inert now but still mysteriously alive, eyes glowing, tail lashing from time to time.

"Hi," Benedict sad softly. "Hi, Ben," he said, and then grinned as the tiger raised its head and looked at him. He had been thinking about how to get the tiger packed and ready to go, but as the great head lifted and the amber eyes glowed at him Benedict knew he would have to get something else for Randolph. This was his tiger. Moving proudly in the amber light, he began getting ready for his trip, throwing clean shirts and drawers into a suitcase, wrapping his toothbrush and razor in toilet paper and slipping them into the shoe pockets.

"I have to go away, Ben," he said when he was finished. "Wait and I'll be back Sunday night."

The tiger watched him intently, face framed by a silvery ruff. Benedict imagined he had hurt Ben's feelings. "Tell you what, Ben," he said to make it feel better, "I'll take the microphone, and if I need you I'll give you a call. Here's what you do. First you go into Manhattan and take the Triboro Bridge . . . "

The microphone fit flatly against his breast, and for reasons Benedict could not understand, it changed his whole aspect.

"Who needs a toy for Randolph?" He was already rehearsing several brave speeches he would make to Uncle James. "I have a tiger at home."

On the train he beat out several people for a seat next to the window. Later, instead of taking a bus or cab to his uncle's place, he found himself calling and asking that someone be sent to pick him up at the station.

In his uncle's dark-paneled study, he shook hands so briskly that he startled the old man. Randolph, knees roughened and burning pinkly, stood belligerently at his uncle's elbow.

"I suppose you didn't bring me anything," he said.

For a split second Benedict faltered. Then the extra weight of the microphone in his pocket reminded him. "I have a *tiger* at home."

"Huh? Whuzzat?" Randolph jabbed him in the ribs. "Come on, let's have it." With a subverbal growl, Benedict cuffed him on the ear.

Randolph was the picture of respect from then on. It had been simple enough; Benedict just hadn't thought of it before.

Just before he left that Sunday night, his Uncle James pressed a sheaf of debentures into his hand.

"You're a fine young man, Edward," the old man said, shaking his head as if he still couldn't believe it. "Fine young man."

Benedict grinned broadly. "Goodbye, Uncle James." I have a *tiger* at home.

Almost before his apartment door closed behind him he had taken out the microphone. He called the tiger to its feet and embraced the massive head. Then he stepped back. The tiger seemed bigger, glossier somehow, and every hair vibrated with a life of its own. Ben's ruff was like snow. Benedict had begun to change too, and he spent a long reflective moment in front of the mirror, studying hair that seemed to crackle with life, a jaw that jutted ever so slightly now.

Later, when it was safe to go out, they went to the park. Benedict sat on a bench and watched his tiger run, delighting in the creature's springy grace. Ben's forays were shorter this time, and he kept returning to the bench to rest his chin on Benedict's knee.

In the first glimmer of the morning Ben raced away once more, taking the ground in flat, racing bounds. He veered suddenly and headed for the lake in full knowledge that it was there, a shadowed streak clearing the water in a leap that made Benedict come to his feet with a shout of joy.

"Ben!"

The tiger made a second splendid leap and came back to him. When Ben touched his master's knee this time, Benedict threw away his coat, yelling, and wheeled and ran with him. Benedict sprinted beside the tiger, careering down the walks, drinking in the night. They were coursing down the last straight walk to the gate when a slight, feminine figure appeared suddenly in the path in front of them, hands outflung in fear, and as they slowed she turned to run and threw something all in the same motion, mouth open in a scream that could not find voice. Something squashy hit Ben on the nose and he shook his head and backed off. Benedict picked it up. It was a pocketbook.

"Hey, you forgot your . . ." He started after her, but as he remembered he'd have to explain the tiger, his voice trailed off and he stopped, shoulders drooping helplessly; then Ben nudged him. "Hey Ben," he said, wondering. "We *scared* her."

He straightened his shoulders, grinning. "How about that?" Then with a new bravado he opened the purse, counted several bills. "We'll make it look like a robbery. Then the cops'll never believe her story about a tiger." He put the purse out in the open, where she would see it, and absently pocketed the bills, making a mental note to pay back the woman some day. "Come on Ben," he said softly. "Let's go home."

Spent, Benedict slept the morning through, head resting on the tiger's silken shoulder. Ben kept watch, amber eyes unblinking, the whipping of his tail the only movement in the silent room.

He woke well after noon, alarmed at first because he was four hours late for work. Then he caught the tiger's eye and laughed. *I have a tiger.* He stretched luxuriously, yawning, and ate a slow breakfast and took his time about getting dressed. He found the debentures his uncle had given him on the dresser, figured them up, and found they would realize a sizable sum.

"Hum," he muttered. "What would I most like to do today?"

When he had put on a bow tie and pocketed the microphone, he went into the city and quit his job. He cashed in the debentures and bought himself a new wardrobe at Rogers-Peet. At home, he tried on each new item to show the tiger before they took their pre-dawn run.

For some days he was content to be lazy, spending afternoons in movies and evenings in restaurants and bars, and twice he even went to the track. The rest of the time he sat and watched the tiger. As the days passed he went to better and better restaurants, surprised to find that headwaiters bowed deferentially and fashionable women watched him with interest—all, he was sure, because he had a tiger at home. There came a day when he was tired of commanding waiters alone, restless in his new assurance, compelled to find out just how far it would take him. He had spent the last of the proceeds from the debentures and (with a guilty twinge) the money he'd taken from the woman in the park. He began reading the business section of *The Times* with purpose, and one day he copied down an address and picked up the microphone. "Wish me luck, Ben," he whispered, and went out.

He was back an hour later, still shaking his head, bemused.

"Ben, you should have seen me. He'd never even heard of me but he begged me to take the job . . . I had him cornered—I was a tiger—" he flushed modestly.—"Meet the second vice president of the Pettigrew Works."

The tiger's eyes flickered and grew bright.

That Friday Benedict brought home his first paycheck, and early the next morning it was Benedict who led the way to the park. He ran with the tiger until his eyes were swimming from the wind, and he ran with the tiger the next morning and every morning after that, and as they ran he grew in assurance. "I have a *tiger* at home," he would tell himself in time of crisis, and then he would forge on to the next thing. He carried the microphone like a talisman, secure in the knowledge that he could whisper into it at any time and call the tiger to his side. He was named a first vice president in a matter of days.

Even as his career advanced and he became a busy, important man, he never forgot the morning run. There were times when he would excuse himself from a party in a crowded nightclub to take his tiger ranging in the park, sprinting beside him in his tuxedo, boiled shirtfront gleaming in the dark. Even as he became bolder, more powerful, he remained faithful.

Until the day he made his biggest deal. His employer had sent him to lunch with Quincy, the company's biggest customer, with instructions to sell him sixteen gross.

"Quincy," Benedict said, "you need twenty gross." They were sitting in a tiger-striped banquette in an expensive restaurant. Quincy, a huge, choleric man, would have terrified him a month before.

"You've got your nerve," Quincy blustered. "What makes you think I want twenty gross?"

" . . . "

For a second, Benedict retreated. Then the tiger-striping touched a chord in him and he snapped forward. "Of course you don't *want* twenty gross," he rumbled. "You *need* them."

Quincy bought thirty gross. Benedict was promoted to general manager.

With his new title resting lightly on his shoulders, he gave himself the rest of the afternoon off. He was springing toward the door on cat feet when he was interrupted in mid-flight by an unexpected silky sound. "Well, Madeline," he said.

The secretary, dark, silk-skinned, unapproachable until now, had come up beside him. She seemed to be trying to tell him something—something inviting.

On impulse, he said, "You're coming to dinner with me tonight, Madeline."

Her voice was like velvet. "I have a date, Eddy—my rich uncle is in town."

He snorted. "The—uh—uncle who gave you that mink? I've seen him. He's too fat," and he added in a growl that dissolved her, "I'll be at your place at eight."

"Why, Eddy! . . . All right." She looked up through furred lashes. "But I should warn you. I am not an inexpensive girl."

"You'll cook dinner of course—then we may do the town." He patted his wallet pocket, and then nipped her ear. "Have steak."

As he rummaged in his sock drawer that night his hand hit something hard, and he pulled it out with a crawly, sinking feeling. The microphone—somehow he'd forgotten it this morning. It must have fallen in among his socks while he was dressing, and he'd been without it all day. All day. He picked it up, shaky with relief, and started to slip it into his tuxedo. Then he paused, thinking. Carefully he set it back in the drawer and shut it away. He didn't need it any more. He was the tiger now.

That night, still rosy with drink and the heady sounds of music and Madeline's breath coming and going in his ear, he went to bed without undressing and slept until it got light. When he woke and padded into the living room in his socks he saw Ben in the corner, diminished somehow, watching him. He had forgotten their run.

"Sorry old fellow," he said as he left for work, giving the tiger a regretful pat.

And, "Got to hustle," the next day, with a cursory caress. "I'm taking Madeline shopping."

As the days went by and Benedict saw more and more of the girl, he forgot to apologize. And the tiger remained motionless in the corner as he came and went, reproaching him.

Benedict bought Madeline an Oleg Cassini.

In the corner of the living room, a fine dust began to settle on Ben's fur.

Benedict bought Madeline a diamond bracelet.

In the corner, a colony of moths found its way into the heavy fur on Ben's breast.

Benedict and Madeline went to Nassau for a week. They stopped at an auto dealer's on the way back and Benedict bought Madeline a Jaguar.

The composition at the roots of Ben's alert nylon whiskers had begun to give. They sagged, and one or two fell.

It was in the cab, on his way home from Madeline's apartment, that Benedict examined his checkbook carefully for the first time. The trip and the down payment on the car had brought his accounts to zero. And there was a payment due on the bracelet the next day. But what did it matter? He shrugged. He was a man of power. At the door he wrote the cabbie a check, grandly adding an extra five dollars to the tip. Then he went upstairs, pausing briefly to examine his tan in a mirror, and went to bed.

He awoke at three a.m., prey to the shadows and the time of day, uneasy for the first time, and in the cold light of his bed lamp, went through his accounts again. There was less money than he realized—he had to get to the bank to cover that check for the cabbie, or the down payment on the Jag would bounce. But he'd written a check for the last installment on the bracelet, and that would be coming in, and the rent was overdue . . .

He had to have money now. He sat in bed with his knees drawn up, mus-ing, and as he thought he remembered the woman he and Ben had frightened that first day, and the money in her purse, and it came to him that he would get the money in the park. He remembered rushing down on the woman, her scream, and in memory that first accidental escapade with the tiger became a daring daylight robbery; hadn't he spent the money? And as he thought back on it he decided to try it again, already forgetting that the tiger had been with him and, in fact, forgetting as he slipped into a striped shirt and tied a kerchief at his throat, forgetting that he was not the tiger, so that he went out without even seeing Ben in the corner, running in low, long strides along side streets and back alleys, hurrying to the park.

It was still dark in the park and he paced the walks, light-footed as a cat, expanding in a sense of power as he stalked. A dark figure came through the gates—his prey—and he growled a little, chuckling as he recognized her, the same sad woman—afraid of a tiger—and he growled again, running toward her, thinking, as he bore down on her, *I will frighten her again.*

"Hey!" she yelled as he rushed at her, and he broke stride because she hadn't shrunk from him in terror; she was standing her ground, feet set wide, swing-ing her handbag.

Eyeing the pocketbook, he circled her and made another rush.

"Hand it over," he snarled.

"I beg your pardon," she said coldly, and when he rushed at her with another growl, "What's the *matter* with you?"

"The pocketbook," he said menacingly, hair bristling.

"Oh, the *pocketbook.*" Abruptly, she lifted the purse and hit him on the head.

Startled, he staggered back, and before he could collect himself for another lunge, she had turned with an indignant snort and started out of the park.

It was too light now to look for another victim. He peeled off the sweatshirt and went out of the park in his shirtsleeves, walking slowly, puzzled over the aborted robbery. He was still brooding as he went into a nearby coffee shop for breakfast, and he worried over it as he ate his Texas steak. The snarl hadn't been quite right, he decided finally, and he straightened his tie and went too early to work.

"The Jaguar dealer called me," Madeline said when she came in an hour later. "Your check bounced."

"Oh?" Something in her eyes kept him from making anything of it. "Oh," he said mildly. "I'll take care of it."

"You'd better," she said. Her eyes were cold.

Ordinarily he would take this opportunity—before anyone else came in—to bite her on the neck, but this morning she seemed so distant (he decided that it was because he hadn't shaved) that he went back to his office instead, scowling over several columns of figures on a lined pad.

"It looks bad," he murmured. "I need a raise."

His employer's name was John Gilfoyle—Mr. Gilfoyle, or Sir, to most of his employees. Benedict had learned early that the use of the initials rattled him, and he used them to put himself at an advantage.

Perhaps because he was off his feed that morning, perhaps because Benedict had forgotten his coat, Gilfoyle didn't even blink. "No time for that now," he snapped.

"You don't seem to understand." Benedict filled his chest and paced the rug in front of the conference desk softly, still the tiger, but noting uneasily that his shoes were muddy from the fiasco in the park. "I want more money."

"Not today, Benedict."

"I could get twice as much elsewhere," Benedict said. He bored in as he always did but there seemed to be a flaw in his attitude (perhaps he was a bit hoarse from running in the early morning air), because Gilfoyle, instead of rising with an offer, as he always did, said, "You don't look very snappy this morning, Benedict. Not like a company man."

" . . . The Welchel Works offered me . . ." Benedict was saying.

"Then why don't you *go* to the Welchel Works." Gilfoyle slapped his desk, annoyed.

"You *need* me," Benedict said. He stuck out his jaw as always, but the failure in the park had left him more shaken than he realized, and he must have said it in the wrong way,

"I don't need you," Gilfoyle barked. "Get out of here or I may decide I don't even want you."

"You . . ." Benedict began.

"Get out!"

"Y—yessir." Unnerved, he backed out of the office.

In the corridor, he bumped into Madeline.

"About that down payment," she said.

"I—I'll tend to it. If I can just come over . . ."

"Not tonight," she sniffed. She seemed to sense a change in him. "I'm going to be a little busy."

He was too shattered to protest.

Back at his desk, he mulled over and over the figures in his notebook. At lunch he stayed in his chair, absently stroking his paperweight, a tiger-striped lump he had bought in palmier days, and as he stroked it he thought of Ben.

For the first time in several weeks he dwelled on the tiger, unexpectedly, over-whelmingly homesick for him. He sat out the rest of the afternoon in misery, too unsure of himself now to leave the office before the clock told him it was time. As soon as he could he left, taking a cab with a five-spot he had found in a lower drawer, thinking all the time that at least the tiger would never desert him, that it would be good to take Ben out again, comforting to run with his old friend in the park.

Forgetting the elevator, he raced up the stairs and into his living room, stop-ping only to switch on a small lamp by the door. "Ben," he said, and threw his arms around the tiger's neck. Then he went into his bedroom and hunted up the microphone. He found it in his closet, under a pile of dirty underwear.

It took the tiger a long time to get to his feet. His right eye was so dim now that Benedict could hardly see by it. The light behind the left eye had gone out. When his master called him to the door he moved slowly, and as he came into the lamplight, Benedict, gulping, saw why.

Ben's tail was lashing only feebly, and his eyes were dimmed with dust. His coat had lost its luster, and the mechanism that moved him in response to Benedict's commands had stiffened with disuse. The proud silver ruff was yel-low, spotted here and there where the moths had eaten it too close. Moving rustily, the tiger pressed his head against Benedict.

"Hey, fella," Benedict said with a lump in his throat. "Hey. Tell you what," he said, stroking the thinning fur, "soon as it's late enough we'll go out to the park. A little fresh air—" he said, voice breaking, "—fresh air'll put the spring back in you." With an empty feeling that belied his words, he settled himself on the couch to wait. As the tiger drew near, he took one of his silver-backed brushes and began brushing the tiger's lifeless coat. The fur came out in patches, adher-ing to soft bristles, and saddened, Benedict put the brush aside. "It'll be OK, fella," he said, stroking the tiger's head to reassure himself. For a moment Ben's eyes picked up the glow from the lamp, and Benedict tried to tell himself they had already begun to grow brighter.

"It's time," Benedict said. "C'mon, Ben." He started out the door and down the hall, going slowly. The tiger followed him creakily, and they began the painful trip to the park.

Several minutes later the park gates loomed reassuringly, and Benedict pushed on, sure, somehow, that once the tiger was within their shelter his strength would begin to return. And it seemed true at first, because the dark-ness braced the tiger in some gentle way, and he started off springily when Benedict turned to him and said, "Let's go."

Benedict ran a few long, mad steps, telling himself the tiger was right behind him and then slowed, pacing the tiger, because he realized now that if he ran at full strength Ben would never be able to keep up with him. He went at a respectable lope for some distance, and the tiger managed to keep up, but then he found himself going slower and slower as the tiger, trying gallantly, moved his soft feet in the travesty of a run.

Finally Benedict went to a bench and called him back, head lowered so the tiger wouldn't see he was almost crying.

"Ben," he said, "forgive me."

The big head nudged him and as Benedict turned, the faint light from the one good eye illumined his face. Ben seemed to comprehend his expression, because he touched Benedict's knee with one paw, looking at him soulfully with his brave blind eye. Then he flexed his body and drew it under him in a semblance of his own powerful grace and set off at a run, heading for the artificial lake. The tiger looked back once and made an extra little bound, as if to show Benedict that he was his old self now, that there was nothing to forgive, and launched himself in a leap across the lake. He started splendidly but it was too late—the mechanism had been unused for too long now, and just as he was airborne it failed him and the proud, flying body stiffened in midair and dropped, rigid, into the lake.

When he could see well enough to make his way to the lake Ben went forward, grinding tears from his eyes. Dust—a few hairs—floated on the surface, but that was all. Thoughtfully, Benedict took the microphone from his pocket and dropped it in the lake. He stood, watching the lake until the first light of morning came raggedly through the trees. He was in no hurry because he knew without being told that he was finished at the office. He would probably have to sell the new wardrobe, the silver brushes, to meet his debts, but he was not particularly concerned. It seemed appropriate, now, that he should be left with nothing.

—*The Magazine of Fantasy and Science Fiction*, 1964

Wherein We Enter the Museum

Spike D'Arthenay

Outstanding, we're the first ones in.

Until today, only authorized personnel made it through the electrified gates to the Museum—builders, painters, plumbers and electricians, tech support and curators. Next month the hundred galleries open for the great American public to look on the works of the mighty and admire.

If the public wants to come.

Today there's nobody here but us. They want us going in all *tabula rasa,* with nobody around to get between us and The Donor's intentions. Like we're his special, expensive, living crash test dummies or the canaries that they drop into mines to test the air. If we come back dead, will he put off the Grand Opening another year?

Stupid gig, but for people like us, success hangs on stupid things. The Donor is intolerably rich and seriously *connected.* He says who gets remembered here, and who ends on the Remainders heap. Do this right and we get our own pedestals. Or our portrait in the 'Oughties hall. Worst-case scenario: a footnote on The Wall of Fame.

In a business built on making something out of nothing, you travel on hope. You hope you can do it, hope it's good, hope to God somebody will take it and you'll get paid, reviewed. Remembered. It's about making it. It's always about making it, but.

Through every gallery in this place? Out alive?

Too soon to tell.

We don't have long. In today, out by Thursday, and the marble monster crouching on the hilltop is enormous. You could land a Learjet on that roof, and on the facade . . . Holy crap. The facade.

Bronze block letters stomp across the marble, shouting:

THE MUSEUM OF GREAT AMERICAN WRITERS

Gasping, Charlee gropes for my hand, but I'm too wild and distracted to grope back.

Stan yips like a virgin *interruptus,* and somebody—Melanie?—goes, "Wow." One of us—me?—says, "It's so big." Thinking: *we are so small.*

Stan glares, thinking whatever Stan thinks.

"All for one." Charlee's voice flutters up. "Right?"

"As if!" In those wide boots, Mel looks like a castaway raised by pirates. Tough girl, she races Stan up the steps and hammers on the bell. I'm not the only one thinking, *me, me!*

Electronically controlled from *somewhere,* the bronze doors swing wide.

Mr. Me-First muscles past. "Onward and upward with the fucking arts."

Our ears pop as the doors snap shut behind us like the doors to a new Rolls-Royce. Charlee says into the hush, "We're here," but we are neither here nor there.

With one exception, all the doors leading out of the Rotunda are locked but one. That one, we are avoiding. For reasons. We're stranded until the docent brings the keys, four wannabes eddying around a mammoth bronze.

The craggy hulk dominates the Rotunda like the centerpiece at an A-list banquet, too bad we're not invited. It's just like the Iwo Jima Memorial but bigger, and those aren't Marines struggling to raise the flag. This sculptor put Thoreau and Emerson and Hawthorne and Louisa May Alcott up there, struggling with the flagpole; the rockets' red glare turns out to be a light show in the dome and, Right. The flag lights up as we approach.

Stan says, "THE TRANSCENDENTALISTS, how over are they?" and frankly, he has a point.

All the statues in niches ringing the Rotunda are of people like that, as in, long dead and too gone to be competition: Theodore Dreiser and Willa Cather and Richard Wright, along with Frank Norris; so, what did he write? Plus Margaret Mitchell that we all know about but face it, she's dead, and a bunch of others I've never heard of, as well as Michael Wigglesworth who, in the posterity sweepstakes, is not what you would call a threat, so, in my career? No problem.

Every museum has to make its manners to the past, but face it. Who cares which hairy old scribblers mattered back in the pen-and-ink days before we had Twitter so everybody knew?

Mel backs off to take a screen shot of the bronze to post at TwitPic, gropes for her phone and smacks her head: DOH! They took our electronics at the checkpoint. The Committee sent us in here with nothing but a floor plan: no equipment, no flashlights, no walkie-talkies or signal flares, not even a ball of string or bag of Goldfish or a Post-it pad to mark our trail in this or any other part of the forest. Which, until they bring the keys, is immaterial.

We do what we have to. We open the door that we've all been avoiding. It leads to the ultimate dead end.

A placard on an easel just inside states our condition. Stan and Mel, Charlee and I are in that very special place the world reserves for writers. It's called:

THE WAITING ROOM

Waiting is all we are.

Stan crashes on this sprawling hydra of a visitors' bench, with seven carved settees fanning out from a central post. Carved busts like figureheads mark the end of every seat.

Portraits, but of—who?

Pacing, Mel studies them. "OK, this looks like Joyce Carol Oates but isn't, and this one looks like what's-her-name that wrote *The Devil Wears Prada*-type memoir about working for J. D. Salinger? And—owait, where *is* Salinger, is he in the main gallery, and does he have a whole hall to himself? He deserves a shrine, and . . . Ack, here's Bret Easton Ellis. So, is this the *salon des refusés*? or what?"

"More like the vestibule of the uncreated." Why am I so tired?

"Don't, Spike."

"No. We belong." Stan goes all crown prince on us, yelling, "INSIDE."

Charlee does her wafting, drifting thing, for she is a poet. "Like we're God's focus group."

"This isn't a temple, Char."

"In a way, it is. And we're . . ."

"Nobody. Until we become somebody." Would I step on my grad school lover's head to be remembered here?

Stan snarls, "Shut up! They could be listening."

"Well, if you're listening, bring the damn keys!"

Posturing for the hidden camera, my Charlotte murmurs, "So much history."

I think, *We are so few.*

The Donor

I had a dream, I have money. I dreamed until I saw it clear, and it was perfect. Then I announced.

They came at me with a committee and everything went to hell.

Six of my billions went into my tribute to our nation's unsung heroes, the place is almost finished, but they came at me with a committee, and nothing is like I thought.

One man's vision counts for nothing in this world.

Our nation's capitol would be the perfect site. We have the Air and Space Museum, we have the National Art Galleries, I found a spot for **The Museum of Great American Writers** right in the middle of the National Mall. I sketched my dream building and paid a guy to paint it in oils. Then I went to see The Man.

The President's man had the temerity to turn me down. "Not right for Independence Avenue," he said, but money talks. The President took an interest. It was flattering. It threw me off my guard, and the next thing I knew, every city and big small town in the country threw its name in the hat, like sub-teens entering a beauty pageant. So before I settled on Boise, I had to visit them all.

Now, I made my money in munitions. I make my own decisions and I make them fast. You know what you've got and when a problem comes up, you don't ask. You tell. The President's man sent me out looking for another city. He appointed a site manager, nothing but the best. He hired an architect. She hired more. The Committee met.

Some fool said, "Let's start by making sure we're all on the same page," and it's been downhill ever since. Do you know what it's like, bombing along in your Learjet with The Committee wrangling until the windows frost over and your brain fries? Do you know what it's like, knowing there are two more planes full of jabbering opinionaters hard on your tail?

I hate them, I hate all the bloviating and I hate this *consensus* thing, like their *Committee* is in charge of making up my mind. *Get the hell out of my mind.*

Look what they did to my dream! All I ever wanted was to honor my idols, Dink Stover and Mark Twain and the guy who wrote *Silas Marner* that we all read in high school that made such a big impression on me. Oh, and Henry Wadsworth Longfellow, the greatest American writer of them all, *By the shores of Gitche Gumee* . . . but The Committee . . .

I give them the classics and they smother me with the new. The pretentious fuckers turned up their noses at everybody but Twain. They tried to tell me this guy George Eliot that wrote *Silas Marner* wasn't American! They had the nerve to claim he wasn't even a guy. I had a dream. It was ten years in the building, and now this. They have boiled down my personal tribute to our country's greatest writers into some kind of Hungarian Goulash. Who is this Gary Shteyngart anyway?

E.g. in the matter of the Rotunda, they railroaded me. What's so great about a bunch of nineteenth-century ditherers instead of the truly great writer I wanted honored here: JAMES FENIMORE COOPER. *The Last of the Mohicans,* do you not agree with me that he is great? Oh, I got my Cooper portrait and a Mohican chief's headdress the dealer told me he'd worn but the COOPER COR-NER is stuck in some alcove at the far end of the Middle American wing, and the statue in the lobby? Not my dream.

When I grew up we read the classics, I mean, "Hiawatha" and William Cullen Bryant, who is this Robert Lowell anyway, did this Amy Lowell, his fat, cigar-smoking mama, rope him into poetry to keep the business in the family? And the Henry James Room? In high school we read "The Wreck of the Hesperus," which I personally wanted in the diorama in the Middle American Wing. Instead The Committee got the entire James family, which does not include Jesse, in wax, and if you ask me, it's an effete piece of crap. Every time I laid out an idea, The Committee came back at me with The Canon, The ostensible Necessary Names, and I never heard of most of them, and the ones I have heard of? I don't approve.

I had a dream, and you fools came at me with all these newfangled-come-latelies that mean nothing to me, but in the course of many arguments and even longer wrangles, The Committee prevailed. A Committee is like a dinosaur. It isn't very fast and it isn't very smart, but when it steps on you, it mashes you flat. The Committee always gets what it wants. Well, not this time. Who, I ask you, is picking up the tab?

Me. It's my money, and money talks. They want newfangled? Well, I'll newfangle them.

I went to one of these sandbox Play-Doh Creative Writing Programs that everybody takes on about, and I got me some shiny new MFAs with the sticker tags still on. In terms of Great American Writers according to The Committee, these kids are the newest-fangled of the new. MFA means Master of Fine Arts, if you want to know.

Like Longfellow and George Eliot and Washington Irving needed any stupid *writing school.*

My four just-hatched MFAs are in there right now, inspecting, so let's see what these *writing students* make of **The Museum of Great American Writers**. What they make of The Committee's idea of greatness, as in whether they think it's inspirational or make fun of it or destroy what's left of my dream. And *You can't hear me, people, but I am watching.*

Depending on how it goes down with them, I decide.

Either the place plays well and I let this sad, corrupted dream of mine stand in the ruined state it got dragged into by The Committee, or I trigger the hundreds fuses set by the workers from my factory, which I can do from here.

I'm a self-made man. I make my own decisions, and I make them fast.

I emptied all my warehouses to prepare. My night people packed the walls in every corridor and gallery in the place with my complete inventory, nuclear and pre-nuclear, and if I don't like the way **The Museum of Great American Writers** plays for these kid writers, I blow the place to hell.

The Docent

Look at them posturing for the hidden cameras, all puffed up and self-important, like it's only a matter of time before their puerile screeds turn into gold and their place in history is assured. They look thirteen! Naive little twards, do they really believe they matter here? Listen to them yelling, "Bring it on!" like I am the dull servant and they are masters of the universe. Do they not know what they are? The Committee's cuddly gerbils, two slick literary GI Joes and one Punk Barbie and one Poet Barbie in their trendy, struggling-writer clothes. They, and not I, will run the literary Habitrail, not because they're good. Because they're cute.

They, and not I, Wilfred Englehart, will be in the Museum's promotional video, stars of the viral podcast, three-minute commercials and a selling five-minute spot scheduled to burst onscreen in every cineplex, airport waiting room, hotel lobby, club and sports bar in the land, because the object of this empty exercise is not what these pretty children think. Nobody wants them to observe and report, nobody cares what they think and they're certainly not on The Committee's Wait List, coming to a pedestal near you. Like their pretentious scribbles will be honored here.

They're nothing but glossy marketing tools, fated to be kicked offstage with half the exhibits in this temple to art. Left behind by the parade of Great American Literature as it marches on, into posterity and beyond.

The Museum advertises Great Writers, but, if you want to know the truth, they aimed for the red-hot center of literature and missed.

Norman Mailer, Gore Vidal, F. Scott Fitzgerald indeed! And whose idea was Louis Bromfield or for that matter, Edwin Arlington Robinson and who, I ask you, is Pearl S. Buck? There are, believe me, millions of unknown, unsung, unread writers far more deserving of places in this Museum.

Such as myself.

When I finish my Perpetual Novel, that I am writing for the ages, which I started in graduate writing school in the Seventies and will continue adding to every mortal day for the rest of my life, the world will know. At ten pages a day it's slow, but sure. I will have a place here. Maybe even a whole hall. Genius is recognized. Unfortunately, posterity is on hold until history discovers me, an event that has to wait until death writes FINIS to my tome, although I keep a safe deposit box with a printout and INSTRUCTIONS TO BE CARRIED OUT ON MY DEMISE.

Ten pages a day, seven days a week, month in, month out, it's been forty years since I wrote THE BEGINNING to my Magnum O, thousands of pages and I'm still in *Era One: The Dawning,* the project is that ambitious, the writing is that grand.

You see, my novel is about the history of the world, told from the point of view of a column of stone.

You wondered about the origins of certain phenomena—the Easter Island faces, the Costa Rican Balls. Add to that my fabulous narrator, the noble, omniscient Colombian Column, which stands a stone's throw from the world's greatest river, the unfathomable Amazon.

My protagonist is brilliant. Mysterious. Column doesn't interact, he's too deep.

He thinks.

Like me. If it wasn't for that wretched buzzer, I'd love to sit down and read you my best bit—it's when the Vikings . . . Oh, never mind. The children down there are impatient. The big, messy one is swinging his arms, hurling small objects around The Waiting Room, and I have to go before he breaks something.

Instead of communing with my noble Column, I have to abandon Art and go downstairs and read the blather printed on this ridiculous card. It's The Committee's insipid *Welcoming Speech.* Gifted, intellectual unsung writer that I am, I have to spout their illiterate platitudes, which are, essentially, a pitch. My position here in **The Museum of Great American Writers** is to sideline Art and waste myself on VIP tours—celebrities who have millions to give, media magnates, rich industrialists, visiting heads of state, day after depressing, despicable day, and instead of working on my Perpetual Novel or saying what I really think of this marble travesty, I have to read it off a card.

Stanley Krakowski

Fuck you, pretentious little fucker in your pretentious five-button vest.

I was not about to stand there listening, I mashed the flat of my hand in his face and grabbed a key. That makes me the first one into one of their holy galleries, and, shit.

Is this as good as it gets?

I mean, why make people run through several stupendously boring rooms before they get to any place that isn't just books, is this a museum or what? In terms of exhibitions, who wants to waste time wading through a bunch of bookshelves to get to the good part?

Books are so boring that I wanted to curl up under a showcase and take a nap, but fortunately I came around a corner and into this great big treasure house of *stuff.*

THE HALL OF LITERARY OBJECTS. So, cool!

It took forever to get here, but I don't care. It's totally worth your dime. Look, they've got Herman Melville's underwear, and here's the typewriter Sinclair Lewis wrote *Main Street* on and holy fuck, that's Grip the Raven, all stuffed and glaring at me with beady glass eyes and they've got its beak open because it's croaking on a loop, you guessed it: "Nevermore," but wait! If that isn't Edmund Wilson's puppet stage over there in that tall glass case . . . OMG, there's a life-sized animatronic Edmund Wilson standing behind that mini-stage, push this button and he does his puppet show. Although, next to the mini-dioramas, e.g. Margaret Mitchell watching Atlanta burn, it kind of palls, to say nothing of the oceanic dioramas with figures sloshing in a perpetual wave in the Nautical Ell. You get to see Hart Crane jumping off a boat, and a mini-Katherine Anne Porter on her Ship of Fools with her hand clamped on her chest like an admiral going down with his ship, and look!

There's Flannery O'Connor's favorite peacock. Dead, but looking real as life, although it doesn't squall when you punch it, and where did they get this roll of toilet paper labeled *notes for On the Road*?

Are those really James Whitcomb Riley's baby teeth, and how did Edward Gorey's shrunken head collection end up here, in hatboxes built to come with? You could spend a lifetime in this place, but, come on. A feather from a head-dress belonging to Louise Erdrich, really? Chopsticks once used by Amy Tan?

Then I find a waxwork of James Patterson standing at his *very special table,* and everything clicks into place. And here's Stephanie Meyer, *very lifelike,* plus Charlaine Harris, *kaftan much?* and Harold Robbins, *he's old, if he isn't dead, but still good,* so these are the bestsellers, but not the ones I admire. I mean, OK, that's the woman who wrote *The Ya-Ya Sisterhood,* but who the fuck are Jackie Collins and Judith Krantz?

No time to waste glomming a bunch of stupid junk left behind by people that don't count. This is the wrong fucking hall for me. I belong right up there in the pantheon, wherever that is in this overgrown pack rat's palazzo, because I am Stanley Fucking Krakowski, right?

To win this, I need to swing wide and take large steps, gut myself with a Bowie knife if I have to, whatever gets their attention. Write flash fiction in my blood, anything to focus this rich, anonymous Donor guy on ME. So get this, peeps.

You're looking at the Next Big Thing. Time to cut through the crap here and get with the real writers, and I am not talking Herman Fucking Melville or any of the old dead guys, they're all over, right? I mean the ones *everybody* knows about because they're hot on the web right now, because in this game, it's all about *branding*, for instance this Snooki has gazillion following on Twitter just like James Franco, everybody in the universe has heard of Chuck Pahalniuk, who is my personal idol that I emulate and owe a huge debt to in my work, which I want him to blurb it when it comes out. See, before this is done, the name of Stanley Krakowski is gonna be right up there on the marquee with Dan Brown and that guy who wrote *The Silence of the Lambs,* and everything and everybody else goes out the window until I see the name *Stanley Krakowski* high above Times Square, I want to see it circling the city's tallest building in big block letters that light up and they should be thirty feet high.

Now, I can beat out good old Spike and Charlee without baring a fang, no problem, but sexy Mel is another thing. We're definitely together, as in, might even get married. Well, we were. Sorry, I'm leaving her behind. I feel bad about it but writing is a dirty business, like, it's dog eat dog, so if I have to, I'll do what I have to, because that's what Great Writers do.

See, I've scoped this situation and I'm pretty sure that this is a Mortal Kombat deal. The one that comes out ahead in this **Museum of Great American Writers** is the only one that makes it out alive, and if Spike and I have to duke it out at the end, knives or bare hands, to keep from getting kicked off the island, no problem. I just cracked Raymond Chandler's pistol out of the Weapons Case and I am locked and loaded for bear.

Destiny's wall is out there somewhere. It has *one thing only* posted on it, and it's my name.

Melanie Lerner

Truth? THE HALL OF READINGS raises questions. Are those the world's best animatronics behind the velvet ropes, or do they have real Joyce Carol Oates and real Toni Morrison really standing up there at lecterns in their own special alcoves, surrounded by their manuscripts and doodles to say nothing of first editions, and are they really reading aloud from their works at this very moment, just for me? It's wonderful and exciting and distracting seeing them like this but frankly, it creeps me out. I wouldn't mind giving a reading for somebody besides my boyfriend and the manager of the bookstore, but the idea of standing up there reading and reading and reading day after day, following with a Q&A for the unwashed masses filing through **The Museum of Great American Writers** . . .

Not so much.

But if that's what it takes to make it up there on the Great American Writers list, I'm down with that. Whatever it takes, and believe me, I've got what it takes. One look at The Wall of Fame in the foyer and I got dizzy, I could hear every bone in me humming, *I want that.* When the docent guy opened the door on THE MEMORY PALACE, I was off like a shot. On my way in to NOBEL-IN-WAITING ROOM with a special niche for Philip Roth, I ran through a corridor called AWARDS ARCADE, which was daunting as hell because every shelf is filled with glittering prizes. I saw everybody's Pulitzers, Presidential medals, National Book Awards, along with all the Edgars, Golden Quills, and you-name-its and won by Great American Writers in the past hundred years, and that's not counting Oscars, Tonies, trophies from other media, but first and foremost, they got the Nobel Prize medal from every American who ever won a Nobel Prize.

Trophies like that make a writer like me all greedy and anxious, and if you think that makes me ashamed?

It makes me sure.

I will damn well be remembered here.

Now, Spike's a contender, but *entre nous* he let himself get all bent and distracted because he *so* wants to play with the cool kids. Poor baby, he doesn't only want to be like them.

Not only does he want to *be them,* Spike wants more.

He wants them to like him.

In his dreams poor Spike sees himself hanging out with the likes of Lethem and George Saunders and Jonathan Safran Foer and them, as if, when Spike finally sells *Fucked All Over Town,* he kind of thinks one of his idols will rip through it at one sitting and tweet about it and text all the others, like he'll call Spike personally to read him the rave review he just wrote about it for *The New York Times.* Like Spike's gonna hear Jay McInerney or somebody reading it to him on the phone, although he also mailed it to Spike and Spike is reading it on his phone instead of listening to The Man's words in his very own voice. In Spike's dreams somebody gives him a book party and all the cool kids come; they'll make friends and pretty soon he'll be out running around with his amazing boon buddies that he wants to have even more than he wants to win, and they'll all get drunk together and talk about how bad they feel about David Foster Wallace being dead. I love Spike but in spite of the title his prose is, face it, a tad too fussy to make the cut, but who am I to tell him that?

Now, Charlee, Charlee is an airhead, ergo no threat, which brings it down to me and my ostensible boyfriend Stan.

Too bad he's a macho jerkoff with an ego so big that he can't see past the end of his dick, which, unfortunately, is his writing utensil of choice.

So Committee/Donor/whoever, keep your eye on *me.*

My name is Melanie Patricia Lerner and I've been writing since I was four years old. Not only am I pretty good at what I do, I'm fit, I work out. I start with pushups and crunches at four a.m. and the gears in my head go running along ahead of every word I type and every mile I swim, both day and night. The Mel-machine keeps rolling 24/7 no matter what you throw in front of it, so get out of my way, I never give up and I never run down. In terms of posterity and my place in **The Museum of Great American Writers,** I'm telling you now and when we're done here I'll put this in writing, just in case I get hit by a truck.

No speeches and no flowers. Display all my books cover out, with plastic sleeves to keep the jackets from fading. In my exhibit, put all the things I care about: sweet little Melly's first laptop, my grandmother's copy of *Catcher in the Rye* and podcasts of every TV and online interview I make after I win the Pulitzer Prize, which. About my prizes. I want them in my own personal author display, not junked in with all the others out there in the hall; also, please hang up my blazing skull headset in the case next to the entrance, along with my favorite pair of boots.

And the plaque you screw to the wall by the door? On the plaque, you should put: MELANIE L. SHE WAS TOUGH AS FUCK.

Charlotte Eberstadt

Oh, Mr. X, who brought all these wonders to life for your people and honored Spike and me and the others with the chance to see it all first and firsthand, I want to thank you, but before that, there are a couple of things. First off, you should know that I am a POET, so a little respect here, please.

I thought your museum would be inspiring. I mean, it's a very great honor, being rescued from downtown Iowa and flown in to serve the arts. I was so excited! I thought I could sit down in your Great Hall and gnaw poetry out of my bleeding fingertips, and Mother would stop nagging about my nails. I thought, OK, there's a lot of history here, and *we* are history.

We are history.

God, I love that. Is that my first line?

Second line: *Look at me!*

Poet-in-waiting, chasing the gemlike flame—this place is so big—I think I see it! Unless that's Tinker Bell twinkling down there at the far end of the Edna St. Vincent Millay gallery, which I must confess I'm finding rather thin. She had a glamorous life but she wasn't a very nice person, you know? Plus, is this her stuff, or is it only copies of her stuff that somebody sold you because you can afford it, and they sold you fakes?

Walt Whitman's shaving mug, really? If it isn't, what am I doing here? Looking for posterity. So, that light down there, is that it?

I sing posterity beckoning. Does that sound OK? Believe me, it had better be beckoning, after what I went through to make it here.

Later:

I look for the day of reckoning . . . OK, Charlee, that blows. You are coming up empty here.

I could spend a lifetime on this poem and never get it right because, between the intention and the act, guess what? There falls the shadow. Something's terribly wrong in this place. Imagine, all the space and time and all that money wasted, I mean, how many of these people does anybody read?

Move over for me.

Face it, Mr. Donor, everything and everybody in your **Museum of Great American Writers** is dead. Except me.

Well, me and Spike. Oh, and Melanie, I guess, and Stan, who, frankly, Stan smells bad, in addition to which, he's mean. So, look. You could make something of this place if it was about living, struggling artists like me. Plus, Is that really Maya Angelou's real writing desk I'm looking at, or did somebody sell you a fake?

I've tried and tried, but I just don't feel the vibe.

I know I sound ungrateful after everything, I expected to sit down here and commit *art,* but I can't wait to get out! I want to be out where it's still happening, not ossified like your dead poets under glass. I want to get down and dirty with Spike, and when he and I are done with each other, I'll tell him good-bye, but in a nice way so I can go somewhere and write without being distracted by dummies of Miniver Cheevy and all them, who, face it, are totally dead.

I'm ready to dive headfirst into the gemlike flame, and I won't come out until I'm famous, OK?

Are you listening, Mr. Donor? This is your last warning. If you don't come get me *right now,* I'll just sit here in wax James Baldwin's lap throwing matches at T. S. Eliot until either he melts or you personally come in and lead me out of this terrible place.

The Committee

"Called to order at 1700. Present are . . ."

"That's enough. We're meeting to resolve a situation."

"What situation?"

"If you have to ask, you can't afford it."

"Shut up, Etherington."

"Four mindless MFAs running wild in the galleries. Donor's focus group."

"Judging our efforts."

"Yes."

"And what are we supposed to do about it?"

"Something. Discuss."

"I'm sick of discussions, I . . ."

"This is a mistake."

"Face it, the whole Museum's a mistake."

"Don't say that!"

"It's true. And now The Donor is . . ."

"Pissed."

"And we are going to do about it . . . What?"

"It didn't have to be this way."

"You said it. For instance, I wanted . . ."

"Yeah, but that's not what I wanted, I . . ."

"Enough."

"If we'd only done what I . . ."

"We did what The Donor wanted."

"That's not what *he* thinks."

"We did too many things that too many people wanted."

"Now, nobody wants it."

"If only we'd done what *I* wanted."

"So, are we supposed to do what these kids want?"

"Is that what he thinks?"

"Nobody knows what he's thinking, only that we made him mad."

"We don't care what he thinks. The issue is making him think he's getting what he wants."

"Trouble is, it isn't!"

"Nobody gets what they want."

"Don't go all existential on us."

"Shut up. Do you not get that The Donor is in charge of this?"

"Then why is he so pissed off?"

"Billions, and it isn't what he really wants."

"Don't be ridiculous. What The Donor wants, The Donor gets."

"He doesn't think so."

"Neither do I. I thought it would be more literary."

"Well, I thought it would be more dignified."

"More commercial."

"More promotable."

"More profitable."

"He thought it would be more Early American."

"Early American?"

"Never mind. Now, about the business at hand . . ."

"Hemingway foyer. Depression Steinbeck. Styron Forties Melancholia room, that kind of thing."

"I thought it would be more contemporary."

"I thought it would have a great manuscript library. Emerson papers. Like that."

"The public doesn't care about manuscripts."

"I thought The Museum would be universal. About art."

"Art isn't universal."

"What is art, anyway?"

"Let's don't go there. Not today."

"The public doesn't care about art."

"What does the public care about?"

"Showmanship."

"You're so smart, you tell us. What is showmanship?"

"Giving the public what it wants."

"What does the public want?"

"We've been through that. Moving on, about the . . ."

"Solution: we give the public what it wants. Discuss."

"We're sick of discussions."

" . . . kid focus group. Shut up and listen."

"No more discussions!"

"Shall we vote on that?"

"THAT'S NOT OUR PROBLEM TODAY. It's this *beta test* The Donor's got going. Who makes up his mind for him, us or these piddling MFAs?"

"Us, us!"

"Which means we have to . . ."

"Don't worry, the Subcommittee's handling it as we speak. We have a . . ."

" . . . present a solid front. Etherington, that's enough!"

"Wait. We have a Subcommittee?"

"Yes, and we've got an . . ."

"I said, Enough! As chair, I'm cutting off discussion. What The Donor wants . . ."

" . . . The Donor gets."

". . . . installation going in . . ."

"And our job is to make him think he's getting what he wants . . ."

" . . . out there in the courtyard as we speak."

"And if these kids come back negative, we take care of it. Agreed?"

"Move to vote on the question."

"Adjourned."

The Donor

I thought it would come out better, but, great new writers of the future or not, they're only kids! The two guys ran into each other at an intersection in the Futurist corridor. **Kersplat!** They tangled and went rolling through the archway into the Wilderness displays, and now they're duking it out with Jack London's pikes and knives on Camera 3. They're in there slashing and poking and destroying history, and not a guard on the place to break them up. Stop, you little bastards, cut it out! This is terrible! They just trashed the Natty Bumppo exhibition, one of my few favorites! Do they not know that they're ruining their chances to join the Great American Writers here? My eager, talented, handpicked focus group is wrecking what little I had left of my original dream!

Meanwhile that willowy poet child is at the far end of the Middle American extravaganza, sobbing her heart out on the Emily Dickinson chaise and I am thinking what God thought when He called the shot on Sodom and Gomorrah. Who, with his hopes crumbling, would not?

Besides, instead of doing what I sent her in there to do, that trashy leather girl is swaggering around in the BOOK TO MAJOR MOTION PICTURE AMPHITHEATER like a rock-and-roll music star while my miserable excuse for a docent sits on his fat butt down there in *my office* with his back to me, scrawling on a legal pad instead of stopping those destructive kids or, for Pete's sake, dialing 911. He just keeps on scribbling with that moronic grin, gnawing on his tongue every time he rips off another page and I can't do a thing about it because I'm 1,693 miles away, in case this goes south and there's a blast. At this distance, all I can do is watch while his crumpled, garbagey prose slithers across my flat screen Navajo 9X12 because here in Chicago, glued to my remotes, I'm essentially helpless, with no staff on site and no way to intervene, so I'm powerless.

Except for the red plunger by my chair, which I'm strongly tempted to push.

Look at those self-important, talented kids I hired, which was a great honor. They're running wild because my docent's asleep at the switch and the only other people in the building are The Committee, whom I *do not trust,* up there in the observation booth, thinking they're perfectly safe. It's egregious. They're disgusting. Every one of them!

Even God would push the plunger. But wait! What's this?

Camera A just picked up activity down in the Realist Writers' Courtyard. Looks like some kind of—wait, it is!

A statue. I didn't order that! Five men are rolling it off a truck onto a forklift as we speak.

Now the man in the bucket truck is attaching padded ropes so the crane operator can hoist the figure to its feet.

As the ground crew tugs the ropes, the felt blankets drop, revealing a rather handsome . . .

It looks like a . . . Why, it's a . . .

I didn't order that!

Handsome bronze. A handsome bronze is going up in the main courtyard without my . . . Not a bad looking fellow, now that I think about it, but this is nothing I approved. I wasn't even consulted. Plunger time! But wait. Who is he, and why did I not see sketches or site plans? It's some great writer, I suppose, although it looks a little bit like . . . but what great writer wears a topcoat like mine and wears a homburg that looks just like mine, and who else carries the Gucci briefcase with a special holster for my click-n-switch sword cane, just in case? This is so . . .

Oh!

Very well, then. Kudos to you, Committee. And thank you very much.

Now, moving on. Camera One: the willowy girl has pulled herself together. Looking around for some paper and something to write with. *Lady, not that manuscript. Lady, not Emily Dickinson's pen!* The young studs are still grappling in the Great American Northwest, the lean one has the one I like in a hammer lock, must send Docent in to pull them apart before they . . .

Rethink. Forget this bunch. There are plenty more where they came from, if these two fight to the death, let them. Which, come to think of it, would make an interesting spectacle for the Grand Opening. Maybe with the next pair . . .

Excellent!

Note to self: order bronze light bulb above that great bronze head in the courtyard, signifying Idea.

I know how to save my museum and guarantee that it will do me credit, and looking at the statue in the courtyard—handsome bronze!—I know it's credit that I deserve.

See, businessmen like me know all there is to know about the Great American Way, and now that I've watched these kids in action, I know exactly what to do. In our great country it's not really about who wins and who loses. It's all about the race.

Tomorrow I dispatch The Committee to cover every writing program, workshop, and small press reading and poetry slam in our great nation, with orders to recruit the attraction I should have put in place on Day One.

The exhibit that makes sense of all the literary things collected here.

At the end of the day, instead of being my dream diluted and deferred, **The Museum of Great American Writers** will be a commercial sensation, and a credit to my name. For the Grand Opening, which I predict will take another year to prepare, we'll have the greatest show on earth. In addition to moldy relics of the great and not-so-great American dead, **The Museum of Great American Writers** will feature a living writer in every room.

We can keep wannabes in every room in all those galleries 24/7, pacing, typing, deleting, whatever writers do. Plenty of cannon fodder in those writing schools. We can throw in some other contests to amuse our paying guests: pair them off in bouts of drinking, dancing and bar-fighting, love triangles and bad breakups, even gladiatorial tilts, because the great American public needs to know everything about the ugly underside of the American writing game.

Millions will stroll past my live exhibits just to handicap the winners, and millions will keep coming back, watching their favorites make it into rooms labeled Submission, Rejection, that kind of thing, and we'll let our public place bets at every step along the way. And if your pick gets axed at Rejection?

Come on down again! You can always get yourself a winner next time, and if we throw in a small cash prize . . . Then there'll be the elimination rounds, with the Publication room for the few and for the *very* few, a spot in the Museum's Awards Corridor, next stop, the Late American Wing. From there, as I understand it, it's only a hop and a skip, some schmoozing and a couple of murders, to the Rotunda and—for the best of the *very* few, a photograph of the winners with yours truly by that handsome statue in the courtyard, and—wait for it—a spot on the Wall of Fame.

—Postscripts, 2011

High Rise High

The situation at the school is about like you'd expect: total anarchy, bikers roaring through the halls pillaging and laying waste; big guys hanging screaming frosh out of windows by their feet, shut up or I let go; bathroom floods and flaming mattresses, minor explosions and who knows how many teacher hostages; this is worse than Attica, and the monster prom that puts the arm on Armageddon is Saturday night. The theme is Tinsel Dreams; expect wild carnage fueled by kid gangs sallying forth to trash your neighborhood and bring back anything they want. Who knows how they got out of the citadel? Who can say exactly how they get back in?

An interesting thing has happened. Nobody's cell phone works inside the walls. Worse. The land lines have been cut so you can't phone in.

Then there is the problem with the baby. See, this Bruce Brill, he tries to get down with the kids, you know, call me Bruce, but the kids call him the Motivator? He's always, like, "Come on, if you want to, you can get a C," big mistake trying that on Johnny Slater: "Why are you holding back like this? You could go to MIT!" Well, that and his stupid play. OK, this is what you get for pissing Johnny off. He and his gang have snatched your pregnant wife, they broke into your house while you were scrubbing your hands in front of English class, we'll Macbeth *you*. Johnny is holding pregnant Jane in the woodworking shop while his seven best buds rig the table saw to rip her fuckin in half. Boy, you should hear her scream. Listen, when Mr. McShy the band teacher begged them to let her go the seven of them did, yes they *did* smash sensitive Eddie McShy's Stradivarius over his sensitive head; while he weeps and the pregnant lady screams for help, Johnny uses the splinters to pick his front teeth.

It's Teach, this eager jerk Bruce Brill, that alerted us in the city. "I tried to tell you but you wouldn't listen." Look up from supper and Teach is on your screen sobbing for Global TV. "Now it's too late."

Hunkered down in his office with a handful of survivors, deposed principal Irving Wardlaw shakes his fist at the TV. Frankly, the riot broke out because Bruce tried to make Johnny play a fairy in his "Midsummer Night's Dream." Fucking Shakespeare, what do you expect?

"It's a jungle in there!" Bruce's eyes are wet with disappointment. "I had such hopes."

Yeah right, Wardlaw growls, observing on the Watchman in his still-smoking office. *You shoulda had a gun.*

Then Bruce completely loses it. "My wife is trapped! My baby's coming even as we speak!" And because Teach made it to the Global studios before the kids or the Mayor's men could bring him down the whole world is watching, so instead of saying "We'll look into it" and back-burnering like he does everything else, the Mayor will have to act.

In any other city conquest and recovery would be a snap. SWAT teams on the roof of the school, they could rappel from there no problem, and end the siege; paratroopers could knife in through the skylight, shattering the stained glass with spiked jackboots to break up the Tinsel Prom; the Feds could plant explosives or the governor could call out the National Guard to crack skulls and restore order, but not here. We are ahead of the wave, second to none in doing what we have to do to keep our sanity.

High Rise High is a fortress unto itself.

Listen, these walls are slicker than glass. No pikes and crampons here! We're talking a hundred stories built on bedrock, nobody tunnels out and no mole gets in. The vertical face is tougher to storm than Masada or the Haunted Mesa, when your enemies can't get a toehold you are proof against siege. The first ten floors are windowless, girdled by coiled razor wire bolted tight to the glossy molybdenum face.

What were they thinking when they built HRH? Keeping you out? No. Keeping your kids *in.*

Listen, you wanted it this way. The teen population is out of control, you said, and believe me, you came begging. You showed us your lip that he split when you wouldn't give him the car and the bruises she left in the fight and you whined, "Our kids won't *do* like they should," when you meant, they won't do like we say. Fine, we said. Let's put them all in a good, safe place, with their dope and their dirty underwear and loud rock music, and let's make the walls thick enough so their speakers won't bother us and while we're at it let's make sure they can't get out. We aren't doing anything, we just want our children in some nice, secure environment where they can be happy, i.e., so if they smoke, drink, pop or snort, and exchange STDs and flaunt their tongue studs and anarchic tattoos, we won't have to see.

Ergo: High Rise High.

The ten stories with the no windows? Security! Perfect, until you need to get in. The power source is self-contained on One. Nine floors are thickly packed with hydroponics and walk-in freezers and stacks of freeze-dried TV dinners and canned foods, so you can forget about starving them out. Living quarters from Eleven on up to the fortieth floor, where you get the RV and rock climbing areas, the Rollerblade floor, swimming pool and football field floors, dirt bike mountains, graffiti heaven and the skateboard park floor, a bunch of you-name-it floors and above that on the top five stories, HRH1Z to HRH5, the school. External faculty elevators that shoot up at tremendous speeds and bypass the kids' dorms without opening so no craven grownup can infiltrate, as in, sneak into your private place, and, like, read your diary, try to break all your bad habits or smell your underwear, in other situations unscrupulous 'rents have been known to creep into your room in spite of the sign that says *Keep Out* and pounce on you like *that*.

Privacy. That's how we baited the trap.

Assurances. How else do you think we got the kids to bite? They filed into the entrance that we sealed behind them like so many dumb animals, crazy to get inside where we couldn't watch what they were doing, probably so they could get high or abuse themselves and each other, or worse.

So. Basically, every teen troublemaker in the greater metropolitan area is socked inside our citadel, free to riot at their round-the-clock raves, plus—surprise!—spill out and sack your neighborhoods and then go home to the high rise and pop, snort or drink themselves senseless while you quake in your quiet, childless, orderly houses and your adults-only condos, and there isn't a law enforcement agency in the greater U.S. that can touch them because nobody can figure out how to get inside, even though from the beginning it was clear that the very worst kids had found a way out. Nobody cared much until the riot started and this Bruce went on TV. "My unborn baby! My wife!"

It seemed like a good idea at the time.

Remember, you mandated this when you voted for High Rise High.

Cheer up. All the best heads in law enforcement are huddling on this problem, they brainstorm around the clock but so far nobody's figured out how to breach the walls so that whichever local or national forces can carry out whatever threats and let us decent, God-fearing grownups restore order so we can get some sleep.

Bruce the idealist has been dragged into The Big Meeting by the Democratic candidate. The Republican mayor wants to stonewall the jerk, but remember Global; they are being watched. Municipal switchboards are flooded; the city server is clogged with gigabytes of protest mails. Crowds are gathering in front of the Mayor's residence and City Hall. The president reaches the unlisted red phone. Mayor Patton has caller ID so he has to pick up. "Yes sir." Our nation's leader cracks the whip. "Global laughing stock." The mayor's teeth clench. "I'll end it, yes. No matter what it takes."

At High Rise High, a bloodstained note hurtles into the crowd, tied to a rock. MY STRADIVARIUS!

The crowd's rumble rises to a roar. "You've got to get them out!"

Heads of State send emissaries to plead with us. *End this terrible siege.*

In the nation's capitol, a prayer vigil begins on the mall.

Because the world is watching, the mayor has to name a blue ribbon task force to investigate. That poor pregnant woman. The Stradivarius! We have no choice.

"It's clear there's a way in," Agent Betsy says at The Big Meeting. "Otherwise, how do they get out?"

The mayor doesn't like this woman much, but single-handed, she quelled the riot at Attica, so he has hopes. Five feet tall and less than a hundred pounds and she terrifies him. He says as smoothly as he can manage, "Good point."

She bites the words off and spits them at him like nails. "Don't. You. Condescend to me."

"Go ahead," he snarls. "You have four days."

The governor makes a better show of it. "May God go with you. You have the thanks of a grateful nation."

Agent Betsy snaps, "Not yet."

Daunted, he turns to his aide. "Take it away, Harry. Help make this thing work."

The governor's aide assesses the woman operative. Plain, with her straight brown hair and no makeup and the standard issue Navy blue suit. Tough, Harry Klein thinks, and fit. Very fit. Her eyes crackle and his catch fire. "What are you going to do?"

"I'm going undercover."

"You?"

Agent Betsy sweeps her hair back into a Scrunchy and pops a wad of gum. "Think I can pass?"

Harry grins. She looks about twelve. "The place is a fortress. You'll never make it past the ground floor."

"You think." Although Agent Betsy carries herself as though she thinks this is going to be easy, it takes all her strength and intelligence to keep her voice from trembling. "I'll need two police matrons and a Juvenile Services van." Her glare is so sharp that it makes even Harry tremble. She hands him a piece of paper: a list. He smiles. In that moment they are bonded. "Get me this stuff. I'm going in."

Specially uniformed for the mission she knows would make her father proud of her if he had lived, Agent Betsy has turned over her ID; she is holding out her wrists for the matrons to put on the cuffs when the mayor comes to wish her well. Using a fake hug to cover his real intentions, he grates into her ear, "Saturday. You have until Saturday to fix this. Then we nuke the place."

Inside the school, things aren't going so well. Before he disappeared, Ace Freewalter the custodian stopped the flooding but there's swash in the halls and smoke from hidden fires curls up from the air conditioning ducts. Although there are random shots and they hear the occasional scream, the survivors in Wardlaw's office can't guess how many colleagues are being held hostage in the gym. Some teachers bailed before the insurrection and the concomitant elevator shutdown, as in, after the riot boiled out of the auditorium and overflowed the halls and the cops were notified, the kids blew up the faculty elevator shafts which, as far as the embattled parents in the city know, are the only way in.

While countless hostages huddle in the gym, the escapees are holed up in here, and Ace? Did the bikers bring him down or is he lying dead at the bottom of the incinerator chute just when they need his military expertise? Who knows what happened to him? Safe, for now: Principal Irving Wardlaw, Harvard PhD, who regrets the day he ever agreed to take this job, never mind the hazardous duty pay, the Hyundai, and the perks. Plump, stately French teacher Beverly Flan—still single, and at her age. To her left is Marva Liu, the beautiful Asiamerican swimming coach. At the window stands the gym teacher Bill Dykstra, a gentleman of color who also taught woodworking until Johnny and his droogs commandeered his immaculate shop and trashed the place. Broken by shock, Edward McShy, who escaped the shop after Johnny's guys smashed his Stradivarius, hunches in a corner where he gibbers and sobs.

"McShy, stop that!"

"I can't!"

Wardlaw sighs heavily. The school he worked so hard to build is a shambles. The shame! He'll never get another job. "What are we going to do?"

At the window Dykstra says, "Come here."

"Paratroopers?"

"Not exactly."

"Helicopter?"

"In your dreams."

"SWAT team? What?"

Dykstra is not looking up; he's looking down. He points. "Special delivery. Get a load."

At this height it's hard to make out what's going on, but Dykstra has liberated the custodian's binoculars from the utility closet. Before he burned out in the Gulf War, Ace Freewalter the don't-call-me-a-janitor was a Green Beret. Wardlaw grabs the glasses and takes a squint. There is a disturbance in the street below. Crowds scatter as a van painted Juvenile Detention Center blue noses in to the razor wire and stops. Two matrons step down, straight-arming a struggling teenager who slashes at their shins with chunky alligator boots. They undo the handcuffs, drop the teen on the sidewalk, and get in the van and leave. Wardlaw says, "What?"

"Looks like a new student to me. Unless it's a diversionary tactic. They open the doors for this kid and Commandos rush in."

"Then we're saved," Beverly Flan flutes with a hopeful smile.

Coach grins. "Not so's you'd notice."

The principal sighs. "The entrance is sealed, we saw it on TV. Dykstra, what's going on?"

"Too soon to tell."

Nothing happens for a very long time. Night falls. Arc lights bathe the main entrance. The Detention Center drop-off sits on the sidewalk, hugging her knees. They see her on TV. She's a girl with silver wire woven into green cornrows and studs everywhere and the greatest of all possible tattoos. The girl shakes her fist at the Fox Nightly News camera, but it isn't us she is talking to. She is talking to *them*. Your children! She says, "Let me the fuck in."

The remaining staff clusters around Principal Wardlaw's Watchman, which doesn't show them much. Later they take turns watching while the others sleep. Near dawn, Dykstra sees it. The razor wire at ground-floor level is stirring. A door opens where even the principal didn't know there was a door.

Dykstra says in a low voice, "They're coming out."

"No, somebody's taking her in."

"Give me those." Beverly Flan looks. "It's Johnny Slater!"

"How do you know?"

"I know Johnny when I see him. Why, I had him in French!"

The group in the office roars, "Get the bastard!"

Edward McShy cries, "My Stradivarius!"

The crowd below begins to part like grain when the rats run through it. They see it on TV. Snipers' bullets strike sparks on the razor wire.

Marva Liu says, "If Johnny's down there, maybe we can sneak over to the shop and rescue poor Bruce's wife!"

Dykstra reaches for her hand. "That's not a job for civilians, dear."

Dear. For the moment, Marva is glad they're under siege. Later, she thinks joyfully, something will come of this. "Oh, Bill."

Below, men in helmets like mushrooms break cover and swarm the entrance steps. Wardlaw's breath explodes into words. "Thank God, Marines!"

But Johnny and his gang yank the girl inside and before the first wave of jarheads can reach the pediment an explosion seals the door.

The new kid is squirming in Johnny Slater's grasp. Johnny is tall, stringy and good-looking with the blond Mohawk and piercing green eyes. *Cute.* The girl snarls, "What took you, meathead?"

She doesn't look so bad herself: Day-Glo green hair, skinny pants and a skimpy, spangled top. He is leading her through a maze of generators and steam pipes to the hidden elevator, the one you in the city don't know about. There's a lot you don't know. These two, alone! It is love at first sight. "We had to be sure. The name is Johnny, you skank."

Agent Betsy thinks for a moment. "I'm Trinket." Johnny slips a silver Scrunchy on her wrist: invitation to the Tinsel Prom. Her voice ripples with surprise. *Yo, Trinket.* "I am!"

They go up a dozen floors. The doors open on a cluttered kid room, the kind we all wanted back then: Indian mirrorwork pillows, Astroturf and Furbys, posters and plastic shit from record stores, eight generations of PlayStation, windup toys and model rockets and action figures, you name it, fox fur with the head and dangling feet and the chattering vinyl skull with skeleton attached, ripped off from the bio lab. Trinket lets her voice go soft with wonder. "Is this your *place?*"

Deep in the school subbasement where you can't go, Lance Corporal Ace Freewalter USA (retired) considers his options. He outran the bike gang on HRH3, but he barely escaped the motorized razor scooters on HRH2; the enemy took out after him with blowtorches, intent on burning him alive. Trained in survival tactics, Ace has gone to ground where even the toughest kids don't have the guts to follow. He is holed up behind the generator on HRH1Z, where he keeps his war diary. Iraq was Kissinger's fault. This defeat is his. Opening a metal chest he keeps concealed here, Ace studies his arsenal. Tactical weapons.

Smart bombs. You name it. Scowling, he blackens his face. The HRH shutdown is his fault. With gritted teeth, he ties a black band around his head, tucking in the ends with a determined glare. It's up to him to win the building back.

"Hakuna Matata." The mayor has been awake for forty-eight hours now and is getting a little schizzy. "Sorry. Good evening. I am taking this opportunity to let you know that the situation at High Rise High is under control and we will make every effort to keep it contained. We have armed guards securing the perimeter and, rest assured, the neighborhood raids have ceased."

Unfortunately the live feed suggests otherwise, but His Honor can't know what the networks have chosen to put on our screens. There are flameouts in the Greenmont and Springdale areas, explosions in Parkhurst, and person or persons unknown have brought down a police helicopter in the park.

"We will not rest until the faculty and Mrs. Um. Bruce's wife and unborn baby are safe." He rests his knuckles on his desk and leans into the camera. "And we will search and destroy if we have to, to rescue the innocent. We will get them out at all costs."

Mayor Patton looks deep into the camera, trying to lock eyes with us. "We have made these young savages an extraordinary offer. A chance to release the hostages and walk free. And we are prepared to back it up with cash. If the students of High Rise High don't settle this peacefully and give themselves up we will be forced to invade, and if the invasion fails . . ."

Rage opens its red jaws and without meaning to, the mayor accidentally tips his hand. He snarls, "Well, we will take drastic steps to stem this human plague."

Somewhere in the city, a thousand mothers groan, but the mayor is too mad at you to hear.

"Explosives. ICBMs. We're prepared to take a few prisoners and kill a lot more but . . ." He is speaking for us, remember, the exhausted parents of these terrible kids, but *in extremis* as he is, Mayor Patton forgets who he's talking to. "If that doesn't work we'll blow the building and everybody in it straight to hell."

Mayor Patton, the city's mothers are listening. "My baby!" a woman in the Hill District shouts and women everywhere take up the cry. Pressed though they were by their children's demands and glad as they were to get rid of them, the mayor's threats bite deep. They remind these women what they used to do.

"Billy, please don't hurt Billy," someone sobs, and a block away another mother cries, "Nobody touches Maryann!" The voices spill out of open windows and fill the streets. "Not Lizzy." "Not my Dave!" The chorus overflows your buildings, it swells until the vibration drowns out thought. *"Don't you dare touch our children!"* You fobbed your teenaged children off on the city but they are still yours, and you are resolute.

In a barren, freshly scoured apartment in the projects, one woman in particular hears. "You better not lay a hand on my kid!" Rolling up her sleeves, she looks around her tiny apartment for weapons. She's a decent woman. Except for a steak knife and sewing shears, there is nothing at hand. Never mind. She picks up her mobile phone and grabs her late husband's safari jacket. Unarmed, Marybeth Slater will take on anybody and everything that threatens her son. "I'm getting Johnny out. If I have to, I'll kill."

The studio switchboard lights up like a fireworks finale. The women get an open mike. "Patton you bastard. Murderer!"

"Ladies and gentlemen, I'm sorry for any confusion. When I say blow them up it isn't an exact meaning." Caught in the act, Mayor Patton is getting shrill. "It's just a matter of speaking." His press officer mutters into his ear: too late. He screeches, "It's a metaphor!"

Agent Betsy looks up from the locket Johnny just gave her. "I guess you're not having school in here any more."

"Not so's you'd notice."

"What, um." She has to make it sound like kid conversation instead of a leading question. "What do you guys want?"

"What do you mean what do we want?"

"I mean, do you have, um, like, demands?"

The answer is too complicated for Johnny Slater to come up with, at least right now. "Everything not sucking, that's all."

"Everything always sucks, it's no big," Trinket says. *Come on, Johnny, give me something I can work with.* Entrance and escape routes, weak spots, ways to get him to back down, Agent Betsy is thinking, but she is also thinking, *he really is cute.* Trinket rubs against him, but only a little bit, "I mean, do you guys want to get out of this stupid place or what?"

He explodes. "I just want them to leave us alone, that's all."

"It looks to me like that, you got."

"This isn't alone, this is . . ." He lifts Bruce Brill's stupid Titania wig that started the whole thing. It looks like a microwaved rat. Words pop out of him like exploding shells. "This asshole Teach tried to put me in a *play.*"

"And you snatched his wife for that?"

"Nobody makes a pussy out of J. Slater." He gestures at the crates that line the room where they are standing. "Look what I got."

What has he got? What doesn't he have. Cases of assault weapons, gravity knives, and mounded six-packs of MACE, a crate filled with Gulf War era grenades. Anthrax pellets, for all she knows. Agent Betsy gulps. "What's the plan?"

He picks up a grenade. "What makes you think there's a plan?"

She knows enough to shrug. "Beats the shit out of me."

He drops it into the crate. It lands with a clank. "You're the new kid and you think I'm gonna tell you the plan? I love ya baby, but sheesh!"

This isn't a job for psychology, she realizes, looking into the open crate. Shit she knew that. Shit this kid is dangerous. The mayor has given her until Saturday to get results; it'll take that long to worm her way into Johnny Slater's head.

"Yo Trinket," he says, and the look he gives her slides between love and hate. Worse. He sees the break in concentration as the agent glances over her shoulder to see who he's talking to, the second it takes her to find and replace *Betsy* with her new name. In a flash he clenches his elbow around her neck. "Come with me."

How did our children get this way? When did they start to fight us over every little thing, and what makes them so judgmental? What turned them mean? They started out little and cute and now they scare the shit out of us.

When something like this comes up everybody has excuses, and with or without one, we scramble for an explanation. Better that than admitting there are things about us that nobody can explain.

Bad parenting, you say, some of you, and the finger you are pointing is never at yourself.

You say, *You didn't listen to them, you always gave them what they wanted/ always said no.*

You say, *You neglected/overprotected them.*

Another theory? *You gave them everything they wanted but you couldn't give them love* or, *You gave them what they wanted when discipline is what they need.* Or: *You gave them too much/you didn't give them enough.*

Television, you say. *It's what you get when kids watch too much TV.*

Poverty, you say, *That's the root cause. They're angry because they grew up poor,* except you know as well as we do that these aren't only ghetto kids rampaging, they are people like us. They come out of upmarket apartments, lots of them, some from posh brownstones and more from shiny tract houses or treelined neighborhoods in the 'burbs, so what's going on here isn't only a function of poverty, although which of us is to say what makes a family poor?

It is, however, a function of rage. Why else would they do everything and hurt everybody and trash the place?

Bad companions, you say, *bad influence. H/she never would have gotten into this all by h/erself, it's all this hanging out with the wrong kind of kids*—you think this, every one of you, even though, hey, *somebody's* kid's gotta be wrong or they'd all be perfect, right? You think, if only we save our nice, nice children from all that bad company and talk sense to them!

Do any of you remember what it's like to be sixteen?

Race, you say, or *religious discrimination,* but if you look at the mix in HRH you will find it is a perfect mix, kids seething like roaches in the same melting pot.

Oh, oh! If only I hadn't refused her the car/made fun of the crush/made rules/ made him wear that purple shirt!

When kids go bad, it's never what you think.

What did she do wrong? What changed? Grimly, Johnny frog-marches Agent Betsy to the elevator and with his arm still locked around her neck, drags her inside. They shoot up, up, and up into the ruined school. When she can speak she asks, "Where are we going?"

"I'm done showing you around." The door opens on HRH1 and he forces her into the hall.

"You didn't show me shit." She wants to try, *Why don't you show me that you like me* but she is strangling as he drags her along. "Where are we really going?"

"Check on things."

"So. What. Are we going to the prom together or not?"

Johnny laughs and tightens his grip. "You're my number one woman, right?"

"Then. Agh." She chokes out the words. "Why are you hurting me?"

Johnny unlocks his arm and turns. He lifts her off her feet by the tightly braided green ponytail, sets her down, and gives her a kiss. "It's just the way I am."

In Wardlaw's office, Beverly Flan whimpers, "We're running out of food."

Coach Dykstra says, "The situation is desperate. We have to get a message out."

Wardlaw pounds on his dead Totalphone and skates his muted cell phone across his desk and into the trash. "How?"

"I have an idea." Patting her gray satin front, Beverly Flan smiles brightly. Wardlaw hates Beverly Flan. "We can open a window and drop a note!"

Wardlaw says through his teeth, "You know as well as I do that these windows can't open. At this altitude the wind would create a vacuum and suck us all to hell."

Huddled in his corner, Edward McShy is shaken by a coughing fit. Remember that note he attached to a rock that almost brained a rubbernecker? MY STRADIVARIUS. What window did he open that he shouldn't have opened, to drop it out, and if that window is still open, what will happen if some kid crashes his way into the music closet, which has formed its own airlock, breaking the seal?

And in the governor's office, with nothing on TV but reruns of the Bruce Brill interview and the mayor's speech, Harry Klein paces and frets. On the surveillance monitor, the silhouette of High Rise High looms, huge in the encroaching dawn. The woman he thinks he loves is undercover somewhere in there, and he's afraid she is in danger. Is she OK? She promised to let him know. The city's phones are dead and the police scanner gives back only background racket, nightmare static from beyond the pale. Betsy has to get in touch, but how? She swore she'd find a way to let Harry know she was all right. He saw her go in, all right, but nothing has come out.

Amazing what happens when systems break down, Trinket thinks as her new boyfriend rushes her along. Order in institutions is always delicately balanced, a masterpiece of tension. Amazing, how long so few could control so many particles. A thousand kids kept at bay for all these months by a hundred teachers at most, few of them particularly physically strong and even fewer armed. Teachers plus the custodian who, the folder they gave her at the briefing told her, had been a Green Beret. Everything running smoothly until . . .

Brill, she thinks. That idiot Bruce Brill.

Now the adults are absent or neutralized in a holding pen, and order has gone out the window. The place is falling apart. The school isn't exactly a charnel house but by this time it's pretty much a mess. Instead of going back to their dorms after the riot, the kids seem to want to hang together. It's either a gut fear of being alone or herd instinct or maybe it's a victory thing. Nerved up and chattering, they've holed up in various classrooms to extend the experience, jittering teenagers on a perpetual roll. Maybe they think if they go home to bed, the adults will swarm them and take over while they sleep. They've dragged mattresses into the school precincts and set up little camps in labs and classrooms—bikers here, ravers there, the tightly knit Geeks and Monsters here in the computer lab on HRH2, wrapped up in a multi-level chess game in which the National Honor Society kids have just checkmated the Science Club in six dimensions, happy and peaceable because they've played for two days straight undisturbed by the need to change classes or leave here to go to Study Hall. *Kids,* Betsy wants to yell, although she's strangling and can't yell anything, *put your eggheads together and come up with a plan to save the school.*

Johnny drags her along past kid fundamentalists ranting in the nondenominational chapel and hard-core druggies zoning in the cafeteria on HRH3 and there is, of course, the Rifle Club holding the hostages at their encampment in the gym on 4. Agent Betsy notes that the HRH gangs have divided according to every possible line a group could draw between itself and another group: racial lines, gender lines, politics; they have divided according to everything from sexual orientation to religion: Muslim Alliance, Baptist Youth, Murray Atheists, Holy Rollers, Bayit, Rosicrucians, to say nothing of the Republican Youth, Young Democrats, Conservative Fucks; you name it, a splinter group is here. Oh yes, and the school chapter of A.A., which is meeting over coffee in the abandoned teachers' lounge. Meanwhile the real drinkers have taken over the school library; as Johnny steers her past, kid drunks reel out to high five him, giggling and happily plotzed.

"These are my people," he says into her ear.

She does not say, *You'd be better off at MIT.*

"And this is my place."

What Agent Betsy doesn't know, rolling down the hall with the school's number one tough guy, is that if Johnny Slater tried to raise an army now, it wouldn't necessarily be *his* army. The kids of HRH would tear each other to pieces trying to decide who should be in charge.

Outside the gym, the silence is impressive. Inside, the hostages—half the faculty—are bedded down on exercise mats while the Rifle Club patrols with M20s and with fatigues tucked into tightly laced boots. There's blood on the floor in a couple of places—that'll teach you to argue with us. Solid as a truck, fat, blue-eyed Chunk MacKenzie goes from mat to mat with a flashlight, turning over huddled teachers with a heavily shod toe. He is looking for the light of his life. She's a tad too old for him but he is meant to be with the only woman whose heft matches his—big as a tub but beautifully dressed with pretty blonde permanent hair and what a pretty face—his love, the one and only French teacher, Ms. Beverly Flan. His heart is breaking. Where is she? Around him, other guys and girls in the Rifle Club are getting off their rocks getting even with the teachers who humiliated them in math or told them to shut up or just plain gave them a D, but Chunk's head is on a different track. Enough hitting and kicking for him, enough pushing teachers to their knees and making them beg. His heart is in the high place. *We can be together when this is over,* he tells himself, unless he is trying to tell Beverly.

Everybody has a dream, and this is Chunk's. *I'll save her and she'll forget I'm too young and start talking to me in French. I'll save her and she'll thank me, you'll see.*

As they reach the end of the fourth floor hall Johnny relaxes his grip slightly, letting Trinket slide down a bit; they're going along like sweethearts now, cute couple walking close. "We took this place down in fifteen minutes," he says. "The school is ours."

Words fail her. "Kewl."

Overhead there is ominous thudding and rumbling: the Decorations Committee hanging pink balloons and Mylar streamers from the rafters under the skylight, decorating the Olympic-sized indoor track with Styrofoam snowmen and silver Kmart Christmas trees for the Tinsel Prom.

They reach the machine shop. Johnny's guys have given up on the table saw and instead are flipping cigarette butts at the Teach's gravely pregnant wife, who turns her head with a cold glare. Even though her eyes are swollen from hours of crying so quietly that nobody will know, when Mrs. Brill sees Johnny coming in with Agent Betsy, she understands. Kids are only kids, but women know. They exchange looks. Agent Betsy's hair is crazy green and she's dressed like a kid; she carries herself like a kid, but women know what's up before men have a clue. Jane Brill's eyes kindle at the sight of her, but Johnny's watching so the pregnant woman quenches them fast. A lesser person would beg for her life but Jane is a lot smarter than her husband the bright-eyed Teach. "Oh," she says with absolutely no inflection. Not surprised. Not scared. Not anything, just observing, the way you'd say, *It's raining.* "You're back."

"Look what I got," Johnny says, putting Agent Betsy in front of him like a prize he won at the carnival. God, is he trying to impress her? The woman is tied to a chair! "This my girlfriend Trinket, Mrs. Teach. In case you thought . . ."

It seems wise to act impressed. Agent Betsy says, "Is that your *hostage?*"

"Hell no. Better. This is my ticket to ride."

Quick as *that*—maybe too quickly for a guy's girlfriend, Trinket asks, "Ride where?"

When you're seventeen sometimes your body takes you places your mind isn't ready to be. Johnny gives her a look of naked doubt, but covers quickly. "Like I'd tell you."

In the chair, Jane Brill sits without moving. Agent Betsy notes that her ankles have begun to swell. Sometimes women can communicate without words. Trinket lowers her voice. "Has this lady, like, been to the bathroom?"

"Who gives a shit?"

"She's no good to you if she croaks." She hisses like something out of a scary movie. "Did you ever hear of *toxemia?*"

"Oh," Johnny says. Smart, remember; in his time this kid has read everything.

"See how her ankles are puffing up?"

"Oh, shit."

"You better let her go before she pops."

Seven louts in black spandex and Army surplus boots converge, all cartridge belts and jangling chains. "Did we win yet?" "What took you?" "What did we get from them?" "You were going to bring pizza." The biggest, the one with Sidekick written all over him, gives Johnny a bearish nudge. "Where's the beer?"

"Fuck off, Dolph," he says. "I'm bringing Trinket for the girls to take care of while I'm busy. He means: *surveill.* He knows the word but he knows not to say it. "But first. Trinket, these are the guys. Guys, Trinket."

The gratifying rumble tells Trinket she is looking good.

"So, the Slaterettes are holed up . . . where?"

"Music room, what's left of it. Susie's putting up a tent."

Dolph mutters, "You're taking your chick to the *girls?*"

Johnny grins. "You got a problem with that?"

"You know how they are with new kids," Dolph says.

Trinket gives him a sharp look. "I can take care of myself."

He bends over Trinket with an amiable leer. "Just watch the fuck out for Mad Maggie."

Then Johnny says something that absolutely terrifies her. "Fuck that shit, she's mine. Mag knows I saw her first."

Think fast, Trinket. "Like, you don't want me to take Mrs. Teach here to the bathroom? If she pops on you, you're screwed."

Jane Brill says, "Especially if I pop right here."

Trinket bores in. "You want dead baby all over the place?"

"Shut up."

Jane's voice is shaking but she says, "Think of the mess."

Ever the cop, Trinket clinches it. "By me, that makes it Murder One."

Jane says, "And they still fry killers in America."

"I said, shut up." Johnny plasters duct tape over Jane Brill's mouth. Then he takes out his knife. Cool as she is, the teacher's wife shrinks as the point touches her front. In a swift gesture, he cuts the tape that keeps her in her chair. "Go with them, Dolph."

Dolph does. About the conversation between these women: there will be no conversation. Dolph lounges while Betsy helps the teacher's wife stagger to the bathroom; he props the stall door open as she sits and without Trinket there to drop one strap of her tank top, creating a distraction, Johnny's sidekick would have watched the pregnant lady peeing like a customer ogling a pole dancer in a topless bar. What he won't see, no matter how carefully he watches, is the look of complicity, or that Trinket has slipped a razor blade into Jane Brill's palm.

Deep in the bowels of the school's heating system, Ace Freewalter has belted on the necessary equipment and snaked into a ventilating duct. Juvenile perps and Saddam wannabes, watch out. The Ace is on the move.

Days pass faster than they should. The prom is almost here! Adults in the city outside are in a righteous frenzy. No school has ever capped its prom with a human sacrifice, but there's always a first.

The time whips by like nothing for the waiting city because we are more ex-cited than we are scared—what a show!—and even faster for the excited kids, who are definitely on a roll, trying on outfits and dragging a lifetime supply of glits and Mylar and phosphorescent tubes up to the fifth floor, burning their favorites on CDs for the prom DJ and rehearsing some live music of their own; Johnny has the idea that they should dress Principal Wardlaw up as a Christ-mas tree and make him sing the kickoff number at the Tinsel Prom.

For the adults trapped inside High Rise High, chomping on graham crack-ers and Pepperidge Farms goldfish in Irving Wardlaw's office or tossing on filthy wrestling mats in the gym while they wait to be rescued, however, the days and nights seem interminable.

Whereas Trinket is like a cat jittering on a fence. Time is whipping by too fast, in terms of Agent Betsy's mission. In the last four days she's tried a lot of things and accomplished zip. She had hoped to undermine the revolution or at the very least open the main doors downstairs for the SWAT team by this time, but when you're in a building this size everything takes longer than you think.

Plus she's heavily surveilled. For Agent Betsy, the clock is ticking and time is running out.

And Trinket? This is taking *forever*. She can hardly wait for the prom! When he isn't with her, Johnny turns her over to the Slaterettes. She was worried about it going in, like this Mad Mag kid would mess her up, but it's cool. This Mad Maggie everybody's so afraid of turned out to be a fat, soft bully with a big voice. When Mag came down on this kid Evie for no reason, Trinket used her police training to deck the two-hundred-pound bitch and all the other Slaterettes clapped. Now she and Evie are best friends. Agent Betsy's expertise has made Trinket something of a hero. To say nothing of her wardrobe sense. With Evie riding post, Trinket and the Slaterettes have raided closets on the dormitory floors for everything from dental mirrors to wing nuts and jewelry and hubcaps to pin onto costumes from the aborted Shakespeare thing. With Trinket as personal shopper, the Slaterettes scored big. Now they're in the music room working on their Look.

"Don't have much time," Trinket says, suddenly confused. She looks up from the black gauze shift she is decorating, surprised. "It's tomorrow night."

Oh, man. Remember the mayor's secret ultimatum? Agent Betsy has forgotten a lot of the things she had in mind but she hasn't forgotten the threat the mayor made right before he patted her on the butt and sent her in. If she can't bring the revolution down by the time they crown the prom queen, he's going to send a plane in to nuke the place.

But tonight is the pep rally, and for a kid in high school, first things come first. It's cool. After all, it's a big world in here, and she still has twenty-four hours.

They like me, Trinket thinks, doing makeup for the pep rally. Makeup: after her drab girlhood as a police officer's orphan child, after rigorous police training to make up for it, hanging out with kids doing makeup is a trip.

And Johnny, she thinks, even though she should not be thinking it, not with Harry Klein parting the razor wire down below and running his laser knife around a sealed opening that you don't know about, not with Harry letting himself into the bottom of the exhaust shaft where he labors upward in spite of fumes and grit-filled smoke. She definitely should not be thinking, *and Johnny,* not with Harry tightening the crampons to climb a hundred stories straight up if he has to, just to get to her, but Agent Betsy is giddy with success and for a dead cop's daughter who's having her first real *girlhood,* this is distracting. If Trinket had a diary, her kid life in HRH has left her in such a state that she'd write, *Dear Diary,* she thinks, because she never had a diary, but instead of writing it down or speaking aloud, she burns the words into the air: *They really like me. And Johnny. Johnny likes me.*

In the streets of the city in crisis, mothers are on the march. They don't know the mayor set the clock ticking, but they do know he has made threats. They think as one: *Not my kid.*

Imagine being in a mothers' march. Someone like you! Time's gone by but you are still a mother and it twists in your gut like a knife. *My baby, my kid!*

Your kids got too big for the nest, you thought, when they went off to school it was a relief. Then why do you find yourselves wandering into their empty rooms on bright autumn afternoons, remembering how cute they were when they were little and (yes, Marie!) satisfied with a little toy and now they are at risk so never mind what they do to you for breaking into their special place, you are out to bring them back. You don't want them at home, really, but you do want them at home sort of, they used to be so *cute,* and you are determined to get them out of that school because no matter what he did to you, you love him, and you love her no matter what she said during the fight because whether or not you intended it, once you have become a mother you are a mother all your life; you have, etched into your consciousness, the legend of the mother's heart. One more time: the thief cuts out his mother's heart for a profit, he's running to the highest bidder to collect the cash when he trips and falls in the dirt and drops the heart and the heart cries out, *are you hurt?*

Mothers, do not hope to get into the building. Do not expect to change the outcome, you are only a mother and mothers can't. Just go to the place and do what you always do. Coursing through the streets, you are joined by others occupying the same head, house cleaners and brain surgeons alike: intent not so much on their occupations or accomplishments or dreams or even maternal duties as on their job description, which is both name and self-fulfilling prophecy. There are thousands of you now.

In the refurbished auditorium. Johnny and Trinket are onstage for the pep rally, him in a red shirt with gazillion safety pins and slashes, her looking cool in a shift she made out of a rug she found.

"This is it, guys," Johnny says but even he must notice that nobody's listening. They are distracted by the threats in the sky outside—warnings from the mayor etched in the clouds in phosphorescent pink smoke. GIVE UP. The ultimatum hinted at. TOMORROW BY MIDNIGHT. The antique plane doing the writing has just put the final flourish on: OR ELSE.

There is, furthermore, the mysterious clanking coming from somewhere deep in the building, as though somebody's running a forklift into the trash chute which, incidentally, is pretty much jammed right now since this Ace Freewalter guy, you know, the supe, disappeared without starting the incinerator and kids are throwing things in at such a rate that the stink is piling up. Still, these are his people and Johnny Slater is on a roll.

By this time he's forgotten how this thing got started; he's forgotten the promises he made to get his people going and he's almost forgotten the Teach's pregnant wife who is by this time sitting in her chair in the shop with a pool of water at her feet—don't ask. What he's thinking about now as he looks out over the assembly is that this is going to be the bitchinest prom ever, he's here with an extremely sweet new woman, even though she still hasn't let him fuck her it's close, and nobody is never, ever gonna make him put on a stupid wig. He raises his hand for silence, which, forget it.

"Guys."

Wait. No great moment gets launched without a slogan, but the uprising at High Rise High was spontaneous, no big moment he can point to, no main reason, just a thousand kids exploding all at once. Now Johnny's people are milling and jabbering and he has to come up with some slogan or he'll blow this deal. "Guys," he says, but it's getting so loud in here that nobody hears.

In the back of the auditorium kids have started throwing ninja blades at the velvet curtains onstage and one of them zips close, maybe too close to Johnny's head. "Guys."

Funny, it's Mayor Patton that gets their attention. Amazing, his geeks have patched a remote into the school's PA system and his voice is booming from every speaker. GIVE UP OR WE NUKE YOU TO SAVE THE INSTALLATION. They think it's a bluff so only Agent Betsy knows it is true. The Mayor booms on, silencing the rally. HAVE YOU CHILDREN EVER HEARD OF NERVE GAS?

All it takes to move mountains is a really good threat. Kids start bumming right and left. Five minutes of this and they'll be storming the secret staircase, swarming out like rats.

"Babe," Johnny whispers into Trinket's Day-Glo hair. "It's you and me to the end."

It's odd, what happens to Agent Betsy then. *He loves me. Johnny **loves** me.*

On the other hand, you can find ways to turn a really good threat, to make people mobilize. At Johnny Slater's side, his girl Trinket starts shaking like a rocket at liftoff. Her thought balloon has a light bulb in it. She pulls a stick of something out of her front and with a wild grin, she lights it off. Johnny flinches but it isn't dynamite Trinket holds overhead like the Statue of Liberty's torch; it's a flare. "That's just shit!" she cries, and in the front row Dolph mutters to the guys, "What did she just say?" and Fred yells, "I think she said *what the shit!*" This rocks so strong that every kid in the place takes it up, and as it passes through the room Agent Betsy's angry outcry morphs into the kickass slogan to end all slogans. Pretty soon the place is rocking with it: "What the shit. What the shit!"

Crouched in the school ventilator system, Ace Freewalter rocks and nods in time to the chant. He is considering his options. With the stuff he's packing, he could blow every kid in the auditorium to smithereens, but you don't get the Congressional Medal for nuking a batch of high school kids when your mission is to bring them in under guard with a white flag to seal the surrender. He could use a Smart Bomb to take out the leader and his girlfriend but like any good soldier Ace knows every group like this has its unsuspected secret agent and he's pretty sure he knows who the city's agent is. All he needs to do, then, is separate this green-haired girl in the ruggy-looking shift from the boyfriend and give her the grip. He needs to get with this woman agent and figure out the best way to liberate this place. He and the agent will exchange passwords and together they'll figure out how to save the day and do it without harming the hair on a single kid.

Onstage with Johnny, cute, popular little Trinket is so caught up in the moment that she forgets who she used to be. The crowd roars and that stringy, unhappy, capable person whose dad died in the line of duty which is why she's such a good cop fades away. She fingers the silver Scrunchy Johnny put on her wrist excitedly because she's about to get everything she wants! In her life outside HRH, Betsy Gallaher went to her high school junior prom alone and her senior prom with a blind date who threw up on her feet, and no matter how smart a woman is, or how accomplished, no matter how smart *you* are, hurts incurred in high school never go away; they just go on hurting. Well, life's unexpectedly turned around for her. Trinket is going to the Tinsel Prom at HRH with the hottest boy in the entire school. It's soon! Overhead, the Decorations Committee thuds back and forth in a crepe paper and Mylar-fueled frenzy. Only one day left to get ready for the prom.

It is a long night, broken only by the mysterious architectural clanks and thuds characteristic of any building under siege. Unless something else is going on.

In the plaza outside HRH the mothers have merged into a solid, slow-moving wedge, pushing into the wall of Marine guards in front of the sealed front door. One has made it to the steps and is hammering angrily, in hopes that she's front and center on the school's surveillance cameras which have, incidentally, gone dead. She shouts in a voice big enough to crack stone, "Rafe Michaels, you come the hell out or I'm coming in."

The mothers won't know that this is like trying to storm a pyramid and if they did know it wouldn't stop them; mothers—even very small ones—have been known to occupy entire cities through sheer force of will. In the ranks, some of you are preparing your speeches. Threats: "Come out or *else*." Expressions of rage: "You'd talk to your *mother* like that?" Invitations to shame: "I'm glad Grandma Jo didn't live to see this." Some of you prepare to make promises—cars, trips to Cambodia, you name it—and some of you have come armed with the most powerful weapon of all. "I've got brownies, the kind with Heath Bar chunks," or the simpler, more powerful, "I baked."

Under orders to protect the perimeter at all costs, the Marines shift and try to close ranks but nobody gets in the way of women once they mobilize and nothing stops mothers on the move. They aren't as strong as the troops and they're relatively slow, but together they can move anything. They come down on the regiment with the force of an avalanche. In minutes the first of them are at the razor wire, watching mutely as some of their number move in with blowtorches, working until the wire at the base falls away from the walls, at least as far up as the tallest of them can reach.

Now it is morning. Everybody's on edge because they were too excited to sleep much. That funny thing where time flies at the same time that it doesn't move an inch. Kids have started wrangling out of sheer tension. Factions have formed and even more are forming.

It is axiomatic that every revolution spawns a counter-revolution, and Chunk Mackenzie didn't give up after Johnny's gang flattened him. If he can crack the captive teachers out, he will be a hero to the woman he loves. Looking for his true love, he found the pocket of holdouts in the principal's office. Now he's come back with his gang because he's convinced his love is inside. Ms. Flan, I mean Beverly, is waiting for him with, like they say in the romance paperbacks he secretly reads, with open arms. His Beverly isn't in the gym and she didn't evacuate with the fifty who got away, so she's gotta be in there. Listen, when Chunk breaks in and rescues her, she'll forget about him being a dull normal and fall in love with him for true.

It's either ESP or behind the door Beverly really is whispering, "Chunk, watch out!"

Then Principal Wardlaw sends Coach Dykstra out with an offer of amnesty. Armed with Marva Liu's can of Mace, to keep himself from falling into enemy hands, he holds it up. Chunk leaps for it like a dolphin surfacing in a tank. He knows the handwriting! The principal told her what words to put, but the flowery writing is all Beverly Flan. He recognizes it from his last French paper. *Not quite C work, Charles but for you, this is **merveilleuse**.*

He reads aloud: *Let us out and you'll all walk free. Plus expense-paid shopping sprees at the Brookdale Mall for all.*

"Go forth," Chunk mutters, "and tell the people." Climbing on a chair he yells, "Let them go and we walk free." He repeats because nobody seems to care: Chunk, who turns out to be the real idealist. Again, louder. "Let them go and we walk free!"

But a girl named Patsy looked on his paper before he got on the chair and she picks up on the real issue. "Listen," she shrieks, "It says let 'em go and it's the mall for all!

Boy, does this bring them running! "The Mall for All."

Pretty soon the halls of HRH (well, the classroom floors, at least) are rattling with colliding slogans. Alerted by the racket, Johnny's people come down in waves, roaring:

"What the shit," while Chunk's buds from the wrestling team try to push them back, yelling,

"WALK FREE, TURN OUR TEACHERS LOOSE,"

intercut with the airheads who picked up on the mall part of the message only and are screaming, "The Mall for All."

While in the library, the forgotten vestiges of the National Honor Society, the chess club and the choir sit among the comatose drinkers, singing so dolefully that you can't hear them, "Let my people go."

At the moment, the mall crowd is prevailing. For kids interned in this high-ticket institution packed with everything they thought they wanted, the call to the mall tugs with a powerful force. It isn't *stuff* they're interested in, the city baited this place with more stuff than they can use, clothes, computer games, cell phones, Rollerblades, you name it—it's the chance to walk free—well not free exactly, but in the place where everybody, like, you know, hangs out?

Where they just might accidentally bump into whoever or whatever it is that will end the boredom and do the magic that changes their life.

See, this is the thing. Our lives don't hang on what happens. Not back then, not now. It doesn't matter how many defeats we suffer or how bad it hurts, the thing that keeps us going is: what *might* happen. Here's what's important to us. It was important back then when we were in high school and it is important now.

Possibilities.

The skirmish outside Wardlaw's office is short and ugly. It ends with Dolph, Fred, and the rest of Johnny's gang on top, and. Wait. What they are on top of? Dolph is standing at the peak of the mound Chunk Mackenzie's gasping body makes with eight guys bearing down on him—yes, Johnny led the charge, he shoulder-checked Chunk and tipped him. Then Dolph and the others pushed him down. Inside, perhaps aware that this cavalry charge led by her dumbest student was a product of true love, Ms. Flan pats her lavender satin bosom and sighs. "That boy who took the note? I think I *know* that boy."

The clanking sound traveling up from the ground floor is nothing to worry about, it's just a pale reflection of the anger and frustration driving Harry Klein. The exhaust tube turned out to be a dead end for him, the sides were too slippery to climb and he was driven back by the fumes. Back at ground level after hours of effort, he used the climber's pick he boosted from his boss's mountaineering pack to hack his way out of the tube. Frustrated at every turn, he bashed the hell out of the clogged incinerator chute because the more he needs to find Betsy, the more frustrations the building hands out. Avenue after avenue turned out to be closed to him: faculty elevator shafts imploded, freight elevator disabled for good and all. In the end Harry threaded the maze of generators on the ground floor, intent on locating the emergency staircase he knew had to be in place somewhere. Before he worked on the governor's first campaign and was rewarded with a staff position, Harry was an architect, and he knows the state board would never approve a building that didn't come up to code.

Working with only the light from a pencil flash, he walked the walls until he found the secret staircase: the emergency exit, which is his emergency entrance, had been Sheetrocked and painted over. In seconds, he pried off the Sheetrock and then, using safecracking tools that happen to be his own from high school, he opens it. The stairs! By his reckoning, to get to HS1X, he will have to go up almost a hundred flights. What remains of the night before the prom will spin out unbroken for Harry Klein. Gnawing on a Power Bar, Agent Betsy's partner and, he hopes, upcoming life-partner, takes a deep breath and begins his climb.

All this coming and going, Doc Glazer thinks crossly, removing the Sheetrock some fool just dropped on the skylight to his place. It might look like a Dumpster to you, but by God it is his home. All this coming and going has turned it into a hellhole. *When am I, a simple hermit, going to get any peace?* When Doc could no longer shave his age and get away with it, hard-hearted Irving Wardlaw let the old English teacher go. The fool hired Bruce Brill, but survival is triumph; witness Doc. As it turns out, younger does not always mean better. Young Brill's stupidity started this whole riot thing, which serves Irv Wardlaw right.

And Doc is here to tell you that being let go doesn't mean you have to let go. When Howard Glazer cleaned out his desk after the farewell party last year and took the faculty elevator down for the last time, he contrived to ride down alone, which means that somewhere en route Doc managed to stop the nonstop elevator and climb on top of one of his less important cartons to get himself and the things he cared about out of the ceiling hatch. He pried open the doors on a storage floor and put his stuff through the opening, one box at a time. It took him six weeks to work himself and his stuff down to One which was important because Doc spied for long enough to find out that kids came and went down here, and then he spied long enough to learn where the kids' secret exit is located, because he likes to go out for an evening walk, although he's so jealous of his spot on the ground floor that he never leaves the grounds. In the months since, he's turned this Dumpster into a showplace, raiding the upper floors as needed for supplies.

Now there are so many people milling in the plaza outside that he can't slip out for his constitutional. He misses the fresh air. Worse, the combination of the mothers' thumping on the facade and the mayor's amplified SURRENDER message is so loud that he can't sleep and the mothers rock the building just enough so he can't rest, either. Worst of all, the ground floor is full of rabble: that pesky custodian, who tramped around all week collecting things instead of setting the incinerator on autostoke, which means the chute is jammed and the whole place is beginning to smell.

Doc can't be sure but he thinks there's a mother loose in here somewhere, and now this.

Sighing, he does what any good scholar does when presented with a problem. As he's alone here, he can't call a committee meeting about it, so Howard Glazer does the next best thing. He pulls out the books he has on riots and begins. When in doubt, he always says, research.

In the woodworking shop, Jane Brill is damn glad she isn't really in labor. She used the razor blade Agent Betsy gave her to slit the gallon water bottle by her chair so she could scare the crap out of Dolph and the rest of Johnny's gang by screeching, "My water broke!" You bet it cleared the room. The seven of them streamed out the door with their funky hair on end, and it won't matter what this Johnny says to them, no way are they coming back. For the first time, she's alone in the shop. Working quickly, she uses Agent Betsy's razor blade to free her other hand and with enormous difficulty, because she's in the ninth month and rather close to the end, does the necessary contortions so she can saw through the duct tape securing her feet.

Where the hell is Bruce, now that she needs him? What was he thinking when he tried to turn this kid Johnny into a surrogate son? This seventeen-year-old is plenty smart, witness his diatribe when they broke into her house, she particularly admired his choice of the words "assaholic pedant," and the imitation of Bruce in high mentor mode was dead on. Hell, he's probably smart enough to run this place, which means the last thing Johnny Slater wants to do is sit down and learn a thousand new words for the SATs, a test about memory tricks and test-taking skills, not smarts. But that isn't really what pissed him off. What pissed him off was Bruce running at him with the Titania wig and one of his gushy speeches about how in Shakespeare's day, all the girl parts went to the smartest and best-looking young men. What probably toppled the kid was the smarmy smile Bruce gets whenever he talks about "the bard." Jane knows kids have an astoundingly low threshold when it comes to sentimental crap.

So yeah, when you come right down to it this whole mess in High Rise High is Bruce's fault.

It's the kind of thing that makes you wonder whether you want your baby, which Bruce is trying to name Hamnet—whether you want your baby growing up under the influence of a chuckleheaded jerk. Oh yes she is angry, and she isn't just mad at Johnny or Dolph or Fred and the others who brought her here and taped her to the chair with only the briefest of pit stops and few chances to lie down. She is stark boiling pissed off at idealistic, boyish and well-meaning but careless, blundering Bruce.

It's a good thing she can't hear the gloppy things he's saying about her on Global TV right now.

Instead she's busy standing up, a project that takes more time than it ought to, and stretching her aching muscles one by one. When she finishes with the case of Devil Dogs Johnny's gang brought upstairs to pass the time in here, she's going to chug the quart of Gatorade they left behind and stretch out somewhere. She needs time for the blood to make its way back to her head so she can come up with a plan.

How odd. It's the morning of prom day and Trinket and Johnny are having a fight. Maybe it's excitement, maybe it's the mayor's ultimatum and the fact that time is getting short. They've been at it for so long that she forgets what started it; the kid part of her thinks something she said made Johnny jealous, in spite of the arrested development she's old enough that clearly, even in the most constricted life, he can't be her first. The mature Agent Betsy is reflecting on the causes of arrested development and the fact that when you let two children, even two children who love each other very much, play together long enough, they get tired and start to fight.

"Go to hell," she says.

"No," he says, "you go to hell and while you're at it lose the hair, it looks like shit."

She ought to find the way down the stairs/chute/elevator, however the kids get out, and exit the building and let what happens happen, it would serve him right. At the same time she can't write Johnny off, she thinks, regarding him from a great emotional distance while Trinket rips off the tinsel Scrunchy and, weeping, says, "Fine, and you can damn well find a new bug to take to the damn prom."

When she settles this riot thing and the attack squad comes in, she'll do everything she possibly can to cut a nice deal for the kid, but by hell she came in here to settle this riot thing and she is going to end it no matter what. On second thought, maybe she should throw a rope over the rafters in the indoor track and watch Johnny and all his sadistic buddies swing. OK he just grabbed her by the green ponytail and threw her in a corner, yelling, "Fine, I will."

She shouts, "So much for you, asshole," but she is thinking: *now I'll never get to wear my dress.*

"Asshole your own asshole," he barks and stamps out of the music room which is empty just now because the girls are in the teachers' bathroom, trying on dress after dress. The Trinket part of her is sobbing angrily, but in there so deep that he can't guess, Agent Betsy is thinking: *Fine.*

Perhaps you have forgotten about the mayor. Fair enough, it's not like he's doing anything to end the occupation here.

He's busy polishing his image as he prepares to give his primetime Prom Night ultimatum for international Webcast as well as worldwide TV satellite relay so that even the most private geeks happily mousing in the school's ruined computer labs will have to acknowledge that something's going on, never mind that the server is down and every kid who tries to connect is pounding on a blank screen. If you must know, Mayor Timothy a.k.a. Timid Tim Patton is grooming himself for a run for the Senate en route to the White House, and this is his first big step on the long road to DC.

Up Harry climbs, exhausted by now but driven by the need to resolve the situation—not so he will be a hero, but because he hates any kind of waste and millions of dollars and hundreds of kids are being wasted here. That and he's afraid Agent Betsy is in danger. Four days and not a sign! Of course he's been climbing the gigantic baffle the stairwell makes and therefore out of radio contact with the gov for the last twenty-four hours, and since he's the governor's man, his is the only information Harry trusts. He has to emerge into the school proper before he can run a sound test and there, he has to be careful because if they spot him, the kids will know at once that his fingernail-sized radio is government issue. Better keep it silenced, he thinks, and hope Betsy's faring forward and together they can put the lid on this riot at the Tinsel Prom. He has a few tactical weapons in his pack; he also has a plan.

In fact, he has a costume.

Once he reaches HRH1 he intends to put on his disguise and do his best to blend in with the panting rowdies and their ditsy girlfriends heading for the prom. Although he's too far north of thirty to make it stick Harry has studied the language, so that's not a problem, and he's devised the perfect costume, which he did by picking up on the Tinsel theme, which is, basically, silver everything. To make things simple, Harry decided to stay with the clothes he has on—plaid shirt, jeans, hiking boots, hell, he'll pass—and concentrate on the mask. For his arrival at the prom, he has chosen an antique. It is riding on his hip right now: a C-3PO mask that's so old it has turned silver, remember *Star Wars?* You may not, but rest easy, Harry Klein does. He's in touch with the zeitgeist. He knows kids, and he knows what they like.

Now, why this prom is so important. The prom is important because no matter where you started out in life or how far you've come since the big night, if you spent four years in an American public high school, you are formed by the way it came down at your prom. Nobody ever gets over it, and one way or another, you will try to get it back—or compensate for how bad it was for the rest of your life. You think you're a grownup, you think you're fine, but it doesn't matter what you've done to yourself between your prom night and now, any more than it matters what you have accomplished; you can lose the weight/tighten the abs and build the pecs/fix the hair/get the lift/have electrolysis/make the fortune, but in the beginning there was that problem with the prom and no matter how fast you've run, we know, and we know you know, that you are the same person.

Even if it was good your prom wasn't good enough. They never are. Even if you go with the hottest kid in the school, even if your hair is perfect, it's built in. It's supposed to be the happiest night of your life, which means no prom can be as good as you want. *All that,* you think, *and this is all I get?*

More likely, it was bad.

Either way, look back and be humbled by the prom you didn't make, the date you didn't get, the chance you missed because you went with the wrong person, or the existential question: why, when you went with the right person and everything went right, you came home feeling so empty and flat.

Mind you, this is not necessarily a bad thing. For the rest of our lives, people like us jump higher, try harder.

Well, Agent Betsy isn't going to get it back. *Instead,* she thinks, dressing for the prom again and getting ready to go without a date—again—*if she can't get it back,* she thinks . . .

She will get even.

In the best stories about high school, it all comes down at the prom.

In that ideal world we invent when we make stories, the prison riot and siege at High Rise High would end in the only possible way: at the prom.

It would end in the indoor track a.k.a. ballroom with all the kid factions and sympathizers present and the key outsiders—the mayor's agent and the governor's agent and the Gulf War vet and the pregnant woman and poor little McShy of the busted Stradivarius working their way through the littered halls or up through the bowels of the school for a gorgeous conflation, and at the height of the excitement probably—when Johnny crowns the wrong girl prom queen (*my man and my best friend: the rat went with Evie!*), when Johnny puts the Mylar crown on Evie Jones, the five valiant outsiders would burst into the ballroom followed by a thousand seething moms led upstairs by a cranky Doc Slater, and said mothers would shame their kids into submission while the mayor and the governor come in through the shattered skylight to declare amnesty and pin hastily engraved medals on Agent Betsy and Harry Klein who would, OK, who would kiss, take *that* Johnny Slater, while Jane Brill fingered

Johnny as her kidnapper and the tardy SWAT team read him his rights and dragged him away.

But remember, even when it goes well your high school prom is never what you thought it was going to be, so don't be surprised.

This one isn't either.

Every high school prom is a symphony of near misses. Maybe it's only the difference between the dress you thought you bought and the way it really looks on you, or the hopes you had for the peach tuxedo you rented with matching shirt and cummerbund, which looked pretty stupid when the cops were taking your particulars after you lost control and crunched it nose and front wheels halfway up the Whites' humongous forsythia; or your near miss may be something bigger, but only slightly bigger because these things never get as big as our hopes. The way proms like this one end is less likely to be a function of old scores settled and dramatic deflowerings and true love and moonbeams and wrongs righted than it is simple fatigue: the relieved sigh as you finally drop her off at her house (she was cute, but she was shrill) or take off your shoes (it was like kissing a cardboard Tom Cruise cutout on a lobby card), which have begun to bite; we all have dreams about the big moments in our lives but trust me, they are only expectations. When it comes right down to it, most things in life as we know it aren't resolved in fireworks or car crashes or explosions, instead they happen simply or accidentally or capriciously; they are settled out of fatigue or ennui or sheer boredom, so the real outcome, the true and final outcome of the stand at High Rise High?

1. The Federal Government was fully aware of the mayor's threats and dispatched local police to arrest him as his unilaterally set deadline neared. There is a full investigation being made of the city's nuclear arsenal, which turns out to be fuller than any state or federal authorities imagined. The mayor himself has been interned and certain irregularities in the matter of the building of High Rise High are under investigation.

2. The prom went just fine, or about the way proms usually do, in spite of the no adult faculty around to supervise. Remember, the riots began a week ago and nobody's slept in a real bed since so everybody arrived excited, but staggering with exhaustion. Eventually everybody at the prom just got tired of dancing and getting high and they straggled home to bed to crash or to the quiet neo-Olmsted park floor of the building to sleep on the artificial beach, or they drifted back into the corners they'd staked out in the library and the

computer lab, in the sentimental wish to spend one last night in the camps they had set up at the beginning of the high school revolution, when they had such hopes. Right now not one of the kids who rioted and took over HRH could tell you what they'd hoped to gain.

3. Emerging in the last minutes of the dance, i.e. at the moment when Dolph, designated standin for Principal Wardlaw, was crowning Johnny Slater prom king, Jane Brill slipped out from behind the bandstand and made a terrified Chunk Mackenzie show her to the single functioning elevator. Stampeding him with a touch of the end-stage breathing she'd learned at Lamaze, you know, the kind you're supposed to use when you bear down at the end? she pressed the button and rode down alone, and . . .

4. at the bottom the mothers milling on the ground floor parted like the Red Sea—she's a mother, like *us*—so Doctor Howard Glazer, HRH (retired), could lead the nice lady to the kids' secret exit (it was behind the incinerator!), open the hatch and usher her outside, so that from the front you saw double doors in the foundation opening and a small, angry, very pregnant woman marching out, spreading her arms to the fresh air. If you were glued to your television or your computer screen like the rest of us you may have seen the Marine lieutenant in charge mutter into the little woman's ear and if you did, you saw her bark a response that made him flinch. Our microphones didn't pick up what either said but apparently the lieutenant offered to take her to her husband, he was worried about her, and that's what set her off.

"Aha," the mayor said from the police van, where the Chief was keeping track on his Watchman while he dealt with the city's most important prisoner. "I was right. They're giving in!"

"Bullshit," the kids would have said, if any of the kids had been awake to see it. They'd partied till they puked and then some. "We're going the hell to bed."

They were bored of the riot anyway.

Which means that in the principal's office, Irving Wardlaw wakes up to daylight and the awareness that the riot is over. The prom is over. The music's stopped and with it, the relentless thump of the bass speakers that vibrated on every floor. So has the thud of a thousand teenagers jumping up and down. The smell of weed has dissipated and the laughter's died. They are gone. The first to wake, he studies his embattled colleagues. The sleeping McShy's fingers are moving on his bony chest as though he's still playing his ruined violin, while Beverly Flan sleeps with her fat mouth pursed in the face she makes when she tries to teach freshmen how to pronounce *le*. Smiling, Dykstra and Marva Liu sleep in each other's arms. It's Sunday morning, which means they have the day off. He needs to decide whether to keep the staff in the office here, along with the teacher hostages sleeping in the gym, so he'll have a skeleton staff in place when classes start on Monday morning, or whether to cancel graduation so he can give them next week off to recover and take the rest of the summer off. Maybe the latter, he thinks, looking at the broken glass in his office door with a sigh. It's going to take at least that long to get this place cleaned up. But then. He feels that little ripple of excitement that comes every time he thinks the word *September*. Then we'll have our second wind by the time school starts in the fall.

Fall, he thinks. Definitely time for a fresh start.

Meanwhile Klein and Agent Betsy have found each other. It happened early in the prom, he came busting out of the woodwork in his c-3po mask and they knew each other at once, which means they were dancing close by the time Johnny gave Evie the tinsel crown which nonetheless snagged what was left of Trinket's girly heart. But it felt so good, slow-dancing with Harry, that Betsy hardly minded. She thinks. She and Harry danced straight through until daylight filtered through the shattered glass overhead and then fell down on a pile of coats. After the weeklong siege, they are too tired to do anything but talk.

He says, "This was supposed to be our big moment."

"Yeah, I guess it was." Looking around at the littered ballroom, the debris of a thousand high school kids' hopes, she says quietly, "Is it always like this?"

"What do you mean?"

"You know, no denouement and no real resolution, no clinch and no ticker tape parade."

"Probably. But you're wrong about the clinch."

"So there's that," Betsy says, beginning to smile.

"Yes," he says, tightening his arm around her wiry little back. Even though there is only one prom, there is always a next time. "There is."

In the tinsel archway looking back, Johnny tightens his hold on Evie's hand until she squeaks. In this light Trinket looks like, she looks like a . . . She doesn't, but now that he knows Trinket is really Agent Betsy, who is thirty-five years old, he can write the thought that will make sense of this. *What, me care about that old hag?*

Oddly, the mothers in the building do not leave the building, even though the matter of the riot is settled and by Presidential order, the mayor's threat is no longer a threat. They're bopping around among the crates and blocks of heavy equipment on the ground floor because like it or not, this thing has brought home the fact that they still care. They miss their kids, they really do; they miss these near-adults their babies and they miss having them at home but now that push comes to shove they are conflicted and confused. Homesick for the way things used to be and fully aware that once puberty hits, nothing is ever the same, they can't decide whether they should stay and see their sons and daughters, at least to find out how they are doing, or whether they should avoid the aggravation (what if h/she wants to come home? what if h/she doesn't want to come home even if I beg?) and go.

Meanwhile, in the military it is axiomatic that there's always one in every organization that doesn't get the word. Ace Mackenzie hunkers down in the ventilator system directly over the girls' locker room. Eventually the revolution is going to boil in here and he can swing down and take control of the sub-group that brings down the leaders of this fucking riot and when he does that he's going to take out all the troublemakers and bring this place to order, and when he does . . .

He doesn't know, but he can think about it. Right now he has nothing but time.

—Dogs of Truth, 2005

Piggy

Theron swore it. A great winged figure swooped out of the sky one night and threw itself on Duchess, the old Percheron.

Theron ran in the house as soon as it happened and tried to tell his Daddy, but his Daddy just pushed him aside and said "Don't talk dirty," and that was the end of it until the mare foaled the next year. The colt was pink, plastic pink, like the thumb-sized baby dolls in the ten-cent store, and Theron's Daddy had to look close to see the light planting of white hair. The mare's pink baby was round as a couple of barrels, and when he finally got up he teetered on legs too spindly to support a puppy dog. Right off the Pinckneys named him Piggy.

Mostly, Piggy was Theron's pet. Before Piggy came, Theron didn't have anybody in the crumbling old house. There was nobody to talk to but his mother and nobody to play with but the twins, who were too small even to sit up alone, so he just naturally took to Piggy, and pretty soon he was keeping Piggy right outside his bedroom window, in a stall made by the caved-in part of the porch. Theron stuffed hay between the carved railings so Piggy could eat lying down, and he hung a grain bucket from one of the marble pillars, where Piggy could poke it with his nose. His mother gave him a big flowered bowl her granddaddy had used to make punch in, so when Piggy wanted water he wouldn't have to go all the way down to the trough.

Cold nights, when winter was frosting the marsh grass, Mrs. Pinckney would look out the window at Piggy shivering, and she'd get a quilt or Mr. Pinckney's Navy parka and throw it over Piggy in his stall. Sometimes she'd let Theron go outside and sit with him, and Theron would light a little fire right under Piggy's nose.

The night of the hurricane, Mrs. Pinckney made Theron bring Piggy inside the big double doors to take shelter in the living room, and after that Piggy used to spend a lot of time inside. Mrs. Pinckney would send Theron after him whenever Mr. Pinckney was shrimping out of Port Royal or spending his money in Beaufort, the nearest big town. He had clean habits when he was indoors, and he'd fold his legs under him by the fire with his head in Theron's lap, and blow little noises through his nose at Luvver and Fester, the twins. Mrs. Pinckney would sit in the chair that Theron's great-great-great-great had brought with him all the way from England, watching Theron tying knots in Piggy's yellowed mane, and she'd think how nice it was for Theron to have a pet. Daytimes, when Theron was gone, Piggy used to call to her, and many's the time when she sat on the porch rail, just looking at him. He even tried to follow her a couple of times, getting unsteadily to his feet, but she made him keep to his stall and wait for Theron, because he belonged to the boy.

Theron's Daddy felt differently about things. He never went near the stall when he could help it, and the very mention of Piggy made him mad. He had a right to be galled. He'd been pouring grain into Piggy for years, hoping he'd get strong enough to pull a plow, or at least to take the twins out in a basket cart, but Piggy went all shivery every time Mr. Pinckney brought the cart around and his legs buckled every time Mr. Pinckney tried to put the harness on. Mr. Pinckney would swear at him and then Piggy would have to eat some more so he could get his strength up again. Even Theron couldn't get him to move. At first Mr. Pinckney put up with it because Piggy was just a colt and the rest of the family liked him a lot.

But by the time Theron was fifteen Piggy was five years old and Mr. Pinckney had had just about enough. He was eating more grain than Duchess and Rollo put together and he hadn't done a lick of work in his whole pink life. Theron got up one morning to see his father sitting on the porch rail and looking down at Piggy, who was all curled up like an oversized tabby cat at his feet.

"Mornin, Theron," Mr. Pinckney said.

"Mornin, Daddy."

"I was just lookin at Piggy here," Theron's Daddy said, and Theron's heart sank.

"Yes, Daddy," Theron said, and he perched his behind on the porch rail and looked at Piggy too. Piggy lowered his white eyelashes and gave him a yellow look.

Mr. Pinckney settled his bristly chin in his collar. "Piggy's eaten enough of my grain. I'm gonna call the dog warden tomorrow and have him put away."

"The *dog* warden." Theron looked hurt.

Mr. Pinckney poked Piggy with his toe. Hairless, porcine, Piggy was nibbling thoughtfully at his hoofs. "You call that thing a horse?"

"Piggy's a *good* horse, Daddy," Theron said.

His Daddy jerked his head at his old coon hound. "So's Archambault."

"I *mean* it, Daddy," Theron said. "You just give me a chance with him and you'll see." Theron mumbled some words around in his mouth till they tasted right. Then his face lit up. "I bet I could have him broke for ridin by tonight."

He ran his fingers through Piggy's sparse yellow mane. "You been sayin Mama shouldn't have to walk all that way to town. Piggy could take her."

"That's right, Eldred." Theron's mother shook Theron's feather mattress out the window by their heads. She didn't care one way or the other about riding him, but Piggy was a special friend of hers.

Archambault came up and licked Piggy on the nose.

"OK," Theron's Daddy said. "You get him broke by tonight and you can keep him."

"Gee, Daddy." Theron was already coaxing Piggy to his feet. "Hey Luvver," he said, and he gave Luvver the special look that meant he'd better hop to it or he'd get what for. Between them, they got Piggy hove to and headed for the back field. Theron was walking in front, pulling Piggy along, looking proud as Lucifer, and for a minute Piggy was really picking up his feet instead of just dragging them along. "You just wait, Daddy," Theron said. "He'll be broke in before you can get to Beaufort and back. Won't he, Luvver?"

Five minutes later Luvver was back. He tugged at his Daddy until Daddy gave him a bucket of grain. "Piggy sat down," he said.

They held the grain out in front of Piggy until he followed it to the pasture. Then they let him lie on his side and eat grass while Theron rode Luvver around and around, pretending to go on all fours, to give Piggy the idea. Then they got him propped up on his four legs and Theron put Luvver on his back. Piggy sat down. Luvver slid off, hollering, "Hey hey, that's the way," and Theron took him by the collar and said, "Don't be fresh."

Next time he slid off, Luvver hollered, "I'll use force, you dumb horse," and "He's too fat up where I sat" the next. Each time he said something he'd hit the ground and look foolish for a minute, and then he'd start swearing at Piggy to beat the band. When Theron shook him he'd say, "Piggy made me say it. I had to talk like that." Theron just said, "Aw Luvver, don't be dumb," but the next time he slid off, Luvver said, "I went dump and hurt my rump," and Theron told him to get back to the house and send Fester out instead.

While he was waiting for Fester, Theron jacked the back end of Piggy up again and pushed him sideways so his belly was over a rock and he couldn't sit down. It was near noon and Fester was slow coming, so he decided to mount Piggy himself. Piggy looked around at him with an injured expression as he scrambled up on the fat back. Then Piggy shimmied his bald rear quarters a bit, trying to sit down, and he curled his lip at Theron when he found he couldn't sit down because of the rock. His eyelids drooped and he whuffled as if he'd been betrayed.

"There, there, Silverhair," Theron said, and patted him on the neck. Then he reared back because a crawly feeling had come over him and he didn't know from one minute to the next what he was going to say. Piggy tried to sit down again and before he could stop himself Theron was poking him with his heels and spouting:

Come on horse,
I got no other.
Gotta break you
For my mother.

It scared him so much that he scrambled off and ran halfway across the field. Piggy didn't look any different. He just stood there watching Theron, wiggling his hind quarters and trying to get his middle off the rock. Theron snuck up on Piggy, from the wrong side this time, and got on again. He sat there for a minute, feeling different about Piggy and the field and the day, and suddenly something started prickling inside him and before he could help it he opened his mouth and sang out:

Life is real, life is earnest
And the grave is not its goal.
Dust thou art, to dust returnest
Black as the pit from pole to pole.

And it was so beautiful that Fester almost caught him crying when he appeared suddenly in the field.

"Hello, little fellow," he said to Fester, who thumbed his nose. Then he slid down off Piggy because he couldn't trust himself to go on. "You get on back to the house, hear? I don't need you here. And you tell Momma and Daddy to come on down here just before it gets dark." He made a shooing motion. "Git."

As soon as Fester had gone he went back to Piggy and looked long into his yellow eyes. Piggy just breathed in and out, not much caring, and let his lower lip droop because it had been a long hot day.

"What you got in you, horse?" Theron said, and when Piggy wouldn't even turn his head far enough to nuzzle Theron's hand, Theron climbed up on him again to see if that strange feeling would come back. As soon as he got on the whole field seemed to turn all green and shimmery and the sky was changing colors like a piece of mother of pearl. He shook his head because all sorts of strange things were buzzing around inside, and before he could stop himself he was talking out loud again, in words that sounded even fancier than the poem they were reading that year in seventh grade. Theron just threw back his head and listened to himself, talking long, rolling musical lines about things he'd never heard of in this world, and he kept it up until he felt Piggy shaking beneath him, getting tired, and then he tumbled off and led Piggy under a shade tree where they could get some rest.

When Theron's mother and Daddy came down to the field that night, there was Piggy, standing up straighter than he ever had in his fat life, and Theron, looking tall and proud, was sitting on his back. He stayed up until he was sure they'd had a good look at Piggy and then he slid down and said, "See, Daddy? He's broke. He carried me just fine."

Mr. Pinckney was just about to open his mouth and say, "If he's so well broke in, let's see him walk," but Mrs. Pinckney was grabbing him by the elbow and dragging him away, saying, "That's wonderful, Theron," with every step she took. When they got out of earshot she told Mr. Pinckney it didn't really matter if Theron had propped Piggy up on a rock. If he cared that much about Piggy let him keep him, and if she saw the dog warden even drive past in his pickup truck she was going to forget the marriage vows and fill Mr. Pinckney full of shot.

Theron came back from the field so late that his parents were already in bed. His mother had left a plate of hoppin' john on the table, but he was too stirred up to eat. He went to bed instead, murmuring verses over and over to himself, so he'd be able to remember them the next day.

Everybody thought Theron was in school the next morning, like he ought to be, but when Luvver and Fester started playing hide-and-seek, and Luvver left Fester hiding his eyes on the tree counting to a million and two, he took off for the back field to find Theron sitting on Piggy in the middle of the field, waving his arms for all he was worth. Luvver said why wasn't he in school, but Theron just said something he couldn't understand and gave him such a ferocious look that he turned and ran for home. He didn't even tell Fester about it when Fester finally found him hiding under the marble-topped pier table, where Theron's Daddy kept his boots.

Long and fine-ringing words were swimming in Theron's head when he came up for dinner that night. He came late, about six, and everybody but his mother was sitting out on the front porch. Theron slid around to the kitchen and pulled up at the table while she had her back to him, working at the stove.

"Mama," he said, and she jumped because she hadn't heard him come in at all. "Mama, don't you think this is beautiful?" and then he said a long, musical piece that ended:

Footprints in the time of sands . . .

Hugging his skinny shoulders, trying to hold the words within himself because they warmed his insides.

His mother touched his head affectionately. "You better eat your grits."

His father wouldn't even listen.

Theron cornered Luvver outside the cold-house after school the next day, and said poetry at him and *said* poetry at him. Luvver was quiet enough, and Theron's heart lightened, until he saw that Luvver was quiet mostly because he was picking his nose.

He kept pretty much to himself after that, going down to the field as soon as he got home from school. He was quiet and edgy most of the time, thinking about the poetry that would come to him as soon as he got on Piggy's back. Piggy still hated standing up, but he seemed to know how much pleasure it gave Theron, because he stood patiently as long as Theron wanted him to.

Once Theron came home from school to find his mother on her knees beside Piggy, running her fingers over his balding neck. She looked up at him and said, "Is there something special about Piggy, son?"

He said, "I tried to tell you, Mama. He makes poetry come."

"These things I hear you say in your sleep?"

"I guess so, Mama." He wished she would let him go. He wanted to get on Piggy's back again.

"It was real strange," she said thoughtfully. "He almost tried to get up a while ago. He kept poking me with his nose like there was something he wanted me to do."

Not long after that Theron built a lean-to down by the field and moved Piggy out of his stall on the porch for good. He snuck out of the house with a Queen Anne chair and a pile of quilts and a Holland vase to make the place look pretty, and he fixed up the shack. When fall came, he used a lever to roll the big rock in the door of the shack, so that they could sit there most of the day, Theron mouthing poetry and Piggy drowsing a little, one hip dropped, listening to Theron's voice. His Daddy was off with the shrimp fleet, looking for better waters, and there was nobody to bother Theron about how much time he spent down at the field.

Daytimes Piggy would let Theron ride him, and some new lines would come to him as he sat, and evenings he would talk to Piggy, reciting as many lines as he could remember, and Piggy would lie on his side with fat flanks heaving. He'd put his muzzle in Theron's lap and look up at him with yellow eyes. One of the twins would come down with a little pail of supper and Theron wouldn't have to go back to the house until late at night. Sometimes his mother would stop him in the halls and look him in the eyes and try to talk to him, but he'd say, "Night, Mama," and go to his room. In bed, he would cross his feet and look at the ceiling, calling the lines as they came to him. Soon there were so many crowding in his mind that he was afraid he'd forget some, and he took to writing them down. He moved into the shack that October, and he and Piggy lived quietly in the haze of autumn, with words flying around their heads like dandelion puffs in the sun.

It was too beautiful not to share. Theron went up to his Daddy's rolltop desk one day and got a magazine and copied the address down, because he thought other people ought to be able to see Piggy's poetry too. He got three cents from his mother, who loved Theron enough to let him go his own way, and he got out one of his favorite poems and mailed it to the *Breeders' Gazette*. He went down to the mailbox every day for a couple of weeks, looking for a letter, and then he forgot about it.

In November Theron's Daddy came home. He dropped his canvas bag and his yachting cap on the floor in the front hall and peeled off the twins, who were climbing up his trousers, and asked Mrs. Pinckney where Theron was.

She chased the twins into the kitchen and said, "Dow't the field."

Theron's Daddy gave her a close look. "He been any help to you since I left?"

"Course he has," she said, edging in front of the dining room door so he wouldn't see the harness Theron was supposed to repair, still waiting on the dining room table.

"He's wasting his time with that—*horse*." Mr. Pinckney pushed his sleeves up above his elbows and looked around for something to threaten Theron with.

"Eldred Pinckney, you lay one hand on that boy . . ." Mrs. Pinckney stood toe to toe with him.

He backed down a little. "It's not Theron, it's *Piggy* I'm after," he growled. "Should've let the dog warden take him right off. I'll drive him down to Beaufort tonight and see what I can get for him . . ." Theron's Daddy was so mad he'd forgotten Piggy wouldn't walk. He grabbed a cane from the elephant-foot umbrella stand and barged for the front door. The screen swung open and banged him in the face and he reared back to see a little man in a sack suit still reeling from his battle with the door.

"It's wonderful. *Wonderful*," he said, sweeping past Theron's Daddy and taking Mrs. Pinckney by both hands. "Where is he?" He readjusted a folder of papers under his arm and started sniffing around the house.

"What's wonderful," Mr. Pinckney said, standing smack in the doorway so the little man couldn't see into Theron's room.

"Why, *this*," the man in the sack suit said. He closed his eyes as if he were in church and started reciting:

Sky of Sky! With clouds all brindle
With the birds that dart between them
And thy sun which doth enkindle
Nightingales before we've seen them
In our nooks . . .

Then his voice trailed off as he saw that Theron's parents didn't think it was wonderful at all, they were just staring, and he said, "Oh, you didn't know about it," his voice getting fainter and fainter, " . . . perhaps-I'd-better-explain . . ."

A little later, while Mr. Pinckney was sulking on the widow's walk, Mrs. Pinckney took the man in the sack suit down to Theron's field. Theron was just taking Piggy into the shed.

"Theron, honey, this is Mister Brooks. He runs a poetry magazine . . ."

Mr. Brooks flushed to his round collar and said, "That's just in my spare time, I'm afraid. Actually I work for the *Breeders' Gazette*. I was down this way doing a story on hogs . . ."

"You got my poem?" Theron said and pulled him inside.

He sat Mr. Brooks down on a marble-topped commode, far enough away from Piggy so that Mr. Brooks wouldn't be frightened of him, and they talked for a long time. Mr. Brooks told Theron the *Breeders' Gazette* didn't exactly take to his kind of poetry, in fact it didn't take to poetry at all, but he happened to be working there ("just to support my poetry magazine") and he saw it and he wanted Theron to know he thought it was great. Then Mr. Brooks gave him a copy of *Fragile*, which was *his* magazine, and then he gave Theron five dollars, which was because his poem was in it. He got down off the commode and came over and took Theron's hand.

"If you could come back to Louaville with me, I bet I could get you a scholarship somewhere. You could write poetry for the reviews, you know, the *Prairie Schooner,* you could win the Bollingen prize . . ." Mr. Brooks's eyes were hazed over with longing. "We'd both be *famous,* son. With your talent . . ."

"———," Theron said through his fingers, blushing red.

"What did you say?"

"It wasn't me, it was Piggy." He said it over and over, but Mr. Brooks didn't want to understand. Theron did get it across to him that he couldn't go to Louaville ever and thank you very much. Then he looked down at the five dollars and he promised to send Mr. Brooks all his poems because Mr. Brooks seemed to feel so bad.

He patted Piggy on the nose and walked Mr. Brooks to the edge of the field. "I couldn't leave Piggy, see," he said, and then he handed Mr. Brooks a big sheaf of poems because he looked like he was about to cry.

On his way back to the house Mr. Brooks must have said something to Theron's Daddy, because he came down to the shack and took Theron's five dollars. After that he never said anything more about getting rid of Piggy, and he stopped talking about sending Theron back to school.

There were little bits of money after that—Theron's Daddy took the checks to keep up the house—and copies of magazines, *Challenge* and *Output* at first, mimeographed just like *Fragile,* and then austere-looking reviews that bored Theron and Piggy because there were no pictures in, and in a few years there were copies of *The Atlantic* and *The Saturday Review.* One year Piggy was a Yale Younger Poet. Sometimes people came down to see Theron, all bright-eyed and loaded down with their own poetry but Theron's Daddy sent them away. Every once in a while Mr. Brooks would send Theron a clipping about a speech he'd given on poetry—Theron's poetry, because Mr. Brooks had appointed himself Theron's literary Goddaddy and his agent (that was the way he explained it to Theron) and he was very famous now. He'd even quit the *Breeders' Gazette.*

In a few years the twins got married and moved away, and there began to be scruffy patches on Piggy's shoulders, and transparent hairs in his mane. Theron only sat on his back two hours a day now, and the words that came to him were all detached and sharp and pure, wheeling like gulls over the river.

His mother brought his food down to him every evening and took the poems to mail to Mr. Brooks. Piggy's longest poem paid for the funeral when Theron's Daddy died. After he was buried and put away, Theron's mother began hanging around the shack door of an evening, too lonely to go back to the big old house. At first Theron was impatient with her for being there, because the words were singing in his brain and he wanted to be alone with them, but one night when she touched his hand as she gave him the bucket, he looked down to see soft, trembly lines around her mouth, and he was so sorry about that and the way her hand shook that he opened the door and sat her down in the Queen Anne chair. Piggy rocked a little until he was lying alongside her, and put his head in her lap. They both sat quiet as marsh-rabbits and listened to Theron make the words ripple in the air.

Theron threw back his head in the glow of the lamp, thinking he'd be perfectly happy if he could die right then. As his mother got up to go something glittered on her cheek, and Theron saw that there were tears in her eyes.

"Son, that was beautiful." She ducked her head and slipped out the door before Theron could say anything to her. Piggy nickered and looked almost as if he'd like to follow her up to the big house and put his head in her lap again. When she came the next night Theron opened the door and motioned toward the Queen Anne chair without a word. After that his mother spent all the long evenings with him and Piggy, listening to Theron in the closeness of the low-ceilinged shack.

One night after she'd left, Piggy nudged Theron, who watched amazed as Piggy struggled to his feet without urging and edged his hind quarters around so that his belly was resting on the rock. He took Theron's sleeve gently in his teeth, tossing his head until Theron climbed up, slowly because Piggy tired easily these days. Then he gave Theron his most beautiful piece of poetry. When he got it in the mail Mr. Brooks was to say that it was the culmination—the pearl—of Theron's late period:

The sun kept setting, setting still,
Because I could not stop for Death.
Great Streets of silence led away—
I took my power in my hand,
As far from pity as complaint.
My life closed twice before its close
I asked no other thing.
Safe in these alabaster chambers
A spider sewed at
Night.

When his mother heard it the next evening she wept.

Days sang and days passed, one like the other, until Theron's mother tapped at the door one night, bright-eyed and quivering. Theron sat quietly without beginning, because he knew she had something on her mind. She ducked her head, pretending to stroke Piggy's sparse mane, and then she saw that Theron wasn't going to begin; he was waiting for her to tell him what was bothering her.

"Mister Gummery was asking after you, Theron," she said.

Theron scratched his head.

"He was in fourth grade the year you quit school." Her hands fluttered in Piggy's mane.

Theron rattled some papers, wondering what she was going to say.

"Theron." She got up abruptly, so that Piggy's chin fell off her lap and bumped on the floor. "He says the church is going to have its hundred-twentieth birth-day next month, and he wants you to write them a play."

Suddenly, Theron's hands were still. "Mama, I don't know if I can. Piggy's getting tired." His voice sounded old. "And so am I. Can't he use some play out of a book?"

Her eyes were hurt. "I never asked you anything before. Your great-great granddaddy went to that church." She touched his arm gently. "Son?"

Theron looked at Piggy, whose skin was almost transparent now under the light fall of his brindled mane. Piggy's white-rimmed eyes were wide open and swimming with love. He began rocking and rocking back and forth gently, back to floor, then belly, until he got his spidery legs under him and began heaving himself to his feet. He almost made it and then he fell, catching splinters in his delicate knees. Theron rushed to him but he was already struggling again, heaving until he got his legs under him. He rose with a massive gesture and with a sigh put his nose on Mrs. Pinckney's shoulder. Theron gave him one tragic look and then turned to his mother.

"You better go now, Mama. Piggy and I have to get to work."

Piggy carried Theron on his back all that night and all the next day and they were still going the next evening, when Mrs. Pinckney scratched at the door of the shack. Theron's eyes were bloodshot and his fingers cramped from scribbling, but Piggy snatched at him with his teeth every time Theron tried to get down. Finally Theron scribbled "The End," so drunk with words that he didn't realize what he was writing, and with a gallant toss of the head Piggy fell sideways away from the supporting rock and sank to the floor. He turned his head toward Theron, and his eyes glazed over with pride.

"Mama," Theron said simply. "The play."

She turned her eyes away because she couldn't stand to see Piggy's rigid fat body with the legs sticking out, or the pain in Piggy's eyes. After the church show, when Mrs. Pinckney sent a copy of the play, *A.B.,* to Mr. Brooks, he sent her a pile of money and told her it was going to Broadway and Theron would certainly win the Poets' Prize. The money came too late. Piggy had already gone into a decline.

Theron called a heart specialist down from Charleston (he'd have nothing to do with a vet, like he'd had nothing to do with the dog warden all those years before) but there was nothing anybody could do. He took to his shack, pining so that he wouldn't even let his mother come in at night. She sat on a step out-side, listening for Piggy's breath.

The prize came the day after Piggy was buried under a wooden marker, down in the soft grass at the end of the field.

Five men in dark suits and black Homburgs and a woman in a lace-trimmed dress and a velvet tam pulled up outside the Pinckney house. Hushed by the brooding trees, they talked in whispers until Mrs. Pinckney opened the front door. She hardly recognized Mr. Brooks, he was so gray and distinguished-looking. She seemed not to understand until, wordlessly, the woman held out a small leather case with the medal, nested in satin, bearing Theron's name.

"Oh," Mrs. Pinckney said. "You want my son."

They followed her around the house, past crumbled garden statues and a sundial that had sunk into itself a hundred years before, nudging each other and whispering as they caught glimpses of ruined chiffoniers and Federalist mirrors through the tall, low windows. Gently, they untangled vines and bushes from their ankles and, single file, looking reverent and austere in the bright daylight, they followed Theron's mother across the hummocked field. They picked their way up the worn little path and stood uneasily at the door to Theron's shack. His mama called to him. There was a rustling inside and Theron poked out his shock-white head.

He stood in the doorway with the sleeves of his blue work shirt rolled up above his gaunt elbows, and looked at the men in the fine black suits. Then he smiled tentatively at Mr. Brooks, who nodded almost shyly, and the ceremony began.

The leader of the delegation gave his speech. Theron heard him say something about "most coveted prize in poetry," and he said, "Piggy'll be glad," but the man in the sack suit gave him a puzzled look and went on with the speech. Theron waited respectfully until he was finished, stepping aside because he could see that the lady in the velvet hat was trying to peek inside his door. He looked over his shoulder and saw that the Queen Anne chair was standing up, just where he'd propped it, and Piggy's place was all swept clean. He whispered, "That's where Piggy used to sleep," but she pretended not to hear.

" . . . pleased to give you this award," the speaker concluded, and he held out the medal so Theron could see where they had engraved his name.

"It wasn't me," Theron mumbled, and they all nodded their heads and twittered to each other about his modesty. "It wasn't me, it was Piggy," Theron said again, as they pressed the leather case with the medal into his hands. "It was Piggy," he said again as they bowed their heads in a moment's respect and turned like nuns in a procession and started single file back across the field. "It was Piggy," Theron said, looking down at the glint of the medal in his hands.

He sat down on the front step of his shack, turning the case over and over, watching the sunlight catch the gold until tears shimmered in his eyes and he couldn't see. Then he went inside and combed his hair and put on a clean shirt. Slowly, as the delegation had walked, he went to the end of the field and put the leather case on Piggy's grave.

—*The Magazine of Fantasy and Science Fiction*, 1962

Song of the Black Dog

"The black dog is not like any other," the forensics officer says. It is a little incantation.

In the journalists' skybox high above the civic auditorium, Bill Siefert strains to see the distant stage, the speaker, and at her back, the beast he is here to deconstruct. That's the way he thinks of it. Siefert hates anything he doesn't understand. If it doesn't make sense, disassemble it. He's always been uncomfortable with the idea of supernatural powers, but this is not his stated reason for sneaking into the press box. He thinks he's here to crack the black dog program and show the people its inner workings. If the wonder dog is just a dog, then the police department are money-grubbing charlatans and the exposé will move him from unemployed to famous.

He'll be all over CNN. Networks will come calling. *Silence the black dog,* he thinks, and wonders where that came from. Stop mizzling and get the story. He needs a job. He needs the attention. He needs the power. He needs to be more than who he is, and before any of this and all of this Bill Siefert needs to figure out why this morning, on a perfectly ordinary day, he woke up screaming.

Get the story, he tells himself and does not know what about this makes him so uneasy. Cell phone for instant screen shots. Notebook, digicorder, nice smile. Seat in the booth. Fake press pass to get him backstage. Piece of cake.

With the black dog, nothing spins out the way you expect.

"The black dog can cut through the welter of visual and olfactory stimuli in a disaster situation and find those most in need of rescue," the forensics officer says matter-of-factly, as though this is a given. She is sleek in the black uniform. Persuasive. It is disturbing. "He is only the first," she says and then she says portentously, "His descendants will save thousands."

Cut to the chase. Startled, Bill shakes himself. *Did I speak? Who?*

The speaker glitters in a cone of light but the wonder dog—if there is one—is nowhere present. Peering into the shadows behind her, Bill looks for the darker shadow signifying a living creature, reflected light pinpointed in the eyes. The darkness gives back only darkness. Nothing to see, he tells himself, and wonders why this comes as a relief. No dog. Another wasted day like so many days in what is shaping up to be a wasted life.

With the black dog, the future is open to question.

In the next second he shivers, transfixed. He can't even guess what just happened, but all the furniture in his head has shifted.

It sees me.

Given that the stage is far, far below this is unlikely, but the sense that he is being watched is so acute that all of Bill Siefert's bones begin to itch. No, he tells himself. No way. He swallows hard but his throat closes. It's just a dog.

Far below, she continues, "Of course the prototype is a genetic fluke, but one that can be exploited for the good of all."

Yeah, he thinks bitterly. *Yeah, right.*

There are a thousand people in the auditorium, city officials and guests, all in some variation on black tie, velvet, opera-length pearls. The gentry have come out for this press conference—the unveiling of the superdog. A thought flies across Bill's mind: *If there is a dog.* Shifting on his haunches, sweating for no apparent reason, he thinks: *what if I kidnap the thing?* Down, boy. Focus. First in his class in Communications Studies, but a tad bit A.D.D. No wonder he can't keep a job.

The woman who discovered and trained the black dog continues thoughtfully. "We're not certain exactly which combination of pheromones alerts the black dog, but we do recognize his singular power. He can rush into a burning building or dig his way into earthquake debris and go like an arrow to the victim most in need."

Fine, Bill thinks, *your basic St. Bernard.* It helps to picture him bounding over the snow with that keg of rum and the pink tongue flapping. Pant pant pant. Hello, I am here to save you. He tries to laugh but his belly is jittering and when he tries to swallow, the spit won't go down. There is something terribly the matter here, and nobody sees it but him.

"The black dog is unique," she says. "He has no interest in the quick or the dead."

Unaccountably, Siefert feels twin points of light like paired lasers, fixed on him. The eyes—why can he not see the eyes? It leaves him jittery and unsettled.

What the forensics officer says next will overturn him.

"His peculiar skill is like no other." Severe in black, with her own offbeat elegance, the tall, bony woman creates a silence so profound that even the mayor gets nervous.

Then she says into the hush: "He can identify the dying."

The journalists mutter among themselves. From the orchestra seats far below comes a muffled cry.

"He has the uncanny ability to smell impending death." In case they still don't get it, she finishes: "The black dog knows who's next to die."

Everything inside Siefert's head skids to a stop. He wants to silence the other journalists, stop them breathing if he has to, so he can hear what comes next. He has to know! He leans forward with his mouth open and his tongue out like a dog hanging out a car window, gulping the words like rushing air. If he could, he would find a way to stop his heart to create the silence he needs to grasp her meaning. Stop the pounding of his blood so he can hear.

"Understand," she says, "he can predict the exact moment."

The audience gasps.

The speaker smoothes her varnished hair with a proud, confident smile. She is in the home stretch now. Explain. Make the pitch. Walk away with an extra million in public funding. "This makes him particularly useful in triage situations, like earthquake and building collapses, when the living and the dead are trapped under tons of rubble and for us, there is no telling which is which. Of course we have instruments to detect body mass as well as warmth and motion and the sound of breathing, but we have no time to waste excavating cadavers and no way of knowing who to rescue first. Only the black dog knows which of the victims is poised at the door to death, and only he can guide us in to pull that victim back from the brink."

Reporters on either side exchange skeptical looks but Bill is beyond questions. He does not so much ignore his colleagues as rise above them like a soul cut loose and floating outside himself, observing from the top left-hand corner of the press both. Did he see the dog's eyes back then or did he only imagine it?

Does it see him?

Do I?

He whirls. Dear God!

"Don't you see?" the officer trills, rolling into the finale. "Now we know who to rescue first!"

All over the auditorium, hands fly up: questions.

"Of course you want to know how we discovered his power. Science is an exact discipline but to tell the truth, it was an accident."

Bill leans forward as she describes a routine training exercise, the black dog going through its paces like all the others until, without prompting, it stops cold. Sits down in front of the trainer. Refuses to budge. In spite of threats it sits like a rock until its original trainer—young man, too young to have a heart condition—clutches his throat and drops like a felled redwood. Infarction, the coroner says. It's nothing, the chief says. It's just coincidence.

"But I," the speaker says, "as an expert, I knew we were on to something big." She whispers into the microphone, "I took him home."

There the ambitious forensics officer devised a series of tests for the black dog . . .

Matter-of-factly, she details visits to hospitals and hospices, in which the dog paces the complex of halls like a moving shadow and then. Sits. Is present at the exact moment when the soul leaves the body. He is unfailing in his accuracy. The black dog is right every single time. Trainer and dog move on to wards where patients are more viable. Some will make it. Some may not. The dog sits down. Doctors send in the crash cart and save the patient, see how valuable this is?

Bill tunes out of her recital. What it took to get the commissioners' approval. Startup money. Training and experiments. The first disaster—factory explosion—in which medics follow the black dog into the ruins and make sensational, last-minute rescues. The building collapse in which at least a dozen are yanked back from the brink of death. Certain fires. The list goes on, but by this time Bill Siefert is thinking of one thing and one thing only.

He has to see the dog.

"In emergency situations like these," she says, "prioritization is imperative. Why rush to help people strong enough to make it until we get around to them when there are cases in which immediate rescue means the difference between life and death? Why lose hours excavating victims who are already corpses?"

Buzzing with pride, she moves on into the pitch. "Therefore, the response time of our disaster relief units and our success rates depend heavily on the services of the black dog. You can see it is essential to breed thousands like him." Now she romances the crowd in that deep, sexy whisper, "And that's where you come in."

As one, they nod. Yes yes. Oh, yes yes.

"At the moment, the black dog is unique, but I am happy to report that our veterinary unit has used genetic material from our black dog to impregnate thirty black bitches. We hope to replicate his genetic set. He is, after all, this year's gold star winner for valor under extreme circumstances in the Vidalia implosion and the West Virginia mine disaster. My triumph." She raises her voice like a ringmaster preparing to bring on the lions: **ta-da**. "The miraculous black dog."

Everybody cranes.

Speakers vibrate with the communal shout, "Bring on the dog."

She raises a hand like a traffic cop. "And with your support . . ."

But the crowd is waiting for the grand entrance. They squirm in their seats, straining to see the animal, but nothing happens.

Smiling, the glossy, imposing speaker dangles the bait. How much will they pay to see? "And once we receive your support . . ."

On the floor of the auditorium, city officials and invited guests shift in their seats, chanting, "Bring on the dog." The cry starts as a ripple but gathers force, "The dog." It rolls in like a long comber, growing until it breaks on the shore. "The dog!"

"Now, we are prepared to take your pledges."

Somewhere outside himself, fixed on something he can not see, Bill Siefert scours the shadows behind her, searching. He thinks he sees . . . He sees . . . No, he doesn't see . . . Where is it, he wonders, changed. What is it?

You don't want to know.

With a start, he returns to himself, shuddering.

Why is this so important to him?

It isn't just the sensational story: *Interview with the Black Dog.* Skeptical Bill Siefert, who came here to debunk, has been sucked in. He is changed and threatened by the possibility of something that he will never understand. Like a thousand others, he wants to see the animal, but the dog is nowhere present. And yet . . .

Yet

Bill's head jerks so abruptly that his neck snaps. He doesn't know it yet but in the realm of colliding fates he has chosen the black dog, or the black dog has chosen him. For whatever reasons they are in communication. In a universe of particles, in an arena of conflating sights and sounds and stimuli, he and the black dog are yoked in a way that both draws and terrifies him. All at once and through no cause Bill Siefert can divine, he comprehends its size and shape, the yellow eyes burning. Without seeing, he knows.

A question boils inside him. **Name. What is your name.**

Words come in from somewhere new and strange. **What makes you think I have a name?**

"My God!"

The video teams on either side of Bill turn to stare. He shoves his knuckles into his mouth, sealing it shut.

The forensics officer is saying, "Now, I know many of you are wondering why we haven't brought our marvelous black dog onstage tonight, and under ordinary circumstances we would, but these are not ordinary circumstances and this is not an ordinary dog."

The audience grumbles.

She raises a stern hand. "You will have to content yourself with the video of his last rescue. As you will see, we fitted him with a collar cam and a pin spot to bring you this remarkable footage. You will not see the black dog today. In a minute my associates will pass among you with hand mikes because of course I am anxious to answer your questions," she says in a way that makes clear that she has no patience with questions. "Especially yours, Mr. Mayor, since I am here to seek your support for this ambitious project. Of course you deserve an explanation. You won't see the amazing black dog today, but if you will direct your attention to the monitors in the arms of the chairs where you are sitting, you can see one of the miracles he performs daily in the line of duty."

Murky videos blink to life on a thousand monitors. Because the camera is mounted on the collar the people who sat here so patiently won't see the dog tonight, not even on video. Still, the audience shivers as the camera rushes into tight spaces and through dark corridors on the back of something huge and powerful. Everybody but Bill Siefert will see, and everybody but Bill will hear the forensics officer's warning.

By that time he's bolted out of the press box ("pardon me, excuse me, excuse me, pardon me") and through the exit at the end of the corridor, down flight after flight of stairs into the belly of the place. He is running hard. Hunting the beast. He wants to lock his hands in its thick, leonine ruff so he can look it in the face while he asks certain questions.

Therefore he will not hear the forensics officer say, in conclusion, "We can not show you the black dog on stage here in the auditorium. This is for his protection. And for yours."

She says, "Believe me, this is for your own safety."

The crowd protests until she raises her hand for silence.

She says, "In a crowd this size, there are bound to be some . . . well, you can imagine. I mean, actuarial tables suggest that several of you are already . . ." Discreetly, she breaks off. "Think what that would do to him! Sensory overload, and before we can perpetuate the breed. And as for you. Well. Think what would happen if he sat down in front of one of you!"

There is a long silence.

"The presence of the black dog has terrible implications."

For the black dog, the responsibility is tremendous. In a ruined building or an arena full of strangers he must go to the feet of the dying like a bullet to the heart. No, to the first to die. He must sit quietly, when more than anything he wants to lift his head and howl to the heavens. Even here, deep in the belly of the building, he is painfully aware of the hundreds of hearts of hundreds of strangers rustling and thrumming in the vast auditorium above, the cumulative pressure of their failing bodies. There are too many to save!

This is the prodigious engine that drives him. Before they know, he knows.

Can the black dog predict the future?

No. The future predicts him.

Now every hair on his huge body shimmers and ripples over powerful muscles as he pads along the corridors toward the space under the stage where his mistress stands. He is heading for the sunken orchestra pit. Above, his mistress is speaking to all the sad, vulnerable humans. He can hear their ruined bellies crying out. Lungs failing. Hearts stuttering. He knows which will falter and stop.

In spite of his size the black dog goes silently with his great head lifted, scanning the corridor with yellow eyes. His jaws are clenched on the necessary.

He is carrying it in his teeth. **For her.**

Bill Siefert is already compromised, and, like Bill, you must proceed with caution. Stay back if you are anywhere in the vicinity. Be still. The black dog is approaching. No matter who you are or how strong or how arrogantly healthy, this is the time when you must be very, very careful. Do not run if you see him coming because no matter what you try, whatever is going to happen next will happen.

Do not be afraid of the black dog. Feel sorry for him.

Imagine the burden of foreknowledge. The pressure. The choices he has to make. In this world there are billions of humans marching toward death, thousands are at the gate at this very moment and he cannot reach them all.

He does what he can.

His mistress does not know that he is racing to save her. Nor can the forensics officer, strutting and preening to massive applause in her best Armani suit, guess that tonight her pet—no, her creation—is coming for her, trotting purposefully through the maze of corridors with the necessary tightly clamped in his soft mouth.

Stand back. Hold still. Stay out of his way. Be grateful he isn't coming for you.

There are so many! Earlier, a voice cried out to him. Nothing, he thinks, just something he heard. Voice. Yes. That will come, but in due time, because more important to the black dog than this new element in his troubling cosmos is doing what the black dog does. The voice cries out. It is the other: searching. The dog's head comes up, but there isn't time. Asking, but the black dog does not brook questions. There are too many. There isn't time. There isn't time! For the black dog tonight, there is only one. Upstairs, she is still talking. Because she is his mistress, because in spite of her commanding, clinical approach, the black dog has grown fond of her in the way of all dogs.

She does, after all, forget sometimes and scratch his ears. Therefore instead of vaulting the ladder and bounding onstage to sit down at her feet, the black dog will wait down here. He will give her a chance to do what she does as he must do what he does. He may want to spare her public humiliation, if that's a concept the noble creature grasps. For the black dog, pride is irrelevant. All that matters is responsibility.

What he must do.

Of all the failing hearts and bodies in departure mode tonight, exuding death smells in the great, echoing coffin above, even in the realm of a hundred simultaneous deaths he would choose her. When his mistress comes down the ladder he will drop the cell phone at her feet so she has a minute to call 911. Then he will sit down. He'll sit with his flag tail thumping the floor and beg her to save herself.

The others, he will not necessarily save.

The black dog is heavy with foreknowledge. He does not exactly see the blood clot floating into his trainer's brain but he knows it. When it strikes its mark and that part of the brain explodes the black dog will sense it in the way he knows what exactly is failing inside of you, which part of the mechanism you wear so proudly will break and cut you loose from whatever you think you are.

Until the black dog's handler began emanating death smells in the house today, the whole last-minute rescue thing was something she asked him to do, and being a good dog, he did as told. Ordinarily he does what he does in his own time and as he has always done it, but it seemed to please her when he did as she said. She and the big, clumsy men she yoked to him on rescue missions rushed in with their medicine and electric paddles, jerking people back from death, and that is their business. The hero thing was her idea.

The black dog does what he does.

Overhead the applause crescendos and the auditorium floor thrums with the footsteps of a thousand people leaving. His mistress has started down, into the cavity. She descends in a funnel of light at the far end of the corridor. Long stretch: not much time. Must reach her. Drop the phone into her hand. Give her a minute. Sit. She'll know.

Running with his head lifted and every muscle taut with urgency, the black dog is fixed on the orderly progression, the necessary timing. First this. Then this.

Then all at once a human blunders out of a side passage and skids to a stop in front of him, flailing like a flagman on train tracks. It is barking and barking. "Is that you?"

The one he knows, and does not know why he knows it. The thing has a bad smell. It has an ugly bark.

The black dog growls. **Not now.**

It goes, bark bark. "Doggie, stop. I have to see you!" Blarg blarg.

The black dog growls again. No time. **Move.**

It just keeps barking. "Doggie, I have to ask you a question."

Shut up so I can hear her breathe!

She's on the ladder! She's halfway down! He growls again but the human in his path is like a balloon, getting bigger and bigger until it fills the corridor. In times like this even a rescue dog must drop whatever he is carrying to bare his teeth.

"Come on, dog." The human's bark falters. "Please." Then it does the unthinkable. It lunges for the black dog's collar.

The black dog does what he has to. He rakes the human's arm with his fangs and grunts in recognition. He tastes blood, but only a little, and it is vile. At least he has distracted it so he can move on. Whining, the creature frets over its wound. The black dog puts his huge paws on its back to push it down, vaults over it and runs on, bent on rescue.

Too late. In the lost time his mistress dropped like a felled redwood; she is unconscious. Worse: while he was grappling with the human, the window of opportunity slammed shut. This isn't the black dog's fault, even though grief and frustration make him throw back his great head and howl his grief. It is the human's.

The creature with his mark on it made him drop the phone.

What was that? What is it? Trembling, Bill tries to sit up. Ahead, the black dog looks up from the body it has been nosing, Bill wonders *What happened? Did it kill somebody?*—whirls, and charges. He cowers as the great beast covers the distance between them in enormous, terrifying leaps. With its red jaws wide and its yellow eyes suffused with blood and turning a murderous orange, it comes.

"Don't! Don't kill me." Bill cries. Still the great beast rushes down on him, and as Bill Siefert collapses and waits for death, the black dog plants one huge paw on his chest, squeezing the breath out of him, and with an efficiency signifying complete indifference, stalks over him and moves on.

The form passing over Bill is huge, warm and heavily muscled, bigger than a Newfoundland with its thick, shimmering black fur soft and rich and every muscle and tendon humming with power. Its passage is swift but the sensation lingers. It is like being overshadowed by a lover.

Aren't you going to kill me? Bill gasps, struggling for breath as the black dog passes over him and goes on running.

Did it answer? Does he imagine it? In the instant when the enormous paw compressed his chest and its full weight landed on his heart, Bill thinks he heard or comprehended what the creature may have told him. **It isn't time.**

Right now no one in the auditorium knows what has happened down here in the pit, but the implications are prodigious. The forensics officer, its mistress, is dead. Nobody else can control the animal.

The black dog is on the loose.

"Wait!" the human barks as the black dog passes over it, but when he plants his paw in the creature's chest there is a shift in the air. He recognizes it at once. It is the human, pleading: *Wait.* He lifts his head, considering. Did it speak? *Oh please, please wait.* Fragile as the human is inside its thin pink skin, the creature is communicating.

A talking human? How? In time he will have to deal with the matter. The human asks, *what are you?* but the black dog has his own imperatives.

*

There is a brief flurry after Bill's story breaks. Since he was there when it happened, since he found the body, since he *saw* the thing, it is a big story. Blood clot to the brain, but that doesn't stop false charges against the animal. "I was there," Bill says breathlessly. "He tried to get me too. I alone am left," he says. "I alone am left to tell the tale," he says and by the time he has told his story on every known talk show, he is temporarily famous and eminently employable.

There will be a statewide search and bogus reports of countless sightings. The spawn of the black dog—litters artificially inseminated and carefully reared—turn out to be depressingly devoid of powers and are destroyed. For a short time Bill makes news with his *Encounter With the Black Dog,* but only for a little while. He quits his job to write an existential book under the same title, but by the time he has it finished the black dog is a dead issue. After a brief memorial service for the city's top forensics officer, felled by a cerebral embolism on the night of her triumph, the mayor and the police commissioner will forget. After corruption hearings and a series of firings, the city will forget. In time Bill Siefert will forget. Almost.

Meanwhile the black dog runs on. He will not forgive the human he left squirming in the corridor that night, nor can he know why he and it are somehow yoked, but they are. Never mind. In the realm of the black dog there are imperatives that supersede all else.

If their fates are intertwined, then everything will come down when it comes down. When is a matter of no particular importance to him. The time will come and when it does, the black dog will know it. Until then, unencumbered by police handlers, harnesses and leashes and the mistress he almost loved, the black dog runs loose in the world. Not free, exactly, because he is still driven by imperatives. Even so he is free, with nobody to answer to.

Loose in the world, he does what the black dog does.

Bill is not a superficial person, but you can't go on dwelling on a mysterious moment in your past.

He used to think the black dog would make him rich, and if it didn't make him rich it would make him famous. All he had to do was figure out how. If he could find it again, if he could catch the thing, then he could follow his big story, *Encounter With the Black Dog,* with *Capture of the Black Dog,* to be followed by *Interview With the Black Dog* and finally, *Secrets of the Black Dog,* but he had no idea how to go about it. Or collect the reward. Then the police department gave up on the case and withdrew the reward, so that was the end of that.

Siefert never caught the black dog and he never got that book contract. His lecture, *Encounter With the Black Dog,* never made him rich and it didn't make him famous, but it did help his career. He is a local television anchor now. He married a nice girl from the valley, ten years younger. They just bought a house on the other side of the hills.

Still, Bill knows he must have tangled with the black dog for a reason. Like most people in the world, he has to proceed on faith, which in his own way, he is doing. He used to think that if the encounter wasn't about fame or money, it must be about power. Years pass. That hope has come and gone, so Bill has to wonder whether whatever happened back there had left him marked in some other way. If only he could figure it out!

A family man now, Siefert tells himself he's finally let it go, but whether or not he knows it, he and the black dog are by no means done.

Even now there are nights when he sits up in bed and wonders. Sitting next to his sleeping wife with his knees drawn up and his arms locked around them, he gnaws on his bare kneecaps and wonders. What happened back then? Was the black dog trying to tell him something that night in the darkened corridor? What? Why were its yellow eyes turning orange, and if they turn red, what happens then? If he and the black dog were thrown together for a reason, it's no reason he can divine.

And the dog. Every year since his collision with the human, everything the black dog does takes a little longer to do. The slowing tempo is gradual but apparent. Whether it is the byproduct of that night, the black dog could not tell you. Is it that unwanted encounter with an unlike animal that is mysteriously linked to him? The unbidden memory of his lost mistress? The other human's bark-bark-bark, its smell, his own resentment? Insofar as it is the function of the black dog to wonder, he wonders.

Alone in his slowing body he lifts his head and howls without making a sound.

Bill Siefert is middle-aged now, father of two, secure in his career and still happily married. There were years when he would have been thrilled to see the black dog because he was ambitious and reckless and too young to be afraid of the creature. Even though he has more to lose now he has become—not careless, exactly, but less vigilant.

Then he goes to the E.R. with a bellyache and wakes up in a hospital room—a double—groggy and minus his appendix. No big. He'll be fine. A lump in the next bed, supported by ticking monitors and a welter of tubes and drains, tells him it's a double.

It is night in the room, and in the shadows, there is a deeper shadow. Twin lights wink and glow yellow.

Bill shudders. *Is that you?*

He gropes for the buzzer to get help but it isn't anywhere he can find. Nice wife, kids, they have a bigger house. He cries, "You can't be here for me, it's just an appendix!"

The black dog blinks but does not move. At least it's still standing.

He doesn't mean to whimper, but he does. "You don't get it, I'm up for the network anchor job!"

Bark bark bark, why won't the human stop barking and communicate? The black dog creates the silence into which thoughts can fall. In time the creature in the bed quits flailing and lets the words out. *Don't take me.* The smell it gives off is feral, frantic. *Not me, I'm young! I have so much to lose.*

Exactly.

The human points to the next bed. *Take him.*

Still standing, the black dog considers. Nothing will happen until he sits down, and he is not ready.

Although his mission is preordained, he does not know what he will do now, now that they have come to the convergence, only that he and the barking human have been brought together for a reason.

Please.

It seems right to wait until he knows. **All right.**

He moves on to the other bed in the room and sits down. He sits until the old soul parts from the old body. For reasons the black dog is not built to contemplate, his bones rattle with foreknowledge.

Bill Siefert emerges from the hospital changed. He can't say what drives him now but he has lost his ambition. His children find him indifferent. His wife says he is drifting.

This is not precisely the case. He is troubled, distracted. He has become cruelly aware of the multitude of scents, miseries, and toxic humors of the people around him: the lump in his wife's breast, the rales in the lungs of his producer.

It makes him frantic. Can he make her get a checkup so soon after the last one, and for no reason he can give her? Can he get his producer to the doctor in time to forestall his death, at least for now? He does not know. The pressure is terrible, the responsibility tremendous.

His narrow escape from the black dog troubles him. He is not so much changed as sensitized. Where he used to be self-contained and live his life however, he hears a chorus of outcries and farewell wails crowding in. It is like coming into a room where a million people are calling out to him.

Still, a man has to live his life and support his family, so painful as it is—the voices multiply, a million fingers clawing at his heart—Bill goes to New York with a DVD of his best newscasts for the last round of interviews with the Manhattan network affiliates. Only a strategic cocktail party stands between him and that spot as weekend anchor. Not what he wanted as a kid, but better than he expected.

The black dog is dying. He knows it now. This explains everything, but in his life in service, the black dog has never stopped for explanations. For now, he will do what the black dog does.

The top of New York. Siefert has retreated to the penthouse balcony at the top of the glittering network tower. He told them he needed time to consider the offer, but it was the pain that drove him out here, the pressure of the unexpected. Alone for the first time since he arrived, he inhales air so cold that it's like breathing distilled brandy. Maybe he is a little drunk. That must account for it. When he sees the black dog sitting on the wide cement rail with the wind lifting its shimmering hair he is not surprised. He isn't even frightened.

The black dog blinks its yellow eyes. **You know why I'm here.**

He does. He doesn't. *Time to die?* In a way, it would be a relief. He waits for the eyes to turn orange. Red. For it to finish him.

In your dreams.

He does not say, *Why are you here?* He doesn't have to.

You're not the agent I would have chosen.

"If it's about that time I ran into you in the hall . . ."

The black dog turns its magnificent head to taste the wind and lets out a wild, exuberant cry. **It's your turn,** the black dog either says, or doesn't say. Then it is gone.

It won't matter whether this last is spoken, dreamed, or imagined. Siefert understands. Grimacing with unspeakable pain, he turns. Goes inside. Sits down in front of a network vice president.

—SciFiction, 2005

Weston Walks

When your life gets kicked out from under you like a kitchen chair you thought you were standing on, you start to plan. You swear: *never again*. After the funeral Lawrence Weston sat in a velvet chair that was way too big for him while the lawyer read his parents' will out loud. He didn't care about how much he was getting, he only knew what he had lost, and that he would do anything to keep it from happening again.

He was four.

Like a prince in the plague years, he pulled up the drawbridge and locked his heart against intruders. Nobody gets into Weston's tight, carefully furnished life and nobody gets close enough to mess up his heart.

Now look.

When your money makes money you don't have to do anything—so nothing is what Weston ordinarily does except on Saturdays, when he comes out to show the city to you. It isn't the money—don't ask how much he has. He just needs to hear the sound of a human voice. He lives alone because he likes it, but at the end of the day that's exactly what he is. Alone. It's why he started Weston Walks.

He could afford an LED display in Times Square but he sticks to three lines in *The Village Voice*:

New York: an intimate view. Walk the city tourists never see.

He'll show you things you'll never find spawning upstream at Broadway and 42d Street or padding along Fifth Avenue in your ear jocks and puffy coats. This is: *The insider's walking tour.*

Nobody wants to be an outsider, so you make the call. It's not like he will pick up. His phone goes on ringing in some place you can't envision, coming as you do from Out of Town. You hang on the phone, humming "pick up, pick up, pick up." When his machine takes your message, you're pathetically grateful. Excited, too. You are hooked by Weston's promise: *Tailored to your desires.*

What these are, he determines on the basis of a preliminary interview conducted over coffee at Balthazar, on him—or at Starbucks, on you—depending on how you are dressed. He is deciding whether to take you on. No matter how stylish your outfit—or how tacky—if he doesn't like what he hears, he will slap a hundred or a twenty on the table at Balthazar or Starbucks, depending, and leave you there. It's not his fault he went to schools where you learn by osmosis what to do and what not to wear. It's not your fault that you come from some big town or small city where Weston would rather die than have to be. Whatever you want to see, Weston can find, and if you don't know what that is and he decides for you, consider yourself lucky. This is an insider tour!

You're itching to begin your Weston Walk, but you must wait until the tour is filled, and that takes time. Weston is very particular. At last! You meet on the designated street corner. You're the ones with the fanny packs, cameras, monster foam fingers, deely bobbers, Statue of Liberty crowns on the kids—unless you're the overdressed Southerner or one of those razor-thin foreigners in understated black and high-end boots. Weston's the guy in black jeans and laid-back sweater, holding the neatly lettered sign.

He is surprisingly young. Quieter than you'd hoped. Reserved, but in a good way. Nothing like the flacks leafleting in Times Square or bellowing from tour buses on Fifth Avenue or hawking buggy rides through Central Park. He will show you things that you've never seen before, from discos and downtown mud baths nobody knows about to the part of Central Park where your favorite stars Rollerblade to the exclusive precincts of the Academy of Arts and Letters—in the nosebleed district, it's so far uptown, to the marble grand staircase in the Metropolitan Club, which J. P. Morgan built after all the best clubs in the city turned him down.

Notice that at the end he says goodbye in Grand Central, at Ground Zero or the northeast corner of Columbus Circle, some public place where he can shake hands and fade into the crowd. You may want to hug him but you can't—which is just as well because he hates being touched. By the time you turn to ask one last question and sneak in a thank-you slap on the shoulder, he's gone.

He vanishes before you know that you and he are done.

You thought you were friends, but for all he knows, you might follow him home and rip off his van Gogh or trash his beautiful things; you might just murder him, dispose of the body and move into his vacant life. Don't try to call; he keeps the business phone set on *Silent*. It's on the Pugin table in his front hall and if you don't know who Pugin was, you certainly don't belong in his house.

The house is everything Weston hoped. Meticulously furnished, with treasures carefully placed. A little miracle of solitude. Leaving the upper-class grid at venerable St. Paul's and Harvard was like getting out of jail. No more roommates' clutter and intrusions, no more head-on collisions with other people's lives. He sees women on a temporary basis; he'll do anything for them but he never brings them home, which is why it always ends. It's not Weston's fault he's fastidious. Remember, he's an orphaned only child. To survive, he needs everything perfect: sunlight on polished mahogany in his library, morning papers folded and coffee ready and housekeeper long gone, no outsiders, no family to badger him, they all died in that plane crash when he was four.

He spends days at his computer, although he deletes more than he types, lunches at a club even New Yorkers don't know about, hunts treasure in art galleries and secondhand bookstores, can get the best table wherever he wants, but, girls?

He's waiting for one who cares about all the same things.

Too bad that Wings Germaine, and not the first tourist he booked, the one with the lovely phone voice, whom he loved on sight at the interview, shows up for the last-ever Weston Walking Tour. While thirteen lucky tourists gather at the subway kiosk on 72d at Broadway, Wings is waiting elsewhere, and for unstated reasons: *down there.*

Weston has no idea what's ahead. It's a sunny fall Saturday—light breeze, perfect for the classic Central Park walk, so what could be easier or more convenient? It's a half-block from his house. All he has to do is collect his group outside the kiosk where they are milling with vacant smiles. They light up at the sight of his neatly lettered placard. Grinning, he stashes it in the back of his jeans, to be used only when for some unforeseen reason he loses one of them.

A glance tells him this is a Starbucks bunch. With their cameras and sagging fanny packs, they wouldn't be comfortable at chic old Café des Artistes, which is right around the corner from his house. It's not their fault their personal styles are—well, a bad match. But they are. He's one short, which bothers him. Where is that girl he liked so much? Too bad he has to move on, but maybe she'll catch up. Nice day, nice enough people, he thinks—with the possible exception of the burly tourist in the black warmup jacket with the Marine Corps emblem picked out in gold, who walks with his shoulders bunched, leaning into a scowl.

Never mind. It's a beautiful day, and Weston is in charge. Happy and obedient, his tourists trot past the spot where John Lennon died and into the park on a zigzag, heading for the East side, where the Metropolitan Museum bulks above the trees like a mastodon lumbering away. He keeps up a lively patter, spinning stories as his people smile blandly and nod, nod, nod, all except the man with the scowl, who keeps looking at his watch.

Weston looks up: *Ooops.* Like a cutting horse, his ex-Marine has the herd heading into a bad place. *Time to get out of here.* He'll walk them south on Fifth, point out houses owned by people he used to know. "All right," he says brightly, "Time to see how rich people live."

"Wait." The big Marine fills the path like a rhino bunched to charge. "You call this the insider tour?"

Smile, Weston. "Didn't I just . . ." He points to a gap in the bushes; Weston knows it too well.

"TAKE US THE FUCK INSIDE."

No! Behind those bushes, a gash in the rocks opens like a mouth. He can't go back! Weston struggles for that tour-guide tone. "What would you like to see?"

"Tunnels."

The ground underneath the park is laced with unfinished city projects—tunnels, aborted subway stations, all closed to them; Weston has researched, and he knows. "Oh," he says, relieved, "then you want City Spelunking Tours, I have their number and . . ."

"Not those. The ones real people dug. Nam vets. Old hippies."

"There aren't any . . ."

The big man finishes with a disarming grin. "Crazies like me. I have buddies down there."

"There's nothing down there." Weston shudders. *He's a client, don't offend.* "That's just urban legend, like a lot of other things you think you know. Now, if you like legends, I can take you to Frank E. Campbell's, where they have all the famous funerals, or the house where Stanford White got shot by Harry K. Thaw . . ."

"No. *Down!*" The renegade tourist roars like a drill sergeant and the group snaps to like first-day recruits. "Now. Moving out!"

Weston holds up his placard, shouting: "Wait!"

Too late. Like a pack of lemmings, the last-ever Weston Walking Tour falls in behind the big man.

They are heading into a very bad place. No, Weston doesn't want to talk about it. He waves his arms like signal flags. "Wrong way! There's nothing here!"

The Marine whirls, shouting, "You fucking well know it's here."

The hell of it is, Weston does. He is intensely aware of the others in his little group: the newlyweds, the dreary anniversary couple, the plump librarian and the kid in the Derek Jeter shirt, a dozen others are watching with cool, judgmental eyes. In spite of their cheap tourist claptrap and bland holiday smiles, they are not stupid people; they're fixed on the conflict, eager to see something ordinary tourists don't see. The authority of their guide is at issue. They are waiting to see how this plays out. There is an intolerable pause.

"Well?"

One more minute and the last Weston Walking Tour will die of holding its breath.

If you knew what Weston knew, you would be afraid.

His only friend at St. Paul's vanished on their senior class trip to the city. One minute weird Ted Bishop was hunched on the steps of the Museum of Natural History, shivering under a long down coat that was brown and shiny as a cockroach's shell and zipped to the chin on the hottest day of the year. Then he was gone.

Last winter Weston ran into Bishop on Third Avenue, with that same ratty coat leaking feathers and encrusted with mud. It was distressing; he did what he could. He took him into a restaurant and bought him hot food, looked away when his best friend stuffed everything he couldn't devour into his pockets with the nicest smile. "I went crazy. I hid because I didn't want you to know."

"I wouldn't have minded." Weston's stomach convulsed.

"At first I was scared but then, Weston. Oh!"

It was terrifying, all that naked emotion, so close. He shrank, as if whatever Ted had was catching.

"Then they found me." Bishop's pale face gleamed. "Man, there's a whole world down there. I suppose you think I'm nuts."

"Not really." Weston reached for a gag line. "I thought you'd gotten a better offer."

"I did!" Ted lit up like an alabaster lamp. "One look and I knew: *These are my people. And this is my place!* You have to see!"

"I'll try." He did; he followed the poor bastard to the entrance; it's right behind these bushes, he knows—and stopped . . . "Wait."

. . . and heard Ted's voice overlapping, "Wait. I have to tell them you're coming. You *will* wait for me, right?"

Weston wanted to be brave, but he could not lie. "I'll try."

He couldn't stop Ted, either. The tunnel walls shifted behind his friend as if something huge had swallowed him in its sleep. Its foul breath gushed out of the hole; Weston heard the earth panting, waiting to swallow him. Forgive him, he fled.

Awful place, he vowed never to . . . But they are waiting. "OK," he says finally, plunging into the bushes like a diver into a pool full of sharks. "OK."

With the others walking up his heels, Weston looks down into the hole. It's dark as death. Relieved, he looks up. "Sorry, we can't do it today. Not without flashlights. Now . . ."

"Got it covered." The veteran produces a bundle: halogen miners' lamps on headbands. Handing them out, he says the obvious, "Always . . ."

Weston groans. "Prepared." He stands by as his tourists drop into the tunnel, one by one. If they don't come out, what will he tell their families? Will they sue? Will he go to jail? He's happy to stand at the brink mulling it, but the Marine shoves him into the hole.

"Your turn." He drops in after Weston, shutting out daylight with his bulk. The only way they can go is down.

All his life since his parents died, Lawrence Weston has taken great pains to control his environment. Now he is in a place he never imagined. Life goes on, but everything flies out of control. He is part of *this* now, blundering into the ground.

Weston doesn't know what he expects: rats, lurking dragons, thugs with billy clubs, a tribe of pale, blind mutants, or a bunch of gaudy neohippies in sordid underground squats. In fact, several passages fan out from the main entrance, rough tunnels leading to larger caverns with entrances and exits of their own; the underground kingdom is bigger than he feared. He had no idea it would be so old. Debris brought down from the surface to shore up the burrow sticks out of the mud and stone like a schoolchild's display of artifacts from every era. The mud plastering the walls is studded with hardware from the streetcar/gaslight Nineties, fragments of glass and plastic from the Day-Glo-skateboard Nineties and motherboards, abandoned CRTs, bumpers from cars that are too new to carbon-date. The walls are buttressed by four-by-fours, lit by LED bulbs strung from wires, but Weston moves along in a crouch, as though the earth is just about to collapse on his head—which might be merciful, given the fumes. Although fresh air is coming in from somewhere, there is the intolerable stink of mud and small dead things and although to his surprise this tunnel, at least, is free of the expected stink of piss and excrement, there is the smell that comes of too many people living too close together, an overpoweringly human fug.

At first Weston sees nobody, hears nothing he can make sense of, knows only that he can't be in this awful place.

Dense air weighs on him so he can hardly breathe: the effluvia of human souls. Then a voice rises in the passage ahead, a girl's bright, almost festive patter running along ahead of his last-ever Weston Walking Tour as though she and the hulking Marine, and not Weston, are in charge.

Meanwhile the mud walls widen as the path goes deeper. The tunnels are lined with people, their pale faces gleaming wherever he flashes his miner's lamp and it is terrifying. The man who tried so hard to keep all the parts of his life exactly where he put them has lost any semblance of control; the orphan who lived alone because it was safest is trapped in the earth, crowded—no, surrounded—by souls, dozens, perhaps hundreds of others with their needs, their grief and sad secrets and emotional demands.

The pressure of their hopes staggers him.

All at once the lifelong solo flier comprehends what he read in Ted Bishop's face that day, and why he fled. Educated, careful and orderly and self-contained as Lawrence Weston tries so hard to be, only a tissue of belief separates him from them.

Now they are all around him.

I can't. Every crease in his body is greased with the cold sweat of claustrophobia. *I won't.*

He has forgotten how to breathe. One more minute and . . . He doesn't know. Frothing, he wheels, cranked up to fight the devil if he has to, anything to get out of here; he'll tear the hulking veteran apart with teeth and nails, offer money, do murder or if he has to, die in the attempt, anything to escape the dimly perceived but persistent, needy humanity seething underground.

As it turns out, he doesn't have to do any of these things. The bulky vet lurches forward with a big-bear rumble, "Semper fi."

In the dimness ahead, a ragged, gravelly chorus responds: "Semper fi."

The Marine shoulders Weston aside. "Found 'em. Now, shove off. Round up your civilians and move 'em out."

Miraculously, he does. He pulls the WESTON WALKS placard out of the back of his jeans and raises it, pointing the headlamp so his people will see the sign. Then he blows the silver whistle he keeps for emergencies and never had to use.

It makes the tunnels shriek.

"OK," he says with all the force he has left in his body. "Time to go! On to Fifth Avenue and . . ." He goes on in his best tour-guide voice; it's a desperation move, but Weston is desperate enough to offer them anything. "The Russian Tea Room! I'll treat. Dinner at the Waldorf, suites for the night, courtesy of Weston Walking Tours."

Oddly, when they emerge into fresh air and daylight—*dear God, it's still light*—the group is no smaller, but it is different. It takes Weston a minute to figure out what's changed. The bulky ex-Marine with an agenda is gone, an absence he could have predicted, but when he lines them up at the bus stop (yes, he is shaking quarters into the coin drop on a city bus!) he still counts thirteen. Newlyweds, yes, anniversary couple, librarian; assorted bland, satisfied Middle Americans, yes; pimply kid. The group looks the same, but it isn't. He is too disrupted, troubled, and distracted to know who . . .

Safe at last in the Russian Tea Room, he knows which one she is, or thinks he knows because unlike the others, she looks perfectly comfortable here: lovely woman with tousled hair, buff little body wrapped in a big gray sweater with sleeves pulled down over her fingertips; when she reaches for the samovar with a gracious offer to pour he is startled by a flash of black-rimmed fingernails. Never mind, maybe it's a fashion statement he hasn't caught up with.

Instead of leading his group to Times Square or Grand Central for the ceremonial sendoff so he can fade into the crowd, he leaves them at the Waldorf, all marveling as they wait at the elevators for the concierge to show them to their complimentary suites.

Spent and threatened by his close encounter with life, Weston flees.

The first thing he does when he gets home is pull his ad and trash the business phone. Then he does what murderers and rape victims do in movies, after the fact: he spends hours under a hot shower, washing away the event. It will be days before he's fit to go out. He quiets shattered nerves by numbering the beautiful objects in the ultimate safe house he has created, assuages grief with coffee and the day's papers in the sunlit library, taking comfort from small rituals. He needs to visit his father's Turner watercolor, stroke the smooth flank of the Brancusi marble in the foyer, study his treasure, a little Remington bronze.

When he does go out some days later, he almost turns and goes back in. The sexy waif from the tour is on his front steps. Same sweater, same careless toss of the head. The intrusion makes his heart stop and his belly tremble, but the girl who poured so nicely at the Russian Tea Room greets him with a delighted smile.

"I thought you'd never come out."

"You have no right, you have no *right* . . ." She looks so pleased that he starts over. "What are you doing here?"

"I live in the neighborhood." She challenges him with that gorgeous smile.

How do you explain to a pretty girl that she has no right to track you to your lair? How can you tell any New Yorker that your front steps are private, specific only to you? How can you convince her that your life is closed to intruders, or that she is one?

He can't. "I have to go!"

"Where are you . . . "

Staggered by a flashback—tunnel air repeating like something he ate—Weston is too disturbed to make polite excuses, beep his driver, manage any of the usual exit lines. "China!" he blurts, and escapes.

At the corner he wheels to make sure he's escaped and gasps: "Oh!"

Following him at a dead run, she smashes into him with a stirring little thud that splits his heart, exposing it to the light. Oh, the chipped tooth that flashes when she grins. "Um, China this very minute?"

Yes, he is embarrassed. "Well, not really. I mean. Coffee first."

She tugs down the sweater sleeves, beaming. "Let's! I'll pay."

By the time they finish their cappuccinos and he figures out how to get out without hurting her feelings, he's in love.

How does a man like Weston fall in love?

Accidentally. Fast. It's nothing he can control. Still he manages to part from Wings Germaine without letting his hands shake or his eyes mist over; he must not do anything that will tip her off to the fact that this is the last good time. He even manages to hug goodbye without clinging, although it wrecks his heart. "It's been fun," he says. "I have to go."

"No big. Nothing is forever," she says, exposing that chipped tooth.

Dying a little, he backs away with a careful smile. To keep the life he's built so lovingly he has to, but it's hard. "So, bye."

Her foggy voice curls around him and clings. "Take care."

They're friends now, or what passes for friends, so he trusts her not to follow. Even though it's barely four in the afternoon he locks his front door behind him, checks the windows, and sets the alarm.

That beautiful girl seemed to be running ahead of his thoughts so fast that when they exchanged life stories she saw the pain running along underneath the surface of the story he usually tells. Her triangular smile broke his heart. "I'm so sorry," she said.

"Don't be," he told her. "It's nothing you did."

"No," she said. "Oh, no. But I've been there, and I know what it's like."

Orphaned, he assumed. *Like me,* he thinks, although she is nothing like him. Named in honor of her fighter-pilot father, she said. Art student, she said, but she never said when. Mystifyingly, she said, "You have some beautiful stuff." Had he told her about the Calder maquette and forgotten, or mentioned the Sargent portrait of his great-grandfather or the Manet oil sketch? He has replayed that conversation a dozen times today and he still doesn't know.

At night, even though he's secured the house and is safely locked into his bedroom, he has a hard time going to sleep. Before he can manage it he has to get up several times and repeat his daytime circuit of the house. He patrols rooms lit only by reflected streetlights, padding from one to the next in T-shirt and pajama bottoms, touching table tops with light fingers, running his hands over the smooth marble flank of the Brancusi because every object is precious and he needs to know that each is in its appointed place.

Day or night Weston is ruler of his tight little world, secure in the confidence that although he let himself be waylaid by a ragged stranger today, although he ended up doing what she wanted instead of what he intended, here, at least, he commands the world.

Then why can't he sleep?

The fourth time he goes downstairs in the dark he finds her sitting in his living room. At first he imagines his curator has moved a new Degas bronze into the house in the dead of night. Then he realizes it's Wings Germaine, positioned like an ornament on his ancestral brocade sofa, sitting with her arms locked around her knees.

"What," he cries, delighted, angry and terrified. "What!"

Wings moves into his arms so fluidly that the rest flows naturally, like a soft, brilliant dream. "I was in the neighborhood."

They are together in a variety of intense configurations until Weston gasps with joy and falls away from her, exhausted. Drenched in sense memory, he plummets into sleep.

When the housekeeper comes to wake him in the morning, Wings is gone.

By day Weston is the same person; days pass in their usual sweet order, but his nights go by in that fugue of images of Wings Germaine, who hushes his mouth with kisses whenever he tries to ask who she is and how she gets in or whether what they have together is real or imagined. No matter how he wheedles, she doesn't explain; "I live in the neighborhood," she says, and the pleasure of being *this close* quiets his heart. He acknowledges the possibility that the girl is, rather, only hallucination and—astounding for a man so bent on control—he accepts that.

As long as his days pass in order, he tells himself, as long as nothing changes, he'll be ok. He thinks.

When Wings arrives she does what she does so amazingly that he's never quite certain what happened, only that it leaves him joyful and exhausted; then she leaves. His nights are marvels, uncomplicated by the pressure of the usual lover's expectations because they both know she will be gone before the sun comes up. She always is. He wakes up alone, to coffee and the morning paper, sunlight on mahogany. Their nights are wild and confusing but in the daytime world that Weston has spent his life perfecting, everything is reassuringly the same.

Or so he tells himself. It's what he has to believe. If he saw any of this for what it is, he'd have to act and the last thing Weston wants right now is for his dizzy collisions in the night to end.

Until today, when he hurtles out of sleep at 4 a.m. Panic wakes him, the roar of blood thundering in his ears. His synapses clash in serial car crashes; the carnage is terrible. He slides out of bed in the gray dawn and bolts downstairs, lunging from room to room, shattered by the certain knowledge that something has changed.

Unless everything has changed.

What, he wonders, running a finger over table tops, the rims of picture frames, the outlines of priceless maquettes by famous sculptors, all still in place, reassuringly *there*. What?

Dear God, his Picasso plates are missing. Treasures picked up off the master's studio floor by Great-grandfather Weston, who walked away with six signed plates under his arm, leaving behind a thousand dollars and the memory of his famous smile. Horrified, he turns on the light. Pale circles mark the silk wallpaper where the plates hung; empty brackets sag, reproaching him.

He doesn't mention this to Wings when she comes to him that night; he only breathes into her crackling hair and holds her closer, thinking, *It can't be her. She couldn't have, it couldn't be Wings.*

Then he buries himself in her because he knows it is.

Before dawn she leaves Weston drowsing in his messy bed, dazed and grateful. His nights continue to pass like dreams; the rich orphan so bent on life without intrusions welcomes the wild girl in spite of certain losses; love hurts, but he wants what he wants. Their time together passes without reference to the fact that when Weston comes down tomorrow his King George silver service will be missing, to be followed by his Kang dynasty netsuke and then his best Miró. *I love her too much,* he tells himself as objects disappear daily. *I don't want this to stop.*

He inspects. All his external systems remain in place. Alarms are set, there's no sign of forcible entry or exit. It is as though things he thought he prized more than any woman have dropped into the earth without explanation.

He can live without these things, he tells himself. He can! Love is love, and these are only objects.

Until the Brancusi marble goes missing.

In a spasm of grief, his heart empties out.

Wings won't know when they make love that night that her new man is only going through the motions—unless she does know, which straightforward Weston is too new at deception to guess. He does the girl with one eye on the door, which is how he assumes she exits once she's pushed him off the deep end into sleep—which she has done nightly, vanishing before he wakes up.

Careful, Wings. Tonight will be different.

To him, Wings is a closed book.

He needs to crack her open like a piñata and watch the secrets fall out.

Guilty and terrible as he feels about doubting her, confused because he can't bear to lose *one more thing,* he can't let this go on. With Wings still in his arms he struggles to stay awake, watching through slitted eyes for what seems like forever. She drowses; he waits. The night passes like a dark thought, sullenly dragging its feet. Waiting is terrible. By the time a crack of gray light outlines his bedroom blackout shades, he's about to die of it. The girl he loves sighs and delicately disengages herself. Grieving, he watches and when she goes, he counts to twenty and follows.

He knows the house better than Wings; she'll take the back stairs, so he hurries down the front. When she sneaks into the central hall and silences the alarm so she can escape with another of his treasures, he'll spring. Sliding into the niche behind the Brancusi's empty pedestal he crouches until his joints crack, echoing in the silent house. He has no idea how she escaped.

Damn fool, he thinks and does not know which of them he's mad at, himself or elusive Wings Germaine.

When they lie down together after midnight Weston's fears have eased: of being caught following—the tears of regret, the recriminations—unless his greatest fear was that she wasn't coming back because she knew. Did she know he followed? Does she?

She slides into his arms in the nightly miracle that he has come to expect and he pulls her close with a sigh. What will he do after he ends this? What will she steal from him tonight and what will she do when he confronts her? He doesn't know, but it's long overdue. When she slips out of bed before first light he gives her time to take the back stairs and then follows. Like a shadow, he drifts through darkened rooms where the girl moves so surely that he knows she must linger here every night, having her way with his treasured things.

With the swift, smooth touch of a child molester she strokes his family of objects but takes nothing.

Damn! Is he waiting for her to steal? What is she waiting for? Why doesn't she grab something so he can pounce and finish this?

Empty-handed, she veers toward the darkened kitchen.

Weston's back hairs rise and tremble as Wings opens the door to the smoky stone cellar and starts down.

His heart sags. Is that all she is? A generic homeless person with a sordid squat in a corner of his dank basement? When Wings Germaine comes to his bed at night she is freshly scrubbed; she smells of woodsmoke and rich earth and in the part of his head where fantasies have moved in and set up house-keeping, Weston wants to believe that she's fresh from her own rooftop terrace or just in from a day on her country estate.

Idiot.

He has two choices here. He can go back to bed and pretend what he must in order to keep things as they are in spite of escalating losses—or he can track her to her lair.

But, oh! The missing furniture of his life, the art. His Brancusi! What happened to them? Has she sneaked his best things out of the house and fenced them or does she keep them stashed in some secret corner of his cellar for reasons she will never explain? Is his treasured Miró safe? Is anything? He has to know.

Oh, lover. It is a cry from the heart. *Forgive me.*

He goes down.

The cellar is empty. Wings isn't anywhere. He shines his caretaker's flash in every corner and underneath all the shelves and into empty niches in Great-grandfather's wine rack, but there is no sign. It takes him all morning to be absolutely certain, hours in which the housekeeper trots around the kitchen overhead making his breakfast, putting his coffee cup and the steaming carafe, his orange juice and cinnamon toast—and a rose, because roses are in season—on his breakfast tray. He times the woman's trips back and forth to the library where he eats, her visit to his bedroom where she will change his sheets without remarking because she does it every day; he waits for her to finish, punch in the code, and leave by the kitchen door. Then he waits another hour.

When he's sure the house is empty, Weston goes back upstairs for the klieg lights his folks bought for a homes tour the year they died.

Bright as they are, they don't show him much. There are cartons of books in this old cellar, bundles of love letters that he's afraid to read. His parents' skis, the ice skates they bought him the Christmas he turned four, the sled, all remnants of his long-lost past. This is the sad but ordinary basement of an ordinary man who has gone through life with his upper lip stiffer than is normal and his elbows clamped to his sides. It makes him sigh.

Maybe he imagined Wings Germaine.

Then, when he's just about to write her off as a figment of his imagination and the missing pieces, up to and including the Brancusi, as the work of his housekeeper or the guy who installed the alarms, he sees that the floor in front of the wine rack is uneven and that there are fingerprints on one stone.

Very well. He could be Speke, starting out after Burton or Livingston, heading up the Zambezi. The shell Weston has built around himself hardens so that only he will hear his heart crack as he finishes: *Alone.*

When she comes back too long after midnight he is waiting: provisioned this time, equipped with pick and miner's light because he thinks he knows where Wings is going; handcuffs and a length of rope. He will follow her down. Never mind what Weston thinks in the hours while he crouches in his own basement like a sneak thief, waiting; don't try to parse the many escalating heartbroken, reproachful, angry escalating to furious, ultimately threatening speeches he writes and then discards.

The minute that stone moves, he'll lunge. If he's fast enough, he can grab her as she comes out; if she's faster and drops back into the hole, then like a jungle cat, he will plunge in after her and bring her down. Then he'll kneel on the woman's chest and pin her wrists and keep her there until she explains. He already knows that eventually he'll soften and give her one more chance, but it will be on his terms.

She'll have to pack up her stuff and move into his handsome house and settle down in his daytime life because he is probably in love with her. Then he'll have every beautiful thing that he cares about secured in the last safe place.

And by God she'll bring all his stuff back. She will!

He's been staring at the stone for so long that he almost forgets to douse the light when it moves. He manages it just as the stone scrapes aside like a manhole cover and her head pops up.

"Oh," she cries, although he has no idea how she knows he is crouching here in the dark. "Oh, fuck."

It's a long way to the bottom. The fall is harder than he thought. By the time he hits the muddy floor of the tunnel underneath his house Wings Germaine is gone.

He is alone in the narrow tunnel, riveted by the possibility that it's a dead end and there's no way out.

He's even more terrified because a faint glow tells him that there is. To follow Wings, he has to crawl on and out, into the unknown.

Weston goes along on mud-caked hands and slimy knees for what seems like forever before he comes to a place big enough to stand up in. It's a lot like the hole where the runaway tourist stampeded him but it is nothing like it. The man-made grotto is wired and strung with dim lights; the air is as foul as it was in the hole where Ted Bishop disappeared, but this one is deserted. He is at a rude crossroads. Access tunnels snake out in five directions and he has to wonder which one she took, and how far they go.

Stupid bastard, he calls, "Wings?"

There is life down here, Weston knows it; *she* is down here but he has no idea which way she went or where she is hiding or, in fact, whether she is hiding from him. A man in his right mind, even a heartbroken lover, would go back the way he came, haul himself up and station his caretaker by the opening with a shotgun to prevent incursions until he could mix enough concrete to fill the place and cement the stone lid down so no matter what else happened in his house, she would never get back inside.

Instead he cries, "Wings. Oh, Wings!"

He knows better than to wait. If anything is going to happen here, he has to make it happen.

The idea terrifies him. Worse. There are others here. For the first time in his well-ordered life careful Weston, who vowed never to lose anybody or anything he cared about, is lost.

The chamber is empty for the moment but there is life going on just out of sight; he hears the unknown stirring in hidden grottos, moving through tunnels like arteries—approaching, for all he knows. The knowledge is suffocating. The man who needs to be alone understands that other lives are unfolding down here; untold masses are deep in their caverns doing God knows what. A born solitary, he is staggered by the pressure of all those unchecked lives raging, out of sight and beyond the law or any of the usual agencies of control.

Encroaching. *God!*

Trembling, he tries, "Wings?"

As if she cares enough to answer.

The tunnels give back nothing. He wants to run after her but he doesn't know where. Worse, she may see him not as a lover in pursuit, but a giant rat scuttling after food. He should search but he's afraid of what he will find. Much as he misses his things, he's afraid to find out what Wings has done with them and who she is doing it with.

Overturned, he retreats to the mouth of the tunnel that leads to his house and hunkers down to think.

There are others out there, too many! Accustomed now, Weston can sense them, hear them, smell them in the dense underground air, connected by this tunnel to the treasures he tries so hard to protect. The labyrinth is teeming with life but he is reluctant to find out who the others are or how they are. They could be trapped underground like him, miserable and helpless, snapped into fetal position in discrete pits they have dug for themselves. They could be killing each other out there, or lying tangled in wild, orgiastic knots doing amazing things to each other in communal passion pits or thinking great thoughts, writing verse or plotting revolution, or they could be locked into lotus position in individual niches, halfway to Nirvana or—no!—they could be trashing his stolen art. He doesn't want to know.

It is enough to know that for the moment, he is alone at a dead end and that in a way, it's a relief.

Surprise. For the first time since the runaway tourist forced him underground and Wings flew up to the surface and messed up his life, Weston has nothing to hope for and no place to go. And for the first time since he was four years old, he feels safe.

After a time he takes the pick he had strapped to his backpack in case and begins to dig.

In the hours or days that follow, Weston eats, he supposes: by the time the hole is big enough to settle down in, his supply of granola bars is low and the water in his canteen is almost gone but he is not ready to go back into his house. In between bouts of digging, he probably sleeps. Mostly he thinks and then stops thinking as his mind empties out and leaves him drifting in the zone. What zone, he could not say. What he wants and where this will end, he is too disturbed and disrupted to guess.

Then, just when he has adjusted to being alone in this snug, reassuringly tight place, when he is resigned to the fact that he'll never see her again she comes, flashing into life before him like an apparition and smiling that sexy and annoying, enigmatic smile.

"Wings!"

Damn that wild glamour, damn the cloud of tousled hair, damn her for saying with that indecipherable, superior air, "What makes you think I'm really here?"

The girl folds as neatly as a collapsible tripod and sits cross-legged on the floor of the hole Weston has dug, fixed in place in front of him, sitting right here where he can see her, waiting for whatever comes next.

It's better not to meet her eyes. Not now, when he is trying to think. It takes him longer than it should to frame the question.

"What have you done with my stuff?"

Damn her, for answering the way she does. "What do you care? It's only stuff."

Everything he ever cared about simply slides away.

They sit together in Weston's tight little pocket in the earth. They are quiet for entirely too long. She doesn't leave but she doesn't explain, either. She doesn't goad him and she doesn't offer herself. She just sits there regarding him. It's almost more than he can bear.

A question forms deep inside Weston's brain and moves slowly, like a parasite drilling its way to the surface. Finally it explodes into the still, close air. "Are you the devil or what?"

This makes her laugh. "Whatever, sweetie. What do you think?"

"I don't know," he shouts. "I don't know!"

"So get used to it."

But he can't. He won't. More or less content with his place in the narrow hole he has dug for himself, Weston says, "It's time for you to go," and when she hesitates, wondering, he pushes Wings Germaine outside and nudges her along the access tunnel to the hub, the one place where they can stand, facing. She gasps and recoils. To his astonishment, he is brandishing the pick like a club. Then he clamps his free hand on her shoulder and with no clear idea what he will do when this part is done or what comes next, he turns Wings Germaine in his steely grip and sends her away. Before he ducks back into his territory Weston calls after her on a note that makes clear to both of them that they are done. "Don't come back."

Behind him, the cellar waits, but he can't know whether he wants to go back to his life. He is fixed on what he has to do. Resolved, relieved because he knows this at least, he sets to work on the exit where he left her, erasing her with his pick.

—*The Naked City*, 2011

How It Works

I see them framed in a Gothic arch, two handsome women caught in mid-confrontation. It's like something out of an old movie, a black-and-white weepie my mother saw as a kid, although she would deny it, *In your dreams. That was way before my time.*

They sit with heads bent under slanting light, one blonde and one—the habit makes it hard to tell. They're both women of a certain age, although Lydia is, face it, farther along in years and worldly experience than the abbess—I think. Mother Therese is younger, but who knows what she was up to back in her days as Terri Gordon, rising starlet? Both have the chiseled profiles, the entitled air of born stars. It's about bony structure, although unlike her holy adversary, my mother has been surgically enhanced.

Lydia spins out her life in terms of **although.** Weighing this against that, bent on making herself look better to the few people who matter in her odd, Lydia-centric world. My mother is the star of her own life, eternally searching for the right man to share the screen with her. And if she defies probabilities and forces this encounter with the abbess? If you're that deep into this failure of the imagination, Mother, go for it.

They are fighting for the soul of Gerard LaPierre. Mother Therese wants it for God, although if Gerard is to be believed, God already has it. My mother could care less about souls. She wants him for herself.

I can't wait to see the movie.

Note to Mother: dood, it's not a movie.

Don't call me mother. If anybody asks, we're dear friends, and if they remark on the resemblance, yes, we're related. We could be sisters, right?

My mother's newest acquisition told her that he just turned thirty, but he looks older to me. In fact, he told her a lot of things.

Lydia's new man has the same big, square head and blunt, handsome features as her comic book idol—what's his name? Captain Marvel—and how long has it been since he flew? Right, Mother, these details date you without leaving a trace, and you don't even know.

This Gerard looks kind of like him, with the same blunt features and empty eyes, same dark hair like a backslash over the brow. He flashes the same bland, sweet smile. Instead of the cape with the lightning bolt, he arrives cloaked in a boyish, vulnerable air, unless that's tragic inevitability.

Practiced, engaging and needy in equal measure, he spins out his story, smiles, and waits. He is quite the storyteller. And what a story! Your heart goes out: poor guy.

"My father was a black Irishman, that's all Mam would say about him, even though I begged to know. He ran out on her as soon as she got pregnant and it made her angry and sad. She tried hard but was bitter every day of her mortal life. She tore up all his pictures but I guess I look like him, why else would she whip me the way she did? Poor little Jennie LaPierre, nobody to love her, no place to go and ugly to boot. Out of a clear sky she'd turn around and smack me for no reason, and I suppose that's why. She was a hard woman, but she tried. God knows she tried.

"In our part of Minnesota, Catholic girls didn't get pregnant and if they did, God forbid, then they had the baby and either she married the guy or she went back to school and her parents brought it up, the town we lived in was that old-fashioned and remote. We lived so far out in the sticks that the only other option was St. Mary's home for unwed mothers, and that's where I lived until I came here.

"See, my mother was a ward of the state. Even I would have to say she was never good looking, I guess she was pretty hard to place, so she landed with foster parents who didn't care a fig about children and acted like she was a great burden. They didn't want her, they did it for the sake of the monthly check from the state. She lived on table scraps and they worked her like a dog and she never heard a kind word or saw a penny from them. Then she got pregnant. She hid it for as long as she could, but they kicked her out as soon she began to show.

"So she ended up with the nuns, and unlike every other girl who went to St. Mary's, my mother stayed. See, the deal is, they take bad girls in when they get in trouble, and take care of them until their babies come, the idea being that after they give the baby up for adoption, they can go back to their lives unencumbered, and most of them do. My poor Mam had nobody and nothing to go back to. She was fifteen!

"The sisters took pity and gave her a kitchen job, at least to start. I was the only child on the place. It was lonely but they made a big fuss over me, which is just as well. Mam wouldn't give me up because she just wouldn't. She probably loved me, but she didn't like me much. The nuns said I'd be better off with a nice family in want of a child but Mam said stop, or she'd throw me in the river and jump in after me. She said I was hers to take care of and she swore she would, by God, take care of me until the day she died.

"I love my mother and she did try, but Lord, she was mean. Thank God for the nuns."

His recital slips out too easily, and the tone? Archaic, like a book you find in your grandmother's house and start reading out of sheer boredom. He probably says "Lord" every time he tells the story, and the story never varies. Where did you get it, man? Masterpiece Theater? Some things are too good to be true, but Mother bought it. Excuse me. Lydia did.

She bought him.

This is how my mother keeps new men in her life. She may flirt to get their attention, but she pays for what follows, and believe me, she can afford it. She co-opts her quarry with intimate dinners by candlelight in adorable country inns, where she seems almost as pretty as she thinks she is. She buys ambience: a wide, deep sofa by the fireplace where she and the chosen can sit after dinner, lulled by the flames before they go upstairs, and they will go upstairs where there are always feather mattresses in big brass beds. These places are not cheap, but for the time being, for as long as she likes, he is hers.

She consolidates her position with gifts: the barn coat Gerard is wearing the day I get my first look at him. The new Leica hanging around his neck, because she's cast this new man as the next Helmut Newton or Annie Leibovitz—typical Lydia, she's bought him everything but a car, although she's only known him since September.

No problem. My mother is a living showcase for subtle excess. Nothing but the best for our Lydia: the newest sports car, with another coming as soon as new models hit the floor; A-list wraparound shades, designer jackets, and top-of-the-line jeans, boots by Gucci or Prada, depending, a gaudy contrast to the nun's medieval-looking habit, although I've tried to warn her off that encounter. A sheepskin coat and a mink vest to wear over her thousand-dollar cashmere sweaters because her newly renovated weekend place is, after all, in the country. As though she would risk breaking a heel hiking in these woods.

Walking into her costly little shack in the woods, I know I'm not here for quality time with Lydia, who always has reasons.

I've been summoned to admire the nice new life she has decorated and furnished in this nice new town. Since then I've learned to hate the country. The monstrous pines and thick greenery give me psychological nosebleeds. The rustic farmhouse and Lydia's antiques are locked in combat: highly polished, fragile tables teeter on weathered floorboards so heavily varnished that they slide on the slant, while her fussy chairs and elaborate side tables cling to the new bearskin rug with their little claw feet. I am alarmed by the profusion of silk cushions in her lavishly enhanced farmhouse boudoir—only Lydia would think of her bedroom as a boudoir.

I want to believe she invites me because somewhere deep, she actually likes me, but for Lydia, I am an accessory with one simple function: I'm pre-set to arrive, exclaim over all her choices, and admire.

And is Gerard an accessory?

It's hard to know. That first day, I mistake him for the last of a series of personal appearances as neatly scheduled as performers waiting to do their turn onstage: Lydia's nice new friends, walking into the perfect setting for the next scene in her nice new life.

Now I'm not so sure. Had she planned this or does Gerard come and go whenever he wants?

Our lunch guests for Lydia's grand opening are her suave Realtor and his wife, the kind of friends she makes every time she sets up another new life. Her next-door neighbors come over from their refurbished farmhouse in time for tea and leave on the stroke of twilight. The couple she'd invited for drinks thank her and go on to the next party and Lydia sighs the way you do when the curtain comes down on Act One. I sit there in her silent, perfect little living room, exhausted and honored. *Finally. It's just us.*

It's scary. She's my mother, but we've never been, well, what you would call close. Oh, it's not her fault that she sent me to live with Grandmother after she and Hal divorced; after all, was *she* supposed to look after me when job-hunting was first on her to-do list?

I remember the cab; I was three. Lydia leaned forward on the seat, intent on delivering me to Bronxville. I remember her rhinestone compact that she handed off to me to shut me up. There were three compartments clasped in the mouth of a fake gold frog. I made the frog's mouth pop open and shut until the hinges snapped. Lydia smacked me and we both burst into tears. I even remember what she said, "It isn't you, I loved that thing and now it's ruined."

I was too little to tell her that I was crying for the little girl.

It's not Lydia's fault that she handed me off but it is her fault that she took her damn sweet time about taking me back. Grandmother forced the issue so she had no choice, but she did decorate a room for me. Pink. By the time I and my two suitcases arrived, Lydia owned a co-op on the West Side and I was

twelve. We moved my things into the converted maid's room and had a stiff
little dinner at Café des Artistes to celebrate. By then her lovelorn column was
syndicated, showing up in all the best papers, and Larry had left her well fixed.
She could afford the best boarding school, the best prep school, and the best
summer camps, and I went to them all. During the holidays, Grandmother
took up the slack.

I think I was something of a shock.

Wait. You have opinions?

Pretty much.

Well, keep them to yourself. I have to work.

*Enough with the imaginary dialogs, lady. We've spent too much time together
in my imagination, and not nearly enough in real life.*

I came up here to west nowhere with *no idea* what my mother and I would
say to each other in adult life, alone in a room, but here we are.

So, will we end up ordering takeout or has she actually laid in groceries? Or
did she schedule one of her usual diversions at her favorite country inn, with
cameos by the manager and neighbors who eat there every night, so we won't
have to face each other? It's the first time in a long time that Lydia and I have
been alone, with no entrances and exits, no scene breaks—our first crack at
being together as adults.

It's almost thrilling. Terrifying. Both.

But here we are.

Then we aren't.

He taps on the window—lingering landscape gardener, I wonder, painter
with a question, paper boy, I don't know—but Lydia jumps up. It's odd. Gerard's
arrival could be staged, as ordered and on schedule, like the other chic little
visitations we've had today. Unless he's embedded, a man who comes in any
old time, any old way he wants.

Whichever, he enters Lydia's fussy little living room and whisks my mother's
mouth with an all-too-casual kiss. All Lydia's lights go on as he kicks off the
lizard Tony Lama boots, stingrays, like hers.

"Sweetie, this is Gerard." As if I need no introduction, she plays to him, but
she is working me. Lydia the director in full cry: this is the superb portrait
photographer I told you about, he took that amazing portrait of me, *protégé*,
really, he comes to me for career advice. All he needs is the right dealer, the
right art house to publish his photos and the world will recognize him as the
first-class artist that he is, in fact I've been making some important contacts
for him.

And me? But she is distracted. That has to wait.

He's brought food. She thanks him with a hug and gets busy setting the drop-leaf table in the dining area with the vintage Willow ware she found at the sweetest little place in the next town. Oh, Marie, note the embossing on the ornamental hinges of the table, she had it specially made to fit, see how nice the teakwood looks against the brass.

Grinning, he jerks his head in my direction. She goes back for a third plate—right, she forgot somebody—and this reminds her to say, "Oh dear, Gerard, you haven't met Marie." Pretending I'm her BFF and not the grown daughter she couldn't possibly be old enough to have.

He uncovers platters from the local caterer—if they hold all Lydia's favorites because she phoned in the order and secured it with her credit card, she covers, gushing the way she does whenever presents come. Then with a look I recognize she opens a bottle of wine and I think, *Oh God, don't let him sleep over.* It is that obvious.

While Gerard assesses me I smile, more for Lydia than for her newest acquisition. So this is her new friend that I've heard so much about. Negotiating this visit, she actually giggled and fluttered on the phone. For her sake, I murmur and nod and make a fuss over the supper Gerard brought and wait to see how this evening with my mother will turn out.

It isn't about me.

It was never about me. What else explains his cashmere V-neck, same this-year's-color, same high-end designer as hers? After dinner she fusses in the kitchen while he sits in the center of my mother's silly velvet sofa like a rajah granting me an audience. Unless I am the audience.

"She was a harsh, angry person, but she's all I have." Gerard corrects himself. "Had. For warmth and kindness, I had the nuns. Mam was who she was, but the sisters were the only mothers I had. They taught me to read and write and do fractions, and when I was big enough to go on the bus alone, they sent me into town to the Christian Brothers' school. I got my high school education in that town; I took art classes at the local university extension and worked full-time, although she didn't need the money, Mam wanted me at home, and I wanted to give something back to the nuns. I worked for a studio photographer on Main Street, yearbook pictures, wedding photographs. I was twenty, twenty-one, twenty-five, twenty-eight, but every night I came home to the housekeeper's cottage where Mam and I lived. I was broke, but that wasn't the real reason. My mother expected it. After all, she said, 'I took care of you. Now it's your turn to take care of me.' She never liked me, but she was one woman alone, and I was all she had." That sigh. "I stayed with her to the end. I couldn't pack up and leave my old life behind until she died."

Note the past tense. Figment or fact, Gerard says his mother is dead, and although she is, frankly, old enough to be his mother, Lydia's girlish heart rushes out to him. Does she not see the differences between them?

Does she not know that he sees it too, and takes it for what it is? Gerard's voice drops, striking a note so sad that even I want to make him feel better. "It was last March. You might as well know, I drove thousands of miles from Minnesota and the Benedictine rule, but I didn't come far. Remember, I grew up with the nuns. I don't know many people, but I've always been at home with the sisters. Mother Ignatia sent Mother Therese a note and they took me in at the abbey here. I do a few things for the community, and in return . . ."

That night, before she releases me to the Hide-a-bed in her guest cubicle, Lydia shows me her boudoir, as if to prove that tonight, at least, Gerard isn't sleeping here. She takes my hands and pulls me down on her lush velvet quilt. "What do you think?"

I don't know what to think. I don't know what to say but it won't matter because in every circumstance, no matter what mess she's walking into, Lydia talks on.

She says, "Gerard is very religious."

"I gathered."

She says, "I think he's in love with me." She means she is in love with him. What to say, what to say? "That's sweet."

"Do you think he's too young?"

North of forty, at the very least. "Depends."

The next time she summons me to the country I table all my excuses and go. People go to NASCAR tracks for some of the same reasons: being at the rail in case there's a crash, but my real reason is, I think, oddly, altruistic. I take the train to the bus that will drop me in that claustrophobic small town because it's time to tell Lydia what I think.

I won't accuse her of robbing the cradle, which is more or less the case. I think the cradle is robbing her.

Turns out Gerard is away, which is probably why she pulled my chain; the woman languishes without an audience and in spite of the growing cast in her farmhouse drama, she doesn't make real friends. Gerard is back with the nuns in Minnesota, settling his mother's affairs, and Lydia has taken this opportunity to open up to me.

We reach her silky boudoir via a short trip from the local bus stop to an exquisite but long, long dinner at the night's designated country inn, with plenty of staff circling, buzzing her table to chat her up, and enough regulars coming in to drop small talk into all the empty places. Note that she staged my arrival so our day together would be short and end mercifully soon.

Oddly, instead of leaving me to put fresh sheets on the Hide-a-bed, she pours two glasses of port and summons me to her boudoir, which occupies the entire second floor. Only Lydia has a boudoir. One more set she can decorate with her exquisite vision of herself. Now she's sitting cross-legged on the velvet quilt, holding her feet like a college drunk just back from the party of her life.

"Oh, Marie. Oooohhh, Marie." She's rosy with self-importance, confiding as though we really are BFFs, "We're so in love."

"I'm glad." I can't be here, listening to this as she slides closer, words boiling over.

"It's just that . . ."

"Do you mind if I?" The bed dips in the middle; if I don't get up now, while I'm close to the edge, I'll slide into the dip. "It's been a long day."

"My heart is breaking."

I do not say, *You're shitting me.* "I have to . . ."

"Gerard wants me to marry him."

"Oh."

"He's gone to Minnesota to bring back his mother's engagement ring."

"She was engaged?"

"Yes. It's a very sad story."

I can't begin to guess what I'm grieving for, but it makes me bitter. "I know."

"How could you possibly know?" Oh, Lydia, the scorn. All this grief and her hair is sleek and her face impossibly smooth. I would like to meet her plastic surgeon. "This is real."

"So what's the big problem?"

"He's in Minnesota, with those fucking nuns."

"I thought he was getting the ring."

The noise inside her breaks out, smashing her slick surface. Her age shows in her voice, every single year of it. "I don't understand it, but I'm a divorced woman and in spite of everything he's some kind of Catholic. He has to choose between me and God."

"Why can't you just."

"Because we're not married!" Oh, that face. Lydia's face, just then. Her voice clots. "He says we'd be living in sin."

Oh, this is so odd. Odd and awful. Whatever is going on with Gerard, she gives lovely presents, he takes from her, he comes as he goes as he pleases, but *oh, Lydia,* whatever is going on with Gerard stops short of this great big bed.

"*Did you hear what I just said?* It's this Mother Therese. Monday I'm going to see this Mother Therese and straighten him out." Lydia is, OMG, on her feet, teetering on the soft mattress in a drunken fighter's stance. Lydia, preparing for a fight to the death. "By the time he gets back this will be settled, so wish me luck."

"Yeah," I say, because she is too drunk to hear anything I say. "Yeah, right."

I don't sleep much. Although Gerard is doing whatever Gerard does a thousand miles from here, I wake up edgy and pissed off, prowling the living room, fingering priceless small objects in the eighteenth-century cupboard in the little dining ell in my mother's house. I can open her desk and discover all her secrets if I want to, or dance naked in the lavish bathroom, studying my profile in her mirrored walls, and Lydia won't know. She's never up before noon. Something in the narrow, depressing kitchen smells so bad that I wonder: *what does this woman eat?* All I find are stale water biscuits, left over from some party. A can of smoked oysters. A banana too old to peel. While I wasn't looking, my aggressively young mother turned into one of those people who, you're afraid to look into their fridge. It yields a bottle of Cuervo and two glasses in the freezer, rimmed in rock salt and on the shelves below, nothing but a half-bottle of olives, some shriveled carrots, and forgotten clamshells filled with dried-out leftovers from dinners out—nothing a person could eat.

Because everything in the nice new town where my mother is staging her nice new life is much too close to everything else, I take my laptop out for coffee as soon as it gets light.

It's easy enough to find the abbey. The place is famous, perhaps because it and the local writers' colony are symbiotically linked. People whose names you'd recognize have gone to the abbey to detox, finish that book, retreat from life long enough to regroup. No wonder the rising starlet came here at the height of her career. No wonder she stayed. Climbing the hill, I wonder. *Is Gerard here to detox or because he's trying to write a book?*

Then I think it doesn't matter whether, or which. I need to suss out the woman Lydia is girding herself to confront.

It's easier than you'd think.

There's a nun in the kitchen garden that runs along either side of the drive, tying up tomato plants and raking between rows. She's wearing the flowing medieval habit that old nuns cling to like the past, but with the sleeves rolled back and the skirts tucked up. Instead of the starched wimple and flowing veil I expected, the white headband and perfunctory veil look like something you'd clamp on a little girl out trick-or-treating as a nun.

"Um, Sister?"

"Hi."

"I'm looking for Mother Therese? I'm here about."

"Gerard." Oh, how fast her face changes! "Tell me you're not one of his."

Don't finish! "No. But my mother is."

"Oh, Gerard. Gerard." Her expression tells me everything. "We're all very fond of Gerard, but you might as well know. I'm losing patience with him."

Monday, and Lydia is girding herself for the encounter. Don't ask me why I stayed the extra night when I expected to escape right after Sunday lunch. Don't ask me what it was like.

Lydia stands in the mirrored bathroom, contemplating the image she's chosen to present when she confronts Mother Therese. Skin-tight leather jeans over her oldest riding boots because they make her feel brave. Missoni cashmere cut on a tricky diagonal. In the Moschino jacket with its braid and brass buttons, she looks like the brave little drummer boy. Oh, Lydia, what do you think you can accomplish at the abbey, even with a thousand dollars on your back?

"Well," she says, "what do you think?"

I pretend she said, *How do I look?* "Terrific."

If I'm still here in my mother's glossy rural showcase on a Monday when I should be back in the city, safe at work, I guess I'm feeling adult and protective. I should be, knowing what I know, but I move aside so she can open the front door. She stands on the stone step with her sleek little French sports car in the background, waiting for me to admire. I should, but she throws that silk scarf around her glossy salon-cut hair to complete the picture, which is what this is. So I am back in that taxi on the day I broke her compact and she made me cry. Shall I tell her? Will I?

Poised, my mother says, in a spasm of uncertainty, "Wish me luck."

I should pick up my bag and escape. I should slam the door hard and never come back. I should hit the mark and run if I have to, and flag the outgoing bus, but here I am. I wander my mother's kitschy-chic and empty, empty house with my hands floating up, like an astronaut in zero gravity. By three, Lydia's had time to drive to the abbey and back a dozen times and she still isn't back. It makes me anxious and guilty. Whatever the abbess tells her, and I know what she'll tell her, Lydia will be furious. She'll come home changed by the encounter, maybe even for the better. I need to see; I need to make sure that I've relieved her of the slick, lying bastard she wants but never needed.

Gerard doesn't bother to tap on the window. He just walks in on me, affronted. "What are you doing here?"

I'm not that little girl any more. I have an MBA. I strike back. "I thought you were in Minnesota."

"I thought you were gone."

"You're here to see my mother." *Take that!*

Nice, the second in which the eyebrows lift—Gerard didn't know. He covers smoothly enough. "I came back early, just for her."

"You know where she went, right?"

"You know we're in love, right? Or did she not tell you?" Gerard has no interest in my answer. He's fooling with her coffee machine, so I can't see his face. I have to wait while coffee brews and wait for him to wash out two cups and wait for him to pour before he speaks again. Handing me one with a sweet, guileless smile, he sits down on that sofa and starts.

"Growing up in a convent is like nothing you can imagine. There are the sisters' expectations, their selfless, blind generosity. The love. I was their puppy, theirs to love and train up in the way of the Lord," he says and for a French Canadian from Minnesota, he lays it on with a surprisingly Irish lilt. "The way of the Lord is a lonely way." I wait for the sigh. He says, "You can take the boy out of the religion, but. You know the rest. But you. You've never married?"

As though I will fall into his hands. "Don't start."

He doesn't have to.

She comes in white-knuckled and blazing, eyeliner smudged and clothes askew as though she's been rending her garments.

Like guilty lovers, we both spring to our feet.

Now, I think, without even a flicker of regret. *Now you'll get it, Gerard. Now she'll tear you a new one and kick you out for good.* In my heart I knew she wouldn't believe anything I said to her just because I said it, and she's never trusted me. I did the right thing, letting her walk into that confrontation. She'd have to hear it from the abbess firsthand, in her own words, before she got mad enough to destroy the man, and now she has. Lydia and I will never be friends but when this is over she'll thank me for letting her hear the truth, and from the source.

Gerard holds his arms out with moist eyes and a squashy smile, expecting her to rush into them, but she rushes past as though he isn't even in the room.

"You," she shouts, raging. "You went behind my back."

"I did," I tell her, *and I am not sorry.*

"Do you know what that woman said to me? Do you have any idea what she said?"

"Yes. No." I don't want her to tell me. By this time I've written all their dialog inside my head.

"The terrible things she said about Gerard. She's trying to come between us!"

I keep my voice low, for emphasis, "She's trying to help you," but it's as if I haven't spoken.

"Stupid bitch with all her sacred, holy orders. I thought we were fighting for his soul, but she flat-out lied to me. She tried to get rid of Lydia Grayson with the thinnest, stupidest tissue of goddamn lies! Does she know who I am?"

Guess not. But I try. "She didn't tell you about the other . . ."

"He finds love for the first time in his life and that woman says . . . You wouldn't *believe* what she said to me. I sure as hell don't believe it."

I have to try, so I finish, " . . . women?"

Lydia is too angry to hear. "Do you want to know what I believe? She doesn't want to save Gerard's soul, Marie. She wants to save him for herself!"

"Mother . . ."

"Don't."

"Mother, about the other . . ."

She swings and misses—anything to stop my mouth. She is something outside and beyond her vain, selfish self. "And you," she finishes when she can speak. "You flounced up there to the abbey talking trash to her, like that would break us up!"

In its own way, her anger is splendid. Gerard moves in and gently takes the hand to stop her from swinging again.

"Then you deliberately shoved me into that den of lies. What did you tell her, anyway? Is your life so boring that you have to break us up?" She steps back into him, rubbing against his flank like an ingratiating cat. "As if anything could ever break us up."

"I didn't say anything, Lydia. She told me, but nobody can tell you anything. You had to see!"

"What, that my life is over? That Gerard and I are doomed? Get out. Just go. Go out there and wait for the goddamn bus."

I want to. I can't. "The bus is gone."

Before she can say the next angry, Lydia-centric thing, Gerard steps in with an expression I don't want to parse. I know what he wants and I will not have this, but I can't be here, so I let him pick up my bag. I have to escape! The Irish lilt kicks in as he opens the door. "It's all right, darlin', I'll drive you to the train."

—*The Yale Review*, 2012

Precautions

"Don't touch that," Mother said, and I didn't. "Don't go near that. You don't know what's going around."

Well, we all knew, or we sort of did. Terrible things. Staph infections that science can't touch, plus Mother said everybody knows you catch cancer off another person, and nobody wants to do that; "AIDS," she said, "don't even *say* it or you'll get sick."

She sounded so scared that Billy and me clung to her legs and bawled until she promised to keep us safe. The world is a hotbed. You've seen the TV. Everybody who's still out there is getting sick. Smallpox is back, to say nothing of bubonic plague. Tuberculosis creeps up on your best friend without you knowing; smile at them wrong and the next thing you know, you've got it too. Quarantine! Triple locked doors, nurses in masks, they take out one lung and you get it in the other.

"I love you," Mother said to us. "I'd rather see you dead."

Pestilence is loose in the land, one day you're fine; run into the wrong person and the next, you are Infected.

"And you can't tell who's sick! They may look like you or me," Mother told us, "but they don't DO like we do." That was the day she cut her friends off except for phone time, even though Margaret and Etta are clean as anybody and her best friends in the world, the world being where Father went that I am not allowed to go.

You could catch It!

"What, Mother? Catch what?"

"Better safe than sorry," Mother said. She loved her friends but she wiped off the mouthpiece every time they talked.

Then Margaret got necrotizing fasciitis and they had to cut off her arm. Mother quit picking up the phone. "Germs," she said, and for a while she was OK with talking on the speaker. "You can get them before you even know." And poor Etta, she was nice to a stranger and caught herpes, so that was that. When Mother left off phoning, Etta and Margaret wrote letters, but you can't be too careful. When you're scared of germs after a while you start getting scared of everything that might have been near germs. You're scared of germs coming off of people and you're scared of germs getting on things like envelope glue, even though the mail person has strict instructions to put your snail mail in the De-con box outside the front door.

We count on De-con to keep us safe. That plus the airlock.

The first De-con box cost us a bundle, Mother ordered it off the web after Uncle Seymour died of strep, he was the first, and the improved De-con Enhanced Support cost a heap of Father's insurance money, but it is a fantastic service that allows us to go on living the way God meant us to, Uncontaminated. Safe.

That and the care Mother took, starting the first day the bad wind blew in from somewhere else and changed the world.

"Flu," Father said when he got in from work that day. "Everybody in the office is sick."

"Daddy, Daddy." Billy and me clamored around his legs.

Mother yelled, "Don't touch him!" and yanked us away.

Father said to her, "What are you doing?"

"Stand back! The whole world is a contagious ward."

"Don't worry," Father said. "I'm fine."

"Don't try and kid me," Mother said. "There was a special report on TV, this is the worst flu ever. Plus, side effects! And you were just out in it."

"I didn't go anywhere, just to the office."

"On the bus. That's another hotbed. All those people, breathing on you. Who knows what you picked up? And the office! Out of the hotbed and into the incubator. The workplace. The TV says the workplace is the worst." She handed Father his walking papers and shoved him out the door, which she locked and bolted.

He cried on the front lawn until Mother rolled a pup tent and a week's worth of food off the roof. For days he camped outside our front window, calling. "Day four, and I'm not even sneezing. Day five, and I'm fine. Day six . . . "

"Not yet," our mother said. "We have to be sure."

Then on the seventh morning, we heard him sneeze. "I didn't mean it," he cried. "It was an acci—achoo!"

"That does it!" Mother screamed, and took the Glock Daddy kept under his pillow to protect us from burglars and started firing from the roof. "I love you, but go," she yelled, being careful to hit the ground behind him as he ran. "And don't come back until you're clean." She fired again, herding him into the street.

We heard a screech. He got hit by a truck.

Of course we cried, but when it's a matter of your own health and safety, you shut up fast. After all, I mean, first things first. Mother pulled herself together. "I'll keep you safe," she vowed. "No matter what it takes."

"OK," Billy said, "Me and Dolly are going out to play."

"Outside!" Mother grabbed him. "Not on your life! Something terrible could happen to you and you wouldn't even know."

"But I want to go out and play." Billy always was rebellious. He looked ready to hit and yell.

"Not now," Mother said. "You neither, Doll," she said to me. She shuttered the windows. Through De-con she ordered and mounted a defense missile on the front porch roof, IN CASE, and showed us how to use it. She sealed us in. "You'll thank me later. This is for your own good."

"When?" I was scared and excited. Less excited than scared.

"Soon, I promise, just as soon as they get all these sick people put away."

It was a little song she sang to keep us safe. AS SOON AS THEY GET ALL THESE SICK PEOPLE PUT AWAY. And every night we had a little party, cookies and ginger ale. We put on costumes and made jokes. Once a month we tested the defenses. Ready. Aim. Everything but fire. If one of Them tries to get in . . . She made paper hats for us. "Aren't we having fun," Mother said. She was laughing and laughing. "Aren't we having fun!"

So Billy and me, we stayed in, and I can tell you we were damn glad. We saw the ravages on TV. "Just as soon as they get all these sick people put away." Truth? There was a whole world out there that we weren't using, and I could hardly wait.

But here's the trick of it. You can't get people put away when you don't know which ones they are.

Mother said we wouldn't be in here long, but she worked on our armaments while we slept. It's been a while, but at least I'm safe.

So we have Mother to thank. And De-con. We never touch anything any sick person touched.

We order from Web-TV, no problem, De-con guarantees that no germs get into your food and none come in on the clothes you ordered off the Web or from the Shopping Channel and what if it's maybe a little lonely you can count on emailing eBay or Amazon.com and they'll mail you back, you might get a computer virus but at least you are safe. Or, and this is great! With the Shopping Channel, you can phone in and sometimes they put your phone call on TV. Imagine. You can tune in and hear yourself talking to the shopping host right there on the air! Plus, you get safe, germ-free delivery of anything you want, from your Albanian Aardvark to a Jivaro shrunken head. Who needs to go out? Our lives were full!

I guess.

It's interesting, sitting there in front of the TV-puter most of the day. You're, like, CONNECTED to all the billions of others for as long as you stay logged on but you can't touch them, and this is weird. I was sitting in here protecting all my senses from contamination and all I wanted was to be touched.

I guess Billy did too. He said, "I want to go out and meet some people I'm not related to."

Mother smacked him. "No way."

Oh, but we were safe. So safe! See, hear, feel, taste, touch, HAVE anything you want. Get excited ordering it and then get excited waiting for it to come. Well, anything that got delivered to the De-con box and made it through the double-sealed de-germified airlock in our front hall. But what's the point of the perfect dress if nobody sees you in it except your brother and your mom? Billy and I would have had friends, I would have had cute guys to go out with, except Mother wouldn't let us go to school.

And I will tell you this about it. Mother did it because she loves us but home education is the pits. The whole world going on outside, we saw it on TV and on the web, and Billy and me stuck in Father's den, which she had converted to the schoolroom, us and Mother. Sitting too close and breathing the same stale air.

"What do you think, class?"

"I don't know. What do you think, Mom?"

It got old. Billy was the first to crack. He got big and started ogling all these women on TV.

"Stop that. That's just *Baywatch,*" Mother said.

"I don't care what it is, I want to go to the beach!" He meant he wanted to go out in the world and consort with jiggly girls.

"That show's so old those girls are probably dead." Mother said, "Girls aren't like that any more."

"Prove it." Oh my gosh he was ogling me.

I started to cry.

Mother smacked him. "You leave your sister alone."

The next morning he was gone.

It's amazing how Billy got out. He made it through the airlock and out of the De-con box. I tried but I was growing hips and boobs and they were getting in the way. Every once in a while he would try to phone but Mother wouldn't let me pick up. "That was your brother," she'd say. "He wants to come back but remember, he made his choice when he left us for the germs. Now I'm warning you, NO MATTER WHAT HE DOES OR SAYS, DON'T LET HIM IN."

It's OK, I didn't miss him too much. I went out on the Internet and met a lot of cool guys. Amazing what people will tell you when they can't see you. Amazing what you tell them.

Then Mother got sick. Except she didn't call it sick. How I knew there was something bad the matter was, she started teaching me how to run the world: where the money was, the PIN numbers for all our accounts, how to make e-transfers to keep the De-con service and how to pay for the food and the clothes she ordered for us and how to accessorize. The jewelry she'd gotten from the Shopping Channel, she divided into two heaps.

"This is for you." She swept one pile my way. The other, she kept. "I'm going to be buried in this."

"What's buried?" I said.

"Don't worry," she said. "It's not contagious. And wherever God takes me, I promise, I'll protect you to the grave."

I did like she wanted. I took the DigiCam and after I did her makeup and laid her out in all her jewelry and the Melissa Rivers caftan with the solid gold trim, I took lots of pictures and I posted them in the right place on the Web. Then I did like she ordered and put her down the Dispos-Al a little bit at a time. The bones I left in the De-con box and the De-con company took them away. He said through the intercom, "Are you OK in there?"

"Never better," I said.

Except it's really quiet in here.

After she died everything was pretty much the same. Stuff kept coming—clean and safe. But safe turned out not to be enough. Except for the necessaries, I left off shopping. Nobody to dress up for, nobody to care. It was quiet as hell. One day at delivery time I left the airlock open and when the De-con signal went off to tell me the outside box was opening, I stuck my head in the hole so the delivery guy would hear me direct. "Come on in!"

"Lady, you shouldn't do this. You could catch something."

"You're bonded," I told him. "It's OK."

"You got no idea what's out here."

"Cute guys," I said. "I saw them on TV."

"But some of them are carrying terrible diseases. Women too!" He sounded muffled; OK he was talking through his De-con filter mask. In the surveill camera, he looked like he was wearing a gigantic rubber glove. Since Mother died I haven't talked to anyone direct and I was starved for it. Just me and one other, naked face to naked face.

"No problem," I told him. I was wearing Mother's Pamela Anderson outfit from QVC. "I'll stay away from them."

"Precautions," the delivery man said. "No telling what you might run into out here."

"At least I'd be running into SOMETHING," I said but I took his word for it and let it go by. Along with the days. Along with a lot of other days.

Until I found the ad on the Web. SEX AND GLORY, the header ran. SAFE AND TOTAL LOVE WITH THE PERFECT PARTNER—GENDER APPROPRIATE.

I read the disclaimers. I gasped at the down payment. I sold everything I had on eBay and took all the money to do it.

I ordered a guy.

The De-con truck pulled up on the morning appointed. The assistant driver ran a forklift around and unloaded the crate. There were air holes in the crate, it was strapped with warning tape: DO NOT BEND. THIS SIDE UP. I saw it on the surveill TV.

The driver said through the intercom, "I got a questionable delivery."

"No questions. I ordered it."

"It won't fit in the De-con box."

"You can set it down out there and leave." Mother taught us to be cautious. "I'll bring it in."

"You shouldn't come out."

"OK, OK," I said. "You can just open it and leave."

"No way! The crate's been damaged. De-con guarantees protection and no way am I going to be liable. God knows what could have gotten inside."

"I don't care."

"Lady, anything that happens to you comes out of my hide. I can't leave you alone with this thing. You could sue the company."

"I'll take the responsibility."

"Sorry, Ma'am." The De-con guy gestured to the assistant and they started to put the thing back on the truck. I armed the defense missiles and blew both of them away.

It took all the tools in the basement to blow the airlock and get the front door open but I finally managed. I pushed it aside and I came tottering out. Me, Dolly Meriwether, alone out in the world. It was weird! The box was sitting right where the delivery men had left it. I thought I heard thumping. It seemed to bulge.

My guy.

There were air holes, all right, and there were plastic kibbles dribbling from one corner where the crate had smashed. There was also a warning label. MAN-

UFACTURER NOT RESPONSIBLE FOR DAMAGED GOODS OR CONTAGION INCURRED IN TRANSIT.

I put my mouth up to the hole. "Can you hear me? Are you in there?"

I thought I heard a voice.

Oh Mother, I was so excited! I could almost hear Mother hissing, "Leave it alone, Dolly. That thing is full of germs!"

"I don't care!" I opened the box with the crowbar. The sides fell away. Plastic kibbles cascaded down. He was standing there smiling in his orange coverall. "Hello."

Mother hissed from beyond the grave. "Don't touch that thing, you don't know where it's been!"

My guy stepped out of the kibbles. He was nice and apologetic. "I'm here on approval. Truth in advertising, I have to tell you this. If the seal on the box is broken, your product may be contaminated. You can return it and get your money back."

I looked at the corner of the crate. "No problem," I said.

"Look," he said. "I was in a warehouse with a bunch of. Um. I'm sorry, I might of caught something."

"No problem," I said. I grabbed his arm and yanked him inside with me. "Kiss me," I said.

"Even if I'm . . . ?"

I shut his mouth with my mouth and it was the best thing I ever tasted in this world. Then sirens started blatting and guns I didn't even know were in the walls around us slipped out of their slots—the automatic firing squad Mother had planted in the middle of some long-dead night. I heard a hundred clicks. The weapons arming. I heard her voice. "I TOLD YOU I'D PROTECT YOU TO THE GRAVE."

"I love you," I yelled at him as a hundred triggers drew back. "Get out!"

But I know it is too late for both of us.

—*F&SF*, 2000

Journey to the Center of the Earth

Jerome is in Nebraska to visit his father.

His dad lives in a model community located in the middle distance, at the point in the road where you think the line of shadows you see ahead is just about to congeal. At this juncture on this particular highway, you think the murky violet ridge along the horizon may be your first sight of the Rocky Mountains, but you can't be absolutely sure. Stay here and you'll never know; drive ten miles and the outline becomes clear.

This is where you make the turnoff for Bluemont. Take a sharp right on the two-track road through the foothills and in forty miles you're there. According to the literature his dad has sent Jerome over the years since he left them, it's going to be some kind of Jerusalem—*We are the future of the world;* to Jerome it sounds crazy, but . . . exciting? His dad would never admit this, is firm in his use of the words *model community.*

It isn't much of a model.

The snapshots show a ring of outsized mobile homes beached on cinder-block foundations, an assembly hall that promises more than it seems to deliver and a nineteenth-century house restored and painted like a wedding cake, and as for the rest? Half-finished foundations and a couple of huge, raw places in the earth, as if from excavations hastily filled and incompletely healed. Is this all? Jerome's dad says that when it's finished they will all live in contemporary houses with jutting redwood decks and crashing expanses of glass, but this will have to wait. Except for the self-styled mayor and leader of the group, the colonists are all stashed in those trailers, waiting for the town to rise. Their money always seems to be going into something else, but on the phone Jerome's father is vague about what. If it isn't the real thing, he thinks, then what's the point?

It's a strange place for Jerome, but here he is.

He has brought this on himself. Mostly he lives a normal life but when he goes home to visit he runs out of things to say. Caught short at Christmas, fresh out of words, he accidentally showed the brochure to his mom: mistake; the clouds around her head turned brown and started to boil.

"Lord," she said, squinting at the pictures as if she expected to find Jerome's dad walking around in them, this high, "what do you think is going on?"

Who was Jerome to tell her they were getting ready for the end of the world? He should have known she would figure it out: the prose, the strange device on the Bluemont sign.

"My God, he's in a religious sect."

"It's his life."

"He's your father," she said. So his mom has sent him to see about it. Although his folks have been divorced since he was ten, Jerome's mom can't stop worrying.

"I can't help it," she said. "It's never over with a person, no matter what you tell yourself."

"What do you want me to do?"

"I just want you to go."

What is he supposed to do, talk his dad out of this thing he's joined and bring him back to life as they know it? He doesn't think so. Is he supposed to be his mom's advance man, preparing the way? Certainly not. She is with Barry now. They're getting married in the spring.

"So, what?"

"A sect," she said, dispatching him. "I just . . ." She was at a loss. "I just want you to see if he's all right."

Maybe, Jerome thinks, she wants to find out if he's being held against his will.

He doesn't think so. The place isn't jail. It doesn't have to be. Jerome reasons, perhaps because he was brought up Catholic, that all religion is a captivity, souls held tight against their will.

So, hey. It may be what they want. And hey, what if they turn out to be right? A strange, almost sexual undercurrent draws him to this outside possibility. So he is here for his own reasons. Probably he spends too much time trying to make sense of things.

The last thing he did before he got here was to check with her. Stopping at a diner outside Ogallala, he'd called his mother collect. "What if these people are right?"

"God is God, but this is crazy," his mother said.

Still. But before he could raise this or demand marching orders she broke his heart with the good mom's farewell formula. Good old Mom, dismissing him: "Be good. Have fun."

Jerome wants to see his father, is afraid. It's been so long; what are they to each other now? Although they have talked, phone calls from pads on the other side of town and in Maine and Morocco and San Francisco, he hasn't seen his dad since the divorce. After years of bopping around, his father has finally landed in one place. After a lot of confusion, his dad seems to be focused on one thing. Jerome is going to feel better about things if it turns out to be the right one.

Will his father be glad to see Jerome?

At least he'll be surprised.

Jerome is less anxious than depressed, driving in. Bluemont does not look good even in brochures; in person, in mud season, it's worse. In the waning spring light it looks not so much deserted as abandoned, the kind of place a reasonable God would turn his back on as too shabby to figure in any divine scheme. The tinny-looking pastel trailers are listing on their foundations, the assembly hall windows are boarded up against the winter cold and the wedding-cake house looks bedraggled and smirched. If these people are really onto something, there are no outward signs. Unless hardship is the whole thing.

My kingdom is not of this world, Jerome thinks. Yeah, right.

Negotiating the guck, he's grateful for the use of Barry's well-kept Jeep Cherokee, which has four-wheel drive. At least he'll be able to pull out of the mud when it's time to leave. Getting out of the car, he's also glad nobody's around. He really doesn't want to have to talk to anybody until he's seen his dad. It seems important to meet this place on his father's terms. He would like to wander around until he runs into his father, like, accidentally? Oh, hi.

When he gets out of the car, he's surprised by a watery feeling in his shins. It turns out Jerome is scared to death of meeting the other colonists, or whatever, is afraid of what he'll see rattling around behind the eyes. Flickering beyond this encounter with his father is the outside possibility of an absolute; the truth of this place, or his dad's life in this place, is strictly between the two of them. Somebody is coming out of the assembly hall—a woman in a big plaid jacket, quilted pants; she has her wool hat pulled way down, so, good. Jerome slouches along the board sidewalk with his chin buried in his shoulder, trying to look as though he comes here every day. He is so preoccupied by the mud squelching between the boards and over the rubber toes of his Nikes that when they pass, he doesn't even know whether the woman speaks. Automatically polite, he says hi and hurries on.

Finding his father turns out to be no problem. He is out behind his trailer splitting wood; at the right time Jerome just looks up and he's there.

"Dad!" The wind, emotion, something takes his voice away. His big moment and he can't make enough noise for his father to hear.

He looks the same, even from behind. In spite of the weather Justin is working with his coat off and his head uncovered, his fine hair is blowing, and where the drooping neck of the sweatshirt exposes it, the skin on the back of his neck is fair. Jerome is unsettled by the change. When he was little his father was too big for him to see whole; now they are the same size.

Then. It is humiliating. Argh. Ghah. Jerome hears himself gabbling, "Hi. Bet you don't know who I am."

His father turns. "Oh, Jerome," he says, as if it's only been ten minutes. His face goes through a number of changes as he considers possible reasons for this visit. Stabbing Jerome in the heart, he lights on the wrong one. "What's the matter, are you in trouble?"

"No, Dad, everything is fine."

"Oh, son. Don't look like that." His father drops the ax and advances, thumping him into a hug.

Jerome is surprised by the force with which they collide. "Oh, hey."

Probably his father wishes he'd said the right thing to him.

Justin grins his same grin. "Come on in."

Inside is reassuring; the trailer is like a captain's cabin, everything trig; his dad's things look the same: books marching across the desktop, clipper ship bookend Justin took with him when he left, baby picture of Jerome. He has added a laptop and a decanter set. Jerome touches one of the crystal stoppers.

"Your mom never forgave me for liberating the Waterford."

His mom never forgave him period.

In the old days his father used to be much heavier and wear a suit. Now he is skinny, mellow, aggressively laid back in the worn, silvery jeans and the baggy sweatshirt. He commands this space like the captain of a submarine. He is watching Jerome.

"Well, what do you think?"

"Nice," Jerome says, "but isn't it kind of small?"

"We're getting used to functioning in tight quarters." Without explaining, his father pulls out two lead crystal glasses Jerome remembers from his childhood. "Port?"

It's like the class reunion of a very small school. They are having alcohol because it's a party; because his dad still thinks of Jerome as ten years old, they are also having candy. The ashtray between them is filling up with little tags and silver foil.

In a strange way this seems perfectly right to Jerome—lounging on the neat convertible sofas with his dad in the late afternoon, eating Hershey's kisses and getting a buzz on. He focuses on the laptop, thinks it's a good sign. In case it turns out these people are crazy, his dad's probably here writing a book about them. Unless something better comes up, it's what he's going to tell his mom. But he stops his mouth with melting chocolate and doesn't ask. For a long time all they talk about are things they both remember from ten years ago, the dog they had, Jerome's troubles learning to ride his first two-wheeler, but the whole time Jerome is sitting with his eyes cracked too wide and his mouth open, listening for something he may not recognize.

He wants to come right out and ask his father, Where were you when you left us? He doesn't mean, Where did you go? He means, Where were you in your head? But hard as he tries to phrase the question, he has to get semi-blitzed before he can ask Justin anything, and when he does, all he can come up with is, "What happened to your house?"

His dad turns bland eyes to him. "What house?"

"I thought you guys were building modern houses."

"In time," his dad says. "Right now, there are more important things."

Jerome is just drunk enough to say, "The end of the world?"

Justin does not answer. "Supplies, for one."

Then while he slouches in the cushions with his mouth full, letting the chocolate melt and run around in there, his dad lays it out for him: how many of them there are in this community, what the arrangement is. They are pooling funds. The houses are not as important as laying in supplies. Like a materiel officer he numbers the things they have shored up against destruction, whether of society or the earth he does not say. At no point does his dad say anything crazy. The plan as he describes it is not religious, but pragmatic. He names some of the things they have: generators, enough food and water for sixty years, medical supplies, weapons, radiation detectors, a shopping list for Armageddon, but: what makes these people so sure it's coming? Jerome is afraid his dad will say God came down and told him. But he doesn't. He just goes on about hydroponics and subsistence farming and the division of chores.

As his father talks, Jerome scours his speech for clues: as to why he's really here, what he thinks Jerome is doing here, because as he gets drunker and drunker, the tension builds until Jerome is squirming with urgency. He has to know what this man believes in. What's going to be expected of him.

"So that's the whole thing," his dad says finally, although it isn't.

When Jerome speaks, spit and chocolate overflow even though he's been careful to swallow beforehand. "I thought you were into something else."

His father does not ask the question.

Jerome can't frame the answer. "You know."

"I'll show you." Shoving a flashlight into his belt, the dad puts on his heavy jacket and throws a down vest at Jerome. "Here. You'll need an extra coat."

They go outside into the weak spring twilight, picking their way between lighted trailers like steaming jack-o'-lanterns that smell of a dozen dinners cooking. The few people caught outside at this hour are heading for their trailers with their heads down. They don't stop and they don't speak, but when father and son pass the wedding-cake house on their way to the periphery, a man comes out on the porch in his shirtsleeves to hail them; is this the leader?

"Justin," he says to Jerome's father.

"Martel."

Jerome wants to dig in his heels and take a good look at this person, but his father has him by the elbow now; all he has time to do is note the absence of beard or dreadlocks, whatever are the hallmarks. This is an ordinary-looking guy with a bland face, trying to get a squint at Jerome.

When they don't stop, Martel calls, "New believer?"

"My son," Justin says, hurrying Jerome past.

Martel raises his hand in what looks like a blessing. Relieved, Jerome thinks, Oh, OK, so it is a religious thing. "Believer," he says. It's the word he's been waiting for but the speaker is in no respect his father, so . . . what?

His father says only, "Martel is in charge."

"Readiness," the man on the porch calls after them.

"Readiness." Jerome whips his head around. "Is that the whole thing?"

The question is imprecise; Jerome's dad doesn't bother to answer. He runs ahead like a big kid calling, Come play. "Come over here. Come on down and you'll see."

When Jerome catches up Justin is standing in the middle of one of the raw places, in the mixture of mud and rubble that covers a recent excavation. A cement mixer leans next to a makeshift railing around an open space. He turns on his flashlight and shines it into the hole. The sides are shored up by cement forms, suggesting that whatever work is going on here is only partly done. From the top Jerome can't see how deep the ladder goes, but his father has already turned on his flashlight and started down.

At the bottom his dad lands on a metal surface with a leaden *klunk*. Planting his feet on either side of a wheel, he begins opening a hatch. Inside, another ladder descends into blackness. Then his dad finds the switch and the place lights up.

"What's this?"

"Shelter," Justin says. "It's not finished yet."

"What for?"

"Protection."

What? "You're *all* coming down here?"

"Half of us. We're fitting out two."

Following him down, Jerome is dizzy with the complications. His mind keeps zigzagging between the two shelters: Will they be able to talk? How will they know if each other are all right? If somebody's left behind? Whether everybody fits? Who's gone to which? Here two minutes and he's already feeling claustrophobic; it's like being inside a cigar case, this funny metal cylinder that smells. How are they going to stand it for a year?

"Took us a long time to work out the best thing to do the job," his father says. "We've buried propane tanks."

"In case of what?"

"Whatever happens," his father says.

He lets Jerome take it in: the double row of bunks at the far end of the enclosure, lights strung like Christmas bulbs, from exposed wires, wooden flooring that must hide the year's worth of rations his father has told him about. The floor orients him. Without it they would be like astronauts in free fall. Jerome is giddy, short of breath; his dad has brought him all this way and showed him all this and told him everything and at no time and in no way has he mentioned the name of God. It would have been so neat, something to hang onto, that Jerome could pin it all on: the persistence or the folly of faith. But his father is done explaining.

When Jerome can't think of anything to say his father says, "We stay down here until it's safe." He runs out of steam, suddenly, and sits down on the wooden flooring with his back hunched to accommodate the curve in the metal wall. The tank seems hollow, leaden and echoing, cold. Jerome sits down next to him. They probably look like refugees hiding from World War II in the British underground.

Cold and silent, Jerome is crowded by misgivings. Maybe he has attached too much to this. He imagined his father would get him down here and explain, at least; tell him some truth. Either that or demonstrate that he's completely crazy, leaving Jerome free to hug him goodbye and walk away.

Instead he just sits here next to Jerome in the dank shelter without saying anything.

It is almost unbearable, the tension between the two of them wedged here in the curve of the cylinder, and yet there is no reason for it that Jerome can see. They're just hanging, adrift in a welter of particles. There's too much going on and none of it resolved; his father has hurt everybody and run away from everything and replaced it with this.

Sitting shoulder to shoulder with his dad Jerome thinks maybe he's come all this way to let it all out and get it over with; raging, he could just let his father have it: How could you do this to us? How could you run away and bust up our family?

"Don't be too hard on your father," his mom said at the time. "He can't help it." Probably he can't, Jerome thinks, and even if he can, there is no way for Jerome to charge him with it now. What would be the point? It's something they can't change that happened years ago. But this whole thing, this awful *place*. Sitting here under tons of earth, Jerome needs, what: to explain or justify whatever his father thinks he's doing here. If he has come here and is doing this because of either sex or religion it may make some kind of sense, but there is no sign of a girlfriend anywhere in the trailer and this is only a bomb shelter.

Jerome would just like to be able to go back home with some real reason that he can lay out for everyone, so he can call it finished. He wants something he can point to and say, OK. There.

His father surprises him. "I suppose you're here to see if I'm crazy."

Caught in the act, Jerome starts; his head bonks the metal wall. "You really think the end of the world is coming?"

The gaze his father turns on him is empty, without guile. "Does it really matter?"

"I think so," Jerome says.

"And if it's true?"

This is a trick question; if Jerome believes it, the true course of logic followed to its absolute limit dictates the shelter, everything. He has to beg the question. "But Dad, we've stopped being scared of the Russians. Getting nuked. The war."

The look his father turns on him is careful, lucid. "That's only one of the names for it."

"Ah." Jerome squirms. The air in here is becoming intolerable; he pushes. "Names for what?" Armageddon? He is intent, squinting as if he can see the answer written in air inside his father's open mouth.

"Whatever."

Jerome is stifling. "For God's *sake*."

Then his father gets as close as he is going to come. "There are worse things than living at the edge of last things."

Jerome says angrily, "That's it?"

"What did you think you were going to get from me?"

Better than this; too much; he doesn't know.

"Whatever it is, whatever threatens us . . ." The look his father turns to him is careful, lucid. "You might as well boil it all down to something you can prepare for. Can do something about. And start doing it." And then his father, who is supposed to be the adult here, gives him a noogie on the shoulder, grinding the knuckles in with a grin. "But, hey. It doesn't matter if I believe in it. I like it here."

"That's all?"

"It's as good as any of the reasons people give for the things they do."

The logic. "God, Dad." Jerome jumps to his feet; the clammy air is killing him; he can hardly stand it. "Are you ever going to let us out of here?"

"I guess I'd better cancel your reservation," Justin says lightly.

At least there is some logic; Jerome lets his breath out all at once. "Damn straight."

His father pushes him up the ladder. "You first. I'm starved."

The stars are out when they reach the top and explode into the evening air. Jerome's dizzy all over again, this time with relief and delight at being released; Justin catches some of his son's joy. "Come on," he says, "we're out of here. The last of the big spenders is going to take you into Ogallala and buy you a steak."

Then at the end, when Jerome has almost forgotten about it, he gets, if not exactly what he thought he came for, this; it's as good as he's going to get.

They are standing in the Bluemont parking area in the pink early morning, getting ready to say goodbye. His dad, with his face full of incomplete good intentions, is looking at Jerome, who's waiting next to Barry's Jeep Cherokee, kicking the cleated tire. They've already hugged and Jerome is about to get in the car and go but he can't just leave it like this; he is sick of being cool.

"God, Dad," he cries—he wants to get it all back: himself, when little, the family he used to have. Belief. "I didn't come all this way for this."

"What do you want?"

He is astounded to hear himself: "I love you. I want you to come with me!"

"Too late." His father shrugs. "You know. But you can come back here any time you want."

His voice sinks so deep only he can hear it. "Oh God. Oh Dad."

So he has to get into the car. He's already shut the door on himself and rolled down the window to catch any last words when his father blunders into it; his smile is beautiful.

"Be good," Justin says, inadvertently recalling the old pattern, this: that their lives together are all of a piece. "Have fun."

—*Voice Literary Supplement,* 1991

Family Bed

—We have to go!

Like a mouse with the cat crouched outside waiting, my sister burrows deeper. There is cocoa on her breath. —Why, when it's so nice?

—I mean it, Beth. I jab her fat flank. We are too old to be in here. Frankly, there are crumbs.

—Niiice. Bethany, who Mother named after something I don't know about, drops into sleep like a stone into a pond.

Oh sure it's nice in here. Too nice. Soft and warm and seductive. —Mom, other kids don't have to go to bed at . . .

—Shh, Sarah. Can a person thunder in a whisper? Mother can. —We're the Dermotts. This is who we are.

The six of us are, like, trapped inside an idea she had. We used to be seven, but Darryl went out one night and that's all I know. Father says Darryl is fighting for our country in Lebanon.

—Sarah? My one remaining brother mutters, —Cover for me, dude.

My heart lurches. —Bill, you're not . . .

He claps his hand over my mouth.

The word comes out in a little puff anyway, —leaving.

But he is. Bill bundles pillows into a guy-shaped heap as Mother shuts the book and turns off the light with that hateful snap, like she is shutting the lid on us. During the ritual night-nights, he slithers out like a ferret; outside a car waits—five cute guys giggling and whispering; they are heading for the mall. I grab his hand. —Don't go.

—Children! Mom's hiss breaks the connection between us.

Am I the only one who hears him snaking across the rug? Outside the car starts up and my heart goes after it. There are kids at the mall, cute guys, skateboards and loud music. I poke Bethany. —We can't go on like this.

But we do. You see us on TV, you see us in the magazines, the happy Dermotts, smiling, smiling, smiling and you think, how wonderful: sweet family, together here in the dark, what closer bond?

Well, listen.

Here in the dark.

Get it?

Lights out after bedtime cocoa, that means, whether or not you are sleepy. No music at bedtime, no iPod, no whispering; no squirming and no humming please, you know it gets on my nerves. No Game Boy, children, and no TV, especially not now, and definitely no talking after the half hour officially designated for sharing in which we each have to say something embarrassing to make it stop, and as for cell calls or instant messaging, forget it. You get grounded, or worse.

—Mom, it's only nine p.m.!

—Finish your cocoa. It's nine o'clock, she says in Channel Five news tones. Grimly, she adds what I know by heart. —and I know where my children are. Night night, children. Kisses, everybody. Mmm, now you. Mmmmm. And you. And you. Is she counting? —Sleep tight.

Mother, I'm sixteen years old!

Nice, you think, but only because our mother has you brainwashed. We have the perfect mother. Everybody says so on TV. We are a media phenom: magazines, supermarket rags. *How perfect,* you think when she gets all gooshy about family stuff, which she does on every talk show between here and East Wherever, *I wish we were close like that. Snug as bunnies in the nest.*

Do you hear yourselves?

—Family bonding, Mother says with that smug, perfect smile, while Daddy nods gravely into whichever camera, yaaas, yaaas. —This is our private, special time.

Mom, everybody I care about is down at the mall!

But I am jabbed by knees and elbows and sandpaper heels on the special big bed Daddy built for us when we outgrew the super King, six Dermotts locked down for the night. Together. Again. Well, all but one, and this is what they are all ignoring, like: under cover of darkness, my one remaining big brother has fled.

I still miss Darryl. I love Billy and I'm scared for him, well, a little bit. But I am also pissed. Why should he have all the fun? He's malling with slutty Jacie Peterson, for all I know they are going to have sex, and me? I love Tommy, why can't I . . . It's for his own good, I think, but I am lying to myself. —Mom.

—Shhhshh, Sarah, night-night.

—Mo-om!

She probably already knows. She'll blow it off just like everything else that doesn't fit her glowing picture, like, pretend it isn't happening. When I grab her toe she says, —Howard . . .

Dad plants one foot on my shoulder. —Sarah, that's enough.

—But Dad! Bill is . . . God only knows what he's doing and it is killing me. —Mother, he's gone!

—Honey, he probably had to . . . Embarrassed pause. —You know.

—Pee? That's crap and you know it, he's . . .

—Sarah, language!

I go on anyway. —down at the mall.

So she has to face the fact. —Not for long. I said, Howard!

He yawns. —Don't worry honey, he'll be back. Sleep tight.

—Howard! When she gets that tone it scares me shit.

—Mom, I was only kidding! *Billy, what have I done to you?*

Dad lunges up in a plume of bedcovers like Moby Dick spouting. —OK, OK!

The minute it's done I feel bad. It's after Lights Out so we don't see our father dress. We don't see what he slides out of the drawer and snaps on his belt and we don't really know what he'll do when he catches Bill, we only know that it's happened before and Bill comes back to bed shaken, but not changed. It happens and we never speak of it. We never speak of anything bad. It would wreck the show. Dad settles into his boots: *thump.*

I jump out of bed. —Daddy, I'll come with. *Save him somehow.*

Mother hauls me back by the hair. —It's a jungle out there.

—But I have to help!

—It isn't safe.

—Mom! I want to hit or yell bullshit but we don't hit or yell in our family. We aren't allowed to whine. —All the other kids . . .

—Lie down. I'll read you all another chapter as an extra treat.

Last month it was *Pilgrim's Progress* and *Moby-Dick,* she has a great reading voice but the quizzes after are hard. Tonight it's *Don Quixote,* after which she reprises the night-nights and kills the light, after which we are expected to lie still until sleep rescues us, at least for now.

Like a person could sleep with Bill gone and Daddy out there, armed with God knows what. Plus. Beth's elbow is digging into my left boob and Dad's toenail scraped my neck when he left. Mom changes the sheets every day so there are never cocoa stains, but there are still crumbs. Probably this bed thing was cute when we were babies, but, Mom! Plus you and Daddy hog the pillows with Baby Ronnie jammed between you; God only knows when you had sex.

For the sake of our mother, we sleep in the belly of the beast, and in exchange for our freedom? We're famous on TV.

Tomorrow Vandella LeSpire is shooting the *Inside Everything* show from our very own bed. Mother's face is creamed to East Judas in preparation, and her hair is tweaked into cornrows on which, let me tell you, the beads and things look pretty lame. I mean, you can see the scalp and her hair is a scrunty, dyed blonde. Cornrows are supposed to show that what we are doing is very next, like: nothing retro about Family Bed. Mother wants people to see us on TV and go, "How wonderful." What a good mother she is, to do this for her kids. See how safe and happy they are, bonding in the Family Bed.

Did I mention that's what she calls it? Family Bed.

Also known as Sleep Sharing. Anything to euphemize this fluffy jail. And you are wondering how a tenth grader like me knows big long arcane words like arcane, and euphemize? Tomorrow you'll hear Mother expatiating (another, and another!), earnestly facing the camera with her cornrows yanked back in a mini-lift that's supposed to make her look young. —The Family Bed is a great vocabulary builder, she'll say, count on it. —Plus the sense of security. My children never doubt that they are loved.

Then she'll quote the Bible. I've stared at this St. Luke guy and I still don't get it:

Then the one inside answers, 'Don't bother me. The door is already locked, and my children are with me in bed. I can't get up and give you anything.'

Sounds pretty mingy to me.

Mother will tell you we Dermotts owe our warm hearts and fantastic vocabularies to our execrable, life-changing private time in this paragon, my prison: the Family Bed.

Have I mentioned the farting and scratching, the nervosity that comes when you're tucked in with your dad and your brothers and one disappears, where *is* Darryl, anyway? To say nothing of the crumbs. It may sound superficial to you but holy Cremora, when the earth's last picture is painted, there are the crumbs.

Later. Dad heaves Bill onto the bed. I hear compressed sobs. I touch his shoulder and he flinches. Is that blood drying? I wait until they are asleep. Then I murmur, —Billy, I'm *sorry.*

—Do you *know* what you did to me? His voice is a dry rasp.

—Oh God, Bill, I didn't know he was going to . . .

Then he scares me. —You know, Darryl wasn't the first.

—*What?*

—You were too little to remember Howie, he says. —Howard Junior. Don't go thinking he was the first.

—The first what, Billy. The first *what?*

But Mother is stirring and he covers my mouth. —Tonight I got the ultimatum, he says in normal tones because he is beyond caring what comes down. Then Dad clears his throat and instead of finishing, Bill rolls over with a little groan; his back is to me and that's the end of that. But he says, like he wants them to hear him, —They're just keeping me here for the TV show.

So weird, sitting here in my jammies, drinking cocoa in the middle of the day.
   —It began, Mother is telling Vandella LeSpire, —when Billy here was eentsy. Isn't Vandella surprised to find us all packed in bed in the middle of the day just to tape this show? Doesn't the woman see the *weird* in Mother's smile? —I love babies, they're so little and helpless and I love having them near. Mother's voice is soft and cozy, like it's bedtime already. —Billy's my oldest, you know.
   Wait a minute. What about Darryl? On TV we kids are not allowed to speak. There's stuff I haven't told you about, like why they won't let us go near the cellar, which to tell the truth I am not exactly clear on, or the welts I saw on Billy's back when it got light.
   —He'll always be my baby, Mother says while next to me, Bill's teeth grind until his molars crack. —Aren't we all helpless babies in this world? My eentsy sweet Billy, all alone in a big, dark crib, of course he cried, wouldn't you? Mother's voice is full, fat and soft. —I brought him into the bed with us and it was beautiful. So you see, that was the beginning. Four lovely children, we all sleep together, and that's what keeps us close.
   I mutter, —What about Darryl, Mom, but—worse: Billy is growling, —*What about Howie and them?*
   Mother mashes us down. Then she gives Vandella that gooshy, luminous mother's smile. —I love my babies, so much!
   Vandella thinks to ask, —What happens when they grow up, Mrs. Dermott?
   Mother is like a lighthouse, beaming radiant love. —They'll always be my babies, no matter what. She tickles Bill's cheek. It is obscene. —So little and helpless and sweet.
   Shuttered in performance quality mascara, Vandella's eyes mist over at the thought. All you poor women with babies are looking at my mother and feeling inadequate, and us? Don't ask.
   —This is our crucial bonding time, Mother tells Vandella in that sweet, level tone that means buy this or you die, —Bad mothers don't care what happens to their children as long as they're quiet. Good mommies keep their babies in the Family Bed.
   Freaks. She has turned us into freaks.
   At school the day after one of these shows there is the ritual shunning. For

Bethy and Ronnie (did I mention "baby" Ronnie is in first grade?) there is also ritual name-calling followed by the ritual sticking of gum into their hair. Moms may fall for this crap because motherhood makes women feel anxious and inadequate, but, kids . . . kids see the dark circles under our eyes and they know. They recognize the cowed look and the pallor of frustration from time served in Family Bed where there's no argument and nobody gets a night off. —If Father and I have to be here every night, Mother says to us, and I feel the sharp edge of her resentment, —the least you can do is be here and be glad!

But none of this is conveyed to Vandella, who can't see past the forced smiles on our shining faces, and none of this filters into the pink fog that occludes the minds of new moms who are so anxious to do everything right that they will do anything, even something this heinously wrong.

When I am old enough to have a psychiatrist I will have one thing to thank Mother for—enough words to express what she's done to us. That is, if I live long enough to get a psychiatrist.

Then my brother Bill rises up on his elbows, grimacing to get Vandella's attention. Dad already has an elbow yoked around his neck so only I hear what comes out: —Ask her about the others. And faster than I can tell you, Bill disappears. Pretending they are in a father-son bear hug, Dad yanks him back under the giant duvet that covers us all. Vandella is extremely gracious. She promises to edit it out of the tape before this airs but I have my suspicions. Don't these people lie, sometimes, to get the story that they want? Vandella thanks us and says she will be back Thursday to finish up live on her early morning show, interviewing the happy Dermotts as they spill out of the house. Mother has already picked out our wardrobes for the show.

Billy is gone. When we woke up he wasn't here. My sisters and I had to wear these hotwired e-bracelets to school today, with angora socks pulled up to hide the bulge: make one wrong step and the screech of pain will rend the ears of a stone lion. When we came to bed tonight nobody took them off. Billy is gone and Mother is pregnant again. Or she's thinking about it. I heard them talking in the night. When I got up to pee I hit something sharp.

—Arghhh!

—Sarah, what's the matter?

—I was only going to the bathroom! Razor wire rings the bed.

—Father will take you, Mother says. She uses her special voice, the one that rots stainless steel. —Howard!

—First Bill and now razor wire. Where is Billy anyway?

Mother gasps as if I've asked where are the space aliens. —Who?

I let Dad lead me through the gap in the wire and see me to the bathroom. I exchange extra night-nights to prove I have returned to the Family Bed but I am thinking. I am thinking hard.

Billy is in the house somewhere, I know it. I found one of his Hyperbolic space shoes under the bed this morning when I got up and I'm not so sure about Mother or Dad but I do know my one remaining big brother. Without his Hyperbolic space shoes, Billy doesn't leave the house. A message for me, I think, when I find it. This is a message for me. Inside there is a scrap of paper. Block letters in Bill's yellow highlighter. DON'T DRINK IT.

I am scared but I am excited. Billy may be gone from the Family Bed, but I know he's somewhere in the house. They've put him in Solitary or something, and all I have to do is find out where. I'll break him out and together he and I will run away.

As it turns out, this kid Tommy at school that I'm in love with? Tommy loves me back. Where I am in Arts he is on the Vocational track, which means he is an electronic genius. Disarms my e-bracelet via his PDA. I am still wearing it so when I check in at the Family Bed promptly tonight at 8:30, nobody knows it no longer works. I feint for the phone and then give Mother a gratifying squeal to prove she's put me in my place. Finesse the cocoa and try not to fall asleep during *Don Quixote*. Snuggle with Beth and Ronnie, who's been moved down to the foot of the bed to make room for the new baby to come.

—Night night. Mother is rosier than a grotto full of Madonnas: pregnant already? She is sweet, sweeter than ever. —Now sleep tight, I want you to look your best tomorrow. Remember, Vandella's going to have us on her show.

She is going to interview the six—er, five of us happy Dermotts in bright sunshine, although I already know that we kids never get to talk, and Darryl? He is fighting for our country in Iran.

I love them best when they're still babies, Mother says, *so little and helpless and sweet.*

It's going to be a long night.

Before Dad falls asleep I make him lead me to the bathroom again. I've seen the gap in the razor wire by daylight but I need to know how to navigate it in the dark. I don't really have to pee. Instead I stick my head under the basin. Ever so quietly, I tap the bathroom pipes. Clinkety *clink*. I hold my breath. Then I know. All I have to do is follow the plumbing down to the basement. That's Bill answering from somewhere deep underneath the house: clinkety *clink*.

I let Dad lead me back to bed. Then I wait. There is some shifting under the covers: Mother. There is some complaining: Dad. She must be hot to get herself that nice new baby.

Uggg. She wants him to Do It with her right here.

—Not tonight, Dad says. Then he uses his motivational voice. —You want to be pretty for the audience tomorrow, right? Just think: *Inside Everything.* Us, live, on global T V.

Ugly, what she says to him next. I stuff Kleenex in my ears and wait for the parents to drop off. It isn't hard to get out of bed, really, once you set your mind to it, that isn't the problem. What I have to do next is very hard.

I have to break into the cellar. It's clear that's where they have him because it's the one part of the house outside the living room (did I mention the white wall-to-wall carpet or the clear plastic slipcovers on the white furniture?), where we kids are forbidden to go.

The kitchen by night is a spooky place. Shafts of moonlight polishing Mother's spotless floor. Naturally I assume the door to the basement will be locked but, surprise, it isn't seriously locked, it's only trip-it-with-your-credit-card locked. I do it with Dad's discarded Discover card. When she decided we were spending too much Mom took it away from him and I happened to see where it went. I pull it out from under the Rubbermaid sheet in the kitchen silver drawer which is also where Mother keeps her Maglite. Good thing. When I slide the Discover card down the door and it falls open I expect the cellar to smell bad, don't know why, just the vibe I guess, all that: *Don't go down there, children, or else.*

Instead the air smells like flowers. Flowers and, as it turns out, my brother's sweat. I flick the Maglite around; it's bigger down there than I thought. At the bottom of the steps I whisper, —Bill?

I locate him by the sound. It's the sound you make when they've duct-taped your mouth.

—My God, Billy, what have they done to you?

I find him at the entrance to the chamber under our living room, they have duct-taped him to a post. He's taped to a post and in the basement room behind him there is a bed that looks a lot like ours and the glow from my Maglite is dim but I make out figures in the bed and they are smiling, smiling, they look like wax replicas of Darryl—Darryl! and two other people I don't recognize.

—Billy, what happened?

He grimaces. I pull the tape off his mouth and he gasps. —I thought you'd never come.

Quick as I can manage, I start unwinding, walking around and around him as the tape peels off his neck, his shoulders. When his arms are free I stop. —What's going on? What's that? I am looking at the bed.

—Oh, that. He gives me this strange smile. —They look perfect, right?

—What is it? Why are you here?

Bill turns on that warm Billy smile: —They haven't gotten to me yet.

—But you look terrible.

—When they do, he says, and this terrifies me, —I'll look like them.

I glance at the trio of statues or whatever they are. So pretty lying in the bed, so still.

—What, Bill. What?

—I told you, they haven't gotten to me yet.

Come to think of it the figures in the bed don't look like statues, they look more like Grandma in the coffin. Perfect. Shiny. Clean. I bite my wrist. —Oh my God, what are we going to do?

—Don't worry, my brother Bill says: brave Billy. —I knew this was coming. I have a plan.

Elsewhere in the house I hear noises, or I think I do. I imagine Mother feeling around for me with those horny feet, I imagine her right foot making a swath over the empty sheet in my sector of the bed: I could swear I hear her growling —*Howard*. I wait for the terrifying *thump* as Dad lands in his boots. I imagine he is crossing the bedroom now, pulling the stun gun out of the dresser, I think I hear him pounding down the stairs and when he finds me, what will happen next? My face drains white all the way down to the knuckles, you bet I am freaking. —What are we going to do?

—Chill, he says. Bill's arms are free and he continues unwinding, but he can't bend over far enough to free his legs and feet. —First you have to get me down.

In spite of the fact that I am scared shit we will be discovered, I do as he says. I turn on the overhead and, as instructed, I unwind the duct tape. As instructed, I start at the feet. They must have used a gallon of it. It is taking forever to unwind and every time I go behind the post I have to look at the bed and the three *whatever they are* lying there in perfect peace and I am so frightened that my whisper sounds more like a wheeze. —They're coming, I know it, they're going to catch us and when they do they'll put us in that bed with poor Darryl and . . . who are the other two?

—Howie, I think. We have been whispering but all of a sudden Bill is talking in normal tones. —And Duane. Did we know we had another big brother?

—Shh, they'll hear you!

Too loud. He is talking too loud. —I think the third one's Duane.

I am jittering, frantic. —Billy, shut up, they'll hear us. Hurry, they're coming!

But with that smile my brother just keeps on unwinding the tape. —No, he says. —No they aren't.

—How do you know?

The smile melts into an amazing, joyful grin. —You didn't drink the cocoa, right?

Smart Bill. My brother the genius. —How . . .

—I told you I knew this was coming. I doctored the cocoa mix yesterday, before they got up.

—Billy, you didn't *kill* them or anything.

—Who, me? My big brother is grinning, grinning; he can't stop. —Hell no, they're *family.* They're sleeping like baby bunnies, or mice in their sweet little nest. Now hurry, he says. —We've got lots to do before Vandella's crew gets here to set up for the shoot.

So we have lots to do but thanks to Mother's 9 p.m. bedtime, we have plenty of time to do it in. By the time Bill and I come up into the kitchen it's barely midnight. It's just that time passes so mortal slowly when you're lying awake in the dark. The first thing we do is pour the rest of the dry cocoa into the DisposAl and turn on every light in the house—well, except in the bedroom, where the four happy Dermotts are in a profound, drugged sleep. In the morning we have to drag our sleeping family downstairs and out through the French doors in the living room and next we'll move what I guess is all that remains of our three big brothers—Duane, we hardly knew ye!—up from the basement and lay them out next to the others on the grass, but before we do that we will pull all the bedding off Father's super-king that he had specially built for us, because the mattress is way too heavy for us to move. We'll lay out the bedding on our front lawn to make a simulacrum—gotta love that vocabulary!—of the bed. This is where the TV crew will find Mother and her *they'll always be my babies,* all of them sweet and clean and sleeping snugly under the duvet with their heads on the fluffy down pillows out in broad daylight right in front of the house. When she comes for the live telecast, Vandella LeSpire will have so many questions to ask Mother about the three big brothers or what's left of them, she'll have so many questions about what Mother and Dad did to Howie and Darryl and Duane, and how they processed them to keep them sleeping like babies, that she won't notice that two living Dermott children are missing. See, once we're done setting up, Bill and I are running away on Dad's Discover card.

We're getting out of this paragon, our prison, this great American institution that mothers everywhere fear and admire and will—in the course of one broadcast—come to excoriate. They won't come looking for Billy and me. Not after they see this ostensibly wonderful mothering tool exposed for what it is. Mother laid out with Dad and her babies in broad daylight, just exactly how she wants them. Inert.

Safe and obedient. Snuggled down in the Family Bed.

—SciFiction, 2004

The Singing Marine

It's so hot in August in that part of Virginia that dogs die standing up and even insects stick to the asphalt. Flies buzz in place. Embedded, an overturned stag beetle waves its legs helplessly. The singing Marine has to move fast to keep his boondockers from sinking in and gluing him to the spot.

He may be singing to take his mind off what's just happened—the tragedy, or is it disgrace that probably marks the end of his life in the service. The accident—his platoon. How many men has he lost, and how can a man facing court-martial ever hope to love the general's daughter?

Putting one boot in front of the other, he goes along as if understanding is a place you can get to on foot, and as he goes, the song just keeps unfurling. "My mother m-m-m . . ."

If anybody asked what he was singing he would look up, surprised; *who, me?*

But he sings ". . . m-m-m-m-murdered me . . ."

The road gets stickier. Heat mirages shimmer in the middle distance and rise up in front of him, thick and troublesome as cream of nothing soup.

Fuddled by the dense air, the Marine bows his head against the heat and goes into the dim rural drugstore. He is not aware he's being followed.

"What's that you're singing?"

The Marine blinks. "Say what?"

It is a woman's voice. "Mister, the song."

Exploding afterimages of sunlight stud the dimness, so he does not immediately see the speaker. "Ma'am?"

The voice blurs suggestively. "Sit down, Lieutenant."

He blunders against a large shape—leatherette booth, he thinks. He can still leave. "Ma'am, you don't want me to sit with you."

The woman's hand closes on his arm and pulls him down. "You don't know what I want until I tell you."

"You haven't told me your name."

It becomes clear she isn't going to. He hears the sound she makes inside her clothes as she crosses her legs; he can't stop blinking. He thinks he can smell the warm air rising from the hollow at her throat.

What he says next, he says because he can't help himself. The old threnody always bubbles up at times like this, when he thinks he's close—to what? He can't say. He just begins. "I was born of blood and reborn in violence. If you can't handle either, you don't want me sitting with you."

She leans across the table. "You haven't told me what you were singing."

"It's an old thing. I used to think it was sad, but now . . ." He's hurtled into a complicated thought that he can't finish. There's no way to tell her he has bigger problems now. Instead he tells the old story: born late to a childless couple, mother dead in childbirth, wicked stepmother Gerda and the inevitable murder, if it was a murder. His father was away, he was never able to get the truth from his frantic half sister: "You were sitting by the door and your head came off; what can I tell you, your *head* came off." They buried him under the linden tree, Marline and the stepmother, but he rose up, or something did, leached of memory and stark blind crazy with love; he thinks that was him flying overhead and singing, singing:

"My mother murdered me;
"My father grieved for me;
"My sister, little Marline,
"Wept under the linden tree . . ."

The woman snaps, "I thought it was an almond tree."

"All depends where you're coming from," he says, blinking until her outlines emerge from the dimness—wedge-shaped face as beautifully defined as a cat's muzzle, long hair falling over long white arms and that neatly composed face veiling her intentions; he thinks she may be beautiful—too early to tell. "Whatever it is, I can't seem to get rid of the song."

"You're still singing?"

He says in some bewilderment, "It sings me."

Even in the shadows the sudden, attentive tilt of her head is apparent. "And what do you think it means?"

But he slaps both hands flat on the table. "Enough. The stepmother got crushed in a rockfall. I came back. When being home got too hard, I joined up. That's all you need to know."

"Yes," she says, perhaps too quickly. "It is."

"So if you don't mind . . ."

"You haven't ordered."

There is nothing on the menu that he wants. This isn't a bar, where you can order something deep enough to disappear into; it's an old fashioned pharmacy with a soda fountain and this is high noon, not the dead of night that lets you go home with the lovely woman who found you. When he goes outside, it will still be hot and bright. "It's not my kind of place."

As he stands she rises with him; they could be executing the first movement in an elegant *pas de deux*. "It's not mine either," she says, drawing her long hands down his arms. "Let me take you someplace where it's cool."

Emerging from the air conditioned drugstore, he is staggered by the heat. When he looks for the woman, she is several paces ahead. "Where are we going?"

Her tone is suggestive; she does not look back, but the words reach him. "Someplace you already know."

The Marine will remember the afternoon as a bizarre, agonizing progress on foot, her striding ahead with those black gauze skirts flying and him struggling along behind, heading for the next town. No cars pass them but he understands that she would not accept a ride. In the outskirts of the big town or large city, she stops at a marked bench just as the bus comes along. DEEP CAVERNS, the marker says. He is about to tell her he's never heard of the place when she turns on the step and pulls him on board.

So they ride out to the caverns side by side on the cracked leatherette back seat with engine fumes boiling up between their knees while the woman thinks whatever she is thinking and the singing Marine finds that even the relentless monotony of the song cannot crowd out the mishap that separated him from his platoon last night and put him on this road. He is grieving for them. "What?"

"I said, when you get there, I want you to go inside for me."

The thick fumes make his eyes water. "Ma'am?"

"I can't," she says. "You have to. Understand, you won't be sorry. In the end, I'll make you very happy."

"You . . . want me to go into the caverns?"

"It's cool," she says. "Believe me, you won't be sorry."

"You want me to go in and get . . ."

"The tinderbox. It's an old fashioned firestarter."

"What would you want a thing like that for?"

Her eyes glow. Something behind them begins to smolder. "Just do what I say. Then you'll see. Get it and I'll start your fires."

"I was on my way back to the base," he says.

Her smile is touched with malicious humor. "What would you want to do a thing like that for?"

He chooses not to catch her tone. Instead he starts telling; like the song he sings, it's something he has to do because he needs to hear it. "I have to report. I have to let them know it wasn't my fault. I have to forestall the court-martial. It was my platoon. I. God, the sergeant!" He stops and starts again. "We were on maneuvers near Ocracoke. He marched them into the marsh." He does not tell her that the marsh gave way underneath them and half his men are still out there somewhere, either mired to the knees or drowned in mud and confusion; he does not tell her that in another few hours he will be AWOL. "I have to report. I do."

Without even looking at him, she divines the rest. She knows what lies at his center. She is brusque, almost matter-of-fact. "Your platoon's OK. They found everyone. It's in all the papers."

His heart leaps up. "You're sure?"

How cleverly she plays on him. "TV this morning. Interviews."

"But I'm not there."

"Oh you," she says. "They think you deserted."

Maybe I have. It's too much to contemplate. "I have to go back and explain it."

"Do this and you won't have to go back at all. You'll be rich enough to buy your way out of anything."

But when Taps sounds tonight the Marine will go back, slouching over the causeway like the returning prodigal in his muddy fatigues and the boon-dockers that won't stop squelching water. When he does, he will be richer. He knows that when a beautiful woman you don't know asks you to do her a favor, you do what she asks soon enough, but you never, ever let her know what you're thinking.

Right now he says, "I'll think about it."

"No time for that. We're getting off."

They are in the woods for more than an hour, during which the lieutenant's boots get heavier in a geometric progression toward eternity. The heat is intolerable. Gnats crawl into his ears and clog his nostrils; mosquitos feed on the exposed back of his neck, sliding down the sweaty surface to feed on his most vulnerable parts. By the time the woman reaches the cave mouth and gestures, he's ready to plunge in without question: anything to escape the humidity that is pressing down on him and steaming in his throat and in the space between his regulation cap and his skull.

She turns as if she's already explained this: "You understand why I can't go in there."

He shakes his head. The shadowed opening at her back lures him; he wants to throw himself down on the worn stone floor and sleep until December.

"The dogs."

He blinks sweat out of his eyes saying politely, "Ma'am?"

She says impatiently, "I can't go in because of the dogs."

"Dogs." Does he hear anything? Smell anything different? The place is still and if there's anything living inside, there is no hint of it. "Are you sure there are dogs in there?"

She turns that neatly feline face at an angle that makes it impossible for him to read her intentions. "Don't worry. There are only three of them. They have big eyes." When she looks up again her eyes gleam. "And they have what you want. Watch out for the last one, though," she adds. "He can make you or break you."

"It will be dark."

She shakes her head. "It's lighted. They were going to turn this into Luray Caverns until they found out the air was toxic."

"Toxic!"

"It won't bother you," she says with such sublime assurance that he believes her. "And what you find will solve all your problems." She lays out the details.

This is how the singing Marine finds himself descending into Deep Caverns while his companion reclines like a figure carved in the rock at its mouth and waits for him to come back with the tinderbox. "My mother m-m-m . . ." Not his mother. Gerda. For the first time since he came back to himself after the business with the linden tree, the song sounds right. The faces of his platoon recede and he is alone, singing in the cavern.

It is as she told him. At the widest point he finds three little niches opening off the tunnel like side chapels in a subterranean place of worship, but instead of religious statuary or mummified corpses they contain bits of blackness that stalk back and forth inside like furred furies; when the animals see the Marine they lunge for him and are hurled back into their niches as if by invisible barriers. Glowering, they mount their mahogany chests like reluctant plaster saints returning to their pedestals.

He does not like the looks of the first animal. Its eyes are big enough but when he says, "Nice doggy," it stirs in a tremendous effort to please him, and scratches up a storm of pennies that lands at his feet like so much gravel. *Pick up that junk and I won't have any room in my suit for the real thing.* Thus he throws out his first set of instructions. "Nothing doing," he says, and goes on to the next. The eyes are even huger, but in its attempt to win his attention the next animal scratches up a shower of dollar bills, shredded by sharp toenails and worthless as confetti.

The third dog does nothing. Sitting on its chest of treasure, it regards him with eyes bigger and more brilliant than anybody's attempts to describe them. The effect is of lemon neon.

It is like looking into the eye of the beholder.

Without knowing what he means, the Marine says, "Then you know."

Although the dog makes no sound, the singing Marine takes its meaning: *Everything.*

Flowing like velvet, the creature jumps off the chest, fixing him with its intense yellow glare. Although the dog is kept in the little cavern by a shield he can't see, the singing Marine climbs up on the ledge and enters easily. Now that they are in the same space he knows that if it wants to, the animal can destroy him.

"I didn't want to come back from the dead, you know." He thinks about his platoon. "You know being dead is easier."

The silence is profound. The Marine stands with his arms at his sides, waiting. There is a stir as if of air masses colliding. Huge and silent, the dog surges into the space between them. Still he does not move. He does not move even when the massive brute pads the last two steps and presses its bearlike head against him. Startled by the warmth, the *weight,* the singing Marine feels everything bad rush out of him: the violent death and burial, the strange reincarnation that finds him both victim and murderer, song and singer, still in the thrall of the linden tree and the spirits that surround it. The great dog's jaws are wide; its mouth is a fiery chasm, but he doesn't shrink from it.

When you have been dead and buried, many things worry you, but nothing frightens you.

"Stay," he says, and without caring whether it attacks him, he opens the chest. On top he finds the object in question—firestarter, she explained, an antique tinderbox, looking crude and insufficient in its bed of thousand-dollar bills. Something glitters—diamonds scattered among the bills as if by some supremely casual hand. He picks up the tinderbox.

"This is what she wants," he says to the dog. The neon eyes won't let him lie; he couldn't. "I'm supposed to take the rest, but it's only money."

The lemon eyes glimmer like paired moons.

"Money isn't everything." The song is back; he can feel the leaves of the linden tree stirring overhead and one more time replays out the perpetual round of death and survival. He is afraid of repeating it into eternity. He slams the lid and looks at the dog. "Money isn't anything." He looks up, puzzled: the box. "But neither is fire."

There is a stir; blacker than shadow, even blacker because of the neon eyes, the creature nudges him again. Its great plumed tail is wagging.

"Good boy." He tries to pat its head; the dense fur is so deep that his hand won't stop sinking into it. "You keep it. But this." Studying the tinderbox, he turns it over in his hand. "I wonder what she wants with it."

There is seismic thunder—a growl so profound that he forgets the eyes. Then the animal becomes a fury of deep fur and warm flesh and compressed muscles. Planting its head in his chest, it pushes the singing Marine to the edge of the little niche and to his astonishment, nudges him so he falls back into the tunnel. Its growl makes the lights flicker. Without knowing how he knows to do this, the Marine slips the tinderbox deep into his fatigues, storing it in a spot nobody can reach without his express permission. Then he looks up at the great moon eyes. Unlike most animals, this one meets his stare; he feels himself disappearing into the glow. Trapped though it is behind invisible bars, the brute makes a low purr, almost like a tiger's. The tail moves like a flight of banners. He doesn't know what it's trying to tell him. Then he does; it is amazing.

Therefore when the Marine comes up from underground and the beautiful woman slips both arms around his neck and thanks him, he is wary. When he realizes she's patting the many pockets of his fatigues, he is even more wary, but he's not surprised when she says, "You didn't take any money."

He shakes his head.

"But you got the box."

"I did," he says.

"Where is it?"

He only shakes his head.

"I see." She is already fumbling in the depths of her black gauze skirt; she pulls something out of her pocket. Because they are beyond apologies or explanations she says, "Gerda didn't die in a rockfall, you killed her," and as she brings out the knife and raises it high he sees that she looks enough like the dead murderess to be her sister.

He has no choice but to kill her. Marines know how to do this without weapons. Inside, not far from the cave's mouth, there's a chasm so deep that when he pushes her in—sexy, but vindictive, *Gerda's sister,* he listens and listens and never hears her hit bottom. The singing Marine, who hears the same old song unfurling, but louder. "That should be the end of it," he says, but it isn't. He takes the box and without much minding that he's left behind the treasure in the cavern, he does what he should have done in the first place. He goes back to the base.

It is night by the time he gets there, and instead of marching through the main gate like a good officer, he turns off the road and runs along the fence. When you've been dead and buried and come back, you are beyond going out looking for trouble. Instead, you go to earth and wait for it to find you.

He snakes under the cyclone fence at the spot his platoon found during exercises early in training. He runs like a fox through the gullies and comes to earth in the deep gulch behind the senior officers' quarters, where he lies down too tired for thought and sobs until sleep comes up from behind and takes him. One by one the houses at the top of the cliff go dark; from down here they all look alike and it will be noon before the singing Marine realizes that the general's daughter must be only a few houses away, in the back bedroom of the biggest house at the end of Officers' Row. She lies north to south in her bed while face down, the singing Marine lies north to south in the rocks and wet earth near the bottom of the gully. Although she doesn't know he exists, their breathing is synchronized. Breath for breath, she matches him.

At reveille he hears the base waking up: the military motor humming, gears meshing so smoothly that he might never be missed here, and for the first time since they buried him under the linden tree, he is profoundly lonely.

Last night he had imagined it was only a matter of hours until the MPs found him, thus relieving him of any decisions. This morning he understands this place is secure; if he wants to, he can live here forever. The idea has a certain appeal to him. When you have been dead and buried you lose your tolerance for changes.

He has not eaten. Crouched in the gulch with his knees up, the singing Marine considers his options. If he sneaks off the base his life as he knows it is over. If he lets them catch him, his life as he knows it is over. But, God, he is hungry. Still he is an officer, and he is not going to be shot while scavenging. Instead he sits with his head between his knees waiting until he gets tired of waiting. Then he pulls out the tinderbox and with a sense of inevitability, opens it.

There is a little flint stick and a surface to strike it on. He does this once. Twice. Three times, and as he strikes it the third time the earth rattles. "It's too soon!" he cries, loud enough that the general's daughter, hanging her stone-washed jeans on the back rail of her father's quarters several houses away, will lift her head. "You called?" But by that time the singing Marine has slammed the box and whatever has been rumbling toward him just beneath the surface of the earth shudders, receding.

Distressed and gnawed by hunger but still humming, *m-m-m-m*, he rolls over and presses himself into the ground. The sensation is not unfamiliar. In the astounding concentration peculiar to certain mystics, he withdraws to sing the song and wait for night to come again. Rousing once, he sees the sun is low and he sets his inner alarm clock for midnight. Then, schooled in resignation, he lies still, waiting.

When it's safe he sits up and strikes the tinderbox three times. This time when sparks fly, he will leave it open. Instead of fire, it brings dense, living blackness out of blackness, huge and silent, warm. The lemon neon eyes regard him.

"I knew you'd come," he says. The dog drops something in his lap and rests its great head on his shoulder. "And I knew you'd bring food. Money isn't anything, but you can die of hunger."

Closer than close, the dog lies next to him while he eats. It is like sitting with a furnace. When he's done eating he leans into the thick, dense fur and without having to tell it anything, he makes the dog know everything. After a moment it gets up and shakes itself until electricity flies in the darkness. Then it wheels, action following intention so fluidly that they are as one, and the gorgeous brute seems to melt into nothing.

Alone, the singing Marine stares into his empty hands and considers his options. His life as he knows it is over here. It's too late for him to explain himself; only a goddess could do it.

A goddess. It's as if the dog has heard. In seconds it's back, coming over the edge of the little cliff and descending, as silent as it is enormous. Its shape has changed—it seems bulkier, and when the Marine gets to his feet to welcome it he sees this is because there is something on its back: the impossible superimposed on the unlikely. Here is the general's daughter, pale in the shift she slept in, lying in the dog's deep fur and sleeping as heavily as if she'd never been separated from the bed she lay down on.

He tells himself he only needs her to hear him out.

He tells himself he's only doing this because he loves her.

He tells himself this is a long dream and in dreams people love and become as one without actually touching.

Murmuring, she stirs in her sleep. This is the real general's real daughter. This is now and in these days you don't take women unless they invite you.

He says, "I love her, but not like this."

There is that rumble, as of thunder. Growling, the dog cocks its head and before the Marine can put out his hand to stay it or to touch the dangling satiny arm of the beautiful sleeper, it turns and vanishes.

For the rest of the night and the next long day, the singing Marine considers. There is the song that will not stop singing. There is the general's daughter, so close that he can climb out of the gulch if he wants to and try to find her. There is the disgrace that has ended his military career and brought him to all this. Is he victim or lover or deserter? He does not know. All he knows is that as soon as it gets dark he will summon the dog again.

And the dog will bring the general's daughter. Tonight she is in a faded T-shirt the color of the ocean and she looks like Undine, sleeping deep under water. His heart staggers. If he lays his head against her will she know everything?

This time he keeps her until morning. And this time, although the singing Marine doesn't know it, her father the general will note that his daughter is missing, and when he summons the dog again tomorrow night and the dog brings the general's daughter, the slashed pockets of the shirt she has worn to bed will begin to dribble sequins, laying a glittering trail to the spot where he has hidden her.

If MPs look and look and can't find the place, at least at first, he will have the dog to thank. In a brilliant flash of comprehension the animal will strip the shirt with its teeth before it descends into the gully, tossing sequins in a dozen different directions. Not its fault that a few spangled bits cling to its fur as it sets its great haunches and slides to the spot where the Marine is hiding. Here they stay, brute and master and beautiful sleeping girl, who stirs and threatens to wake as the Marine shakes off whatever has been holding him back and too near dawn for anything to be realized, he moves to kiss her.

He can't know whether it's the dog or something inside himself asking: *Why don't you just take what you want?*

When you have been dead and buried you operate in a different context.

Still he tells himself she knows what she's doing; he tells himself her eyes are really open. Awake or not, she raises her arms and they fall into a long embrace made sweeter by the inevitability of interruption.

Almost at once the sun comes up and woman and dog, burden and bearer, recede so quickly that they might as well have vanished, leaving the singing Marine cooling in the dirt with his heart so torn by the pressure of guilt and sorrow and the excruciating pain of these near misses that he sings, too loud:

My mother murdered me.
My father grieved for me.
My sister, little Marlene . . . "

Yes, he probably wants them to find him.

Which they do in the middle of the bright afternoon, sturdy, clean-shaven jarheads, earnest and spiffy in full uniform in spite of the heat, with polished boots and puttees and the inevitable white armbands, standing over him, and at attention. The hell of it is that as they march him out in the smelly fatigues and the squelching boondockers, they will call him Sir and they will treat him with the courtesy appropriate to a ranking officer even though he no longer deserves it.

When night falls in the maximum security wing of the brig, the commanding general comes to see him. He posts his aides outside and comes in alone. It is a surprise to both of them. He looks surprisingly like his daughter, but much tougher. They will not exchange words, exactly. Instead the general will ask him:

"Why?"

and the singing Marine will not be able to answer.

Then the general will ask him, "How?"

and once again, he will not be able to answer. What comes out of him now is "m-m-m-m" because his heart is breaking and the song he sings will not stop singing itself. Even lost out of his mind in love, he is going to hear it. He will go to his grave hearing it.

Then he thinks perhaps when he is in the grave, he won't have to hear it any more.

"You know what I can have done to you," the general says.

The singing Marine does know. He also knows without needing to be told that tradition says he can end all this and make it a happy ending. When he left behind the money in DEEP CAVERNS and took the tinderbox, he came out with the real treasure. If he strikes it once and leaves it open, the first dog will come; if he strikes it twice and leaves it open, he will have the first two dogs here to do his bidding. If he strikes it three times and leaves it open, the finest animal, his champion, his first real *friend* will surge into the room and together they can make anything happen.

But dogs have teeth and they will use them. No matter how fine they are, or how brilliant, necessity makes them savage, and like it or not the singing Marine is never far from the grave under the linden tree; he can see its dirt under his fingernails and smell the earth all these decades later.

Tradition tells him if the dogs kill everybody in charge the personnel on the base will beg him to become the general. He'll go to live in the general's quarters and when he goes into the girl's bedroom this time she'll be awake, and he will have her, but he is sad now, sobered by so many deaths and other losses that when he looks into himself, he discovers that he doesn't want to be that person. Crazy, but so was taking the girl and then not using her a different kind of crazy.

Perhaps because he is an officer, the MPs spared him the strip search, which means that he can feel the corner of the tinderbox digging into the soft flesh of his flank. All he has to do is take it out. But he can also hear himself. "M-m-m-m," and, "m-m-m-murdered me . . ."

And he understands that only when he is in the grave again will the song stop singing. "Sir," he says in a soft voice, "If I tried to attack you now, would you have to shoot me?"

Astounded, the general looks up just as he launches himself, and because Marines know how to kill in self defense the general does exactly what is expected, but because Marines know how to kill without weapons he does it completely differently. It is so swift that the lieutenant has no time for last words or even regrets; he slips away into what he discovers with such gratitude that it obscures all love, all loss, all grief and the thought of anyone who might mourn him is silence. The song of love and death and rebirth and violence that he has heard all his life since the linden tree is ending. Ends. Has ended.

—*F&SF*, 1996

In the *Squalus*

He was under water for too long; lying in the shell of the submarine for more than thirty hours, he left his body and his living mates and became at one with the dead floating on the other side of the bulkhead. In the last seconds before the lights failed a few men had scrambled into the control room to join the living; Larkin and the others in the bow let them through and then, facing the rushing ocean, they were forced to close the door against the rest, so that there were twenty-six dead sealed in the flooded engine room. The survivors lay together under the great weight of the ocean, Larkin alive with the rest but already cut adrift from them.

If he was waiting for rescue he was not aware of it; he heard only vaguely the SOS the others tapped out on the metal hull. When he took his own turn he was not aware that he did so and he was not listening for a reply. Instead he imagined he heard the voices of the dead reverberating in the metal; he heard the dead in his own ship, in all the drowned ships of all time in growing volume, making a remote but ceaseless boom against the hull.

As a child Larkin had looked out across flat New Mexico and dreamed of water. In all those dusty summers he prepared his eyes for the ocean, superimposing that great, watery horizon on the desert. With other landlocked boys he would choose the Navy, going to sea with a thirst he did not yet understand. Married, he would take Marylee and their little girl for vacations at one beach after another, lifting his daughter high above the water and bringing her down quickly, so they would both laugh at the shining splash. He may have been certain he would die by drowning, that in the end he would let the water take him; he would be muffled and shrouded by water, water would carry away all his doubt and pain so that in the end there would be nothing left but water, washing over his own skull's bright, eternal grin.

Instead Alvah Larkin found himself safe in the *Squalus*, freezing in the dark. It was only a matter of time before the diving bell clanked against the hull and he would have to begin the tortuous escape. It would kill them if I stayed here, he thought in the last minutes before he gave himself to darkness. Janny, he thought, seeing the child and Marylee arrested in attitudes of waiting: on the rocks looking out to sea, pleading at the main gate of the base, poised, white-faced on the dock. They would always look to the horizon; Marylee would not let the girl look down, into the water. If Larkin stayed where he was they would remain fixed like that forever; still death seduced him and for some hours it seemed as though he would not have to go back. Numbed, he was able to lose track of time and project eternity.

In the last freezing hours he may have thought he had seen Jonah, or had been Jonah, or was that the face of Christ hovering just beyond the lights streaking his closed eyelids? There was a clang on the hull, the bell, and so he would not find out this time. Instead he had to pull himself back and join the others. When the hatch opened to let them into the bell he would hesitate only a second before going, blinking, into an uncertain birth.

Inside the bell he heard himself saying, "Yeah, I'll be glad to get back to the wife and kid."

When they were all safe in sick bay, President Roosevelt talked to them; his voice was full of static but sad, expressing national relief. Everybody was going right back into submarines, they told the president; Larkin wanted to get back on duty as soon as possible but he knew it wouldn't make any difference; it was too late. He could see in Marylee's eyes that it was too late.

"Oh Alvah," she said. "Those poor men."

Janny hugged him hard. "Daddy, you were gone too long."

He buried his face in her. "But I came back."

Marylee said firmly, "Daddy always comes back."

So he put Janny down and kissed his wife, understanding as she shrank for a split second that he was surrounded by the dead of the *Squalus,* he would walk with the twenty-six drowned men at his back for the rest of his life; even as Marylee threw herself on him in all her warmth, murmuring and pretending nothing had changed, he knew how cold his touch must seem to her, cold as the touch of Lazarus; he had been to death and back and it separated them. Without ever talking about it he had been preparing Marylee for years; he had chosen the Navy, he was no better than anybody else and so one day he would probably be lost at sea. She'd never admitted she understood what he was trying to tell her; after all, submarines were safer than surface ships, there was no war, he was Alvah, not just anybody. She had changed in the hours he was entombed in the *Squalus.* Comprehending, she had accepted; she may even have known that it would be easier for both of them if he hadn't come back up. She could stop pretending she wasn't afraid for him. She would never have to lose him again; instead she could grow old with the memory of a husband perpetually in his early thirties, always smiling and sure; returned, he saw all this in her eyes.

In the car going home from the base he said, "Do you still want your new baby?" Marylee kept her eyes on the road but he thought she said "Yes" and he said with urgency, "Then let's have your baby."

It didn't keep the drowned ship out of their bed. She had to know why he was always cold and anxious and couldn't sleep. He put his face close and tried to tell her everything: how the skipper had kept them quiet and organized after they closed the last watertight door; how they were put on watches, keeping order in the timeless chaos of the dark; why the skipper could not let anybody mention their shipmates, trapped a few inches away, any more than he could let them contemplate the ocean, separated from them only by the metal hull. His dead shipmates. He was trembling in the dark bedroom. "But they were there."

"You heard them pounding and calling."

"Nobody heard them. They were all dead."

She tried to comfort him. "Then there was nothing you could do. There was nothing anybody could do."

He turned away from her. *But I knew they were there.* How could he explain?

Marylee filled the house with friends, trying to crowd out the dead. She was pregnant again; she would fill the house with his children, sending them clattering into his silence to diffuse his memories. But he knew they were still there, and the knowledge marked him. Even after the boat was raised and the bodies were taken out and returned to their families, they were still in the *Squalus* for Larkin; even after the salvaged boat was renamed and recommissioned, the twenty-six men were in the *Squalus* and the *Squalus* lay in the dark waters off Portsmouth, so that whenever Larkin met another of the survivors they got too drunk and talked too much, neither listening to the other but talking because they had to; together they had to shut them out.

It was important that he stay in subs. After Pearl Harbor he would take command of his own S-boat; immuring himself in the close air and the smell of heavily oiled machinery, he would dive and look for them. During the war he managed each patrol by the book, performing perfectly; he was aggressive and cautious in appropriate measure, never jeopardizing his crew. Nobody aboard could know that once he was alone in his cubicle he would sit on the edge of his bunk, pale and sweating in his khakis, and drop his head into his two hands and draw within himself and listen, offering his own life and theirs too, if necessary, for the lives of those who were already lost. Toward the end of the war he would begin to drink too much, beginning another kind of immersion.

At home the summer after the bell brought him to the surface, he would take Janny down on the rocks by the water and sit while she played. Because he knew she wasn't listening, he talked about all of it, and when she said nothing in response he was able to imagine that she understood everything he told her.

"I had to come back."

"Daddy, look at the bird."

"I had to come back for you and Mommy, I had to keep faith. Does that make any sense to you?"

He imagined that she turned to him, saying, *Daddy, you had to come back for us. Otherwise we would have died.*

That's what I thought.

We were waiting and waiting.

I knew you were. That's why I had to come.

There was nothing else you could have done.

He said, "It was for you."

"What, Daddy?" She had disorderly curls and her freckled skin was so white that he could see the blue veins running underneath; she was too beautiful to have come from him and Marylee, she was their hope.

"I said, come here and let me tuck in your shirt."

As it turned out it was she who was faithless; Janny fell through the ice and drowned on the longest night of the winter. Larkin went out to look for her in the deep midnight pitch of five p.m., and in the swirl of dank air knew he had never left the *Squalus.* Marylee was with him, already sobbing; when she stumbled he grabbed her arm and caught her up but his gloves were thick and his fingers cold and even though he saw them closed around her arm, he felt nothing. After a while the police found them and took them home; somebody had located Janny finally by the book bag frozen to the ice next to the black hole she had made, plunging through. Now they would break the news to the Larkins, setting them down in the midst of arrangements, the first sympathy calls, visitors leaving them each with a firm push that meant: *continue.* If Larkin had known, trapped in the *Squalus,* that this would happen, he would have offered his life for her, but when he thought about it he would always wonder if instead, in some occult foreknowledge, he had offered her life for his, whether he had in some way sent the child down to look for the others, if not to redeem them then to join them in some pledge of his own faith and ceaseless grief.

When the rituals were over and her tears were finished at last Marylee put her head against him, saying, "She told me she would be at Dorothy's. If only I had checked."

"She *was* there, right up to the last minute," he said, and then he went on with the formula which would make it possible for her to keep on living; he went on even though he was not convinced of it. "There was nothing anybody could have done."

It will be enough for her, he thought. *She has the baby.* He was ready to let go but Marylee saw him drifting and reached out.

"Alvah." She had him by the hand and she was looking sharply into his face. "Alvah, I'm going to need you."

He answered automatically. "I'm right here." He could feel the increasing pressure; he had a choice; he would not look at her.

She let go. "I'll always love you anyway."

He said, without answering, "I'll be right here."

The baby was to be born in March, and Marylee would pin her life to it. Larkin would give her three more children to replace the dead one, leaving her almost satisfied, but the new ones were nothing of his; they would swirl around him without realizing how remote their father had become because they had never known anything else. Only the dead child was really his, and he would spend most of his life with her and the others; he had been there once and he belonged with them; he would go down in dive after dive to look for them. When he was no longer in submarines he would swim, going fierce, dogged, unremitting lengths in the base pool.

He kept a picture of Janny on his desk wherever he went but never looked at it; instead he would withdraw into himself and rehearse the afternoons they'd spent together on the rocks. He would feel her in his arms, angular and smelling a little, because all living children smell; he'd imagine her on the dock, flinging herself on him again and again. He belonged with Janny and the others; he belonged with all his classmates who had died at Pearl or in the Coral Sea and he imagined that eventually he would join the child and all the others would surround them: tableau. He could not think beyond that moment, but imagined peace. All this seemed more real to him than his wife or his living children, whom he would kiss abstractedly, so that he remained a solitary in the busy house Marylee kept in an attempt to lure him back to life.

By the end of the war Larkin was drinking too much and his men knew it; eventually his superiors became aware of it. They put him on shore duty so they could keep an eye on him; they sent him to sea where he wouldn't have so many opportunities; they put him in a Navy hospital in an attempt to dry him out; eventually they had to survey him, so that in his forties he was retired for medical reasons, living in New London because he couldn't leave the water or the rocks or any of the rest of it; he used to take his tackle and go fishing off a point where he could watch the base. Once in that first winter of his retirement he took his tackle and walked to the middle of the bridge that spanned the Thames, looking for a long time at the black surface of the water. If he jumped it would be over in a minute, but first he would have to go through the awkward business of getting rid of his tackle box and making it over the guardrail, or if he hung on to the box because it would make it quicker, then he would have a hard time getting over the rail at all. The problem could have been solved, but he was held back not so much by the weight of his clothes, his boots, his accoutrements as by the fact of Marylee; he owed her something, if only freedom from another vigil by the water, another funeral. Instead he went to his usual place and fished, finishing the fifth of rye from his tackle box, so blurring the days that it was months before he thought about what he had almost done. Looking over at Marylee at dinner one night, he could not be sure whether he was grateful or resented her because he was still here. He went out to a bar and was gone overnight. Marylee greeted him late the next day; she was pale and taut but she didn't say anything. He was still working at part-time jobs in this period, trying to stave off his desperate boredom, but none of them lasted for long. After a while there weren't any more jobs; he and Marylee both marked it, but neither of them would say anything.

As he moved into his fifties, Larkin would go off for days at a time, disappearing on desperate binges. He would always mark the first time, not because of any place he went or any thing he did but because of Marylee, who came for him and found him. There were two policemen with her, they made him understand they had been looking for him for a week, they'd been about to drag the river, but the words had no particular meaning; the only meaning he saw was in Marylee's face. For the first time he was aware of all the accumulated pain and fatigue of several years; he saw with regret how much he had aged her. He reached out, longing to make everything all right for her and his living children, but he was appalled by the changes life had made in them all. Only Janny remained unchanged, with her face forever bright.

After that he was able to trace the progress of his life by the lines in his wife's face, by the looks of reproach in the faces of his growing children; he marked it by the aches in his own bones and his compounded boredom and loneliness, the pain which would not be drowned in rye, and in his periodic attempts to stop drinking he would thank God that he was getting older, knowing that eventually time would put an end to this—it was the best he could hope for. For the first time he thought with resentment of the dead, who would remain unchanged.

After the first few absences Marylee stopped calling the police; she knew it wouldn't do any good to ask his friends to look for him. It wasn't really necessary. Eventually somebody would telephone—he was passed out sick in the back of a waterfront bar, would she please come and take him home; he had gotten involved in a six-day poker game and gentle as he was when he was sober, he was raging now; if she didn't come get him, he was going to hurt himself or somebody else; he was in the hospital, he'd stepped in front of a slow-moving car. The last time he was gone for three weeks. He came to himself in the hospital, God knew what had happened in the time which had dropped out of his memory; there had been a fight, something worse had happened, he'd been hurt and he seemed to recall being stuck to the pavement, sleeping in a freezing rain. Marylee was by the bed, looking older than he could have imagined, and he could read his own death in her face. They didn't know yet that he had come back, so the doctor continued to talk to Marylee: Heart failure, among other things. His lungs are filled with fluid, it's so far along I don't know how much we can do for him. Larkin knew that he couldn't get his breath; it was almost like drowning and he thought, *God, how appropriate.*

He did get better for a while as it turned out, and on a morning illumined by pallid winter sunlight he and Marylee began to talk. "I'm sorry for everything."

"Don't be."

"I have to make it up."

"You don't need to make anything up," she said. "This is my life, I'm satisfied."

"I should have stayed down there. It would have been better for everybody."

"Alvah, you didn't have to do anything. All you had to do was talk to me."

"I couldn't."

"I know."

"I couldn't . . ." He was groping, trying to explain. "I just couldn't go on."

He understood then that what he had foreseen in the belly of the *Squalus* was not his own death or the guilt he expected to bear for the death of the others, but rather the prospect of having to continue, of having to face the unending, relentless possibilities for change. What he had resisted was not the death of the other men or even the death of Janny, whose young, perfect face he could see to this day, but the fact that he would have to continue and so descend, or decline, so that he may never have felt any guilt for the others but only resentment because they were fixed as they were, bright and young. They would never have to suffer, or age. He could feel his lungs filling again; he knew he was drowning at last. They would bring oxygen but it wouldn't help; he waited with satisfaction.

Larkin was weary, ready to go, but he had to complete the formula. "I made us all suffer."

She said with unexpected bitterness, "Somebody has to."

And so, waiting for oxygen, he understood that it must be the function of all the living to redeem the dead. He could see Janny's face but he said, with some urgency, "I have to get better."

Marylee said, "If only you'd talked to me."

—*The Transatlantic Review*, 1972

Perpetua

We are happy to be traveling together in the alligator. To survive the crisis in the city outside, we have had ourselves made *very small*.

To make our trip more pleasant the alligator herself has been equipped with many windows, cleverly fitted between the armor plates so we can look out at the disaster as we ride along. The lounge where we are riding is paneled in mahogany and fitted with soft leather sofas and beautifully sculpted leather chairs where we recline until seven, when the chef Father engaged calls us to a sit-down dinner in the galley lodged at the base of our alligator's skull. Our vehicle is such a technical masterpiece that our saurian hostess zooms along unhampered, apparently at home in the increasingly treacherous terrain. If she knows we're in here, and if she guesses that tonight we will be dining on Boeuf Wellington and asparagus terrine with Scotch salmon and capers while she has to forage, she rushes along as though she doesn't care. We hear occasional growls and sounds of rending and gnashing over the Vivaldi track Father has chosen as background for this first phase of our journey; she seems to be finding plenty to eat outside.

Inside, everything is arranged for our comfort and happiness, perhaps because Father knows we have reservations about being here. My sisters and I can count on individualized snack trays, drugs of choice and our favorite drinks, which vary from day to day. Over our uniform jumpsuits we wear monogrammed warm-up jackets in our favorite colors—a genteel lavender for Lily, which Ella apes because she's too young to have her own ideas; jade for Cynthia and, it figures, my aggressively girlish sister Anna is in Passive Pink; Father doesn't like it, but I have chosen black.

"Molly, that color doesn't become you."

"Nobody's going to see me, what difference does it make?"

"I like my girls to look nice."

I resent this because we all struggled to escape the family and made it too. We'd still be out there if it wasn't for this. "Your girls, your girls, we haven't been your girls in years." Father: "You will always be my girls." That smile.

OK, I am the family gadfly. "This crisis. Is there something funny going on that we don't know about?"

"Molly," he thunders. "Look out the windows. Then tell me if you think there's anything funny about this."

"I mean, is this a trick to get us back?"

"If you think I made this up, send a goddamn email. Search the Web or turn on the goddamn TV!"

The chairs are fitted with wireless connections so we can download music and email our loved ones although we never hear back, and at our fingertips are multimedia remotes. We want for nothing here in the alligator. Nothing material, that is. I check my sources and Father is right. It is a charnel house out there while in here with Father, we are pampered and well fed and snug. It is a velvet prison, but look at the alternative! Exposure to thunderstorms and fires in collision, vulnerability to mudslides and flooding of undetermined origin; our alligator slithers through rivers of bloody swash and our vision is obscured by the occasional collision with a severed limb. We can't comprehend the nature or the scope of the catastrophe, only that it's all around us, while here inside the alligator, we are safe.

Her name is Perpetua. Weird, right? Me knowing? But I do.

So we are safe inside Perpetua, and I guess we have Father to thank. Where others ignored the cosmic warnings, he took them to heart. Got ready. Spared no expense. I suppose we should be glad.

If it weren't for the absence of certain key loved ones from our table and from our sumptuous beds in the staterooms aft of the spiny ridge, we probably would.

It's Father's fault. Like a king summoning his subjects, he brought us back from the corners of the earth where we strayed after we grew up and escaped the house. He brought us in from West Hollywood (Cynthia) and Machu Picchu (Lily) and (fluffy Anna) Biarritz and Farmington, for our baby sister Ella attends the exclusive Miss Porter's School. And Father reached me . . . where? When Father wants you, it doesn't matter how far you run, you will come back.

Emergency, the message said, *Don't ask. Just come,* and being loyal daughters, we did. With enormous gravity he sat us down in the penthouse.

"My wandering daughters." He beamed. Then he explained. He even had charts. The catastrophe would start here, he said, pointing to the heart of the city. Then it would blossom, expanding until it blanketed the nation and finally, the world. Faced with destruction, would you dare take your chances outside? Would we?

He was not asking. "You will come."

"Of course, Father," we said, although even then I was not sure.

Anna the brownnose gilded the lily with that bright giggle. "Anything you say, Father. Anything to survive."

Mother frowned. "What makes you think you'll survive?"

"Erna!"

"What if this is the Last Judgment?" She had Father's Gutenberg Bible in her lap.

He shouted: "Put that thing down!"

She looked down at the book and then up at him. "What makes you think anybody will survive?"

"That's enough!"

"More than enough, Richard." She raked him with a smile. "I think I'll take my chances here."

He and Mother have never been close. He shrugged. "As you wish. But, you girls . . ."

Anna said, "Daddy, can we bring our jewelry?"

Cynthia laid her fingertip in the hollow of Father's throat. "I'm fresh out of outfits, can I go to Prada and pick up a few things?"

I said, "It's not like we'll be going out to clubs."

"Daddy?"

"Molly, watch your tone." Cynthia is Father's favorite. He told her, "Anything you want, sweet, but be back by four."

Little Ella asked if she could bring all her pets—a litter of kittens and a basset hound. The cat is the natural enemy of the alligator, Father explained; even in miniature—and we were about to be miniaturized—the cats would be an incipient danger but the dog's all right. Ella burst into tears.

"Can I bring my boyfriend?" Lily said.

Our baby sister punched her in the breast so hard she yelled. "Not if I can't take Mittens."

"Boyfriends?" We girls chorused, "Of course."

Father shook his head.

You see, because we are traveling in elegant but close quarters, there's no room for anybody else. This meant no boyfriends, which strikes me as thoughtless if not a little small. When we protested Father reminded us of our choices: death in the disaster or life in luxury with concomitant re-knotting of family ties. He slammed his fist on the hunt table his decorator brought from Colonial Williamsburg at great expense. "Cheap at the price."

I was thinking of my boyfriend, whom I had left sleeping in Rangoon. Never guessing I was leaving forever, I stroked his cheek and slipped out. "But . . . Derek!"

"Don't give it another thought."

"Daddy, what's going to happen to Derek?"

"He'll keep."

Cynthia, Anna and Lily said, "What's going to happen to Jimmy/David/Phil!"

"Oh, they'll keep," he said. Perceiving that he had given the wrong answer, he added. "Trust me. It's being taken care of."

"But, Daddy!"

Perceiving that he still hadn't said enough, he explained that although we were being miniaturized, his technicians would see to it that all our parts would match when we and our boyfriends were reunited, although he did not make clear whether we would be restored to normal size or the men we loved would be made extremely small. He said whatever it took to make us do what he wanted, patting us each with that fond, abstracted smile.

"I've got my best people on it. Don't worry. They'll be fine."

Anna did her loving princess act. "Promise?"

Now Father became impatient. "Girls, I am sparing no expense on this. Don't you think I have covered every little thing?"

None of us dares ask him what this all cost. Unlike most people in the city outside we are, after all, still alive, but the money! How much will be left for us when Father dies?

Of course in normal times the brass fixtures, the ceiling treatment, and luxurious carpeting that line our temporary home would be expensive, but the cost of miniaturizing all these priceless objects and embedding them in our alligator? Who can guess!

One of us began to cry.

"Stop that," Father roared. "Enough is enough."

It probably is enough for him, riding along in luxury with his five daughters, but what about Cynthia and Anna and Lily and Ella and me?

The first few days, I will admit, passed pleasantly as we settled into our quarters and slipped into our routines. Sleep as late as we like and if we miss breakfast Chef leaves it outside our doors in special trays that keep the croissants moist, the juice cold and the coffee hot. There's even a flower on the tray. Late mornings in the dayroom, working puzzles or reading or doing needlework, a skill Father insisted we learn when we were small. Looking at what he's made of us, I have to wonder: five daughters at his beck and call, making a fuss over him and doing calligraphy that would have pleased blind old Milton; we all nap after lunch. We spend our afternoons in the music room followed by cocktails in the lounge and in the evening we say grace over a delicious meal at the long table, with Father like the Almighty at the head: is this what he had in mind for us from the first?

I have never seen him happier.

This poses a terrible problem. Is the catastrophe outside a real raveling of society and the city as we know it and, perhaps, the universe, or is it something Father manufactured to keep us in his thrall?

My sisters may be happy but I am uncertain. I'm bored and dubious. I'm bored and suspicious and lonely as hell.

The others are in the music room with Father at the piano, preparing a Donizetti quartet. I looked in and saw them together in the warm light; with his white hair sparkling in the halogen glow of the piano lamp, he looked exalted. As if there was a halo around his head. Now, I love Father but I was never his favorite. There's no part in the Donizetti piece for me. Why should I go in there and play along? Instead I have retreated to the lounge where I strain at the window in hopes. For hours I look out, staring in a passion of concentration because Derek is out there somewhere, whereas I . . .

If I keep at this, I think, if I press my face to the glass and stare intently, if I can *just keep my mind on what I want,* then maybe I can become part of the glass or pass through it and find Derek.

With my head pressed against the fabric of our rushing host, I whisper:

"Oh, please."

Outside it is quite simply desolate. Mud and worse things splash on my window as the giant beast that hosts us lunges over something huge, snaps at some adversary in her path, worries the corpse and takes a few bites before she rushes on. God, I wish she'd slow down. I wish she would stop! I want her to lurch onto a peak and let me out!

Can't. On autopilot.

Odd. The glass is buzzing. Vibration or what? I brush my face, checking for bees. If I knew how, I'd run to the galley at the base of her skull and thump on the brushed steel walls until she got my message. Crucial question: do alligators know Morse code?

No need.

"What?"

My God. She and I are in communication.

"Lady!"

The windowpane grows warm, as though I have made her blush. *It's Perpetua.*

"I know!"

I thought you did.

"Oh, lady, can you tell me what's going on?

Either more or less than you think.

In a flash I understand the following: we are not, as I suspected—hoped!—being duped. Father has his girls back all right, he has us at his fingertips in a tight space where he has complete control, but this is his response to the warnings, not something he made up. Although my best-case scenario would confirm my suspicions and make it easy to escape, we are not captive inside a submarine in perfectly normal New York City, witlessly doing his bidding while our vehicle sloshes around in a total immersion tank.

There really is a real disaster out there.

Soon enough tidal waves will come crashing in our direction, to be followed by meteorite showers, with volcanic eruptions pending and worse to come. As for Father's contrivances, I am correct about one thing: the cablevision we watch and the Web we surf aren't coming in from the world outside, they are the product of the database deep in the server located behind our alligator's left eye.

"But what about Derek?"

I don't know.

"Can you find out?"

You have to promise to do what I want.

I whisper into the window set into her flank: "What do you want?"

Promise?

"Of course I promise!"

Then all that matters is your promise. It doesn't matter what I want.

"I need to know what's happening!" Maybe Mother is right, maybe it really is the hand of God. Wouldn't you get sick of people like us and want to clean house?

Not clear.

"Whether God is sick of us?"

Any of it. The only clear thing is what we have to do.

"What? What!" She lets me know that although I left him in Rangoon, Derek is adrift somewhere in New York. Don't ask me whether he flew or came by boat or what I'm going to do. Just ask me what I think, and then ask me how I know.

You have to help me.

"You have to stop and let me out!"

I know what's out there because, my God, Perpetua is showing me. Images spill into my head and cloud my eyes: explosions mushrooming, tornadoes, volcanic geysers, what? In seconds I understand how bad it is although Perpetua can't tell me whether we are in the grip of terrorists or space aliens or a concatenation of natural disasters or what; she shows me Derek standing in the ruins of our old building with his hand raised as if to knock on the skeletal door, I see looters and carnivores and all the predictable detritus of a disaster right down to the truck with the CNN remote, and I see that they won't be standing there much longer because the roiling clouds are opening for a fresh hailstorm unless it's a firestorm or a tremendous belching of volcanic ash.

You won't last a minute out there, not the way you are.

She's right. To survive the crisis in the city outside, we have had ourselves made very small.

You got it. You don't stand a chance.

"Oh, God," I cry.

Not God, not by a long shot.

"Oh, Lady!" I hear Father and the others chattering as they come in from the music room. I whisper into the glass. My mouth leaves a wet lip print frosted by my own breath. "What am I going to do?"

Our saurian hostess exits my consciousness so quickly that I have to wonder whether she was ever there. My only proof? I have her last words imprinted: *Find out how.*

Chef brings our afternoon snack trays and my sisters and I graze, browsing contentedly, like farm animals. Father nods and he and Chef exchange looks before Chef bows and backs out of the room.

It comes to me like a gift.

Passionately, I press my lips to the glass. "It's in the food."

Find the antidote. Take it when you get out.

"Are you? Are you, Perpetua?" I am wild with it. "Are you really going to stop and let me out?"

She doesn't answer. The whole vehicle that encloses our family begins to thrash. I hear magnified snarling and terrible rending noises as she snaps some enemy's spine and over Vivaldi I hear her giant teeth clash as she worries it to death.

We bide our time then, Perpetua and I, at least I do. What choice do I have?

But while I am waiting her history is delivered to me whole. It is not so much discovered as remembered, as though it happened to me. Sleeping or waking, I can't say when or how Perpetua reaches me; her story seeps into my mind and as it unfolds I understand why she and I are bonded. Rather, why she chose me. Rushing along through the night while Father plots and my sisters sleep, our alligator somehow drops me into the tremendous ferny landscape of some remote, prehistoric dawn where I watch, astonished, as her early life unfolds under a virgin sun that turns the morning sky pink. Although I am not clear whether it is her past or a universal past that Perpetua is drawing, at some level I understand. She shows me the serpentine tangle of clashing reptiles and the emergence of a king and she takes me beyond that to deliver me at the inevitable: that all fathers of daughters are kings. I see Perpetua's gigantic, armored father with his flaming jaws and his great teeth and I join his delicate, scaly daughters as they slither here and there in the universe, apparently free but always under his power.

So you see.

I have the context, if not the necessity.

Then over the next few days while we float along in our comfortable dream world she encourages me to explore.

While the others nap I feel my way along the flexible vinyl corridors that snake through Perpetua's sinuous body, connecting the chambers where we sleep and the rooms where we eat and the ones where we entertain ourselves. The tubing is transparent and I see Perpetua's vitals pulsing wherever I flash my light. Finally I make my way to the galley—quietly, because Chef sleeps nearby. It's a hop, skip and a jump to the medicine chest, where I find unmarked glass capsules sealed in a case. I slip one into my pocket, in case. From the galley, I discover, there are fixed passageways leading up and a flexible one leading down. I open the hatch and descend.

Yes, Perpetua says inside my head and as I get closer to her destination, repeating like an orgasmic lover, *yes, yes, yes!*

I have found the Destruct button.

It is located at the bottom of the long stairway that circumvents her epiglottis; opening the last hatch I find my way into the control center, which is lodged in her craw. And here it is. Underneath there is a neatly printed plate put there by Father's engineers:

IN CASE OF EMERGENCY, BREAK GLASS.

Perpetua's great body convulses. *Yes.*

Trembling, I press my mouth to the wall: "Is this what you want?" I can't afford to wait for an answer. "It would be suicide!"

We have a deal.

"But what about me?"

When it's time, you'll see.

The next few days are extremely hard. Perpetua rushes on without regard for me while Chef bombards us with new delicacies and Father and my sisters rehearse Gilbert and Sullivan in the music room. I can't help but think of Mother, alone in the ruins of our penthouse. Is she all right, is she maybe in some safe place with my lover Derek or did she die holding the Gutenberg Bible in an eternal *I told you so?* Mother! Is that the Last Judgment shaping up out there or is it simply the end of the world? Whatever it is, I think, she and Derek are better off than I am trapped in here.

Father asks, "What's the matter with you?"

"Nothing. I'm fine."

My sisters say, "Is it Derek? Are you worried about Derek? This is only the beginning, so get over it."

"I'm fine."

"Of course you are, we're terribly lucky," they say. Father has given them jewels to match their eyes. "We're lucky as hell and everything's going to be fine."

I can hardly bear to be with them. "Whatever you want," I whisper to Perpetua. "Let's do it."

When it's time.

Relief comes when you least expect it, probably because you aren't expecting it. Perpetua and I are of the Zen Archer school of life. She summons me out of a stone sleep.

It's time.

The alligator and I aren't one now, but we are thinking as one. Bending to her will, I pad along the corridors to the galley and descend to the control room. She doesn't have to explain. Predictably, the Destruct button is red. At the moment, it is glowing.

I use the hammer to break the glass.

Now.

I push the button that sets the timer. The bottom falls out of the control room, spilling me into her throat and she vomits me out. I crunch down on the breakable capsule that will bring me back to normal size.

My God, I'm back in the world! I'm back in the world and it is terrible.

As I land in the muck Perpetua rushes on like an express train roaring over me while I huddle on the tracks or the Concorde thundering close above as I lie on my back on the runway, counting the plates in its giant belly as it takes off. I have pushed the Destruct button. Is the timer working? Did it abort? Our alligator hostess is traveling at tremendous speeds and as she slithers on she whips her tail and opens her throat in a tremendous cry of grief that comes out of her in a huge, reptilian groan: *Noooooooo . . .*

Rolling out of her wake I see the stars spiraling into the Hudson; in that second I think I see the proliferation and complexity of all creation dividing into gold and dross, unless it is light and dark, but which is which I cannot tell.

A black shape on the horizon advances at tremendous speeds; it resolves into a monstrous reptile crushing everything in its path. The great mouth cracks wide as the huge beast approaches, blazing with red light that pours out from deep inside, and all at once I understand. This vast, dark shape is the one being Perpetua hates most but she is helpless and rushing toward it all the same, and the terror is that she has no choice.

This is by no means God jerking her along, it is a stupendous alligator with its greedy jaws rimmed with blood, summoning Perpetua and its thousand other daughters into its path, preparing to devour them.

The thought trails after her like a pennant of fire. *The father is gathering us in.*

So I understand why the alligator helped me.

And I understand as well the scope of her gift to me: in another minute I will become an orphan, as the monster alligator lunges for Perpetua and she stops it in its tracks, destructing in an explosion that lights up the apocalyptic skies. And because I am about to be free, and free of Father forever . . .

I understand why I had to help her die.

Scared now.

It's ok.

I'll be fine.

—*Flights: Extreme Visions of Fantasy,* 2004

Pilots of the Purple Twilight

The wives spent every day by the pool at the Miramar, not far from the base, waiting for word about their men. The rents were cheap and nobody bothered them, which meant that no one came to patch the rotting stucco or kill centipedes for them or pull out the weeds growing up through the cracks in the cement. They were surrounded by lush undergrowth and bright flowers nobody knew the names for, and although they talked about going into town to shop or taking off for home, wherever that was, they needed to be together by the pool because this was where the men had left them and they seemed to need to keep claustrophobia as one of the conditions of their waiting.

On good days they revolved slowly in the sunlight, redolent of suntan oil and thorough in the exposure of all their surfaces because they wanted the tans to be *right* for the homecoming, but they also knew they had plenty of time. If it rained they would huddle under the fading canopy and play bridge and canasta and gin, keeping scores into the hundreds of thousands even though they were sick of cards. They did their nails and eyebrows and read Perry Mason paperbacks until they were bored to extinction, bitching and waiting for the mail. Everybody took jealous note of the letters received, which never matched the number of letters sent because mail was never forwarded after a man was reported missing. The women wrote anyway, and every day at ten they swarmed down the rutted drive to fall on the mailman like black widow spiders, ravenous.

Most of the letters were for the wretches whose husbands had already come *home,* for God's sake, whisking them away to endlessly messy kitchens and perpetual heaps of laundry in dream houses mortgaged on the GI Bill. Embarrassed by joy, they had left the Miramar without a backward glance, and for the same reason they always wrote at least once, stuffing their letters with vapid-looking snapshots of first babies, posting them from suburbs on the other side of the world.

At suppertime they all went into the rambling stucco building, wrenching open the rusting casements because it seemed important to keep sight of the road. Just before the shadows merged to make darkness they would drift outside again, listening, because planes still flew out from the nearby base every morning and, waiting, they were fixed on the idea of counting them back in. Most of their men had left in ships or on foot but still they waited. To the women at the Miramar every dawn patrol hinted at a twilight return, and the distant Fokkers or P-38s or F-87s seemed appropriate emblems for their own hopes, the suspense a fitting shape to place on the tautening stomachs, the straining ears, the dread of the telegram.

They all knew what they would do when the men came back even though they had written their love scenes privately. There would be the reunion in the crowded station, the embrace that would shut out everybody else. She would be standing at the sink when he came up from behind and put his arms around her waist, or she would be darning or reading, not thinking about him just for once, when a door would open and she would hear him: Honey, I'm home. There would be the embrace at the end of the driveway, the embrace in plain view, the embrace in the field. None of them thought about what he would be like when they embraced, what he must look like now, the way he really smelled, because their memories had been stamped with images distilled, perfected by the quality of their own waiting, the balance they tried to keep between thinking about it and not thinking about it. *If I can just not think about it,* Elise still told herself, *then maybe he will come.*

Watching the sky, even after all these years, she would be sure she heard the distant vibration of motors drumming, or maybe it was the jet sound, tearing the sky like a scythe; she had been there since Château-Thierry, or was it Amiens, and she knew the exact moment at which it became too dark to hope. "Tomorrow," she would say, and because the others preferred to think she was the oldest and so was the best at waiting, they would follow her inside. They all secretly feared that there was an even older woman bedridden in the tower, and that her husband had sailed with Enoch Arden, but nobody wanted to know for sure. They preferred to look to Elise, who kept herself beautifully and was still smiling; she had survived.

They were soft at night, jellied with anticipation and memory, one in spirit with Elise, but each morning found them clattering out to the chaises with Pam and Marge, hard and bright. Pam and Marge were the leaders of a group of self-styled girls in their fifties, who had graying hair and thickening waists. They liked to kid and whistled songs like "Praise the Lord and Pass the Ammunition" through their teeth. They shared a home-front camaraderie that enraged Donna, who was younger, and who had sent her husband off to a war nobody much remembered. She and Sharon and a couple of others in their forties would press their temples with their fists, grumbling about grandstanding, and people who still thought fighting was to be admired. Anxious, bored, frazzled by waiting, these two groups indulged in a number of diverting games: who had the most mail and who was going to sit at the round table at supper, who was hogging all the sunlight. They chose to ignore the newcomers, mere slips of things who had sent their men off to—where was it—Nam, or someplace worse.

Pam and Marge were tugging back and forth with Donna and Sharon this particular morning, wrangling over who was going to sit next to Elise, when Peggy walked in. Her shoes were sandy from the walk up the long driveway and her brave going-away outfit was already rusty with sweat. Bill had put her in a cab for the Miramar because, as he pointed out, he wasn't going to be gone for long and she would be better off with other service wives, they would have so much in common.

"Bitch," Marge was saying, "look what you did to my magazines."

Donna dumped her makeup kit and portable radio on the chaise. "It serves you right."

Marge was red-faced and hot, she may not even have heard herself lashing out. "I hope it crashes."

Even Pam was shocked. "Marge!"

"It would serve her right."

Peggy dropped her overnight bag. "Stop it."

Donna had gone white. "Don't ever say that."

"Stop." Peggy set her fist against her teeth.

"Girls." Elise stood between them, frail and ladylike in voile. "What would Harry and Ralph think if they could see you now?"

Donna and Marge stood back, pink with shame.

"What is the new girl going to think?"

"I'm sorry," Marge said, and she and Donna hugged.

Elise saw that Peggy was backing away, ready to make a break for it. The perfect hostess, she put a hand on her arm. "Come and sit by me, ah . . ." She inclined her head graciously.

"Peggy."

"Come, Peggy." She patted the chaise. "I want you to meet Donna, her Ralph is in the Kula gulf, and Pam and Marge both have husbands at, yes, that's it, Corregidor."

"But they couldn't."

Elise said, serenely, "Won't you have some iced tea?"

Peggy was gauging the distance between her and the overnight bag, looking for a gap in the overgrown greenery. "I can't stay."

"You'll have to excuse the girls," Elise said. "Everybody is a little taut, you understand."

"I don't belong here, I'm . . ."

Elise spoke gently, overlapping, " . . . only here for a little while. I know."

"Bill promised."

"Of course he did.

Later, when she felt better, Peggy let Elise lead her inside the cavernous building. She unpacked her things and after she had changed into her bikini she went out to take her place by the pool. She thought she would join the other girls in bikinis, who looked closer to her age, but they sat in closed ranks at the far end of the pool, giving her guarded looks of such hostility that she hurried back to her place by Elise.

"Don't mind them," Elise said. "It takes time to adjust."

Going down to dinner, Peggy understood how important it was to be well groomed. The room was bright with printed playsuits and pretty shifts in floral patterns chosen in fits of bravery. Although there were only women in the room, each of them had taken care with her hair and makeup, pressing her outfit because it was important; if they flagged, the men might discover them and be disgusted, or else the word would get out that they had given up, and there was no telling what grief that would bring. Either way they would never be forgiven. Whether or not the men came they would face each dinner hour tanned and combed and carefully made up and no matter what it cost, they would be smiling.

That night Pam and Marge were never better; they had on their sharkskin shorts and the bright jersey shirts knotted under their breasts to expose brown bellies, and when Betty joined them at the end of the dining room they went into their Andrews Sisters imitation with a verve that left everybody shouting. Jane played the intro again and again, and even though they were spent and gasping, they came tap dancing back. There was a mood of antic pleasure which had partly to do with the new girl in the audience, and partly with the possibility that the men just might come back and discover them at a high point: *See how well we do without you. Look how pretty we are, how lively. How could you bear to leave us for long?* They imagined the men laughing and hooting the way they did for USO shows; at the finale, the women would bring them up on the stage.

Bernice was next with "I'll be seeing you," and they were all completely still by the time Donna took the microphone and sang, "Fly the Ocean in a Silver Plane." Then it was time to go outside.

"Tell me about him," Elise said, leading Peggy through the trees.

Peggy said, "He has blue eyes."

"Of course he does. Gailliard has blue eyes."

"Who?"

"Gailliard. He crushed my two hands in one of his, and when I cried out he said, Did I hurt you, and I had to let him think he had pinched my fingers because I didn't want to let him know I was afraid." She whimpered. "I'm still afraid."

This old lady? Peggy wanted to support her. *Oh Lord.*

"Harry always kisses me very sweetly," Pam was saying to Marge. "He only opens his mouth a little."

Marge said, "Dave promised to bring me a dish carved out of Koa wood. Have you ever seen Koa wood?"

Donna and her group muttered together; they had been schooled to believe it was important not to let any of it show.

None of the young things seemed to know what they thought about the parting. Still they came out into the evening with all the others, straining as if they too were convinced of the return. Marva knew they didn't even speak the same language as the old ladies, who would talk about duty and patriotism and, what was it, the job that had to be done. She and Ben and a whole bunch of others had been together in the commune, like puppies, until they came for him because he had thrown away the piece of paper with the draft call, the MP kicked him and said, Son, you ought to be damn glad to go. Now here was this new girl not any older than Marva but her husband was what they called a career man, she probably believed in all that junk the old ladies believed in, so she could learn to play canasta and go to hell.

At first Peggy was afraid of the shadows; then the figures in the field sorted themselves out so that she could see which were trees and which were women running across the grass like little girls, stretching their arms upward, and she found herself swallowing rage because this place was worse than any ghetto. The women were all either stringy and bitter or big-assed and foolish and Bill had dumped her here as if she were no better than the rest of them. When Elise tried to take her hand she pulled away.

"It's going to be all right."

"This is terrible."

"You'll get used to it."

"Listen." Marge's voice lifted. "Do you hear anything?"

Waiting, they all stood apart because each departure shimmered in the air at this moment of possible return.

Elise remembered that Gailliard had taken her to the balcony at the Officers

Club. He had set her up on the rail in her gray chiffon with the gray suede slippers and then he stood back to regard her, so handsome that she wanted to cry out, and she remembered that at the time they were so steeped in innocence that each departure of necessity spelled victory and swift return. She wondered if old ladies were supposed to feel the hunger that stirred her when she remembered his body. She wondered if he was still loyal, after all these years. In retrospect their love was so perfect that she knew he would always be beautiful, as she remembered him, and true.

Pam and Marge had said goodbye in peacetime; when Harry and Dave flew out from Pearl in April of that year it had seemed like just another departure. Marge could remember dancing with Dave's picture, relieved, in a way, because the picture never belched or scratched its belly, although she and Pam stoutly believed that if they had known there was going to be a war they could have surrounded the parting with the right number of tears and misgivings, enough prayers to prepare for the return. Their fears would have been camouflaged by bright grins because, when you were a service wife, you had to treat every parting like every other parting. Still . . .

Bernice's husband Rob enlisted in the first flush of patriotism after Pearl Harbor. "Go," she said, clenching her fists to keep from grabbing him. He looked back once: "At least I'm doing the right thing." *He's off there accomplishing things with a bunch of other guys, they're busy all day and at night they relax and horse around while I am stuck here, getting older, with nothing to do except sing that song on Saturday nights . . .* Donna remembered her and Ralph on the bed, wondering what sense it made for him to go into the mess in Korea. There was no choice and so, laying resignation between them like a knife blade, they made love one last time. Marva remembered being stoned in that commune near Camp Pendleton, Ben would come in looking like Donald Duck in that uniform and all the kids would laugh, but the last time he made her pick up her bedroll and he brought her here, he told her he would be back and maybe he would.

Peggy nursed a secret hurt: what Bill said to her in a rage right before he dumped her at the Miramar: "If you can't wait more than five minutes, why should I bother to come back," and her riposte: "Don't bother," so when Marge yelled, "I think I hear something," she had to run to the edge of the clearing with the rest of them; at the first sound they would light the flares. She heard herself calling aloud, thinking if anything happened to Bill it would be her fault, for willing it, and that if she spread her arms and cried, "They're coming," it might bring them.

She discovered that the days were exquisitely organized around their waiting; no one sunned or played cards or read for too long in any one day because it would distort the schedule; they had to keep the division between the segments because it made the hours keep marching. Although fights were a constant, no quarrel could be too violent to preclude a reconciliation because they had to continue together, even as they had to silence any suggestion that even one of them might be disappointed; when the men came back they were all coming, down to the last one. Unless this was so, there was no way for the women to live together.

Pam and Marge organized a softball team, mostly thick-waisted "girls" from their own age group. They got Peggy to play, and after some consideration Donna joined them.

"Wait till you meet Dave," Marge said, sprawling in the grass in the outfield. "I would see him at the end of the walk in his uniform and that was when I loved him most. He'll never change."

"Everybody changes," Donna said gently.

"Not my Dave."

"Now, Bill . . ." Peggy began, but when she tried to think of Bill there was a blur and what she remembered was not what he looked like but what she wanted him to look like because she had always been bothered by the hair growing in his nostrils, his wide Mongol cheekbones, covered by too much flesh, so she recomposed his face to her liking: *If I can't have what I had, then at least let me make it what I want.* "Bill looks like something out of the movies."

Somebody decided it would be a good idea to have bonfires ready; if the planes should come by daylight they would see the smoke columns. Every few weeks the women could rebuild the heaps of firewood, taking out anything that looked wet or rotten. Bernice organized a duplicate bridge tournament. Marva and some of the younger girls meditated for half an hour before breakfast and again before supper and, grudgingly, asked Peggy to join them.

She and Peggy were the first at the chaises one bright morning and they exchanged stories, grumbling about being stuck with all these old biddies, no better off than anybody else.

"I don't know," Marva was saying, "at least the meals come regular. I got sick of granola."

Peggy said, "I never had a tan like this before."

"But they act like we're going to be here forever." Marva looked at Marge, wobbling out on wedgies. "It's obscene."

Peggy said bravely, "We're not like them."

"We'll never be like them."

"We just have to hang in here for the time being." Peggy settled herself, feeling the sun on her belly. "For the time being we're in the same boat."

Elise seemed especially drawn to Peggy; she would pat the chaise next to her and wait for Peggy to join her. Then she would put the name, Gailliard, into the air between them and sit contemplating it, assuming that Peggy shared some of the same feelings. She told herself Peggy was young enough to be her daughter but that was a lie; she could be Peggy's grandmother, and knew it. Still it seemed important to her to keep the pretense of youth, even as it was important to keep herself exquisitely groomed and to greet each morning with the same generous smile, the same air of hope because to the others she was a fixed point, which they could sight from, and until she flagged they would not waver. She did her best to suspend Peggy in that same network of waiting, to keep her safe along with the rest.

"You ought to talk to Donna," she said, "I think you have a lot in common."

"I'm afraid of her because she seems so sad."

"You could learn from her," Elise said. "She keeps herself well."

Peggy knew what Elise meant. Pam and Marge and their group played records over and over and mooned and dithered like a bunch of girls but Donna kept her dignity, fixed in a purity of waiting which Elise would admire because it resembled her own. There was no way for Peggy to explain that she and Bill had parted in anger, that she was pledged to wait but she had already jeopardized everything she was waiting for, that in her failure of will she might already have wished Bill to his death.

Please bring him back, she thought. *I would give anything to have him back.* By the time she thought this she had already been there longer than she realized; time blurred, and as she sent out her wish she heard the distant drumming of engines and the sky darkened with planes returning, the message running ahead of them, singing in the air at the Miramar, hanging before them as clearly as anything in writing:

I'M BACK

so that Peggy had to hide her head and rock with anxiety and it was Donna who was the first to acknowledge it, addressing the sky gently, her voice soft with several lifetimes of regret.

She said, so nobody else heard her: "I'm afraid it's too late."

Elise found her hands fluttering about her face and her loins weak and her head buzzing in panic. Even with her eyes closed she was aware of Gailliard shimmering before her, beautiful and unscathed, and she pulled a towel up to cover her, murmuring, "He'll see me, he'll *see* me," because she knew that he would come to her with his beauty preserved at the moment when his life went out like a spark and she was well past seventy now, beautifully groomed but old, wrinkled, with all her systems crumbling, diminished even further by his relentless beauty, and if he recognized her at all he would say, You're so *old*. She pulled the towel closer, like a shroud, whispering, "Please don't let him see me."

HONEY, IT'S ME

(Donna murmured, "There's nothing left here.")

"You bastard, wasting me like this, while you stayed young." Bernice went to her room and pulled the curtains and slammed the door.

Marge was ablaze with love, and she sang, or prayed: Dave, let me keep you out there, perfect and unchanged. If you come back you will have a beer belly, just like me, you will have gotten gray. As she sang, or prayed, she imagined she heard him responding: How could I, I've been dead, and she said, aloud, "Dave, let me keep you the way I thought you were."

DON'T YOU HEAR ME

(In the tower, the oldest lady turned milky eyes to the ceiling; she could no longer speak but she made herself understood: *It was all used up by waiting*.)

Peggy cowered; they were supposed to light the flares or something—set off fires. Remembering the story of the monkey's paw she thought her last wish had come true and that Bill was struggling out of some distant heap of wreckage at this very minute, and he would be mangled, dreadful, dragging toward her . . .

"The meals aren't bad," Marva was saying, doing her best to override the thunder of the engines; the sky above was black now but she pushed on, "And Ben, he never really gave a damn." Shrugging as if to brush aside the shadows of the wings, she said, "Hey, Peg, do you hear anything?"

. . . either that or he would try and yank her away from this place that she loved just to go on making her unhappy. He would be Enoch Arden, at the window, and she would turn to face him: Oh, it's you.

"No," Peggy said firmly, as the planes passed over, "I don't hear anything."

—*Other Stories and: The Attack of the Giant Baby*, 1981

Sisohpromatem

I, Joseph Bug, awoke one morning to find that I had become an enormous human. I lay under the washbasin in the furnished room which heretofore had been my kingdom, an unbounded world, and saw first that the bottom of the washbasin dripped only a few inches above my face and that from where I lay I could see all four walls of the room.

Then I realized I was lying on my back. At first I thought I would die there unless someone came and nudged me over, and then, as I began kicking my legs, I discovered that the forelegs clung to the edge of the washbasin and with a certain amount of manipulation I would be able to regain my belly. Even then I hoped that once turned, so, I would be able to crawl away and lose myself in the woodwork that I loved.

As you must have gathered, I had not yet grasped the enormity of my plight. So eager was I to regain my legs that I grappled with the basin, scrambling and then losing purchase, falling back at last to rest.

It was only then, as I lay with these new, pink legs sprawled about me, that I understood how repulsive I had become. The new appendages were huge and disgustingly pink, bloated like night crawlers, and they were only four in number. My back, which pressed against the rotting floorboards, was uncommonly tender. Gone was my crowning beauty; gone was the brave carapace which had glittered in the dim light, protecting me from the thousand perils that threaten a young roach. Gone were my brilliant antennae and the excellent legs which supported my waist. In place of a body which moved like quicksilver I was left with a series of huge mounds and excrescences; my quick form had been replaced by an untidy, ungainly, hideous mound of flesh.

I would have despaired then, had it not been for the instinct stronger than reason which told me that I must struggle to regain my belly, for only then would the world look right to me.

Gathering all my strength, I grappled with the washbasin again, thinking longingly of the slime which once I had gloried in, knowing that never again would I frolic in those pipes. Once again I was reminded of those revels, the races in the cracks around the bottom of the toilet, our gallant disregard for the pellets put down by the room's human occupant, the pride one felt in escaping a clumsy human foot. And because I was, after all, an insect, I drew myself together and attempted to regain my feet. Using my strange forelegs I embraced the washbasin, pulling myself up until my upper half rested upon it, inadvertently standing as I now remembered that humans did, coming abreast of a reflecting surface, and so inadvertently into what I would take to be my face.

I screamed for a full minute, so overcome by tremors that I fell to what I know must have been my knees, pressing my new face against the cold porcelain. Trembling, I crumpled, noticing in transit that I bent now in several directions, most notably at the waist. Instinct guided me so that I fell in a series of stages, bending and folding and coming to rest at last on my belly, and the simple fact of lying as the gods intended gave me some small cheer.

Still I might have died then, of simple horror, if a new hope had not presented itself. As I lay with my head under the washbasin I was aware of a small progress going on in the baseboard near my head. Even though my ears had been sadly dulled I could hear them coming—bold Hugo and grumbling Arnold, with Sarah and Steve and Gloria chittering behind. They must have been drawn by my cries—surely they were coming to rescue me.

Arnold came first, looking brightly from the murk beneath the baseboard. Because I could not interpret his expression I lay silent, waiting to see what would come. Hugo pushed up beside him, studying my left elbow, and the others came out, rank on rank, looking at me and talking among themselves. They looked so familiar, all those beloved faces, so concerned that I was sure they had come to help me and so, speaking softly so as not to flatten them with my huge voice, I said:

"Hugo. Arnold. Thank heaven you have come."

But they didn't answer. Instead they bowed their heads together, antennae intertwining, and although I could not make out what they were saying I was sure they were talking about me as they would never talk in my presence if I were myself again.

Pained by this, I turned at last to Gloria, who had been close to me in the way of a cockroach with another cockroach, and because she was not chattering with the rest but instead looked at me with a certain concentrated expression, I whispered, full of longing:

"Gloria, surely *you* will . . . "

Gloria laid an egg.

Before I could help myself, I had begun to weep. Now this itself was a new experience, and so fascinated was I by the sensation, by the interesting taste of the liquid I excreted, that I forgot for a minute about the little delegation along the baseboard.

In the next moment, they attacked. Uttering cries of hatred and revulsion, taking advantage of me in my weakened state, they marched on to me, crawling along my foreleg, heading toward my vulnerable face. They may even have thought to feed upon my eyes.

I cannot explain what happened next. Perhaps it was my pain and resentment toward these, my former brethren, perhaps it was only a sign of my metamorphosis; I only know that my pale flesh began to crawl and I rose, cracking my skull on the washbasin, nevertheless striking out, flailing, trying to scrape them off.

Landing in a cluster about my knees, they regrouped, and in the pause I tried to explain, to apologize, to beg them to recognize and accept me, but in the next second they attacked again. And so, goaded, I did what one cockroach has never done to another; I lashed out, first at Gloria, sending her flying against the baseboard; I could tell she was injured, but I was too angry to care. Then I squashed Sarah with my fist.

The others fled then, leaving me alone next to the basin, and as they left, a strange new feeling overtook me. I had for the first time power, and as I thought on the injuries the others had done me, this new power tasted sweet. Almost without effort I rose once more, coming quite naturally to my feet. Then, because it seemed the reasonable thing to do, I struck the faucet until water came and washed what was left of Sarah off what I now know to be my hands.

In the next few hours I discovered my kingdom anew. The room which I had always assumed to be the world was rather small, bounded on four sides by walls and filled with appurtenances which I gradually identified according to their functions. Experimenting with my joints, I applied part of myself to a chair. In time, remembering what I knew of humans, I took up some of the rags laid over the back of the chair and put them on my person, working my head and arms into a large, stretchy garment designed for that purpose, and grandly tying another garment around my waist.

Troubled, I went about the room again and again and again, finding at last an object with pictures on bits of paper bound together, understanding from the pictures that I had done something wrong and then re-garbing myself according to what I saw.

From time to time I would go back to the basics and if I saw so much as a sign of one of my fellows, I would poke at the crevices with my shoe.

I was occupied thus when there was a sound on the other side of the door and before I could gather myself to hide, the door opened and another human—a female—let herself into the room.

She spoke, and so complete was my transformation that I understood her. "Where's Richard?"

Because I was afraid to try my voice, I answered her with a shrug.

"You must be one of his thousand cousins."

I nodded. I was somehow comforted by her phrase; I had always taken humans to be isolated, and it made me feel somehow secure to know that their families were as big as ours.

"Well, when is he coming back?"

I shrugged again, but this time it did not satisfy her. She came closer, apparently studying me, and she said, finally, "What's your name?"

"J-Joseph." Even I was pleased with the way it came out.

"Well, Joseph, perhaps we can go out for a bite and when we get back maybe Richard will be here."

I didn't know why, but I knew I wasn't ready. "I—I can't do that."

"Oh, you want to wait for him. Well, that's your business." She looked at me through a fall of red hair and for the first time I found hair attractive. She was soft all over and, inexplicably, that was attractive too.

"But I am—hungry." I had not had anything since morning, when I found something behind the toilet bowl.

"I'll bring you a hamburger," she said. "If Richard comes while I'm gone, bring him down to Hatton's." She studied me for a moment. "You know, you're not bad looking. But why on earth do you have your shirt buttoned that way?"

I will never forget what happened next. She stepped forward and fumbled with my upper garment, yanking it this way and that, patting it into place, and when she was satisfied she stepped back and said, "Not bad. Not bad at all." In the next second, too fast for me but not for my heart, which followed her, she was gone.

How I exulted then! I whirled around the room like a spider, rejoicing in my many joints, knowing for the first time a certain pride in all my agile parts and the soft flesh that covered them, thinking that I would have the best of both worlds. I had been the largest and finest in the insect kingdom; now I would be the handsomest in the human world: a prince among cockroaches, a king among men. I spun and danced and celebrated my new body and then, in an orgy of release, I went back to the corner by the washbasin and with one of Richard's shoes I battered all the antennae which came at me from that miserable little crack.

"You, Ralph. Hugo. Now I understand. The lesser will always hate the great."

I was talking thus when a strange weakness overcame me, so that I had to stand suddenly because my beautiful joints had betrayed me and would not bend. Instead I stayed on my feet next to the room's one window, looking out on the world below and thinking that once I had eaten, my strength would return and I would go out into it, a man among men.

And I would take the female with me. Now that she had seen me she would have no more use for this shabby Richard, who lived in this tiny, wretched room. She and I would find a nest of our own, and then . . . The thought dizzied me and I backed into a soft place set on four legs and because I could no longer remain upright without a tremendous effort I settled back in the softness, lying with a certain degree of discomfort on my back.

I was lying, so, noticing a certain strangeness about my mandibles, when a male, probably Richard, opened the door and came into the room.

In the next second he saw me lying in what I assume is his bed and some new transformation must have overtaken me for the face of which I was so proud did not please him at all, nor did my shape, lying among his bedcovers, nor did the limbs which I waved, calling out for him to stop screaming and wait . . .

I can hear his voice downstairs now, screaming and screaming, and I hear a female bellowing the alarm and I hear the voices of many men and know that they are armed. They are on the stairs now with chains and clubs and to my fear I find that large as I am I can move again, half this, half that, and I make my way to the basin and try to fit beneath it, and I cry out, pleading with my brethren to let me join them.

"Hugo, Arnold, let me come back."

I am trying desperately to make myself small against the baseboard but part of me still protrudes from underneath the basin—I can feel the air against my naked, hardening carapace. They have broken down the door now, they are upon us.

Hugo, Arnold. It's me.

—*New Worlds,* 1966

On the Penal Colony

Notebook found in candy bin
General Store,
Old Arkham Village, Arkham, Mass.

Friend, if you are reading this, I am already dead. I, Arch Plummer, am giving this notebook to Hester Phyle with instructions to burn it as soon as she knows Gemma and I and our friend are safe. The truth must out. Unspeakable secrets fester here. Atrocities. If the three of us don't make it, Hester knows what to do. The horror must be exposed!

If we make it, Gemma and Laramie and I will hold a press conference and blow the lid off this place. If we don't, Hester has promised to leave this where you will find it. Whoever you are, the future depends on you.

If you pulled this out of the barrel in the General Store instead of Olde Arkham™ candy corn or packaged pemmican or arrowheads or that cornhusk doll your daughter wanted, then Gemma and Laramie and I are already dead. I beg you. Call *The Times* and *Hard Copy* now. Leave no stone unturned. Contact the network anchors whether or not they can pronounce the language. Bring *The National Enquirer.*

*

"And on your right note the authentic eighteenth-century architecture. Every house in Old Arkham Village is more than two hundred years old! Now count the windowpanes. Every window is 12 over 12."

"Mom, can we leave now?"

"Quit hitting your brother!"

"I want to watch TV."

" . . . paints made from natural substances. Blueberries. Buttermilk. Now, the village tavern. Our colonists will be happy to answer any questions you have."

"Harry, that one is smiling at me."

"It's his job. Don't get too close." Dad lights a match and winks. "Watch this."

The "colonist" rips off the flaming wig. "Eeeowwww!"

＊

You come for the day and you say "Ohhh, quaint." You have no idea what's really happening just below the surface in our idyllic colonial village, deep in the Massachusetts hills. Underneath the mobcaps. Underneath the earth. You're all malled out so you bring the kids, drop your candy papers and Ziploc sandwich bags, deface the property, take your snapshots, and go. You cart in foreign guests to impress them with your nation's heritage—eighteenth-century houses and shops; oh, wow, these things are *old!* Or you bring Gran because she is old.

Or something shakes loose inside you and starts rattling around. You get hungry for your past. Not necessarily your past. A past. Any past. Some commercial visionary resurrected all these old buildings and moved them here to supply an early American past for all of you late Americans to enjoy even though you never had one. At twenty bucks a pop, it's your past too.

So you pack up the kids and throw grinders and a six-pack of brewskis into the cooler and come rolling our way as if this is some kind of Colonial Mecca, God's own solution to two problems: crime and rootlessness. Well I can't tell you about rootlessness—who cares whether your great-greats hit Plymouth Rock or Ellis Island or rolled in hanging from the axle of a truck? But I can tell you a thing or two about crime.

＊

"*. . . scheme for a model prison." Bullfinch Warden hocks; the sound is heard clear to the back of the tram. "As our country's leading penologists you can see what we have accomplished here. Forget license plates. Forget telemarketing and Readers' Clearing House as revenue producing activities for prisoners who turn back the proceeds to the state. We are at the apex here. The prison of the future. Convicts as capital.*"

＊

Crime? You want to see crime? This place is a crime. Maggoty food and floggings in the picturesque village square, torture so deep that you never hear the screams. Murderous trusties, sadistic screws. But what do you know anyway, you stuff home made gingerbread into the kids and buy them the thirteen-star flag and you lead them onto the scaled-down replica of the *Bonhomme Richard* and you go, "Oh, wow, these are my people."

You trudge through the landlocked whaler, humming to the canned gabble on the Auditron, and no matter where you came from, you're all, like, *these are our forefathers.* You get to feeling all-American even if you just landed on a raft. Correction. Early American; you ride Paul Bunyan's blue ox and you bong your knuckles on the genuine authentic half-sized Liberty Bell and if the screws aren't looking maybe you try to scratch in your initials, but only a little bit, and you feel as American as hell.

And, wuoow, you think, what a cool solution to America's problems. Punishment and restitution, all in one place! Symbiosis. Patriotism and profit. Plus rehabilitation, us hard-timers in tricorns or aprons and mobcaps answering your stupid questions about beef jerky and square-headed nails. And we are so fucking polite! You push a button and the National Anthem plays and the replicated flag goes up over the to-scale replica of Fort McHenry. Your heart swells up like the Barney balloon in the Macy's Day parade and you're like, America, wow!

*

"Note the presentation. It's based on a revolutionary new concept. It's not what you're doing, it's what it looks *like you're doing that shapes society. Hence the ideal village. Happy villagers."*

*

Happy! What do you care about us? What do you know?

You see us sweating in our period costumes and you think, fine. Hardened criminals working their way back into the fabric of American life. How heartwarming. When they get out they'll be all-American, yes!

*

"I don't know, I turned the other way and the prisoner just . . ." The guard produces two bloody ears.

"Shut up, they'll hear you."

"But Warden, what are we going to do?"

"Shut up. The state examiners!" Bullfinch Warden snarls, *"Get him out of here."*

"He's so deep in solitary that . . ."

"Not the perp. The tourist who got hurt. We can't have this getting out."

*

You think we look charming. If you think about us at all. Hester lays out bay-berry candles and you get all mushy: I love America. Delightful. You note the glint in the 12-over-12s that us hard-timers clean every day at dawn and you get all proud. American ingenuity. Quaint.

Well, you don't have a clue. See, you can watch us cobble or pot until you get bored and then you can buy your barley sugar sticks and take the Ethan Frome or Hester Prynne shuttle back to the Molly Pitcher or the Crispus Attucks Parking Lot and get in your RVs and go. We stay.

I could tell you about charming. I could show you the underside of cute. Old Arkham Village is our nation's heritage all right, but it's not what you think. Rehabilitation, sure: let cons do time in pretty-pretty early America. Whittle by the fireplace with the mantel painted in authentic imitation cranberry-and-buttermilk paint, except we can't have knives. Press criminals through the all-American grid. They come out the other side like potatoes, mashed. Homogenized. You can mold them into anything you want. It's America all right, America straight out of Lizzie Borden by Simon Legree. We, your model prisoners, live by the numbers. Bullfinch Warden has thumbscrews and a gift for hurting people so the marks don't show. Then there are the trusties with their Red Devils and their cattle prods. And at night, stalking the catwalks in our dormitory hundreds of feet below Betsy Ross Lot 3, the screws.

*

"Honey, let's fuck here."

"Eeek, what would our forefathers think?"

"Our forefathers are off duty. The place is closed."

The tourists are lying together on the greensward. A noise comes out of the ground like a great, communal groan. She leaps out of her lover's arms with a shriek. "Ernie, somebody's listening, let's get out of here!"

*

I am writing in my own blood, by what light sifts through the bars in the sub-terranean part of Old Arkham Village that you never see. This is our home nights until dawn, Thanksgiving and Christmas, when even public parks in the State of Massachusetts close.

And if we look all right to you in the daytime, bowing and smiling, answering your questions in eighteenth-century quaint—well. You don't see the hidden monitors, trusties ready to rat if the smile slips even a half inch. Sonic barriers at the perimeters and electrified razor wire in the woods. The anklets and the belt.

I'll come to the belt.

Meanwhile, my credentials. To prove that this is no political tract and definitely not a gag. It isn't even a cry for help.

It's a record of how things are. What it's like in this tarted-up, chintzy, early American penal colony, me to you. I, Arch Plummer, am a lifer here in Old Arkham Village; for years I have been your friendly village blacksmith, answering your stupid questions as I hammer horseshoes and craft cheesy rings for your kids out of genuine, authentic replicas of eighteenth-century square-headed nails. You've seen me pull glowing metal out of the forge and bong horseshoes into shape to the voice of Jason Robards reading, "Under the spreading chestnut tree . . ." *The Village Blacksmith,* piped in here on a loop, and you've seen me hammer them on to the Percherons' hooves and finish them off with the hasp while on the same loop some old mid-American broad named Jo Stafford belts out "The Blacksmith Blues." Well I could tell you a thing or two about blacksmith blues.

Right, I am the village smithy. For my crimes. If you knew how many times I've heard that track or what would happen to me if I trashed the speakers or tried to walk away from the racket, you'd understand. Burn scars on my ankles where the anklets zapped me; mossy cracks in my skull from the beatings in solitary and beginning marks around my waist from the belt. I am a lifer.

A life sentence to Old Arkham Village, when all I did was steal a loaf of bread.

OK, OK, it was a Lexus, but I didn't know about the toddler in the back until we reached Cuernavaca, by which time the only logical thing to do was send the ransom note. I never laid a finger on him! I bought him the Pancho Villa serape and matching Mexican hat and put him on the bus home before I even mailed the note. And here I am with the hard-timers. Quiven, the decoy duck carver (murder One), and Roland the town printer (arson), Gemma the gingerbread maker (crime of passion, don't ask; her husband was *shtupping* her mom), sweet Gemma—whom I happen to be in love with—and Laramie the cobbler (armed robbery, which I happen to know was a frame).

*

"It is well known that society's dregs are recidivists beyond all hope of rehabilitation." The warden fills the eighteenth-century meeting house, roaring like a frustrated warthog, and thirty visiting penologists flinch. "If we are going to warehouse them, let's do it creatively. There is no enterprise without its profit."

*

If you find this. When you read this. Know this. Everything I've done I did for Joanna. And Quiven. Because of what happened to them when the only wrong thing they did was falling in love.

See, when the screws turn us out of the rack and march the work details out four hours before Old Arkham Village opens, nobody cares who walks next to who in the double line. Hard-timers, all of us, groggy from the pills, belching oatmeal and miserable in our pointed shoes and scratchy linsey-woolsey period costumes, shambling like the dead.

The screws are zoned out on these grim mornings; hung over from the orgy and bitter about being stuck on the predawn shift. Nobody notices if you're marching with guys from your tier or sidling closer to the women in the foggy dawn, and if you do collide with her—Oh, Gemma . . . if Quiven collides with Joanna!—if you mutter to each other under cover of the guards' shouting and get to know each other, everybody thinks what you two say to each other leads to zilch. The vise of a maximum security prison is too tight for love.

But Quiven got close to Joanna and fell in love anyway.

*

"Mommy, that lady doesn't like me."
"Of course she does, dear. It's her job."
"Then why is she crying?"
"Shut up. Shut up and eat your horehound drops."

*

I didn't even see it happening; I was conditioned to march on, like Pavlov's dogs or the chicken that dances on the electrified turntable, like, soft-shoe like crazy to keep from getting shocked. Want to break and run? Want to kill and burn? Light some weed or relieve yourself behind a tree? Forget it. We look free to you, but we are not. Hidden by the costumes, there are the anklets, with an extra added incentive for us. Under the shirts and leather jerkins, we wear the belts.

Electronic control. Now and ever. Day and night. We prisoners are reined in tight. We eat rotten meat and weevily bread and belch misery and resentment; we crawl out of boxes on these dank mornings and break rocks before we don our costumes for the Early American Card Shoppe or tickety-boo little Scrimshaw Junction, folding our hands underneath leather aprons and putting on prim Colonial smiles. But what do you tourists care?

We look all right to you.

*

"And to keep order we give them the illusion of rehabilitation. That they are learning new careers. Movement is not action, but we make them think it is. A true belief in movement can prevent action," Bullfinch Warden says.

*

Appearances. Happy colonists. Model prisoners. If you look at all, you don't see past the costumes and bland faces, but there is rage scorching the sweaty gauze under our wigs and murder in our hearts. Be careful what you do when you come into our shops and houses; be careful what you say! Rebellion etches the insides of our bellies; pry open our jaws and you'll see fire. We mean to destroy Bullfinch Warden, but you happen to be closer. Beware. We could just rip a hole in your face.

Some days one of us forgets himself and strikes out or makes a break for it, but it never lasts long: the belts. The monitors. The drugs. No sleep. Debilitating food.

By the time you come at ten a.m. we're so deep into it that we look right at home in the confected past. And if Quiven and Joanna fall in love and begin to plan, I don't guess it, so how could you? I am in love with Gemma, but it's only since the *auto-da-fé*.

Quiven was in love with Joanna. He couldn't leave it alone. Notes dropped in with the laundry, sweet Gemma slipped Joanna's notes into the pockets of his fatigues for her, and in the men's supply room Laramie Beckam did the same for Quiven. Quiven and Joanna had seconds to cherish and devour each other's notes; the screws turn out the beds and check the toilets on the hour. Their love fed on messages in the code that desperate prisoners send, endearments tapped out on prison pipes. They kept in touch! Love grew on the most insubstantial communication—veiled looks, those endearments murmured standing in line; one day I saw Quiven and Joanna lock fingers. I whispered, "Careful. You'll get hurt!" but a trusty heard me and instead of working at the smithy I logged the twelve hours until the park closed with my head and hands clamped in the village stocks. I tried to warn him!

*

"But let's face it, ladies and gentlemen. These people are animals. We are a warehouse here. Good penology is optimizing it."

*

Quiven knew it would kill them both but he was in love. Still, love might have died of starvation if Bullfinch Warden hadn't caught Joanna dreaming over her spinning wheel: a complaint. Family of Latvians, in the hand-worked shirts and aprons with the lambs embroidered on the front. When lovesick Joanna was too distracted to answer their hundred questions they went to the warden for a refund. Mind you they thought he was the historic curator. Yeah, right. "We come so far. She look asleep!" They claimed the hostess in the Cotton Mather house was not only dumb, but deaf.

The next day Joanna was ashen and drawn. Bullfinch Warden had activated her anklets. Not big-time torture, just enough voltage to keep her on her toes. Safe. But seeing Joanna suffer drove Quiven nuts. It was around then that we had the Indian corn pudding riot, with Quiven standing up on the table in the dining hall and us chanting and banging our cups until they zapped all the anklets and belts and we fell out senseless from the pain. When we came to, Quiven was in solitary and we were under lockdown on short rations, bread and water and fried pork rinds, don't ask.

It wasn't bad food that drove Quiven. It was compression. When he cleared solitary he was assigned to the Old Stone Jail. Then he heard Joanna scream. Fury drove him to crack the leg irons and wrench off the cell door. Compression sent him out of the jail and across the Village Green to the Cotton Mather house. He went in spite of the fact that the belt's secret workings intensified as he got farther from his designated post.

Quiven was in agony by the time he reached Cotton Mather house. Screaming Joanna was bent backward over her spinning wheel by a sex-crazed tourist in a FUCK ME I'M AMERICAN T-shirt and an International Harvester cap. In spite of the teeth of pain Quiven pulled her away from the horrified tourists and took her upstairs. Security programming sent a couple of jolts into her anklets to keep her in place but love overrode the pain.

"Oh, Quiven," she said, or so Gemma reports.

Quiven looked at her with his own death written in his face. "I love you." They both knew that this was not only the first time for them, it would be the last time.

It was excruciating, but they didn't care. The anklets wouldn't kill her, only scar her, and when push comes to shove in prison, it is the moment you strive for, not the terrible aftermath or punishments to come.

So Quiven and Joanna locked themselves into a bedroom where they murmured and touched for as long as they could manage until the gnawing scorpions in the belt overrode even Quiven's compressed love and grief and he fell out of himself, never to return.

*

"*Because of its nature, a democracy is obligated to pretend to rehabilitate. To work, rehabilitation has to be voluntary. Since it is mandatory it never works. Therefore, the state's only obligation is to make it look as if we have tried.*"

*

By the time Bullfinch's cadre in their Revolutionary war uniforms broke in on them, pain ruled. Quiven was dead. And Joanna? Joanna had gone so far back inside herself that not all the Thorazine in the world could retrieve her. She was lost to us.

No deed goes unpunished and nothing in prison passes without note. Bullfinch took off the belt and strung Quiven's body up in the underground cellblock. He made us file by to see the exact cost of rebellion. They hung him upside down, so we walked by the body cranksided with our heads resting on our shoulders so we could see into his face.

*

"*Sometimes you can only teach by example. That's why the state gives us the death penalty. Sometimes the example itself is more powerful than the threat of death.*"

*

Bullfinch Warden actually said, "Look on my works, ye mighty."

And we saw. Incised around Quiven's naked waist by the constant jackhammering of a million tiny needles was the warning: LOVE IS DEATH . . . FREEDOM IS SUICIDE . . . FREEDOM IS SUICIDE . . . LOVE IS DEATH, words chasing each other around and around dead Quiven's waist, a warning to us all etched in pain, and if the needles penetrated Quiven's vitals, it's a testimony to physical strength and to the power of his love that he had his moment with Joanna before his heart faltered and he died.

In case you're interested, Warden Bullfinch wasn't about to leave it at that.

He stood up on the catwalk while we filed past what was left of Quiven and he made a speech. I'll spare you the details. It was worse than the anklets and the belts, and the punch line? Instead of sending Joanna to Quincy for retrial, Bullfinch Warden was conducting a witchcraft trial, special event for the Labor Day Weekend visitors to Old Arkham Village, us on time-and-a-half rations since prisoners are never paid, and the state makes overtime provisions when they need you around the clock. The trial was slated to take place in front of high-ticket audiences at special evening showings so we could continue with business as usual during the day.

*

"The lessons we teach here are for the ages. They are lessons for us all."

*

But what do you care? You loved the trial. It went live on CNN. *Hard Copy* came in on it, along with *Inside Edition,* and Ted Koppel interviewed William F. Buckley Junior on the witch hunts of the 1950s in a special *Nightline* telecast direct from here.

Because you thought it was contrived just for your entertainment, you even loved the *auto-da-fé.* It's a good thing Joanna was already catatonic; she didn't feel a thing. At least we don't think she did, although *Entertainment Tonight* reported agents from William Morris and CAA were trying to sign her up on the basis of her performance, up to and including her dying screams.

And because you were excited and distracted by how real the flames looked and how eloquently Joanna writhed, and because the screws were busy keeping you from mobbing the stake, Gemma's body and mine touched in the crush:

"Arch." "Gemma!" We fused, bonded by instant love. And as reflected flames licked our faces and we moaned in the heat, my friend Laramie Beckam, who knows every duct and pipe in the bowels of our underground cellblock because he is a trusty, Laramie fell in with us and we hatched the plan.

*

"The only effective facility is the maximum security facility. It has to look civil from the outside, but it must shut off all possibilities of escape."

*

Now our plan is complete. We've assembled civilian wardrobes and kited them over the electronic barrier. After I plant this note I give the signal. Laramie starts the fire in the paint locker. By the time it's extinguished he's shorted out the E-barrier and we're out of here. And if we don't make it; if they see us escaping in spite of the fire and confusion; if they shoot us dead, no matter. It's better than one more day in the smithy, with Gemma suffering behind the Visitors' Center desk or giving her monologue on Colonial spinning in the repaired and refurbished Cotton Mather house.

*

"Effective prevention is predicated on the impossibility of escape."

*

Quiet. You don't hear me. If our plan works, you will never read this. Instead you'll see me on all 1,000 Primestar channels, telling our story to the world. All that remains is to slip this account into my jerkin and, when the shift changes and the screws march us, the early detail, to the holding pen to draw breath before they put us back into the Colonial petting zoo, I'm going to slip away. I'll stick this notebook into the cornhusk doll barrel in the Bayberry Candle corner of the General Store. Although Hester is afraid to come with us, she's volunteered to risk her life if necessary to preserve this testament. At my signal that we're home free, she'll destroy it for our own protection as well as hers.

Live free or die.

We go tonight.

—*F&SF*, 1998

The Food Farm

So here I am, warden-in-charge, fattening them up for our leader, Tommy Fango; here I am laying on the banana pudding and the milkshakes and the cream-and-brandy cocktails, going about like a technician, gauging their effect on haunch and thigh when all the time it is I who love him, I who could have pleased him eternally if only life had broken differently. But I am scrawny now, I am swept like a leaf around corners, battered by the slightest wind. My elbows rattle against my ribs and I have to spend half the day in bed so a gram or two of what I eat will stay with me for if I do not, the fats and creams will vanish, burned up in my own insatiable furnace, and what little flesh I have left will melt away.

Cruel as it may sound, I know where to place the blame.

It was vanity, all vanity, and I hate them most for that. It was not my vanity, for I have always been a simple soul; I reconciled myself early to reinforced chairs and loose garments, to the spattering of remarks. Instead of heeding them as I plugged in, and I would have been happy to let it go at that, going through life with my radio in my bodice, for while I never drew cries of admiration, no one ever blanched and turned away. But they were vain and in their vanity my frail father, my pale, scrawny mother saw me not as an entity but a reflection on themselves. I flush with shame to remember the excuses they made for me. "She takes after May's side of the family," my father would say, denying any responsibility. "It's only baby fat," my mother would say, jabbing her elbow into my soft flank. "Nelly is big for her age." Then she would jerk furiously, pulling my voluminous smock down to cover my knees. That was when they still consented to be seen with me. In that period they would stuff me with pies and roasts before we went anywhere, filling me up so I would not gorge myself in public. Even so I had to take thirds, fourths, fifths and so I was a humiliation to them.

In time I was too much for them and they stopped taking me out; they made no more attempts to explain. Instead they tried to think of ways to make me look better; the doctors tried the fool's poor battery of pills, they tried to make me join a club. For a while my mother and I did exercises; we would sit on the floor, she in a black leotard, I in my smock. Then she would do the brisk one-two, one-two and I would make a few passes at my toes. But I had to listen, I had to plug in, and after I was plugged in naturally I had to find something to eat; Tommy might sing and I always ate when Tommy sang, and so I would leave her there on the floor, still going one-two, one-two. For a while after that they tried locking up the food. Then they began to cut into my meals.

That was the cruelest time. They would refuse me bread, they would plead and cry, plying me with lettuce and telling me it was all for my own good. My own good. Couldn't they hear my vitals crying out? I fought. I screamed, and when that failed I suffered in silent obedience until finally hunger drove me into the streets. I would lie in bed, made brave by the Monets and Barry Arkin and the Philadons coming in over the radio, and Tommy (there was never enough; I heard him a hundred times a day and it was never enough; how bitter that seems now!). I would open the first pie or the first half-gallon of ice cream and then, as I began, I would plug in.

Tommy, beautiful Tommy Fango, the others paled to nothing next to him. Everybody heard him in those days; they played him two or three times an hour but you never knew when it would be so you were plugged in and listening hard every living minute; you ate, you slept, you drew breath for the moment when they would put on one of Tommy's records, you waited for his voice to fill the room. Cold cuts and cupcakes and game hens came and went during that period in my life but one thing was constant: I always had a cream pie thawing and when they played the first bars of "When a Widow" and Tommy's voice first flexed and uncurled, I was ready, I would eat the cream pie during Tommy's midnight show. The whole world waited in those days; we waited through endless sunlight, through nights of drumbeats and monotony, we all waited for Tommy Fango's records, and we waited for that whole unbroken hour of Tommy, his midnight show. He came on live at midnight in those days; he sang, broadcasting from the Hotel Riverside, and that was beautiful, but more important, he talked, and while he was talking he made everything all right. Nobody was lonely when Tommy talked; he brought us all together on that midnight show, he talked and made us powerful, he talked and finally he sang. You have to imagine what it was like, me in the night, Tommy, the pie. In a while I would go to a place where I had to live on Tommy and only Tommy, to a time when hearing Tommy would bring back the pie, all the poor lost pies . . .

Tommy's records, his show, the pie . . . that was perhaps the happiest period of my life. I would sit and listen and I would eat and eat and eat. So great was my bliss that it became torture to put away the food at daybreak; it grew harder and harder for me to hide the cartons and the cans and the bottles, all the residue of my happiness. Perhaps a bit of bacon fell into the register; perhaps an egg rolled under the bed and began to smell. All right, perhaps I did become careless, continuing my revels into the morning, or I may have been thoughtless enough to leave a jelly roll unfinished on the rug. I became aware that they were watching, lurking just outside my door, plotting as I ate. In time they broke in on me, weeping and pleading, lamenting over every ice cream carton and crumb of pie; then they threatened. Finally they restored the food they had taken from me in the daytime, thinking to curtail my eating at night. Folly. By that time I needed it all. I shut myself in with it and would not listen. I ignored their cries of hurt pride, their outpouring of wounded vanity, their puny little threats. Even if I had listened, I could not have forestalled what happened next.

I was so happy that last day. There was a Smithfield ham, mine, and I remember a jar of cherry preserves, mine, and I remember bacon, pale and white on Italian bread. I remember sounds downstairs and before I could take warning, an assault, a company of uniformed attendants, the sting of a hypodermic gun. Then the ten of them closed in and grappled me into a sling, or net, and heaving and straining, they bore me down the stairs. I'll never forgive you, I cried as they bundled me into the ambulance. I'll never forgive you, I bellowed as my mother in a last betrayal took away my radio, and I cried out one last time, as my father removed a ham bone from my bra: I'll never forgive you. And I never have.

It is painful to describe what happened next. I remember three days of horror and agony, of being too weak, finally, to cry out or claw the walls. Then at last I was quiet and they moved me into a sunny, pastel, chintz-bedizened room. I remember that there were flowers on the dresser and someone was watching me.

"What are you in for?" she said.

I could barely speak for weakness. "Despair."

"Hell with that," she said, chewing. "You're in for food."

"What are you eating?" I tried to raise my head.

"Chewing. Inside of the mouth. It helps."

"I'm going to die."

"Everybody thinks that at first. I did." She tilted her head in an attitude of grace. "You know, this is a very exclusive school."

Her name was Ramona and as I wept silently, she filled me in. This was a last resort for the few who could afford to send their children here. They prettied it up with a schedule of therapy, exercise, massage; we would wear dainty pink smocks and talk of art and theater; from time to time we would attend classes in elocution and hygiene. Our parents would say with pride that we were away at Faircrest, an elegant finishing school; we knew better—it was a prison and we were being starved.

"It's a world I never made," said Ramona, and I knew that her parents were to blame, even as mine were. Her mother liked to take the children into hotels and casinos, wearing her thin daughters like a garland of jewels. Her father followed the sun on his private yacht, with the pennants flying and his children on the fantail, lithe and tanned. He would pat his flat, tanned belly and look at Ramona in disgust. When it was no longer possible to hide her, he gave in to blind pride. One night they came in a launch and took her away. She had been here six months now, and had lost almost a hundred pounds. She must have been monumental in her prime; she was still huge.

"We live from day to day," she said. "But you don't know the worst."

"My radio," I said in a spasm of fear. "They took away my radio."

"There is a reason," she said. "They call it therapy."

I was mumbling in my throat, in a minute I would scream.

"Wait." With ceremony, she pushed aside a picture and touched a tiny switch and then, like sweet balm for my panic, Tommy's voice flowed into the room.

When I was quiet she said, "You only hear him once a day."

"No."

"But you can hear him any time you want to. You hear him when you need him most."

But we were missing the first few bars and so we shut up and listened, and after "When a Widow" was over we sat quietly for a moment, her resigned, me weeping, and then Ramona threw another switch and the Sound filtered into the room, and it was almost like being plugged in.

"Try not to think about it."

"I'll die."

"If you think about it you *will* die. You have to learn to use it instead. In a minute they will come with lunch," Ramona said and as The Screamers sang sweet background, she went on in a monotone: "One chop. One lousy chop with a piece of lettuce and maybe some gluten bread. I pretend it's a leg of lamb, that works if you eat very, very slowly and think about Tommy the whole time; then if you look at your picture of Tommy you can turn the lettuce into anything you want, Caesar salad or a whole smorgasbord, and if you say his name over and over you can pretend a whole bombe or torte if you want to and . . ."

"I'm going to pretend a ham and kidney pie and a watermelon filled with chopped fruits and Tommy and I are in the Rainbow Room and we're going to finish up with Fudge Royale . . ." I almost drowned in my own saliva; in the background I could almost hear Tommy and I could hear Ramona saying, "Capon, Tommy would like capon, *canard à l'orange,* Napoleons, tomorrow we will save Tommy for lunch and listen while we eat . . ." and I thought about that, I thought about listening and imagining whole cream pies and I went on, " . . . lemon pie, rice pudding, a whole Edam cheese. . . . I think I'm going to live."

The matron came in the next morning at breakfast and stood as she would every day, tapping red fingernails on one svelte hip, looking on in revulsion as we fell on the glass of orange juice and the hard-boiled egg. I was too weak to control myself; I heard a shrill sniveling sound and realized only from her expression that it was my own voice: "Please, just some bread, a stick of butter, anything. I could lick the dishes if you'd let me, only please don't leave me like this, please . . ." I can still see her sneer as she turned her back.

I felt Ramona's loyal hand on my shoulder. "There's always toothpaste but don't use too much at once or they'll come and take it away from you."

I was too weak to rise and so she brought it and we shared the tube and talked about all the banquets we had ever known, and when we got tired of that we talked about Tommy and when that failed, Ramona went to the switch and we heard "When a Widow," and that helped for a while, and then we decided that tomorrow we would put off "When a Widow" until bedtime because then we would have something to look forward to all day. Then lunch came and we both wept.

It was not just hunger: after a while the stomach begins to devour itself and the few grams you toss it at mealtimes assuage it so that in time the appetite itself begins to fail. After hunger comes depression. I lay there, still too weak to get about, and in my misery I realized that they could bring me roast pork and watermelon and Boston cream pie without ceasing; they could gratify all my dreams and I would only weep helplessly, because I no longer had the strength to eat. Even then, when I thought I had reached rock bottom, I had not comprehended the worst. I noticed it first in Ramona. Watching her at the mirror, I said, in fear:

"You're thinner."

She turned with tears in her eyes. "Nelly, I'm not the only one."

I looked around at my own arms and saw that she was right: there was one less fold of flesh above the elbow; there was one less wrinkle at the wrist. I turned my face to the wall and all Ramona's talk of food and Tommy did not comfort me. In desperation she turned on Tommy's voice, but as he sang I lay back and contemplated the melting of my own flesh.

"If we stole a radio we could hear him again," Ramona said, trying to soothe me. "We could hear him when he sings tonight."

Tommy came to Faircrest on a visit two days later, for reasons I could not then understand. All the other girls lumbered into the assembly hall to see him, thousands of pounds of agitated flesh. It was that morning that I discovered I could walk again, and I was on my feet, struggling into the pink tent in a fury to get to Tommy, when the matron intercepted me.

"Not you, Nelly."

'I have to get to Tommy. I have to hear him sing."

"Next time, maybe." With a look of naked cruelty she added, "You're a disgrace. You're still too gross."

I lunged but it was too late; she had already shot the bolt. And so I sat in the midst of my diminishing body, suffering while every other girl in the place listened to him sing. I knew then that I had to act; I would regain myself somehow, I would find food and regain my flesh and then I would go to Tommy. I would use force if I had to, but I would hear him sing. I raged through the room all that morning, hearing the shrieks of five hundred girls, the thunder of their feet, but even when I pressed myself against the wall I could not hear Tommy's voice.

Yet Ramona, when she came back to the room, said the most interesting thing. It was some time before she could speak at all, but in her generosity she played "When a Widow" while she regained herself, and then she spoke:

"He came for something, Nelly. He came for something he didn't find."

"Tell about what he was wearing. Tell what his throat did when he sang."

"He looked at all the *before* pictures, Nelly. The matron was trying to make him look at the *afters* but he kept looking at the *befores* and shaking his head and then he found one and put it in his pocket and if he hadn't found it, he wasn't going to sing."

I could feel my spine stiffen. "Ramona, you've got to help me. I must go to him."

That night we staged a daring break. We clubbed the attendant when he brought dinner, and once we had him under the bed we ate all the chops and gluten bread on his cart and then we went down the corridor, lifting bolts, and when we were a hundred strong we locked the matron in her office and raided the dining hall, howling and eating everything we could find. I ate that night, how I ate, but even as I ate I was aware of a fatal lightness in my bones, a failure in capacity, and so they found me in the frozen food locker, weeping over a chain of link sausage, inconsolable because I understood that they had spoiled it for me, they with their chops and their gluten bread; I could never eat as I once had, I would never be myself again.

In my fury I went after the matron with a ham hock, and when I had them all at bay I took a loin of pork for sustenance and I broke out of that place. I had to get to Tommy before I got any thinner: I had to try. Outside the gate I stopped a car and hit the driver with the loin of pork and then I drove to the Hotel Riverside, where Tommy always stayed. I made my way up the fire stairs on little cat feet and when the valet went to his suite with one of his velveteen suits I followed, quick as a tigress, and the next moment I was inside. When all was quiet I tiptoed to his door and stepped inside.

He was magnificent. He stood at the window, gaunt and beautiful; his blond hair fell to his waist and his shoulders shriveled under a heartbreaking double-breasted pea-green velvet suit. He did not see me at first; I drank in his image and then, delicately, cleared my throat. In the second that he turned and saw me, everything seemed possible.

"It's you." His voice throbbed.

"I had to come."

Our eyes fused and in that moment I believed that we two could meet, burning as a single, lambent flame, but in the next second his face had crumpled in disappointment; he brought a picture from his pocket, a fingered, cracked photograph, and he looked from it to me and back at the photograph, saying, "My darling, you've fallen off."

"Maybe it's not too late," I cried, but we both knew I would fail.

And fail I did, even though I ate for days, for five desperate, heroic weeks; I threw pies into the breach, fresh hams and whole sides of beef, but those sad days at the food farm, the starvation and the drugs have so upset my chemistry that it cannot be restored; no matter what I eat I fall off and I continue to fall off; my body is a halfway house for foods I can no longer assimilate. Tommy watches, and because he knows he almost had me, huge and round and beautiful, Tommy mourns. He eats less and less now. He eats like a bird and lately he has refused to sing; strangely, his records have begun to disappear.

And so a whole nation waits.

"I almost had her," he says when they beg him to resume his midnight shows; he will not sing, he won't talk, but his hands describe the mountain of woman he has longed for all his life.

And so I have lost Tommy, and he has lost me, but I am doing my best to make it up to him. I own Faircrest now, and in the place where Ramona and I once suffered I use my skills on the girls Tommy wants me to cultivate. I can put twenty pounds on a girl in a couple of weeks and I don't mean bloat. I mean solid fat. Ramona and I feed them up and once a week we weigh and I poke the upper arm with a special stick and I will not be satisfied until the stick goes in and does not rebound because all resiliency is gone. Each week I bring out my best and Tommy shakes his head in misery because the best is not yet good enough, none of them are what I once was. But one day the time and the girl will be right—would that it were me—the time and the girl will be right and Tommy will sing again. In the meantime, the whole world waits; in the meantime, in a private wing well away from the others, I keep my special cases: the matron, who grows fatter as I watch her. And Mom. And Dad.

—*Orbit 2*, 1967

In Behalf of the Product

Of course I owe everything I am today to Mr. Manuel Omerta, my personal representative, who arranged for practically everything, including the dental surgery and the annulment, but I want all of you wonderful people to know that I couldn't have done any of it without the help and support of the most wonderful person of all, my Mom. It was Mom who kept coming with the super-enriched formula and the vitamins, she was the one who twirled my hair around her finger every time she washed it, it was Mom who put Vaseline on my eyelashes and paid for the trampoline lessons because she had faith in me. Anybody coming in off the street might have thought I was just an ordinary little girl, but not my mom: why, the first thing I remember is her standing me up on a table in front of everybody. I had on my baby tap shoes and a big smile and Mom was saying, Vonnie is going to be Miss Wonderful Land of Ours someday.

Even then she knew.

Well, here I am, and I can't tell you how happy I am to be up here, queen of the nation, an inspiration and a model for all those millions and billions of American girls who can grow up to be just like me. And this is only the beginning. Why, after I spend a year touring the country, meeting the people and introducing them to the product, after I walk down the runway at next year's pageant and put the American eagle floral piece into the arms of my successor, and she cries, anything can happen. I might go on to a career as an internationally famous television personality, or if I'd rather, I could become a movie queen or a spot welder, or I could marry Stanley, if he's still speaking to me, and raise my own little Miss Wonderful Land of Ours. Why, the world is mine, except of course for the iron curtain countries and their sympathizers, and after this wonderful year, who knows?

I just wish Daddy could be here to share this moment, but I guess that's just too much to hope, and I want you to know, Daddy, wherever you are out there, I forgive you, and if you'll only turn yourself in and make a public confession, I know the authorities will be lenient with you.

And that goes for you too, Sal. I know it was hard on you, always being the ugly older sister, but I really don't think you should have done what you did, and to show you how big I can be, if the acid scars came out as bad as I think they did, Mom and I are perfectly willing to let bygones be bygones and sink half the prize money into plastic surgery for you. I mean, after all, it's the least we can do. Why, there aren't even any charges outstanding against you; after all, nobody was really hurt—I mean, since Mr. Omerta happened to come in when he did and bumped your arm, and the acid went all over you instead of me.

I know I am the center of all eyes standing up here, I am the envy of millions, and I love the way the silver gown feels, slithering down over me like so much baby oil. I even love the weight of the twenty-foot-long red, white and blue velvet cloak, and every once in a while I want to reach up and touch the rhinestone stars and lightning bolts in my tiara but of course I can't because I am still holding the American eagle floral piece, the emblem of everything I have ever wanted. Of course you girls envy me. I used to get a stomachache just from looking at the pageant on T V. I would look at the winner smiling out over the Great Seal and I would think: Die, and let it be me. I just want you girls to know it hasn't all been bread and roses, there have been sacrifices, and Mom and Mr. Omerta had to work very hard, so if you're out there watching and thinking: What did she do to deserve that? let me tell you, the answer is, Plenty.

The thing is, without Mr. Omerta, poor Mom and I wouldn't have known where to begin. Before Mr. Omerta we were just rookies in the ballgame of life; we didn't have a prayer. There we were at the locals in the Miss Tiny Miss contest, me in my pink tutu and the little sequined tiara, I even had a wand; it was my first outing and I came in with a fourth runner-up. If it had been up to me I would have turned in my wand right then and there. Maybe Mom would have given up too, if it hadn't been for Mr. Omerta, but there must have been something about me, star quality, because he picked me out of all those other little girls, *me.* He didn't even give the winner a second look, he just came over to us in his elegant kidskin suit and the metallic shoes. We didn't know it then but it was Mr. Manuel Omerta, and he was going to change my life.

I was a loser, I must have looked a mess; the winner and the first runner-up were over on the platform crying for the camera and pinching each other in between lovey-dovey hugs, it was all over for the day, Mom and I were hanging up our cleats and packing away our uniforms when Mr. Omerta licked Mom's ear and said, "You two did a lot of things wrong today, but I want to tell you I like your style." I said, Oh thank you, and went on crying but Mom, she shushed me and hissed at me to listen up. She knew what she was doing too; she wasn't just going to say, Oh, thank you, and take the whole thing sitting down. She said, "What do you mean, a few things wrong?" and Mr. Omerta said, "Listen, I can give you a few pointers. Come over here." I couldn't hear what he said to her but she kept nodding and looking over at me and by the time I went over to tell them they were closing the armory and we had better get out, they were winding up the agreement; Mr. Omerta said, "And I'll only take fifty percent."

"Don't you fifty percent me," Mom said. "You know she's got the goods or you never would have picked her."

"All right," he said, "forty-five percent."

Mom said, "She has naturally curly hair."

"You're trying to ruin me."

First Mr. Omerta pretended to walk out on Mom and then Mom pretended to take me away and they finally settled it; he would become my personal representative, success guaranteed, and he would take forty-two point eight percent off the top.

"The first thing," he said. "Tap dancing is a lousy talent. No big winner has ever made it on tap dancing alone. You have to throw in a gimmick, like pantomime. Something really different."

"Sword swallowing," Mom said in a flash.

"Keep coming, I really like your style." They bashed it back and forth for another few minutes. "Another thing," Mr. Omerta said. "We've got to fix those teeth; they look kind of, I don't know, *foreign.*"

Mom said, "Got it Mr. Omerta, I think we're going to make a winning team."

It turned out Mr. Omerta was more or less between things and besides, to do a good job he was going to have to be on the spot, so he ended up coming home with us. Dad was a little surprised at first but he got used to it, or at least he acted like he was used to it; he only yelled first thing in the morning, while Sal and I were still hiding in our beds and Mr. Omerta was still out on the sun porch with the pillow over his head, stacking Zs. We fixed the sun porch up for Mr. Omerta; the only inconvenience was when you wanted to watch TV you had to go in and sit on the end of the Hide-a-Bed and sometimes it made him mad and other times it didn't; you were in trouble either way. Sal used to hit him on the knuckles with her leg brace; she said if you just kept smacking him he would get the idea and quit. He didn't bother me much. I was five at the time, and later on I was, you know, the Property; in the end I was going to be up against the Virginity Test and even when you passed that they did a lot of close checking to be sure you hadn't been fooling around. If you are going to represent this Wonderful Land of Ours, you have to be a model for all American womanhood, I mean, you wouldn't put pasties on Columbia the Gem of the Ocean or photograph the Statue of Liberty without her concrete robe, which is why I am so grateful to Mr. Omerta for busting in on Stanley and me in Elkton, Maryland, even if we *were* legally married by a justice of the peace. We could have taken care of the married part, but there was the other thing; it isn't widely known but if you flunk the Test in the semifinals you are tied to the Great Seal in front of everybody and all the other contestants get to cast the first stone.

I cried but Mr. Omerta said not to be foolish, I was only engaging in the classic search for daddy anyway, just like in all the books. I suppose he was right, except that by the time Stanley and I ran away together Daddy had been gone for ten years. We were sitting around one night when I was eight. I had just won the state Miss Subteen title and Mr. Omerta and Mom were clashing glasses; before he put the prize check less his percentage into my campaign fund, Mr. Omerta had lost his head and bought us a couple of bottles of pink champagne. Then Daddy got fed up or something, he threw down his glass and stood up, yelling, "You're turning my daughter into a Kewpie doll." Sally started giggling and Mom slapped her and let my father have it all in one fluid motion. She said, "Henry, it's the patriotic thing to do." He said, "I don't see what that has to do with anything, and besides . . ."

I got terribly quiet. Mom and Mr. Omerta were both leaning forward, saying, "Besides?"

I tried to shut him up but it was too late.

"Besides, what's so wonderful about a country that lets this kind of thing go on?"

"Oh, *Daddy*," I cried, but it was already too late. Mr. Omerta was already on the hot line to the House Un-American Activities Committee Patrol Headquarters; he didn't even hear Daddy yelling that the whole thing was a gimmick to help sell the war. By that time we could hear sirens. Daddy crashed through the back window and landed in the flower bed and that was the last anybody ever saw of him.

Well, we do have to go and visit the troops a lot and we do lead those victory rallies as part of our public appearance tour in behalf of the product, but it's not anything like Daddy said. I mean, any girl would do as much, and if you happen to be named Miss Wonderful Land of Ours, it's an honor and a privilege. I keep dreaming that when I start my nationwide personal appearance tour I will find Daddy standing in the audience in Detroit or Nebraska, he will be carrying a huge UP AMERICA sign and I can take him to my bosom and forgive him and he'll come back home to live.

Now that I think about it, Stanley does look a little bit like Daddy, and maybe that's why I was attracted to him. I mean, it's no fun growing up in a household where there are no men around, unless, of course, you want to count Mr. Omerta, who did keep saying he wanted to be a father to me, but that wasn't exactly what he meant. I was allowed to go to public high school so I could be a cheerleader because that can make or break you if you're going for Miss Teen-Age Wonderful Land of Ours, which of course is only a way station, but it's a lot of good personal experience. As it turned out I only got to the state finals. I could have gone to the nationals as an alternate but Mr. Omerta said it would be bad exposure and besides, we made enough out of the state contest to see us through until it was time for the main event. Anyway, Stanley was captain of the football team the year I made head cheerleader, and at first Mr. Omerta encouraged us because he could take pictures of us sitting in the local soda fountain, one soda and two straws, or me handing a big armful of goldenrod to Stanley after the big game.

The thing I liked about Stanley, he wasn't interested in One Thing Only, he really loved me for my soul. When I came in after a date Mr. Omerta would sneak upstairs and sit on the end of my bed in his bathrobe while I told him all about it: you would have thought we were college roommates after the junior prom. Stanley loved me so much I know he would have waited but I decided there were more important things than being Miss Wonderful Land of Ours so the night of graduation we ran off to Elkton, Maryland, and if Mr. Omerta had gotten there five minutes later it would have been too late.

Whatever you might think about what he did to Stanley, you've got to give him credit for doing his job. He was my personal representative, he got me through the Miss Preteen and the Miss Adolescent with flying colors, and saw me through Miss Teen-Age Wonderful Land of Ours; he got me named Miss Our Town and it was all only a matter of time, I was a cinch for Miss State, and once I got to the nationals, well, with my talent gig, I was a natural, but here I was in Elkton, Maryland, I was just about to throw it all away for a pot of marriage when Mr. Omerta came crashing in and saved the day. What happened was, I was just melting into Stanley's arms when the door banged open and there were about a hundred people in the room, Mr. Omerta in the vanguard. I could have killed him then and there and he knew it. He took me by the shoulders and he looked me in the eye and said, "Brace up, baby, you owe it to your country. I will not let you smirch yourself before the pageant. Death before dishonor," Mr. Omerta said, and then he yelled, "There he is, grab him," and they dragged poor Stanley away. I'll never know how he managed to tail us, but he had the propaganda squad with him and before I could do a thing they had poor Stanley arrested on charges of menacing a national monument, they threw in a couple of perversion charges so Mr. Omerta could push through the annulment, and now poor Stanley is on ice until the end of next year. By that time my tour as Miss Wonderful Land of Ours will be over and maybe Mr. Omerta will let bygones be bygones and clear Stanley's name so he and I can get married again; after all, that's the only way I will ever be eligible to become *Mrs.* Wonderful Land of Ours, and you can't let yourself slip into retirement just because you've already been to the top.

But I haven't told you anything about my talent. I mean, it's possible to take lessons in Frankness and Sincerity, but talent is the one thing you can't fake. Mr. Omerta told us right off that tap dancing alone just wouldn't make it, but every time I tried sword swallowing (Mom's idea) I gagged and had to stop, but the trouble with fire eating was that the first time I burned my face, so naturally after that they couldn't even get me to try tapping and twirling the flaming baton. We thought about pantomime but of course that would rule out personal charm and just then Mr. Omerta had an inspiration; he got me an accordion. So I went into the Miss Tiny Miss contest the next year tapping and playing the accordion, but there was a girl who sang patriotic songs and tapped the V for Victory in Morse code, and that gave Mr. Omerta an even better idea.

To make a long story short, when I got up here tonight to do my talent for the last time, it was a routine we have been working on for years, and I owe it all to Mr. Omerta, with an extra little bow for Mom, whose idea it was to dress me in the Betsy Ross costume with the cutouts and the skirt ripped off at the crotch, our tattered forefathers and all that, and if you all enjoyed my interpretation of "O Beautiful, for Spacious Skies" done in song and dance and pantomime with interludes on the accordion, I want to say a humble thank you, thank you one and all.

I guess not many of you wonderful people know how close I came to not making it. First there was that terrible moment in the semifinals when we went back to find that my entire pageant wardrobe had been stolen, but I want you to know that Miss Massachusetts has been apprehended and they made her give me her wardrobe because between the ripping and the ink she had more or less ruined mine, and I have begged them to go easy on her because we are all working under such a terrible strain. And then there was the thing where they wouldn't let my mom into the rehearsals but they settled that very nicely and she is watching right now from her very own private room in the hospital and they will let her come home as soon as she is able to relate. Thanks for everything, Mom, and as soon as we get off TV I'm coming over and give you a great big kiss even if you don't know it's me. Then there's the thing about Mr. Omerta, and I feel just terrible, but it had to be done. I mean, he just snapped last night, he got past all the chaperones and came up to my hotel room. I said,

"Oh, Mr. Omerta, you shouldn't be here, I could be disqualified," and the next thing I knew he had thrown himself down on my feet. He said, "Vonnie, I love you, I adore you." It was disgusting. He said, "Throw it all over and run away with me." Well, there I was not twenty-four hours from the big title; it was terrible. I said, "Oh, come on, Mr. Omerta, don't start that now, not after what you did to Stanley," and when he wouldn't stop kissing my ankles I kicked him a couple of times and said, "Come on, all you've ever thought about is money, money," and when he said there were more important things than money I started screaming, "Help me, somebody come and help me, this man is making an indecent advance," and the matrons came like lightning and carried him off to jail. Well, what did he expect? He's spent the last thirteen years training me for this day.

So when the big moment came tonight I was the one with the perfect figure, the perfect walk, the perfect talent, I wowed them in the charm department and . . . I don't know, there has just been this guy up here, the All-American Master of Ceremonies; you thought he was kissing my cheek and handing me another bouquet but instead he was whispering in my ear, "OK, sweetie, enough's enough." There seems to be something wrong; it turns out I am not reaching you wonderful people out there, my subjects. You can see my lips moving but that's not me you hear on the PA system, it's a prerecorded speech. He says . . . he says I'm perfect in almost every respect but there's this one thing wrong, they found out too late so they're going to have to go through with it. I guess they found out when I got up here and tried to make this speech. I am a weeny bit too frank to be a typical Miss Wonderful Land of Ours, he says I have too many regrets, but just as soon as I get down from here and they run the last commercial, they're going to take care of that. He says I'll be ready to begin my nationwide personal appearance tour in behalf of the product just as soon as they finish the lobotomy.

—*Bad Moon Rising,* Thomas M. Disch ed., 1973

Songs of War

For some weeks now a fire had burned day and night on a hillside just beyond the town limits; standing at her kitchen sink, Sally Hall could see the smoke rising over the trees. It curled upward in promise but she could not be sure what it promised, and despite the fact that she was contented with her work and her family, Sally found herself stirred by the bright autumn air, the smoke emblem.

Nobody seemed to want to talk much about the fire, or what it meant. Her husband, Zack, passed it off with a shrug, saying it was probably just another commune. June Goodall, her neighbor, said it was coming from Ellen Ferguson's place; she owned the land and it was her business what she did with it. Sally said what if she had been taken prisoner. Vic Goodall said not to be ridiculous, if Ellen Ferguson wanted those people off her place, all she had to do was call the police and get them off, and in the meantime it was nobody's business.

Still there was something commanding about the presence of the fire; the smoke rose steadily and could be seen for miles, and Sally, working at her drawing board, and a number of other women, going about their daily business, found themselves yearning after the smoke column with complex feelings. Some may have been recalling a primal past in which men conked large animals and dragged them into camp, and the only housework involved was a little gutting before they roasted the bloody chunks over the fire. The grease used to sink into the dirt and afterward the diners, smeared with blood and fat, would roll around in a happy tangle. Other women were stirred by all the adventure tales they had stored up from childhood; people would run away without even bothering to pack or leave a note, they always found food one way or another and they met new friends in the woods. Together they would tell stories over a campfire, and when they had eaten they would walk away from the bones to some high excitement that had nothing to do with the business of living from day to day. A few women, thinking of Castro and his happy guerrilla band, in the carefree, glamorous days before he came to power, were closer to the truth. Thinking wistfully of campfire camaraderie, of everybody marching together in a common cause, they were already dreaming of revolution.

Despite the haircut and the cheap suit supplied by the Acme Vacuum

Cleaner company, Andy Ellis was an underachiever college dropout who could care less about vacuum cleaners. Until this week he had been a beautiful, carefree kid and now, with a dying mother to support, with the wraiths of unpaid bills and unsold MarvelVacs trailing behind him like Marley's chains, he was still beautiful, which is why the women opened their doors to him.

He was supposed to say, "Good morning, I'm from the Acme Vacuum Cleaner company and I'm here to clean your living room, no obligation, absolutely free of charge." Then, with the room clean and the Marvelsweep attachment with twenty others and ten optional features spread all over the rug, he was supposed to make his pitch.

The first woman he called on said he did good work but her husband would have to decide, so Andy sighed and began collecting the Flutesnoot, the Miracle Whoosher and all the other attachments and putting them back into the patented Bomb Bay Door.

"Well thanks anyway . . ."

"Oh, thank *you*," she said. He was astounded to discover that she was unbuttoning him here and there.

"Does this mean you want the vacuum after all?"

She covered him with hungry kisses. "Shut up and deal."

At the next house, he began again. "Good morning, I'm from the Acme Vacuum Cleaner company . . ."

"Never mind that. Come in."

At the third house, he and the lady of the house grappled in the midst of her unfinished novel, rolling here and there between the unfinished tapestry and the unfinished wire sculpture.

"If he would let me alone for a minute I would get some of these things done," she said. "All he ever thinks about is sex."

"If you don't like it, why are we doing this?"

"To get even," she said.

On his second day as a vacuum cleaner salesman, Andy changed his approach. Instead of going into his pitch, he would say, "Want to screw?" By the third day he had refined it to, "My place or yours?"

Friday his mother died so he was able to turn in his MarvelVac, which he thought was just as well, because he was exhausted and depressed, and, for all his efforts, he had made only one tentative sale, which was contingent upon his picking up the payments in person every week for the next twelve years. Standing over his mother's coffin, he could not for the life of him understand what had happened to women—not good old Mom, who had more or less liked her family and at any rate had died uncomplaining—but the others, all the women in every condition in all the houses he had gone to this week. Why weren't any of them happy?

Up in the hills, sitting around the fire, the women in the vanguard were talking about just that; the vagaries of life, and woman's condition. They had to think it was only that. If they were going to go on, they would have to be able to decide the problem was X, whatever X was. It had to be something they could name, so that, together, they could do something about it.

They were of a mind to free themselves. One of the things was to free themselves of the necessity of being thought of as sexual objects, which turned out to mean only that certain obvious concessions, like lipstick and pretty clothes, had by ukase been done away with. Still, there were those who wore their khakis and bandoliers with a difference. Whether or not they shaved their legs and armpits, whether or not they smelled, the pretty ones were still pretty and the others were not; the ones with good bodies walked in an unconscious pride and the others tried to ignore the differences and settled into their flesh, saying: Now, we are all equal.

There were great disputes as to what they were going to do and which things they would do first. It was fairly well agreed that although the law said that they were equal, nothing much was changed. There was still the monthly bleeding. Dr. Ora Fessenden, the noted gynecologist, had showed them a trick which was supposed to take care of all that, but nothing short of surgery or menopause would halt the process altogether; what man had to undergo such indignities? There was still pregnancy, but the women all agreed they were on top of that problem. That left the rest; men still looked down on them, in part because in the main, women were shorter; they were more or less free to pursue their careers, assuming they could keep a babysitter, but there were still midafternoon depressions, dishes, the wash; despite all the changes, life was much the same. More drastic action was needed.

They decided to form an army.

At the time, nobody was agreed on what they were going to do or how they would go about it, but they were all agreed that it was time for a change. Things could not go on as they were; life was often boring, and too hard.

The youngest housewife watched the smoke, thinking hard. Then she wrote a note:

> Dear Ralph,
> I am running away to realize my full potential. I know you have always said I could do anything I want but what you meant was, I could do any-

thing as long as it didn't mess you up, which is not exactly the same thing now, is it? Don't bother to look for me.

No longer yours,

Lory

Then she went to join the women in the hills.

I would like to go, Suellen thought, *but what if they wouldn't let me have my baby?*

Jolene's uncle in the country always had a liver-colored setter named Fido. The name remained the same and the dogs were more or less interchangeable. Jolene called all her lovers Mike, and because they were more or less interchangeable, eventually she tired of them and went to join the women in the hills.

"You're not going," Herb Chandler said.

Annie said, "I am."

He grabbed her as she reached the door. "The hell you are, I need you."

"You don't need me, you need a maid." She slapped the side of his head. "Now let me go."

"You're mine," he said, aiming a karate chop at her neck. She wriggled and he missed.

"Just like your ox and your ass, huh." She had gotten hold of a lamp and she let him have it on top of the head.

"Ow," he said, and crumpled to the floor.

"Nobody owns me," she said, throwing the vase of flowers she kept on the side table, just for good measure. "I'll be back when it's over." Stepping over him, she went out the door.

After everybody left that morning, June mooned around the living room, picking up the scattered newspapers, collecting her and Vic's empty coffee cups and marching out to face the kitchen table, which looked the same way every morning at this time, glossy with spilled milk and clotted cereal, which meant that she had to go through the same motions every morning at this time, feeling more and more like that jerk, whatever his name was, who for eternity kept on pushing the same recalcitrant stone up the hill; he was never going to get it to the top because it kept falling back on him and she was never going to get to the top, wherever that was, because there would always be the kitchen table, and the wash, and the crumbs on the rug, and besides she didn't know where the top was because she had gotten married right after Sweetbriar and the next minute, bang, there was the kitchen table and, give or take a few babies, give or take a few stabs at night classes in something or other, that seemed to be her life. There it was in the morning, there it was again at noon, there it was at night; when people said, at parties, "What do you do?" she could only move her hands helplessly because there was no answer she could give that would please either herself or them. *I clean the kitchen table,* she thought, because there was no other way to describe it.

Occasionally she thought about running away but where would she go, and how would she live? Besides, she would miss Vic and the kids and her favorite chair in the television room. Sometimes she thought she might grab the milkman or the next delivery boy, but she knew she would be too embarrassed, either that or she would start laughing, or the delivery boy would, and even if they didn't she would never be able to face Vic. She thought she had begun to disappear, like the television or the washing machine; after a while nobody would see her at all. They might complain if she wasn't working properly, but in the main she was just another household appliance, and so she mooned, wondering if this was all there was ever going to be: herself in the house, the kitchen table.

JOIN NOW

It was in the morning mail, hastily mimeographed and addressed to her by name. If she had been in a different mood she might have tossed it out with the rest of the junk mail, or called a few of her friends to see if they'd gotten it too. As it was, she read it through, chewing over certain catchy phrases in this call to arms, surprised to find her blood quickening. Then she packed and wrote her note:

> Dear Vic,
> There are clean sheets on all the beds and three casseroles in the freezer and one in the oven. The veal one should do for two meals. I have done all the wash and a thorough vacuuming. If Sandy's cough doesn't get any better you should take him in to see Dr. Weixelbaum, and don't forget Jimmy is supposed to have his braces tightened on the 12th. Don't look for me.
> Love,
> June

Then she went to join the women in the hills.

Glenda Thompson taught psychology at the university; it was the semester break and she thought she might go to the women's encampment in an open spirit of inquiry. If she liked what they were doing she might chuck Richard, who was only an instructor while she was an assistant professor, and join them. To keep the appearance of objectivity, she would take notes.

Of course she was going to have to figure out what to do with the children while she was gone. No matter how many hours she and Richard taught, the children were her responsibility, and if they were both working in the house, she had to leave her typewriter and shush the children because of the way Richard got when he was disturbed. None of the sitters she called could come; Mrs. Birdsall, their regular sitter, had taken off without notice again, to see her son the freshman in Miami, and she exhausted the list of student sitters without any luck. She thought briefly of leaving them at Richard's office, but she couldn't trust him to remember them at the end of the day. She reflected bitterly that men who wanted to work just got up and went to the office, it had never seemed fair.

"Oh hell," she said finally, and because it was easier, she packed Tommy and Bobby and took them along.

Marva and Patsy and Betts were sitting around in Marva's room; it was two days before the junior prom and not one of them had a date, or even a nibble, there weren't even any blind dates to be had.

"I know what let's do," Marva said, "let's go up to Ferguson's and join the women's army."

Betts said, "I didn't know they had an *army*."

"Nobody knows what they have up there," Patsy said.

They left a note so Marva's mother would be sure and call them in case somebody asked for a date at the last minute and they got invited to the prom after all.

Sally felt a twinge of guilt when she opened the flyer.

JOIN NOW

After she read it she went to the window and looked at the smoke column in open disappointment: *Oh, so that's all it is.* Yearning after it in the early autumn twilight, she had thought it might represent something more: excitement, escape, but she supposed she should have guessed. There was no great getaway, just a bunch of people who needed more people to help. She knew she probably ought to go up and help out for a while, she could design posters and ads they could never afford if they went to a regular graphics studio. Still, all those women . . . She couldn't bring herself to make the first move.

"I'm not a joiner," she said aloud, but that wasn't really it; she had always worked at home, her studio took up one wing of the house and she made her own hours; when she tired of working she could pick at the breakfast dishes or take a nap on the lumpy couch at one end of the studio; when the kids came home she was always there and besides, she didn't like going places without Zack.

At the camp, Dr. Ora Fessenden was leading an indoctrination program for new recruits. She herself was in the stirrups, lecturing coolly while everybody filed by.

One little girl, lifted up by her mother, began to whisper: "Ashphasphazz-zzzz-pzz."

The mother muttered, "Mumumumumummmmmm . . . "

Ellen Ferguson, who was holding the light, turned it on the child for a moment. "Well, what does *she* want?"

"She wants to know what a man's looks like."

Dr. Ora Fessenden took hold, barking from the stirrups, "With luck, she'll never have to see."

"Right on," the butch sisters chorused, but the others began to look at one another in growing discomfiture, which as the weeks passed would ripen into alarm.

By the time she reached the camp, June was already worried about the casseroles she had left for Vic and the kids. Would the one she had left in the oven go bad at room temperature? Maybe she ought to call Vic and tell him to let it bubble for an extra half hour just in case. Would Vic really keep an eye on Sandy, and if she got worse would he get her to the doctor in time? What about Jimmy's braces? She almost turned back.

But she was already at the gate to Ellen Ferguson's farm, and she was surprised to see a hastily constructed guardhouse, with Ellen herself in khakis, standing with a carbine at the ready and she said, "Don't shoot, Ellen, it's me."

"For God's sake, June, I'm not going to shoot you." Ellen pushed her glasses up on her forehead so she could look into June's face. "I never thought you'd have the guts."

"I guess I needed a change."

"Isn't it thrilling?"

"I feel funny without the children." June was trying to remember when she had last seen Ellen: over a bridge table? at Weight Watchers? "How did you get into this?"

"I needed something to live for," Ellen said.

By that time two other women with rifles had impounded her car and then she was in a jeep bouncing up the dirt road to headquarters.

The women behind the table all had on khakis, but they looked not at all alike in them. One was tall and tawny and called herself Sheena; there was a tough, funny-looking one named Rap and the third was Margy, still redolent of the kitchen sink. Sheena made the welcoming speech, and then Rap took her particulars while Margy wrote everything down.

She lied a little about her weight, and was already on the defensive when Rap looked at her over her glasses, saying, "Occupation?"

"Uh, household manager."

"Oh shit, another housewife. Skills?"

"Well, I used to paint a little, and . . ."

Rap snorted.

"I'm pretty good at conversational French."

"Kitchen detail," Rap said to Margy and Margy checked off a box and flipped over to the next sheet.

"But I'm tired of all that," June said.

Rap said, "Next."

Oh it was good sitting around the campfire, swapping stories about the men at work and the men at home; every woman had a horror story, because even the men who claimed to be behind them weren't really behind them, they were playing lip service to avoid a higher price, and even the best among them would make those terrible verbal slips. It was good to talk to other women who were smarter than their husbands and having to pretend they weren't. It was good to be able to sprawl in front of the fire without having to think about Richard and what time he would be home. The kids were safely stashed down at the day care compound, along with everybody else's kids, and for the first time in at least eight years Glenda could relax and think about herself. She listened drowsily to that night's speeches, three examples of wildly diverging cant, and she would have taken notes except that she was full, digesting a dinner she hadn't had to cook, and for almost the first time in eight years she wasn't going to have to go out in the kitchen and face the dishes.

Marva, Patsy and Betts took turns admiring each other in their new uniforms and they sat at the edge of the group, hugging their knees and listening in growing excitement. Why, they didn't *have* to worry about what they looked like, what wasn't going to matter in the new scheme of things. It didn't *matter* whether or not they had dates. By the time the new order was established, they weren't even going to *want* dates. Although they would rather die than admit it, they all felt a little pang at this. Goodbye hope chest, goodbye wedding trip to Nassau and picture in the papers in the long white veil. Patsy, who wanted to be a corporation lawyer, thought: *Why can't I have it* all.

Now that his mother was dead and he didn't need to sell vacuum cleaners any more, Andy Ellis was thrown back on his own resources. He spent three hours in the shower and three days sleeping, and on the fourth day he emerged to find out his girl had left him for the koto player across the hall. "Well shit," he said, and wandered into the street.

He had only been asleep for three days but everything was subtly different. The people in the corner market were mostly men, stocking up on TV dinners and chunky soups or else buying cooking wines and herbs, kidneys, beef liver and tripe. The usual girl was gone from the checkout counter, the butcher was running the register instead, and when Andy asked about it Freddy the manager said, "She joined up."

"Are you kidding?"

"Some girl scout camp up at Ferguson's. The tails revolt."

Just then a Jeep sped by in the street outside, there was a crash and they both hit the floor, rising to their elbows after the object that had shattered the front window did not explode. It was a rock with a note attached. Andy picked his way through the glass to retrieve it. It read:

WE WILL BURY YOU

"See?" Freddy said, ugly and vindictive. "See? See?"

The local hospital admitted several cases of temporary blindness in men who had been attacked by night with women's deodorant spray.

All over town the men whose wives remained lay next to them in growing unease. Although they all feigned sleep, they were aware that the stillness was too profound: the women were thinking.

The women trashed a porn movie house. Among them was the wife of the manager, who said, as she threw an open can of film over the balcony, watching it unroll, "I'm doing this for us."

So it had begun. For the time being, Rap and her cadre, who were in charge of the military operation, intended to satisfy themselves with guerrilla tactics; so far, nobody had been able to link the sniping and materiel bombing with the women on the hill, but they all knew it was only a matter of time before the first police cruiser came up to Ellen Ferguson's gate with a search warrant, and they were going to have to wage open war.

By this time one of the back pastures had been converted to a rifle range, and even poor June had to spend at least one hour of every day in practice. She began to take an embarrassing pleasure in it, thinking, as she potted away:

Aha, Vic, there's a nick in your scalp. Maybe you'll remember what I look like next time you leave the house for the day.

OK, kids, I am not the maid.

All right, Sally, you and your damn career. You're still only the maid.

Then, surprisingly, *This is for you, Sheena. How dare you go around looking like that, when I have to look like this.*

This is for every rapist on the block.

By the time she fired her last shot her vision was blurred by tears. *June, you are stupid, stupid, you always have been and you know perfectly well nothing is going to make any difference.*

Two places away, Glenda saw Richard's outline in the target. She made a bullseye. *All right, damn you, pick up that toilet brush.*

Going back to camp in the truck they all sang "Up Women" and "The Internationale," and June began to feel a little better. It reminded her of the good old days at camp in middle childhood, when girls and boys played together as if there wasn't any difference. She longed for that old androgynous body, the time before sexual responsibility. Sitting next to her on the bench, Glenda sang along but her mind was at the university; she didn't know what she was going to do if she got the Guggenheim because Richard had applied without success for so long that he had given up trying. What should she do, lie about it? It would be in all the papers. She wondered how convincing she would be, saying, Shit, honey, it doesn't mean anything. She would have to give up the revolution and get back to her work; her book was only half-written, she would have to go back to juggling kids and house and work, it was going to be hard, hard. She decided finally that she would let the Guggenheim Foundation make the decision for her. She would wait until late February and then write and tell Richard where to forward her mail.

Leading the song, Rap looked at her group. Even the softest ones had calluses now, but it was going to be some time before she made real fighters out of them. She wondered why women had all buried the instinct to kill. It was those damn babies, she decided, grunt, strain, pain, *Baby*. Hand a mother a gun and tell her to kill and she will say, *After I went to all that trouble? Well, if you are going to make sacrifices you are going to have to make sacrifices*, she thought, and led them in a chorus of the battle anthem, watching to see just who did and who didn't throw herself into the last chorus, which ended: kill, kill, *kill*.

Sally was watching the smoke again. Zack said, "I wish you would come away from that window."

She kept looking for longer than he would have liked her to, and when she turned she said, "Zack, why did you marry me?"

"Couldn't live without you."

"No, really."

"Because I wanted to love you and decorate you and take care of you for the rest of your life."

"Why me?"

"I thought we could be friends for a long time."

"I guess I didn't mean why did you marry *me*, I meant, why did you *marry* me."

He looked into his palms. "I wanted you to take care of me too."

"Is that all?"

He could see she was serious and because she was not going to let go he thought for a minute and said at last, "Nobody wants to die alone."

Down the street, June Goodall's husband, Vic, had called every hospital in the county without results. The police had no reports of middle-aged housewives losing their memory in Sears or getting raped, robbed or poleaxed anywhere within the city limits. The police sergeant said, "Mr. Goodall, we've got more serious things on our minds. These bombings, for one thing, and the leaflets and the ripoffs. Do you know that women have been walking out of super-markets with full shopping carts without paying a cent?" There seemed to be a thousand cases like June's, and if the department ever got a minute for them it would have to be first come first served.

So Vic languished in his darkening house. He had managed to get the kids off to school by himself the past couple of days. He gave them money for hot lunches but they were running out of clean clothes and he could not bring himself to sort through those disgusting smelly things in the clothes hamper to run a load of wash. They had run through June's casseroles and they were going to have to start eating out; they would probably go to the Big Beef Plaza tonight, and have pizza tomorrow and chicken the next night and Chinese the next, and if June wasn't back by that time he didn't know what he was going to do because he was at his wits' end. The dishes were piling up in the kitchen and he couldn't understand why everything looked so grimy; he couldn't quite figure out why, but the toilet had begun to smell. One of these days he was going to have to try and get his mother over to clean things up a little. It was annoying, not having any clean underwear. He wished June would come back.

For the fifth straight day, Richard Thompson, Glenda's husband, opened *The French Chef* to a new recipe and prepared himself an exquisite dinner. Once it was finished he relaxed in the blissful silence. Now that Glenda was gone he was able to keep things the way he liked them; he didn't break his neck on Matchbox racers every time he went to put a little Vivaldi on the record player. It was refreshing not to have to meet Glenda's eyes, where, to his growing dissatisfaction, he perpetually measured himself. Without her demands, without the kids around to distract him, he would be able to finish his monograph on Lyly's *Euphues*. He might even begin to write his book. Setting aside Glenda's half-finished manuscript with a certain satisfaction, he cleared a space for himself at the desk and tried to begin.

Castrated, he thought half an hour later. *Her and her damned career, she has castrated me.*

He went to the phone and began calling names on his secret list. For some reason most of them weren't home, but on the fifth call he came up with Jennifer, the biology major who wanted to write poetry, and within minutes the two of them were reaffirming his masculinity on the living room rug, and if a few pages of Glenda's half-finished manuscript got mislaid in the tussle, who was there to protest? If she was going to be off there, farting around in the woods with all those women, she never would get it finished.

In the hills, the number of women had swelled, and it was apparent to Sheena, Ellen and Rap that it was time to stop hit-and-run terrorism and operate on a larger scale. They would mount a final recruiting campaign. Once that was completed, they would be ready to take their first objective. Sheena had decided the Sunnydell Shopping Center would be their base for a sweep of the entire country. They were fairly sure retaliation would be slow, and to impede it further, they had prepared an advertising campaign built on the slogan: YOU WOULDN'T SHOOT YOUR MOTHER, WOULD YOU? As soon as they could they would co-opt some television equipment and make their first nationwide telecast from Sunnydell. Volunteers would flock in from fifty states and in time the country would be theirs.

There was some difference of opinion as to what they were going to do with it. Rap was advocating a scorched-earth policy; the women would rise like phoenixes from the ashes and build a new nation from the rubble, more or less alone. Sheena raised the idea of an auxiliary made up of male sympathizers. The women would rule, but with men at hand. Margy secretly felt that both Rap and Sheena were too militant; she didn't want things to be completely different, only a little better. Ellen Ferguson wanted to annex all the land surrounding her place. She envisioned it as the capitol city of the new world. The butch sisters wanted special legislation that would outlaw contact, social or sexual, with men, with, perhaps, special provisions for social meetings with their gay brethren. Certain of the straight sisters were made uncomfortable by their association with the butch sisters and wished there were some way the battle could progress without them. At least half of these women wanted their men back, once victory was assured, and the other half were looking into ways of perpetuating the race by means of parthenogenesis, or, at worst, sperm banks and AI techniques. One highly vocal splinter group wanted mandatory sterilization for everybody, and certain extremists were demanding transsexual operations. Because nobody could agree, the women decided for the time being to skip over the issues and concentrate on the war effort itself.

By this time word had spread and the volunteers were coming in, so it was easy to ignore issues because logistics were more pressing. It was still warm enough for the extras to bunk in the fields, but winter was coming on and the women were going to have to manage food, shelters, and uniforms for an unpredictable number. There had been a temporary windfall when Rap's bunch hijacked a couple of semis filled with frozen dinners and surplus clothes, but Rap and Sheena and the others could sense the hounds of hunger and need not far away and so they worked feverishly to prepare for the invasion. Unless they could take the town by the end of the month, they were lost.

"We won't have to hurt our *fathers,* will we?" Although she was now an expert marksman and had been placed in charge of a platoon, Patsy was still not at ease with the cause.

Rap avoided her eyes. "Don't be ridiculous."

"I just couldn't do that to anybody I *loved,*" Patsy said. She reassembled her rifle, driving the bolt into place with a click.

"Don't you worry about it," Rap said. "All you have to worry about is looking good when you lead that recruiting detail."

"Okay." Patsy tossed her hair. She knew how she and her platoon looked, charging into the wind; she could feel the whole wild group around her, on the run with their heads high and their bright hair streaming. *I wish the boys at school could see,* she thought, and turned away hastily before Rap could guess what she was thinking.

I wonder if any woman academic can be happy. Glenda was on latrine detail and this always made her reflective. *Maybe if they marry garage mechanics.* In the old days there had been academic types: single, tweedy, sturdy in orthopedic shoes, but somewhere along the way these types had been supplanted by married women of every conceivable type, who pressed forward in wildly varied disciplines, having in common only the singular harried look which marked them all. The rubric was more or less set: if you were good, you always had to worry about whether you were shortchanging your family; if you weren't as good as she was, you would always have to wonder whether it was because of all the other duties: babies, meals, the house; if despite everything you turned out to be better than he was, then you had to decide whether to try and minimize it, or prepare yourself for the wise looks on the one side, on the other, his look of uncomprehending reproach. If you *were* better than he was, then why should you be wasting your time with *him?* She felt light years removed from the time when girls used to be advised to let *him* win the tennis match; everybody played to win now, but she had the uncomfortable feeling that there might never be any real victories. Whether or not you won there were too many impediments; if he had a job and you didn't, then tough; if you both had jobs but he didn't get tenure, then you had to quit and move with him to a new place. She poured Lysol into the last toilet and turned her back on it, thinking: *Maybe that's why those Hollywood marriages are always breaking up.*

Sally finished putting the children to bed and came back into the living room, where Zack was waiting for her on the couch. By this time she had heard the women's broadcasts, she was well aware of what was going on at Ellen Ferguson's place and knew as well that this was where June was, and June was so inept, so soft and incapable that she really ought to be up there helping June, helping *them;* it was a job that ought to be done, on what scale she could not be sure, but the fire was warm and Zack was waiting; he and the children, her career, were all more important than that abstraction in the hills; she had negotiated her own peace—let them take care of theirs. Settling in next to Zack, she thought: *I don't love my little pink dish mop. I don't, but everybody has to shovel some shit.* Then: *God help the sailors and poor fishermen who have to be abroad on a night like this.*

June had requisitioned a Jeep and was on her way into town to knock over the corner market, because food was already in short supply. She had on the housedress she had worn when she enlisted, and she would carry somebody's old pink coat over her arm to hide the pistol and the grenade she would use to hold her hostages at bay while the grocery boys filled up the Jeep. She had meant to go directly to her own corner market, thinking, among other things, that the manager might recognize her and tell Vic, after which, of course, he would track her back to the camp and force her to come home to him and the children. Somehow or other she went right by the market and ended up at the corner of her street.

She knew she was making a mistake but she parked and began to prowl the neighborhood. The curtains in Sally's window were drawn but the light behind them gave out a rosy glow, which called up in her longings that she could not have identified; they had very little to do with her own home, or her life with Vic; they dated, rather, from her childhood, when she had imagined marriage, had prepared herself for it with an amorphous but unshakeable idea of what it would be like.

Vic had forgotten to put out the garbage; overflowing cans crowded the back porch and one of them was overturned. Walking on self-conscious cat feet, June made her way up on the porch and peered into the kitchen: just as she had suspected, a mess. A portion of her was tempted to go in and do a swift, secret cleaning—*the phantom housewife strikes*—but the risk of being discovered was too great. Well, let him clean up his own damn messes from now on. She tiptoed back down the steps and went around the house, crunching through bushes to look into the living room. She had hoped to get a glimpse of the children, but they were already in bed. She thought about waking Juney with pebbles on her window, whispering: Don't worry, mother's all right, but she wasn't strong enough; if she saw the children she would never be able to walk away and return to camp. She assuaged herself by thinking she would come back for Juney and Victor Junior just as soon as victory was assured. The living room had an abandoned look, with dust visible and papers strewn, a chair overturned and Vic himself asleep on the couch, just another neglected object in this neglected house. Surprised at how little she felt, she shrugged and turned away. On her way back to the Jeep she did stop to right the garbage can.

The holdup went off all right; she could hear distant sirens building behind her, but so far as she knew, she wasn't followed.

The worst thing turned out to be finding Rap, Sheena, and Ellen Ferguson gathered around the stove in the main cabin; they didn't hear her come in.

" . . . so damn fat and soft," Rap was saying.

Sheena said, "You have to take your soldiers where you can find them."

Ellen said, "An army travels on its stomach."

"As soon as it's over we dump the housewives," Rap said. "Every single one."

June cleared her throat. "I've brought the food."

"Politics may make strange bedfellows," Glenda said, "but this is ridiculous."

"Have it your way," she said huffily—whoever she was—and left the way she had come in.

Patsy was in charge of the recruiting platoon, which visited the high school, and she thought the principal was really impressed when he saw that it was her. Her girls bound and gagged the faculty and held the boys at bay with M-1s while she made her pitch. She was successful but drained when she finished, pale and exhausted, and while her girls were processing the recruits (all but one percent of the girl students, as it turned out) and waiting for the bus to take them all to camp, Patsy put Marva in charge and simply drifted away, surprised to find herself in front of the sweetie ship two blocks from school. The place was empty except for Andy Ellis, who had just begun work as a counter boy.

He brought her a double dip milkshake and lingered.

She tried to wave him away with her rifle. "We don't have to pay."

"That isn't it." He yearned, drawn to her.

She couldn't help seeing how beautiful he was. "Bug off."

Andy said, "Beautiful."

She lifted her head, aglow. "Really?"

"No kidding. Give me a minute. I'm going to fall in love with you."

"You can't," she said, remembering her part in the eleventh-grade production of *Romeo and Juliet*. "I'm some kind of Montague."

"OK, then, I'll be the Capulet."

"I . . ." Patsy leaned forward over the counter so they could kiss. She drew back at the sound of a distant shot. "I have to go."

"When can I see you?"

Patsy said, "I'll sneak out tonight."

Sheena was in charge of the recruiting detail that visited Sally's neighborhood. Although she had been an obscure first-year medical student when the upheaval started, she was emerging as the heroine of the revolution. The newspapers and television newscasters all knew who she was and so Sally knew, and was undeniably flattered that she had come in person.

She and Sally met on a high level; if there is an aristocracy of achievement, then they spoke aristocrat to aristocrat. Sheena spoke of talent and obligation; she spoke of need and duty; she spoke of service. She said the women needed Sally's help, and when Sally said, Let them help themselves, she said, They can't. They were still arguing when the kids came home from school, they were still arguing when Zack came home. Sheena spoke of the common cause and a better world. She spoke once more of the relationship between gifts and service. Sally turned to Zack, murmuring, and he said:

"If you think you have to do it, then I guess you'd better do it."

She said: "The sooner I go the sooner this thing will be over."

Zack said, "I hope you're right."

Sheena stood aside so they could make their goodbyes. Sally hugged the children, and when they begged to go with her she said, "It's no place for kids."

Climbing into the truck, she looked back at Zack and thought: *I could not love thee half so much loved I not honor more.* What she said was, "I must be out of my mind."

Zack stood in the street with his arms around the kids, saying, "She'll be back soon. Some day they'll come marching down our street."

In the truck, Sheena said, "Don't worry. When we occupy, we'll see that he gets a break."

They were going so fast now that there was no jumping off the truck; the other women at the camp seemed to be so grateful to see her that she knew there would be no jumping off the truck until it was over.

June whispered, "To be perfectly honest, I was beginning to have my doubts about the whole thing, but with *you* along . . ."

They made Sally a member of the council.

The next day the women took the Sunnydell Shopping Center, which included two supermarkets, a discount house, a fast-food place and a cinema; they selected it because it was close to camp and they could change guard details with a minimum of difficulty. The markets would solve the food problem for the time being, at least.

In battle, they used M-1s, one submachine gun, and a variety of sidearms and grenades. They took the place without firing a shot.

The truth was that until this moment, the men had not taken the revolution seriously.

The men had thought: *After all, it's only women.*

They had thought: *Let them have their fun. We can stop this thing whenever we like.*

They had thought: *What difference does it make? They'll come crawling back to us.*

In this first foray the men, who were, after all, unarmed, fled in surprise. Because the women had not been able to agree upon policy, they let their vanquished enemy go; for the time being, they would take no prisoners.

They were sitting around the victory fire that night, already aware that it was chilly and when the flames burned down a bit they were going to have to go back inside. It was then, for the first time, that Sheena raised the question of allies.

She said, "Sooner or later we have to face facts. We can't make it alone."

Sally brightened, thinking of Zack. "I think you're right."

Rap leaned forward. "Are you *serious?*"

Sheena tossed her hair. "What's the matter with sympathetic men?"

"The only sympathetic man is a dead man," Rap said.

Sally rose. "Wait a minute."

Ellen Ferguson pulled her down. "Relax. All she means is, at this stage we can't afford any risks. Infiltration. Spies."

Sheena said, "We could use a few men."

Sally heard herself, *sotto voce.* "You're not kidding."

Dr. Ora Fessenden rose, in stages. She said, with force, "Look here, Sheena, if you are going to take a stance, you are going to have to take a stance."

If she had been there, Patsy would have risen to speak in favor of a men's auxiliary. As it was, she had sneaked out to meet Andy. They were down in the shadow of the conquered shopping center, falling in love.

In the command shack, much later, Sheena paced moodily. "They aren't going to be satisfied with the shopping center for long."

Sally said, "I think things are going to get out of hand."

"They can't." Sheena kept on pacing. "We have too much to do."

"Your friend Rap and the doctor are out for blood. Lord knows how many of the others are going to go along." Sally sat at the desk, doodling on the roll sheet. "Maybe you ought to dump them."

"We need muscle, Sally."

Margy, who seemed to be dusting, said, "I go along with Sally."

"No." Lory was in the corner, transcribing Sheena's remarks of the evening. "Sheena's absolutely right."

It was morning, and Ellen Ferguson paced the perimeter of the camp. "We're going to need fortifications here, and more over here."

Glenda, who followed with the clipboard, said, "What are you expecting?"

"I don't know, but I want to be ready for it."

"Shouldn't we be concentrating on *offense?*"

"Not me," Ellen said, with her feet set wide in the dirt. "This is my place. This is where I make my stand."

"Allies. That woman is a marshmallow. *Allies.*" Rap was still seething. "I think we ought to go ahead and make our play."

"We still need them," Dr. Ora Fessenden said. The two of them were squatting in the woods above the camp. "When we get strong enough, then . . ." She drew her finger across her throat. "Zzzzt."

"Dammit to hell, Ora." Rap was on her feet, punching a tree trunk. "If you're going to fight, you're going to have to kill."

"You know it and I know it," Dr. Ora Fessenden said. "Now try and tell that to the rest of the girls."

As she settled into the routine, Sally missed Zack more and more and, partly because she missed him so much, she began making a few inquiries. The consensus was that women had to free themselves from every kind of dependence, both emotional and physical; sexual demands would be treated on the level of other bodily functions, any old toilet would do.

"Hello, Ralph?"

"Yes?"

"It's me, Lory. Listen, did you read about what we did?"

"About what *who* did?"

"Stop trying to pretend you don't know. Listen, Ralph, that was us that took over out at Sunnydale. *Me.*"

"You and what army?"

"The women's army. Oh, I see, you're being sarcastic. Well listen, Ralph, I said I was going to realize myself as a person and I have. I'm a sub-lieutenant now. A sub-lieutenant, imagine."

"What about your novel you were going to write about your rotten marriage?"

"Don't pick nits. I'm Sheena's secretary now. You were holding me back, Ralph, all those years you were dragging me down. Well now I'm a free agent. Free."

"Terrific."

"Look, I have to go; we have uniform 9 inspection now and worst luck, I drew KP."

"Listen," Rap was saying to a group of intent women, "You're going along minding your own business and wham, he swoops down like the wolf upon the fold. It's the ultimate weapon."

Dr. Ora Fessenden said bitterly, "And you just try and rape him back."

Margy said, "I thought men were, you know, supposed to protect women from all that."

Annie Chandler, who had emerged as one of the militants, threw her knife into a tree. "Try and convince them it ever happened. The cops say you must have led him on."

Dr. Ora Fessenden drew a picture of the woman as a ruined city, with gestures.

"I don't know what I would do if one of them tried to . . ." Betts said to Patsy. "What would you do?"

Oh, Andy. Patsy said, "I don't know."

"There's only one thing *to* do," Rap said, with force. "Shoot on sight."

It was hard to say what their expectations had been after this first victory. There were probably almost as many expectations as there were women. A certain segment of the group was disappointed because Vic/Richard/Tom-Dick-Harry had not come crawling up the hill crying, My God how I have missed you, come home and everything will be different. Rap and the others would have wished for more carnage, and as the days passed the thirst for blood heaped dust in their mouths. Sheena was secretly disappointed that there had not been wider coverage of the battle in the press and on nationwide TV. The mood in the camp after that first victory was one of anticlimax, indefinable but growing discontent.

Petty fights broke out in the rank and file.

There arose, around this time, some differences between the rank-and-file women, some of whom had children, and the Mothers' Escadrille, an elite corps of women who saw themselves as professional mothers. As a group, they looked down on people like Glenda, who sent their children off to the day care compound. The Mothers' Escadrille would admit, when pressed, that their goal in banding together was the eventual elimination of the role of the man in the family, for man, with his incessant demands, interfered with the primary function of the mother. Still, they had to admit that, since they had no other profession, they were going to have to be assured some kind of financial support in the ultimate scheme of things. They also wanted more respect from the other women, who seemed to look down on them because they lacked technical or professional skills, and so they conducted their allotted duties in a growing atmosphere of hostility.

It was after a heated discussion with one of the mothers that Glenda, suffering guilt pangs and feelings of inadequacy, went down to the day care compound to see her own children. She picked them out at once, playing in the middle of a tangle of preschoolers, but she saw with a pang that Bobby was reluctant to leave the group to come and talk to her, and even after she said, "It's Mommy," it took Tommy a measurable number of seconds before he recognized her.

The price, she thought in some bitterness. *I hope in the end it turns out to be worth the price.*

Betts had tried running across the field both with and without her bra, and except for the time when she wrapped herself in the Ace bandage, she definitely bounced. At the moment nobody in the camp was agreed as to whether it was a good or a bad thing to bounce; it was either another one of those things the world at large was going to have to, by God, learn to ignore, or else it was a sign of weakness. Either way, it was uncomfortable, but so was the Ace bandage uncomfortable.

Sally was drawn toward home but at the same time, looking around at the disparate women and their growing discontent, she knew she ought to stay on until the revolution had put itself in order. The women were unable to agree what the next step would be, or to consolidate their gains, and so she met late into the night with Sheena, and walked around among the others. She had the feeling that she could help, that whatever her own circumstance, the others were so patently miserable that she must help.

"Listen," said Zack, when Sally called him to explain, "it's no picnic being a guy, either."

The fear of rape had become epidemic. Perhaps because there had been no overt assault on the women's camp, no army battalions, not even any police cruisers, the women expected more subtle and more brutal retaliation. The older women were outraged because some of the younger women said what difference did it make? If you were going to make it, what did the circumstances matter? Still, the women talked about it around the campfire and at last it was agreed that regardless of individual reactions, for ideological reasons it was important that it be made impossible; the propaganda value to the enemy would be too great, and so, at Rap's suggestion, each woman was instructed to carry her hand weapon at all times and to shoot first and ask questions later.

Patsy and Andy Ellis were finding more and more ways to be together, but no matter how much they were together it didn't seem to be enough. Since Andy's hair was long, they thought briefly of disguising him as a woman and getting him into camp, but a number of things: whiskers, figure, musculature, would give him away and Patsy decided it would be too dangerous.

"Look, I'm in love with you," Andy said. "Why don't you run away?"

"Oh, I couldn't do that," Patsy said, trying to hide herself in his arms. "And besides . . ."

He hid his face in her hair. "Besides nothing."

"No, really. Besides. Everybody has guns now, everybody has different feelings, but they all hate deserters. We have a new policy."

"They'd never find us."

She looked into Andy's face. "Don't you want to hear about the new policy?"

"OK, what?"

"About deserters." She spelled it out, more than a little surprised at how far she had come. "It's hunt down and shave and kill."

"They wouldn't really do that."

"We had the first one last night, this poor old lady about forty. She got homesick for her family and tried to run away."

Andy was still amused. "They shaved all her hair off?"

"That wasn't all," Patsy said. "When they got finished they really did it. Firing squad, the works."

Although June would not have been sensitive to it, there were diverging feelings in the camp about who did what, and what there was to do. All she knew was she was sick and tired of working in the day care compound and when she went to Sheena and complained, Sheena, with exquisite sensitivity, put her in charge of the detail that guarded the shopping center. It was a temporary assignment but it gave June a chance to put on a cartridge belt and all the other paraphernalia of victory, so she cut an impressive figure for Vic, when he came along.

"It's me, honey, don't you know me?"

"Go away," she said with some satisfaction. "No civilians allowed."

"Oh for God's sake."

To their mutual astonishment, she raised her rifle. "Bug off, fella."

"You don't really think you can get away with this."

"Bug off or I'll shoot."

"We're just letting you do this, to get it out of your system." Vic moved as if to relieve her of the rifle. "If it makes you feel a little better . . ."

"This is your last warning."

"Listen," Vic said, a study in male outrage, "one step too far and, *tschoom,* federal troops."

She fired a warning shot so he left.

Glenda was a little sensitive about the fact that various husbands had found ways to smuggle in messages, some had even come looking for their wives, but not Richard. One poor bastard had been shot when he came in too close to the fire; they heard an outcry and a thrashing in the bushes but when they looked for him the next morning there was no body, so he must have dragged himself away. There had been notes in food consignments and one husband had hired a skywriter, but so far she had neither word nor sign from Richard, and she wasn't altogether convinced she cared. He seemed to have drifted off into time past along with her job, her students, and her book. Once her greatest hope had been to read her first chapter at the national psychological conference; now she wondered whether there would even be any more conferences. If she and the others were successful, that would break down, along with a number of other things. Still, in the end she would have had her definitive work on the women's revolution, but so far the day-to-day talk had been so engrossing that she hadn't had a minute to begin. Right now, there was too much to do.

They made their first nationwide telecast from a specifically erected podium in front of the captured shopping center. For various complicated reasons the leaders made Sally speak first, and, as they had anticipated, she espoused the moderate view: this was a matter of service, women were going to have to give up a few things to help better the lot of their sisters. Once the job was done everything would be improved, but not really different.

Sheena came next, throwing back her bright hair and issuing the call to arms. The mail she drew would include several spirited letters from male volunteers who were already in love with her and would follow her anywhere; because the women had pledged never to take allies, these letters would be destroyed before they ever reached her.

Dr. Ora Fessenden was all threats, fire and brimstone. Rap took up where she left off.

"We're going to fight until there's not a man left standing . . ."

Annie Chandler yelled, "Right on."

Margy was trying to speak. " . . . just a few concessions."

Rap's eyes glittered. "Only sisters, and you guys . . ."

Ellen Ferguson said, "Up, women, out of slavery."

Rap's voice rose. " . . . you guys are going to burn."

Sally was saying, " . . . reason with you."

Rap hissed, "Bury you."

It was hard to say which parts of these messages reached the viewing public, as the women all interrupted and overrode each other and the cameramen concentrated on Sheena, who was to become the sign and symbol of the revolution. None of the women on the platform seemed to be listening to any of the others, which may have been just as well; the only reason they had been able to come this far together was because nobody ever did.

The letters began to come.

"Dear Sheena, I would like to join, but I already have nine children and now I am pregnant again . . ."

"Dear Sheena, I am a wife and mother but I will throw it all over in an instant if you will only glance my way . . ."

"Dear Sheena, our group has occupied the town hall in Gillespie, Indiana, but we are running out of ammo and the water supply is low. Several of the women have been stricken with plague, and we are running out of food . . ."

"First I made him lick my boots and then I killed him but now I have this terrible problem with the body, the kids don't want me to get rid of him . . ."

"Who do you think you are, running this war when you don't even know what you are doing, what you have to do is kill every last damn one of them and the ones you don't kill you had better cut off their Things . . ."

"Sheena, baby, if you will only give up this half-assed revolution you and I can make beautiful music together. I have signed this letter Maud to escape the censors but if you look underneath the stamp you can see who I really am."

The volunteers were arriving in dozens. The first thing was that there was not housing for all of them; there was not equipment, and so the woman in charge had to cut off enlistments at a certain point and send the others back to make war in their own hometowns.

The second thing was that, with the increase in numbers, there was an increasing bitterness about the chores. Nobody wanted to do them; in secret truth nobody ever had, but so far the volunteers had all borne it, up to a point, because they sincerely believed that in the new order there would be no chores.

Now they understood that the more people there were banded together, the more chores there would be. Laundry and garbage were piling up. At some point around the time of the occupation of the shopping center, the women had begun to understand that no matter what they accomplished, there would always be ugly things to do: the chores, and now, because there seemed to be so *much* work, there were terrible disagreements as to who was supposed to do what, and as a consequence they had all more or less stopped doing any of it.

Meals around the camp were catch as catch can.

The time was approaching when nobody in the camp would have clean underwear.

The latrines were unspeakable.

The children were getting out of hand; some of them were forming packs and making raids of their own, so that the quartermaster never had any clear idea of what she would find in the storehouse. Most of the women in the detail that had been put in charge of the day care compound were fed up.

By this time Sheena was a national figure; her picture was on the cover of both newsmagazines in the same week and there were nationally distributed lines of sweatshirts and tooth glasses bearing her picture and her name. She received love mail and hate mail in such quantity that Lory, who had joined the women to realize her potential as an individual, had to give up her other duties to concentrate on Sheena's mail. She would have to admit that it was better than KP, and besides, if Sheena went on to better things, maybe she would get to go along.

The air of dissatisfaction grew. Nobody agreed any more, not even all those who had agreed to agree for the sake of the cause. Fights broke out like flash fires; some women were given to sulks and inexplicable silences, others to blows and helpless tears quickly forgotten. On advice from Sally, Sheena called a council to try and bring everybody together, but it got off on the wrong foot.

Dr. Ora Fessenden said, "Are we going to sit around on our butts, or what?"

Sheena said, "National opinion is running in our favor. We have to consolidate our gains."

Rap said, "Gains hell. What kind of war is this? Where are the scalps?"

Sheena drew herself up. "We are not Amazons."

Rap said, "That's a crock of shit," and she and Dr. Ora Fessenden stamped out.

"Rape," Rap screamed, running from the far left to the far right and then making a complete circuit of the clearing. "Rape," she shouted, taking careful note of who came running and who didn't. "Raaaaaaaaape."

Dr. Ora Fessenden rushed to her side, the figure of outraged womanhood. They both watched until a suitable number of women had assembled and then she said, in stentorian tones, "We cannot let this go unavenged."

"My God," Sheena said, looking at the blackened object in Rap's hand. "What are you doing with that thing?"

Blood-smeared and grinning, Rap said, "When you're trying to make a point, you have to go ahead and make your point." She thrust her trophy into Sheena's face.

Sheena averted her eyes quickly; she thought it was an ear. "That's supposed to be a *rhetorical* point."

"Listen, baby, this world doesn't give marks for good conduct."

Sheena stiffened. "You keep your girls in line or you're finished."

Rap was smoldering; she pushed her face up to Sheena's, saying, "You can't do without us and you know it."

"If we have to, we'll learn."

"Aieeee." One of Rap's cadre had taken the trophy from her and tied it on a string; now she ran through the camp swinging it around her head, and dozens of throats opened to echo her shout. "Aieeeeee."

Patsy and Andy were together in the bushes near the camp; proximity to danger made their pleasure more intense. Andy said, "Leave with me."

She said, "I can't. I told you what they do to deserters."

"They'll never catch us."

"You don't know these women," Patsy said. "Look, Andy, you'd better go."

"Just a minute more." Andy buried his face in her hair. "Just a little minute more."

"Rape," Rap shouted again, running through the clearing with her voice raised like a trumpet. "Raaaaaaaape."

Although she knew it was a mistake, Sally had sneaked away to see Zack and the children. The camp seemed strangely deserted, and nobody was there to sign out the Jeep she took. She had an uncanny intimation of trouble at a great distance, but she shook it off and drove to her house. She would have expected barricades and guards: state of war, but the streets were virtually empty and she reached her neighborhood without trouble.

Zack and the children embraced her and wanted to know when she was coming home.

"Soon, I think. They're all frightened of us now."

Zack said, "I'm not so sure."

"There doesn't seem to be any resistance."

"Oh," he said, "they've decided to let you have the town."

"What did I tell you?"

"Sop," he said. "You can have anything you want. Up to a point."

Sally was thinking of Rap and Dr. Ora Fessenden. "What if we take more?"

"Wipeout," Zack said. "You'll see."

"Oh Lord," she said, vaulting into the Jeep. "Maybe it'll be over sooner than I thought."

She was already too late. She saw the flames shooting skyward as she came out of the drive.

"It's Flowermont."

Because she had to make sure, she wrenched the Jeep in that direction and rode to the garden apartments; smoke filled the streets for blocks around.

Looking at the devastation, Sally was reminded of Indian massacres in the movies of her childhood: the smoking ruins, the carnage, the moans of the single survivor who would bubble out his story in her arms. She could not be sure about the bodies: whether there were any, whether there were as many as she thought, but she was sure those were charred corpses in the rubble. Rap and Dr. Ora Fessenden had devised a flag and hoisted it from a tree: the symbol of the women's movement, altered to suit their mood—the crudely executed fist reduced to clenched bones and surrounded by flames. The single survivor died before he could bubble out his story in her arms.

In the camp, Rap and Dr. Ora Fessenden had a victory celebration around the fire. They had taken unspeakable trophies in their raid and could not understand why many of the women refused to wear them.

Patsy and Andy, in the bushes, watched with growing alarm. Even from their safe distance, Andy was fairly sure he saw what he thought he saw and he whispered, "Look, we've got to get out of here."

"Not now," Patsy said, pulling him closer. "Tonight. The patrols."

By now the little girls had been brought up from the day care compound and they had joined the dance, their fat cheeks smeared with blood. Rap's women were in heated discussion with the Mothers' Escadrille about the disposition of the boy children: would they be destroyed or reared as slaves? While they were talking, one of the mothers who had never felt at home in any faction sneaked down to the compound and freed the lot of them. Now she was running around in helpless tears, flapping her arms and sobbing broken messages, but no matter what she said to the children, she couldn't seem to get any of them to flee.

Sheena and her lieutenant, Margy, and Lory, her secretary, came out of the command shack at the same moment Sally arrived in camp; she rushed to join them, and together they extracted Rap and Dr. Ora Fessenden from the dance for a meeting of the council.

When they entered the shack, Ellen Ferguson hung up the phone in clattering haste and turned to confront them with a confusing mixture of expressions; Sally thought the foremost one was probably guilt.

Sally waited until they were all silent and then said, "The place is surrounded. They let me through to bring the message. They have tanks."

Ellen Ferguson said, "They just delivered their ultimatum. Stop the raids and pull back to camp or they'll have bombers level this place."

"Pull back, hell," Rap said.

Dr. Ora Fessenden shook a bloody fist. "We'll show them."

"We'll fight to the death."

Ellen said, quietly, "I already agreed."

Down at the main gate, Marva, who was on guard duty, leaned across the barbed wire to talk to the captain of the tank detail. She thought he was kind of cute.

"Don't anybody panic," Rap was saying. "We can handle this thing. We can fight them off."

"We can fight them in the hedgerows," Dr. Ora Fessenden said in rising tones. "We can fight them in the ditches, we can hit them with everything we've got . . ."

"Not from here you can't."

"We can burn and bomb and kill and . . . What did you say?"

"I said, not from here." Because they were all staring, Ellen Ferguson covered quickly, saying, "I mean, if I'm going to be of any value to the movement, I have to have this place in good condition."

Sheena said quietly, "That's not what you mean."

Ellen was near tears. "All right, dammit. This place is all I have."

"My God," Annie Chandler shrieked. "Rape." She parted the bushes to reveal Patsy and Andy, who hugged each other in silence. "Rape," Annie screamed, and everybody who could hear above the din came running. "Kill the bastard, rape, rape, rape."

Patsy rose to her feet and drew Andy up with her, shouting to make herself heard. "I said, it isn't rape."

Rap and Dr. Ora Fessenden were advancing on Ellen Ferguson. "You're not going to compromise us. We'll kill you first."

"Oh," Ellen said, backing away. "That's another thing. They wanted the two of you. I had to promise we'd send you out."

The two women lunged, and then retreated, mute with fury. Ellen had produced a gun from her desk drawer and now she had them covered.

"Son of a bitch," Rap said. "Son of a bitch."

"Kill them."

"Burn them."

"Hurt them."

"Make an example of them."

"I love you, Patsy."

"Oh, Andy, I love you."

Sally said softly, "So it's all over."

"Only parts of it," Ellen said. "It will never really be over, as long as there are women left to fight. We'll be better off without these two and their cannibals; we can retrench and make a new start."

"I guess this is as good a time as any." Sheena got to her feet. "I might as well tell you, I'm splitting."

They turned to face her, Ellen being careful to keep the gun on Dr. Ora Fessenden and Rap.

"You're what?"

"I can do a hell of a lot more good on my new show. Prime time, nightly, nationwide TV."

Rap snarled, "The hell you say."

"Look, Rap, I'll interview you."

"Stuff it."

"Think what I can do for the movement. I can reach sixty million people, you'll see."

Ellen Ferguson said, with some satisfaction, "That's not really what you mean."

"Maybe it isn't. It's been you, you, you all this time." Sheena picked up her clipboard, her notebooks and papers; Lory and Margy both moved as if to follow her but she rebuffed them with a single sweep of her arm. "Well, it's high time I started thinking about me."

Outside, the women had raised a stake and now Patsy and Andy were lashed to it, standing back to back.

In the shack, Rap and Dr. Ora Fessenden had turned as one and advanced on Ellen Ferguson, pushing the gun aside.

The good doctor said, "I knew you wouldn't have the guts to shoot. You never had any guts."

Ellen cried out, "Sheena, help me."

But Sheena was already in the doorway, and she hesitated for only a moment, saying, "Listen, it's *sauve qui peut* in this day and time, sweetie, and the sooner you realize it, the better."

Rap finished pushing Ellen down and took the gun. She stood over her victim for a minute, grinning. "In the battle of the sexes, there are only allies." Then she put a bullet through Ellen's favorite moose head so Ellen would have something to remember her by.

The women had collected twigs and they were just about to set fire to Patsy and Andy when Sheena came out, closely followed by Dr. Ora Fessenden and a warlike Rap.

Everybody started shouting at once and in the imbroglio that followed, Patsy and Andy escaped. They would surface years later in a small town in Minnesota, with an ecologically alarming number of children; they would both be able to pursue their chosen careers in the law because they worked hand in hand to take care of all the children and the house, and they would love each other until they died.

Ellen Ferguson sat with her elbows on her knees and her head drooping, saying, "I can't believe it's all over, after I worked so hard, I gave so much . . ."

Sally said, "It isn't over. Remember what you said, as long as there are women, there will be a fight."

"But we've lost our leaders."

"You could . . ."

"No, I couldn't."

"Don't worry, there are plenty of others."

"As Sally spoke, the door opened and Glenda stepped in to take Sheena's place.

When the melee in the clearing was over, Dr. Ora Fessenden and Rap had escaped with their followers. They knew the lay of the land and so they were able to elude the troop concentration, which surrounded the camp, and began to lay plans to regroup and fight another day.

A number of women, disgusted by the orgy of violence, chose to pack their things and go. The Mothers' Escadrille deserted *en masse,* taking their children and a few children who didn't even belong to them.

Ellen said, "You're going to have to go down there and parley. I'm not used to talking to men."

And so Sally found herself going down to the gate to conduct negotiations.

She said, "The two you wanted got away. The rest of them—I mean us—are acting in good faith." She lifted her chin. "If you want to go ahead and bomb anyway, you'll have to go ahead and bomb."

The captain lifted her and set her on the hood of the Jeep. He was grinning. "Shit, little lady, we just wanted to throw a scare into you."

"You don't understand." She wanted to get down off the hood but he had propped his arms on either side of her. She knew she ought to be furious, but instead she kept thinking how much she missed Zack. Speaking with as much dignity as she could under the circumstances, she outlined the women's complaints; she already knew it was hopeless to list them as demands.

"Don't you worry about a thing, honey." He lifted her down and gave her a slap on the rump to speed her on her way. "Everything is going to be real different from now on."

"I bet."

Coming back up the hill to camp, she saw how sad everything looked, and she could not for the life of her decide whether it was because the women who had been gathered here had been inadequate in the cause or whether it was, rather, that the cause itself had been insufficiently identified; she suspected that they had come up against the human condition, failed to recognize it and so tried to attack a single part, which seemed to involve attacking the only allies they would ever have. As for the specific campaign, as far as she could tell, it was possible to change some of the surface or superficial details but once that was done things were still going to be more or less the way they were, and all the best will in the world would not make any real difference.

In the clearing, Lory stood at Glenda's elbow. "Of course you're going to need a lieutenant."

Glenda said, "I guess so."

Ellen Ferguson was brooding over a row of birches that had been trashed during the struggle. If she could stake them back up in time, they might re-root.

June said, "OK, I'm going to be mess sergeant."

Margy said, "The hell you will," and pushed her in the face.

Glenda said, thoughtfully, "Maybe we could mount a Lysistrata campaign."

Lory snorted. "If their wives won't do it, there are plenty of girls who will."

Zack sent a message:

WE HAVE TO HELP EACH OTHER.

Sally sent back:

I KNOW.

Before she went home, Sally had to say goodbye to Ellen Ferguson.

Ellen's huge, homely face sagged. "Not you too."

Sally looked at the desultory groups policing the wreckage, at the separate councils convening in every corner. "I don't know why I came. I guess I thought we could really *do* something."

Ellen made a half-turn, taking in the command shack, the compound, the women who remained. "Isn't this enough?"

"I have to get on with my *life*."

Ellen said, "This is mine."

"Oh, Vic, I've been so stupid." June was sobbing in Vic's arms. She was also lying in her teeth but she didn't care, she was sick of the revolution and she was going to have to go through this formula before Vic would allow her to resume her place at his kitchen sink. The work was still boring and stupid but at least there was less of it than there had been at camp; her bed was softer, and since it was coming on winter, she was always grateful for the storm sashes, which Vic put up every November, and the warmth of the oil burner, which he took apart and cleaned with his own hands every fall.

Sally found her house in good order, thanks to Zack, but there were several weeks' work piled up in her studio, and she had lost a couple of commissions. She opened her drawer to discover, with a smile, that Zack had washed at least one load of underwear with something red.

"I think we do better together," Zack said.

Sally said, "We always have."

In the wake of fraternization with the military guard detail, Marva discovered she was pregnant. She knew what Dr. Ora Fessenden said she was supposed to do, but she didn't think she wanted to.

As weeks passed, the women continued to drift away. "It's nice here and all," Betts said apologetically, "but there's a certain *je ne sais quoi* missing; I don't know what it is, but I'm going back in there and see if I can find it."

Glenda said, "Yeah, well. So long as there is a yang, I guess there is going to have to be a yin."

"Don't you mean, so long as there is a yin, there is going to have to be a yang?"

Glenda looked in the general direction of town, knowing there was nothing there for her to go back to. "I don't know what I mean any more."

Activity and numbers at the camp had decreased to the point where federal troops could be withdrawn. They were needed, as it turned out, to deal with wildcat raids in another part of the state. Those who had been on the scene came back with reports of incredible viciousness.

Standing at their windows in the town, the women could look up to the hills and see the camp fire still burning, but as the months wore on, fewer and fewer of them looked and the column of smoke diminished in size because the remaining women were running out of volunteers whose turn it was to feed the fire.

Now that it was over, things went on more or less as they had before.

—*Nova 4*, 1974

Winter

It was late fall when he come to us, there was a scum of ice on all the puddles and I could feel the winter cold and fearsome in my bones, the hunger inside me was already uncurling, it would pace through the first of the year but by spring it would be raging like a tiger, consuming me until the thaw when Maude could hunt again and we would get the truck down the road to town. I was done canning but I got the tomatoes we had hanging in the cellar and I canned some more; Maude went out and brought back every piece of meat she could shoot and all the grain and flour and powdered milk she could bring in one truckload, we had to lay in everything we could before the snow came and sealed us in. The week he come Maude found a jackrabbit stone dead in the road, it was frozen with its feet sticking straight up, and all the meat hanging in the cold-room had froze. Friday there was rime on the grass and when I looked out I seen footprints in the rime, I said Maude, someone is in the play-house and we went out and there he was. He was asleep in the mess of clothes we always dressed up in, he had his head on the velvet gown my mother wore to the Exposition and his feet on the satin gown she married Father in, he had pulled her feather boa around his neck and her fox fur was wrapped around his loins.

Before he come, Maude and me would pass the winter talking about how it used to be, we would call up the past between us and look at it and Maude would end by blaming me. I could of married either Lister Hoffman or Harry Mead and left this place for good if it hadn't been for you, Lizzie. I'd tell her, Hell, I never needed you. You didn't marry them because you didn't marry them, you was scared of it and you would use me for an excuse. She would get mad then. It's a lie. Have it your way, I would tell her, just to keep the peace.

We both knew I would of married the first man that asked me, but nobody would, not even with all my money, nobody would ask me because of the taint. If nobody had of known then some man might of married me, but I went down to the field with Miles Harrison once while Father was still alive, and Miles and me, we almost, except that the blackness took me, right there in front of him, and so I never did. Nobody needed to know, but then Miles saw me fall down in the field. I guess it was him that put something between my teeth so I wouldn't bite my tongue, but when I come to myself he was gone. Next time I went to town they all looked at me funny, some of them would try and face up to me and be polite but they was all jumpy, thinking would I do it right there in front of them, would I froth much, would they get hurt, as soon as was decent they would say Excuse me, I got to, anything to get out of there fast. When I run into Miles after that day he wouldn't look at me and there hasn't been a man near me since then, not in more than fifty years, but Miles and me, we almost, and I have never stopped thinking about that.

Now Father is gone and my mother is gone and even Lister Hoffman and Miles Harrison and half the town kids that used to laugh at me, they are all gone, but Maude still reproaches me, we sit after supper and she says, If it hadn't been for you I would have grandchildren now and I tell her I would of had them before ever she did because she never liked men, she would only suffer them to get children and that would be too much trouble, it would hurt. That's a lie, Lizzie, she would say, Harry and me used to . . . and I would tell her You never, but Miles and me . . . Then we would both think about being young and having people's hands on us but memory turns Maude bitter and she can never leave it at that, she says, It's all your fault, but I know in my heart that people make their lives what they want them, and all she ever wanted was to be locked in here with nobody to make demands on her, she wanted to stay in this house with me, her dried-up sister, cold and safe, and if the hunger is on her, it has come on her late.

After a while we would start to make up stuff: Once I went with a boy all the way to Portland . . . Once I danced all night and half the morning, he wanted to kiss me on the place where my elbow bends . . . We would try to spin out the winter, but even that was not enough and so we would always be left with the hunger; no matter how much we laid in, the meat was always gone before the thaw and I suppose it was really our lives we was judging but we would decide nothing in the cans looked good to us and so we would sit and dream and hunger and wonder if we would die of it, but finally the thaw would come and Maude would look at me and sigh: If only we had another chance.

Well now perhaps we will.

We found him in the playhouse, maybe it was seeing him being in the play-house, where we pretended so many times, asleep in the middle of my mother's clothes or maybe it was something of mine; there was this boy, or man, some-thing about him called up our best memories, there was promise wrote all over him. I am too old, I am all dried out, but I have never stopped thinking about that one time, and seeing that boy there, I could pretend he was Miles and I was still young. I guess he sensed us, he woke up fast and went into a crouch, maybe he had a knife, and then I guess he saw it was just two big old ladies in Army boots, he said, I run away from the Marines, I need a place to sleep.

Maude said, I don't care what you need, you got to get out of here, but when he stood up he wobbled. His hair fell across his head like the hair on a boy I used to know and I said, Maude, why don't you say yes to something just this once.

He had on this denim shirt and pants like no uniform I ever seen and he was saying, Two things happened, I found out I might have to shoot somebody in the war and then I made a mistake and they beat me so I cut out of there. He smiled and he looked open. I stared hard at Maude and Maude finally looked at me and said, All right, come up to the house and get something to eat.

He said his name was Arnold but when we asked him Arnold what, he said Never mind. He was in the kitchen by then, he had his head bent over a bowl of oatmeal and some biscuits I had made, and when I looked at Maude she was watching the way the light slid across his hair. When we told him our names he said, You are both beautiful ladies, and I could see Maude's hands go up to her face and she went into her room and when she came back I saw she had put color on her cheeks. While we was alone he said how good the biscuits was and wasn't that beautiful silver, did I keep it polished all by myself and I said well yes, Maude brings in supplies but I am in charge of the house and making all the food. She come back then and saw us with our heads together and said to Arnold, I guess you'll be leaving soon.

I don't know, he said, they'll be out looking for me with guns and dogs.

That's no never mind of ours.

I never done anything bad in the Marines, we just had different ideas.

We both figured it was something worse but he looked so sad and tired and besides, it was nice to have him to talk to, he said, I just need a place to hole up for a while.

Maude said, You could always go back to your family.

He said, They never wanted me. They was always mean-hearted, not like you.

I took her aside and said, It wouldn't kill you to let him stay on. Maude, it's time we had a little life around here.

There won't be enough food for three.

He won't stay long. Besides, he can help you with the chores.

She was looking at his bright hair again, she said, like it was all my doing, If you want to let him stay I guess we can let him stay.

He was saying, I could work for my keep.

All right, I said, you can stay on until you get your strength.

My heart jumped. A man, I thought. A man. How can I explain it? It was like being young, having him around. I looked at Maude and saw some of the same things in her eyes, hunger and hope, and I thought, *You are ours now, Arnold, you are all ours. We will feed you and take care of you and when you want to wander we will let you wander, but we will never let you go.*

Just until things die down a little, he was saying.

Maude had a funny grin. Just until things died down.

Well it must of started snowing right after dark that afternoon, because when we all waked up the house was surrounded. I said, Good thing you got the meat in, Maude, and she looked out, it was still blowing snow and it showed no signs of stopping; she looked out and said, I guess it is.

He was still asleep, he slept the day through except he stumbled down at dusk and dreamed over a bowl of my rabbit stew, I turned to the sink and when I looked back the stew was gone and the biscuits was gone and all the extra in the pot was gone, I had a little flash of fright, it was all disappearing too fast. Then Maude come over to me and hissed, The food, he's eating all the food and I looked at his brown hands and his tender neck and I said, It don't matter, Maude, he's young and strong and if we run short he can go out into the snow and hunt. When we looked around next time he was gone, he had dreamed his way through half a pie and gone right back to bed.

Next morning he was up before the light, we sat together around the kitchen table and I thought how nice it was to have a man in the house, I could look at him and imagine anything I wanted. Then he got up and said, Look, I want to thank you for everything, I got to get along now, and I said, You can't, and he said, I got things to do, I been here long enough, but I told him You can't, and took him over to the window. The sun was up by then and there it was, snow almost to the window ledges, like we have every winter, and all the trees was shrouded, we could watch the sun take the snow and make it sparkle and I said, Beautiful snow, beautiful, and he only shrugged and said, I guess I'll have to wait till it clears off some. I touched his shoulder. I guess you will. I knew not to tell him it would never clear off, not until late spring; maybe he guessed, anyway he looked so sad I gave him Father's silver snuffbox to cheer him up.

He would divide his time between Maude and me, he played Rook with her and made her laugh so hard she gave him her pearl earrings and the brooch Father brought her back from Quebec. I gave him Grandfather's diamond stickpin because he admired it, and for Christmas we gave him the cameos and Father's gold-headed cane. Maude got the flu over New Year's and Arnold and me spent New Year's Eve together, I mulled some wine and he hung up some of Mama's jewelry from the center light, and touched it and made it twirl. We lit candles and played the radio, New Year's Eve in Times Square and somebody's Make-believe Ballroom, I went to pour another cup of wine and his hand was on mine on the bottle, I knew my lips was red for once and next day I gave him Papa's fur-lined coat.

I guess Maude suspected there was something between us, she looked pinched and mean when I went in with her broth at lunch, she said, Where were you at breakfast and I said, Maude, it's New Year's Day, I thought I would like to sleep in for once. You were with him. I thought, *If she wants to think that about me, let her,* and I let my eyes go sleepy and I said, We had to see the New Year in, didn't we? She was out of bed in two days, I have never seen anybody get up so fast after the flu. I think she couldn't stand us being where she couldn't see what we was up to every living minute.

Then I got sick and I knew what torture it must have been for her just laying there, I would call Maude and I would call her, and sometimes she would come and sometimes she wouldn't come and when she finally did look in on me I would say, Maude, where have you been, and she would only giggle and not answer. There was meat cooking all the time, roasts and chops and chicken fricassee, when I said Maude, you're going to use it up, she would only smile and say, I just had to show him who's who in the kitchen, he tells me I'm a better cook than you ever was. After a while I got up, I had to even if I was dizzy and like to throw up, I had to get downstairs where I could keep an eye on them. As soon as I was up to it I made a roast of venison that would put hair on an egg and after that we would vie with each other in the kitchen, Maude and me. Once I had my hand on the skillet handle and she come over and tried to take it away, she was saying, Let me serve it up for him, I said, You're a fool, Maude, I cooked this, and she hissed at me, through the steam, It won't do you no good, Lizzie, it's me he loves, and I just pushed her away and said, You goddam fool, he loves me, and I give him my amethysts just to prove it. A couple of days later I couldn't find neither of them nowhere, I thought I heard noises up in the back room and I went up and if they was in there they wouldn't answer, the door was locked and they wouldn't say nothing, not even when I knocked and knocked and knocked. So the next day I took him up in my room and we locked the door and I told him a story about every piece in my jewel box, even the cheap ones, when Maude tapped and whined outside the door we would just shush, and when we did come out and she said, All right, Lizzie, what was you doing in there, I only giggled and wouldn't tell.

She shouldn't of done it, we was all sitting around the table after dinner and he looked at me hard and said, You know something, Arnold, I wouldn't get too close to Lizzie, she has fits. Arnold only tried to look like it didn't matter, but after Maude went to bed I went down to make sure it was all right. He was still in the kitchen, whittling, and when I tried to touch his hand he pulled away.

I said, Don't be scared, I only throw one in a blue moon.

He said, That don't matter.

Then what's the matter?

I don't know, Miss Lizzie, I just don't think you trust me.

Course I trust you, Arnold, don't I give you everything?

He just looked sad. Everything but trust.

I owe you so much, Arnold, you make me feel so young.

He just smiled for me then. You look younger, Miss Lizzie, you been getting younger every day I been here.

You did it.

If you let me, I could make you really young.

Yes, Arnold, yes.

But I have to know you trust me.

Yes, Arnold.

So I showed him where the money was. By then it was past midnight and we was both tired, he said, Tomorrow, and I let him go off to get his rest.

I don't know what roused us both and brought us out into the hall but I bumped into Maude at dawn, we was both standing in our nightgowns like two ghosts. We crept downstairs together and there was light in the kitchen, the place where we kept the money was open, empty, and there was a crack of light in the door to the cold room. I remember looking through and thinking, The meat is almost gone. Then we opened the door a crack wider and there he was, he had made a sledge, he must of sneaked down there and worked on it every night. It was piled with stuff, and now he had the door to the outside open, he had dug himself a ramp out of the snow and he was lashing some homemade snowshoes on his feet, in another minute he would cut out of there.

When he heard us he turned.

I had the shotgun and Maude had the ax.

We said, We don't care about the stuff, Arnold. How could we tell him it was our youth he was taking away?

He looked at us, walleyed. You can have it all, just let me out.

He was going to get away in another minute, so Maude let him have it with the ax.

Afterwards we closed the way to the outside and stood there and looked at each other, I couldn't say what was in my heart so I only looked at Maude, we was both sad, sad, I said, The food is almost gone.

Maude said, Everything is gone. We'll never make it to spring.

I said, We have to make it to spring.

Maude looked at him laying there. You know what he told me? He said, I can make you young.

Me too, I said. There was something in his eyes that made me believe it.

Maude's eyes was glittering, she said, The food is almost gone.

I knew what she meant, he was going to make us young. I don't know how it will work in us, but he is going to make us young, it will be as if the fits had never took me, never in all them years. Maude was looking at me, waiting, and after a minute I looked square at her and I said, I know.

So we et him.

—London, *Winter's Tales,* 1969

The Weremother

Often in that period in her life, when she least expected it, she would feel the change creeping over her. It would start in the middle of an intense conversation with her younger son or with her daughter, behind whose newly finished face she saw her past and intimations of her future flickering silently, waiting to break cover. Black hairs would begin creeping down the backs of her hands and claws would spring from her fingertips. She could feel her lip lifting over her incisors as she snarled: "Can't you remember *anything?*" or: "Stop picking your face."

She had to concentrate on standing erect then, determined to defeat her own worst instincts just once more, but she knew it was only a matter of time before she fell into the feral crouch. In spite of her best efforts she would end up loping on all fours, slinking through alleys and stretching her long belly as she slid over fences; she would find herself hammering on her older son's window, or deviling him on the phone: Yes we are adults together, we are even friends, but do you look decent for the office? Even when he faced her without guile, as he would any ordinary person, she could feel the howl bubbling in her throat: Did you *remember to use your face medicine?*

Beware, she is never far from us; she will stalk us to the death, wreaking her will and spoiling our best moments, threatening our future, devouring our past. Beware the weremother when the moon is high and you and the one you love are sinking to earth; look sharp or she will spring upon you; she will tear you apart to save you if she has to, bloodying tooth and claw in the inadvertency of love.

Lash me to the closet pole she cried, knowing what was coming, but she was thinking what might happen to the older son if he married the wrong girl, whom he is in love with. Who would iron his shirts? Would she know how to take care of him? It's his decision now; he's a grown man and we are adults together, but I am his mother, and older. I have a longer past than he does and can divine the future.

This is for your own good.

She and the man she married were at a party years before they even had children. Someone introduced the identity game. Tell who you are in three sentences. After you finished, the woman who started the game diagnosed you. She said you valued what you put first. Somebody began, My name is Martha, I'm a mother. She remembers looking at that alien woman, thinking, A mother? Is that all you want to be? What does that make of the man sitting next to you? She thinks: *I know who I am. I know my marriage. I know my ambitions. I am those three things and by the way I am a mother. I would never list it first in this or any other game.*

On the other hand, she can't shake the identity.

Here is an old story she hates. It is called The Mother's Heart. The cherished only son fell into debt and murdered his adoring mother for her money. He had been ordered to tear out her heart and take it to his debtors as proof. On the way he fell. Rolling out of the basket, the heart cried: "Are you hurt, my son?"

Damn fool.

Nobody wanted that. Not him, not her.

As a child she had always hated little girls who told everybody they wanted to grow up to be mothers.

She goes to visit her own mother, who may get sick at any moment and need care for the rest of her life. She comes into the tiny apartment in a combined guilt and love that render her speechless. On these visits she slips helplessly into childhood, her mind seething with unspoken complexities while her lips shape the expected speeches.

What was it like for you?

"How are you feeling?"

Did you and he enjoy it and how did you keep that a secret?

"That's too bad. Your African violets look wonderful."

Why won't you ever give me a straight answer?

"Do you really want Kitty up there with the plants? I wish you'd get someone in to help you clean."

I wish I didn't have to worry. I went from child who depended to woman struggling for freedom to this without ever once passing through a safe zone in which neither of us really needed the other.

"That dress is beautiful, Mother, but you don't look warm enough."

I know you think I dress to embarrass you.

The aging woman whose gracious manner comes out of a forgotten time says, "As long as it looks nice, I can put up with being chilly."

Just before the mother looks away, her daughter sees a flash of the captive girl. The old lady's flesh has burned away, leaving the skin quite close to her skull. Stepping off the curb, she is uncertain. Caged behind her mother's face is her own future.

As they go out the door the old mother tries to brush a strand of hair off her grown daughter's forehead; the old lady would like to replace her daughter's wardrobe with clothes more like her own.

Stop that. Please don't do that.

She thinks, *Mother, I'm sorry your old age is lonely*, but something else snags at the back of her mind. Why was my childhood lonely? She will lavish her own children with company: siblings, people to sleep over. She will answer all their questions in full.

She will never insist on anything that isn't important.

All her friends have mothers. In one way or another all those mothers have driven their grown daughters crazy.

"She pretended to know me," says Diana, who had flown all the way to Yorkshire to be with her. "Then on the fourth day we were in the sitting room when she showed me a picture. I asked who it was and she said this was her daughter Diana, who was married and living in America. She had erased me."

Another says: "When I was little she praised everything I did, even if it wasn't any good. She praises everything so much that you know she means, Is that all?"

"She says, You can't do that, whatever it is, when what she means is that she couldn't do it. When I told her in spite of the family and the job I'd made the Law Review she said, 'You're doing too much,' when what she meant was: 'It's your funeral.'"

"The world has gone past her, and at some level she is jealous."

Every one of the women says, "She thinks my house is never clean enough."

"She thinks families always love each other and dinners are delicious and everything is always fine, and if it isn't, then it's my failure."

We are never going to be like that.

As their children grow older they try to remain open, friendly, honest, tolerant, but behind their eyes the question rises and will not be put down. Will we be like that after all?

Beware for she is lurking, as the full moon approaches she will beg her captors to lock the cell tightly and chain her to the bars, but when the moon completes itself she will break through steel to get to you and when she does she will spring on your best moments and savage them, the bloody saliva spraying for your own good for she never does anything she does except out of love.

And she does love you.

Says her own mother, whom she has just asked what she's going to do when she gets out of the hospital:

"We'll see."

It is the same answer her mother gave when she was a child and asking, Are we going to the movies? Can I have some candy? Is my life going to come out all right? It infuriates her because it means nothing.

(She will always give her own children straight answers. She will tell them more than they want to know about things they may not have asked.)

She is trembling with rage. The aging woman looks at her with that same heedless smile, magnificently negligent. How will she manage alone with a mending hip?

We'll see. That smile!

She cannot know whether this is folly or bravery. In her secret self she can feel the yoke descending.

I will never be like that.

Can she keep her hand from twitching when she sees her daughter's hair flying out of control? Can she be still when the oldest flies to Europe and his brother wants to leave school/move away/ hitchhike to Florida and sleep on beaches? Will she be able to pretend these decisions are theirs to make or will she begin to replicate those maternal patterns of duplicity? Kissing the cheek to detect fever, giving the gift designed to improve the recipient, making remarks that pretend to be idle but stampede her young in the direction she has chosen. She never wants to do that.

She wants to be herself, is all.

Is that such a big thing to want?

Her problem is that she wishes to believe she has more than one function.

Lash me to the . . .

Are you sure you know what you're doing?

Are you all right?

I was just asking.

Beware the weremother, for even when you have hung the room with wolfs-bane and sealed the door and bolted it with a crucifix, even as you light the candles she is abroad and there is no power to prevent her; cross yourself and stay alert for she will spring upon you and her bite has the power to transform even the strongest. Barricade yourself and never take anything for granted even when you think you're safe, for even in that last moment, when you think you have killed her with the silver bullet or stopped her once for all with the stake at the crossroads her power lives; when everything else is finished there will be the guilt.

—1979

Voyager

In *Now, Voyager* . . . The hell of it is he can't remember exactly what in *Now, Voyager*. Not important. Bill is sharp. He walks two miles every morning, reads the paper, does the taxes, writes regularly to the children, keeps track of the bills. People treat him the same. But Sara. Sara is like one of those scraps you cut out of magazines and present at the supermarket register, in hopes—a blank coupon, waiting to be redeemed.

People ask, "Is she OK out here in the open like this?" when they mean, Is she going to fall down in our store? Their look says *you poor bastard.* "You must be . . ."

Don't tell me what I must, or how I am.

They go to the South-side Publix in St. Petersburg, Florida on Thursdays, Bill dresses Sara nicely in his favorite figured silk that didn't used to be so loose on her and clamps her hand over his elbow like a sheaf of quills so he can lead her to the Graymont van.

If the sky has turned silver and a morning breeze tatters the palm fronds and disturbs the water off the point, he is too intent on his task to see. Let go of her elbow for a minute and Sara will veer, falling off the curb or blundering into the treacherous, springy Bermuda grass where she'll collapse in the little sigh of air that escapes from under her skirt. It irritates him that she can see these hazards just as plain as he does and walk right into them. Although the others sitting in the van simmer and hiss he takes his time with her, and although he might as well be walking her into a closet or a meat locker for all Sara knows, she smiles at him and gets on. You look up one day to discover the person that you think you know is no longer that person; she's drifting out to sea, drawn by the tides into an unknown ocean while you stand, helplessly ranting, as she bobs away.

Hesitating in the cereal aisle he tries to return her to the shore of the familiar. "Is it Wheat Chex that we like with bananas or is it Rice Krispies?" A flicker is all he hopes for, anything to remind him who she once was. With his heart thudding he tries heavy lifting: "Oh look, that cereal Willy's kids used to like so much when they came to our house. Lucky Charms." My God, she turns and smiles, but he has no way of knowing whether it's their son's name or the

Hershey bar he's given her that makes her face so bright, all shimmering eyes and teeth brown with sweet milk chocolate.

Sara is postverbal. "Oh look," Bill says, because when they don't talk it makes you talk too much. "Here are cookies just like the ones we used to have at home."

That smile goes on like the light in a refrigerator: because you're looking in. He would put a pillow over her face and have done with it; no, he'd put her into the health center where the nurses want her and move into town but for that radiant, indiscriminate smile. *I'd walk a million miles . . .* Bill's memory goes back too far, which is how to your astonishment you end up old. He doesn't feel like an old guy but he sees it in the way people look at him. Their spot judgments as he sits her down next to him in the movies and plies her with candy to keep her in place, or pretends Sara is choosing the new dresses he buys for her: why are you wasting your time?

Listen. You can bring back even patients who have spent months in a coma through patterning. He's done a lot of reading about this. Surround them with familiar objects and keep talking and you can teach them just the way a baby learns. You can restore atrophying muscles, you can even reconnect synapses through exercise. Bill has read that through patterning, autistic children can be made to speak and recognize the speaker; they can even learn to hug back, and God, if he gets impatient it is because he still believes if not in happy endings then in convergence, that effort is rewarded and everything you try, no matter how futile it looks to others, has effect.

But when he puts her on the bed and moves her arms and legs in the exercises on the physical therapist's sheet Sara smiles as if she gets it, and when he stops it's as if none of this has taken place. It's like dropping a pebble into deep water; for the moment you disturb the surface. Look back and the last traces are gone.

Deteriorating is a medical name for something you don't necessarily see from up close. Live with a person and you note without remarking them the increasing degrees of difficulty—things you didn't used to have to clean up after; that when you're dressing her—when did you start dressing her?—it's a little harder to bend that intractable right arm, and without being able to help it you touch your own shriveling face. Sometimes he gets too close and yells; forgive him, sometimes he wants to hit that face, to see it charged with shock, pain, anything but that unalterable, uncomprehending smile.

Exasperated, he shouts, "Sara if you would just." Come back.

"I, Sinue the Egyptian . . ." Yes. Wander, forever damned. I will find my lover no matter how far she's traveled or how completely she's lost; I will bring her back even if I have to broach the Nile at ebb tide and scour the putrid hollow where the Pharaoh's intestines coiled and fill it with spices, earning my freedom in the bowels of the City of the Dead. But he and Sara are like the prisoners at the end of *Land of the Pharaohs* listening as giant stones slide in to seal the pyramid.

Today she does her exercises just the way you tell her, dutifully counting when you count, and if she tugs against you it could just be the mirror image, Sara distracted because whatever she does, she does with her eyes fixed on your face as if you are—not the sun, exactly, but something she needs to watch.

"I thought maybe here." He coughs and starts over. "I thought if we could just get someplace where you'd have a little help . . ."

If he agreed to sell the house and move to Florida; if he agreed to buy an apartment at Graymont and eat the goddamned communal evening meal with all those old fuds it was for Sara's sake—laundry and maid service on Tuesdays and Thursdays at a time when he told himself that was all she really needed, regular meals that spared them both the knowledge that when they sat down to eat at night, if they sat down at all, Sara would have managed boiled chicken breasts. Applesauce from the jar. Two spoons. The move spared them the bleak refrigerator with forgotten ground beef freezer-burned to death and it spared them the sticky floor and overlapping burns on the loose, bleached skin hanging from her wrists. They were also spared—if Sara was still alert enough to respond to things he took to be obvious—her chagrin at the failure, the tears. It's been a long time since she cried.

Are you still in there? Whether he begs or shakes, thinking to shock her back into herself, she only blinks and blinks.

Yet at night when he touches her Sara stirs against him as though still in need, and this stops him. It would be like raping a child. He holds her close so he won't see her incomprehension—no. He holds her close so he won't have to see the pearly skin incandescing as she smiles at him like a baby at the moon.

Take your vitamins and do your morning exercises. Stay strong, because you are the beacon or is it the Judas goat leading her forward, or are you the torchbearer in the cave? If your light gutters out, she plunges to her death.

After the war he was dispatched to Parris Island; he couldn't get quarters on the base so Sara stayed in Beaufort, jammed into a studio apartment where their two little girls slept in the window seat. They paid a high school girl to take them to the Saturday movie at the Breeze, and gave her extra to sit through it twice. Try not to bring back the way Sara looked in those days, with her quick, quick mouth and that dark hair.

A month before Bill was discharged a drill sergeant on a night march ordered his platoon of boots into the marsh where currents are swift and the mud can swallow you whole. Marsh shifts and tides can suck the ground out from under you but next to Iwo this was nothing, and if the D.I. was ready to give everything in war, he expected as much of his men in peace. The night was thick and black but orders are orders and by the time the first boot stepped in quicksand, gargling for help, it was too late. Five men were lost. Base personnel were mobilized for a search that went on long after it was clear there was no point; even though he was a supply officer, Bill put on boondockers and flotation gear and waded out.

The next day he staffed the emergency command post, fielding phone calls from the press and marking areas covered on a chart of those waters, and as the first body was found, dispatching a junior officer to break the news to the family. Movement is not action but it gave him the illusion that he was doing something, methodically moving those pins across the grid.

The other bodies were never retrieved. For weeks afterward he couldn't sleep. In civilian life he would have pulled Sara close and lost himself in her, but she was stacked like a log next to their two girls on the divan in Beaufort, ignorant of most of this, and he was in the rack in the B.O.Q. listening for anything—sirens, shouts, a quickening of the tempo of traffic—anything that would tell him the lost men had been found.

The waters that surround Parris Island are murky and the mud apparently bottomless and Bill already knew as well as the D.I. did what had become of his men. Later the drill instructor would be court martialed and the matter declared closed, but such matters are never closed. Four boys lost out there with their mouths wide and their hair streaming, submerged in mud! Bill still sees them marching in lockstep, blind eyes wide and feet moving in unison, because lost is lost and death is terrible but orders are orders, even in the muck at the deepest part of the channel where strong currents have carried them. Yes he knows better. After all these decades the lost platoon is well and truly dead, and if he cherishes the idea that they crawled ashore on the mainland and spent the rest of their lives AWOL, it's because nobody wants to give up hope for good.

Thank God he was just about to be mustered out of the service. "Oh, Bill," Sara said, forgetting for once that their own flesh was sleeping on the far side of the veneered coffee table. "This is so terrible."

Death! Hugging her, he agreed.

Neither of us knew what terrible was.

But in a life without change, or without changes that Bill is willing to admit to, things will sometimes happen. Do. At dinner that night the Advent screen is wheeled into the Graymont dining room so residents and servers can keep track of an approaching storm. This morning it looked like nothing but now it's an event, which the local weather watch covers like the invasion at Normandy, with advisories and status upgrades and gaudy visual aids, tracing flood tides and the movement of the storm center in contrasting colors on a computer generated map. Dauntless reporters in slickers lean into sheets of rain on thunderous waterfronts to shout for the cameras—bulletins from the front. In the absence of news, weather is news.

From his assigned place at their assigned table Bill watches the TV with gratitude because it spares him the nightly responsibility to his assigned tablemates.

New to Florida, some of the residents are worried.

"It's nothing," says the overblown woman at the next table, a longtime Floridian whose children put her here. "I've survived worse."

This isn't good enough for the smart aleck who comes to Bill and Sara's table in the ersatz captain's cap. "What's this place built on, anyway?"

He and the fourth at their table watch Sara with mean, judgmental eyes; they are like crows waiting for the unprotected moment. Let Bill look away for a second and they'll peck her to death. He hates the smart aleck less than he hates the plump widow who beggars Sara with her lavish flesh, but in a way he is grateful. Without them to push against there would be nothing—no talk, no action, just Sara with her sweet, unremitting smile.

As they leave the dining room a nice old guy just about his age stops him under the canopy. "You have to crack a window on the lee side of the house or the storm makes a vacuum. I've seen plate glass windows sucked clean out." Like Sara, this man's wife Elsa is postverbal but she's managed to keep one word. "Blazing blazing blazing blazing." It is strange and beautiful. "Blazing blazing . . ."

Patting Elsa's arm, Bill groans. "I know." Blazing. Like the skies in the black-and-white *Hurricane,* an entire Polynesian island leveled by the storm, villagers flying like pennants from palm trees until they are torn loose by the wind and swept out to sea.

His heart makes a secret, savage leap. He can almost see it: his life, the present, Sara, everything torn loose and cleansed and blown away and if he is blown out to sea along with her—well.

The last hurricane Bill was this close to was his last week in the service. When the winds died high tides obliterated the perimeters of Parris Island; as is often the case in coastal South Carolina, land and water became one. He and the others paddled inflatable boats up and down Officers' Row like large children, when he should have been trying to get through to Sara on the mainland to tell her to keep the kids inside. In all he and Sara had three. They had Willy after he was discharged. When Sara told him she was pregnant they made love as if to raise the dead, and Bill was astounded by how easy it was to pick her up and turn her around. Sara had begun by wailing, "What are we going to do?" while in fierce, secret triumph he considered the ledger and made a check mark on the credit side. When he set her down again she was smiling; what had he said? "Love him, I guess."

"Blazing."

"I heard you," Bill says, and with impatient hands hurries Sara past. He always reads the paper to her after dinner. He makes her watch the TV evening news.

At ten he gets a call from Ellie at the Health Center, offering to keep Sara for the duration of the storm. She tells him what he already knows; regular services here are probably going to be interrupted, Graymont has an auxiliary generator but they may still lose power. If the water broaches the top of the seawall, they'll have to evacuate. Ellie says gently, "She'll do better here."

"We can handle it."

"Sometimes these old people get disoriented." The nurse uses a word he resents but is no longer surprised to hear. "She's pretty frail."

When they were in their sixties they vowed never to get like that. No. Like this. Sara's sitting in her chair looking frail, if that's what they want to call it, but just as pretty as she ever did in the new dress. He's like the prince contemplating Sleeping Beauty: *If only you could speak.* He tells Ellie, "Thanks, but we can handle it." Clinging to royal palms at right angles like Terangi and his love, if they have to—athletic feats in which he and Sara wave like banners, brilliant in the wind.

Athletic feats are not out of the question. Once Sara flew, but only for a moment. Drunk on spring, they left the supper dishes and went tumbling into the fresh grass behind their postwar house. The little girls hung close, but Willy hitched across the grass and lunged behind a bush where only a protruding scrap of nightgown located him, like the tail of Casper the Friendly Ghost. Bill's oldest girl pushed her father down on his back in the grass. "Make me a flying angel." She leaned forward to take his hands. He planted his feet firmly in her midsection, raising her until she was horizontal, floating above the earth. At first she wavered and gasped, but eventually she let go and lifted her head and her arms as if in a swan dive, soaring, with Bill's supporting feet her only contact with earth. "Me," somebody cried and Bill let her down gently and held out his hands to the next angel, thinking it would be his younger girl. "Oh, please. Me."

And this was how, that evening in Newton, Mass., with his children jiggling and crowding and her sweet breath damp on his face and her face framed by the heartbreaking violet light, he held his wife Sara in midair, suspended for the moment before his legs buckled under her weight and with a little shriek of rage, she pitched off. Before she landed she lashed out at him, "Fool!"—kids, Sara, everybody in a tumble, with the little girls murmuring "Oh mommy," while his wife picked Willy up and clamped him to her like a shield.

Over the baby's head she shot Bill a look that suggested this was no better than she expected, that she might love him forever, but this failure she could never forgive.

It makes him sad to see his grown children getting old; touch your face and think: *am I.* The house he bought to raise their family was the house he sold for the down payment here; in other circumstances he would have willed it to their kids. If the superintendent at Graymont said, "Sometimes people show remarkable improvement after they move here," it was a factor.

Things you have to believe so you can do what you have to do.

When she wakes in the night he goes to the pocket fridge just the way he always does at this hour. He gets her a vanilla Jell-O pudding, prodding her lips with the spoon until she flinches at the pressure of the cold metal and begins to eat. She'd rather sleep; so would he, but this is important. She eats so little during the day that it's important to give her these little meals whenever he can get her to eat. Sleepy, he says automatically, "You've got to get your strength back," where he used to say, "You have to keep up your strength." Frail. *She looks all right to me.*

After they had their Schnauzer put down, he dreamed he and the dog were at the top of a stone tower and the dog was flying, dipping and wheeling around his head. He woke reluctantly. Sara was shaking his arm, and breathless from being dragged out of sleep he gasped, "What's the matter?"

"How am I supposed to know what's the matter? You were laughing," she said.

To his shame he dreamed last month that Sara was lying in her bed and at the benevolent distance dreams sometimes grant the dreamer, he also saw that she was severely altered by whatever change is marching over her in jackboots, pushed so far that she might never make it back. Then he saw his wife leave her body, Sara transfigured. No. Sara restored, dark-haired again, with that sweet, quick mouth; real Sara, that he knows. She separated herself and lifted, departing—it was so perfect. He was so glad. Then just before she disappeared from the upper right-hand corner of the room he saw her turn back and blow a kiss at the figure on the bed. It made him feel happy, terrible.

Sometimes it's simpler to go on being a fool. Pretend everything's OK until they rub your nose in it. Evacuate. You have a hard enough time taking care of her in a place she knows, and the last thing you want is to pry her out of Graymont like a snail out of a shell and set her down someplace new. Pretend you can stick it out here. When he wakes to a power failure he sees no need to panic Sara and no need to keep calling the desk, but he is prepared. He puts Sara's night things and all her medications in a bag, and as a precaution adds food: cheese, fruit and the chocolate granola bars his kids had sent, imagining they can get their mother to eat. He fixes her cold cereal for breakfast and peanut butter sandwiches for lunch.

When the aide doesn't come he reconciles himself to the fact that services are interrupted, but he can't help anticipating dinnertime, when he and Sara can join their assigned tablemates at that wretched assigned table for hot food and he can compare notes on the storm. Sara's restless; usually they take a walk now. Pretend. They paddle in the halls, Sara stumbling even on industrial strength carpeting. By midafternoon even though the winds have died, water is crashing over the breakwater, creeping closer to the Garson building where they live.

From the window he sees handicapped vans and ambulances removing patients from the health center, and as he watches, neighbors with overnight bags start coming out of the main door below. There's a procession of cars snaking out of the parking lot in water almost up to the axles—old models, mostly, but most of them top of the line. Motors flood out and won't start again. Watching, Bill decides that if the time comes he and Sara will be better off leaving by bus. When the faucet belches muddy salt water, he knows it's time. Even before the desk calls to alert them, they are standing out front with the others in the continuing rain. He's surrounded by poor old people in straw hats and plastic rain hats, hunched and miserable; as the bus pulls up and they bump each other in the rush to hoist themselves on he thinks she may not talk, but Sara's no worse than the rest.

There's more storm damage than he thought. Power is out all over town and flooded streets are clogged with shorn branches and felled trees. The bus driver says they're only going a short way; Bill was a fool to imagine they'd be taken to some nice safe motel where he could just check in and try to make Sara think nothing's changed. Instead they are delivered to a downtown church where the patients from the health center are already being rolled into little clusters in their wheelchairs or bedded down on pews. These old people look terrible. Until you see them together like this, until you see them yanked out of context and jammed in here in the aggregate, milling in escalating confusion, you don't know how bad it is. Here are his erstwhile neighbors, here are the lame, the halt, and tottering next to him, some old wreck—*mon semblable*—no, he has to stop himself. He has to distinguish Us from Them. He has to ignore the change disruption wreaks in people who looked OK to him in the cushioned safety of the Graymont dining room; in this context it is essential to make the separation. My God, these people look like all those wounded soldiers laid out in Atlanta just before the intermission, you know, in *Gone With the Wind*.

Every old person in the place seems to need something—the drenched, the hungry, the bed and wheelchair patients who need their medications, bedpan, fresh Attends. There isn't enough staff to go around. Bill can see the superintendent helping an old man toward the sacristy; there's only one bathroom on this floor. In spite of the staff's best efforts the nave is filling up with complaints; voices roll in on top of voices—hungry, anxious, querulous, disturbed. He thinks he hears Sara beginning to whimper; wouldn't you? And just as she tugs at his elbow another batch comes in. In ordinary times Bill would whirl and stare into her face, trying to catch the ghost of an expression. She's been so free of emotion for so long that he needs to see Sara altered by circumstance, even Sara distressed, but here's Ellie from the health center, saying in confidential tones, "This is awful. I don't know what we're going to do with them."

It's like Parris Island. "We've got to get organized."

The nurse is so pressed by circumstance that she simply accepts the *we*. "I could use a little help."

"Wait." Now he does turn to Sara, who smiles that smile. No. It's the smile she gave him that night in Beaufort, brave: *this isn't so bad*. Yes, he tells himself. She's all right. "Now you stay here." He kisses her on the forehead and sits her down in a pew next to a nice old lady who's perched like a confused pigeon, clinging to her purse. "This is my wife, Sara Penney. We're neighbors." As she gives him a wary scowl he says, "She won't be any trouble. Look, she's smiling at you."

Then he looks for Ellie. She's at the door, where newcomers are pooling like tadpoles in a storm drain. "Give me your clipboard. At least I can check these people in."

Through the night Bill works, helping these old folks slog in from the bus and try to dry themselves, rounding them up when they start to wander, serving coffee, carrying trays, and if a part of him knows that Sara has drifted out of the pew where he left her, he tells himself Ellie has an eye on her and besides, he's needed here. He has work to do.

He's of more use here than he was at Parris Island. He acknowledges now that was only busy work. At Parris Island he needed to think he was doing something for the dead boys when he knew there was nothing anybody could do for them. Here he hands out food and people thank him; he brings medicine to the ones who need it on a regular schedule and they take it; he boils water on the gas stove in the basement and brings it up for the nurses to pour in the paper cups he takes around with the meds. He has the pleasure of doing something that gets results.

In a way it was a relief to him when Willy caught up with the dead recruits in age and passed into the safety of his late twenties. If in fact you do some things because of certain other things, you can't afford to make too much of it, or think of the events as tightly linked. Not Willy's fault that as he grew Bill had to suppress images of his son marching with the dead boys. He was just grateful that Willy wanted to be a doctor and had no interest in the service. Thank God he was exempt from the draft.

And just when he is busiest, clicking on all . . . Just when he is at his most effective, Bill discovers that Sara has wandered off. She isn't anywhere. At first he thinks she's gotten lost in the choir loft or one of the basement bathrooms, but when he's looked in all those places he has to admit to himself that she is gone. Distraught, he goes from one attendant to another: "Have you seen her?" "Have you?" Vivian Leigh in Atlanta, looking for . . . oh stop. Nobody has. He can't ask them to stop what they're doing just to look for one old lady who may have wandered off. Even Ellie, who has designs on her, is too caught up in the exigencies. He can't even ask one of the old people to go out in the rain and help him look. Bill is exhausted by this time, surprised by the fact that his efforts have left him so shaky, but he can't sit down. Sara's gone. It's raining again, but not enough to keep him from going out, and, terrified that he'll lose her—no, that he won't lose her—galvanized by a spasm of guilty love, he rushes out of the church and goes looking for his wife.

Terangi, watch out. He blunders along the rain torn streets and although in the dark like this everything is confusing, finds that he's wading along the main road back to Graymont. From Graymont, town seems so far, but it's such a short walk! Struggling against the water that covers the toes of his shoes, he rounds the last corner without any sense of how long it's taken him to make it this far. Leaning against the carved Graymont sign with a strangely fated feeling, he can't know whether it's because he's so impoverished, so bereft of imagination that this is the only place he can think of to look for her, or whether he's trying to second-guess Sara, who is beyond guessing, because he hopes blind instinct has led her back to the one place she may know.

Just maybe the waters are receding; debris and dead palm fronds clog the walks in a pattern left by high tide. He can't see much; it's raining hard. If he calls her, will she know her name? If she hears him, will she come? He's too drained and guilty to call very loud. Terangi vowed love forever, but what can you do? What can you do?

Then he sees her under the canopy in front of the main building, standing with the security guard who just found her and the charge nurse who left her post in the health center at the guard's call. Recognizing Bill as he emerges from the rain, the guard, who locks the Garson building at night and unlocks it in the morning, touches his wet cap and turns away as if what happens next is going to be so private that he is embarrassed. The nurse stands with her arms around Sara as if trying to dry her out and get her warm at the same time. Bill doesn't have to hear her say, *How could you?* Too pressed to speak, he holds out his hands. With a scowl the nurse releases his wife and delivers her to him, sodden and desperate, frail Sara, his nemesis, his love—Sara, who turns to him with her lovely face leached to the skull and beautiful, drenched eyes that hold not an intimation, not even a ghost of recognition. The nurse is angry, Sara terrified and trembling; she does not have to say: *She can't go on like this.*

This is true.

He puts his hand on top of his only wife's head like a cop handing a prisoner into a patrol car and thus he relinquishes her, perhaps releasing all of them. It's raining too hard for Bill even to hear the farewell words that ambush him as the nurse takes his wife, his only love, and leads her inside.

—*The Yale Review*, 1996

Old Soldiers

It's supposed to be pretty in the place where Jane's grandmother lives; it says so in the Palmshine brochure. The pages are filled with photos of nice old ladies in the bright Florida sunlight, laughing and flirting with spunky old men in airy rooms. The sun is always high when Jane goes to visit Gram, but shadows fall as soon as she walks in the front door.

She's here because her mother can't bear to come. If Jane asks why, her mother starts crying. She says, "She isn't who she used to be," but that isn't the real reason.

"She isn't dead either," Jane snaps. "Oh, Mom, it is so awful there."

"Don't say that! It's the best we could find."

"I just wish we could . . ."

When her mother's lips tighten like that she looks a lot like Gram. "Well, we can't."

Palmshine Villa should be sunny and bright inside, after all, this is Florida, but no matter how fast Jane strides along the halls, at her back she hears the rushing shadows. She comes so often that she knows the regulars, although none of them knows her. Does being old make you forgetful or is it that when you're their age all people Jane's age look alike?

In the brochure everything is supposed to be nice. On the surface everything is. The coiffed and rouged wheelchair patients playing nerf ball in the lobby are smiling, but from the remote Extended Care wing, a voice so old that Jane can't gender it cries out.

She should be used to it by now but she whirls. "Ma'am," she says to the nearest aide. "Ma'am!"

Oblivious, the aide trots on. She is carrying the richest lady's Shih Tzu; every day Kiki and its owner frolic on the kingsized bed in the Villa's best room. Once when Jane begged she brought the dog into Gram's room and put it into Gram's arms. It licked her face. She was so happy! Jane said, "Will you bring it in sometimes, when I'm not around?" She already knew it was money that made these things happen and Gram will never have enough.

The aide is Barbie perfect, buff and agile; the rich lady who owns the Shih Tzu is old. Unlike Gram and the others, who have fallen away, the rich lady has hung on to both her money and her flesh—did money make the difference? Pink, powdered and sweetly rounded, she stays in bed because her knees can't support her weight. Even though she's rosy and better dressed than the others, she is just as frail. With her firm butt bouncing, the aide walks into her employer's room. Doesn't she notice the disparity? The diamond rings embedded in the fat fingers and her fleshy, entitled smile say no. Roiling shadows collect on her ceiling just the way they do on Gram's, but the rich old lady doesn't see; she never looks up.

Nobody here can afford to look up. For all they know, the place is lovely and everything's fine.

At the nurses' station a covey of early risers leans on walkers, waiting for the balloon lady to come. In the breakfast room five women warble, "My Bonnie Lies Over the Ocean," while the recreation director beats time. Four old ladies with Magic Marker red mouths sit around a card table, waiting for the attendant to deal. Cheerful enough, Jane supposes, considering they're all going to die soon, but she can't afford to dwell.

Instead she hurries because she can't shake the idea that something new has entered the place. Jane is aware of some new element, a difference in the air. She's almost used to the shadows but today, there's something more—an extra density that makes her eyes snap wide. She imagines it taking shape.

Has death come to visit? If only. But no, she thinks. Just, no. It isn't the cumulative pressure of old age that makes her twitch and it isn't the sound that time makes when God pulls the plug. There is a difference in the shadows that drift in the sunlit building and come rushing in her wake.

She passes the old lady whose vocabulary got away, all but one word. "Good morning," Jane says to her even though it won't make any difference.

When she turns at the sound the old lady's eyes are leached of light. "Dwelling, dwelling, dwelling, dwelling," she says in conversational tones, inching toward the dayroom in her flowered muumuu with the pastel webbed belt. Her leash is attached to the rail the management put in so old people who tip over won't fall far.

She used to be somebody, Jane thinks. They all did. It makes her move a little faster because Gram's failing. Every time she comes into the room at Palmshine Villa she comes wondering how much of her grandmother is still left.

In the room across the hall from Gram the old soldier shouts. He's been shouting for years. *Harmless,* the nurses said when Mom begged them to move Gram to another room so she wouldn't have to hear. They looked condescendingly at Gram. *Remember, he doesn't have a nice family like Mrs. Trefethen here. Do they, Gram?* Gram smiled, happy as a dog at the pound, eating its last meal. Mom protested. "But he scares her." Gram wasn't scared, Mom was. *Paraplegic,* they said, *even if he wanted to he couldn't hurt a flea.* "He's making threats." *No he isn't, he's fighting Nazis. The war,* they said. They said, *So sad. Nobody comes even at Christmas, nobody phones and they never come.* "That's not my problem," Mom said, "it's his problem." They said, *If your mother isn't happy here you can always* . . . Jane's heart leaped up but Mom recovered in a flash. "Oh no," she said in that tired, tired voice, "This is perfect. Everything's just fine." *He only shouts when he hears you coming,* they said. *When you're not here he's quiet as a clam.*

Even though Jane tiptoes he knows. The dry voice cracks the air above her head like a whip. "I know you're out there. Come here!"

This is what she hates most about these Sundays. "Oh, please. Not today."

God damn you God look what you've done to me, me in the bed and Vic dead and I can't get out until I find out who. Vic is dead God damn you. Dead and nobody will help.

It is in the building now. **You**

"Who killed Vic?"

"Oh, please." Jane looked in once and saw a sheaf of white hair, a profile like the face on a medal. He heard her breathing and turned, a blur of red rage—a glaring mouth with that savage flash of teeth but his expression was both so blind and so angry that she fled before she could find out whether he saw her and if he did, whether he knew who she was. That day she closed Gram's door as nearly as she could and leaned against the inside, terrified that he'd lurch into the wooden panels in his rage and send her and the door crashing into the room. Today his dry, hard voice knifes into her. "Who killed Vic?" This is how it always begins. Once he gets started the shouter will rant for hours. "Come on, you bastard bastards, who did it?"

Half of Jane wants to confront the old wreck and shut him up, but she's afraid to go in. "Shut up."

"It had to be one of you." His shout cuts through everything. It's like being within range of a heat-seeking missile. It doesn't matter who you are today. It wants to find you and destroy. As she dives into Gram's doorway the accusations follow. "Now, God damn you. Who?"

"Beats me," she says and dodges into the room.

Odd. Behind her, something in the shadows stirs.

The room is nicely kept and so is Gram, but she's always anxious, going in. What does she expect to find in the sweet little room with its ruffled bed, a lip-sticked skeleton? Gram gone, with the bed stripped and her belongings rolled on top like the bedding of an army moving out? Or is she afraid of Gram rising out of her velour recliner to scold her for being late, the way she did when Jane was young.

The old man isn't done. "God damn your shit," he cries. "Tell the truth or I'll eat your face and spit out the teeth."

"Gram, it's me."

Never mind, Gram is glad to see her. Gram is always glad to see her, it's a given that when Jane walks in the old lady's smile lights up the room. She knows her granddaughter, too, it's not like she forgets. "Jane," Gram says with that smile that the complications of old age can't turn off and not even pain can dim.

She flinches. Is Gram in pain? Gram won't tell her or she can't tell her, so Jane has never known. She still has words, but a lot of important ones have gone away.

"Smear your shit in your eyes," he howls. "Now, tell."

"Hello," she says, bending to kiss that transparent cheek. "Hello, Gram."

She looks so sweet sitting there in the recliner where the aides put her after they sponged the oatmeal off her mouth and dressed her for the day; Jane thinks Gram is in fact sweeter than she ever was in real life. Something in the water, she wonders? Something they give her at night? Or is it just that Gram has finally let herself lay back and let go? After a lifetime of keeping a perfect house, washing and ironing for a family that she controlled and fed for years, along with the multitudes, after all that *taking care,* she's on vacation from her life.

"I brought blueberry muffins, Gram."

"Of course you did." That smile!

"And the shit in your eyes." So loud, so ugly.

Jane gestures in the direction of the shout. "Oh Gram, I'm so sorry about that."

Gram smiles and blinks politely the way she always does when she doesn't understand, which is most of the time lately. Age has left her with a few macros—boilerplate speeches that kick in whenever Jane says anything but she knows who Jane is, she does! "You were lovely to come."

Does it hurt, Gram? How much does it hurt? She wants to ask but Gram looks so happy that she's afraid to bring it up. She responds by rote, "Lovely to see you, Gram."

The television is going—it always is—Sally Jessy, Oprah, Rosie, Ricki, makes no difference, the daylight voices are interchangeable. The psychic Muzak and emotional screensaver supply everything Gram needs now that she's lost everything else. Jane is grateful that the old lady's lost it, so she doesn't know how awful this is. She may not know she's in this pale blue room in this pretty place in her oversized aqua recliner because this is the bottom line. Gram isn't getting well. She's here for good; except for her birthday and Christmas, when an ambulance brings her to her daughter's house for dinner and takes her away before the pie, she is going to be in this chair in this room in Palmshine Villa for whatever's left of her life. It's good Gram likes TV so much. Good thing poor Gram's protective mechanism kicked in when her hard disk overloaded and crashed.

Gram looks nice in aqua: aqua muumuu, fluffy aqua robe. It complements the chair.

Gram looks nice and the room is nice but the words barreling in from across the hall are ugly and sharp. "And sleep in your shit because you won't tell me who killed him."

Oh stop.

"Oh, look," Gram says. "Doesn't Rosie have on a pretty red shirt today."

But she can't drown out the old soldier. "Who killed Vic? Was it you?"

"And doesn't she dress the child nice," Gram says because he can't drown out her sweet voice.

This is her life now, these daily TV people are closer to Gram than her family, Jane realizes. She's a little hurt and at the same time happy for Gram, who looks frail but clean and pretty and well taken care of, with her white hair nicely waved and a bobby pin with a blue butterfly clinging to the spot where the pink scalp shows through. "Nice, Gram. It's a nice color. Would you like me to get you one like that?"

He is still shouting. "Was it me?"

"Don't worry," Gram says, beaming. "Just get me the box tops. I can always send away."

"Help me," he screams. "I have to find out."

I don't know who did it but I may, he is lying dead somewhere but if I can get back the memory I may find out. Solomons I was fighting on, or was I at Tobruk?

Was that Vic running along beside me, did I push him ahead and did he take the bullet that was meant for me, is it my fault he was killed in the first wave? Is that what happened to you, old shitface, is it my fault you got blasted out of your life?

Something is shimmering out there. **I am coming for you.**

"Who killed Vic?"

Jane murmurs, "I wish he'd stop."

Rosie's theme music makes a cheerful sound in the room. The ambiance is cheerful, and so is Gram. Although massed shadows roll down the halls like thunderclouds before a terrible storm, the room is bright. There are stuffed animals the great-grandchildren gave, marine blue curtains to match the nice comforter and ruffled bolster that Mom bought when they moved Gram out of the house she couldn't keep. Her hospital bed has a dust ruffle just like a little girl's. Books she can't read any more line the little bookshelf like the ghosts of old friends. Family photos stand on the top in Plexiglas frames. Gram with Mom and Jane and the others in Gram's better days. She looks so pretty! Like somebody else. You wouldn't know her if it wasn't for the smile that travels from one snapshot into the next into the studio portrait made on her 80th birthday, into this room and onto the face of the wraith in the recliner chair. There isn't much left but the smile.

It's enough, or it would be except for the scary business in the halls. What is it, exactly, that makes Jane anxious today, and fearful for Gram?

It could be nothing, she thinks, as across the hall the old man accuses the world at large: "You know who killed Vic. Who was it? Was it you?"

"Who's Vic?" she says to Gram.

The old lady turns sweet, empty eyes on her. "Who?"

"The old man across the hall says somebody got murdered." She shouldn't be talking about this but it's better than what she really wants to say: *Don't you ever want to get out of here, Grammy? Are you happy or sometimes do you think you want to die?* Disturbed, she finishes, "This guy Vic."

"Oh," Gram says, blinking the way she does when she doesn't have the fog-giest, which is all the time now. "Vic," she says with that midrange pleasant smile that means nothing. It is nothing like the welcoming blaze when Jane enters the room but it's the best she can do. Lips like a shriveled rosebud, with that genteel, vacant tone. "Of course," Gram says without knowing what she's saying. "Vic."

"Who was he, Gram? Was Vic his son and did you meet him, do you know?"

What did the nurses say? *He has a family. They used to come. Now nobody comes and the checks come straight from the bank.*

"Who?"

"Vic!" She doesn't want to scare her grandmother but she does want an answer.

Bemused, the old lady murmurs because it's expected, "Poor Vic. Oh look, Janie, look what Rosie's doing now."

It's useless to ask her but Gram's the only person she can ask. "What happened to him, Gram?"

What happened to me? Wife I had before I went away, two boys I had, Timmy and little, did we name one of them Vic My friend Angus had little girls, he was the first over the top and I promised to follow but his belly blew up in a fountain of fire and blood Pull me back *he was begging would he not have died? I couldn't, not with that hole in the belly, guts blooming, twitching wet parts of him slithering into my arms it's not my fault he went first dead like my point man and when I try to sleep they blossom all over again they found his penis in the dirt next to my face keep your head down men . . .*

In the building now, and coming down the hall. **It's nothing you did in the war.**

"Somebody killed Vic and you know it . . ."

"Oh God." Jane groans. "What if this is the wrong place?"

"It's so sweet," Gram says, "Rosie bringing up her own baby all by herself."

"You have to move out of this place," Jane says wildly. Is she trying to get the old lady out of this room for the afternoon or for good? She doesn't know. The old soldier's voice rises and she shouts to cover the sound, "It's not out of the question."

"Rosie's just a wonderful mother, just like Oprah and those wonderful people in *The Partridge Family* . . . "

She grabs Gram's shoulders. "What if something happened to you?"

"And that nice girl who took care of the Trapp children, they are an inspiration for us all." This is a lot for Gram to say at one time but she is all worked up now. Her lips are trembling and her eyes glisten with approval. "It's fine mothers like them and that lovely Ma Walton who make America great."

Jane tries, she tries! "I don't think Oprah has any children, Gram."

At least Gram has a nice family, unlike that poor bastard across the hall. Who will not stop shouting, "No. He didn't kill Vic. You know he didn't and you know who did."

"Oh, shut up."

Gram gasps.

"No no, Gram. Not you!"

"And I know it too." Querulous. "Did you kill Vic?"

"I didn't kill anybody, Janie, I didn't." Gram's face shrinks like crepe paper; she's about to cry.

"Shh. Shh, Gram. Don't worry about him, really."

"Who?"

"You know. You do! He's just a crazy old man."

But Gram's face is working. She's caught on an old memory that won't surface. She can't tell Jane what it is but Jane can see from her face that it hurts. There is something buried back there unless something is happening to her in the room right now. Whatever it is, it hurts. Gram's lap robe falls away and she sees her grandmother's feet are cased in plastic lined with sheepskin. Why? *Oh, Gram.*

Meanwhile the old man rails, "Did you kill him?"

If he would only stop *shouting.*

"Did you?"

Jane rises to close the door.

"Why, no." Gram is terribly upset. "Of course not. No."

But the doors in this place are jiggered so they won't really close. Regulations, Jane thinks. Health care centers have to come up to code. She soothes her grandmother with bits of blueberry muffin. The old lady chews and chews but when she spreads her mouth in a new smile, the bits of blueberry muffin are still there.

Suddenly the old man's tone changes. "Why, you didn't kill Vic, you tried to save him."

Uneasy, Jane glances at her grandmother, but Gram is fixed on the television now. She smiles on as though she doesn't hear.

"But he died anyway!"

"Oh, look, Gram." Jane warbles. Her voice is shaking. It sounds sweet and false. "Look at Rosie."

"Do you want to know who killed Vic? Do you?"

"Isn't that a pretty red shirt?"

Anguished, the old man finishes. "I killed Vic."

"My God." Jane shoots a look at her grandmother. Did she hear? Is she afraid?

I didn't kill Angus and I didn't kill my point man, I got a citation for what I did, the Purple Heart and a Bronze Star but it was shit because I couldn't get an erection and I couldn't get a job. I was shit and my life was shit and I hated them, because before the war ever happened it already was. Alana left me for that Hunky refugee and took the kids but I showed her, I did, I showed them all.

All except me.

"I know who killed Vic," the old man cries.

"Pretty red shirt. Your mother ought to wear red," Gram says. "It would take people's minds off the wrinkles and the fat."

"Gram!"

Gram goes on in the unruffled tone she uses when Mom cracks during one of these lectures and starts to yell. Just when you love her best she gets a little mean and you remember she always was. "If only she'd get herself up nice, like my girls Rosie and Oprah do."

From across the hall, the news comes in on a sob. "I killed Vic."

"They're just television, Gram." What if the old man really is a murderer?

"Lose her looks and she'll lose her handsome man and then what will she do?"

"Mom looks fine." What if he kills Gram?

"Aaaaaahhh." His throat opens in grief. "Aaaaaah."

"Shh," Jane murmurs, "please don't."

And with that brilliant smile that lights up Palmshine, Gram burbles, "Poor Vic."

"Shh, don't worry. It's just crazy talk, Gram."

Nothing to worry about, Jane tells herself. Veteran, Congressional Medal of Honor or something, all that. Even if he could walk, what would he use? No scissors and no razors allowed here, plastic silverware.

But Jane worries. She's worried ever since they moved Gram. In a play she knows, street cleaners came for you with rolling garbage cans. You heard the tin whistle just before they took you away. In one story, it's the Dark Men who come. They live in the mortuary and work by night. When they finish with you, you are another store dummy in the window at Wanamaker's, and nobody knows. What if evil really is out there, not things you are afraid of, but something real? What if the doctors are ranching organs and selling them by night? What if some Svengali in white tries to bilk Gram out of her money and starts pinching when she says no? Secret beatings and spiteful bruisings go on in places like this, sexual abuse and worse. Anything can happen when you're old and frail and can't get out of your chair. Should she stay here and protect Gram? But Jane has a life and a day job. She can't sleep at the foot of Gram's bed every night, even though Gram's so small now that there's plenty of room. Besides, Mom researched. Palmshine is run by staunch Methodists with big dependable feet, good, kind Methodist faces, and capable Methodist hands. Palmshine is the best of its kind, Mom researched it. It says so right there in *Consumer Reports.*

Then why is she so upset?

Mostly, it's the shouting. "Who killed Vic?"

"Look, Gram," Jane says, pointing to a branch outside the window. "Look at the pretty bird."

Gram turns her head obediently. She looks right at it but does not see. "Pretty," she says with that lovely, undiscriminating smile.

In the next second she's asleep. It happens. Jane's used to it. She's also pledged to stay until six. If she's not here when Gram wakes up—if she doesn't stay until the supper tray comes—"Oh look, Gram, it's lovely Sunday dinner, turkey and apple crisp, again" her grandmother won't eat. If she doesn't stay her grandmother will wake up alone in her pretty room on a Sunday night and start to cry.

Nobody can stand living with the dead I know that stink of decay, when they pull back the robe to wash me I see in their faces how it smells, well stick your face in it put your hands into it and inhale, take me the way I am if I can't stand it how can you so wallow in your own stink and stay the fuck away I don't want you but I won't let go until I get my revenge on you God damn you, it's all your fault unless it was Alana's, she was gone and the boys were gone when I got back so it's her fault unless Angus started it, why didn't you just say no, unless it was the Lieutenant for putting me in charge or those candymouthed shitfaced sons I had with their greedy shiteating smiles you can all just go to hell and stay there and leave me alone and I'll stay here

Let me in.

As long as Gram keeps smiling, Jane can handle it. She can live with the shadows and the shouting, but Gram isn't in right now. Jane is alone with it.

"You didn't kill Vic."

"Oh, stop it." She turns up the TV.

The puchline rolls in. "I killed Vic," he cries again. Again.

Trembling, Jane pats the air above Gram, she apologizes to Rosie—are these shows on a loop? Spilling into these cheery rooms even on Sundays when real

TV is showing something else? "I'll be right back," she says, and even though at Gram's age sleep is tenuous and leaving her is risky, she slips into the hall.

"Do you know who killed Vic?" The old man's shout meets her at the door. "Do you?"

"Stop it." She slams into his room. "Just stop it!"

"What?" His head turns at the sound. "What?" he shouts, glaring at nothing. His mouth is a furnace fueled by hatred. "Go away!"

But Jane is angry now. "I'm not going anywhere until you shut up."

"It's you." For a moment his voice softens. "Is it really you?"

"Who do you think I am?"

Something changes. "Thank God you've come."

A part of Jane knows you shouldn't walk into things you don't know about, but it's too late. Besides, the shadows are massing outside the door and if she stands here long enough they will come rolling in. Something is out there waiting, whether for her or for Gram or for this old veteran, she does not know. There is more at issue here than Jane's sanity or her grandmother's comfort and safety. The trouble—and this is what strikes her dumb and leaves her cracked open, vulnerable and waiting—is that she can't say what. Because the old soldier's tone has changed she says gently, "Just be quiet now, OK?"

"And now that I have you here. It's Anzio, don't you see?" He clears his throat like a lecturer about to start. "Tobruk." Big voice for a man in his what, eighties, nineties. The old veteran looks well and handsome, considering—flowing white hair, square jaw, sharp brow, knife-blade nose.

"You're hurting people out there. That's all."

"Don't you see what I'm talking about?"

"That's enough!"

"Stand still, Alana. Don't you dare walk out while I'm talking to you! Bizerte, don't you get it? Monte Cassino. Normandy. Tobruk."

"I said, that's enough." Jane puts up her hand as if to ward him off but the battlefield names keep rolling out on a current of rage and it is too much. It's just too much.

"You know you were fucking him, you bitch, and all the time . . . Don't you see where I was?"

"Just stop!" It's his health that angers her, the strong arms and firm jaw and the forearms like blades; there are dumbbells crossed on the side table and a metal triangle hangs above the bed. This old man is so strong that he can go on forever. He can shout on and on unless somebody stops him. "Shut up."

He is raging at a world of people she can't see and never was, people that she won't see and can't help and it is terrible. "That's all you know, Sergeant." Then, "Shut up, you unfaithful bitch. Shut up or they'll shave all your hair and rape you to death for being a collaborator. They'll lock you up."

She shouts back, "Shut up or they'll lock you up!"

This is how he silences her. "I was locked up. Who do you think killed Vic?"

"Who *are* you?"

"You weren't there, Sergeant. None of you were, so you don't know what became of us. What do you know about it?"

Jane throws back her head like a horse that's been spooked; eyes wide, whites showing all the way around. "Oh, stop it. Just *don't!*"

"What do you know about Vic?" The eyes the old man turns toward her are like milk glass, shining and opaque. There's a chance that he still doesn't know that Jane is here. It doesn't matter whether she's here or not or who she is or even whether she's listening. The harangue is etched into his mind. "You didn't crawl through shit and you didn't see your buddy's face blown off or your best friend's belly torn up by a grenade. You didn't see anything, you little bitch," he says. So he does see her. And now that he sees her his face splits open and she looks into the agony. He is crying for both of them. "You careless, careless bitch."

The pain is so obvious and so powerful that her voice shakes. "I'm so sorry it hurts!"

"Who did this to us? Whose fault is it then?"

Trembling, she backs away. "I'll go get somebody."

"Don't! I'm not finished with you."

"I'm only trying to help."

"Shit on that. Shit on your help." The old soldier rolls his head from side to side on the pillow, looking here, there, nowhere, tossing hopelessly like a child who's never been rocked. He is struggling. "Don't go." Words back up in his throat and he strangles on them.

I said, let me in!

"I'll get a doctor."

His face writhes in a series of conflicting expressions. "Fuck that shit. Get out!"

"They'll give you a shot."

"You bitch, you're just like all the rest of them." The old veteran is so filled with grief and hatred that the words come out in puffs like exploding shells. "Alana, the kids. Now go away."

Jane is stumbling backward to the door when his expression changes. There is a stir at her back. It's more than a shadow, she thinks, but can't be sure. There is something new in the room. Whatever it is, it keeps her in place while the old man's words blur with pain and stop being speech. He groans aloud. She tries again, "Please let me get someone."

"Just go away! Take the kids and get out of here." He can hardly breathe. "Get out before you get hurt."

Trapped in the bed like that, how could he . . . Still she's afraid. Her voice trembles. "Just don't hurt my grandmother."

"You have no idea what I can do."

"Nurse! The bell, Mr. ah."

"That's classified!"

"OK, OK." Shaking, she advances. "Ah. Don't hurt me, I'm just going to reach over here and ring the . . ."

"No! You have no idea what I can do."

"I'm only trying to help!"

"Stay back!" The force of his hatred overturns her, "You have no idea what I can do to you!"

"You did it," she murmurs, frozen in place. "You killed Vic."

"I did. I kill everything I love!" The rest comes out in a spray—his story, Jane guesses, but so distorted by resentment that she can't make it out—a dozen voices fill the room: allies and enemies, traitors, everyone, the story that came before everything else in his life comes tumbling out so fast that nobody in this life could sort it out, and as he rambles, shadows begin rolling into the room. He rasps, "Yes I killed him, and I'll kill you too."

At her back something moves and she wheels, startled, and looks into its face. He looks so *nice.* "Who are you?"

"I'll kill everyone who . . ." But the furious old soldier sees it too. He bares his teeth, thundering: "Go away!"

But the gnashing, outraged old man can't frighten the young one no matter how loud he shouts. The young soldier is smiling, fresh-faced and handsome and easy in the fatigues, with his combat boots hanging down from laces knotted around his neck, hitting the dogtags that dangle from a chain until they clink. The muddy helmet swings from one hand. With the other, he makes a cross on his lips as the old man in the bed goes on railing:

"It serves him right, you know. God damned Vic . . ."

"What?" she cries.

"It serves you right."

This nice young man; she asks, "What did you do to him?"

Shh. The newcomer shakes his head and without speaking he tells her, **Shh. You don't need to know.**

"Who are you?" she asks. Then she knows. It's Vic, he is this patient's long-dead victim and now he's come back to confront the man who murdered him all those years ago. She turns to the young soldier. "Oh, Vic. Poor Vic!"

The old man sits bolt upright. "You called?"

"Vic?" She turns from one to the other. The profile, the eyes . . . She covers her mouth and points at the veteran in the bed. "You're Vic!"

"This is all your fault!" The milk glass eyes snap wide. His voice overflows the room and roars down the hall. "You brought him, you bitch. Get out."

Jane hears footsteps approaching—the nurse, orderlies—but she says, "Oh my God, I'm sorry." She doesn't know why she's crying, but she is.

"Die, you bastard." Propped on trembling arms he snarls at the young man, "Finish it!"

The air in the room shimmers. There is a decision hanging fire.

Not now.

"Die, God damn you. Go ahead and get it over with!"

Jane wheels to protect the young soldier—Vic? But he shakes his head. *No.* In the next second, he is gone.

"Get out!"

As the head nurse comes into the room. "Victor Earhart, you stop that! You stop abusing people around here! I'm sorry," she says to Jane. "He has a history."

"I'm sorry."

"Bitch, you bitch. You get the fuck out!"

"Don't worry," she says to Jane, "he does that to everybody, he just drives people away." With the heel of her hand she straight arms the old veteran, pushing him down on the pillow. "Keep it down, Vic, or I'll have to give you a shot."

Vic?

"Shut up, Vic, she's going."

Vic.

"Go away." He is howling now. "Go away, God damn you, go!"

"I am!" Sobbing, she runs. Jane retreats to Gram's room, to nice Gram who has been stripped of her possessions, her flesh, of all the old, bad complications, so the sweetness is the only thing left. And the pain, she sees now. The pain.

"Oh," Gram says, extending her arms to Jane. Her smile turns on with the force of a thousand halogen lamps. "Oh, how nice!"

"Oh, Gram." Jane advances with her arms out, she can hug Gram and even though Gram has lost her powers, she can still make it all right. In the next second she realizes her grandmother isn't looking at her. The old lady's thin arms fan out in a welcoming hug and her face lights up, but it isn't her granddaughter she's reaching for and it isn't Mom. It isn't anybody in this world, Jane understands. Gram is reaching for somebody else.

Turning, she sees that the shadows have followed her out of the old veteran's room and gathered in Gram's nice place, and with them, the new force that came into the building today to effect—not revenge, a rescue? Young Vic is standing here in Gram's room in his fatigues with boots around his neck and the helmet dangling. He's taken off his dogtags and he carries them in the other hand. Grinning, he tosses them to Gram.

Across the hall, the old veteran starts. "Who killed Vic?" Old man, old man! He can't shut up. Now he'll never shut up.

I came for you. Come with me?

"Oh Gram, please don't . . ."
With that smile blazing, she does.

—*Infinity Plus One*, 2001

Incursions

Lives go to pieces incrementally, not all at once, although it may take some of us a while to notice. Man wakes up in the middle of an empty field with his arms swinging; his heart is doing cartwheels while his head struggles to catch up. *Over,* he thinks, with the hammer behind his eyes thudding against his frontal bone: dawning terror, followed by recognition. *My life is over.*

His head jerks and hits plastic. Oh. Dream. I'm on the train. He unfolds his crumpled ticket and holds it up for the waiting conductor. Get hold of yourself, Travers. You're not crossing the Styx or anything, you're going to the city for a meeting.

But he can't stop the sound of the mallet pounding inside his skull, unless it's the thunder of his own blood: Duh. Duh-duh-duh-duh. Duh.

Travers clutches his Nokia and cell phones home. "I'm on the train."

The woman keyboarding next to him growls, "We know."

"Can you hear me? I'm on the train."

There may be sound at the other end but it isn't loud enough to make out.

"Sandra? It's me, Dave. Can you hear me?" He raises his voice, in case. He really means, do you love me, but he's afraid to ask.

Around Travers, the regulars reading newspapers or tap-tapping on notebooks and PDAs frown and clear their throats. The passenger shouting into his cell phone is disrupting the flow. They all have their habits and know each other on sight. They are easy here because they do this every day; they muse or work or sleep on the train and time disappears, whereas Travers is new and every second has an edge. He doesn't *do* like they do, he is uncoordinated and gauche; he's talking too loud. He should learn to keep his head down and his elbows close to his sides.

It isn't Dave's fault; he doesn't know. Dave Travers isn't your ordinary commuter. In fact, he hasn't been to the city since he took Sandra to the World Trade Center on their anniversary, the year before the fall. He doesn't fit in with the regulars on this morning milk run; he isn't a broker or a banker or a lawyer who chose to commute so the kids could grow up in a town with grass, he's a junior college professor doing everything within his power to bring himself up in the world. He's only teaching college because his folks said he was too smart to work at Kmart and he can't think of anything else to do.

He's never wanted to teach. He doesn't like it and he hates his middle aged night-schoolers with their moist, uncomprehending stares. He hates not being any better than he is. It's not as though he ever will be, either, except in one respect. Unlike most people, he knows it. Still there are changes he can make.

He has a meeting in New York today, a travel agency interviewing possible on-site people they can post to Mexican Hat to lead their Monument Valley tours, tailor made for a guy who is sick of his life. At least that's what Travers tells himself. He does, after all, know a little something about the West, having read about it for years. What's it really like in Mexican Hat? Would Sandra like it there? He doesn't know. All he knows is that they both need a change.

"Sandra?" He's calling her all the way from this train, roving charges and all that implies, and so far she hasn't even said hello. "I know you're there Sandra, can you hear me!"

Around him the regulars look up, annoyed.

He just can't go on the way he is. He taps the phone and says, louder: "Can you hear me?"

Six passengers chorus, "If we can hear you, they can hear you."

"Oh, Sandra." He presses his open mouth to the Nokia as though he can inhale her response and save it to examine later.

The phone is dead empty.

He says anyway, "I'm on the train."

If that's all he is, why won't the mallet stop thumping behind his frontal bone?

I'm only on the train, going to the city. Then why does it feel like a trip to the end of the world?

Then Travers thinks, What if I just got off at Greens Farms and ran away? Sandra wouldn't miss me, I don't think, and I know the students wouldn't. I could cut out for the high country and start over in some new place where nobody knows.

What, he wonders. His life is so dull and so simple that there aren't very many things about it. What have I got that I don't want anybody to know?

He taps the Nokia. "It's me. I'm on the train." He is still trying to reach Sandra even though they don't like each other very much. The unspoken part of the message is, Aren't you glad?

It doesn't matter what he says to the bright plastic instrument. It won't matter what the woman on the other end is saying, if indeed she is saying anything. The phone is just as dead.

This is more or less how Dave Travers finds himself getting off Metro North somewhere outside Greens Farms, Connecticut, and disappearing from the face of the earth. He isn't there yet, but he will be soon.

Greens Farms is one of those station stops that annoys New York–New Haven/New Haven–New York commuters because it is just one more delay on a trip that already has too many stops. To Metro North longtimers anxious to get where they are going, it's a place there's no point in stopping; nobody gets on and nobody gets off at Greens Farms because as far as they know, there's nothing there. Coming out after a hard day in the city, Greens Farms is the definition of eternity. All this time on the train and we're only at Greens Farms. At the Greens Farms stop most travelers raise their newspapers and refuse to look out the window—even Travers, the few times he's been this way. To look is to acknowledge the length of the trip and the size of the chunk it is gnawing out of their lives. Like the regulars, Travers has never read or heard anything about Greens Farms and he's certainly never been there, which as much as anything explains why he has drawn a picture of it in his head.

Even the conductor sounds weary as he reports that they are approaching Greens Farms. Again.

In his head Travers sees the field where he whirled in the long dream he was having before the conductor woke him. It was so green! Scary, but he'd like to get back to that place. There he was free, dislocated as he was. Startled, he jumps to attention. It's as though some great voice out there has just invited him to jump off the edge of the world.

That might not be such a bad idea.

"Did I say that?"

He doesn't know. Around him, passengers glare; why is the idiot shouting when he's holstered his phone?

It's important to pretend that wasn't him they heard, or that he wasn't really yelling. Travers spreads both his hands with a foolish grin. Look folks, you've got me wrong, it was somebody else. To confuse them Travers hums: *Show me how to get out of this world 'cause that's where everything is.*

He isn't depressed, exactly, just interested in voids and what it would be like to be suspended in one—no demands, no expectations, no humiliations—just the restful dark and silence that should come with the long-awaited and by no means certain-to-show-up-for-the-concert personal appearance of the last big thing, the cataclysm guaranteed to get top billing in this circus, the End of the World.

Something happens outside Rowayton and all the train doors pop open. Travers feels his heart hit a bump and soar like a racer bouncing into a crash. The doors to the car are only open for a moment but he sees his opportunity. For all he knows, everything lies beyond. Abandoning his briefcase, he gets up and slips out. He hits hard, rolling in the gravel as he lands. He doesn't remember which station was last or what's next but he imagines this must be Greens Farms.

He gets up gasping. He won't remember running across the tracks or scuttling under a fence and taking off with his arms flapping and his breath coming fast. He has to come to a stop before he can come to his senses at all. By the time his breathing and his heart rate return to normal, Travers is in the middle of a late-summer field flanked by thick and smelly Ailanthus, the rank, ambiguous growth that is neither weed nor tree. The deep grass in the field where Travers is standing sways in the breeze coming up from water he can not see. The late summer sun is bright but the air is cool and sharp, hinting at fall. It isn't perfect but in his present frame of mind, it'll do. If Travers can't reach the edge of the world from here, he can certainly go someplace he's never been. If he likes it, he thinks with his heart lifting, he'll never go back. Nobody who smells escape wants to go back to being what he was.

Now, he thinks for no reason in particular. He never really intended to disappear, but now he has a chance.

Yep. Now. All I have to do is find the road. If I keep walking I can walk out of Greens Farms and out of Connecticut and out of my life in New Haven, where I was doing OK but not well. Tomorrow I can wake up in some new big town or small city and start fresh. You read about this kind of thing all the time. Man disappears and years later they find him, upstanding pillar of some new community and surrounded by a fresh batch of loved ones, happy and prosperous, maybe even successful, as somebody else. Amnesia, he can tell the people who catch up with him, unless he is hunted for some crime, in which case he says, Witness protection. Listen, he could develop amnesia at any time. When you get right down to it, who's to know? Travers sees himself idealized in a Realtor's photo, a happy homeowner in a neat shirt and a tiny moustache, standing with his nice new family in front of his shiny black car, showing off his high ticket nouveau Colonial house.

It would solve a lot of problems, he thinks.

The field seems to stretch in all directions without boundaries. It's harder going than he thought. Once he starts moving the sawgrass whips his trousers and the ground is uneven and spongy under his feet. He walks for longer than seems right for a guy who wants simply to get to the nearest road so he can hitch a ride to some more exciting place.

At the moment the field seems endless. Travers has read enough French writers to think: I suppose this is symbolic. Existential whatever. It's probably about where I am in life.

But it isn't. He is really standing in a field, but where? In fact, he isn't much of anywhere, but he has no way of knowing. To the east there's a shape that may turn out to be a house. If it is a house and he goes inside, will he find a trap door in the living room and stairs leading to an underground universe, like the one in the computer game he used to play? No. This kind of experience doesn't play itself out like **Zork** or any other interactive game, although **Zork** is the perfect model for what's happening here. At the moment there is just Dave Travers, truly alone for the first time since he can remember, alone and standing in a field.

He doesn't know it but the geography isn't the only thing that eludes him. He's going to sit down to rest in a minute and when he gets up he'll know where he is. He will be less certain *when* it is. More: he won't know who he is.

Strangely, even though he forgets who he is, Travers will remember **Zork1,** the text-based computer game he played obsessively the summer when he was twelve.

Zork1: The Great Underground Empire

West of House

You are standing in an open field west of a white house, with a boarded front door.

There is a small mailbox here.

You were standing in the field but even there at the beginning with only three lines on your screen, you had options; you could open the mailbox and hope there was some usable scrap of information on the note inside (there wasn't) or you could go west toward the woods and mountains or you could go east and try to get into the house. Each time you made a choice you were presented with a new set of decisions, and it is this that Travers used to love—the sense of infinitely unfolding options and the knowledge that he could thwart the roving thief and bring back treasures if only he chose the right ones.

Everything rushes out of him in a sigh. He knows that so far, at least up to the moment when the train stopped, all his choices have been wrong. Why else would the details of his life slip away from him?

When he gets to his feet again he is still standing in a field, but it has changed. There is a mailbox here, and to the east he definitely sees a white house. From here he can see the front door is boarded up but he knows he will find a window open if he walks around the house. He is standing in a field, but who he is in the game and what he's doing here eludes him. *Kind of like life,* he thinks, although he has no idea what his life is supposed to be like right now. *I wonder what I'm supposed to do next.*

Travers already knows there's nothing substantive in the note in the mailbox so he turns, wondering exactly how many moves he has coming before the inevitable thief pounces and takes everything, which he's programmed to do when a player collects one too many treasures. When Travers reaches the house the windows are boarded up too, as in **Zork,** but he understands this is nothing like **Zork.** The back door stands open and even though it's nowhere near time for the thief to show up, there are people inside.

In the kitchen, three men sit around the table. He hears other men mumbling upstairs and men moving around in the living room. Travers should be afraid but he isn't, probably because they are well dressed and obviously middle class and in this light they look sweetly bemused.

He says the first thing he can think of: "I'm new around here." He's afraid to ask *where are we?* so he says, "Who are you?"

The first stands with a polite smile. "Dave Isham."

"Dave Caverness," the second says pleasantly.

"Dave Blount." The third of them says, "And who are you?"

Here it comes: the astonishment. "I don't know." Travers thinks for a minute. "Dave," he says. He doesn't want to remember, but he does. "Dave Travers."

Dave Blount grins. "Just goes to show, the nicest guys are always named Dave."

"Or the biggest losers." Dave Winters wanders in from the living room where there are other men on sofas and kicked back in Barcaloungers, muttering pleasantly over beers. "Welcome to the Island of Lost Boys."

Dave Isham says, "Don't scare him."

"Kidding!"

"Is that where I am?" Travers means, is that what I am? Lost?

Dave Blount shrugs. "Give or take. One way or another we're all taking a time out. You go along and you go along and then one day you just get sick of it, you know?"

The shrug ripples through the room like a wave. In another minute the others will begin to tell their stories and since he has lost any sense of what his story might be, Travers doesn't really want to be expected to pay back in kind. "Who pays the rent, and how?"

"It comes from somewhere," Dave Winters says.

Intent on making him feel welcome, Blount says, "We all kick in, but don't worry. It doesn't amount to much."

Travers pats his pockets. Wallet in place. He can't remember where he was going on the train but he remembers the train now. He remembers that in spite of Sandra's protests that he was cutting into the paycheck he banked to cover their monthly expenses, he took an extra hundred dollars to spend. OK, he remembers Sandra too. He remembers trying to talk to her and he remembers hearing her breathing into the phone. He asks, "Where does the money come from?"

One of the Daves says, "Odd jobs. We come and go as we like here and feed the kitty with money we pick up doing odd jobs."

So this is not like **Zork**, he understands, there is no trap door under the rug in the living room and no trophy case for storing captured treasures because there aren't going to be any treasures. There is no rich subterranean chamber waiting at the bottom of the stairs and there may not even be any stairs leading down. This isn't a game, it's a mundane setting, in which . . . what? The wild hubbies hide out? The Daves sitting in the kitchen and in the living room and the Daves collecting in the doorway are all smiling pleasantly; they seem happy enough, but when the doors popped open and Travers skipped the train—ok, he remembers skipping the train—he expected something more or better to come from his escape. This is too much like a kids' clubhouse, snug but shabby and overcrowded. Squinting, Travers tries to make it make sense. "I don't get it. This is a real place and I'm really in it?"

"Pretty much."

That shrug again. Dave Blount repeats, "Give or take. Listen, Dave, we're all on the run from something, one way and another. This works for us and if you like it, you're welcome to join us here."

"I don't know."

"You don't have to like it," Dave Winters says.

"Don't worry." Dave Blount will not stop smiling. "We'll do everything we can to make it pleasant for you here."

Travers looks around warily. "This isn't one of those places where when you try to leave they won't let you, is it."

The Daves shake their heads.

"Certainly not."

"No way."

"We're easy here."

"It's *sauve qui peut*," Dave Isham says with a look that tells Travers he isn't exactly sure what that means. "We were just about to eat. Grab a bowl and pull up a chair."

"Mi casa su casa."

"Thanks."

The chairs are comfortable. The soup they serve him is good. As if Travers has asked, they take turns explaining what they're doing here. In its own way the talk that surrounds him is as empty as the field he woke up in. The various Daves all got sick of their lives one day in different ways for various reasons but all more or less at the age Travers is now, which is thirty-five. One way or another they all woke up one morning to the sameold sameold and simply maxd out, but all on a different lover or a different line of work or a different family situation in a completely different place from all the others, although the stories seem interchangeable. Each presents the circumstances as brand-new. Each of them knows there are a million stories like the one he tells and every one of them insists that his story is different. This is what every man honestly believes. The Daves all got sick of their lives and started looking for ways out: the faked death so the survivors would get the insurance money to see them through; the explained runaway, with farewell note (DON'T LOOK FOR ME) pinned to the pillow or neatly folded on the kitchen table; the simple disappearance, although with fingerprints on file online and Missing Persons divisions in abundance, no disappearance is simple. Escaping the sameold sameold, the Daves all seem the same.

How long have they been here? The answers vary. How long are they going to stay and what do they want to do next? No one can say.

"We're cool," Dave Isham says, "who wants to do anything next?"

Travers feels his head jerk. Was he nodding off or did something sneak up behind him and smack him with a rolled-up newspaper? He isn't sure. He stands abruptly. "I can't be here."

"Where are you going?"

"Out."

"What are you going to do?"

Too soon to tell. "I need to think." He sticks his head back in the door and tells the polite lie. "Back soon."

"Take your time," Dave Blount says genially.

Somebody else calls after him, "It's the one thing we've got plenty of."

The surrounding field is even emptier than before. It is like surfacing in a vacuum. When Travers skims the horizon looking for landmarks to ground himself, the banked Ailanthus look dauntingly the same. No tree stands out from any other tree. If he doesn't start walking, he'll never find the road out of here, but he's reluctant to push off. If he turns his back on the house and starts walking he may never find it again. The changing light is so gradual that he is surprised to see that it's getting dark. When he looks back, there is smoke curling enchantingly out of the chimney and there are lights glowing in every window, although he remembers them as boarded up. It makes him think of long walks after supper on December nights in New London. When he was old enough to go out alone he used to leave the house as soon as it got dark and roam the neighborhood, waiting for lights to pop on in other people's windows. He knows now that he was window-shopping for other lives, checking out the displays in his neighbors' brightly lighted houses as though what he saw could be his, any time he was willing to pay the price. Did he want to live here, where a high school boy sits over his computer in his very own room or over there, where a couple with a flock of children bend their heads over grace before meals at the kitchen table or does he want to be like this old, old man in the orange stucco and live in silence in a place where nobody comes?

He needs to get moving but nostalgia hobbles him. The lives he used to spy on fuse with the life he thinks he and Sandra were living, bending their heads over nuked chicken dinners on the few nights when they ate together, slouching together on the sofa to watch TV while they emptied the identical foil trays, down to the bake-in-place apple cobbler. Sweet, he thinks. From the outside other people's lives usually look sweet.

OK, time to decide. Travers has three choices here. He can go back into the house and settle down with the Daves for as long as it takes. He can look for the road and head out into a more productive disappearance or he can do what he already knows he has to do—head back for the tracks—that way, he thinks. The morning train is long gone but if he can find the tracks he can get another train. Head for the tracks and follow them to the next station where, he thinks, his ticket is probably still good. After all, he bought a fare from New Haven to New York and didn't get the good of it because he jumped off somewhere around halfway. Worst case scenario, he can forget about the city and use his return ticket. He checks. Yep, he's still holding his return.

OK. Right. Time to pull up his socks and go back. He thinks: I owe it to my boss and my students, even though none of them ever gets anything above a C. I owe it to Sandra. After all, he thinks, not necessarily correctly, Sandra needs me. Get home, he thinks, walk in and she'll be so glad to see me that everything will be better for us. He should call ahead, but his phone isn't necessarily working and he doesn't want to find out for sure. Besides, he wants it to be a surprise. Things will change if she was really worried and she's really glad to see him.

If this field was really like the field in *Zork*, Dave's return would involve a measured number of trials and errors, ordeals and decisions, but it isn't. If this disconnected state Travers is in was in fact an ordinary crisis, his decision to go back would certainly resolve it. All this would turn out to be one of those dreams that evaporates as soon as the sleeper wakes up.

Travers would wake up on the same train he was riding this morning, surrounded by the same passengers and sitting next to the woman keyboarding with the morning paper folded on his lap and his briefcase at his feet and he would wake up with no actual time elapsed. Waking, he'd discover that although it's almost night here in the field where he is standing, on the train he was riding to the city, it is still ten a.m., seconds before he jumped.

There's also the possibility that he fell out: some kind of seizure—an attack of *petit mal* or a sugar crash that knocked him flat. In that case Travers will come to on the rattling metal floor just over the car's rear wheels, surrounded by horrified commuters who don't know what to do because he's choking on his tongue. *Step back,* one of the passengers will say, brandishing a pencil for him to clench between his teeth. *I'm a doctor.* Worst case scenario is a heart attack, unless it is the best: Travers returning to consciousness in an emergency room in Stamford or Bridgeport because much as the white light beckoned, at the last minute he lost heart and ran away from it. He hopes it doesn't spin out that way because he knows that people who almost die and come back from the white light spend the rest of their lives in perpetual mourning. They felt so calm, they say with that catch in the breath that masks a bereaved sob.

It was so peaceful there that they will never be happy again.

Travers should be so lucky. As it turns out, once he starts walking away from the house, he has to walk for hours. With no sun to steer by and no sliver of moon to light his way, he has no idea whether he's going east, toward the water and the tracks, or whether in fact he has circled in the dark and is accidentally heading for the mountains in the west where—if this could only be *Zork!*— where he'd go through the mountain pass and broach the gorge to find the miserable dam and, with any luck, the lost Atlantis which reveals itself when a player pushes the right buttons and the river drains. When he looks back in hopes of sighting his only landmark, Travers can no longer see the lights of the house glowing behind him. He thinks the breeze is a little damper and he catches a hint of salt on his tongue, so there is a chance he's really going toward Long Island Sound and the tracks.

Then a string of lights streaks along just above the horizon: the train, he thinks, lucky people staring at nothing out of all those lighted windows. It's so late here that he has no way of knowing whether it is his train. Probably not. It would appear that this journey is not the product of a temporary fainting fit and he isn't dreaming, either. His train is long gone. It really is night and it's getting late. After midnight the Metro North schedule thins to a trickle. Few trains go by at this hour, so he has to wait. There is the additional problem of getting any train to stop for him.

When a train does come its lights pick up Travers standing in the middle of the tracks with his white face glowing like a surrender flag. He wigwags his arms wildly, trying to get the engineer's attention, but the thing comes roaring down on him anyway. For a second he wavers, considering. It is an opportunity, and it is tempting. He jumps out of the way, but only at the last minute. When you decide to get back on the train you don't give in and get trashed by one.

He shrugs. Sighing, he starts walking along the tracks.

It is a long night.

The landscape is barren and the tracks seem endless. Even in gathering daylight the engineers won't stop for him. The stations, if there are stations where he is heading, must be closed for the night. Eventually, he supposes, he'll come to at least one crossing where the tracks intersect a major road instead of taking the bridge over it or disappearing into yet another underpass. Then he can take the road and hope drivers are better at the Samaritan thing than the night engineers on Metro North. Hopeful, he looks ahead, but as far as he can tell, it's unbroken track all the way down the line.

Come on, he thinks. *I can't go on this way.* As it turns out, he can. He walks for another hour and except for detritus stirred up by the breeze from passing trains, nothing changes. It's getting tired out. He's hungry now.

Defeated, he taps his phone. "Sandra? It's me. I'm on the train."

He's not but it won't matter. Either his battery's dead or the nearest relay tower is so far out of range that she won't hear him.

"I never should have gotten off that train," he says anyway.

—The Texas Review, 1986

The Bride of Bigfoot

Imagine the two of us together, the sound of our flesh colliding; the smell of him. The smell of me.

At first I was afraid. Who would not be frightened by stirring shadows, leaves that shiver inexplicably, the suspicion that just outside the circle of bug lamps and firelight something huge has passed? If there was a Thing at all it was reported to be shy; the best photographs are blurred and of questionable origin; hunters said it would not attack even if provoked, but still . . . The silence it left behind was enormous; I could feel my heart shudder in my chest. With gross figures roaming, who would not be afraid?

We did not see or hear it; there was only the intimation. It had been there. It was gone. Thomas, whom I married six months ago, said, Listen. I said, I don't hear anything. Roberta said, I'm cold. Thomas persisted: I thought I heard something. Did you hear anything? I did not speak but Malcolm, who was torturing steaks on our behalf, spoke politely. Everybody's so quiet, it must be twenty of or twenty after. Then Roberta said, Something just walked over my grave. I tried to laugh, but I was cold.

This was the night of our first cookout of the summer, shortly before I found certain pieces of my underwear missing from the line.

Our house is on the outer ring of streets here, so that instead of our neighbors' carports and arrangements for eating outside we look out at a wooded hillside, dense undergrowth and slender trees marching up the slope.

If it weren't for dust and attrition and human failure our house would be picture perfect. I used to want to go to live in one of our arrangements; the future would find me among the plant stands, splayfooted and supporting a begonia; I would be both beautiful and functional, a true work of art. Or I would be discovered on the sofa among the pillows, my permanent face fixed in a perpetual smile. I would face the future with no worries and no obligations, just one more pretty, blameless thing. It's a long road that knows no turning but an even longer one we women go. Each night even as I surveyed my creation I could see fresh dust settling on my polished surfaces, crumbs collecting on my kitchen floor, and I knew soon the light would change and leaves drop from my plants no matter what I did. Each night I knew I had to turn from my creations and start dinner because although Thomas and I both worked, it was I who must prepare the food. Because women are free and we are in the new society I was not forced to do these things; I had to do them by choice.

But it was summer, we opened all the windows and went in the yard without coats. We had that first cookout and maybe it was the curling smoke that wakened it, or maybe it saw me in my bathing suit . . . All I can tell you is that I lost certain underthings: my satin panties, my gossamer sheen bra. When I came home from work at night I went directly into the back yard. I tried to penetrate the woods, staring at the screen of leaves for so long that I was certain I had seen something move. The summer air was already dense with its scent, but what it was I did not know; I could not be sure whether that was a tuft of hair caught in the wild honeysuckle or only fur. Every night I lingered and therefore had to apologize to Thomas because dinner was late.

Something dragged a flowering bush to our back stoop. Outside our bedroom the flowers were flattened mysteriously. I got up at dawn and listened to the woods. Did I imagine the sound of soft breath? Did I catch a flash of gold among the leaves, the pattern of shadows dappling a naked flank?

In midsummer something left a dead bird with some flowers on my kitchen table and I stopped going outside. I stopped leaving the windows open too; I told Thomas we would sleep better with the air conditioning. I should have known none of our arrangements are permanent. Even with the house sealed and the air conditioner whirring I could hear something crashing in the woods. I ran to the back door to see and when I found nothing I stood a moment longer so that even though I could not see it, it would see me. When we went to bed that night it was not Thomas I imagined next to me, but something else.

In August I retreated to the kitchen; with the oven fan going and the radio on, the blender whizzing and all my whisks and ladles and spatulas laid out I could pretend there was nothing funny happening. We had seafood soufflé one night and the next we had veal medallions, one of my best efforts. When we went to bed Thomas turned to me and I tried to be attentive but I was already torn. I was as uneasy as a girl waiting for somebody new to come in to the high school party—one of those strange, tough boys that shows up unexpectedly, with the black T-shirt and the long, slick hair, who stands there with his pelvis on the slant and the slightly dangerous look that lets you know your mother would never approve.

On Friday I made salmon mayonnaise, which I decorated with cress and dill, and for dessert I made a raspberry fool, after which I put on my lavender shift and opened the back door. In spite of the heat I stood there until Thomas came in the front door. Then I touched the corners of the mats and napkins on my pretty table and aligned the wineglasses and the water tumblers because Thomas and I had pretty arrangements and we set store by them.

Honey, why such a big kiss?

I missed you, I said. How was your day?

Much the same.

So we sat down at the little table with all our precious objects: the crystal candle holders, the wedding china, the Waterford, him, me. I asked if he liked his dinner.

Mmmm.

All right; I tried to slip it in. Am I doing something wrong?

I'm just a little tired.

Tell me about your day, you never do.

Mmm.

Outside, the thing in the woods was stirring. Thomas, love is to man a thing apart, it's woman's whole existence.

Mmmmm.

In the woods there was the thunder of air curdling: something stopping in mid rush.

I love you, Thomas.

I love you.

Honey, are you sure?

Mmmmm.

I put out a dish of milk for it.

No, Lieutenant, there were no signs of a struggle, one reason I didn't think to call you right away. I thought she had just stepped out and was coming back. When I got home from work Monday she was gone. Nothing out of order, nothing to raise your suspicions, no broken windows or torn screens. The house was shining clean. She had even left a chicken pie for me. But there was this strange, wild stink in the bedroom, plus which later I found *this* stuck in the ornamental palm tree on our screen door, your lab could tell you if it's hair, or fur.

I wish I could give you more details, like whether the Thing knocked my wife out or tied her up or what, but I wasn't too careful looking for clues because I didn't even know there was a Thing. For all I knew she had run over to a neighbor's, or down to the store to pick up some wine, which is what I thought in spite of the heap of clothes by the bed, thought even after it got dark.

By midnight when I hadn't heard I called her folks. You can imagine. Then

I checked the closet with my heart going, clunk, clunk. Nothing gone. Her bankbook and wallet were in her purse. All right, I should have called you but to tell the truth I thought it was something I could handle by myself. Ought to handle. A man has a right to protect what's his, *droit de seigneur,* OK? Besides, I didn't think it was kidnappers. That gray fur. The smell. It had to be some kind of wild animal, an element with which I am equipped to cope. I used to hunt with my father, and I know what animals do when they're spooked. Your cordon of men or police helicopter could panic it into doing something we would all be sorry for. I figured if it was a bear or wolf or something that got in, and it didn't kill her right here, it had probably carried her off to its lair, which meant it was a job for one man alone. Now I have my share of trophies, you might as well know back home I was an Eagle Scout and furthermore I am a paid-up member of the N.R.A. Plus which, this is not exactly the wilds. This is suburban living enhanced by proximity to the woods. If something carried off my wife I would stalk it to its lair and lie in wait. Then when it fell asleep or went off hunting, I would swarm in and carry her out.

All right, it did cross my mind that we might get an exclusive. Also it was marginally possible that if I rescued her we might lure the creature into the open. I could booby-trap the terrace and snare it on the hoof. Right, I had guessed what it was, imagine the publicity! The North American serial rights alone . . . After which we could take our sweet time deciding which publisher, holding the paperback auction, choosing between the major motion picture and an exclusive on TV. I personally would opt for the movie, we could sell backward to television and follow up with a series pilot and spinoff, the possibilities are astronomical, and if we could get the Thing to agree to star . . .

But my Sue is a sentimental girl and I couldn't spring this on her all at once. First I had to get her home and then I was going to have to walk her through it, one step at a time, how I was going to make it clear to the public that she was an unwilling prisoner, so nobody would think she was easy, or cheap. You know how girls are. I was going to have to promise not to take advantage of her privileged relationship with the Thing. But what if we could train it to do what we wanted? What if we taught it to talk! I was going to lay it out to her in terms of fitting recompense. I mean, there is no point being a victim when you can cash in on a slice of your life.

Lord, if that was all I had to worry about! But what did I know? That was in another country and besides . . . Right, T. S. Eliot. I don't want you to think of me as an uncultivated man.

I got up before dawn and dressed for the hunt: long-sleeved shirt and long trousers, against the insects; boots, against the snakes. I tied up my head for personal reasons and smeared insect repellent on my hands and face. Then I got the rest of my equipment: hunting knife, with sheath; a pint of rye, to lure it; tape recorder, don't ask; my rifle, in case. A coil of rope.

It took less time to track it than I thought. You might not even know there was anything in the woods because you're not attuned to these things, but I can tell you they left a trail a mile wide. Broken twigs, twisted leaves, that kind of thing. So I closed in on their arrangement while it was still light; I came over the last rise and down into a thicket and there it was. I had expected to have a hard time locating her once I got to the lair; the Thing would have tied her in a tree, say, or concealed her under a mass of brush or behind a pile of rocks.

This was not the case. She was right out in the open, sitting on a ledge in front of its lair just as nice as you please. Except for the one thing, you would think she was sunning in the park. Right. Except for the dirt and the flowers in her hair, she was *au naturel*. There was my wife Susie sitting with a pile of fruits in season, she was not tied up and she was not screaming, she wasn't even writing a note. She was—good Lord, she was combing her hair. I went to earth. I had to be careful in case the Thing was using her for bait. It could be in its cave lying in wait, or circling behind me, ready to attack. I lay still for an hour while she combed and hummed and nothing happened. There was nothing, not even a trace. I got up and showed myself.

I guess I startled her. She jumped three feet. I said, Don't be frightened, it's me.

Oh, it's you. Where did you come from?

Never mind that now. We have to hurry.

What are you doing?

Suze, I have come to take you home.

Imagine my surprise. All this way to rescue my darling helpmate, the equipment, precautions, and all she could find to say was: You can't do that.

What do you mean?

So she was trying to spare my feelings, but that would take me some time to figure out. You have to go for your own good, Thomas. He'll tear you limb from limb.

Just let him try. I shook my rifle.

Thomas, no!

I did not like the way this was going. Not only was she not thrilled to see me but she showed signs of wanting to stay put. I was not sure what we had here, whether she was playing a game I had not learned the rules to or whether she had been unhinged by the experience. You should only have to court a woman once. What I did at this point was assert my rights. Any husband would have done the same. I said, Enough is enough, honey, now let's get home before it gets dark. Listen, this is for your own good. Susie, what are you doing with that rock?

To make a long story short I had to bop her on the head and drag her out. I don't know how we made it back to the house. Halfway down the hill she woke up and started struggling so I had to throw her on the ground and tie her up, in addition to which the woods were filled with what I would have to call intimations of the creature. There was always your getting pounced upon from the shadows, or jumped out of a tree onto, to say nothing of your getting grabbed from behind and shaken, your neck snapped with one pop. I kept thinking I heard the Thing sneaking up behind me, I imagined its foul breath on my neck. As a matter of fact I never saw hide nor hair of it, and it crossed my mind that there might never have been a Thing, a thought I quickly banished. Of course there had. Then I figured out that it was afraid to run after what it believed in, which meant that it was craven indeed, to let her go without a fight.

As soon as we got inside I locked all the doors and windows and put Susie in the tub with a hooker of gin and a pint of bubble bath, after which, together, we washed all that stuff out of her hair, including the smell. I guess the gin opened the floodgates; she just sat there with the tears running down her cheeks while I picked the flowers out of her hair. Somehow I knew this was not the time to bring up the major motion picture. What we had here might turn out to be private and not interesting to anybody but us.

There there, Suze, I said. Don't feel bad.

She only cried louder.

Now we know who loves you the most.

She just kept on crying.

I tried to cheer her up by making a joke. Maybe it found a cheap date.

She howled and wouldn't speak to me.

So I looked at her naked, heaving shoulders and I thought: *Aren't you going to apologize?* I was afraid to ask but I had to say something; after all, she was my wife.

Don't be ashamed, Suze. We all get carried away at least once in our life.

When she would not stop crying I thought it must have been one of those one-night stands, if the Thing cared about her at all it would be tearing the house down to get to her. She would get over it, I thought. But she would not be consoled. There there, I said, there there. When this blows over I'll buy you a car.

Fat lot I knew. It was a tactic. All the Thing had to do was lay back and wait for her to get loose. Which I discovered shortly before dawn when I woke to an unusual sound. I sat up and saw her moving among the bedroom curtains, trying to unlock the sliding door. Was the Thing in the bushes, waiting? Would she run outside with cries of delight? I was afraid to find out. I sprang up and tackled her, after which I laid down the law. She didn't argue, she only wept and languished. It was terrible. I had tried to arm against the enemy outside and all the time I had this enemy within. I called us both in sick at work after which I marched her with me to the hardware store and surveilled her the whole time I was buying locks. Then I barred the doors and put extra locks on all the windows. The Thing was so smart it wasn't going to show itself. It was just going to sit tight and wait. Well, two could play at that game, I thought. When it got tired of waiting and showed itself I would blow it apart.

I suppose I was counting too much on her. I thought sooner or later she would clean herself up and apologize and we could go back to our life. Not so. We went from vacation time into leave without pay and she was still a mess. She would not stop crying and she wouldn't speak to me. She just kept plastering herself to the windows with this awful look of hope. In addition to which, there was the smell. It would fill the room when I least expected it. My Susie would lift her head and sniff and grin and if I tried to lay a hand on her, look out! It was enough to make a grown man weep.

I had to act.

So what I did was put her in the cellar and lock her up, after which I put on my hunting clothes and located the equipment; rifle, knife, rope. The tape recorder, she had smashed. I didn't know how far I would have to stalk the Thing or what I would have to do to make it show itself but I was sick of the waiting game. Damn right I was scared. I took the double bar off the back door and went down the steps.

I tiptoed across the night garden, and over to the trees. I know you're in there, I said in a reasonable tone. If you don't come out I'm coming in after you.

There was nothing, only the smell. I thought I would pass out.

Homewrecker. Bastard, come on. Right, I was getting mad. I cocked the rifle. In another minute I was going to spray the trees.

Then it showed itself. It just parted the maples like swinging doors and walked out.

Huge? Yes, and that fetor, wow! The hair that covered it, the teeth . . . You've heard tales brought back by hunters. You can imagine the rest. The Thing stood there in the moonlight with its yellow teeth bared while I kept my rifle trained on its chest. It just stood there snuffling. I was, all right, I was overconfident. I yelled: Are you going to leave Susie and me alone or what?

At which point it sprang. Before I could even squeeze the trigger this great big monstrous Thing sprang right on top of me after which I don't remember much except the explosion of my rifle, the kick. So it must be wounded, at least, which I suppose means it has left a trail of blood, but Lieutenant, I don't want to press charges. The thing is, my Susie left me of her own free will and now that all is said and done I understand.

No, I can't explain, not exactly, except it has to do with the thing, no, I mean, *Thing*: the stench, the roar, the smack of its prodigious flesh. It must have squeezed the daylights out of me and thrown me into Malcolm's grape arbor, which is where I woke up. They were gone and he was calling the police.

I'm letting her go, Lieutenant, and with my blessings, because I learned something extraordinary in that terrible embrace. There are things we don't *want* to want but that doesn't stop us wanting them, even as we beg forgiveness. Life lets us know there is more than the orderly lines we lay out, that these lines can flex so we catch glimpses of the rest, and if a thing like this can happen to my Susie, who am I to say what I would do if it happened to me?

—*Asimov's* SF, 1984

The Zombie Prince

What do you know, fool, all you know is what you see in the movies: clashing jaws and bloody teeth; raw hunger lurching in to eat you, thud thud thud. We are nothing like you think.

The zombie that comes for you is indifferent to flesh. What it takes from you is tasteless, odorless, colorless, and huge. You have a lot to lose.

The incursion is gradual. It does not count the hours or months it may spend circling the bedroom where you sleep. For the zombie, there is no anxiety and no waiting. We walk in a zone that transcends disorders like human emotion. In the cosmos of the undead there is only being and un-being, without reference to time.

Therefore your zombie keeps its distance, fixed on the patch of warmth that represents you, the unseemly racket you make, breathing. Does your heart have to make all that noise, does your chest have to keep going in and out with that irritating rasp? The organs of the undead are sublimely still. Anything else is an abomination.

Then you cough in your sleep. It is like an invitation.

We are at your bedroom window. The thing we need is laid open for us to devour.

For no reason you sit up in bed with your heart jumping and your jaw ajar: what?

Nothing, *you tell yourself, because you have to if you're going to make it through the night.* Just something I ate.

Hush, if you enjoy living. Be still. Try to be as still as me. Whatever you do, don't go to the window! Your future crouches below, my perfect body cold and dense as marble, the eyes devoid of light. If you expect to go on being yourself tomorrow when the sun comes up, stay awake! Do it! This is the only warning you'll get.

One woman alone, naturally you are uneasy, but you think you're safe. Didn't you lock the windows when you went to bed last night, didn't you lock your doors and slip the dead bolt? Nice house, gated community with Security patrolling, what could go wrong? You don't know that while you sleep the zombie seeks entry. This won't be anything like you think.

Therefore you stumble to the bathroom and pad back to your bedroom in the dark. You drop on the bed like a felled cedar, courting sleep. It's as close as you can get to being one of us. Go ahead, then. Sleep like a stone and if tonight the zombie who has come for you slips in and takes what it needs from you, tomorrow you will not wake up, exactly.

You will get up. Changed.

When death comes for you, you don't expect it to be tall and gorgeous. You won't even know the name of the disaster that overtakes you until it's too late.

Last night Dana Graver wished she could just bury herself in bed and never have to wake up. She'd rather die than go on feeling the way she does.

She wanted to die the way women do when the man they love ends it with no apologies and no explanation. "I'd understand," she cried, "if this was about another girl." And Bill Wylie, the man she thought she loved—that she thought loved her! Bill gave her that bland, sad look and said unhelpfully, "I'm sorry, I just can't do this any more."

Her misery is like a bouquet of broken glass flowers, every petal a jagged edge tearing her up inside. She would do anything to make it stop. She'd never put herself out—no pills, no razor blades for Dana Graver, no blackened corpse for Bill to find, although he deserves an ugly shock.

She'd never consciously hurt herself but if she lies on her back in the dark and *wills* herself to die it might just accidentally happen, would that be so bad? Let the heartless bastard come in and find his sad, rejected love perfectly composed, lovely in black with her white hands folded gracefully and her dark hair flowing, a reproach that would haunt him for the rest of his life. *Look what you did to me.* Doesn't he deserve to know what it sounds like to hear your own heart break?

Composed for death, Dana dozes instead. She drops into sleep like an ocean, wishing she could submerge and please God, never have to come back up. She . . .

She jerks awake. *Oh God, I didn't mean it!*

There is something in the room.

With her heart hammering she sits up, trembling. Switches on the light.

The silent figure standing by the dresser looks nothing like the deaths a single woman envisions. No ski mask, so this is no home invasion; no burglar's tools. It isn't emblematic, either, there's no grim reaper's robe, no apocalyptic scythe. This isn't SARS coming for her and it isn't the Red Death. The intruder is tall and composed. Extremely handsome. Impeccable in white. The only hint of difference is the crescents of black underneath the pale, finely buffed fingernails.

She shrieks.

In ordinary incursions the victim's scream prompts action: threats or gunshots or knife attack, the marauder's lunge. This person does nothing. If it is a person. The shape of the head is too perfect. There is something sublime in its unwavering scrutiny.

Chilled, Dana scrambles backward until she is clinging to the bedstead. She throws the lamp at it, screaming. "Get out!"

It doesn't move. It doesn't speak.

There is only the crash as the glass lamp base shatters against the wall behind the huge head. The light itself survives, casting ragged shadows on the ceiling. The silence spins out for as long as Dana can stand it. They are in stasis here.

When she can speak, she says, "What are you doing here?"

Is it possible to talk without moving your lips? The stranger in her room doesn't speak. Instead, Dana knows. Uncanny. She *knows*.

—**Good evening. Isn't that what you people say?**

She does what you do. She opens her throat and screams to wake the dead.

—**Don't do that.**

"I can't help it!"

—**I'm sorry. I'm new at this.**

"Who are you?"

—**You mean the name I used to have? No idea. It left me when I died . . .**

"Died!"

The intruder continues —**and I would have to die again to get it back, and you know what death brings. Dissolution and decay. Sorrow.**

"*What* are you?"

—**For the purposes of this conversation, you can call me X. Every one of us is known as X.**

"Oh my God. Oh, my God!"

The great head lifts. —**Who?**

"Get out." Higher. Dana sends her voice high enough to clear the room and raise the neighborhood. "Get out!" When she uncovers her face the intruder hasn't advanced and it hasn't run away.

It hasn't moved. It is watching her, graceful and self-contained. As if her screams are nothing to it. —**No.**

"Get out or I'll . . ." Groping for the empty pistol she keeps under the pillow she threatens wildly. "I'll shoot!"

—**Go ahead.** So calm. Too calm! —**It won't change anything.**

"Oh." Noting the fixed, crystalline eyes she understands that this is true. "Oh my *God*."

The bedroom is unnaturally still. So is the intruder. Except for the trembling Dana can't control, except for her light, irregular breathing, she too manages to stay quiet. The figure in white stands without moving, a monument to patience. There is a fixed beauty to the eyes, a terrifying lack of expression. They are empty and too perfect, like doll's eyes: too pale to be real, blue as blown flowers with stars for pupils. —**Don't be afraid. That won't change anything either.**

Dana isn't afraid, exactly, she is too badly hurt by the breakup with Bill to think much about anything else, and this? What's happening here in her bedroom is too strange to be real. It's as though she is floating far above it. Not an out-of-body experience, exactly, but one in which everything changes.

The intruder is impeccable in a white suit, black shirt, bright circle of silver about one wrist—silver wire braided, she notes in the kind of mad attention to detail that crisis sparks in some people. The rapt gaze. Like an underground prince ravished by its first look at the sun. The attention leaves her more puzzled than frightened. Flattered, really, by that gaze fixed on her as if she really matters. As if this strange figure has come to break her out of the jail that is her life. Bill's betrayal changed her. She was almost destroyed but even that is changing. She can't forgive Bill but with this magnetic presence in her room, for seconds at a time she almost forgets about Bill.

The dark hair, the eyebrows like single brushstrokes, the pallor, are eerie and sinister and glamorous. She doesn't know whether to flirt or threaten. Better the former, she thinks. *Let Bill come in and find us, that will show him.* Unless she's stalling until her fingers can find bullets and load the gun. As if she could make a dent in that lustrous skin. "What is this?" she asks, overtaken. "Why are you here?"

The answer takes too long coming. It is not that the stranger has stopped to choose its words. It exists without reference to time. When the answer comes, it isn't exactly an answer. —**You are my first.**

"First what?" First what, she wonders. First love? First kill? The stranger is so gorgeous standing there. So courteous and so still. Impervious. None of her fears fit the template. If Dana's clock is still running, she can't read the face. Unnerved by the absence of sound—this intruder doesn't shift on its feet, it doesn't cough or clear its throat; she doesn't hear it breathing!—she whispers, "What are you?"

—**Does the word undead mean anything to you?**

"No!" It doesn't. Nice suit, cultivated manner, he's a bit of a mystery, but the handsome face, the strange, cool eyes lift him so far out of the ordinary that the rules don't pertain here. He's here because he's attracted to her. "You don't look like a . . ."

—**Zombie?**

Then it does! Images flood the room, blinding her to everything but the terror. Dana flies out of bed, rushing the door, ricocheting off the stranger's alabaster facade with her hands flying here, there. Screaming, she hurls herself at the sealed bedroom window, battering on the glass.

—**Or walking dead.**

"No!" A zombie.

—**If you prefer.**

This is a zombie. "No, no! Oh my God, don't touch me!"

—**Hold still.** It has an eerie dignity. —**I'm not going to eat you.**

Idiot human. If you're afraid of getting your face gnawed off or your arm ripped out of its socket and devoured, you've seen too many movies. Your body is of no interest to us, not me, not any. We don't hunt in packs nor do we come in pairs. The zombie travels alone and the zombie takes what it needs without your knowing it. What I take can be extracted through the slightest opening; a keyhole, the crack under your bedroom door. Like a rich man the morning after a robbery, you may not even know what is missing.

"Don't." Sobbing, Dana retreats to the bed, pulling the covers up in a knot. All her flailing, her failed attempts to escape, all that screaming and the intruder hasn't advanced a fraction of an inch. So calm and so very beautiful. In a way it's everything she wants, she thinks, or everything she wants to be. Unless it's everything she's afraid of. She is a tangled mass of conflicting emotions—grief and terror and something as powerful as it is elusive. "What do you want?"

—**Zombies do not want. They need.**

"You're not going to . . ." She locks her arms across her front with an inadvertent shudder.

—**Do you really believe I want to chew your arm off?**

"I don't know what I believe!" This is not exactly true. In spite of what it says, Dana is afraid it's here to devour her. *Doesn't have to be me,* she thinks cleverly. Odd what rejection does to you; her heart congeals like a pond in a flash freeze. Why not pull a switch and buy her safety with a substitute? In a vision of the fitness of things she sees Bill broken in two for his sins; she hears Bill howling in pain as the zombie's pale, strong hands plunge into his open chest, and when this happens? Maybe she and her elegant zombie will make love while Bill dies and that'll show him, that will damn well show him. "If you want to eat," she says in a low voice, "I can feed you."

—**If that was what I came for you'd be bare bones by now.**

She does what you do in ambiguous situations. She asks a polite question. "How . . . How did you get this way?"

—**No idea. Zombies do not remember.**

This brings Dana's head up fast. "You don't remember anything?"

—**No.**

Thoughtfully, she says, "So you don't remember how it happened."

—**No. Nothing from before.** The silence is suddenly empty, as though the thing in her bedroom has just walked out and closed the door on itself.

Nothing, it is the nature of our condition. There was a name on my headstone when I got up and walked, but I had no interest in reading it. There was this silver bracelet on my wrist that must have meant something to me once. Engraving inside, perhaps, but I don't need to read it. Who gave it, and what did I feel for her back when I was human? Human I'm not. There is no grief in the zone where I walk, There is no loss and no pain, and yet . . .

I came out of the grave wiped clean. I came out strong and powerful and insentient. Yet there is this great sucking hole at my center. It burns. I need. I need . . . What?

"But all this time you've been dead. I mean, undead. You must be starved." Clever Dana's fingers creep toward the phone. She can't imagine what she needs to say to please him. "I can get you somebody. Somebody big. Practically twice my size."

—**No thank you.**

"Really." All she has to do is tell the bastard she's OD'd on sleeping pills. Guilt will have him here in a flash. "Tall. Overweight." Fat, she thinks, Bill is fat and now that she thinks about it, probably unfaithful. "Fleshy. Just let me make this call."

—**You don't understand.** Terrifying but beautiful, in a way, the flat blue gaze. That grave shake of the head. —**Flesh is anathema to us.**

Idiot woman, do you imagine I came here to feed? Flesh-eating monsters may exist, botched lab experiments or mindless aberrations raised from the grave by toxic spills, but they are only things *with no awareness of outcomes and this is the difference between them and us.*

When you have been dead and buried, outcomes are everything to you.

Eat and the outcome is inevitable. Gorge on flesh—take even one bite!—and it all comes back: life, memory and regret, rapid, inexorable decay, and with it, an insatiable desire for the fires of home.

Gnawing anxiously at her lower lip, Dana is too distracted to feel her teeth break the skin. She sees the intruder's eyes shift slightly. They are fixed not on her throat, but on her mouth. She shakes her head, puzzled. "You're really not hungry?"

—**When you have been dead and buried, mortal concerns are nothing to you.**

"So you really don't have to eat."

—**If we do, we lose everything.**

"But when you die you lose everything," she says, shivering.

—**If you mean little things like pain and memory, yes.**

This brings Dana's head up. "Nothing hurts?"

—**Nothing like that. No.**

"Wait," she says carefully. "You don't feel anything?"

—**We are above human flaws like feeling . . .**

"And you don't remember anything. Oh. Oh!" The truth comes in like a highway robber approaching in stages. She says in a low voice, "I can't imagine what that's like."

—**. . . and mortality.**

Her breath catches and her heart shudders at the discovery. Her hand flies to cover it. "Oh," she cries. "Oh!"

Easy. This is easy. Greedy, vulnerable girl. I knew you before you saw this coming. Who wouldn't want to forget and who doesn't love oblivion? Who would risk all that for a scrap of meat, the taste of blood? Knowing flesh can destroy us.

Topple and your former self comes back to you. All the love and pain and terror and excitement and grief and intolerable suspense that come with mortality. All you want to do is go home. You want to go home!

Aroused and terrified, you set out. With your restarted heart thudding, you approach the house. You are burning to rejoin the family. Walk into the circle: am I late? *as though nothing's happened. Do not expect to find them as you left them. You have changed too. Are changing as your body begins to decay—too fast, all that lost time to make up for.*

It will be harsh.

Do not imagine that—wherever you come from, no matter how sorely you are missed—they will be glad to see you. Didn't they drop dirt and roses on your coffin a dozen years ago when they put you away? They sobbed when you slipped into a coma and fell dead, no cause the doctors could find, so sad. They loved you and begged God to bring you back to them, but they didn't mean it.

Not like this.

Your body is no longer in stasis. You are in a footrace with decay. The changes begin the minute your heart resumes beating so hurry, you are on fire. If only you can see them again! Hurry. Try to make it home while they can still recognize you! You will decompose fast because, face it, you died a long time ago. You've been around too long. In the end, you'll die again, and the family? Look at them sitting around the supper table in the yellow light, photo of you on the mantel, pot roast again. God in His heaven and everything in its place. Do you really want to blunder in and interrupt that?

You should hang back, but now that you remember, now that you feel, you are excited to see them, you can't wait! Be warned, nothing is as you remember. Not any more. With your arms spread wide in hopes you will come surging out of the darkness, incandescing with love, but do not be surprised when they run screaming. Your loving face is a terror, your gestures are nightmarish, they are horrified by the sounds you make, your heartfelt cries that they can't quite decipher bubbling out of your rotting face.

Pray to God that your home is so far away that you won't make it even though you are doomed to keep going. Sobbing, you will forge ahead on bloody stumps, heading home until the bones that hold you up splinter and you drop. Now hope to God that what's left of you decomposes in a woods somewhere, unseen by the loved ones you're trying so desperately to reach. You need to see them just once more and you need it terribly, but be grateful that they are spared this final horror. You will die in the agony of complete memory, and you will die weeping for everything you've lost.

Time passes. The silence is profound. It is as though they are sharing the same long dream. Certain things are understood without having to be spoken. At last Dana snaps to attention. Like a refrigerator light set to go on when the door opens, the handsome figure in her bedroom remains motionless, with its great hands relaxed at its sides and crystal eyes looking into something she can only guess at. Alert now, excited by the possibilities, Dana tilts her head, regarding him. Carefully, she resumes the catechism. "You really don't feel anything?"

—**No.**

Dana studies the beautiful face, the graceful stance. Absolute composure, like a gift. She says dreamily, "That must be wonderful."

Sometime during the long silence that has linked them, she stopped thinking of the zombie who has come for her as an it. This is a man, living or dead or undead, a beautiful man in her room and he is here for her. Without speaking he tells her, —**When you have been dead and buried there is no wonderful . . .**

"I see." Not sure where this is going, Dana touches her speed dial. On her cell phone, Bill has always been number one. Her zombie notes this but nothing in his face changes. If he hears the little concatenation of beeps and the phone's ringing and ringing cut short by Bill's tiny, angry "What!" it makes no difference to him. When she's sure Bill is wide awake and listening Dana opens her arms to the intruder, saying in a new voice, "But we can still . . ."

— **. . . and no desire . . .**

"But you're so beautiful." She expects him to say, *So are you.*

— **. . . looks are nothing to you . . .**

"That's so sad!" The phone is alive with Bill's angry squawking.

— **. . . because you never change.**

"Oh!" This makes her stop and think. "You mean you never get old?"

—**No.**

For Bill's benefit she continues on that same sexy note. Oddly, it seems to fit the story that's unfolding. "And nothing hurts . . ."

—**No, nothing hurts.**

Far out of reach, Bill shouts into the phone. "Dana . . . "

As Dana purrs like a tiger licking velvet. "But everybody wants."

—**Zombies don't want. They need.**

She is drawn into the rhythm of the exchange, the metronomic back and forth. God he is handsome, she would like to run her hands along that perfect jaw, down the neck, and inside the shirt collar to that perfect throat. "And you need . . ."

Without moving he is suddenly too close. She sees green veins lacing the pale skin. —**Something elusive. Infinitesimal. You won't even miss it. And when it's gone . . .**

"Dammit, Dana!"

"But when it's gone . . ."

—**You will be changed.**

"Changed," she says dreamily, "and nothing will hurt any more."

—**When you have been dead and buried pain is nothing to you.**

"Will I be like you?"

—**In a way.**

She says into the growing hush, "So I'll be immortal."

—In a way.

There is an intolerable pause. Why doesn't he touch her? She doesn't know. He is close enough for her to see the detail on the silver bracelet; he's next to the bed, he is right *here* and yet he hasn't reached out. Unaccountably chilled as she is right now—something in the air, she supposes—Dana is drawn. Whatever he is, she wants. She has to have it! Her voice comes from somewhere deep inside. "What do you want me to do?"

His cold, cold hand rises to her cheek but does not touch it. —**Nothing.**

"Are we going to, ah . . ." Dana's tone says, *make love.* She is distantly aware of Bill Wylie still on the phone, trying to get her attention.

"Dana, do you hear me?"

"Shut up, Bill. Don't bother me." She wants to taunt him with the mystery. She doesn't understand it herself. She wants to make love with this magnetic, unassailable stranger; she wants to *be* him. She wants him to love her as Bill never did, really, and she wants Bill to hear everything that happens between them. She wants Bill Wylie to lie there in his outsized bachelor's bed listening as his seduction unfolds, far out of sight and beyond his control—Bill, who until last night she expected to marry and live with forever. Let this night sit in Bill's imagination and fester there and torture him for the rest of his life. Whatever she does with this breathtaking stranger will free her forever, and Bill? It will serve him right. "Come take what you want."

"Damn it to hell, Dana, I'm coming over!"

—**When you have been dead and buried you do not know desire.**

Yet there is a change in the air between them.

The mind forgets but the body remembers. Bracelet glinting on my arm. What's the matter with me? *Zombies know, insofar as they know anything, that you extract the soul from a distance. Through a keyhole, through a crack in a bedroom window. Always from a distance. This is essential. This knowledge is embedded: get too close and you get sucked in. And yet, and yet! It is as though the bracelet links X to the past it has no memory of. Interesting failure here, perhaps because this is its first assault on the precincts of the living. Zombies come out of the grave knowing certain things, but this one is distracted by unbidden reminders of the flesh, the circle of bright silver around the bone like a link to the forgotten.*

"Then what," Dana cries as destiny closes in on her; she is laughing, crying, singing in a long, ecstatic giggle that stops suddenly as all the breath in her lungs—her *soul*—rushes out of her body and into his, along with the salty blood from her cut lip, the hanging shred of skin, "what will you take?"

—Everything.

Dana . . . can't breathe . . . she doesn't have to breathe, she . . . Lifeless, she slips from his arms as her inadvertent lover—if he is a lover—staggers and cries out, jittering with fear and excitement as emotion and memory rush into him. Shuddering back to life, he will not know which of them performed the seduction.

"Oh my God," he shouts, horrified by the sound of his own voice. "Oh my God."

That which used to be Dana Graver does not speak. It doesn't have to. The word is just out there, shared, like the air Dana is no longer breathing. **—Who?**

My God, my God, I am Remy L'Heureux, and I miss my wife so much! For my sins, I was separated from my soul and with it, everything I care about. For my sins I was put in the grave and for my sins, my empty body was raised up, and what did I do that was so terrible? I ran away from the hounfort *with the only daughter of the* houngan, *God help me, I did! We met at Tulane, we fell in love and believe me, I was warned! My Sallie's father was Hector Bonfort, they said, a doctor they said, very powerful. A doctor, yes, I said, but a doctor of what? And without being told I knew, because this was the one question none of them would answer. I should have been afraid, but I loved Sallie too much. I went to her house. I told him Sallie and I were in love. Hector said we were too young, fathers always do. I said we were in love and he said I would never be good enough for her, so we ran away. I laughed in his face and took her out of his house one night while he was away at a conference.*

My Sallie left him a note: Don't look for us, *she wrote.* We'll be back when you accept Remy as your own son. *The priest we asked to marry us begged us to reconsider; he warned us.* "You have made a very grave enemy, and I . . ." *He was afraid. We went to City Hall and the registrar of voters married us instead. Silver bracelet for my darling instead of a ring. Hector did not swear vengeance that I heard, but I knew he was powerful. Nobody ever spelled out what he was. I knew, but I pretended not to know. Sallie and I were so much in love that I took her knowing he would come for me. God, we were happy. God, we were in love.*

Sallie, so bright and so pretty with her whole heart and soul showing in her face, we were so happy! But we should have known it was not for long. When Jamie came he was the image of both of us. Our little boy! The three of us were never happier than we were in New York, as far away from New Orleans as we could go. I couldn't stay at Tulane, not with Hector's heart turned against me. In New York, we thought we could be safe. There are always flaws in plans cobbled out of love. Hector found out. Then he, it . . . Something came for me. I got sick.

I fell into a coma, unless it was a trance. I didn't know what was happening, but Sallie did. She prayed by my bedside. She cried.

We were torn apart by my death, I could hear her sobbing over my bed in the days, the weeks, after I fell unconscious but I couldn't reach out and I couldn't talk to her. I heard her sobbing in the room, I heard her sobbing on the telephone, I heard her begging her father the houngan *to come and release me from the trance. I tried to warn her but I couldn't speak.* Whatever you do, don't tell him where we are. *Then I felt Hector in the city. On our street. In my house. Deep inside my body where what was left of me was hiding. I felt the intrusion, and that before he ever came into my room. It was only a matter of time before his hand parted me down to the center, and I was lost. I was buried too deep to talk but I begged Sallie:* Don't leave me alone! *Then Hector was in the room and in the seconds when Sallie had to leave us alone—our son was crying, Jamie needed her, she'd never have left me like that if it hadn't been for him—when Sally left I felt Hector approaching—not physically, but from somewhere much closer, searching, probing deep. Reaching into the arena of the uncreated.*

Sallie came in and caught him. "Father. Don't!"

"I wasn't doing anything."

"I know what you were doing. Bring him back!"

"I'm trying," *he said. It was a lie.*

Then he put his mouth to my mouth, my mouth *and my God with the sound of velvet tearing, my soul rushed out of me.* "Father," *Sallie cried and he thumped my chest with his big fist:* CPR. *Then he turned to her.*

"Too late," *he said.* "When I came into the house Remy was already dying."

She rushed at him and shoved him aside. Before he could stop her she slipped her silver bracelet on my wrist. I was almost gone but I heard her sobbing, "Promise to come back."

The grief was crushing. It was almost a relief to descend into the grave with my sweetheart's tears still drying on my face and the bracelet that bound us rattling on my wrist, forgotten. Until now. My God, until now!

What have I done?

I was better off when I was no more than a thing, *like that beautiful, cold woman rising from the bed but it's too late to go back. Where I felt no pain and no desire, desire is reawakened.*

I want to go home!

I have to go home to Sallie, the love of my soul, and I want to see Jamie, our son. I miss them so much, but I can't! I have been dead and buried and I don't know how long it's been. I would give anything to see them but for their protection, I have to stay back. Sallie wants to see me again, but not like this. The hand

I bring up to my face is redolent of the grave and when I open my mouth I taste the sweet rot rising inside of me.

I can't go back to them, not the way I am,

I won't.

I have to. I can't not go because with the return of life comes the awful, inexorable compulsion. Better I throw myself in front of a train or into a furnace than do this to the woman I love. I know what's happening, the rushing decay because to live again means you're going to die, and when you have been dead and buried, death comes fast. I have to stop. I have to stop myself. I . . .

The creature on the bed does not speak. It doesn't have to.

—**Have to go home.**

I have to go home. In a return of everything that made him human—love, regret, and a terrible foreboding and before any of these, compulsion—in full knowledge of what he has been and what he is becoming, Remy L'Heureux turns his back on the undead thing on the bed, barely noting the fraught, anxious arrival of Billy Wylie, who has no idea what he's walking into.

That which had been Dana Graver sits up, its eyes burning with a new green light and its pale skin shimmering against the black nightgown. —**Then go.**

I'm going now.

—*The Magazine of Fantasy and Science Fiction*, 2004

Grand Opening

It's brilliant. The Bruneians have bought Yankee Stadium. The team went bust last year—it was the boredom. There's nothing at issue in baseball, face it. Where's the suspense? It's only a game. Today we expect more from our entertainment: love and death, fire and blood. Lives at stake. Who wouldn't get tired of going out to see people in the same old outfits going through the moves? Fans did, even the most committed ones. The times demand narrative. We do! If the Yankees can't supply it, someone better will.

The team failed and with it, commerce in the city: restaurants and hotels went under and with them all those providers who brought you baseball caps and Yankees mugs and diamonds and furs, filthy pictures and china Statues of Liberty and high-end leather jackets that rich foreigners paid too much for because it's important to travel but even more important to take something home. Like dominoes falling in a Japanese stadium, businesses went under, threatening the infrastructure, and the Sultan's advisors saw the opportunity and pounced. Face it. Without the revenue from Brunei your metropolis would be a tent city in a parking lot. All praise to the Sultan.

Unlike the national imagination that stopped short at baseball, the Sultan had a dream. A vision that would beggar Kubla Khan. It's enough to point to the models the Bruneians sent ahead to prepare us for the offer, and the projections they sent when we refused and they tripled it. Magnificent, even in the miniature it took the imperial architects weeks to complete. Imagine it now. Before the deal was even struck, advance teams took down the stands and leveled two miles surrounding for the armature and the diorama, as well as excavating for parking. While New Yorkers made a desperate last-minute pitch for all-American backers, crews moved in to complete UNIVERSE, the Bruneian Mall of the World, which opens tonight at the outskirts of the bankrupt city.

For months, UNIVERSION has telecast the preparations to a rapt audience of billions. We all watched the story unfold. Would UNIVERSE be done in time to save our bacon? Would we be among the first to see it? The suspense is unbearable and remember, we live for suspense.

We have been waiting for months for this day.

We don't know it yet, but Ahmed Shah has been waiting all his life.

Ah, but when the time is right we'll see it on TV. We have been watching from our homes and the luckiest of us are watching on the monitors lining the way in from the parking lots where we have been waiting for so long. When we first catch sight of Ahmed, it will be on TV. And the rest? Soon. We will see everything soon. The grand opening is almost upon us. It's today.

Last night at midnight the Sultan's emissary and the Mayor of New York City broke the seal on the main gates, although only the Sultan's party will enter there. The thousand special delegates are entering through designated portals. The Sultan's dream is so vast that they won't reach the Grand Glass Escalator at the heart of UNIVERSE much before noon. It will take hours for them to find their places inside the ceremonial dome—and longer still for the rest of us to filter into the rotunda. The best seats will be gone! What if we get stuck behind some overweight New Yorker who's too big to see over or peek around!

Meanwhile the privileged, the invited delegates—Ahmed!—pad happily along miles of Bokhara runners, gasping at the sights of the surrounding diorama. They pass through exquisite landscapes where great moments of history bloom like gaudy flowers—everything from the fall of the Tower of Babel to the showiest nuclear explosions replicated in polyvinyl resin, a magnificent panoply that beggars Singapore's previously renowned Tiger Balm Gardens. Excited by the World's Fair with its glittering visions of the future? Regard the monstroplex!

In RVs and trailers, in massed sleeping bags and hastily erected tents outside UNIVERSE, the public waits. The crowd has been gathering for weeks. We want to be first! Every one of us!

But none so much as Ahmed Shah, who is here on a sacred mission. Ordinary people wait like sheep. Through a combination of luck and trickery, Ahmed has made his way inside.

To survive our lives we must divine the story of our lives, and this is Ahmed's.

Never mind how he infiltrated the throng of dignitaries at the A-list metal detectors while we were forced to wait. The gold brocade robe says it all. The diamond set into his forehead tells the world that Ahmed Shah is special. Expensive forgeries certify him as the delegate of an obscure but potentially useful oil-rich country. Let the hoi polloi wait submissively. Ahmed is in the first wave of delegates entering the monstroplex.

And when the ceremonies begin, Ahmed will . . . well, never mind. When you spend your life plotting, you know the best-laid plans are the ones you keep secret.

At twilight the heads of both states—Brunei and Manhattan—will meet in the rotunda to cut the ribbon and declare this Perspex-and-steel Nirvana open to the world. The Sultan's monstroplex outstrips everything humanity has ever devised for profit and pleasure. The future is yesterday. Welcome to UNIVERSE.

As a palliative to Native Americans—New Yorkers to you—the ceremonies will begin with a ritual reenactment of Yankee baseball triumphs. Trained entertainers will re-create the Yankees' last game—before the cutting of the ribbon.

Salman Rushdie is throwing out the first ball.

Perfect.

Ahmed has been waiting all his life for this moment.

So, he thinks, has Rushdie. He never dreamed it would take so long, or that he would be so old, and he is old; last September Ahmed Shah turned ninety. So, of course, did Rushdie, which makes them kindred.

They are, after all, in this together. Hunter and hunted. Instrument and destiny, for every great pursuit demands the cooperation of both parties. For every Jean Valjean there is a Javert and if either died the other would be desolate. Imagine Ahmed and Rushdie, the perfection of pursuit and flight. Neither exists without the other.

Ahmed has pursued Rushdie through war and peace, mind you, through riots and confusion, through the nights and days and over the years. He has spent his adult life on this and he's come close, he has! But never close enough. Is it fate that steps in Ahmed's way at the last minute, or some suppressed will to fail? Ahmed would tell you that he has spent all his money and all his strength running toward this encounter. Once he got within firing range but the rented pistol failed; once he saw Rushdie leaving a party for Amy Tan and Stephen King, but his quarry's entourage people crowded him out before Ahmed could whip the silk thugee's cord around Rushdie's neck and tighten the knot. For years he was insulated by fame, but people forget. Like Ahmed's physical powers in his ninety-first year, Rushdie's fame has dwindled.

In a way, Ahmed feels sorry for him. *Lo how the mighty, eh Salman?*

How odd, to be so committed to the mission and yet so fond of the man. After all, they have a lot in common. Together yet stupendously separated by accidents of birth and fame, Ahmed and Rushdie have written dozens of books. They have outlived wives and lovers and numerous exes; all this Ahmed knows because he stays informed; he watches TV; he reads the papers and has Meena print new bulletins from the Internet. In their lifetime he and Rushdie have outlived Madonna and Brad Pitt and most world rulers; they have outlived, in fact, everything but the *fatwah*. Rushdie's fault, for offending Allah with that profane best seller. *Fatwah* made Rushdie celebrated and it made him rich while Ahmed's poor little book went out of print before it ever made it into the stores. Rushdie must die, it is kismet.

How sad, that none of his women have understood this sacred charge.

"Don't," Meena begged only last night, clinging to the golden robe to keep Ahmed from leaving; "you have me to think of."

Lovely Meena. His fourth wife loves him even though she is only twenty-three. Leaving at dawn, he told the story of his life. "Before anything, I have my mission."

Which brings Ahmed into UNIVERSE, surging past the metal detectors as though it is fated. In fact it is fated. What Allah ordains, Ahmed will execute, and if he dies in the act then he will bypass Mecca and be lifted into Paradise to walk in the garden with Allah, hand in hand.

Better yet, when Ahmed has done what he's waited so long to do, when he has killed Salman Rushdie, the Ayatollah will reward him with one million dollars.

Justice. Who hopes for more? Rushdie's outrageous screed overshadowed Ahmed's poetic tribute to the Prophet, it smothered it in the cradle. Rushdie got famous while Ahmed's *Sacred Verses* was stillborn. Rushdie got paid for his obscenity while Ahmed paid dearly, starting with the cost of the printing. Ah, but once he is dead and Ahmed is paid they will be even.

He is so fixed on his mission that the eight-hour trek into the heart of the monstroplex passes like minutes. Carpeted sidewalks move delegates along through the diorama that surrounds UNIVERSE like the rings around Saturn. They glide through the Fall of Carthage and the lifelike veldt and the Rise of Industrialism to the inner circle of synthetic jungle that gives onto the megamall proper with its magic, glassy territory of a hundred thousand shops. There are plentiful snacks for the honored guests in the monstroplex, chaises for those who tire and tented facilities for every conceivable bodily need. Lovely attendants provide massages for the weary. The hours pass in a heartbeat, unless it is a lifetime. Oh but the crystal flowers, the plastic trees along the way are distracting to the pilgrims, the way stations where perfumes fill the air, the transparent vaulted ceiling! It is magnificent. Music floods the space, Rimsky-Korsakov booming as fountains play and perfume blossoms in the air at the glassy, convex margins. Ahmed would like to linger but he's given up too much to come this far. The professional ambitions he's set aside to pursue his quarry, the children he's outlived, the company of women . . .

And that's another thing. While Rushdie swans around at celebrity affairs on the arms of attractive popsies who as the man ages gets younger and younger, Ahmed has lost every woman he ever had: first sweet Mrinal and then Lakshme and his pearly American girl Stephanie and dark-haired Sujeeta and only yesterday the last wife he'll probably ever find, plump Meena with her sad almond eyes. Oh, his lovers and wives all said different things when they packed the children and left but Ahmed knows what they meant:

You said you loved me but all you care about is this Rushdie thing.

Crafty, sacrilegious Rushdie takes all, leaving nothing for Ahmed. One million dollars. Who wouldn't want to kill him?

Who knew it would take so long! When the *fatwah* came down Ahmed accepted the Ayatollah's mandate without question. He has spent his life trying to discharge it. Not that he hasn't come close. That time in London, twice in New York. Fans, lovers, groupies, TV—the trappings of fame get between him and his mission. He hates Rushdie for being famous. He hates him for his cars and his women but what Ahmed hates most about Salman Rushdie is his own obscurity.

Ah but tonight, Rushdie is a sitting target.

Ahmed is ready. His preparations are exquisite: the blue-and-white baseball uniform Meena hand sewed, hidden by the golden mantle he chose for the long trip inside, the cleated shoes with poison transfused into every cleat, and finally the sleek, undetectable weapon—a glass kris! Access to the dugout, don't ask. As the Yankees strut out in their quaint uniforms Ahmed doffs the robe and slips onto the bench like one of the team, reliving the glory days for an audience of billions. When the Star Spangled Banner ends and the band begins the Bruneian Anthem, when the Yankees trot onto the field and Rushdie hauls back to throw the first ball Ahmed will take advantage of the festivity and stab him.

But there is something funny going on.

Ahmed feels it before he comprehends it. A change in the air. He is aware of it before the band begins its medley of themes from the Bruneian anthem. A difference. A deviation from the expected. Most ceremonies go as scripted but something new is happening.

We are aware of it, watching on TV or climbing to sky seats in the rotunda. The hell of it is, we'll never agree on what happened. Multiply any event by the number of witnesses and you won't come close to the number of diverging stories. There is the event, yes.

There is what we bring to it.

Then there is what we make of it.

Add to that our weakness for worst-case scenarios, because narrative is fueled by our collective paranoia.

You bet there's something funny going on. If it wasn't, where would we find the story that enriches our days? And in a continuum this bizarre, in a world where a Rushdie gets rich and famous and an artist like Ahmed is discarded, in a society where commerce rules and nothing you expect can be expected, it could be almost anything. Today's story could end in:

Armageddon; as the monstroplex opens, leaders of twin states nobody's even heard of simultaneously push the red button that starts the war; above the great dome the sky blossoms . . .

Invasion by space aliens; the transparent panels that enclose the rotunda snap open like a giant iris to reveal . . .

Revolution, a million valet parking attendants and decorators and grounds-people take up their weapons to overthrow the rich . . .

Economic conquest: the Sultan of Brunei hands an enormous check to the acting U.S. president and buys us, U., S. and A. . . .

Are you afraid yet? Do you want to be? Play with the possibilities. Turn the ratchet one more time. Today's story may end with:

Extermination: with the leaders of the known world assembled for the grand opening all the vents snap shut and yellow vapor pervades the amphitheater, thousands of the unsuspecting willingly assembled for the ultimate genocide . . .

Subsumption by a superpower none of the delegates and weekend shoppers even imagined existed . . .

Divine intervention.

Now, this, Ahmed could have lived with. Allah's emissary shooting into the arena like a meteor to forgive Rushdie.

Or could it be all in Ahmed's mind? Or all in your mind, or mine? Remember, the *fatwah* was called off decades ago, although Ahmed doesn't know it. And remember, the Yankees tanked because there are no love affairs and no murders in baseball games, there is no story: one more proof that to survive our lives, we must have narrative. We build stories like traps to capture incident and turn it into Event.

And where there is no narrative, we have to supply it. For every story, there are a thousand possible endings. The two most obvious:

It was only a dream.

It's all in Ahmed's mind.

Really.

Rather, it is in yours, because for every observer there is a different interpretation, and when all accounts are settled, this particular event is what you make of it.

You can make whatever you want.

As it turns out we were all there when it happened, half a million of us, swarming into the rotunda. We saw the encounter between Ahmed and his target. There isn't time or space to tell you what we made of it—there was too much going on. There are too many of us. Too many interpretations. To say nothing of yourself, along with all the baggage you bring to this.

To simplify, let's stick with Ahmed.

Rushdie is behind the velvet ropes, waiting for the signal. His lips are trembling; he has grown old in the service, the pursued, who, face it! Was overexposed to the point where he has become invisible. Except to Ahmed.

Time is suspended.

It's the moment in the story when anything could happen.

Shark attack.

Alien abduction.

In fact, something even stranger happens.

It is both stranger and harder to understand, at least in this version, and remember this is Ahmed's version, Rushdie-specific and not pertaining to you, for this is Ahmed's story.

The teams come out and the throng applauds. Rushdie trots out onto the field, ancient but spry in his favorite outfit. At the sight of him every muscle in Ahmed's groin tightens but the applause trails off and the music fades.

The emcee's voice fails along with it. "Who's that?" he squeaks, confused.

Rushdie throws his arms wide—to the Ayatollah? to Allah himself or to fickle fate or to us, the public that's forgotten him?

The collective breath rushes out. *Who are you?*

"It is I." He grabs the hand mike and the words boom, the forgotten man crying to an unheeding heaven. "It is I, Salman Rushdie."

Silence.

"You know," he shouts in a failing voice, whirling until his scrawny arms fly out from his sides like scarves on a dervish. His lips move but only Ahmed hears the dying fall . . . "*Satanic Verses?* Rushdie, that awful book? The *fatwah?* You know."

Only Ahmed is listening.

On the quaint old baseball diamond, there are two events unfolding. Ahmed's. Ours, which is somewhat bigger. Figures at Rushdie's back play out the larger drama of life and death and finance and speculation as U.S. Marines march out under the flag, platoon after platoon of them in close order drill, with each platoon circling gorgeously under its red guidon in a formation more intricate and beautiful than anything devised for the fabled Dallas Cowgirls . . .

U.S. Marines march out and surround the velvet ropes that mark the Sultan's place and in a silent coup subdue the Sultan's bodyguards . . .

And the Sultan himself is under military arrest, oh, *yes* he is raging and—*mirabile!*—the monstroplex and properties surrounding are returned to the City of New York in a bloodless *coup,* a gift to Manhattanites from the combined forces of our saviors the financial giants: Disney, Bertelsmann and Microsoft.

That fast.

The band segues into "The Star Spangled Banner."

While on the abandoned baseball diamond, Salman Rushdie dithers, forgotten.

Well, almost forgotten.

"Allah *bismallah,*" Ahmed cries. It's time! With upraised kris he breaks through the crowd and with all the strength left in his ninety-year-old body, he lunges at Rushdie.

His mark's eyes grow wide with excitement as Ahmed bears down on him. He beams, delighted. "You!"

Caught in midlunge, Ahmed is transfixed, thunderstruck and rattled to the foundations. "You." He has waited all his life for this moment.

"Yes!" Rushdie wags his head in delight at being recognized.

"You look just like all your pictures." Ahmed falls on him and they grapple. Never mind that the *fatwah* was called off dozens of years ago. Never mind that Ahmed is the last man standing who failed to get the word. This is fated, fated. "Yes."

Locked in a mortal embrace, Rushdie sighs as if to a lover, "I thought you'd never come."

—*The Barcelona Review,* 2005

Special

Ashley Famous is coming to town and we're all excited and a little apprehensive. Ours is the last unspoiled village on the Hudson, one of those quiet places where nobody important ever comes, and the last thing we want is gawking disciples trampling our flower beds, to say nothing of gift shops and roadside shrines popping up all along Route 9. Still we get the shivers, thinking, *Ashley Famous. Here.*

Bill Anthony says although she's world renowned it's in a good way, no YouTube antics to embarrass us, no scandal, no paparazzi implied, she can only bring honor to Schuylerton. "Think people like us, but with the sheen of greatness"—Bill actually said that!—"when all she wants is to blend in and disappear." Well, she's picked the right place. We all mind our own business here.

She writes those sexy little books about God, so crowds collect like flies on a road kill because, who wouldn't want to touch the hand that's been in touch with God? People do it, but not people you know. She can walk down our streets undisturbed, although when Gloria saw her out in front of Tazewell's Realty that first day, she could swear the woman had *look at me* written all over her.

Of course Gloria is not our most reliable witness. Even though she's a published writer, she is not all that popular, while Ashley Famous has all those fans driving her into seclusion. They follow her everywhere with misty eyes and wide, wet smiles. Bill says everybody has a cross and this is hers.

Our Reverend Anthony wrote a book about her, which is how they got friends. Bill fought his way to the platform when she got that medal, waving the book with her picture on the front. "Oh," she shouted, "how lovely," but by that time fans were stampeding like a herd of leeches and Bill had to rescue her. She thanked him with the saddest smile and said, "Sometimes you just get tired."

The thing is, if you've touched the hand and God just happens to drop in on you, the last thing He wants is to fight off gangs of rapt admirers, Bill says, so she's going into seclusion—here!

Bill is dean over at the college so he stepped up and invited her, to do what, we aren't certain, but there you are.

She's bought the Eversons' boathouse which is odd, since we will do anything to keep our houses in the family; we owe it to our children to say nothing of the generations that came before, but you'd have to be one of us to understand. We're not pointing any fingers, but this is the first piece of riverfront property to pass out of family hands in two centuries and Grant didn't consult Bunk Schuyler at Historical Preservation before he sold.

Never mind. Schuylerton could use a little pizzazz, and it is well known that celebrities like Ashley Famous have creative, fascinating friends who would probably love a weekend in the country, especially with summer coming on. She'll want to invite gangs of poets and artists, who are bound to be more exciting than certain people around here, which will definitely perk up our social lives. We can't wait to be invited—that is, if she takes to us.

The question is, where to start with her? We won't intrude and we never, ever overstep—no screen captures in the IGA parking lot, we promise, no cell phone shots at Luther's Drug Store even though we're dying for our friends to know. Uninvited drop-ins and cold calls are out; when a person's keeping the line open for God, who are we to interrupt? We don't go where we're not invited and our kind doesn't gawk, it's just not done.

When we do meet her we'll be discreet, we will! *Guess what. We have a secret. Guess what. It's you.*

Oh, but she said something odd to Jack Tazewell when he was showing the boathouse. "I think the most interesting things in the world are sex and religion, don't you?"

So, should we lock up our husbands or what?

We don't mean to fret, but if we happen to run into her, is it all right to say hello?

It's hard to know. But we *are* looking forward to meeting her, however it comes about, Ms. Famous and whichever husband she has this time around. We hear that there have been several, but never mind. We're very forgiving here. We'd let you into our hearts quicker than we'd let you into our homes.

We just haven't figured out how to let her know she has friends here in Schuylerton.

Beth and Gloria and Jeannie Chandler and I have been going home by the river road after lunch at the club, checking for signs of life. So far all we've seen is Grant Everson glowering over his rose bushes as we come through his gate; when he pops up with the hedge clippers we wave our fingers and laugh: la-la, Grant, you're the one who sold the boathouse, now look. Evanoaks is not your private property now.

Rich as she is, you'd think Ashley Famous would have the boathouse crawling with painters and decorators, God knows those books make millions, but the new mailbox and fresh geraniums in the cut-out truck tire planter are pretty much it. Well, that will all change once we're friends; we can tell her where to shop for all the best things. If only we'd come upon her planting something in the front yard; if only she'd hear our car in the turnaround and stick her head out the front door to see who's coming, then we could all smile and wave, hel-*looo*. Of course she'd wave back and if we caught her smiling we'd pile out of the car and make friends, but we've cruised the boathouse four times this week and we haven't seen a trace.

With anybody else, we'd start with the chess pie or the hot cross buns, but you don't take food to a star, not even the apple basket from Creech's Orchards with Elva Creech's jams and homemade maple sugar leaves; usually casseroles and deep dish pies are great conversation pieces, but even the mocha cheese-cake from Tempest's Teapot is just wrong.

With a best-selling author who can't stop winning prizes, where do you start? It's not like Gloria would know.

We hear she's very reclusive. Maybe she's like us, standoffish, but only with people she doesn't want to know.

We hear she's a lot of fun at parties, if you can only get her to come.

We hear that sometimes she can get a little wild.

Then why is she so damn difficult, when all we're trying to do is welcome her to Schuylerton?

Bill warned us that she doesn't warm up to just anybody, but Bill is infuriat-ingly smug just because he happened to write a book. We're not *just anybody*, which he knows, and if he won't tell Ashley Famous who we are in this town, then how do we let her know?

Should we sidle up to her in the supermarket and start the discussion about cheeses or tell her which produce to avoid? A few words and she'll understand who we are. So, can we get friends by showing her the farmers' market or should we offer her our cleaning lady or should we just come right out in the open and give a party for her?

What if she hates parties and doesn't want to come?

What if she loves parties and doesn't want to come?

What if she wants to come, just not to our house?

Would she come if we gave it at the club? Does she really hate parties, and does she know what an honor that would be? Outsiders can live here for gen-erations without seeing the inside of the Schuylerton River Club. Bill says the last thing she wants is to feel crowded and we don't want to make her self-conscious so it should sound casual, "If you happen to be around," even though we're putting on the dog. When she gets to the club and sees how much fun we're all having she'll know how lucky she is: *we know you're big and important but in our own way we're important too.* Of course she'll invite us back, if we can only get her to come.

We could probably start by reading her books, but who has the time? Should we fake it and send her admiring notes? Naturally we'll have them laid out on our end tables when she comes over and after she notices, of course we'll ask her to sign—unless that's gauche. We bought them all, what more does she expect?

Unlike my friends, who dropped theirs in the tub or left them out on the clubhouse porch in the rain, at least I tried. My Richard thought it was foolish, sitting up in bed improving my mind when he thought we should be doing something else, and was it my fault I got bored and fell asleep between the pages, or hers? To tell the truth, her stuff is all too airy-fairy for me—beautiful, but neither here nor there. So it just won't do to barge up to her on Broad Street with that gooshy Ashley-fan smile, babbling, "I just loved your book." I hate being false even when it's working, and if there was a quiz, I'd die.

Mirabile, Stephanie Parrish makes the big breakthrough. Yesterday our Ms. Famous tripped on the old boot scraper outside Fanueil Flowers and all her shopping bags went whoosh, so Stephanie got down and helped her pick up her stuff.

Of course she was grateful, and all the while Stephanie was taking note of the items: which face creams, what shade of lipstick, whose bread; hand-knit sweater from Erdrich's with those lambs on the front plus, from Ezekiel's of all things, canned smelts. She thanked Stephanie three times, but that was it. It wasn't like Ashley Famous invited her back to the boathouse for coffee, or to have lunch at Tempest's before she headed home.

In fact Beth was the first to speak to her, and it wasn't exactly a conversation. She saw her in Ezekiel's, lined up for bagels on Sunday morning just like every-body else but with dark glasses and a kerchief pulled down, so we wouldn't know. Beth just went right up to her. She smiled as nicely as she could without being smarmy and spoke. "Excuse me, but aren't you . . ."

And in the name of Edith Wharton, who used to live around here and I'm sure was a lot more gracious, Ashley Famous said, "No."

That set us back.

But we have discovered that she is a very sweet person and tremendously vulnerable, which Mariel Edmunds learned when she braved the Hudson in Jake's little boat after Beth told us about it at brunch. She cut the motor and glided in tactfully, so to look at her, you'd think she was quietly fishing in the marsh and accidentally drifted in without noticing how close she was, which is how she caught our world-class new neighbor weeping out on the end of Grant Everson's dock.

Well, one thing led to another—empathic grimaces, little waves—and Mariel scooted up the ladder and, respecting her privacy, sat on the end of the dock next to Ms. Famous, but not too close. She stayed quiet as the tomb while they both stared out at the channel until finally the sight of this *star* sitting there with tears streaming was more than Mariel could bear and she had to ask, "Are you all right?"

Imagine all that and then guess what this person with a brilliant career and gobs of honors and every man she ever wanted revealed in that thrilling, smoky voice she uses on TV. Not a damn thing. She said, "It's just so beautiful."

Although she's not one of our nearest and dearest Mariel is a masterpiece of self-control; without turning a hair she dropped her own voice six feet to wherever Ashley Famous keeps hers and said, "Yes."

We all know you don't cry along, it's hypocritical. Mariel just sat there and Ashley Famous just sat until she got over it and sprang up like a cat after a shower. She went skipping back to the house in her pink sneakers, calling back so carelessly that Mariel couldn't believe her ears. "Come again."

Mariel did not gush, "Oh, thank you." We're better than that. She put on our best Schuylerton River Club drawl, "But never without calling first."

So we were in. Well, not all of us and not that minute, but this was the start. Mariel waited a good long time and then she dropped by the boathouse and asked Ashley Famous to the River Club for brunch this Sunday after church, don't dress up, we're just country people here.

We'll all drift into church the way we do every week but we're a little twitchy: what to wear, what to wear? In addition to his duties at the Episcopal college, where nobody knows what Ashley Famous will be doing for all that money, Bill Anthony is the rector here. When we told him she was coming he said of course, she'd already promised because it was his loaves-and-fishes sermon this week. So we could have seen her up close anyway, and without being beholden to Mariel, but who knew?

Besides if it hadn't been for Mariel, we wouldn't know that Ashley Famous and religion are . . . how did she put it? "Boy, is that a contradiction in terms."

When she dropped by to invite ("I would have called, but I went off without your number . . .") she scoped the boathouse interior, and she's not part of our foursome but Mariel is very good at detail. Tacky was only the beginning, she moved on to "neo-Goodwill." Patchwork quilts covering a multitude of sins, she said, inspirational motto painted on velvet, nicely framed and hanging over the fireplace and, oh my God, a pillow needlepointed with the praying hands. Plus, she told us, for an icon, she doesn't dress very well. She wore more or less what we wear except in all the wrong colors, Mariel said, borderline shabby, who would have guessed? Nothing went with anything else, and that was the least of it.

She positively exuded pheromones, how did Mariel put it? "She may be all about God but she talked like a sailor rolling into a bordello after years at sea, all that with her nice husband sitting right there!"

Indeed, we have to wonder. That tight T-shirt and flowered jeans she wore to church and to the club after, never mind the straw cartwheel hat and pink lizard clutch. She's the kind who can't tell when she's pitifully underdressed, and the husband was cute. Younger, in that obvious way, with a sensitive mouth and cultivated hair. There were so many people on the lawn around Ashley Famous that day, half my friends and all our men fetching this, offering her that, that I couldn't help feeling sorry for the husband, so I sat down next to him on the porch.

It didn't take much to draw him out.

A poet, he told me, smoldering nicely, he's one of those sandy boys who tan so fast that the body hairs shimmer, no question what she saw in him. He's adorable. I probably shouldn't have asked where to buy his books but when I saw his face I made up for it by reading the one poem he had tucked in his shirt pocket. Something to occupy him while Ashley holed up in the loft because, he said, and he wasn't complaining, she needs to get with God before she can face church. It's clear he adores her but I could see how hard it is for him to write with that big old shadow of greatness looming over him. At the end he invited me to come over and he'd read to me and I promised I would. His name is Archbold, from some fine old family, which is interesting because now that we see her up close it's clear that Ashley Famous comes from somewhere south of quality. Arch, he said, just call me Arch. Sweet boy, but who knows how soon she will tire of him, or what he will do then.

We think certain thoughts about handsome young men but we always go home to bed with our husbands, most of us, even so. But among our tennis foursome, I alone had been invited, even though it was by Arch and not his first-ever and only wife, at least so far. Whatever happens, he's entitled, the woman has been married four times.

In fact, Gloria was next to visit, and she wasn't even invited. Of course Gloria thinks of herself as a fellow professional, which gives her the right. She just bellied up to the door and introduced herself to Ashley Famous, writer to writer as it were, as though they were equals and Ms. Famous had to ask her in.

In Schuylerton, maybe they are equals; in local matters Gloria has the edge, but otherwise, no. The prizes alone, money, passionate fans in droves, but it wasn't very kind of Ms. Famous to point it out.

Which—we finally got it out of Gloria, who is livid—she did. She told it like a sad story, but Gloria knew. Oh, Ashley Famous was dripping with self-pity, but Gloria knew.

She'd have to be drunk out of her mind or beaten senseless not to know. She says a little of both. Too much wine in strong sunlight bouncing off the river, it put her off her guard. She let herself imagine they were friends. Gloria is a giving person so she said kindly, "My contact at Valley TV would love to come talk to you, he's doing a show on writers living on the Hudson and I thought . . ."

Then wasn't she surprised. Gloria was knocking herself out to be helpful, and Ashley Famous rose right up and bit her in the ass.

"I don't like being famous," she said, sudden as a slap in the face.

"It's only local TV."

It was too late. This Ashley's voice went back to that deep place. Her face got all pink and she went on like an angry kindergarten teacher explaining to a stupid child. About that time Arch, who had been hovering, faded away like a painter's wet wash of a failing sky. "I don't like it at all," Ashley Famous said to his back, and there were tears standing in her eyes.

Gloria tried for a snappy comeback but all she managed was, "I just thought." Then she read that face and gave up.

"People keep writing books on me, they're making a whole movie about my life, they want me to narrate the Bible on PBS; they won't leave me alone! Everybody wants to send me presents and force me to take their prizes; they all want me to bless them or something, when all I want is to be left alone!"

Gloria was about to go there-there when Ashley Famous got all holy and condescending. "But you wouldn't understand."

Gloria blinked the way you do when a strobe light flashes and you have no idea where it's coming from.

"You wouldn't know," she said to Gloria. Unfortunately, that's true, but she didn't have to rub it in. "You would have no way of knowing how very, very hard it is to be as famous as me. The things people tell you, the things they ask you to do."

By the time she was finished laying out the tribulations of a literary icon, she had Gloria backing away on her hands and knees, anything to get out of there. She clamped the insides of her mouth until they bled so she didn't accidentally apologize for something she hadn't done, and when she could manage, she stood up. "Oh," she told Ashley Famous when she could bring herself to speak without screaming, "I would never give him your number without permission." Then she more or less tugged her forelock and left without ever once losing her temper and telling the truth, which was that she only said it to be nice.

Gloria says that behind all that sacred, holy stuff Ashley Famous is not a nice person, but of course Gloria is biased. People say mean things about Mother Teresa too.

Beth and I are here to tell you that Gloria is wrong. Ms. Famous is an inspiration, as we discover as soon as we and Ashley start spending quality time. I personally have been invited, and I take Beth along to ride post so Arch won't get in trouble for inviting me.

I just don't want Ashley to think there's anything funny going on between her husband and me and there isn't, attractive as he is. Even though she isn't expecting us she's glad to see us because naturally any friend of her Archie's is a friend of hers but as it turns out, her Arch just left for a reading in New York.

She waves us inside with an industrial-strength smile. It's bright enough to be seen from the back of any hall and Beth and I can't help thinking, *No wonder everybody loves her* because this time, it's shining for us.

Then we get inside and it's: *Hasn't she ever heard of* IKEA?

I *mean*, Mariel barely scratched the surface here. It's all about vintage shag rugs in bad colors and milk crates stuffed with magazines and board-and-brick bookcases like kids make in graduate school, which makes me wonder whether all her taste is in her mouth or if she downplays the decor to make Archie feel at home. Jacket photos notwithstanding, Ashley Famous is no kid either, now that we see her up close. But she ushers us in glowing as though she is completely unaware. Then dear God she says, "Things of this world are only things of this world so why bother," so we know she knows.

She sits us down and brings us steaming cups of cambric tea which our grandmothers remember vaguely and used to offer when we were small.

You don't exactly talk to Ashley Famous, you listen, which is how we find out why people fall down and worship her and follow her anywhere. It's a foregone conclusion, *voilà, tout de suite,* when she starts going on in that thrilling voice. Actually, although it's a little embarrassing, we follow her upstairs into the loft. It's her meditation room, she says, and somehow the three of us end up sitting on that hard, hard floor in lotus position—or something like it for Beth and me—it's a little harder for Beth as certain parts of her have begun to spread. We sit facing the new Sheetrock wall Arch put up for her and we meditate, or Ashley Famous does, while Beth and I stare at the wall as instructed and try to empty our minds and see into the beyond, which is what she seems to expect. It's not easy to do when you're wondering if she's gone out of her mind and into the Presence while you're still sitting there worried about how long you can be on this floor in a fixed position without screaming and offending her and whether if you got up and tried to leave, she'd know.

Can you really meditate with us watching?

Still, it is an honor to be hunched in a row like this, contemplating eternity. Imagine, contemplating. Us!

Just being here makes Beth and me feel special, and definitely close to the source—although of what—well, it's pretty ineffable. We're only beginners, after all. I guess we're expected to stare at that wall until we're cross-eyed, which if you do for long enough actually does move you to a higher plane unless that's all the blood leaving your head and pooling in your butt. Whatever it is, I could swear that *something* happened, so when Ashley Famous says, in hushed tones, "Can you feel it?" Beth and I both manage a breathy, "Yes" and for the moment and after we go limp and it stops hurting, we believe.

Then she kind of flows up while Beth and I creak and groan miserably and struggle to our feet, humiliated because we've failed. But, how glorious. Whatever we are suffering, Ashley Famous must be mysteriously transcending, because she says, "Wasn't that wonderful!" and rakes us with that white-light smile.

Ergo, voilà, mirabile, we are friends. We're invited back tomorrow, Ashley says she sees great promise in us, which is borderline divine. I'm sitting right down and reading every one of her books as soon as I get home.

When we come back on Wednesday Arch is there; I can't help hoping he'll come up in to the loft with us because once I get the hang of this, maybe we can meet on some astral plane. Failing that, I'll have something good to look at while our minds are traveling out and beyond. But when she asks him, "Are you?" his face shuts up shop, so I know I'm right about them, although Beth doesn't pick up on it.

Then Arch goes off wherever he goes to write and we're back on that wretched floor maintaining fixed positions until I think I see paisley lights, unless I'm on the first step to the next level as Ashley promised and my life is about to change. I can't help it, I have to peek.

Surprise, Beth is peeking too and if you believe in that kind of thing, Ashley Famous looks pretty much transfixed, unless we're both giddy with hunger because she didn't give lunch before she sat us down to meditate. It's like seeing one of those intricate Chinese ivories with the light bulb inside, my God! She looks lit from within, but only for a second. In the next she yips and hits the floor like a felled log. Beth and I are gnawing our knuckles and reaching for our phones when she sits up with her eyes blazing and asks, "Did you see it? Were you there?"

We don't know what to say, exactly, so we don't.

"Well," she says in that breathy tone that enchants thousands, "there you are."

Who are we to say otherwise?

On the way home Beth says, "Did she just . . . "

"I don't know."

"Did we?"

It's amazing, I am thinking *not really* but I have to say, "I don't know!"

"I don't either," Beth says, "but wasn't it grand." Her voice drops so it's more a statement than a question, and we leave it there.

We get out of the car feeling somewhat exalted, and go back to our lives. I'd love to tell Richard, but there's no way to explain it so he'd understand. Instead Beth and I go around feeling special, *special,* whether because of the experience or because of all Schuylerton society we alone are designated friends of Ashley Famous, it's hard to say. We don't talk about it because this is precious and we owe it to Ashley not to tell. Also, it pisses certain people off. Mariel and Stephanie of course, but they were never part of the inner circle. Jeannie because she wasn't invited, and Gloria for sure.

To make it up to them we decide to give a party at my house, nothing fancy: champagne with Gloria's crudités and the satays and teriyakes the chef from Kang's restaurant does on his row of hibachis, Jeannie's chocolate cheesecake, Japanese lanterns in the woods, and to double-atone for being best friends with her and leaving Jeannie and Gloria and the others outside the loop, I get Arch to make sure Ashley Famous comes.

We do these things so well that naturally she'll understand this is nothing special, we give beautiful parties all the time. Beth and I are looking out at the terrace just before the first guests come and everything is perfect: glowing hibachis, LED lights winking in the trees and Japanese lanterns glowing in the woods beyond; the peonies are out and I tell her, "Look hard, Beth, so you'll never forget what this party looks like. We're going to remember this night for the rest of our lives."

Ashley and Arch come in late, and look at her! My, isn't that the transformation? And don't our men, who had zero interest in the matter until the party, collect like mosquitoes around the bug zapper on a summer night? Where she came to church in a T-shirt and those tawdry flowered jeans, tonight she walks in barefoot in a beautiful diaphanous thing that I swear is by Issy Miyake, and a wreath of gold on her head with bachelor's buttons woven in. Her hair is flying and she looks like what she is: an ornament to the community, our star.

Instead of pleasing one and all with our own personal famous writer, we've alienated quite a few, because the only men who aren't glued to her are Bill Anthony, who foolishly wore the clerical collar, a turnoff for both of them, apparently, and the fourth Mr. Famous, who stalks the fringes looking every inch the poet, like Lord Byron under a cloud, but without the club foot.

Still it's a beautiful party, everyone has to agree. Beth and I knock ourselves out running around mingling, pulling outsiders from Hyde Park and Rhinebeck and Red Hook into the circle, mixing up couples with people they already knew; we are a storm, a flame of congeniality that seems to go out as soon as we turn our backs because Ashley Famous is sitting on the steps to the fountain barefoot, holding forth, and that's where everyone is.

This seems like the time to let Richard know that the gauzy Ms. Famous and I are kindred so I make my way through the throng and say "Ashley, dear!" Then she gives me the strangest look and does a one-two take. *Who **are** you* is quickly replaced by a manufactured smile and oddly, since Beth and I are, after all, giving the party—I mean does she not recognize us or what?—oddly she says, "How lovely, running into you here." And practically in the same breath Richard—my Richard!—shushes me: "Please, honey. Ashley is in the middle of a joke."

Not that anybody notices when I storm away. At my back I hear her trilling, "I think the two most interesting things in the world are sex and religion, don't you?"

Then, what is it the woman said to Bill Anthony, that hooked him and brought all this down on us? Right.

Sometimes you. Just. Get. Tired.

What I hate most is that I'm trying not to feel wounded, but I'm hurt. Feeling perhaps a tad bit guilty, Richard puts an arm around me and tries to pull me back into the social mainstream, but I do what any woman would do. I float out of the mainstream and drift along in the backwaters, among dropped napkins and abandoned plates. One of the Japanese lanterns in the woods has caught fire—nothing serious, it's May, and too wet to burn long; Kang's chef is gone and the hibachis have burned out. As I bob along I hear Gloria grumble, "You'd think being famous would be enough," but I let it pass and drift on in the shallows until I fetch up against Arch, the lonely fourth husband, beached on the bank. I don't do much. When we collide I plant my fingers on that broad, strong wrist, warm in spite of the fact that the night just turned cool.

I want to draw his attention to the clump of men and ask him *who's next* but in our circle we don't say the unspeakable and for all I know the poor boy has no idea that his time with Ms. Famous is growing short. I try, "Is she always like this?"

He turns, blinded by misconception and glowing with God knows what. "You mean, radiant?"

"Radiant, yes." I am too well bred to say, *Radiant, no. Voracious.*

"Ashley is . . . Well, Ashley."

He may be dazzled but he has not moved and my fingers are still on his warm, warm wrist, and I am thinking: *well, I'll show her!* I make them curl to make a bracelet for him, like a gift. "Would you like to take a walk?"

Look at our men, all gathering like cultists about to paint themselves blue and perform extreme acts. Look at my women friends, stewing in their own bitter juices. Look at me, bent on subversion, and look at Arch, grinning at me like a dirty boy. "Of course."

We push off from the ship of fools and head out along the driveway to Mill Road and I have to wonder if she even saw us go; well, when her man comes home smirched and guilty, she will damn well know it. He recites yards of free verse as we walk, and I make appreciative noises and we both feel good enough about ourselves, going along in the moonlight. Then I think: *Now,* and nudge him until we're facing so I can take his hands. I tell him, "They aren't all like her."

Then, oh! Heedless boy; when he says, "There's nobody like her," he is glistening all over again. I'm about to despair when he says, as if to redeem it, "You know, there is one thing."

This could still go the other way so I leave my answer wide open. "Yes?"

"Ashley isn't happy here." He frees one hand and we turn back.

"Oooooh. She isn't?" When he doesn't pick up on it I say, "That's too bad."

"When she's unhappy, it makes it hard for me."

"Unhappy. Hmmm . . ." I do this carefully, leaving a hole big enough for him to drive a forklift into, but he doesn't follow up, he just trudges along even after I prompt him with, "And?" One unkind word and we can start on her.

It's maddening, walking hand in hand with an attractive kid who is too stupid to know what's happened to him let alone what's possible here, and too obtuse to explain why.

The silence drags on until I am forced to say in tones controlled as tightly as I can squeeze them, "What. Ah. What's gone wrong?"

"It's hard to explain."

I hate this. "Is it something we did?"

"In a way. Sort of. Oh, this is embarrassing."

Right. He has been deputized. I try to make it easy for him. "What is?"

It appears that when you're the fourth Mr. Ashley Famous, nothing is easy for you. After a struggle he gets it out—well, part of it. "It's something you haven't done!"

Try playing twenty questions on a country road in the middle of the night. Make that forty questions. It takes too long, but I manage to ask them all.

As it turns out, Arch isn't embarrassed; where you or I would be humiliated, fishing on behalf of somebody who doesn't love you enough to stay by your side at parties, Arch says as though pointing out the obvious, "Your little party is nice and all, but Ashley . . . She's very upset." By this time he is strongly aware that I am done asking polite questions so he explains. "Usually when she comes to a new town people do something special, a concert, a dinner or a dance, something big, in her honor."

"Something big."

"Right. When Ashley Famous comes to town people get together and throw a great big party for her."

"Even though she hates parties."

"Oh, you know Ashley. She only says she does."

"At the club."

"Could it be black tie?" Even by moonlight there's no missing the grateful smile and I still can't say whether it's triumph he's exuding, or relief. "She loves to dress up."

Oh, we'll give her a party all right, if that's what she expects, and it will be the biggest and most beautiful party ever to go down in the annals of the Schuylerton River Club. Before we're done it will rival the best efforts of the Vanderbilts and the first Roosevelts back in the day, a masterpiece of planning and execution, all in honor of our brand new local celebrity, **Welcome, Ashley, now you are one of us,** and naturally it will be black tie so the bitch can come in high drag without putting the rest of us in the shade, for we clean up nicely and put on our diamonds for events like this. Then the lovely Ashley Famous can float into the room in her most expensive designer-Whatever, and I hope she has the good grace to blush at Bill Anthony's welcoming speech, after which she will truly be in our midst, surrounded by admirers, secure in the knowledge that where apparently we've been remiss without knowing it, we're pulling out all the stops, including picking out her name in dwarf roses on top of one of Tempest's most beautiful cakes. We will show Ashley Famous every way we know how that this whole beautiful, expensive evening is all about her. Before we're done, she will have drunk from champagne fountains and danced to the Tippy Little orchestra and cracked lobsters in the driveway with the heel of her most elegant shoe; on her big night she will wine and dine and whirl around the dance floor at the center of attention in spite of her reclusive qualities, the cynosure of all eyes, and when that soft pink glow in the sky above the Hudson warns us that sunrise comes next we will by God do what you do for the GOH at any bacchanal; we'll chase our maiden up into the woods overlooking the River Club and push her backward over a slab of granite and cut out her heart.

—*The Kenyon Review,* 2009

Monkey Do

Every writer wants to be famous, at least just once. I've been at it since before the dog died, but it's an animal planet, so what do you expect? If a hundred monkeys typing for a thousand years would probably produce a novel, what could one monkey do with a computer and the right software?

That is, a computer-literate monkey like Spud.

I never liked the monkey. I brought it home because I was stuck on certain points in my monkey planet novel and needed a specimen to observe first hand. In a one-room apartment, gorillas are out of the question and chimps are too annoying to have around. Plus, baboons are evil incarnate, which you'd know if you'd ever looked one in the eye. Ergo, Spud.

He was quiet, he was small enough to fit in a shopping bag, if he scrunched, so what could go wrong?

He had bad habits, his breath was vile but I thought, cool. Bestseller at any cost. Instant movie. Fame! I finished the book OK, I even got paid. I did all the right things to promote it even though they weren't paying squat. I touched all the miserable bases, up to and including being snubbed at cons and sitting at bookstore tables for hours waiting to sign *Rhesus Planet* for fans who never showed up. Nice poster featuring Spud attracted a few ladies, but they awwww-ed and moved on.

My novel tanked but the monkey is still around.

It's not like I wanted to keep the monkey. It sat around scratching its belly and mocking me, and I could swear it was grunting, failure. I saw pity in its eyes.

You bet I was over Spud. In fact the first thing I did after the book was done was take him back to the pet store for a refund but the dealer said he didn't accept returns. I tried to trade him in for an anaconda, but a sarcastic, second hand rhesus monkey with white eyebrows and a white goatee and white hair on its butt like a second beard around its asshole turns out to be a drug on the market.

So I donated him to the local zoo. They took him on a trial basis. We hugged goodbye. I thought good riddance but he was back on my doorstep in less than a week. There was a note attached to his carrier: BAD INFLUENCE. I was embarrassed, but not surprised.

I tried to take him out in the wild and set him free, and he was OK in the car until I turned off the freeway. Stupid jerk, he started to cry. Never mind, I found him a nice field with lots of growing things that he could eat if he wasn't so fussy, a nice pond and trees he could jump around in. God knows I tried to turn him loose. I put him down and gave him a little pat on the butt. "Go, be free!" Instead he locked his arms and legs around my shin and no matter how hard I kicked to shake him off he clung, going ook-ook-oook so pathetically that I picked him up and we went home.

As a result Spud is still around, a constant reminder of whatever is the most recent failure and believe me, there have been a few too many since *Rhesus Planet,* the unsuccessful *Cockatoo Nation* being one. At least the dealer let me turn in the bird for a goldfish, which mysteriously disappeared the day I brought it home.

Never mind. I did what you do in the wake of failure, which pretty much happens every time I try. I sat down at the computer and started another novel, but when nobody likes you it's hard, thinking up new words to push around the screen.

You get distracted, and the monkey was no help. Spud got bored or jealous or some damn thing whenever I sat down to write. Worse, every time I walked away to get coffee or look out the window for inspiration, which was often, he hopped up on the table and started bopping away at my keyboard with his little fists, bonka-bonka-bonka, and one day when I came back from gazing into the bathroom mirror, I found words.

HELO BILY

Well, he spelled it all wrong, but I'm here to tell you: never condescend to a monkey. It turns out the little fuckers are clever. Plus they are easily bored and idle hands can delete an entire chapter just while you're in the bathroom, examining your zits.

I had to come up with a distraction if I was ever going to finish this rotten book. If I could just get Spud on to something that kept him busy, he wouldn't have to spring up on my keyboard every time I turned my back, like, when I came back to work I wouldn't have to deal with him crouching on top of the bookcase with that reproachful look, oook-oooking every time I quit typing because I was trying to think.

It was inhibiting, all that judgmental hopping and oooking and worse, knowing that he was watching my every move with those sober eyes. I could swear he knew every time I switched screens to see if my Amazon figures had improved or went looking for signs of life on my Facebook page; if I started to blog the ook-ooking slipped into a positively spiteful screeeee.

The monkey was judging me. If I wanted to get anywhere with *Koala Galaxy,* I needed to get Spud the sententious rhesus monkey off my case. Monkey see, monkey do? Fine. I would create a diversion.

I dragged out the laptop Mom bought me when she first found out that I was going to be a famous writer. If it takes a hundred monkeys a thousand years to type a novel and I only had one, how wrong could it go?

I gave my old klunker to the monkey.

Oh, he bonked out a few words but he was no threat to me, for I am an artist. While he was plinking away I managed to crank out *Gibbous Moon,* 3,000,004 on Amazon last time I looked, and *Screaming Meemies,* my first horror novel which, in case you're interested, is in its fifth year on offer, for mysterious reasons, and therefore still available.

And Spud? Oh, he banged out a few hundred words, no big deal, but pretty damn good for a monkey. At least his spelling improved. His little screeds weren't worth squat, but seeing how lame they were compared to my work absolutely cheered me up. I would pat him on the back and praise him and I don't think he knew for a minute that my tone was maybe a little bit condescending, for he is the monkey and I am the pro.

He got good enough that I started printing out some of his stuff and at night, after we'd both eaten and I was sick of playing World of Warcraft and fluffing up my MySpace page, I workshopped the stuff with him, or I tried to. If you want to know the truth, Spud's always been a little too thin-skinned about criticism to be a real writer. One harsh word out of me, one little suggestion and he started ook-oook-ooooking so loud that we had complaints from the neighbors and the super gave me an or-else speech.

"Very well," I said to the monkey finally, and I'm sorry to say that he took it very badly, "if you can't handle a little constructive criticism, shut up,or get out of the kitchen."

How was I supposed to know he was so thin-skinned that he would sulk? When I next looked at his laptop screen the ungrateful brute had typed—never mind what he typed, it was insulting and unprintable. I shouted, "Language!" but he didn't care.

I told him what he could do with his copy and went back to work, and if the next time I peeked Spud had written a villanelle, well—never mind. "Oook-oook-oook," I said to him after I printed it. "This is what I think of your villanelle." He cried when I tore it to bits and threw the pieces away. At least I think that's what he was doing. I sneaked a peek at his screen, which is how he usually communicates, but it was blank, so I never found out what he was thinking.

For the next few days he pretty much abandoned the laptop. Whether I was working or not, he sat in a corner and kept his back to me. He wouldn't eat, at least not while I was watching, and he wouldn't touch the keyboard—plus, every once in a while I could swear I heard him moan, but with monkeys, you never know. He was sulking for sure.

In a way, it was a relief. It was a lot easier to work without him watching. I managed to finish *Dam of the Unconscionable,* my first literary novel. My feeling is, I never sold many copies because I've always been a hybrid and the world resents a literary novelist, but I could gain respect. I thought *Dam of the Unconscionable* would make me famous. I wrote my heart out on that book! It was so intense that I just knew it would win a couple of prizes; this was going to be the novel that would break me out.

Meanwhile Spud was languishing. He wouldn't type, didn't write, wouldn't celebrate with me when a small press gave me a contract for my novel. He wouldn't touch the laptop even though I gave him inspiring speeches about perseverance. Frankly, it was depressing, seeing him dragging around with his shoulders hunched, and I would do anything to buck him up. I even told him he showed promise and slid the open laptop in front of him, hoping to lure him back to his escritoire. The ungrateful bastard just sat on the windowsill, looking into his paws. I hate the sober little jerk but that expression made me feel bad for him and a tad bit guilty too, for letting him type away on that laptop with nary an honest or even a hypocritical kind word.

"You're good," I told him, and I tried my best not to sound condescending this time. "You're really good." But he just looked at me the way he did and I knew that he knew.

Then *Dam of the Unconscionable* tanked. The small press wouldn't even give my money back. I brought home the only copy they printed and I shook it in Spud's face. I'm afraid I shouted: "Well, are you happy now?" I could tell he was still sulking. He wouldn't even oook for me.

So for months Spud sat around and brooded; he was shedding, like every clump of fur was a little reproach. Have you ever tried to sit down and get serious about your novel in the presence of a living reproach? It's like typing on the deck of the Ark the day it starts raining in earnest. Everything shorts out.

If I was ever going to finish *Screed of the Outrageous* and get famous, Spud was a problem that had to be solved.

I couldn't get rid of the guy, too much has gone down between us, so I had to make him happy. Whatever it took.

Then inspiration struck. I was surfing—ok, I was mousing along thinking, the way you do when things aren't going well inside your head, and I came upon this amazing product. I clicked on this page and it said in big letters all the way across the top, NOVEL WRITING WAS NEVER EASIER. I thought, oh boy, lead me to it, for if I haven't mentioned it, a writer's life is consummate hell. The ad read:

Create and track your characters.

Invent situations that work.

Consummate climaxes.

Triumph over conclusions.

Pay for our software out of your first royalty check.

Everything you need to be a successful novelist for five hundred dollars.

Naturally I clicked through to find out more about this miracle and on the next opening in Ta-DAAA print I got its name:

Success guaranteed with . . .

STORYGRINDER

Lead me to it, I thought. Of course electronic miracles are not for me, for I am an artist, but given that Mom had just sent me one of her inspiration bonus checks I thought it might be just the thing for Spud. Plus, if I downloaded it for him I could look over the monkey's shoulder and see if **Storygrinder** knew any tricks, like: five hundred dollars, is there anything in that black bag for me?

So I read the fumpf out loud, thinking to get Spud's attention. "Success guaranteed," I read. "Spud, get a load of this. They can show you how to write *Bright Lights, Big City,*" I told him, which, unfortunately, didn't get a rise out of him, not so much as an ooook.

Then I said, "Or if you wanted, maybe even *The Bible.*"

Nothing. "Or . . . Or . . ." Then I was inspired. "A book like *Animal Farm.*"

Bingo. Spud's head came up.

I thought, if a hundred monkeys typing take a thousand years to write a novel, this software ought to be enough to keep this one off my back for thirty years, which is about as long as these labor-intensive rhesus guys are supposed to last.

I bought **Storygrinder** for the monkey. One look and it was clear the software was not for me. It was, frankly, simplistic. One click and I could write *The Last of the Mohicans,* which, hel-LO, has already been done.

"Here you go, dude," I told him, and on the premise that monkey see, monkey do, I walked him through the first stages.

"It was the best of times, it was the worst of times," I wrote, like Charles Dickens, although the application gave me options that would let me write like one of the Brontes. A flag popped up:

DID YOU MEAN TO REPEAT YOURSELF? FIX.

So I wrote, "Call me Ishmael." Naturally it questioned my spelling, but what the hey, Spud sidled over to watch.

Then I started writing a book that began, "It was love at first sight. The first time Yossarian saw the chaplain he fell madly in love with him," and the monkey's interest in life came back with a jerk.

"Oook!" Spud said and he hurtled in and shoved me out of the way with the force of his entire body. "Oook-ooook!"

"Good boy." Although it would have been fun to play with the software at least a little bit I backed off, relieved and delighted to see him distracted and busy for a change. "Go to it, little dude. Onward," I said, "and upward with the arts."

His eyes lit up.

I said helpfully, "I'd click on the button that says, **start my book**."

For the first time since I brought him home to my apartment, Spud sounded positively joyful. "Oook!"

It did my heart good to see him pounding away with both fists, and better yet, given the nature of the buttons and whistles attached to this new application, which not only tracks your spelling and punctuation but also tells you when you're depending too heavily on certain verbs or using an adjective like "magnificent" more than once in your whole entire novel, the little bugger is a genius with the mouse.

A month with **Storygrinder** and Spud bounded past the pound-and-click method and into proper keyboarding before I noticed what was up. For the first time since I gave him the laptop he started using his tiny fingers. To my surprise the animal has a stretch that any concert pianist would envy and, man, you ought to see his attack! After a month he was up to speed and the next thing I knew he had outrun me, typing so fast that there was no telling where it would end. Next time I checked, his output almost matched mine, and as I was in the final third of my next attempt after *Screed of the Outrageous* and, frankly, my best shot at going for the gold, what I had thought of as a gimmick to keep Spud out of my hair ended up with us in a footrace for fame.

He was hard at it and instead of being relieved by my first weeks of freedom from his constant sulking—to say nothing of the fierce, judgmental attention I got back in the days when I was working well and he was bored—I was proud, but I was also a little bit afraid.

The worst part was that where we used to print out every night and talk about what he'd done, now at night when Spud was done for the day he would slam the laptop shut with this don't-even-think-about-it glare. And do you know, he had the thing password-protected? I ask you, who taught him that?

Either he was jealous of **Storygrinder** and afraid I'd siphon off a copy and get the jump on him, or he didn't want me finding out what his novel looked like.

What it looked like, it looked like it was a thousand pages long and I had to start wondering whether it was *War and Peace* he was writing, only with rhesus monkeys instead of Russians, or this century's answer to *Gone with the Wind*. Monkeys, you never know, and he wasn't tipping his hand. Naturally I'd started out with this thinking I would keep close tabs on him, of course he'd want me to print out so we could workshop what he was writing the way we did in the good old days, but I'd do it better this time around. Like, more praise for what he was doing, but definitely constructive criticism over cookies and cocoa like we used to do, late at night.

How sharper than a serpent's tooth is the ungrateful protege. The one time I tried to hook up his laptop to the printer cable, Spud latched on to me like that thing out of *Alien* and plastered his smelly body to my face. I went lunging around blindly with his legs in a stranglehold so tight that I couldn't breathe and his fists clamped on my ears. I had to stagger into the kitchen and duck my head in the dirty dishwater to make him let go. After that I had to make certain promises, like you do when you have to get somebody off your case because they're all up in your face.

I retreated to my corner and he stayed in his forever typing, typing, typing, and when I tried to make things better with a tactful smile or an inoffensive remark—even when I came at him with bananas and candy he would get all defensive and slam the laptop shut with that look. He was what you'd have to call vindictive, so after a while I backed off and tried my best to get back to *Deranged All Over Town* which will rival *Bright Lights, Big City* if I can ever get it back on track which, given what happened with the monkey's novel, gets harder and harder to do.

The little bastard sent it off to an agent without even telling me it was done.

I'd just as soon spare myself the details of what happened next, but since the monkey can't open bank accounts or deposit checks, not to mention endorsing them convincingly, I've benefited a bit. Prada and Gucci everything, as Spud could care less about outfits and frankly, he's careless about his looks. A specially fitted car seat for trips to public appearances and book signings, where he has generously allowed me to stand in for him. In fact, as far as the world knows it is I, Billy Masterton (that's the renowned W. B. Masterton, Pulitzer Prize winning author) who did the deed. The monkey has nothing to complain about. He has his very own room in our Brooklyn town house and I bought him three computers loaded with **Storygrinder** in his own special work area that I've fitted out so he can write his miserable, best-selling potboilers three at a time for all I care. Between us, the monkey and I put James Patterson so far behind in the popularity sweepstakes that the man can put his entire staff to work 24/7 and still never catch up on any bestseller list. And if I get the money and the credit?

What Spud doesn't know, he doesn't have to know.

The trouble is, this whole mad success up to and including bestsellerdom has me working day and night on the little bastard's behalf, which means that since it all hit the fan and sprayed money on us, my cherished *Deranged All Over Town* is advancing at the rate of one line a day, and I'm sad to say, the line I finally manage is one I'm so pressured that I don't get time or space in my head to think it through, which means first thing next morning, I have to delete.

Plus, Spud has me answering every single piece of his fan mail, sending thank-yous for those endless and insultingly expensive gifts and maintaining his pages on MySpace, where he has ten thousand friends, and on Facebook, where he has a mere eight thousand, although my carpals are seriously tunneled just from scrolling through the stuff, never mind the hours I spend virtually sitting in front of W. B. Masterton's virtual bookstore on Second Life.

And the monkey? I think he just finished this century's answer to *The Brothers Karamazov,* but with more sex and a lot more guilt. Where does he get off, thinking he knows anything about guilt? He, who smothered my brilliant career like an infant in its crib.

But what's killing me, if you want to know what kills me, is the blog. I don't get to see what the monkey writes until he posts it. I sneak looks at his printed works while I'm waiting for his platoons of fans to flood the auditorium where I am speaking, or for booksellers to unbar the doors to let the next wave of frantic admirers in, but that isn't enough. His work is pretty good, which, frankly, is depressing, but not half as depressing as discovering from one of these gooshy-eyed teenagers or inspired surfer dudes that the son of a bitch has been dissing me on his blog.

If you want to read what Spud says about me, go ahead and read it, you'll find more than you want to know about our relationship plastered in the pages at: http://www.wbmastertonauthor.net.

I only looked the once. After everything I've done for Spud, the software and the encouragement and the plush cover for his rotten car seat in the Beemer and the patent leather evening slippers because after he saw mine he wouldn't stop oook-oooking until I had some especially made for him; in spite of me buying him his very own organ grinder the ungrateful little bastard had the nerve to write this very day:

Those of you who think I know the way to happiness might as well know that success isn't everything. You may think I am happy because of the American Book Award and all, but as long as I am the prisoner of a shitty writer, happiness is forever and eternally out of reach and if any of you care about me ever, you have to come to my house and GET ME OUT.

That to his eight million hits a day, forwarded to all their friends and acquaintances all over the English-speaking world!

OK, if that's how it is, that's how it's going to be.

Well, if that's what he thinks of me . . .

I'll show him.

The ape's got four more novels banked in those computers, and even if I can't crack his passwords, he's already raking in so much that it's no skin off my butt if he crashes and bursts into flames, so, cool. I'm fixed for life. I don't want to hurt the monkey, really, and I won't hit him with a bill of particulars. I won't even do the gratifying thing and smash his head in with an ax.

Given the pillow, which I've soaked in chloroform, the little fucker won't feel a thing.

—Asimov's SF, 2010

The Outside Event

I'm supposed to come down and sit in your, like, confession box and spill my . . . what? Wait! I have to do makeup. So, is this judged more on looks, or is it a performance thing?

All right, all right, this is *not* a contest, but. Really. Gazillion writing samples, audition demos, personal interviews and you only picked twenty of us, how is this not competitive? I am very close to someone who didn't make it, and believe me, there are feelings . . . Davy, I love you, think of me as doing it for you!

Hello out there, Audience? Judges? Whatever you are. This is Cynthia La-Mott, speaking to you from The Confessional in the re-purposed Gothic chapel on my very first day at Strickfield. What a rush! First I want to thank Dame Hilda for founding the colony in memory of Ralph Strickler, her son, who died. Nobody will say how, but it was awful. Greetings from the great stone castle where many are called but few are, oh, you know.

Mom, they chose me, bad Cynnie, and not Leon, family crown prince and bum playwright, for this expense-paid summer in the castle; if you have to ask you can't afford it, and fuck you.

Davy was very sweet about it when I got the callback because until last week, he thought we were equals. He's a poet so it shouldn't be a problem, but it is. A guy in a white suit hand-carried the invitation up four flights to our front door. By the time Davy and I opened it he was down in the street, getting into a cab. Davy made me jump for the envelope like this was a game, which it definitely is not.

I think.

Mom, it was for me! Time, place and dates engraved, with a note added in that farty, rich-girl handwriting you see in raised silver foil on every Aline Armantout best seller:

Welcome, writer-in-waiting. At Strickfield, you'll do great things, and this year we're starting something new! Do come. Your future depends on it.

xxxx   A.A.

That's all.

Aline herself followed up with a phone call, which is how Davy and I knew it wasn't a joke. I wanted to ask about the *something new* but she said, "Congratulations, you are chosen." Period. Davy gave me Swarovski crystals to prove he isn't mad. Real writers don't have day jobs so Davy maxed out his plastic to cover the rental car plus gas and snacks along the way to keep me sharp so I can sparkle at the Opening Night Banquet. Everybody, it's black tie!

We drove forever to get here. Strickfield is in the middle of, like, the Black Forest. Who knew it was also shopping hell? No malls anywhere, you can't even order online. In woods like these, delivery kids get hunted down and eaten by bears, and all the pretty things in their packages ripped to shreds. Riding up here, I could swear I saw wolves running along behind the car. They didn't peel off until the castle gates opened up and then clanged shut behind Davy's Zip car like a giant bear trap.

In spite of which this place is beautiful, although there are weird noises coming from the attic and rumors about the Thing in the Lake. Three months, all expenses paid, what could go wrong?

Well, one thing. Nobody warned me *every single dinner is black tie.* If I do this right I'll be famous, my whole life is at stake and I'm sitting here thinking, *what to wear, what to wear?*

See, for dress up, I brought exactly one sexy dress and my Jimmy Choos that I got off a stall, I saw the guy glue in the label himself. Oh, and my present Davy bought to prove he's OK with this—which was big of him, as, whatever the game is, we both know he just lost.

Entre nous, it's just as well Strickfield's just for the chosen, so he's not allowed to stay. When you're in love with a guy, the last thing you want is you and him both fighting over the same prize.

I hope Davy gets home all right.

I hope he won't dump me if I lose.

Unless I'm scared he'll dump me if I win.

Do I love being a writer more than I love my boyfriend, are we lovers or rivals or what? Not clear. I'm not a poet like he is, so we thought it was OK but it isn't, and that's just bad.

Which is more important, really, my one-and-only or this thing that I don't even know what it is, that I have to do? Does wanting something bigger than I am make me a writer or is there more? It's not like I can make out the size and shape of my ambition, all I know is that I want this, and I want it BAD.

Writers work alone but here I am, batched with people who fought, bled and died to make it here, so what's that all about? Probably we'd rather hang out than work, so we're putting off the hard part, where we have to sit down and bash our heads against a wall of words with nobody around to cheer us on. See, at rock bottom what goes on between you and your work is strictly private, in spite of which we cluster in these places, and it scares the crap out of me. Like we're all in a footrace or a beauty contest, with only one prize.

"*We expect great things from you.*" They do. It was on the invitation, but what, exactly, is not written, here or anywhere.

So, are colonies like Strickfield really part of the process? You hear about one person every year when a Strickfield summer ends, and that person starts winning prizes, fame and fortune implied, but what happens to the rest?

I guess you stop hearing about them because the world only wants to hear about winners, right?

Which is why I have to win this thing! No prob. All I have to do is figure out the object of the game—and play the game, but, wait. What if the object of the game is finding out what is the object of the game?

Oooh, camera, I think I know how my novel starts!

Emerging from the dressing room, Stephanie was sweating thumbtacks that penetrated every soft spot in her body. The regulation satin thong gave her a humiliating wedgie. Her heart constricted under the mandated mini-bra. Her perfume stank and her head wobbled under the weight of her towering hair but she had agreed to enter the Miss Universe pageant and now, next-to-naked, she was heading into the blinding light, exposed like this, on the cavernous stage.

Oh, sorry. I was just. Never mind.

It was scary, coming up the walk, like the electrified razor wire on top of the wall was the only thing holding back those monstrous trees. Gnarly bushes loomed like predators crouched to spring. Then Miss Nedobity opened the great front door and everything got worse. Strickfield's successes publish smarmy thank-you notes to this woman; they dedicate books to her, but she's famous for being mean and nobody can figure out why sweet Dame Hilda left her in charge.

This pair of heavily armored boobs came out first, closely followed by the lady herself, with her fierce diamond dog collar and her fuck-you smile. She was all, "Welcome, welcome."

Then she wasn't. *Wham,* she slammed her clipboard into Davy's chest. "Not you," she said, and ticked my name off. "LaMott. You're the last. Now, keep this sheet with you at all times."

It was pink. It was headed: HOUSE RULES, which Miss Nedobity recited in case I couldn't read. "No cell phones at Strickfield, we have a signal blocker so don't even try. In case of emergency, there's a pay phone in the office, computers but no Internet, no wandering in the halls after Lights Out and *no outsiders.*"

She snarled at Davy. "And no fraternizing with outsiders either, under pain." She didn't say on pain of what. "And you. You keep to the path when you go to your individual studios in the woods and you stay there until the dinner bell. Don't even think about leaving the grounds. If you're caught trying, you're OUT, and believe me, the ride away from Strickfield is not pleasant, and whatever you do, never *ever* go down to the lake."

"Not even to swim?"

"No! Read this sheet carefully, memorize it, and keep it on your person at all times because you must never forget even one of these important rules. Your room is on four, it's 13A, take the rear stairwell, it's down that hall and remember, you don't interface with the others until the banquet. Cocktails at six. Now, go."

Davy and I stood there blinking, like, *Whatever happened to hello?* He dragged my stuff inside in spite of her, while I studied the portrait of Dame Hilda above the fireplace and wished to hell she hadn't died. See, Dame Hilda did all the intake interviews, and Davy looks like that portrait of her son. They say she was a sucker for cute guys, although they also say if you happened to be one and she asked you up for coffee in the Morning Room, *watch out.*

Now it's this Miss Nedobity in her don't-fuck-with-me diamonds and black polyester dress, and she could care less that Davy and I are in love. She a-*hem*med until we kissed goodbye, and ripped us asunder so fast that I heard the pop and slammed the door on him. So I had to lug all my stuff up four flights because Strickfield rejects don't get past the foyer, Or Else.

The Or Else is spelled out in very small print. There are outdoor strobes and sirens so don't even think about sneaking out, and if your boyfriend or girlfriend makes it over the razor wire . . . Well, there are Dobermans. Like they're scared one of us will be caught having sex with, shudder, an *outsider,* although they don't spell out which of us does what with which others after the gates clang shut.

You read books about Strickfield's famous writers and their famous affairs, but is it, like, mandatory or optional? Miss Nedobity's poop sheet doesn't say. So, is one of the elimination rounds about the sex? Wait. Do you win if you have a lot of it and I should find someone—or if you don't have it at all?

There's a lot I don't understand, like weirdness I hear overhead, or the hastily scrawled note on my door.

Results may be affected or determined by Outside Event. Outside Event? Affected or determined? Just tell me. Which is it? Is Strickfield really about art for art's sake or is it something I didn't know about?

Dear Davy, This place is big and creepy and I miss you already.

Department of conjecture:

1. Writers' colony as first rung on the ladder to success, in which case I'm lucky I'm here.
   Note to self: *What makes you so sure?*
2. Writers' colony as penal colony like in Kafka, and we get tortured if we don't produce?
3. Writers' colony as Olympics, with elimination rounds based on number of pages we crank out?
4. Writers' colony as pressure cooker of human emotions
   a. Unexpected love affairs and concomitant infidelity
   b. Artistic meltdowns
   c. Jealousy and petty quarrels
   d. Food fights
   e. Potential violence sparked by honest opinions of rival's work.
5. Writers' colony as test match, the prize goes to the best?
   Note to self: What *is* best?
6. Writers' colony as narrative petri dish, as in:
   You may wonder why I have gathered you together here.

Which?

None of the above?

All of the above?

Will I go home changed?

Will I go home at all?

—Oh, I know, I think I know how to start my book!

Now that she was at the destination she'd struggled all her life to reach, lovely Dahlia Eastwood shuddered, thinking: Something is not right. *As she approached the manor, the outline of the monumental heap shifted slightly, as though without the occupants knowing it, something profound had changed. From somewhere within came a sound that might have been taken for a prodigious groan, as though the entity inside knew how beautiful she was, and that she had come here alone. The most frightening thing about it was that although she was afraid, she was not surprised.*

I'm sorry, I got distracted. I was thinking about my. Um. Novel, which I'm writing this summer right here in my studio at Strickfield, right? Um, right?

Look. I have to go do wardrobe and makeup for the Opening Night Banquet, first impressions are so important. So, if you're actually shooting this and it isn't just a surveillcam, are we graded more on promptness or more on our personal look? Charm or number of words produced? Do I have to sell a whole novel to win, or what?

Look. Why don't you just tell me? Like, is the winner the first one to make it to the top?

Or the last one still standing at the end?

The faces you meet are false faces we put on to meet you, and it isn't just me wearing an expression that's not my own. What the twenty of us are doing and what you think we're doing aren't the same.

Smile, girl. Put on your Swarovski earrings and crystal flash drive lavalier and go down and show yourself to the people. And suss them out.

Behold Cynthia LaMott on the grand staircase at Strickfield, beholding all the other wannabes milling outside the sliding doors to the Great Hall. Down I go in my simple, drop-dead little black dress. I put on Davy's crystals to signify that not only am I better than the others, I am also different, although how I can make this dress look new and exciting every single night . . .

The people I have to beat are milling around down there in the foyer, talking and laughing like they belong, and! The clothes! Did every single woman bring designer dresses but me? I should be draining my debit card at Nordstrom Rack right now, because every single one of them is dressed to kill or maim.

To tell the truth, that foyer is a lot like the mezzanine at Nordstrom's, with a pianist tinkling while people you'd kill to get friends with mingle in evening clothes.

You see the outfit. The smile, and nothing of the engine that drives me, not even a hint of what's going on underneath the hood. While we scope each other I'm considering:

Is this a death match?

Dog show, with prizes for looks and grooming?

Arena, where we're matched like gladiators?
Coliseum, with lions TK, outcome TBA?
Or is this really only about words?
It's too soon to tell.

Idea: *In the grand foyer all but one of the gifted, chosen ten fluttered like trapped pigeons, plucking at each other with anxious fingers. Maribel ran among them, asking, "Where's Brad?" Here for less than a week, and she and Brad Fairchild are lovers, separated since lunch with no hint of where he went. Frantic, she starts the others buzzing, "Has anyone seen Brad?" They were already uneasy, ten strangers summoned to the dismal mansion for a reason, here because of Aunt Matilda's mysterious note.*

The day was ending like all the others, until the rhinoceros housekeeper shrieked, "Stay out of the library. Something terrible has happened."

They were no longer ten.

Dear Davy, If only you'd seen me tonight, sexy and dressed to kill.

OK booth, I'm not supposed to be here, but if I don't tell *somebody,* I'll explode. One night at Strickfield and the pressure is intense. Standing right there on the stairwell, I started my **watch** list, and five hours later, it's only half done.

People to watch out for:

Edwine Evergood, with her sweet Pre-Raphaelite smile and a bunch of stories I totally don't get, in spite of which she's *actually published,* but it's a very small press. Wardrobe A+, potential hard to measure because her stuff is obscure but she already has a book. Is *obscure* a good thing and I should try it? Yuck!

Fred Fisher, he has a story under consideration at *The New Yorker* and he got his hunting memoir into *Esquire,* looks like a lumberjack even in black tie, either too nice or totally confused. *Confused is good, but:* **Watch out for too nice.** I could never write like Fred. Every page drips testosterone.

And then there's The Great Profile. Suave. Way too suave. Sleek Mark Armitage is older, but not so old that it's creepy, head of some bigtime ad agency and, wow, he got an MFA from Columbia nights, and wrote *Trash* in his spare time, slick but arty, already on the AWP short list. Plus, he's too short to be trusted, it's hard to explain. Stingray cowboy boots with the tux and he looks, I don't know. Relentless. Like he could knock you down and walk right over you.

Serena Soleil. I don't care what she writes, she's tall and silky and so gorgeous that you'd just as soon she died.

By dinnertime I'd made some contacts, although it's hard to figure out who matters here. I picked this old guy Cecil to eat with because he's friendly, and too creaky to be a threat, like IBM gave him the gold watch so with nothing to do, he might as well write a book. Well, good luck with that. Unlike certain others who shall remain nameless I'm strong and the youngest if you don't count Alvin Gelb, who is, face it, fourteen and easily confused, which means that whatever it takes, I can beat him out.

I kind of have to. The kid's on the bestseller list.

Cecil says Andover let Alvin out before exams for this, probably because his father is Ted Gelb. He's here in a hand tailored Armani tux, thanks to his famous dad, I bet that's how he got published in the first place and I know it got him on that bestseller list, I mean, whose newspaper is it, anyway? He comes on all cute and preppy but if you ask me, the kid is shifty and way too smart to be nice.

Dear Davy, I wish I was back at our place, where I can work!

Explain to me please how being thrown together with others, everybody out for the same thing, can help me get good enough at what I do to matter in the world. I work at home! Alone, so how? Contacts, maybe. A big plus on my resume, that's for sure, but in terms of free time and limiting distractions, a month in Solitary with no visitors and no Internet, no phone and no TV would be a lot less distracting. What does sorting out this jumbled mess inside my head have to do with anything we say to each other in this big, intimidating place?

At dinner Dame Hilda's fat nephew Leslie gave the opening speech—Cecil says it's sad that poor Ralph wasn't here to cut the cake, terrible about what happened to him, whatever it was.

This Leslie used to come to Cecil's birthdays when they were little, but he cried and went home before the cake. Miss Nedobity cut this one; it was bitter, like her. Every year bakers replicate the castle with all its turrets and crenellations, plus marzipan chimneys and slate roofs paved in chocolate, if I sleep on my cake will I have nightmares or can I dream this novel, and win?

We toasted Dame Hilda with pink champagne and everybody got a little drunk. Then Aline Armantout, who gushes like a game show host, led us down to the Garden of Forking Paths and turned us loose to find our studios in the woods. After breakfast tomorrow that's where we go. Lunch comes in a basket under a checkered napkin, no fraternizing, and don't even think about coming back to the big house before six. They want us to lock ourselves in and think Big Thoughts.

Turns out, if you can't find your studio you're OUT, so this really is a contest and that was the first event.

Poor Cecil. I guess I should have picked a friend with more staying power. He got lost in the woods and we never saw him again. I don't know what they did to him, but Aline says he gave a sweet exit interview in the Confessional and the world will see it when this show finally airs. OMG, we're on a show! We didn't ask her where Cecil went, and she didn't say. It's not like we had a tribal council and everybody got to vote. Aline and Leslie call the shots.

But, hey. Win and it's the Strickfield Wall of Fame! They carve your name into the marble and you get famous, like every winner since this place started. The future is ahead, but what about Davy, will he resent me if I win?

I don't get to see him again until I win or I lose and they kick me out of the colony, and this is what scares me. Right now I don't know which would be worse. What do I have to do to win this?

Meanwhile I hear eerie noises in the attic every night. Unless it's my imagination.

We're all here because of our vivid imaginations, right?

Frightened as she was of the darkness overhead, Gemma knew that sooner or later she had to find out who or what was suffering on the floor above, Every fiber in her body shrieked, "Don't go up there, don't go up there," but if she didn't, she might spend the rest of her life wondering, and never sleep. She would, she thought, go up there, but not until she found somebody she trusted to stand watch while she entered the cavernous maw of the unknown, so that was the issue. Finding someone she can trust.

Dear Davy, I'm just so very, very sorry they made you leave, and I . . .

Memory, imagination, anxiety, that deep, what-if paranoia—everything feeds this question I'm trying so hard to satisfy: what I want, really, and what I want to do. Which is cool, except instead of coming up with answers, I come up dry. Not knowing terrifies me. That and these formal dinners, me up against the others on wardrobe, on style, everything, all of us gauging the others' level of confidence, all of us asking, all *faux naive*, "How did it go today?"

This is what I'm most afraid of. Silence. Not the terrible, silent woods or the cutesy rustic studio where I'm expected to work all alone—no water cooler, no coffee shop—until nightfall, but the silence inside my head.

It's been a long week. I've made kind-of friends with Elly Tarbell, she's a crap poet and therefore not that big of a threat. And I really like Roger Adair, who I hardly noticed last week. His studio is the next one on the hill and when I am staring out the window, which is mostly, I see origami water bombs stuck in the bushes and if I look up at the right time, I see paper airplanes flying out. Until yesterday I thought they were made out of old pages of Roger's most recent, but heading back to the house for dinner I picked one up, and, cool! When I unfolded it, all there was on the paper were two crossed-out lines and a penciled note:

FUCK I'M BORED.

Then last night at dinner . . . (I spent Thursday night making a shift out of Cecil's bedspread—watch out curtains, beware bedsheets, mattress cover, you're next. I can always vary the outfits with a jerkin cut out of that shag rug and when I run out of rug I'll start on the slipcovers in my studio, where I am trapped from nine a.m. to five, like if I sit there long enough, I can create . . .)

Listen, you overdressed bitches, including Aline Armantout, is this "Project Runway" or are we serious about our work?

Anyway, last night at dinner, I had the paper airplane tucked under a spaghetti strap on my slinky shift, which if I do say so, came out really well. Roger saw it and, zot! We bonded. You should have seen his face when Barton Freeman bragged that he'd knocked out ten thousand words before lunch and Melanie Fangold, who's out-and-proud-of-it said so what, she's halfway through her novel, *Jillville*, it's a sensation and it's going to be a smash.

A bunch of others weighed in, swapping word counts like jocks comparing sexploits in some cosmic locker room. Roger stuffed his fist in his mouth to keep from laughing. I couldn't help it, I was laughing too because everybody who is anybody knows that in this game, it isn't how *much* you do, it's how good it is.

I think.

But guess what. Elly Tarbell, who I thought was a dependable summertime friend, said, too loud, "Well, *I* only wrote one page and . . ." Maybe she should have kept it to herself. Her voice shook, but she was so smug that I hated her for saying, "Then I tore it up."

Let that be a lesson to me, although I don't know if it's about not bragging or shutting up until my book is done. Elly was gone by breakfast, and nobody, not even Miss Nedobity, would tell us where she went.

DEAR DAVY, BORROW IF YOU HAVE TO, I NEED YOU. COME BACK. LOVE

Nobody in the colony knew about the Thing in the lake, not even the overbearing housekeeper who herded the colonists like cattle. She harassed them unchecked until the morning that they found the ethereal Wanda Loveland's drenched body on the path that ran downhill from the studios where the chain gang was unhitched every morning and incarcerated separately until she marched them back to the big house every night. Although Miss Finnerty and the other administrators called it suicide by drowning, nobody could dispute the seaweed that shrouded the body and filled the muddy tracks left by whatever dragged poor Wanda's sodden, ravaged body uphill to the spot where she was found.

OK, Cynnie, don't go there. There isn't any Thing in the lake at Strickfield and if there was one and I wrote about it, with my luck, it would turn out **that's** the elimination deal, that you were stupid, you fell for the myth. I want to win this thing! I tried to pump Miss Nedobity but after Ellie left, the Witch of Endor went somewhere inside herself and she won't come out.

Dear Davy, I miss you, you're the only man I trust, but you have your work and we're so busy here . . .

Plus certain people are getting better lunches, is that a reward for something I don't know about, or some kind of sign? Mine today was Velveeta spread on Ry Krisp with an apple. To keep me regular? At what? Meanwhile Melanie and Barton Freeman came to dinner belching paté and Alvin Gelb wore a chicken bone in his lapel like a merit badge and of course his second novel (he has a contract) is going like wildfire, and this is only Week Two. I don't like Edwine, but I have to admire Edwine. She gave them a sour scowl and said ever so sweetly, loud enough for even flabby, fatuous Leslie Strickler to hear, "Quantity doesn't mean quality, does it?" Then she raked us with that sickly sweet, superior smile.

Gotta love Roger. He and I were both breaking up.

Then after dinner Aline gave a little speech about how lucky we were to be still in the running and things will be harder from here on. I thought at least Miss Nedobity would snort derisively, but she just sat there looking moodily into her hands while Aline went on and on about how proud we were making her and Leslie, who hasn't exactly spoken since that first night. "So far so good," she finished, "but, remember. Success is unpredictable."

Now, what the hell was that?

Was she, like, foreshadowing the Outside Event?

Then her voice dropped. After way too long, it popped up in a new, perky place. "Work is work but Strickfield is about colleagueship. Which is why Dame Hilda instituted our famous Crit Nights."

Aline was beaming, but I swear I heard somebody groan. "Now, ask your best friend here to tell you the truth about your work."

She said, "Tonight," after which people began to drift away in pairs, at which point I noticed that of the twenty, there weren't twenty of us any more, just enough to pair off neatly, girl-boy, girl-boy, all but Melanie, who went off to her room with a triumphal, above-it-all grin because as a lesbian, she'd won the immunity prize.

Roger made a *get it?* face. I nodded and we paired off. By that time everybody had found somebody, even Alvin Gelb, despite only being fourteen—but, with Serena?

Serena! So sleek. So intent on meeting Alvin's famous dad.

Well, everybody paired off except some dweeb so lame that I never learned his name and Florence Klamm, who has nice clothes and the sparkle of a hermit crab. They straggled off to their single rooms alone and this morning they were gone. Into obscurity, I suppose, no better than they deserve. Strickfield winners make headlines and the rest? Who cares what happens to the rest?

I checked Florence's room today and—score! She left in such a hurry that she forgot her party dresses which, OK. Frankly, they look way better on me.

So, if these confessions we're all making *do* get aired? Davy, I want you to know nothing went on between Roger and me except some honest literary criticism, I read his chapter and he read an old story I brought along as backup so chill, Davy, we're just good friends.

Dear Davy, Crit Night was gruesome. You're my best first-reader and the only one I trust . . .

What's risky and more terrifying than showing another writer your unborn work?

Finding the right thing to say about theirs.

We enter the treacherous land of envy and unbidden admiration that we're too choked by anxiety and ambition to express, compounded by the fear that what we read will be so awful that accidental truths will pop out of our rivals' mouths. That resentment will smolder, building until it ignites. Outbursts surface like flash fires, leading to threats and slashed tires, depending on how much we've had to drink; camaraderie can morph into hurt feelings, irremediable rifts, but in the seconds before the flare-up, we were so *close!* Last night started well but it ended with Roger and me on the outs: awful, I only had one friend here and now I don't.

It's easier to say something nice about even a close friend's work than to hear him say anything that pleases you.

I want to go home.

Oh, your crit sessions are a great idea. When this show airs, I want the audience to know how useful they are, although of course we'll spare them the gories, like, I'll sign the confidentiality agreement when I win. This is going to air, right? I figured it out! We're shooting the pilot for *Strickfield*, the greatest-ever reality show, um, aren't we? If not, why am I confessing here?

Really. I just wish Roger hadn't gotten so mad at me before I showed him the new opening of my novel, I'm sorry it was only a half-page but there are way too many distractions to get anything done. I wish I'd had time to rewrite it, but. Oh never mind.

I just wish we could write our own futures, but even that's out of our hands and, about the attic. I only saw that door open once, when Miss Nedobity took Fred Fisher's bedding upstairs the day *Esquire* blew the whistle on him. Plagiarism. One phone call and he was gone. It makes me feel bad. And anxious. And bad.

Part of me wants to go down to Roger's room and throw myself on his mercy and beg him to like me again so I'll have at least one friend. I need him to sit by the attic stairs while I try to find out what's going on up there, and come up after me if something gets me and I don't come down. It's the least he could do after what he said about my work, but Roger's so pissed off about my crit that he probably wouldn't notice if I packed up and left right now, sobbing my heart out in the night.

Is that moaning I hear, is it the wind or is it remorse blowing around inside my empty head? OK, Roger. I'm sorry I said your chapter needed work. I am!

In the woods Martha trails Dennis like a shadow of herself. Dying leaves rustle like old women wringing their hands, whether in grief or anticipation, she can not say. "Dennis." Before last night they were as one but that changed; she can't find the reason they are here. What if she loses him? What if he abandons her? The thought sours in her mouth. "Wait up!"

"It's this way." Dennis hurries as though he doesn't care whether she follows or not.

> **In the room, my desires come and go**
> **weeping, because they do not know**

"Oh, Dennis." She begins but when he turns, can't find a way to finish the sentence.

"Be patient," he tells her with a look like a perfunctory farewell kiss.

I've come too far to give up now, she thinks and in the next second regret blows into her like a cyclone through an unfinished house.

I shouldn't have come.

> **. . . weeping, because they'll never know**
> **what might have been on other days**

Excitement quickens her steps. Hopes send her pelting after her lover like a schoolgirl after a soccer ball as the last line comes to her whole.

> **Unless she stays.**

That's it! Wow, talk about your *coup de foudre.*

Unless she stays. I don't need Davy. I know what I'm doing now! All I have to do is get it done, and if Roger and I *both* could win . . .

You bet I feel better, and I have this to say to your peeps before I go down to yet another horrible breakfast where everybody is either too sleepy or too depressed or too hung over to talk.

I don't have enough on paper to make Roger smile at me like he did before terrible Crit Night, but by the end of the week I will.

I think.

Was it *so* bad that I said his prose was too big for the story? I was only trying to help him, and as for me?

I've scuttled projects X, Y and Z for this exciting new idea I got in the night. I'm channeling smug, pimply Alvin Gelb, and my novel is just pouring out!

Last week Roger found out that the wonder kid is writing a book about Strickfield and all of us. The nerve! Alvin's hero is, like, gushing out his puerile thoughts day by day as the summer unwinds. Roger pulled a printout out of the kid's trash while Alvin was outside his studio getting loaded in the woods—so much for rules—and gave it to me, but of course that was before we had Crit Night and Roger stopped speaking to me.

It was still on my desk when I choked down toast and dragged my grieving, wounded self downhill to the shack. Excuse me. Studio, where we're supposed to write. Alvin's first chapter was lying there like a gift. I won't bore you by quoting Alvin's ostensible book, it's stupid and callow and mean, but for me? One look and . . . Wow!

It was the moment when they zap the corpse with the paddles and the patient comes back to life.

A writers' colony is like a foreign country. Not the right place for paranoid, inner-directed people—introverted, most of us, with careers built on failed efforts to bring order out of the chaos inside our heads. We do what we do in hopes of . . . In hopes. In territory like this we are all xenophobes: touchy, paranoid. Every little thing said or done by the others sinks into sensitive ground, takes root and grows. Like foreigners, we assess the others. Are we the only outsider and they're all native to this place? We're uneasy. Aliens, feeling our way, timidly trying to master the language and to make sense of the currency, calculating everything we do, trying it this way, that, in hopes nobody will find out how foreign we are, rehearsing our lines in perpetual fear of saying something wrong.

Dear Davy, I'm sorry I haven't written. It's been busy here . . .

You bet I am a smug little bastard, I, Alphonse Frankenstein, son of the most notable critic in the whole fucking country, head and shoulders above every single writer in this entire fucking place which they sent me into like a babe unto the wilderness because Dad said my head was getting too big for my body and I was out of control. Well, fuck that, one look and I know I write better than every single one of these half-baked old writer wannabes in this fucking colony, oh not you, Thalia Fineheart, for you are my best friend in this weird, weird place where Dad planted me like a fucking guidon, like a Crusader in one of his old black-and-white movies that he looks at 24/7, you know, "In the name of God I claim this land for France."

I've found my voice! I came to dinner last night with two thousand words under my belt, and I loved it. Everybody changed color when I told them, which makes me think all those suppertime scorecards flashed by certain people are a lie.

I could win this. I could!

Two writers were eliminated during the campfire sing and six more were gone after the staged readings of Serena's astonishing play. Four more lost on wardrobe, deportment, last week's fox trot contest, which was if you ask me, totally unfair. Leslie Strickler announced it and Miss Nedobity made us practice at cocktail time every night. I wore Florence's handkerchief point dress and everybody thought I'd flown it in from Bergdorf's or Neiman's, I got points for my look, so, cool, but the contest was a put up job. Leslie's been taking lessons and puffy as he is, turns out to be quite the twinkler in his patent leather loafers. He danced everybody into the ground except Serena, Alvin, Roger and Melanie and me.

There are so few of us left that I'm getting scared. So far everything's been— well, unpredictable but not unexpected, but we're all strung tight over the Outside Event. Will it be dangerous? Targeted? Specific to each player, which is, face it, what we are, or something bigger and worse?

I should bond with whoever's left because by God it is strange out, and getting stranger. Even the dreadnought in the diamond dog collar is getting strange. I caught Miss Nedobity on her knees in front of the portrait of the late Ralph Strickler, and the monster of the manor was in tears! Upset much? I couldn't help it, I freaked. And worst part is, now that Roger isn't speaking to me, I don't have anybody to tell. I need somebody I can sit with at these dinners so we can talk and laugh—you know, like friends. I need a friend!

DEAR DAVY I NEED YOU. DROP EVERYTHING. COME!

All any of us wants is to *belong*. We try, but we're always a little off. Hypersensitive. Judgmental. Jumping to conclusions inside our heads: occupational hazard, right? Every little thing we say comes out wrong, or it's taken wrong. Even small gestures are misconstrued and although we try to hide it, at every turn we are assessing: *are you a winner? Am I?*

As if the worst thing that can happen is losing. Unless it's taking sides and finding out that we chose wrong. Is that why I'm here? Because fiction is the only work I know how to do, but all I really want is to belong?

It's getting weird here. Dinners are weird, just us five and the staff, everybody at the same table, everybody but Roger on edge, no bragging, just nervous bla-blabla like rain dropping into the hush. We toasted Ralph Strickler's birthday, and everything got even weirder. How could I sleep? I'm in the Confessional at, what is it? Dawn. If I don't win this thing and get on TV, *somebody* needs to know.

It was four a.m. when it started up overhead—shuffling, moaning, I guess—but instead of fading, it intensified. Grief outgrew the attic and poured downstairs. I heard it in the hall, so I had to look, and, OMG. There was a great, quivering blob crouched at the bottom of the attic stairs, OMG, I mean *really*, it was Miss Nedobity in her diamond choker! Slipcovered like a Strickfield sofa in her white canvas nightie. She had her hands over her face and she was crying so hard that I was scared to touch her.

She was sobbing, and I was like: *Is this the Outside Event?*

I said, "Are you all right?"

"I'm so tired. I'm just so tired." I can't afford to get on her bad side so I patted her shoulder. She spread her fingers and peeked through them. "Oh, it's you." Then she wailed, "I wasn't *always* this big!" and cried so hard that I was afraid the others would hear and come out into the hall and, what. Get in on this. "It wasn't always this way."

I kept pat-patting and shushing until she nodded and swallowed hard. Her whole body was heaving but she managed, "I'm sorry, it's his birthday. Again, and I have to make sure he has enough . . . Agh!"

Score. That's *her* in the attic every night. Grieving, like every day is Ralph Strickler's birthday to her.

For a minute I wondered if this show of weakness put me ahead in the run for the finish line, but reason kicked in. Her freaking was in no way organized. Patting and there-there-ing, I rethought.

No, this is not the Outside Event.

I tried to go but she grabbed my wrist and sobbed out her story, which, Wow. I need sleep to win this, but I showed solidarity and heard her out. Good thing I did. Her first line was a zinger.

"Ralph and I were in love." By the time she finished I knew more than I want to know, and exactly what I needed to know. If I want to get home in one piece, I have to win!

At the end she deflated and went comatose. I tucked in her feet and the tail of her canvas nightshirt and shut the attic door. If somebody else wins this, if I don't make it, I want the world to know.

What happened to Ralph Strickler was her fault! It bound her to Strickfield with hoops of steel, and now that Dame Hilda's dead, she's the one keeping him under control.

It isn't just the guilt.

They were in love, and she still isn't over it. In fact, she . . . OK, Long story short, Miss Nedobity was having sex with Ralph in the elevator; at the bottom the doors opened he tumbled partway into the hall. She was so scared of Dame Hilda firing her that she pushed the wrong button and the doors slammed shut on the heir of Strickfield's bare neck, blood started gushing out and then . . . What happened to Ralph happened on her watch, but that isn't the worst thing. The worst thing is what she did about it, and what things are like here as a result. She said it was terrible, but if you want to know the truth, it was *disgusting,* what she swore, to keep from losing him . . .

I'll never tell, if I want to win I can't tell you. No! I have to win or I . . .

I have to go. *Really.* See, Miss Nedobity confided that two heads will roll today, unfortunate metaphor, right? I have to hang in until I win. Or Else and no, I won't tell you about the Or Else, it's my big advantage, but I can say this much. It's a matter of life and death. Right now I'm the only player who knows the Or Else and I will damn well win.

DAVY: IGNORE FIRST TELEGRAM. LETTER FOLLOWS.

Melanie went this morning. Aline was poisonously sweet about it. Before breakfast she read Dame Edna on "attitude" straight out of her will. What she really meant was, Melanie's sharp, she's stylish and a great writer, but way too feisty to win Miss Popularity which, OMG, is one of the things they're judging us on! Plus, her sexual persuasion is not popular with rich fuddy duddies on the Strickfield board. Which leaves just four of us, Roger and Alvin and Serena with her fantastic wardrobe and her surefire blockbuster. And me.

Gorgeous Serena's a definite threat, especially if they're scoring our videos. If it wasn't for that business between her and Alvin on Crit night, I'd be a lot more worried than I am. The affair's still going on and it will bring them down, leaving only Roger and me. They'll get expelled for moral terps. I mean, if the judges freaked over Melanie, no way will they have a winner who gets brought up on charges. It's illegal to have sex with a minor in this state. Now, Alvin's big for his age, but, hey. He's fourteen!

We had special breakfast: rashers of bacon and individual omelets. It was because today was Pitch Day.

Aline said, "As you may have guessed, this is a very special day. You four have been chosen on the basis of staying power, and although some of you think production is the main issue here, you might as well know that there's a lot more to writing a book than writing it." Aline Armantout, first-ever Strickfield winner and international best seller, loved this! She went on with that convicted winner's fuck-you glow.

"There's more to publishing your book than just getting published." I would swear she went: a-*hem*. "Starting with the pitch. Futures hang on promotion. Who makes it and who won't . . . " Then she scared me. "You aren't just selling a book. Who wants a book? There are billions of them out there begging for people's time. They don't need your book."

I looked at Roger. We were both freaking. *OMG, OMG, OMG!*

"You're selling *yourselves*. Today, we work on the pitch." She flashed a savage smile. "Now, you need to pound protein. Caffeinate, add lots of sugar. Dextrose for energy, darlings. Sparkle! If you put on writing clothes, go put on something CLASSY. Not you, Roger, that craggy look will help you sell, sell, sell."

"Think marketing. Think saturation. Think, SALES." Then she said the scariest thing since Miss Nedobity sobbed out her story last night, including the Or Else. "Your futures depend on it."

Interesting, they downloaded Web components for us to work on, for judging only. Aline said, "Understand, you won't see your postings uploaded, you have to *win*. Only the winner's postings go up on the Web." Then on the way into the next meeting, she grabbed my elbow so tight that I squeaked and she whispered. The words came into my ear in splinters, like truth squeezed through a cheese grater: "*Understand, the winner will be sworn to secrecy, under pain of—you don't want to know.*" But she only told *me*, so, wow, wow!

I aced them all, including photo upload and necessary links, OMG I'm posting a new eyecatcher that, the minute they decide I'm the winner, this .jpg of me in Florence's backless shift goes up on my blog! Besides, I've had FB, MySpace, Friendster pages since I was ten, so when I win, Cormac McCarthy and Junot Diaz and all my other invisible friends will be the first to know; before I came to Strickfield and lost my connection I texted gazillion people daily, I've tweeted squatrillion tweets that got re-re-tweeted around the world, and if I need to give lap dances on Second Life to sell me as a writer, Aline has my demo, although maintaining my Internet presence may cut into work time once I'm famous, and the rest?

I scored at dinnertime schmoozing, wardrobe less so, but if I sell *anything* that will change, unless they expect me to steal to stay gorgeous, which I am totally prepared to do. Personal interview: I used the pitch that got me into Strickfield, although I haven't exactly written the novel: Score! Video presentation: Score. So I'm sitting here in the Confessional after a long day on no sleep saying OK, guys, so far so good, and I'd like to thank you all for . . .

OK, I did what I had to, to make it this far.

Bottom line. I ratted out Alvin and Serena at dinner. Alvin left screaming, but tonight it's boiled down to Roger and me.

Only two of us left, and if Roger won't concede so we can be together, I'll . . . Eeek, is this really me? Promotion means a lot more in this world than I thought when I wrote my very first story in first grade, and the world is bigger and a harder place for artists like me than I thought. When I won grad school prizes for CREATIVE WRITING I thought my dreams had come true. Then I got into Strickfield and I thought I had it made!

Yeah, right. After Pitch Day I *know*. It doesn't matter how good you are, it's how you sell it. The world is a harsh, judgmental place. If I can't make it here, I won't make it anywhere.

I love making words do what I say, and I love making things up, but if I have to win this to get them out there, then fine. Whatever it takes.

Dear Davy, Turn back. I mean it. There are some things you have to do alone.

Writers try to tell the truth, but some things are too terrible to tell. Fiction expresses what we know, but are reluctant to admit. Sooner or later the things too terrible to talk about, things we're ashamed of and all the things that frighten us transform themselves, and surface in our work.

Davy, you can't be here!

Barking dogs split the night. Sirens. Flashing strobe lights, proscriptions in place and threats carried out exactly as warned, inscribed, memorized and forgotten along with the crumpled green RULES *sheet. Ivy LaMont, nearing the top of the Hartfield colony shortlist, is* BANG: **awake** *without knowing what woke her or what brings her to her feet in a single bound. She finds herself teetering in front of the bedroom window. Blinking, she leans out into the glare, afraid of what she will see.*

She hears a tortured roar. Billy! Her boyfriend Billy is on the near wall of the enclosure, he came all this long way to rescue her. He really loves her; he does! Now he is suspended, halfway in, halfway out, caught on the razor wire, with the great jaws of the leaping Dobermans clashing all too close to his hands yet in extremis *as he is, Billy isn't yelling for help. He's calling her name.*

"Ivy!"

Oh, Billy, not now.

The boy Ivy loves and left behind has come this long, hard way to get her back. He's risked everything to rescue her, signifying that this is true love. Ivy LaMont, methodically climbing the Hartfield colony shortlist, is up against it now.

"Ivy!"

What she says and does now determines whether she stays or goes and where she should be running downstairs and out into the garden to beg them to call off the dogs and save the boy she thought she loved. If she does, she loses. Miss Trefethen will keep the promise she made to the devil that keeps Hal Harter alive and for so many years, has kept the colony at Hartfield safe. She will feed Ivy, this year's last remaining loser, to what's left of her huge, mangled lover, the greedy, raging Thing in the Lake.

*Poleaxed, Ivy thinks: **The Outside Event is nothing like I thought. It comes out of nowhere and it is, as it turns out, specific to me.***

Not for the first time, she has to make a decision. If Ivy, who began colony life without guessing how much it would demand of her, pushes through to win the title, and she will or die in the attempt, she'll make such decisions tonight and again and again every day for the rest of her working life.

—Asimov's SF, *2011*

The Legend of Troop 13

The Lost Troop

In the mountains tonight, in the jagged hills below the observatory, the Girl Scouts' voices ring— just not where you can hear, for the missing girls of Troop 13 are as wary as they are spirited.

"Beautiful," Louie says. He paints the observatory dome, top to bottom on his revolving scaffold, so he's in a position to know. He says, "It's a little bit like angels singing."

It would lift your heart to hear them, tourists claim, because tourists believe everything they hear, whether or not they actually heard it.

Although they've been missing for years, some people think the legendary lost Girl Scouts of Troop 13 are still out there on Palamountain, camping in the shadow of the great white dome. We don't know how it happened or where our girls went when they went missing, but tourists come to the mountain in hopes, and business is booming.

They claim they came to see the cosmos through the world's largest telescope, but the men's wet mouths tell you different.

As for our girls, there have been signs, e.g.: surprise raids on picnic tables, although it could be bears. Outsiders swear the Last Incline is booby-trapped with broken glass and sharp objects, but they can't prove it. They have to lug their ruined tires downhill to Elbow and by the time the wrecker brings these tourists back uphill with their new tires, the road is clear—no Scouts, no sign of Scouts, but their cars have been rifled.

So there's a chance our girls are running through the woods in their green hats at this very minute, with their badge sashes thrown over items missing from our clotheslines. It's like a party every night, twelve Girl Scouts on their Sit-Upons around the campfire—feasting on candy and s'mores, judging from supplies stolen in midnight break-ins at Piney's Store. Our sheriff and the State Police looked for months; the FBI came, but the cold trail just got colder. It's been so long that even their mothers have stopped looking.

Now, you may come to Palamountain expecting to find dead campfires, skeletal teepees, abandoned Sit-Upons; you may think you spotted little green hats bobbing up there on the West Slope, but don't expect to catch up with them. You won't find our lost girls, no matter how hungry you are for love or adventure, so forget about easing whatever itch you thought you'd scratch here. They haven't been seen or heard from since the day Tracie Marsters threw the gaudy Troop Leader Scarf around her throat and led them up the mountain.

What happened to the Scouts in Troop 13, really? Why did they not come back from that last patrol, when we patted their little green hats and kissed them goodbye so happily? Did they not love us, or are there things on Pala-mountain that we don't know about? Were they wiped out in a rockfall or kid-napped by Persons Unknown, or are they just plain lost in the woods, and still trying to find their way back to us? Our Scouts couldn't be carried off against their will, that's unthinkable. Their motto is "Be Prepared," and they'd know what to do. We would have found markers: bits of crumpled paper on the trail, blazes on the trees, to signify which way they were taken.

We're afraid they went looking for someplace better than the settlement at Elbow, halfway up the East Grade on Palamountain, or our boring home town in the foothills. Prepared or not, we don't want to think about them running around in some big city. Unless they were running away from home and us personally, which is even worse.

Better to think of them as still up there, somewhere on Palamountain.

Listen, there have been sightings!

A tourist staggers into Mike's bar in the Elbow and he is all, *I alone am left to tell the tale, I alone am left to tell* . . . At this point words desert him; it was that intense. No, he can't tell you where, or what, exactly, and that's the least of it.

We need to shush him, so we shush him. That kind of talk is bad for business.

If they're still up there, they're too happy to hurt you. They're probably fine, running along to: "Ash Grove" or "Daisy, Daisy, we honor your memory true," that's the Girl Scout version, "We are Girl Scouts, all because of you . . . " won-derful songs. You won't hear them singing as they bound along, because Scouts are trained to be careful, they'd be trilling.

It's a pretty sound but it chills your blood, according to Louie, who has heard it. He says, "If you hear them coming, *run.*"

No, we think. Not our girls. How could those sweet things be dangerous?

Edwin Ebersole III

Five a.m., and we've been on this bus for so long that the babies are panick-ing, not all at once, but more or less sequentially. Yow, one cries. Wawww, goes the next; uuuck and aaah aaah aaaa; and the big ones erupt in counterpoint, **Are we there yet,** wawww, **are we there yet,** aaaah aaaah aaaa, **Are we there yet?** Bwaaaaaaa, **Are we** . . . it's like a class project on chain reaction. The racket is exponential and we're all too anxious and depressed to make it stop and the only thing that keeps me going on this excursion is the glittering secret in my pocket and the chance that I can get what I want out of this trip, up there at the top. It's taking too long!

Fifty movers and shakers with wives and kids, riding into the experience of a lifetime in a stinking, overloaded repurposed Greyhound bus, and why? Evanescent Tours sold us on the trip of a lifetime. It was the card. Triple cream stock. Engraved. Gold ink.

EVANESCENT TOURS PRESENTS:
THE TOP OF THE WORLD, VIA LUXURY COACH.
PALAMOUNTAIN OBSERVATORY EXCLUSIVE

And the kicker?

by invitation only

Who wouldn't bite? No riffraff, just us, the business elite, and, better? Every man on this tour is like me, tough, successful, rich. No ordinary guys on this bus. They can't afford it, and for us, top of the world, with more T.K. See, these pretty little Girl Scouts vanished up there when they were small, nobody knows how. The lost little girls must be big girls by now. Every man on this bus has stated reasons for riding up the mountain, but at bottom, there are babes in those woods and they need us.

We're going up the mountain to hunt. Like we can get back something we lost before we even knew it was missing.

The hell of it is, Serena's on to me. I plugged this trip as our second honeymoon, that I'd booked especially for her, but she knows. Nowhere is it written but she knows we've never been happy. She jumped up in the middle of the night and dragged our girl Maggie off to sit in the back, and for what? All I did was move on my wife in the dark because she is after all my wife, and we've been traveling for so long that my want ran ahead of me.

Dammit, the bus was dark. They were all asleep.

I thought, 2 a.m., OK, let's make the time go by a little faster—you know.

Serena slapped my hand away. "Back off, you horny fuck!" and I went, "I was just . . ." which devolved into the usual.

Serena: You always . . .

Me: I never, and besides, you . . .

Her: I always, and you say you love me but you never . . .

This happens to couples in enclosed situations: the vacation house, the Carnival Cruise. This bus.

Thousands I spent to get us here, high-end launch party at a luxury hotel on the coast, with us done up like kings: for me, Gucci shoes, the Hugo Boss tux with the Armani vest. I even bought Serena a Valentino gown. Champagne smashed across the prow of our private vehicle, full access to the Observatory, satisfaction guaranteed, I bought front row seats for the spectacle of the century, and where are we?

Nowhere.

We've been rolling for days, all the toilets are stopped up and the video player is kaput. We're running out of food, probably because the driver got us lost back there. Worse yet, he isn't speaking to us.

We don't know if he's sworn to secrecy by Evanescent Tours or if he's pissed at us for bitching or just plain out of control.

I personally think the captain is mad. This Clyde Pritchard is one hostile hick. He drives without stopping except for gas, at which point, given the sticker price on this extravaganza, he should let us get out, relieve ourselves at the Roaming Mountains Dine and Dance that we whizzed past an hour ago instead of in one of his rolling cesspools, he should let us visit our luggage for necessaries and eat hot food for a change, instead of the freeze-dried dinners Evanescent Tours Incorporated vacuum-packed for the days or is it weeks we'll be in this rat trap.

—Later

Last night the judgmental knuckle-dragger threw packs of beef jerky and rattler pate at us, one each, and warned us to limit fluids because, well, you don't want to know. Today it was oyster crackers, one miserable packet each, stamped with the name of some crap diner in the flatlands. Are we low on food? What if he runs off the road out here where I can't get a signal? What if we have to kill and eat each other, in hopes somebody will see the vultures circling and rescue whoever's left?

I parleyed with the guys. "Does he know who we *are?* Nobody treats us like trailer trash. We're *rich.*" A bunch of us got together and went up there to stick it to the slack-jawed hick. At least he could tell us which route is he taking, the East Slope Road, or the West Slope Incline, which is, like, our polite way of asking, *Do you know what the fuck you're doing?*

He won't answer. He jerks his thumb over his shoulder and when we don't back off, he pulls a sidearm out of his belt. "Back to your seats or I fire," he says, and he's not kidding.

I pass a note to Serena, and watch it going hand over hand to the bench seat in the back, where she is braiding fishermen's lures into our daughter's hair. Without bothering to open my heartfelt apology, she tears it to shreds and braids paper butterflies in with all the other junk in Maggie's hair.

My son Eugene the felon drags his paw across my arm. "Dad."

"Shut up, Eugene."

Kid goes, "I saw a sign!"

A sign. Like we're pilgrims, looking for the golden calf or something. O wait. It says . . . but this pissed-off fool is whipping around curves so fast that I catch it out of the corner of my eye. *Mount Palamountain.* "Guys!"

Our heads snap back on our necks so fast that nobody hears. We take a sharp turn and start the climb. Our hearts rise up.

We are going to the mountain! The mountain, where I get mine.

Clyde Pritchard

I thought you'd be excited, but you don't give a crap. I stop at the Overlook to let you look up at Palamountain and around at territory surrounding, it's a perfect 360 but you don't care, you just circle like bears fixing to take a dump right here on Overlook Point and the next thing I know, you're wandering across the road sniffing for something in the woods, this Ebersole guy in the lead. Look at you, with candy wrappers stuck to your camp shorts and pork rinds ground into your big, white Jell-O thighs, drooling red because of the gummy rattlesnakes I threw you after lunch. Cover those legs, they're disgusting! If I left you off right here I'd be doing you a favor, you wouldn't be smarter by the time you made it back downhill to the highway exit ramp, but by God you'd be thinner.

I show you the nth wonder of the world, the full 360, and . . .

OK, Clyde, try. "Friends, look up! From here, you can see the monster telescope move! At this height, critters you've never seen before streak by so fast that you don't even know they're stalking you, these woods bristle with undergrowth that you don't see anywhere, winding suckers around petrified trees, and . . ." *Oh shit.* "Wait a minute. Where are you going?" *Uncouth fuckers.* "Come back!"

But you run for the woods with your pants on fire, like you'll find those girls hiding behind the next tree, so I do what I have to, it's company regulations. I yell.

"OK then, watch out! There's rattlesnakes in those ferns and the last thing you want is for one of those mean suckers to bite you, they can strike up to six feet high," *but nobody stops.*

"OK, dammit. **Go ahead and get bit.**" *I'd be glad, but I have to read off the warning card anyway: Evanescent policy.*

"When it happens, do not make a cross and try to suck the venom out. You have to raise the part that got bit higher than your head and hightail it for the observatory gift shop. Agatha can help you . . . if you get back on the goddam bus. Do you hear me? There's antivenin in the gift shop and Agatha can call 911 for you on the land line, that is, **if** we get there before closing time . . .

"I warned you."

Like you care. You crunch after Ebersole, loaded for bear. Agatha's visiting her great-granddaughter in Scottsdale at the moment, and she might not get back until Thursday, but I did what I could, and you brought it on yourselves.

"OK, fuckers. Be careful out there."

The Lost Girls

Oh yay hurray, another great day, running along in our badge sashes and deerskin shoes for we are, first of all, Girl Scouts, and so very proud! Melody Harkness is our leader now, and she's the best! Moira's put Girl Scout trefoils on the moccasins she made for us, for with the needles Stephanie carved from bones cut out of the last deer we brought down, and beads sewn on with hair pulled out of Delia, who has plenty to spare because it grew until it was long enough to sit on, Moira can make anything. For wild girls we're pretty well dressed, considering. Scouting makes you resourceful. Steal a bed-sheet or two from the line behind the P.O. when Miss Archibald's out delivering the mail and, man, Nancy will whip up a sweet outfit, and if anything rips, Ella will patch it, that's her job.

There's tons of food for girls who know how to find it, you can kill it in the woods or dig it out of the dirt, plus, there's food in gangs of places you wouldn't think to look, like, there's food in the day tripper's cars and summer cabins and down at Piney's store in Elbow; there's food on picnic blankets and food on windowsills just asking for it so don't you moms worry about us.

In spite of what you think happened, your Scouts that used to be so little and cute are fat and sassy now, and we're doing fine, fine, fine. We run along singing, just not so anybody but us can hear, we are that fine, and our songs are wonderful! We move fast and keep it low, so you can't hunt us down and catch us, and the fun will never end. If it did, that would be the end of us so if you were thinking of catching us, forget it or it will be the end of you. Nobody sneaks up on Troop 13, our motto is **Be Prepared**, don't even try.

We get what we want and we keep what we have which is fun, fun, *fun*, Troop 13 is forever, so beware.

Ida Mae Howells

19—

I'm so lucky! I'm a happy, lucky girl, running free with my sister Scouts, and all because I chased a kitty in the woods when I was little, and got lost for good which was lucky, *lucky* because it was so awful at home.

It was the day our grade came up Palamountain to see the stars.

I got so lost!

I wouldn't of, if everybody wasn't so mean to me, so I guess that was lucky too. We were up to stars in first grade so Mrs. Greevey brought us all the way uphill in the school bus to see stars through the giant telescope. Ahead of time I was very excited to come, but it was awful on the bus. Betty Ann and them said eeeww, dirty underpants, when I fell down getting on the bus. They wouldn't sit with me, which, it's not my fault Uncle Martha's always gone and never did the wash, so I had to ride all the way up the mountain in my dirty underpants sitting all by myself. Also it was loud and ugly in the bus, because of all those boys yelling at you and rubbing stuff in your hair and them all fighting in the aisles. Mrs. Greevey yelled that she would buy us all ice cream sandwiches at Piney's Store when we got to the Elbow if we would only shut up, she yelled and yelled but it only got worse.

Mrs. Greevey made the driver stop at Piney's anyway, either it was them ganging up on her or she forgot. Kids jumped down and ran into Piney's so fast that Mrs. Greevey fell down and hurt herself, I think she even cried. She was too upset to count when we went into the store and I guess she wasn't counting when they all came back after, except not me.

They left without me, and you know what? I was glad!

See, Gerald pushed me down the back steps and my ice cream all squoze out of the sandwich and got mooshed into the dirt. They all laughed, so I had to get down and play like I had a rock in my shoe until they got bored of waiting for me to get up and forgot. Then Jane threw a rock at Billy Carson and Gerald and them piled on her, which pretty much served her right. I ran into the woods while nobody was looking so I wouldn't have to mess, I went way, way up there on the hill where it was quiet, so I never even saw them get back on the bus.

The cutest little kitty came up to me!

I tried to pet it, but it ran away so I ran after it, it looked so cuddly and soft. By the time I gave up, I was lost and it was getting dark. Well, I could of screamed and hollered until somebody down at Piney's store would of heard me and they came up and found me, but then I would of had to go sit in the store and wait for the bus to come back down and I'd have to go home to Uncle Martha and them. I'm not never going back, I'd rather die. So I just set there doing nothing and waiting for the kitty to come back, and my bones would still be sitting there waiting except there were noises in the woods like kids trying not to laugh and the next minute, they came.

It was this wonderful lady Miss Tracie, with a special scarf around her hair.

I found out later that meant she was the troop leader, and those cute things on the girls were badge sashes and Girl Scout pins with three gold leaves, so just when I could of starved to death or died of loneliness, Troop 13 found me and I went home with them.

They didn't ask who was I or was I lost or what was I doing up there. They just brought me back to their camp and fed me on pigs in the blanket and s'mores until I couldn't eat any more so when I felt better, I explained. Miss Tracie said be glad that kitty was too fast for me because there are no kitties in these woods, just mountain lions, and if the mother had found me I would be dead by now.

She said I should thank my stars, but I was already thanking my stars because by the time the fire went out and everybody sang "Day is done . . ." Miss Tracie decided I could stay. She called Council and they voted me in. This girl Myrna whispered that it was either that or, but she never told me the or. I was way happy because nobody voted to send me downhill to Piney's, so I would never, ever have to go back to Uncle Martha and the bike gang, they said Piney would of sent me home and they might torture me until I told on Troop 13.

Now this is my home! Wherever we set down our Sit-Upons and build a fire and put up our tents. Camp is so, so much nicer than Uncle Martha's big old shed on the freeway down at the tippy bottom of the hills, where they were so mean to me, plus I had to do all their dirty dishes and they made me sleep in the loft.

The first week Miss Tracie taught me the Girl Scout Promise and a bunch of other Girl Scout things, then she asked did I want to be one. Yes! So by Saturday I was a brand new member of Troop 13 although I was only in first grade. See, Miss Tracie was a great, great troop leader, and they don't have Brownies here. Plus something happened to this other girl in the troop and they needed one more.

That was so wonderful, they *needed* me!

That night we all stood around the fire saying the Girl Scout Promise, "On my honor I will try . . ." where we promise to follow the Girl Scout Law. Miss Tracie and them and me, we all put our hands over our hearts and swore to "make the world better and be a sister to every Girl Scout," and that is what we do.

Clyde Pritchard

"Here we are, people. It's a short walk to the top from this point, but you have to stay in line and follow me. It's steep."

So what if the bus broke down on the West Grade and we're here after closing time? I left voicemail so Gavin and Lionel will hang in long enough to give you the tour.

This is all your fault and I want you off my back. Eli had to truck new parts uphill from Elbow because you fat fucks overloaded my bus and it blew a Thing and now you're bitching because we got here late, when it was you that ditched the wives and kids at the Overlook, two hours wasted sitting on our thumbs. Like your lost girls would be in there rubbing up against trees, all hot and ready to give you what you want. Believe me, you don't want to tangle with them.

Two hours, and you come back empty-handed, red in the face and pissed off at me, and Ebersole reams me out for making you late.

Shut up, asshole. We're here.

*Look at you looking back, like you'll spot them flitting through the woods at the bottom of Observatory Hill. One of your women goes to look over the edge before I can head her off. She jams her fists in her mouth, all, **eek** and I have to grab her elbow and help her pull herself together before the others freak, but you don't care. You don't even see. The air is so thick with your desire that it's hard to corral you and aim you toward the stone steps to the top.*

*Time to grab the walkie and start the spiel. I bang on the mouthpiece. "A-**hem**."*
I heard that dirty laugh.

"Welcome to the Palamountain observatory, crown jewel of the western range. We usually walk up from the parking lot, but I parked on the Last Incline because we're late. Excited much?"

Parking up here on the narrow ledge is risky, given that we're nosed into an eight thousand-foot drop, but so is shoving you up the long, windy path from the parking lot at this hour, when tourists are more likely to stray and get lost or snakebit or worse.

I funnel you into the straight and narrow, a hundred stairsteps to the brass double doors as daylight thins out and starts to go. I think up mountain gods so I can pray that Gavin and Lionel are still on deck when we hit the top. "Light's going, so watch your step."

You're all mutter grumble, mutter mutter, "...food in this place," "... restaurant," "fucking starving," "... restaurant," Ebersole, belching, "...food!"

The sun is in a nosedive and you're thinking food? "There's plenty to see once we get into the rotunda, plus the amazing Palamountain gift shop has snacks." Yeah, I hear you snarling, "snacks!" OK, Clyde, think fast. "Fountain pens and snow globes with the Palamountain dome. Observatory patches, spyglass miniscopes. Sky's the limit, you can get meteorite fragments, powerful pills for what ails you, moon rocks! Baseball caps and warmup jackets with the Palamountain emblem, show the people where you've been!"

Like that works. *". . . fucking starving."*

"Food."

*The nth wonder of the universe and you're all, **food**. "There are marvels in the rotunda, and you can get food and drink in the gift shop on the exit side. Beef jerky, volcanic stew, moon pies." I invent, to keep you quiet. "Whiskey singles, Palamountain wines . . . "*

*("**Restaurant!**")*

*About the restaurant. There is no restaurant, which is not my problem. And there's more, and this is what I'm dreading, laying out the **more**.*

*I could tell you outright, but you don't want to hear. You bang on your chests like uncaged gorillas in the fading light, yelling "Top of the world," and "Bring it on," like our lost girls will hear what big men you are and swarm out of the woods all warmed up **down there** and waiting for you to come out when the tour is done. Well, I can tell you about that. Your women are over you, and our girls . . . You don't want to know. You don't need to know that there have been Incidents, not to mention the lawsuit, so whatever you thought you heard about Troop 13, you're wrong.*

There is no Troop 13, trust me, there are no wild girls out there, get it? But if you see them coming, run! Shit, who am I to tell you rich fucks what to look out for when you can't even be bothered to field strip your cigarettes? Fuck you and your hidden desires. I waste my life hauling you up here by the busload, with your fat wallets and I-can-buy-and-sell-you squints and I am done with you.

Ebersole straight-arms me. "I want in!"

I want him dead. "And on this level, the Waiting Room."

This is bad. The observatory's dark, just the one light over the keyhole to the double doors to the Waiting Room. I check my phone: no texts, no missed calls. Usually I unlock the doors and give a little speech in the Waiting Room while you file in, saying this is the air lock, the last chamber between you and the wonders of space, which is Gavin's cue to come out and give his speech and unlock the rotunda, but the observatory is dark and Gavin isn't here.

Where is everybody?

So I stall. "Before we go in, you need to take the circular staircase up to the observation deck and get your vanity shots. Snap the wife and kids in front of the mighty Palamountain dome." Good thing you're easily distracted. Every one of you tenses up, like, where to pose them and who's first. Like the family matters. You're all about getting off your crap screen shots so the homefolks can start feeling bad **right now** *because you're here, and they can't afford it. I pretend to consult my watch. "And be back here in um. Oh, fifteen."*

By that time, Gavin had better be here. There's the Evanescent regulation for late arrivals like us, and I want you toured and gift-shopped before I break the news.

As soon as you guys tramp up the steps to the observation deck, I pull out my phone, but even Lionel isn't picking up.

Where is everybody anyway?

"Problem?" Ebersole is back, all suspicious and mean.

"No problem." I lock my face up tight and throw away the key. "Better hurry or you'll lose the light."

Randy motherfuckers you're back in five, agitating to get inside the rotunda and get your tour because you can't wait to get out and go hunting. You expect to ditch me and the family when you're done and go have your way in the woods. Well, good luck with that. I hear it in your ugly laughter and your muttered asides, all rank and gross. I can smell it on you. I want to yell into the microphone, but, company regulations: I'm not allowed to say shut up, **shut up.** *Whether or not Gavin shows, I need you inside, where I can keep track, so I say, "Welcome to the world-famous Palamountain Observatory, the largest and finest in the world." I unlock the doors and herd you into the Waiting Room with a tired "Ta-DA."*

You damn near trample me, getting in. Good thing you don't hear the clang as the doors behind you shut. I switch on the lights and the women relax a little bit but you guys bang on the doors to the rotunda like you bought and paid for it, "Open up!"

"Sorry for the delay, folks. The keys . . . "

"Let's get this over with." You turn into a monster with twenty heads, teeth bared in angry growls and your flabby bodies bunched like that's all muscle: big men. Used to getting what you want.

Sooner or later, I have to break the news.

Nobody gets into the rotunda unless Gavin shows up with the keys and nobody leaves until Lionel fires up the telescope after which the docents talk, after which there's the light show so when I explain that we're stuck here until morning, at least you got your money's worth. See, after the tour I let you into the gift shop so you can load up on junk food before I lock you into the Waiting Room. If you're eating when I tell you what happens next, it will soften the blow. Except Agatha's in New Mexico and we're waiting for Gavin, and Gavin isn't anywhere.

I've looked.

The Lost Girls

—Now

My my, where did the time go?

Day is done, gone the sun and we're still rollicking, laughing and frolicking in our special place, eating the catch of the day while Marcia toasts a yummy batch of s'mores over our sweet little fire. We're down to our last mini-marshies but nobody really cares, nobody worries because that cute Claude from the valley brought another busload up the mountain today. They stopped at the Overlook, and . . . Melody saw. You can see practically everything from there!

Melody's the oldest, but she wears the tattered badge sash with pride, over a sweet pink dimity something she snatched from a clothesline back in the day. Melody sees everything, and Melody knows. That girl runs these woods.

"Freeze dried eggs and fresh orange juice on that bus," she says, "Lots of good things!"

"And Clyde'll leave them off when he goes."

He will. He's never seen us but he must love us, he always puts leftovers on the rock at the Overlook when the bus goes back downhill.

Patsy giggles. "Plus whatever they're carrying, if . . . "

"If . . . " It's catching, like music. "Whatever they're carrying if . . . " If we happen to *want*.

Day is done, yay for fun!

It's not Ida Mae's fault how she talks, she didn't get much education; she goes, "And whoever they brung."

Stephanie is all, "Girls, let's hold back on this one," but nobody listens, because she's only been in this troop since her folks' car broke down and she replaced Sallie Traub that was in the bear trap accident.

Marcia is like, "Stephanie, shut up," and Steph goes, "No, you shut up," which is not to say that Girl Scouts fight among themselves, because that would be a violation of the Girl Scout code, so Melody goes, "Girls, shhhh!"

Melody is in charge and for a minute, we do.

But Stephanie's all this and Marcia's all that, and people are taking sides because when we finished the BBQ tonight, enough wasn't, well, quite enough. Melody's extra worried because there'll be tourists at the observatory tonight, and it's after hours.

If anything happens, she has to say who and what we take and if we take somebody, what we do with them, which is a lot, so she sings:

"Day is done . . . "

And we all sing, "Gone the sun," and by the time we finish we're pretty much chill, because that's what Melody really means when she starts singing, she means, "Chill."

We all lay back with our heads on our Sit-Upons and Melody's all happy to see us settled in the firelight so she starts our most favorite, favorite story to keep us settled. It's "The Bloody Finger of Ghostine Deck," about something awful that happens on a boat. She strings it along and *strings* it along until the moon is high and everyone but Ida Mae Howells is snuggled down in the canebrake and sound asleep because Melody put Ida Mae on guard. She has to wake us all up if one of them strays down here, it's so exciting!

She kind of whispers, just like this, it's so low and so *sharp* that we know it even in our sleep:

"They're here."

Clyde Pritchard

Back off, assholes. It's hard to breathe with you all up in my face. Rich fat pricks closing in, all puffed up and pushy with your needs, you're too fucking big for the space.

"Sorry for the delay, folks. In the old days the telescope was hand operated, staff here around the clock. These days it's all computerized, and our research assistant . . . " *I don't know where Lionel is, but I can tell you what Lionel is. Lionel is late.* " . . . will be with you after he does a couple more things."

I fill some time with a little spiel about the Bleeding Heart restaurant on down in the Elbow, at which point you all perk up because you've been agitating about the no-restaurant ever since we arrived. You finished your last pork rinds and candy bars on the Overlook and I can hear you gulping drool. I hit the high spots on the Bleeding Heart menu, from Mountain Ash Venison all the way down to Palamountain Passion, Mag's sensational dessert, to distract you until Gavin comes, which should be any minute now except it isn't and yeah, I know where your minds are wandering, it's stuffy in here and it's getting late.

Too late. OK *then. Break the news. Tour or no tour, you will not be leaving the observatory tonight. Whatever you think you heard about Troop 13 and those* **wild girls***, for your safety and mine, you're socked in here until it gets light. I pull out the card and read the Evanescent Night-time Regulation:* **Late arrivals must remain on the premises until 8.a.m.** *It's my job to lug forty bedrolls out of the lockers when the tour's done and we're back in the Waiting Room, show you the toilets and vending machines and lock you in for the night.*

Break it gently.

"OK *folks, you'll eat well at the Bleeding Heart, but it won't be tonight. Trust me, you'll get your tour tomorrow morning as soon as Arnold comes in. We'll be back in Elbow by noon, but right now . . . For your comfort and safety, we're bunking here." The women groan but you . . .*

"The fuck we are."

"Where it's warm and safe."

*Ebersole. "We're not paying for **safe.**"*

I know what you want. You stink of it. "Bathrooms and vending machines down the hall to your left, soft drinks, Slim Jims and Pocky Sticks so you won't starve. Arnold's always here by eight. You'll get private tour."

*The noise you make is ugly, **ugly.***

" . . . the fuck out of here."

Oh hell, I go, "I know you're sick of waiting, but trust me, it's worth waiting for."

Your minds go running along ahead to the dirty place. There are things I could tell you about Troop 13, but you don't like me any more than I like you, so why should I? As the Evanescent tour driver, I am forced to add, "People, it's not safe out there!"

But you're all stampeding, threatening legal action or worse.

OK, in situations like this, the foyer is the safest place to sleep, but no way am I bedding down with you ignorant, flatulent, loud-mouthed fools. You want out? OK, you asked for it.

You'll bitch when I fill your pockets with food from the machines and frog-march you down the steep staircase to the ledge, but the bus is almost as safe as the Waiting Room, so get used to it. See, I don't mind your women or the kids but I can't stand another minute of you, and don't go thinking I don't have the power. You backed off when I pulled my gun? Now the Evanescent Taser shows its teeth. You'll let me shovel you back onto the bus and lock you in for the night, which I am obligated to do, because even though you signed off on the liability clause before you came on this tour and I don't like you, I am responsible, so sleep safe and fuck you.

By the time you look for me I'll laying out my bedroll back here in the Waiting Room, drunk on the silence, happy as a rat in a barrel of rum.

Edwin Ebersole III

One more sleepless night on that toilet of a tour bus, one more dinner of crap freeze-dried packets supplied by Evanescent Tours, no way am I walking back into that.

Why are we still here? I'll tell you why. The technician never showed up. Docents never showed up. We jammed that retard driver's face into the sur-veillcam and an old lady came. It took forever and she was mad as fuck, but she unlocked the gift shop so this Clyde could herd us out past astronaut T-shirts and bogus moon rocks, shoving us through like a bunch of mountain mice. Six figures blown on this excursion and not one shot of us looking through the giant telescope or any other damn thing and Serena is even more pissed at me because I can't call a taxi and I damn well won't fake a heart attack so Lifestar will come and lift us out of here.

As if this dumb hick marching us down a hundred steps in the dark could get Lifestar to do anything but take a piss on him, and besides, how's Lifestar landing on this Godforsaken crag which I don't mind, because . . .

I am damn well not leaving until I get what I came for. Just watch me fake-walking down the steps with you, marking time while everybody follows this Clyde like lemmings to the slaughter. Well, fuck you Clyde, while you herd my family *down* the steps I'm fake-walking, i.e. going backward, *up* the steps, and I'll hide at the top until you've loaded them on and locked everybody in. No way am I piling into that rolling garbage can they call a luxury coach. I'll luxury you, Evanescent Tours Incorporated, I'll sue your brains out as soon as I get what I came for and bring her back at which point you might as well know, Serena, you and I are done.

I came up the mountain to get me a sweet, sexy, grown-up Girl Scout. I know she's out there, like, you think a babe like her wants to stay up here all funky in the woods when she can have me, and everything that comes with? E.g. the little diamond something-something that I brought to lure her out of the hills. It's in the security pocket in my cargo pants, and in case you were worried about me hunting sweet pussy all alone out here in the dark, I came prepared. Cavalry boots laced up to the knees under the leg extensions I zipped on while you were all flopping around the Overlook, so if there are snakes out there, no worries, This beekeeper's hat with a see-through veil thing will keep me safe.

I rolled it down like a theater curtain as soon as the hick led us out into the dark. Winners get what they pay for, and I'm here to get mine, so don't think you can stiff me. The minute you slam the door on that death trap and run for the waiting room I hum a few bars to let her know that I am here and I love her already, and everything good will happen, all she has to do is show herself.

Do you hear me sweetheart?

This is me not-singing, not-crooning this love song that I wrote inside my head on those long, terrible nights in the luxury coach, I'm rolling it out right now, for you.

"Are you lonely, do you miss it, do you want it, do you hate running wild and sleeping in the dirt, would you like something pretty, see I brought it, just for you . . . " going into a sort of ooo oooo ooooo . . . as I come down the steps and I let it get a little bit louder after I pass that stinking sardine can full of losers and head downhill into the parking lot by the woods where I happen to know you're hiding out. I get a little bit louder because I love you already and I want to hear, how old are you now, sweetheart, twenty? Eighteen?

Babe, listen to me singing, see me crouching low like a tiger romancing his mate, come to me, sweet baby, let me show you diamonds, and if you like them, I'll buy you a diamond collar and lead you out of these filthy woods on a diamond leash, and the first thing we'll do when we get off this stupid mountain is get you into a nice hot shower and scrub you down until your nipples lift and all your skin turns pink and then, you and I can . . . and then . . .

Ida Mae Howells
—Now

I'm a Scout and I have sisters now, and Uncle Martha and them can go to hell. It's sad what happened to Miss Tracie, but they gave me her Girl Scout pin after it happened because she didn't need it any more, and then we sang "Day is done" and gave her a really nice funeral before we put her in next to Ellie DeVere and some girl named Sallie inside the lime cave under the ledge on the Last Incline.

I love my troop and, you know what? After Uncle Martha and all, I love that there's only us *sisters* around. We live together and we play together and we belong together and when one of us gets too big for what we were wearing, Melody sees to it, and Martha makes alterations and if there's nothing on hand Stephanie goes out with the raiding party and they bring back such cute things! Melody's the oldest, and Melody knows what we need and who gets what when we're one short, and she knows if a girl is lost in the woods and she knows if that lost girl needs us, and after we find her or if she finds us, Melody decides whether or not this girl belongs, and if not, Melody knows what to do about it, and if something worse happens, she knows what to do, and *how,* and Melody decides *when.*

Melody decided and now it's my turn to be up on the hill all by myself, she gave me the Midnight Watch. This is so cool! Me, Ida Mae Howells, hiding on the slope by the parking lot keeping watch, so my sister Scouts can sleep safe.

She trusts me to stay awake and be vigilant, so they can't sneak up on us while we sleep.

Like, these guys come crunching into the woods in the dead of night acting all heroic, like they're here to be nice, but we know they all want to Do Things to girls in the woods up here where nobody sees it and nobody can hear. Twice we caught men hunting us for the reward, like they could drag us back down the mountain in their teeth, back to our boring, stupid old lives. Well, we took care of them.

Sleep safe, girls. Nobody gets past me. I'm watching them people in the bus away up the Last Incline, no problem. Clyde marched them down and locked them all in the bus. They're asleep, so I can relax.

Wait! What's that? Did I dream it? did I accidentally fall asleep? Who's out there anyway?

Ooooh nooooo!

And why am I all weird right now, thinking about all those outsiders, *this close*. We all hung back today when the bus left the Overlook, and when Clyde drove past, up the Last Incline, we were glad. See, in the parking lot, they get out and bop around and sometimes one gets lost. Then Stephanie warns us so low that only we can hear, "Run!" So we pick up and run.

We can't let them find us. If they find us, it will be bad.

Except this time it isn't them, it's only me.

And he's singing. Somebody is out here singing, I can hear him, it's for me!

Are you lonely, do you miss it, do you want it, it's so weird, and then, in the bushes something sparkles just above my head in and the sneaky, nice-nasty sound comes with, too low for anybody but Ida Mae to hear, *it's so pretty, would you like it,* and the sparkle hangs closer, *do you want it, see I brought it just for you* and all of a sudden I don't want to move, I don't jump, I don't sound the alarm because I want to listen, I have to see, *if you want it you can have it . . .* and I should hoot to warn my sister Scouts but instead I just let the song happen until I see him through the leaves, he's singing and singing, he's close!

He looks huge in *all that stuff*, and, oh! Miss Tracie, I talked to him, I did! I kept it low, so as not to rouse the others, I whispered, "Oh, you can take off the hat, our rattlers are all curled up sleeping in their holes," which is a lie, but I had to see what he looked like in the face behind the veil.

"Oh," he said, "are you in there? Let me see you, come out and look at me, and let me look at you." If he Tried Something I would of bopped him but he didn't move, he just waited in what was left of the moonlight, dangling this sparkly thing and singing his long, sweet song thing that made me squirm Down There, *if you want it you can have it, I brought diamonds just for you . . .*

And they're so shiny and he's so close that I almost, almost betrayed the spirit of Miss Tracie and Melody and Stephanie and all my other sister Scouts sleeping under my watch. I'm weak! I think: *It's OK, I don't even have to warn.*

I tell myself: *I just want to see him. Then I'll decide.*

I tell myself: *be careful, careful, Ida Mae, there are gangs of big city folks asleep on the ledge up there, right there, in the bus*, but his song is so sweet, so soft and so all about me and my chain of diamonds that I squirm forward on my elbows like a rattler in heat and at the last second I rear up so he sees me and like he promised, he takes off the veil hat and I'm all, "Oh, crap."

"You," he says, in a different voice, he's so *ugly*, and this is awful. He says it like: *ewwwww*. "You aren't . . . "

And I think: *fine!* so I say, too low to rouse my sister Scouts, "Well neither are you. Go away!" but I keep coming at him because I want the sparkly. I'll just grab it and let him go.

But he snaps off a branch and starts swinging at me like I'm a monster that he has to kill but it's OK, I have my rock.

I really think I can just bop him and roll him off the edge before my sisters come but he yells "Get away from me" mean enough to scare the whole mountain and I vomit one last warning, "shut up, shut *up!*"

But he howls in my face, "Get away from me, you ugly dirtbag." Then he shouts out the worst thing ever. "You're too *old!*"

So I smash him with the rock. Then I bash his head and bash it and bash it, I have to wipe that disgusting, hurtful word off his disgusting face. By the time my sister Scouts are wide awake and charging uphill to join, there's not much left to bash but, oh boy, he screamed so loud that up there on the ledge, lights pop on all over Clyde's bus and we hear them hammering to get out. Usually we're such good Scouts that we come and go without anybody knowing, but this time it got loud, and it's all my fault.

"Ohhhh, Melody, I'm so *sorry.*"

Her voice goes hard. "Don't worry, I heard."

"Old." This is awful, it comes out in a sob. I'm so *embarrassed.*

Everybody in Troop 13 is mortified and raging, "Old!"

Stephanie looks down at what's left of the man like he's a rattler we had to squash. "We all heard."

"OK girls, Scout Council." Melody points and we squat in a circle around what's left of what we just did, wondering what to do.

Sisters, worrying. "Tomorrow they'll find out."

"They don't have to." Melody is the one who decides *whether.*

This is so *hard*. I say, "They can't find out."

We shudder. "Nobody can."

"They might." Even Stephanie is scared.

Melody comes down on that like a hammer, "They won't find out," and we all feel better because Melody also decides *when.*

Day and night, summer, winter, year after year for a really long time, we have protected our sweet life on the mountainside. Nothing gets between Troop 13 and our freedom, and nothing will.

"OK" Melody says, "Council," Melody says, and we squat in a circle and begin. After Council, she will say *how.*

Either we do what we usually do, break camp and fade away to the East Grade and do like it says in the Girl Scout prayer, "Help us to see where we may serve / In some new place in some new way," praying that nobody looks out the window when the sun comes up and Clyde backs that bus around and comes downhill and that Louie doesn't care what the vultures are eating when he cranks himself up the dome . . .

Or we go up to the ledge and do something else about it tonight.

Clyde never unlocks the bus until the sun comes up. There are enough of us to get it rolling, all it takes is one little push.

—*Asimov's SF*, 2013

The Wait

Penetrating a windshield blotched with decalcomanias of every tourist attraction from Luray Caverns to Silver Springs, Miriam read the road sign.

"It's Babylon, Georgia, Momma. Can't we stop?"

"Sure, sweetie. Anything you want to do." The little, round, brindle woman took off her sunglasses. "After all, it's your trip."

"I know, Momma, I know. All I want is a popsicle, not the Grand Tour."

"Don't be fresh."

They were on their way home again, after Miriam's graduation trip through the South. (Momma had planned it for years, and had taken two months off, right in the middle of the summer, too, and they'd left right after high school commencement ceremonies. "Mr. Margulies said I could have the whole summer, because I've been with him and Mr. Kent for so long," she had said. "Isn't it wonderful to be going somewhere together, dear?" Miriam had sighed, thinking of her crowd meeting in drugstores and in movies and eating melted ice cream in the park all through the good, hot summer. "Yes," she'd said.)

Today they'd gotten off 301 somehow, and had driven dusty Georgia miles without seeing another car or another person, except for a Negro driving a tractor down the softening asphalt road, and two kids walking into a seemingly deserted country store. Now they drove slowly into a town, empty because it was two o'clock and the sun was shimmering in the streets. They *had* to stop, Miriam knew, on the pretext of wanting something cold to drink. They had to reassure themselves that there were other people in the town, in Georgia, in the world.

In the sleeping square, a man lay. He raised himself on his elbows when he saw the car, and beckoned to Miriam, grinning.

"Momma, see *that* place? Would you mind if I worked in a place like *that?*" They drove past the drugstore, a chrome palace with big front windows.

"Oh, Miriam, don't start that again. How many times do I have to tell you, I don't want you working in a drugstore when we get back." Her mother made a pass at a parking place, drove once again around the square. "What do you think I sent you to high school for? I want you to go to Katie Gibbs this summer, and get a good job in the fall. What kind of boyfriends do you think you can meet jerking sodas? You know, I don't want you to work for the rest of your life. All you have to do is get a good job, and you'll meet some nice boy, maybe from your office, and get married and never have to work again." She parked the car and got out, fanning herself. They stood under the trees, arguing.

"Momma, even if I *did* want to meet your nice people, I wouldn't have a thing to wear." The girl settled into the groove of the old argument. "I want some pretty clothes and I want to get a car. I know a place where you only have to pay forty dollars a month, I'll be getting thirty-five a week at the drug-store"—

"And spending it all on yourself, I suppose. How many times do I have to explain, nice people don't work in places like that. Here I've supported you, fed you, dressed you, ever since your father died, and now, when I want you to have a *nice* future, you want to throw it out of the window for a couple of fancy dresses." Her lips quivered. "Here I am practically dead on my feet, giving you a nice trip, and a chance to learn typing and shorthand and have a nice future"—

"Oh, Momma." The girl kicked at the sidewalk and sighed. She said the thing that would stop the argument. "I'm sorry. I'll like it, I guess, when I get started."

Round, soft, jiggling and determined, her mother moved ahead of her, trotting in too-high heels, skirting the square. "The main thing, sweetie, is to be a good girl. If boys see you behind a soda fountain, they're liable to get the wrong idea. They may think they can get away with something, and try to take advantage . . ."

In the square across the street, lying on a pallet in the sun, a young boy watched them. He called out.

" . . . Don't pay any attention to him," the mother said. " . . . and if boys know you're a *good* girl, one day you'll meet one who will want to marry you. Maybe a big businessman, or a banker, if you have a good steno job. But if he thinks he can take advantage," her eyes were suddenly crafty, "he'll never marry you. You just pay attention. Don't ever let boys get away with anything. Like when you're on a date, do you ever"—

"Oh, Momma," Miriam cried, insulted.

"I'm sorry, sweetie, but I do so want you to be a *good* girl. Are you listening to me, Miriam?"

"Momma, that lady seems to be calling me. The one lying over there in the park. What do you suppose she wants?"

"I don't know. Well, don't just stand there. She looks like a *nice* woman. Go over and see if you can help her. Guess she's sunbathing, but it *does* look funny, almost like she's in bed. Ask her, Mirry. Go *on!*"

"Will you move me into the shade?" The woman, obviously one of the leading matrons of the town, was lying on a thin mattress. The shadow of the tree she was under had shifted with the sun, leaving her in the heat.

Awkwardly, Miriam tugged at the ends of the thin mattress, got it into the shade.

"And my water and medicine bottle too, please?"

"Yes Ma'am. Is there anything the matter, Ma'am?"

"Well." The woman ticked the familiar recital off on her fingers: "It started with cramps and—you know—lady trouble. Thing is, now my head burns all the time and I've got a pain in my left side, not burning, you know, but just sort of tingling."

"Oh, that's too bad."

"Well, has your mother there ever had that kind of trouble? What did the doctor prescribe? What would *you* do for my kind of trouble? Do you know anybody who's had anything like it? That pain, it starts up around my ribs, and goes down, sort of zigzag . . ."

Miriam bolted.

"Momma, I've changed my mind. I don't want a popsicle. Let's get you out of here, please. Momma?"

"If you don't mind, sweetie, I want a Coke." Her mother dropped on a bench. "I don't feel so good. My head . . ."

They went into the drugstore. Behind the chrome and plate glass, it was like every drugstore they'd seen in every small town along the East Coast, cool and dim and a little dingy in the back. They sat at one of the small round wooden tables and a dispirited waitress brought them their order.

"What did Stanny and Bernice say when you told them you were going on a big tour?" Miriam's mother slurped at her Coke, breathing hard.

"Oh, they thought it was all right."

"Well, I certainly hope you tell them all about it when we get back. It's not every young girl gets a chance to see all the historical monuments. I bet Bernice has never been to Manassas."

"I guess not, Momma."

"I guess Stanny and that Mrs. Fyle will be pretty impressed when you get back and tell 'em where all we've been. I bet that Mrs. Fyle could never get Toby to go anywhere with her. Of course, they've never been as close as we've been."

"I guess not, Momma." The girl sucked and sucked at the bottom half of her popsicle, to keep it from dripping on her dress.

In the back of the store, a young woman in dirty white shorts held onto her little son's hand and talked to the waitress. The baby, about two, sat on the floor in gray, dusty diapers.

"Your birthday's coming pretty soon, isn't it?" She dropped the baby's hand.

"Yeah. Oh, you ought to see my white dress. Golly Anne, hope I won't have to Wait too long. Anne, what was it like?"

The young woman looked away from her with the veiled face of the married, who do not talk about such things.

"Myla went last week, and she only had to stay for a couple of days. Don't tell anybody, because of course she's going to marry Harry next week, but she wishes she could see Him again . . ."

The young woman moved a foot, accidentally hit the baby. He snuffled and she helped him onto her lap, gurgling at him. In the front of the store, Miriam heard the baby and jumped. "Momma, come *on*. We'll never get to Richmond by night. We've already lost our way twice!" Her mother, dabbling her straw in the ice at the bottom of her paper cup, roused herself. They dropped two nickels on the counter and left.

They skirted the square again, ignoring the three people who lay on the grass motioning and calling to them with a sudden urgency. Miriam got into the car.

"Momma, come *on! Momma!*" Her mother was still standing at the door by the driver's seat, hanging onto the handle. Miriam slid across the front seat to open the door for her. She gave the handle an impatient twist and then started as she saw her mother's upper body and face slip past the window in a slow fall to the pavement. "Oh, I *knew* we never should have come!" It was an agonized, vexed groan. Red-faced and furious, she got out of the car, ran around to help her mother.

On their pallets in the park, the sick people perked up. Men and women were coming from everywhere. Cars pulled up and stopped and more people came. Kneeling on the pavement, Miriam managed to tug her mother over onto her back. She fanned her and talked to her, and when she saw she wasn't going to wake up or move, she looked at the faces above her in sudden terror.

"Oh please help me. We're alone here. She'll be all right, I think, once we get her inside. She's never fainted before. Please, someone get a doctor." Then, frantically, "I just want to get out of here."

"Why, honey, you don't need to do that. Don't you worry." A shambling, balding, pleasant man in his forties knelt beside her and put his hand on her shoulder. "We'll have her diagnosed and started on a cure in no time. Can you tell me what's been her trouble?"

"Not so far, Doctor."

"I'm not a doctor, honey."

"Not so far," she said dazedly, "except she's been awfully hot."

(Two women in the background nodded at each other knowingly.) "I thought it was the weather, but I guess it's fever." (The crowd was waiting.) "And she has an open place on her foot—got it while we were sightseeing in Tallahassee."

"Well honey, maybe we'd better look at it." The shoe came off and when it did, the men and women moved even closer, clucking and whispering about the wet, raw sore.

"If we could just get back to Queens," Miriam said. "If we could just get home, I know everything would be all right."

"Why, we'll have her diagnosed before you know it." The shambling man got up from his knees. "Anybody here had anything like this recently?" The men and women conferred in whispers.

"Well," one man said, "Harry Parkins's daughter had a fever like that, turned out to be pneumonia, but she never had nothin' like that on her foot. I reckon she ought to have antibiotics for that fever."

"Why, I had somethin' like that on my arm." A woman amputee was talking. "Wouldn't go away and wouldn't go away. Said I woulda died if they hadn't of done this." She waved the stump.

"We don't want to do anything like that yet. Might not even be the same thing," the bald man said. "Anybody else?"

"Might be tetanus."

"Could be typhoid, but I don't think so."

"Bet it's some sort of staphylococcus infection."

"Well," the bald man said, "since we don't seem to be able to prescribe just now, guess we'd better put her on the square. Call your friends when you get home tonight, folks, and see if any of them know about it; if not, we'll just have to depend on tourists."

"All right, Herman."

"B'bye, Herman."

"See ya, Herman."

"'G'bye."

The mother, who had come to during the dialog and listened with terrified fascination, gulped a potion and a glass of water the druggist had brought from across the street. From the furniture store came the messenger boy with a thin mattress. Someone else brought a couple of sheets, and the remainder of the crowd carried her into the square and put her down not far from the woman who had the lady trouble.

When Miriam last saw her mother, she was talking drowsily to the woman, almost ready to let the drug take her completely.

Frightened but glad to be away from the smell of sickness, Miriam followed Herman Clark down a side street. "You can come home with me, honey," he said. "I've got a daughter just about your age, and you'll be well taken care of until that mother of yours gets well." Miriam smiled, reassured, used to following her elders. "Guess you're wondering about our little system," Clark said, hustling her into his car. "What with specialization and all, doctors got so they were knowin' so little, askin' so much, chargin' so much. Here in Babylon, we found we don't really need 'em. Practically everybody in this town has been sick one way or another, and what with the way women like to talk about their operations, we've learned a lot about treatment. We don't need doctors any more. We just benefit by other people's experience."

"Experience?" None of this was real, Miriam was sure, but Clark had the authoritative air of a long-time parent, and she knew parents were always right.

"Why, yes. If you had chicken pox, and were out where everybody in town could see you, pretty soon somebody'd come along who'd had it. They'd tell you what you had, and tell you what they did to get rid of it. Wouldn't even have to pay a doctor to write the prescription. Why, I used Silas Lapham's old nerve tonic on my wife when she had her bad spell. She's fine now; didn't cost us a cent except for the tonic. This way, if you're sick we put you in the square and you stay there until somebody happens by who's had your symptoms; then you just try his cure. Usually works fine. If not, somebody else'll be by. 'Course we can't let any of the sick folks leave the square until they're well; don't want anybody else catchin' it."

"How long will it take?"

"Well, we'll try some of the stuff Maysie Campbell used—and Gilyard Pinckney's penicillin prescription. If that doesn't work we may have to wait until a tourist happens through."

"But what makes the tourists ask and suggest?"

"Have to. It's the law. You come on home with me, honey, and we'll try to get your mother well."

Miriam met Clark's wife and Clark's family. For the first week she wouldn't unpack her suitcases. She was sure they'd be leaving soon, if she could just hold out. They tried Asa Whitleaf's tonic on her mother and doctored her foot with the salve Harmon Johnson gave his youngest when she had boils. They gave her Gilyard Pinckney's penicillin prescription.

"She doesn't seem much better," Miriam said to Clark one day. "Maybe if I could get her to Richmond or Atlanta to the hospital"—

"We couldn't let her out of Babylon until she's well, honey. Might carry it to other cities. Besides, if we cure her she won't send county health nurses back, trying to change our methods. And it might be bad for her to travel. You'll get to like it here, hon."

That night Miriam unpacked. Monday she got a job clerking in the dime store.

"You're the new one, huh?" The girl behind the jewelry counter moved over to her, friendly, interested. "You Waited yet? No, I guess not. You look too young yet."

"No, I've never waited on people. This is my first job," Miriam said confidentially.

"I didn't mean *that* kind of wait," the girl said with some scorn. Then, seemingly irrelevantly, "You're from a pretty big town, I hear. Probably already laid with boys and everything. Won't have to Wait."

"What do you mean? I never have. Never! I'm a *good* girl!" Almost sobbing, Miriam ran back to the manager's office. She was put in the candy department, several counters away. That night she stayed up late with a road map and a flashlight, figuring, figuring.

The next day the NO VISITORS sign was taken down from the tree in the park and Miriam went to see her mother.

"I feel terrible, sweetie, you having to work in the dime store while I'm out here under these nice trees. Now you just remember all I told you, and don't let any of these town boys get fresh with you. Just because you have to work in the dime store doesn't mean you aren't a nice girl and as soon as I can, I'm going to get you out of that job. Oh, I *wish* I was up and around."

"Poor Momma." Miriam smoothed the sheets and put a pile of movie magazines down by her mother's pillow. "How can you stand lying out here all day?"

"It isn't so bad, really. And y'know, that Whitleaf woman seems to know a little something about my trouble. I haven't really felt right since you were nine."

"Momma, I think we ought to get out of here. Things aren't right"—

"People certainly are being nice. Why, two of the ladies brought me some broth this morning."

Miriam felt like grabbing her mother and shaking her until she was willing to pick up her bedclothes and run with her. She kissed her goodbye and went back to the dime store. Over their lunch, two of the counter girls were talking.

"I go next week. I want to marry Harry Phibbs soon, so I sure hope I won't be there too long. Sometimes it's three years."

"Oh, you're pretty, Donna. You won't have too long to Wait."

"I'm kind of scared. Wonder what it'll be like."

"Yeah, wonder what it's like. I envy you."

Chilled for some reason, Miriam hurried past them to her counter and began carefully rearranging marshmallow candies in the counter display.

That night she walked to the edge of the town, along the road she and her mother had come in on. Ahead in the road she saw two gaunt men standing, just where the dusty sign marked the city limits. She was afraid to go near them and almost ran back to town, frightened, thinking. She loitered outside the bus station for some time, wondering how much a ticket out of the place would cost her. But of course she couldn't desert her mother. She was investigating the family car, still parked by the square, when Tommy Clark came up to her. "Time to go home, isn't it?" he asked, and they walked together back to his father's house.

"Momma, did you know it's almost impossible to get out of this town?" Miriam was at her mother's side a week later.

"Don't get upset, sweetie. I know it's tough on you, having to work in the dime store, but that won't be forever. Why don't you look around for a little nicer job, dear?"

"Momma, I don't *mean* that. I want to go home! Look, I've got an idea. I'll get the car keys from your bag here and tonight, just before they move you all into the courthouse to sleep, we'll run for the car and get away."

"Dear," her mother sighed gently. "You know I can't move."

"Oh Mother, can't you *try?*"

"When I'm a little stronger, dear, then maybe we'll try. The Pinckney woman is coming tomorrow with her daughter's herb tea. That should pep me up a lot. Listen, why don't you arrange to be down here? She has the best-looking son! Miriam, you come right back here and kiss me goodbye."

Tommy Clark had started meeting Miriam for lunch. They'd taken in one movie together, walking home hand in hand in an incredible pink dusk. On the second date Tommy had tried to kiss her but she'd said, "Oh Tommy, I don't know the Babylon rules," because she knew it wasn't good to kiss a boy she didn't know very well. Handing Tommy half her peanut-butter sandwich, Miriam said, "Can we go to the ball game tonight? The American Legion's playing."

"Not tonight, kid. It's Margy's turn to go."

"What do you mean, turn to go?"

"Oh." Tommy blushed. "You know."

That afternoon right after she finished work, Tommy picked her up and they went to the party given for Herman Clark's oldest daughter. Radiant, Margy was dressed in white. It was her eighteenth birthday. At the end of the party, just when it began to get dark, Margy and her mother left the house. "I'll bring some stuff out in the truck tomorrow morning, honey," Clark said. "Take care of yourself." "Goodbye." "B'bye." "Happy Waitin', Margy!"

"Tommy, where is Margy going?" Something about the party and something in Margy's eyes frightened Miriam.

"Oh, you know. Where they all go. But don't worry." Tommy took her hand. "She'll be back soon. She's pretty."

In the park the next day Miriam whispered in her mother's ear, "Momma, it's been almost a month now. Please, please, we *have* to go! Won't you please try to go with me?" She knelt next to her, talking urgently. "The car's been taken. I went back to check it over last night and it was gone. But I sort of think, if we could get out on the highway, we could get a ride. Momma, we've got to get out of here." Her mother sighed a little, and stretched. "You always said you never wanted me to be a bad girl, didn't you, Momma?"

The older woman's eyes narrowed. "You aren't letting that Clark boy take advantage"—

"No, Momma. No. That's not it at all. I just think I've heard something horrible. I don't even want to talk about it. It's some sort of law. Oh, Momma, please. I'm scared."

"Now, sweetie, you know there's nothing to worry about. Pour me a little water, won't you, dear? You know, I think they're going to cure me yet. Helva Smythe and Margaret Box have been coming in to see me every day, and they've brought some penicillin pills in hot milk that I think are really doing me some good."

"But Momma, I'm scared."

"Now dear, I've seen you going past with that nice Clark boy. The Clarks are a good family and you're lucky to be staying with them. You just play your cards right and remember: be a good girl."

"Momma, we've got to get out."

"You just calm down, young lady. Now go back and be nice to that Tommy Clark. Helva Smythe says he's going to own his daddy's business some day. You might bring him out here to see me tomorrow."

"Momma!"

"I've decided. They're making me better, and we're going to stay here until I'm well. People may not pay you much attention in a big city, but you're really *somebody* in a small town." She smoothed her blankets complacently and settled down to sleep.

That night Miriam sat with Tommy Clark in his front porch swing. They'd started talking a lot to each other, about everything.

" . . . so I guess I'll have to go into the business," Tommy was saying. "I'd kind of like to go to Wesleyan or Clemson or something, but Dad says I'll be better off right here, in business with him. Why won't they ever let us do what we want to do?"

"I don't know, Tommy. Mine wants me to go to Katherine Gibbs—that's a secretarial school in New York—and get a typing job this fall."

"You won't like that much, will you?"

"Uh-uh. Except now I'm kind of anxious to get back up there—you know, get out of this town."

"You don't like it here?" Tommy's face clouded. "You don't like me?"

"Oh Tommy, I like you fine. But I'm pretty grown up now, and I'd like to get back to New York and start in on a job. Why I got out of high school last month."

"No kidding. You only look about fifteen."

"Aw, I do not. I'll be eighteen next week—oh, I didn't want to tell you. I don't want your folks to have to do anything about my birthday. Promise you won't tell them."

"You'll be eighteen, huh. Ready for the Wait yourself. Boy, I sure wish *I* didn't know you!"

"Tommy! What do you mean? Don't you like me?"

"That's just the point, I *do* like you. A lot. If I was a stranger, I could break your Wait."

"Wait? What kind of wait?"

"Oh"—he blushed "—you know."

A week later, after a frustrating visit with her mother in the park, Miriam came home to the Clarks' and dragged herself up to her room. Even her mother had forgotten her birthday. She wanted to fling herself on her pillow and sob until supper. She dropped on the bed, got up uneasily. A white, filmy, full-skirted dress hung on the closet door. She was frightened. Herman Clark and his wife bustled into the room, wishing her happy birthday. "The dress is for you." "You shouldn't have," she cried. Clark's wife shooed him out and helped Miriam dress. She started downstairs with the yards of white chiffon whispering and billowing about her ankles.

Nobody else at her birthday party was particularly dressed up. Some of the older women in the neighborhood watched Tommy help Miriam cut the cake, moist-eyed. "She hardly seems old enough"— "Doubt if she'll have long to Wait." "Pretty little thing, wonder if Tommy likes her." "Bet Herman Clark's son wishes *he* didn't know her," they said. Uneasily, Miriam talked to them all, tried to laugh, choked down a little ice cream and cake.

"G'bye, kid," Tommy said, and squeezed her hand. It was just beginning to get dark out.

"Where are you going, Tommy?"

"Nowhere, silly. I'll see you in a couple of weeks. May want to talk to you about something, if things turn out."

The men had slipped, one by one, from the room. Shadows were getting longer but nobody in the birthday-party room had thought to turn on the lights. The women gathered around Miriam. Mrs. Clark, eyes shining, came close to her. "And here's the best birthday present of all," she said, holding out a big ball of brilliant blue string. Miriam looked at her, not understanding. She tried to stammer a thank you. "Now dear, come with me." Clark's wife and Helva Smythe caught her by the arms and gently led her out of the house, down the gray street. "I'm going to see if we can get you staked out near Margy," she said. They started off into the August twilight.

When they came to the field, Miriam first thought the women were still busy at a late harvest, but she saw that the maidens, scores of them, were just sitting on little boxes at intervals in the seemingly endless field. There were people in the bushes at the field's edge—Miriam saw them. Every once in a while one of the men would start off, following one of the brilliantly colored strings toward the woman who sat at the end of it, in a white dress, waiting. Frightened, Miriam turned to Mrs. Clark. "Why am I here? Why? Mrs. Clark, explain!"

"Poor child's a little nervous. I guess we all were, when it happened to us," Clark's wife said to Helva Smythe and Helva nodded. "It's all right, dear, you just stand here at the edge and watch for a little while, until you get used to the idea. Remember, the man must be a stranger. We'll be out with the truck with food for you and Margy during visitors' time Sunday. That's right. And when you go out there, try to stake out near Margy. It'll make the Wait nicer for you."

"*What* wait?"

"The Wait of the Virgins, dear. Goodbye."

Dazed, Miriam stood at the edge of the great domed field, watching the little world crisscrossed by hundreds of colored cords. She moved a little closer, trying to hide her cord under her skirts, trying not to look like one of them. Two men started toward her, one handsome, one unshaven and hideous, but when they saw she had not yet entered the field they dropped back, waiting. Sitting near her, she saw one of the dime-store clerks, who had quit her job two weeks back and suddenly disappeared. She was fidgeting nervously, casting her eyes at a young man ranging the edge of the field. As Miriam watched, the young man strode up her cord, without speaking threw money into her lap. Smiling, the dime-store girl stood up, and the two went off into the bushes. The girl nearest Miriam, a harelip with incredibly ugly skin, looked up from the half-finished sweater she was knitting.

"Well, there goes another one," she said to Miriam. "Pretty ones always go first. I reckon one day there won't be any pretty ones here, and then I'll go." She shook out her yarn. "This is my fortieth sweater." Not understanding, Miriam shrank away from the ugly girl. "I'd even be glad for old Fats there," she was saying. She pointed to a lewd-eyed old man hovering near. "Trouble is, even old Fats goes for the pretty ones. Heh! You ought to see it, when he goes up to one of them high school queens. Heh! Law says they can't say no!" Choking with curiosity, stiff, trembling, Miriam edged up to the girl.

"Where . . . where do they go?"

The harelip looked at her suspiciously. Her white dress, tattered and white no longer, stank. "Why, you really don't know, do you?" She pointed to a place near them, where the bushes swayed. "To lay with them. It's the law."

"Momma! Mommamommamomma!" With her dress whipping at her legs, Miriam ran into the square. It was well before the time when the sick were taken to sleep in the hall of the courthouse.

"Why, dear, how pretty you look!" the mother said. Then, archly, "They always say, wear white when you want a man to propose."

"Momma, we've got to get out of here." Miriam was crying for breath.

"I thought we went over all that."

"Momma, you always said you wanted me to be a good girl. Not ever to let any man take advan"—

"Why, dear, of course I did."

"Momma, don't you see! You've got to help me—we've got to get out of here, or somebody *I don't even know* . . . Oh, Momma, please. I'll help you walk. I saw you practicing the other day, with Mrs. Pinckney helping you."

"Now, dear, you just sit down here and explain to me. Be calm."

"Momma, *listen!* There's something every girl here has to do when she's eighteen. You know how they don't use doctors here, for anything?" Embarrassed, she hesitated. "Well, you remember when Violet got married, and she went to Dr. Dix for a checkup?"

"Yes, dear—now calm down, and tell Momma."

"Well, it's sort of a *checkup,* don't you see, only it's like graduating from high school too, and it's how they . . . see whether you're any good."

"What on earth are you trying to tell me?"

"Momma, you have to go to this field, and sit there, and sit there until a man throws money in your lap. *Then you have to go into the bushes and lie with a stranger!*" Hysterical, Miriam got to her feet, started tugging at the mattress.

"You just calm down. Calm down!"

"But Mother, I want to do like you told me. I want to be good!"

Vaguely, her mother started talking. "You said you were dating that nice Clark boy? His father is a real-estate salesman. Good business, dear. Just think, you might not even have to work"—

"Oh, Momma!"

"And when I get well I could come live with you. They're very good to me here—it's the first time I've found people who really *cared* what was wrong with me. And if you were married to that nice, solid boy, who seems to have such a *good* job with his father, why we could have a lovely house together, the three of us."

"Momma, we've got to get *out* of here. I can't do it. I just *can't.*" The girl had thrown herself on the grass again.

Furious, her mother lashed out at her. "Miriam. Miriam Elise Holland. I've fed you and dressed you and paid for you and taken care of you ever since your father died. And you've always been selfish, selfish, selfish. Can't you ever do anything for me? First I want you to go to secretarial school, to get a nice opening, and meet nice people, and you don't want to do that. Then you get a chance to settle in a good town, with a *nice* family, but you don't even want that. You only think about yourself. Here I have a chance to get well at last, and settle down in a really nice town, where good families live, and see you married to the right kind of boy." Rising on her elbows, she glared at the girl. "Can't you ever do anything for *me?*"

"Momma, Momma, you don't *understand!*"

"I've known about the Wait since the first week we came here." The woman leaned back on her pillow. "Now pour me a glass of water and go back and do whatever Mrs. Clark tells you."

"Mother!"

Sobbing, stumbling, Miriam ran out of the square. First she started toward the edge of town, running. She got to the edge of the highway, where the road signs were, and saw the two shabby, shambling men, apparently in quiet evening conversation by the street post. She doubled back and started across a neatly plowed field. Behind her, she saw the Pinckney boys. In front of her, the Campbells and the Dodges started across the field. When she turned toward town, trembling, they walked past her, ignoring her, on some business of their own. It was getting dark.

She wandered the fields for most of the night. Each one was blocked by a Campbell or a Smythe or a Pinckney; the big men carried rifles and flashlights, and called out cheerfully to each other when they met, and talked about a wild fox hunt. She crept into the Clarks' place when it was just beginning to get light out, and locked herself in her room. No one in the family paid attention to her storming and crying as she paced the length and width of the room.

That night, still in the bedraggled, torn white dress, Miriam came out of the bedroom and down the stairs. She stopped in front of the hall mirror to put on lipstick and repair her hair. She tugged at the raveled sleeves of the white chiffon top. She started for the place where the virgins Wait. At the field's edge Miriam stopped, shuddered as she saw the man called old Fats watching her. A few yards away she saw another man, young, lithe, with bright hair, waiting. She sighed as she watched one woman, with a tall, loose boy in jeans, leave the field and start for the woods.

She tied her string to a stake at the edge of the great domed field. Threading her way among the many bright-colored strings, past waiting girls in white, she came to a stop in a likely-looking place and took her seat.

—*F&SF*, 1958

ABOUT THE AUTHOR

Kit Reed's most recent novel is *Enclave;* her next, *Son of Destruction*, is coming out this year. Other novels include *J. Eden, Catholic Girls*, and *Thinner Than Thou*, which won an ALA Alex Award. Often anthologized, her short stories appear in venues ranging from *The Magazine of Fantasy and Science Fiction, Asimov's SF*, and *Omni* to *The Yale Review, The Kenyon Review,* and *The Norton Anthology of American Literature.* Her short story collections include *Thief of Lives; Dogs of Truth;* and *Weird Women, Wired Women,* which, along with *Little Sisters of the Apocalypse,* made the short list for the Tiptree Award. Her 2011 collection, *What Wolves Know,* was nominated for the Shirley Jackson Award. A Guggenheim Fellow and the first American recipient of a five-year literary grant from the Abraham Woursell Foundation, she is Resident Writer at Wesleyan University.